The Temporal Void

Peter F. Hamilton was born in Rutland in 1960, and still lives near Rutland Water. He began writing in 1987 and sold his first short story to *Fear* magazine in 1988. He has also been published in *Interzone* and the *In Dreams* and *New Worlds* anthologies, and in several small press publications. His previous novels include the Greg Mandel series: *Mindstar Rising*, *A Quantum Murder* and *The Nano Flower* and the bestselling Night's Dawn trilogy: *The Reality Dysfunction*, *The Neutronium Alchemist* and *The Naked God*. Also published by Macmillan (and Pan Books) are *A Second Chance at Eden*, a novella and six short stories set in the same brilliantly realized universe, and *The Confederation Handbook*, a vital guide to the Night's Dawn trilogy. His recent novels are *Fallen Dragon*, *Misspent Youth*, *Pandora's Star*, *Judas Unchained* and *The Dreaming Void*.

Also by Peter F. Hamilton

The Greg Mandel series

Mindstar Rising

A Quantum Murder

The Nano Flower

The Night's Dawn trilogy

The Reality Dysfunction

The Neutronium Alchemist

The Naked God

In the same timeline

A Second Chance at Eden

The Confederation Handbook
(a vital guide to the Night's Dawn trilogy)

Fallen Dragon

Misspent Youth

The Commonwealth Saga

Pandora's Star

Judas Unchained

The Void trilogy

The Dreaming Void

Peter F. Hamilton

THE TEMPORAL VOID

PART TWO OF THE VOID TRILOGY

PAN BOOKS

First published 2008 by Macmillan

This paperback edition published 2009 by Pan Books
an imprint of Pan Macmillan Ltd
Pan Macmillan, 20 New Wharf Road, London N1 9RR
Basingstoke and Oxford
Associated companies throughout the world
www.panmacmillan.com

ISBN 978-0-330-50788-2

9 8 7 6 5 4 3 2 1

A CIP catalogue record for this book is available from
the British Library.

Typeset by SetSystems Ltd, Saffron Walden, Essex
Printed in the UK by CPI Mackays, Chatham ME5 8TD

Visit www.panmacmillan.com to read more about all our books
and to buy them. You will also find features, author interviews and
news of any author events, and you can sign up for e-newsletters
so that you're always first to hear about our new releases.

THE TEMPORAL VOID

1

Strangely enough, it was the oak trees which Justine Burnelli always remembered from the day Centurion Station died. She was hurrying towards the safety bunker doors along with everyone else in the garden dome when she glanced back over her shoulder. The thick emerald grass was littered with the debris of the party, mashed canapés stamped into the grass, broken glasses and plates juddering about as the colossal gravity waves washed across the station in fast unrelenting succession. Overhead, the timid light emitted by the nebulas surrounding the galactic core was now smeared into pastel streaks by the dome's misty emergency force fields. Justine felt her weight reducing again. Yells of surprise and near-panic broke out from the staff pressed against her as they all fought for traction on the glowing orange path. Then a *crack* like a thunderbolt echoed across the dome. One of the huge lower boughs on a two-hundred-year-old oak tree split open close to the thick trunk, and the bough crashed down. Leaves swirled upwards like a flock of startled butterflies. The whole majestic tree sagged, with further fissures opening along the length of the trunk. It twisted as it started to fall into its neighbour. The elegant little tree house platform which the band had been playing on barely a minute ago splintered and snapped apart. The last glimpse Justine had of the trees was a couple of red squirrels scampering out of the toppled giants.

The malmetal safety bunker doors contracted behind her, and

for a moment she was enveloped within an oasis of calm. It was a bizarre image, everyone still dressed in their best party clothes, breathing heavily with dishevelled hair and anxious faces. Director Trachtenberg was standing beside her, looking round wild-eyed.

'You okay?' he asked.

She nodded, not quite trusting her voice.

Another of the gravity waves swept through the station. Once again Justine felt her weight lessen. Her u-shadow accessed the station's net, and she pulled out the sensor images of the sky above. The Raiel's DF spheres were still accelerating across the star system to their new positions. She checked that the *Silverbird* was unaffected by the weird gravity waves which the DF spheres were throwing off. The starship's smartcore told her it was maintaining position just above the dusty lava field which served as the station's landing area.

'I've just conferred with our alien colleges,' Director Trachtenberg announced. He smiled wryly. 'Those that talk to us, anyway. And we all agree the gravity shifts are beyond anything the safety systems were designed for. With regret I am ordering an immediate evacuation.'

Several people groaned in dismay.

'You can't,' Graffal Ehasz complained. 'This is what we're here for. Dear Ozzie, man, the data this event is spewing out. What we can learn is unprecedented! We can't just crawl away because of some safety restriction imposed by a committee back in the Commonwealth.'

'I understand your concern,' Trachtenberg said calmly. 'If the situation alters we will return. But, for now, please embark your designated ship.'

Justine could see most of the staff were relieved; while Ehasz and a small hard-core science clique radiated resentment. When she opened her mind to the local gaiafield the clash of emotion was pronounced. But Ehasz was definitely in the minority.

Trachtenberg leaned in close to Justine and quietly asked, 'Can your ship cope with this?'

'Oh yes,' she assured him.

'Very well, if you would please depart with the rest of us.'

'Of course.'

Through her link with the smartcore she saw the safety bunkers break surface, titanium-black spheres bubbling up out of the dusty lava plain. They started to glide smoothly towards the waiting starships.

With the evacuation procedures obviously working, Justine's nerves calmed considerably. She asked the *Silverbird*'s smartcore to open a link along the tenuous Navy communication relay all the way back to the Commonwealth, thirty thousand lightyears away. 'Dad?'

'You're okay, then,' Gore Burnelli said. 'Thank Christ for that.'

Leaking along the minuscule bandwidth was the faintest sensation of a smile. Warm Caribbean sunlight was shining on his lips. It was a comfort that delivered a completely unexpected emotional jolt to Justine. She felt her throat muscles tensing up as her eyes filled with tears and her cheeks flushed. *Goddamn this stupid body*, she raged at its weakness. But she smiled back weakly, ignoring the way people in the shelter were looking at her. 'Yeah, I'm okay.'

'Good, then get a load of this. I've been monitoring the Navy relay link to Centurion Station. Your new friend Trachtenberg just called the Cleric Conservator to tell him about the expansion phase. He did that before he even bothered to warn the Navy what was happening.'

Justine was proud of the way she managed to avoid glancing in Trachtenberg's direction. *Okay, maybe this old body's not quite so useless after all.* 'Really. How interesting.'

'It gets better. About five hours ago the Second Dreamer told his Skylord pal that he wasn't going to lead anyone into the Void. Next thing we know, this expansion begins. I don't know what your take is, but nobody back here thinks it's a coincidence.'

'The Second Dreamer caused this?'

'It wasn't deliberate. At least I seriously hope it wasn't. Cause and effect, I guess. The Skylords exist to ferry souls into the Heart of the Void, and someone tells them that their new supply is going to be cut off. Junkies tend to get irritated and irrational about such things.'

'The Skylords aren't junkies.'

'Don't take everything so literally. I'm doing metaphors, or allegories, some shit like that. Point is, now they know we're out here waiting to be guided, if we don't come to them . . .'

'They come to us,' she whispered.

'Looks like it.'

'But nothing can survive the boundary.'

'The original ship did. Somehow.'

'Has the Second Dreamer said anything?'

'Not a goddamn word, not even "ooops, sorry". Conceited little turd. I thought I was arrogant, but Jeezus!'

'Well, he's going to have to do something.'

'That's the consensus back here, too. The thing is, Living Dream is closing in on him. That's going to make serious trouble if they get their hands on him; our friend Ilanthe will make sure of that.'

Justine accessed the data coming from the station, watching with concern as their life support equipment was stressed close to its limit by the gravity waves. 'It doesn't get much worse than this, Dad.'

'Shit, I'm sorry, angel. Are you going to get out all right?'

'You know you don't have to worry about me. Hang on for a moment, we've reached the starships.'

People were activating their personal force fields as the airlock's outer door parted. Some of them were also taking pressure suits from the bunker's lockers, making doubly sure they were safe. Justine knew she could depend on her biononics to protect her from anything the unnamed planet could throw at her. Her integral force field strengthened round her. She slipped her heeled pumps off and followed the others out through the triple pressure curtain. Ten aluminium steps and she was standing on the lava in bare feet and a completely incongruous little black cocktail dress. Tremors managed to shake the soles of her feet through the protective cushion of the force field. A gentle argon breeze fluttered round her, raising short-lived twisters of dust that never came above her knees.

The bunker had come to rest a hundred metres beyond the squat building holding the base's main airlock. Two of the five Navy ships were poised on either side of her, hanging a few metres above the ground on ingrav, rocking slightly as they compensated for the treacherous gravity. Justine hastened round the nose of one to see the *Silverbird* waiting a further twenty metres beyond it. A welcome sight, its simple purple ovoid shape floating casually over the lava, holding a lot steadier than the Navy ships. She grinned in relief and scuttled underneath. The airlock at the base of the fuselage bulged inwards, opening into a dark funnel leading to the heart of the ship. The smartcore was already countering gravity to pull her inside when she saw something moving on the horizon. An impossible sight.

'Stop,' she commanded.

Her feet paused ten centimetres above the lava. Retinal inserts zoomed in. It was a mounted Silfen. The elf-like hominoid was clad in a thick cobalt-blue coat embroidered with the most fabulous stipple of jewels that sparkled in the wavering pastels of starlight. His black hat was tall and pointed, with a simple gold ribbon fluttering from the tip. A gloved hand gripped a long phosphorescent spear which he held aloft, as if in salute. It might have been such a gesture, for he was leaning forward in his saddle, half standing on the stirrups. As if his appearance wasn't astonishing enough, she was dumbfounded by his mount. The creature most closely resembled a terrestrial rhinoceros, except it was almost the size of an elephant, and had two flat tails that swept from side to side. Its long shaggy fur was bright scarlet, and the four horns curving from the side of its long head were devilishly sharp. Justine, who had once ridden on the Charlemagnes which the old Barsoomians had produced on Far Away, knew that this fearsome beast was a true warrior-animal. Her ancient body instinctively produced a flood of worry hormones just at the sight of it.

The Silfen simply shouldn't have been here. She'd never known one of their paths had led to this remote, desolate planet. And he was an oxygen breather; so, she suspected, was his lethally regal mount. This tenuous, radiation-saturated argon atmosphere was deathly to living things. Then she grinned at herself and her silly affront. Who was she to make such a claim, standing exposed to the eerie energy emissions of the Wall stars in nothing more than a disgracefully short cocktail dress?

So it wasn't an absolute impossibility to find a Silfen here. Nor that he was using some technological protection from the environment.

But . . . 'Why?' she whispered.

'The Silfen live to experience,' Gore told her, equally absorbed by the alien's presence. 'Face it, my girl, you don't get a much bigger experience than watching the end of the galaxy crashing down around you.'

She'd forgotten she'd left the link open. 'A very short experience,' she retorted sourly. 'And what is that thing he's riding?'

'Who knows? I remember Ozzie saying the Silfen he encountered on a winter planet rode to the hunt on odd creatures.'

'Odd, not terrifying.'

'Does it matter? I imagine he's here on the toughest steed he can find in honour of the event. After all, you've got the butchest starship in that section of the galaxy.'

'A *butch* starship?' But it broke her enchantment with the strange alien. She bowed her head formally at him. He dipped the spear in return, and sat back on his small saddle.

The *Silverbird* drew her up into the small luxurious cabin. Once inside, she relaxed into a deep curving chair that the deck extended. Within the ANA-designed craft she was now as safe as it was possible for any human to be. The starship's sensors showed her the last of the station staff hurrying into the airlocks of the Navy ships. Another two Silfen had joined the first watcher. Her father was right, she acknowledged, they would only come here for something momentous. For her, their presence served only to amplify the whole deadly panorama unfolding outside.

'Let's go,' she told the smartcore.

The *Silverbird* rose from Centurion Station ahead of all the other starships. As the rest of them began to surge up after her they made for a strangely varied flock: Commonwealth Navy ships sleek beside the cumbersome Ticoth vessels, while the glittering purple spheres of the Ethox danced nimbly round the big tankers containing the Suline. In another time she would have enjoyed travelling in the elegant avian-like artificial-life constructs that soared and swooped to carry the Forleene away from danger. Despite the devastation raging all around them, few of the departing species could resist a quick scan in the direction of the metal cube housing the Kandra. None, therefore, were wholly surprised when the whole mass simply lifted cleanly from the dusty ground and accelerated smoothly away from the collapsing structures of the observation project.

Justine was ridiculously proud of the way that none of them seemed able to match the *Silverbird*'s acceleration. It had taken the ultradrive ship just a few seconds to reach an altitude of five hundred kilometres, where it stopped to scrutinize the last minutes of Centurion Station. Another gravity wave shook the hull so violently the onboard gravity generator could barely counter it. Justine felt a distinct shiver run through the cabin. The unnamed planet curved away below the fuselage, its ancient geology stubbornly resistant to the worst effects of the awesome gravity waves washing invisibly through its mantle. Underneath her, the hot Ethox tower was the first to succumb; rocking from side to side until the undulations became too great for the safety systems to compensate for. It toppled with slow grace to shatter against the unyielding lava. Big waves of water cascaded out from splits in the Suline tanks, pushing a spume of debris ahead of them. Flying spray quickly solidified into sharp needles of hail, to be re-absorbed by the dark water. Inevitably, the cold won, producing a rumpled ice lake three kilometres across. Thin grey clouds streamed out of cracks in domes of both the human and the Forleene, quickly dissipating in the weak gusts of argon.

In an astonishingly short time the structures were flattened, joining the greater enclave of ruins which marked the site where hundreds of alien species had spent millennia observing the terrible, enigmatic Void at the centre of the galaxy. Justine switched her attention to the wounded sky above. As if they could feel what was happening beyond the Wall stars, the massive ion storms were seething with a rare angry sheen, brighter than she'd seen in her brief time at the station.

The *Silverbird* was tracking the Raiel's gas giant-sized DF spheres as they continued their flight across the star system. Gravity waves spilled out from them with astonishing force, distorting the orbits within the main asteroid rings. A couple of small moons caught in the backwash had also changed inclination. All nine of the DFs were heading in towards the small orange star which Centurion Station's never-named planet was in orbit around. As the ship watched, the photosphere started to dim.

'Holy crap,' Justine yelped. The DFs must be drawing power directly from the star. She wondered how they would manifest it. The effect was fascinating, almost countering the anxiety she felt. There had been a few minutes after the emergency began that she'd seriously thought Centurion Station was where her body would finally die.

As if sharing her thought, Lehr Trachtenberg opened a channel to all the human starships. 'Status report please, is everyone all right?'

'I'm fine,' she reported back to the CNE *Dalfrod*, where he was embarked, along with the senior staff.

Once he'd established all his own staff were safe, the director exchanged messages with the alien craft ascending out of the atmosphere. They all confirmed that everyone had escaped intact; though they had to assume the Kandra were safe as the enigmatic cube didn't respond to any communication.

'We'll return to the Commonwealth immediately,' Trachtenberg announced. 'From what the observation systems can ascertain, we should manage to stay ahead of the boundary. It's expanding at about three or four lightyears an hour. That gives us a huge safety margin.'

'Is the data still coming in?' Justine asked.

'Some of it. It's patchy now, there's a lot going on in the Wall we don't understand. I expect most of the disturbances we're registering are coming from the Raiel defence systems, but even so we can keep a reduced watch until the sensors are overcome. We're relaying as much as we can to the Navy Exploration Division centre back home.'

'I see.'

Justine watched the other starships reach her altitude, feeling strangely annoyed with them and herself. Surely there was something else to be done other than simply flee? It smacked of not a little cowardice, ignorant peasants cowering from the lightning storm, howling that the gods were angry, looking for a sacrifice to appease them. *And we stopped that nonsense millennia ago. Yet for all our enlightenment we're right back there sheltering from the onslaught in our nice dry cave.* Then the ships were accelerating past her, starting to disperse as they headed back towards their own home stars. The Forleene were the first to go ftl, slipping down into wormholes which closed immediately, a last farewell hanging in the ether from their pack leader.

The *Silverbird*'s cabin rocked again. Eighty million miles away the DFs were streaking into a low orbit against the darkening star. The motion hardened her determination. *This is not the way it should be.*

'Dad?'

'Still here.'

'What have the Raiel said about the expansion?'

'Sweet fuck all. The *High Angel* is a lifeboat, remember. Their defence systems are all concentrated round your part of the galaxy. Anyway, we can hardly blame them for not telling us anything. Right now every sentient species in the galaxy is pissed at us over the Pilgrimage, and who can blame them. I'm pissed at us.'

'I know. That's why I'm going in,' she said, surprising herself at the speed of the thought.

'You're doing *what*?'

'Heading in to the Void.' Even as she told him she was instructing the smartcore, laying down the course. Fast. *Before I chicken out.*

'You're doing no such thing, my girl.'

The *Silverbird* dropped smoothly into hyperspace, heading in towards the Wall stars at fifty lightyears an hour. 'Tell him,' she said to her father. 'Tell the Second Dreamer. Get him to ask the Skylord to let me in. Once I'm in, once I'm talking to the Skylord direct, I'll try to explain the situation, the damage their boundary is causing.'

'Get your ass back here right fucking now!'

'Dad. No. This is our chance at a diplomatic solution. The Raiel have tried force for a million years. It doesn't work.'

'Come back. You can't get in. This thing is killing the whole fucking galaxy. Your ship . . .'

'Humans can get in, we already know that. Somehow we can do it. And if the Second Dreamer helps me, I'll stand a really good chance.'

'This is insane.'

'I have to do this, Dad. Somebody has to make the effort. We have to try a human method. We're part of this galaxy now, a big part. It's our turn to attempt our way. We have the right.' The blood was pounding in her ears as she hyped herself up. 'I'm going to carry the torch for all of us. If I fail, then . . . we try something else. That's being human, too.'

'Justine.'

Over thirty thousand lightyears she could feel his anguish. For a split second, she shared it. 'Dad, if anyone can get to the Second Dreamer, if anyone can make them see reason, it's you, it's *the* Gore Burnelli. All he has to do is tell the Skylord I'm out

12

here. Ask him. Beg him. Offer him riches. Whatever it takes. You can do it. Please, Dad.'

'God-*damn*, why are you always so fucking difficult?'

'I'm your daughter.'

Bitter laughter echoed across the stars. 'Of course I'll ask. I'll do a damn sight more than that. If he doesn't get down on his knees and beg that Skylord he'll wish all he faces is oblivion in the expansion.'

'Now don't start threatening people,' she rebuked immediately.

'Yeah, yeah.'

'I'll try to keep a channel open to Centurion Station's relay as long as I can. The Navy systems are tough, they should hold out a while yet.'

'Okay, I'll go find me the little tit responsible for this almighty screw-up.'

'Thanks, Dad.'

'Godspeed.'

*

At three o'clock in the morning Chris Turner left the staff canteen on the east side of Colwyn City's docks and grimaced at the rain splattering on to his face. He'd hoped the unseasonal weather front would blow over while he was taking his break. But no, the thick clouds showed no sign of relenting. His semi-organic jacket rolled a collar up round his neck, and he hurried back to the maintenance depot.

Chris couldn't see anything moving in the docks tonight. Not that other nights were much different. Night-time staffing levels were low. Bots were off line for maintenance, which was why he'd pulled this grotty shift – it wasn't popular but it paid well. Trans-ocean barges stayed moored to the quay while their crews slept or clubbed the night away in town. Warehouses were shut.

There wasn't any activity in the city, either. The rain had put a halt to the usual nightlife. Capsules and ground vehicles had hauled the last optimistic revellers back to their homes a long time ago. He could just make out the huge single-span arch bridge over the Cairns, its lights a hazy smear through the rain. Normally there would be something driving over it, or a few taxis sliding along its metro rail. But not tonight. He shivered. The city like this was actually kind of spooky. To counter the feeling of isolation he reached down into the gaiafield to gain some emotional comfort from the eternal thoughts whirling within. The usual busy background babble slithered round him like noisy spectres; thoughts that called, mournfully and eagerly, feelings which intrigued, though he shied away from the sadder ones.

A little more comfortable now he knew there were other humans still alive and awake, Chris quickened his pace. There were another eight general purpose bots that needed an overhaul before morning. Even with the company smartcore interfaced with the engineering bays back in the maintenance depot, he'd be hard pressed to finish on time. Yet again he wondered if the pay for late shift was truly worth the cost. His friends only ever got to see him at the weekends, and then his sleep pattern made him lousy company.

He walked along the long line of landing pads, boots splashing in the puddles that were expanding over the vast apron of concrete. Gentle green-tinged ripples reflected the luminescence given off by the lighting globes on their high posts overhead. Thick droplets splattered down noisily from the dark hulls of parked starships.

Up in front and ten metres above the slick concrete a small star flared blue-violet. Chris's mouth dropped open in astonishment. You couldn't work in the starship business, even in a peripheral position like his, without knowing the signature spectrum of Cherenkov radiation. 'That's wrong,' he said dumbly.

The star vanished, and the air where it had been rippled. Chris was suddenly staring at a perfect black circle whose base touched the ground. The blackness changed again, lightening to blue-grey, then *receding* at a speed which made him giddy. Instinct brought his arms up for balance, he was certain he was falling forwards. When he steadied himself he was looking along an infinite tunnel. Its soft-glowing fabric brightened intolerably as dazzling sunlight streamed out. Not Viotia's sun, he knew. This was another star altogether.

The light dimmed for a moment as a big capsule slipped out of the opening. Chris scurried away to one side. He could see the wormhole had lowered itself so the bottom quarter was now below ground level, giving the long line of armour-clad figures a broad flat path to march through from their world. Above them, capsules slid through nose to tail. Boots were hitting the wet concrete in a steady rhythm, echoing round the high walls of the dock buildings. It was an eerily brutal sound, Chris thought. Over a hundred of the soldiers were on the Viotia side already. *Soldiers?* But what else could he call them?

Finally, the impossibility he was witnessing started to register. His u-shadow was throwing out frantic emergency calls to his family, friends, work-colleagues, company offices, the police, the mayor, government . . . His mind let loose a powerful wail of shock into the gaiafield, which drew some instant reactions of surprise from local sharers, who immediately became curious indeed as his vision opened to them.

'You there!' an amplified voice boomed from the first rank of the marching figures. There must have been thirty capsules in the air now, starting to accelerate out across the city, and still more were rushing through. From his angle, the wormhole provided Chris with a narrow window out across the vast field on the other side. Warm afternoon sunlight shone down cosily on row after row of armoured figures, thousands of them – tens of thousands. Most of them were in shadow from the armada of regrav capsules suspended in the air above.

Chris Turner turned and started to run.

'Halt,' the harsh voice commanded. 'We are the legitimate police of Viotia, accredited by your Prime Minister. Halt now or face the consequences.'

Chris kept on running. This couldn't be happening. This was the Commonwealth. It was safe and it was comfortable. People with guns didn't invade from other planets, not even in troubled times like these. *Not happening!*

'Last warning. Halt.'

His family was starting to respond to his frantic calls. Those he shared himself with through the gaiafield were producing the same dismayed reaction as his own. Then the jangle pulse struck, and Chris was unconscious before he hit the wet concrete.

*

Elvin's Payback was only an hour out from Viotia when the shit hit the fan. Everyone on board went quiet at more or less the same time as their u-shadows reported the news that was breaking into the unisphere. They accessed in astonishment as images of armoured paramilitary police and their support capsules poured out of the wormhole in Colwyn City's docks. In a carefully choreographed political sequence the Cleric Conservator's office on Ellezelin formally issued a public invitation to Viotia to join the Free Trade Zone. It was swiftly followed by Viotia's Prime Minister accepting on behalf of her planet. One minute later the wormhole had opened.

So Oscar Monroe wasn't the least surprised when Paula called him on a secure link a couple of minutes later. 'We knew they were planning annexation,' Paula said. 'The trigger factor has to be the Second Dreamer.'

'That figures,' Oscar said. 'Everyone's scared crapless over the devourment phase. If we do manage to get hold of him, I'd like to shake some sense into the stupid bastard myself.'

'I think the devourment has taken Living Dream by surprise as much as everyone else. The dream simply confirmed his location for them. They're acting on that.'

Oscar reviewed some of the images relayed by reporters who'd gathered around the edge of the docks. 'So we can safely assume he's in Colwyn City.'

'Yes, but they don't know exactly where. If they had an accurate fix, their embedded agents would have simply run a covert snatch operation. This is an indicator of Ethan's desperation. Our sources on the ground indicate they're shutting down all traffic in and out of the city – ground, air and space.'

'Closing the noose.'

'Exactly.'

'That doesn't make our mission any easier. We'll have to infiltrate through the perimeter.'

'Don't complicate things. I'd suggest you simply fly straight down into the docks.'

'You're kidding me, right?'

'Not at all. Get the smartcore to display the ship's stealth function to you. I don't believe that Living Dream has anything on Viotia which can detect you at night in the rain.'

'Oh, crap. All right.'

The link ended, and he turned to his shipmates to explain.

'I can insert some software that will help cover our approach,' Liatris McPeierl said. 'Their network is already growing out from the docks, I'm monitoring its development through the unisphere, but I can crack the junction nodes. That'll let me into their sensors and command links.'

'The docks will be a good position,' Tomansio said. 'It puts us in right at the heart of their operation. I don't care how dense their network is, or how powerful their smartcores are, it will be chaotic down there to start with. That provides us with a golden opportunity.'

'All right,' Oscar said, 'you guys are the experts. Tell me what approach route you want.'

Forty minutes later *Elvin's Payback* emerged into real space a thousand kilometres above Colwyn City. It was already fully stealthed, capable of avoiding the most advanced military-grade sensors. A huge case of overkill. Viotia's civil space detectors could barely locate a starship out at geosynchronous orbit when its beacon was signalling. As yet, the Ellezelin forces pouring into the docks hadn't established any kind of sensor coverage above the atmosphere. They were concentrating on tracking capsule traffic in the city, and apprehending anyone who tried to leave.

Nobody was looking for craft coming into the area. The commercial starships which had arrived after the annexation began were staying in orbit, awaiting developments and clear orders from their owners.

Following Tomansio's directions, Oscar brought the starship straight down above the estuary a couple of miles outside the city. It was still raining, the swollen river covered by rolling cloud. With a high intensity optical distortion shimmering round its fuselage, the ovoid starship looked like a particularly dense patch of drizzle in the few wisps of sombre starlight that defused through the cloud. Electronic sensors simply lost focus, mass scanners were unable to find anything heavier than air in the space it occupied. Even Higher field functions, had there been any operating, would have been hard pressed to find anything. If it had been broad daylight on a clear morning, then maybe someone might have spotted something. But not this dreary shadowed night.

Oscar took them down to three metres above the muddy water, and steered upriver using passive sensors alone. Several of the large Ellezelin forces' support capsules streaked across the sky above them, on their way to intercept fleeing citizens. *Elvin's Payback* remained invisible, though that didn't stop Oscar holding his breath and foolishly staring up at the cabin ceiling as the capsules passed overhead. He remembered the war films he used to watch in his first life, already ancient then, which depicted silent running in submarines. The principles here were comparable. He was even tempted to take the starship underwater to make their approach, completing the similarity. Tomansio had talked him out of it, pointing out that the noise and displacement they'd make breaking surface would probably give them away.

So they drifted in over the deserted quays like a ghost through mist. According to the information Liatris had hacked from the invaders' network, several paramilitary squads had been deployed round the perimeter of the docks, supported by ten armed capsules, to secure their immediate footprint. Nobody was watching the dock's long river frontage.

Beckia McKratz had infiltrated the dock's original commercial network, skilfully manipulating the nodes with software that opened up channels without the management monitors being aware of anything untoward. Even before they reached land she'd assumed complete command of a giant cargo warehouse belonging to the Bootel & Leicester import agency. As they passed above an empty barge repair bay just outside she opened one of the plyplastic doors, and the starship slipped into the dark enclosed space beyond, dripping cold rain onto the enzyme-bonded concrete floor. The door shut silently behind them, and five rounded pedestal legs swelled out from the base of the hull. Oscar landed them next to a tall stack of yellow and green cargo crates containing civil engineering excavators manufactured offworld.

'Down and safe,' Oscar said, letting out a long breath of relief.

'We're safe,' Tomansio said cheerfully. 'I don't fancy anyone else's chances.'

*

When *Mellanie's Redemption* dropped out of hyperspace four thousand kilometres above Sholapur, Troblum looked down on a continent rolling slowly into the dawn. The bright new light illuminated a wide monsoon building just off the subtropical coast where the city state of Ikeo squatted amid spectacularly craggy landscape. He studied the weather with interest. There weren't many monsoons on Sholapur, but those that did materialize tended towards the fierce. It would reach the land in less than two hours.

On the chair opposite him in the starship's cabin, the solido of Catriona Saleeb lounged back, smiling contentedly. She pushed a hand through her curly black hair, a languid movement he always found sensual. 'That storm could help us,' she said in her husky voice.

Trisha Marina Halgarth's solido walked across the small floor space to Catriona. She wore a pair of tight black leather jeans, and a small pure-white T-shirt to show off a nicely athletic body.

Green butterfly-wing OCtattoos quivered slowly across her cheeks as she wriggled herself on to the cushioning beside Catriona. The two girls put their arms comfortably round each other; Trisha flexed her bare toes. 'Do you think so?' she asked Catriona.

'It's going to take hours to pass across Ikeo. That'll mess up sensors, no matter how sophisticated they are. There will be force fields on over most estates, which will block a lot of low-angle scanning. That's to our advantage, isn't it Troblum, darling?'

'Could be,' he admitted. What he would have liked was Isabella Halgarth's opinion on the situation, but he'd lost her I-sentient personality program when he'd left the Accelerator Faction station, using it in a projector to convince the sensors his starship was still sitting passively in the docking bay. Isabella had an altogether more devious outlook than the other girls, which would have made her ideal to analyse forthcoming events.

'Not if you try and arrive during the storm,' Tricia said. 'Even with this ship's ingrav you'll be struggling to hold level in the winds. Best you leave it to provide cover if you have to leave in a hurry.'

Troblum accessed the external sensor imagery again. It was a large storm. Even from this height he could see flashes of sheet lightning ripping through the dark clouds. At his request the smartcore overlaid the sensor patterns guarding Ikeo from uninvited intruders. The *Mellanie's Redemption* could sneak through unnoticed. Probably. But it would be a close fought electronic battle. And Tricia was right, the storm would produce a particularly difficult environment to fly through. He ran a passive scan for orbiting ships, but there was no inbound or outbound traffic that he could detect, just Sholapur's small band of geosynchronous satellites. 'Activate our full stealth suite and take us down,' he told the smartcore; then pulled up a map of the city, and designated a small valley five miles from Stubsy Florac's home, just outside the estate's official boundary.

*

Troblum was sweating with worry as they descended through the last levels of cloud. Then they were past the cold vapour, and the rugged land was only two kilometres below. In the wan pre-dawn light the starship blended perfectly into the grey overcast sky as it sank fast through the clear air. He landed it next to some tall palm-equivalent trees that were already starting to wave about as the wind built up.

To visit Stubsy Florac he selected an armoured fabric one-piece he could wear under his toga suit. Then he ran a fast check on the biononics which produced his integral force field to make sure of their functionality. In combination, the armour and shielding should be able to stop a great many weapons, but he didn't delude himself about their ultimate ability if a fully enriched Accelerator agent cornered him. For a moment he considered taking a weapon. There were two jelly guns stashed away in a locker. Both of which would need charging. But he didn't have any experience in physical combat, his biononics could produce a respectable distortion pulse if pushed, and besides Stubsy wouldn't like him carrying that kind of hardware into his home. It was going to be bad enough turning up unannounced and then asking for a further favour. So he left the guns in the locker and went into the airlock.

There was a one-man regrav scooter stowed in a midship cargo hold. Troblum gave it a suspicious stare as it floated out to hover a couple of centimetres above the thick blue-tinged grass. He hadn't used it in decades. It looked uncomfortably small now, and it bobbed about alarmingly under his weight as he tried to lift his leg over the saddle. It took three attempts, but he eventually managed to sit astride it, wincing at what he was sure was a pulled muscle just above his hip. Biononics went to work tracking down and repairing the cells in his overstrained flesh. A transparent plyplastic visor unfurled from the front of the scooter, producing a streamlined hemisphere to shield the rider from the slipstream, though it had to curve outwards to enclose Troblum. He directed the little craft towards Stubsy's grand villa just outside the valley, keeping his speed to a prudent fifty kilometres an hour at a three-metre altitude.

While he was travelling, his u-shadow analysed all the space-ports whose networks were connected to the sparse planetary cybersphere. It produced a list of starships currently on the ground, none of which were Earth-registered. Hardly complete, he acknowledged, but then he was fairly sure that Paula Myo wouldn't draw attention to herself here, which is undoubtedly what an Earth registration would do. Nor was there a ship that fitted the profile of an Accelerator agent. If anyone was here for him, they weren't out in the open.

His scooter arrived at the line of slim silver pillars which marked out the boundary of Stubsy's estate. His field functions reported several sensors locking on as he slowed. He called Stubsy's code. It took a disconcertingly long time for the dealer to answer.

'Troblum, man, is that you out there?'

'Of course it's me. Will you let me through your perimeter, please.'

'I didn't know you were on Sholapur. You didn't land at Ikeo spaceport.'

'I told you I needed discretion for our last transaction.'

'Yeah, yeah, right.'

Troblum gave the silver pillars an uneasy glance. He was feeling very alone and exposed out here. 'Are you going to let me in?'

'Right. Yeah. Sure. I've cleared you through the defence systems. Come on in.'

The top of the two pillars in front of him turned green. Troblum eased the scooter forward between them, tensing up as he passed over the line. When nothing happened he breathed easier.

Beyond the big white villa, a dense curtain of rain was heading in across the steel-grey sea. As he settled in front of the high glass doors, Troblum looked down the long slope to the lovely little cove below. There was no sign of Stubsy's glide-boat anchored offshore.

Stubsy opened the door, and gave Troblum a nervous grin. 'Hey, big man, how's it going, huh?'

'No change,' Troblum said. His gaze swept across Stubsy, who was hanging on to the side of the door, preventing any glimpse of the big hallway beyond. The man was wearing his usual expensive and tasteless garb, too-tight gold sports trousers and a shirt with a vivid black and orange flower pattern, open to the waist. But his face looked haggard, as if he was suffering the mother of all hangovers, with dark circles under his eyes, and at least two days' stubble. He looked flushed as well, his skin hot and sweaty.

'I'm here to pick up my collection.'

'Yeah,' Stubsy said, scratching the base of his neck. 'Yeah. Yeah. That's it. You are.' Somewhere in the house behind him was the sound of bare feet running on tiles.

Troblum had to consult his social interaction program. 'Can I get them now, please?' he read off his exovison script.

'Okay,' Stubsy said reluctantly. He swung the door open and stood aside.

The open area in the middle of the house was exactly as before, with waterfalls bubbling swiftly down the surrounding boulders to top up the pool. Green and yellow flowering plants twice Troblum's height waved in the gusts that were starting to spill over the low roof. Nobody was swimming. Three of Stubsy's Olympic warrior women companions were waiting in the patio area, with one lying on a sun lounger while the other two stood motionless beside the long bar. Troblum's mild field scan showed him that all their enrichments were inactive.

The sound of thunder rolled through the sky. All three companions looked upwards at the noise.

'Are you going to put up a force field?' Troblum asked Stubsy as he sank his bulk into a sun lounger. The wood and fabric creaked as it accepted his full weight. He'd chosen the one next to the companion in the emerald green bikini. She was gripping the edges of her own sun lounger very tight, as if she was holding herself down against a gravity inversion. 'That storm looked big.'

'Force field,' Stubsy said. 'Yeah. Good idea, man. Uh, yeah, we can do that, sure.'

'Did my collection arrive okay?'

Stubsy nodded his head, and perched himself on a sun lounger beside the companion in the green bikini. 'Yeah,' he said slowly. 'It's here. We ferried it over from the freighter as agreed. The captain was very curious, you know. I had to slot some extra cash his way. I've got it all downstairs. Man, I wasn't expecting so much junk, you know.'

'I have been collecting for a long time. And it is not junk.' Troblum glanced up as a force field came on above the villa. The sound of the wind shrank to nothing. 'I'd like to get it loaded on my starship today.'

'Where is your starship, man?'

'Close,' Troblum said. He wasn't going to give anything away until he'd sorted out payment and the collection was ready to move. 'Do you have a cargo capsule?'

'Sure, sure.'

'There's something else I need from you if you don't mind. I'll pay for the trouble, of course.'

Stubsy drew down a loud breath, as if he was having trouble swallowing. 'What's that, then, man?'

'I want to meet someone here in private. Someone you wouldn't ordinarily have at your house. You'll have to clear them with the city's defence system.'

'Who?'

'Think of her as a police officer.'

'Police?' Stubsy grimaced a smile. 'Ho boy. Well, what the hell, we're all going to die in the Void boundary anyway, right?'

'Possibly,' Troblum said. He didn't know what to make of the expansion phase yet. If it really couldn't be stopped then fleeing to a colony world was going to be no use at all. He'd have to travel all the way to another galaxy, as Nigel Sheldon had been rumoured to do. It would be a huge challenge for the *Mellanie's Redemption*. Fortunately, the hardware he'd taken from the Accelerator station should make such a flight achievable, if he could ever assemble the myriad components and make it work.

'So I can call her and arrange a meeting?'

Stubsy produced a strange little laugh, his eyes crinkled up. 'Sure.'

'Thank you,' Troblum said. He used the secure link he was maintaining to his starship to call ANA:Governance's security division.

'Yes, Troblum,' ANA:Governance said.

'Connect me to Paula Myo, please.'

'As you wish.'

Paula Myo came on line. 'Are you ready to meet?'

'I told you not to stealth your ship.'

'I haven't.'

'Then where are you?'

'Close to Sholapur.'

'All right. I'm at Ikeo city, Florac's villa, I've arranged for him to let you through the city's defences. How long will it take you to reach me?'

'I can be there within a couple of hours.'

'Fine, I'll be waiting.' Troblum ended the call. He glanced over at Stubsy, who hadn't moved. 'She'll be here in two hours.' Which wasn't exactly what she'd said, a pedantic section of his mind acknowledged. Paula would never lie, but there were a lot of ambiguities in the way she'd phrased it.

'Cool,' Stubsy said.

'Can I see the collection?'

'Sure thing, man. It's downstairs.'

Stubsy led the way back into the villa. The three companions stayed beside the pool, though their eyes followed Troblum like targeting sensors as he walked after Stubsy.

One of the arching doors in the hallway opened to a set of concrete stairs leading down. Stubsy stood at the top as the polyphoto strips came on. He seemed reluctant to go down.

'Down here?' Troblum asked.

'Yeah,' Stubsy whispered.

The dealer was sweating again, Troblum saw. Whatever excess he'd indulged in last night must have been substantial for his body to take so long to flush the effects out.

Stubsy started down the stairs. Troblum was right behind him, keen to make sure his precious collection of Starflyer War memorabilia was unharmed. Everything had been in an individual case with a stabilizer field, but he'd had to rely on chartered commercial carriers to get it all to Sholapur without any supervision on his part – it was the only way to avoid Marius's attention. So much could have gone wrong.

There was a broad passage at the bottom of the stairs, carved into the naked rock, with smaller corridors branching off every few metres. They were lined with malmetal doors. Stubsy's vaults were a lot larger than the villa above.

Troblum nearly asked, *What do you keep down here?* But his social interaction program told him that Stubsy was likely to get upset by that kind of question.

Stubsy turned off into one of the side passages. A malmetal door opened for him. Lights came on in the chamber beyond. Troblum walked into a large circular chamber filled with low tables. His collection was there waiting for him. Every priceless case, their surfaces shimmering with protective shielding. It was going to be tough squeezing everything into *Mellanie's Redemption*, he acknowledged, some of the larger items might even have to be discarded. His u-shadow performed a fast inventory, checking case logs. They'd been banged around more than Troblum liked, but the cases had protected their contents perfectly. Smiling, he ran his hand over the case containing the handheld array with a foxory casing; the expensive unit had belonged to Mellanie Rescorai herself, a gift from her lover Morton before his trial. Troblum could just discern its outline below the shimmer.

'Thank you,' Troblum said. 'I know you didn't have to do

this.' When he glanced up at Stubsy Florac he saw an expression his emotional context program interpreted as anger and con tempt.

The villa nodes relaying his secure link to the *Mellanie's Redemption* went dead.

'All this makes me feel quite at home,' the Cat said.

Shock ran through Troblum's body in the same way as physical pain. His knees almost gave way, forcing him to clutch at the table. She stepped out from behind a huge casing containing the blunt nose cone belonging to a Wessex-based exospheric combat aerobot. Her lean body was dressed in a simple white suit that emitted a hazy glow as if she were some historical saint; it was wreathed in black bands which undulated slowly; ten of them formed a bizarre cage around her head. Troblum knew the suit had to be some kind of armour. Even now with fear so strong it threatened to reduce him to tears, he acknowledged she looked quite magnificent.

'Troblum, my dear,' she said brightly as if she'd only just caught sight of him. 'How lovely to see you again. You're really a lot of fun. It was a brilliant game we played. Well, I thought so.'

'Game? he said weakly. His integral force field had come on instantly, though he knew it would be no use against *her*.

The Cat took a few paces towards him. Troblum lurched backwards in near panic. Even now he couldn't resist admiring her movements; they really were feline.

'Why yes, darling,' the Cat said. 'How funny you couldn't work it out. Marius was right, wasn't he? You don't connect with humans on an emotional level. You marched in here completely oblivious to dear old Stubsy and his naughty little posse. Didn't you see their faces, Troblum? Take a look now.'

Troblum gave Stubsy a wild glance. The dealer's face was a rigid mask, teeth clamped together so hard his lips were quivering. Two of the companions appeared at the chamber door, tall and powerful. Troblum recognized them from his last visit:

Somonie, wearing a scarlet dress with a high hem; while Alcinda's taut muscles stretched her shiny black bikini fabric to near bursting point.

The Cat let out a mocking wolf-whistle. 'Aren't they gorgeous? And they play nasty, too, which is really fun.' She cocked her head at Troblum. 'You still don't get it, do you? Fantastic. You are interesting. Run an emotional context recognition program, my dear. It'll tell you they're all very, very pissed off. They were when you came through the front door, and sadly they still are. All because of little old me.'

'Okay,' Troblum said. 'You're right, I didn't get it. Congratulations.'

'I know.' The Cat gave a fulsome pout. 'Me and Stubsy here had a small wager going. I thought you'd realize by the time you reached the pool, Stubsy said it would be as soon as you arrived and saw him. We both lost. Your fault.'

'How did you find me?' Troblum said. He didn't really have any tactical programs to run, no smart way to work out how to escape from an underground room with only one door and no communications. But then he was pretty sure even the best tactical program would tell him he was going to die. His own knowledge unfortunately supplied him with a host of extremely unpleasant methods she was known to use to kill her enemies (and friends), and that was before he called up her file to check. If he could just keep her talking . . . He glanced at the door again.

'Oh my!' The Cat's delighted laughter rang across the chamber as she caught his unsubtle motion. 'Troblum, darling, are you going to make a run for it? Tell you what, I'll give you a five minute head start. Do you think your fat legs can reach the bottom of the stairs by then? Will you need to sit down and take a breather?'

'Fuck you.'

'Troblum! How jolly rude!'

From anyone else it would have been ridiculous. From her, it frightened him even further.

'How did you find me?' he repeated.

The Cat batted her eyes. 'It was so difficult. You're such a master covert agent. Let me see, could it be all the illegal money your Accelerator friends pay into your External world bank accounts, which is rather easily traceable to Stubsy here? Or was it when you called ANA:Governance and told my dearest old chum Paula Myo to meet you here? Humm, which was it now? My memory is not what it was.'

'Oh.' It wasn't often Troblum felt foolish, but the way she said it made him realize what an idiot he'd been. He'd suspected that the unisphere might be compromised to a Faction, yet he still hadn't taken adequate precautions. And as for the money, well any half-rate e-head could trace money.

'Where's your ship?' the Cat said.

Troblum shook his head. 'No.' The smartcore had some very specific instructions should his secure link be broken. A timer was counting down in his exovision. It was a small glimmer of hope, though he suspected the kind of ship which the Accelerators had supplied her with would be able to burn the *Mellanie's Redemption* out of the sky with a single shot. More bad planning. That just left one chance.

'Troblum,' she said as if chiding a child, 'I'd like to know where your ship is, and I want the command codes. And I believe that you of all people know you really shouldn't annoy me.'

'I know. Why do you want the ship?'

'Oh, come on, you know that, darling. Marius might be slightly peeved you made him look like a complete dickhead in front of his masters, but that hardly motivates me, now does it, Mr Me-expert?'

'Paula. You want to use it to catch Paula.'

She clapped her hands delightedly. 'She and I are going to be together for a very long time. I have plans, you see. Big plans for our shared future. And I need her intact. Which you're going to help me achieve, by convincing her that everything here is just hunky dory.'

'There's no point. Nobody has a future any more. The galaxy is being eaten alive. We're all going to die within a few years.'

A flicker of annoyance passed over the Cat's face. She gave Troblum a long stare. 'I want her to walk in here expecting to see you. Moderately unsuspecting, though she is a paranoid little bitch. So . . . Ship. Now.'

'No.'

'What do I do to people I don't like?'

He shrugged, not wanting to think of the details he'd so laboriously extracted from various police reports over the decades.

'You will help me,' she said. 'Don't make me threaten you. I'm only being this patient because I know you don't understand the consequences of your stupidity. So ask yourself this, how come Stubsy and his friends are being so cooperative?'

Troblum turned to the dealer. It wasn't something he'd considered. Another mistake, he thought.

'Just help her,' Stubsy said brokenly.

'I cheated,' the Cat said, and rested a finger on her lips. 'Bad lady that I am. I used a small insert.' She grinned at the companions, who glared back at her with clenched teeth. 'And it was quite difficult to insert, wasn't it, girls? You know, I actually had to hold them down to do it there was so much girly squealing and wiggling. And look at them now, happy to do as they're told.'

Troblum thought he might be sick. His biononics had to work hard at keeping his hormone glands suppressed. And finally he didn't need any programs to interpret the expression both Somonie and Alcinda registered, their fear and loathing. Somonie had a tear squeezing out of her right eye.

'The girls are going to hold you down for me now, Troblum,' the Cat said. 'Even their silly little weapons enrichments can overcome your pitiful force field. Higher culture,' she said with a shake of her head. 'Where do you people get off calling yourselves that? Talk about insecurities. And you think I've got psychological flaws.'

The two companions started to walk towards Troblum. He ordered the shields on all the cases to switch off, as well as his own integral force field. The Cat's response was instantaneous. She vanished inside a silver glow, as though she'd been encased in moon-washed silk.

'Stop,' Troblum told the companions.

They hesitated, looking at the Cat's glowing shape for instruction.

'Troblum?' the Cat's smooth voice issued out of the protective aurora. 'What are you doing? You haven't got any defences now.'

'Remember this?' he asked and pointed at a grey ovoid on a table close to the door.

'No,' the Cat said. Her tone was one of dangerous boredom.

'It was on the Ables ND47 you rode through into Boongate,' Troblum explained, wishing he wasn't trembling and sweating so much. 'Somebody salvaged it and took it with them to their planet's new world. I never found out why, maybe they thought it would give them some kind of edge over their fellow settlers. But the government confiscated it, and then it got lost in evidence archives for several hundred years. Then a museum found it and—'

'Troblum!' The Cat's angry voice snapped across the chamber.

'Yes, sorry: it's a zone-killer dispenser,' Troblum said meekly. 'And I was really lucky when I bought it, the museum had kept it in a stabilizer field so it's still functional and active. The thing's about as antique as you can get, but in a confined space like this one I don't rate anyone's chances, not even in a force field like yours. What do you think?'

There was a short pause. 'Are you trying to threaten me, darling?' the Cat asked.

'I've got it on a double activation switch,' Troblum said. 'I can trigger it if I think you're going to try to hurt me. Or if you're too quick for me, and I'm exterminated, that'll trigger it as well.'

'Oh, fuck me backwards with a power blade,' Stubsy wailed. His legs were giving way, sliding him on to the floor. 'I can't take any more.' His hands went over his head, and he started sobbing. 'Just fucking do it, man. End this, for fuck's sake. Kill us.'

'He won't,' the Cat said. 'He's not the type. If you fire that thing, fat boy, we all die, not just me. If you do as I say and help me capture Paula, I might even overlook this little misdemeanour. Carry on, Alcinda,' she ordered.

Troblum sent an order into the dispenser's management array; its malmetal surface rippled, opening fifty small portals. 'No.'

Alcinda had taken one step towards him. Now she stopped again.

'Do it,' the Cat said.

'They don't understand,' Troblum said. 'It's not just the insert that helps you control them, they have hope. I don't. I know how stupid that is. I know you. You're probably one of the few people I actually do understand. That's why I turned my force field off. So there's no chance of me surviving the explosion. I know you're going to kill me no matter what. And we both know that I'll never get re-lifed even if the galaxy does survive. This is it for me, the end. Not just bodyloss, but real death. So I might as well do the human race a favour and take you with me.'

'What about Stubsy and the girls?' The Cat asked.

'Do it, you fucking bastard!' Stubsy screamed.

'Yes,' Alcinda growled. 'Take us—' Her body stiffened, her back arching convulsively. Her spine bent so far Troblum thought it might snap. She clamped her hands to her head, elegant fingernails clawing long bloody streaks in her scalp as she tried to tear out the source of her agony. She screamed silently as her legs gave out.

'Let's not confuse the issue with other people's poor advice,' the Cat said lightly. 'You still think you can get out of this, otherwise you would have fired the zone killer straight away. What's the deal?'

'I don't know,' Troblum said. 'I don't have a tactical program.

This doesn't have a logical outcome. I'm just waiting for you to do something scary, then I fire it. We both die together.' He stared at Alcinda, who was writhing helplessly on the floor. Things like furry mushrooms were emerging from her eyes, mouth, and ears; then another one bloomed from her belly button. They began to spread wide, swelling.

The Cat laughed. 'Oh, darling, you are delectable. I'm the only person you understand, and because of that you're going to kill yourself. How about you walk out the door and rush into your starship while I wait here for Paula?'

Troblum couldn't stop staring at Alcinda, who had begun to shake in a convulsive fit. Her head was now half-covered in the furry growths, with additional ones pushing out around the edges of her bikini bottoms. Tiny clear fluid drops glistened at the tip of each strand of fur. The shaking grew more violent. Troblum was seriously considering trying to kill her with a disruptor pulse if his biononics could put one together. 'I'd never make it to the stairs,' he said, trying desperately to focus on what the Cat was saying. Alcinda's death would be a mercy, and she'd definitely have a secure memory store and re-life insurance. 'Stubsy's other companions would make sure of that.'

The Cat made a small gesture with her hand. Alcinda stopped shuddering, her body collapsing limply to the rock floor. 'See. If that's all you're worried about, the girls are easily disposed of.'

Troblum thought he was going to collapse himself. A stricken Somonie was gazing at Alcinda's body. The grey fur continued to spread outward. He'd never seen anyone die before, and certainly not in such a terrible fashion. 'Don't do that,' Troblum gasped.

'Why? I thought you were going to kill us all, anyway.'

Troblum began to accept that he really was going to die. In a way it was kind of fitting that he would do it eliminating one of the most horrifying human beings who'd ever existed.

The villa nodes abruptly came on, flashing a short encrypted message he couldn't decode. He tried to use them to reconnect to his starship, but they wouldn't acknowledge his u-shadow.

'She's here,' the Cat snarled happily. 'Was this why you were stalling, my dear? I thought she wasn't due for another couple of hours.'

'Sorry,' Troblum said. He couldn't help grinning.

'I won't let her save you, darling.' The Cat brought an arm up, bulging through the aurora.

'You can go,' Troblum said quickly.

'What?'

'Go. Have your battle. If anyone can defeat you, it'll be Paula. I'll wait down here. Leave Somonie to guard me if you want. I can't get a message out to warn Paula. If you win I'll fire the zone killer. If she wins, well, you don't get to call the shots then, do you?'

'Clever boy,' the Cat said in an admiring tone. 'I accept. Stubsy, get up. You're going to have to be the bait now Troblum isn't playing.'

'No!' Stubsy howled. His body jerked madly, and he scrambled to his feet as if the floor had turned white hot. Troblum didn't like to dwell on that idea.

'Do it, you almighty shit,' Stubsy cried at Troblum. 'Kill us all. Kill *her*.'

'Tut tut,' said the Cat. 'Is that gratitude?'

Stubsy's mouth slammed shut. A trickle of blood dribbled down from the corner of his lip.

'Somonie, you stay here,' the Cat instructed as she walked out of the chamber. Stubsy Florac hobbled after her, throwing one last desolate glance at Troblum. Somonie stood in the doorway as the malmetal contracted shut, framing her with a dark circle.

'I'm sorry,' Troblum told her. She didn't say anything, though he could see her jaw muscles working silently.

The Cat must be remote controlling her, he guessed, which didn't leave him much time. Then he noticed the way her eyes kept switching from him to Alcinda's body. The vile grey growth had covered her flesh completely; now it was starting to spread across the floor, sending out fronds that moved like a spilled liquid.

Troblum activated his integral force field again, and hurried across the chamber until he came to the longest case in his collection. He was sure he heard some kind of bang from outside, maybe more than one, but the door was an effective seal and he didn't want to turn off his force field again. Paula must have arrived at the villa itself.

He had to use biononic reinforcement for his muscles so that he could lift the elongated cylinder out of its cradle mountings. The weapon was incredibly heavy, but then designers of the old Moscow-class warships didn't have to worry about mass. He just managed to lever it vertical, feeling like some pre-history knight hoisting up a lance. The cylinder's tip was barely a couple of centimetres from the cavern roof, wavering as he fought to keep it steady. There was no guarantee its ancient components would hold together if he switched it on; nor was he convinced his integral force field would withstand either a malfunction explosion or a successful discharge. But the Cat had eliminated certainty from his life, he was flying on logic and fatality now.

He looked directly at Somonie, whose right eyelid flickered. For the second time in a day Troblum didn't need a program to interpret a human emotion. He nodded back, and fired the ship-to-ship neutron laser.

For Paula it really hadn't been difficult to discover who was Troblum's ally on Sholapur. Troblum's clandestine money transfers had been subject to forensic accounting by an office at the Commonwealth Senate Treasury ever since Justine reported on his strangely empty hangar at Daroca spaceport. The Treasury office had quickly determined that Stubsy Florac's accounts had been the beneficiary of a great deal of money over the years, and ANA Security had accumulated a large file on the dealer's activities. An irritant rather than any kind of threat, Florac moved objects around the Commonwealth, which he had no legal right to do. The majority were basically harmless like Troblum's War relics, though he did supply weapons to agitator groups. As far as ANA knew he didn't involve himself with any Factions or their agents. Despite what he liked to imagine, Stubsy was very small-time in relation to the real political and economic subversives operating on the edges of Commonwealth society.

So she arrived in her ship, the *Alexis Denken*, a day before the agreed meeting. Descended through the atmosphere in stealth mode at night, easily evading the sensor sweeps run by Ikeo's defence system, and sank under the water twenty miles away from Florac's villa. When she arrived just offshore, she was interested to find the wreckage of a high-performance glide-boat resting on the sand close to Florac's charming white-sand beach. An examination by sensorbots showed it had been cut apart by a disruptor pulse. Paula guessed that she wasn't the only one who wanted to meet the elusive Troblum. It would be difficult for a Faction to intercept calls to ANA:Governance security, but hardly impossible. And Troblum had promised to divulge what he considered important activity concerning the Accelerators. Ilanthe would inevitably send a representative to intercept him. Possibly even Marius himself. Paula would enjoy arresting him, though he would probably self-destruct before he allowed any such humiliating indignity to prevail.

Five small passive sensor remotes slipped out of the sea to take up position on various high points around the estate, and she settled down to wait. Her piano slid out of its padded storage alcove; three hundred years old, made out of fiwood that glimmered with a soft red-brown sheen in the cabin's subdued lighting. The instrument had been handcrafted in a workshop on Lothian by a Higher artisan who'd taken a hundred and fifty years to perfect his craft, exceeding even the quality of Earth's legendary piano makers. Paula had commissioned it new, and the lush sound was well worth the ninety-year waiting list.

She sat at the velvet stool, pulled the sheet music out, and once again tried to play 'Für Elise'. Her trouble was the lack of practice time. It would be all too easy to use a music program linked with a dexterity function. But Paula wanted to be able to play the piece *properly*. A piano as beautiful as this one deserved that level of respect and commitment. Fingers ruled by a program would be no better than simply playing a recording.

Curious native fish nosing round the unusual ovoid resting on the sandy seabed were subjected to the ancient melody repeated dozens of times, interrupted, and begun again with relentless determination.

A day later, when she was playing with a lot more confidence, Paula had to admit Troblum's ship was extremely well shielded. She was caught off guard by the large figure in a shabby old toga suit riding a small scooter out of the forest on the far side of the Florac estate. None of her sensors had caught the *Mellanie's Redemption* coming down out of orbit. Her fingers hung motionless above keys of vat-grown ivory as she waited to see what would happen.

The scooter stopped just outside the estate boundary posts. It wobbled oddly as Troblum opened a link to Florac. Then the perimeter disarmed, and Troblum flew on unsteadily to the villa.

Soon after he arrived at the front door and went inside, a force field came on over the villa. The leading edge of the monsoon had arrived.

Troblum called ANA:Governance security division, who relayed the call to Paula. Her remote sensors couldn't quite get close enough to the villa boundary to give her a clear image of him standing beside the pool, but she could certainly see the line of exotic yellow and green flowering plants that hedged in the one open side of the pool area as she talked to him. She didn't lie. She would definitely be at the villa within two hours.

Paula told the smartcore to retract the piano back into its alcove, climbed into her armour, activated three of the combatbots stowed in the starship's forward hold, and stepped out through the airlock. The suit's regrav lifted her straight to the surface, emerging into driving rain as the heavy storm clouds raced overhead. She flew in a low fast curve to the top of the cliff above the white beach, landing beside one of the estate boundary's silver pillars. The three combatbots hovered protectively overhead, difficult to detect in the deluge. Lightning flashed constantly. Sensors locked on to her, and the villa's smartcore demanded she identify herself.

'You are expecting me. I am Paula Myo, an ANA representative on official business. Let me in now.'

There was no reply. The boundary posts remained active, so she used a proton laser to kill the eight nearest to her. Her suit flew her towards the villa, keeping five metres above the ground. Ahead of her, the force field was hardening. She curved around until she was facing the open end of the three-sided building. Water rippled down the force field, blurring direct visual observation. However, she saw three Amazon-like women in bikinis hurrying round the pool to take up positions behind the waterfall boulders. The small intelligence file on Florac had mentioned the kind of bodyguards he favoured.

'Oh, *come on*,' she muttered. They weren't even wearing armour. Stupid amateurs.

Their formation was a standard one, protecting access to the centre of the villa. Paula guessed that would be where their boss was cowering, along with Troblum.

Two of the combatbots dropped a flock of energy-dumps onto the top of the villa's force field dome. The small dark spheres skidded and slithered down the curve. Bright energy flares whipped out around each contact point, and the dumps began to slow as if the dome had somehow become tacky. Lightning flashed out from the clouds overhead, attracted by the brawny spray of ions fizzing out from each dump to slam into the force field. The darkness surrounding the dumps began to expand and slowly sink through the force field, which was now sparkling a dangerous stressed crimson.

Hot, steaming water began to seep through the force field to splatter the pool area. The villa's protective force field shone like a red dwarf sun that was being eaten by black cancers. Paula's full field function scan was burning its way through the faltering dome. She could make out several weapons enrichments powering up in the Amazon women. But there was no sign of Troblum.

'Where are you?' she muttered. Another heavily enriched human was moving slowly inside the villa. Hard to pinpoint with the tormented force field still obstinately functional. Her field function still couldn't locate Troblum, he must be deeper inside, possibly underground.

Lightning lashed down again. The combatbots added three proton laser strikes to the impact. It was too much. The force field collapsed in a devastating sonic shockwave that ripped the pool plants to shreds, sending a plume of smouldering leaves cascading up into the sodden sky. Windows burst apart, flinging long shards of glass across the paving slabs.

Paula swooped into the pool area as the downpour saturated the villa. The Amazon women fired a barrage of X-ray lasers and disruptor pulses at her. Jelly gun shots slashed harmlessly across her armour's force field. She was puzzled by that. Surely Stubsy or whoever had blown apart the glide boat had stronger weapons that this?

'Deactivate your enrichments right now,' Paula commanded. The combatbots streaked through the deluge towards the women. Two of them fired at the hulking bots as they withdrew back into the villa. Paula pushed a disruptor pulse into one of the waterfall boulders just as the one in the bright green bikini left it to scamper through a ruined patio door. The boulder detonated into thousands of fragments which embedded themselves in the villa walls. 'Halt,' she yelled. But the women scattered inside what she took to be a long lounge. Again they were in a defensive formation. 'Troblum, come out. I'm here at your invitation for heaven's sake.'

Another fusillade of energy shots hammered into her force field. Dazzling purple static webs roared out from the impact points, vaporizing the rain pouring down her shoulders. Paula sighed, it was going to be difficult to neutralize the stupid women without damaging them. Her field function swept through the villa. The enriched person she'd spotted before was creeping along the back of the room the women were protecting. She still couldn't locate Troblum.

'Enough of this,' Paula decided. The armour's regrav lifted her off the ground, starting to power her forward. She fired a disruptor pulse, blasting apart the wall in front of her and half of the roof above, opening up the lounge. A cascade of debris came tumbling down along with the rain. The women dived for cover, immediately reorganizing their fire pattern.

The sensor remotes outside the villa reported something approaching the estate through the torrent of rain. A large craft, keeping very low, flying the same route as Troblum's scooter out of the forest. *His starship*. Paula slowed abruptly, uncertain of the ship's ability.

In front of her, yellow and purple petals of exotic energy erupted from the floor of the lounge. Eight of them, curving up like the jaws of some vicious predator. They swept past barely a metre from her armour, clashing together to form a broad column. It began to twist, the petals separating out again, stretching out towards her, elongating *fast*.

Paula's suit regrav shoved at her violently, pushing her backwards as she gasped in shock. She and the three combatbots unleashed a torrent of firepower at the base of the exotic energy manifestation. Trying to kill the generator. The tip of exotic energy stroked the front of her armour's force field. Weird warning symbols erupted across her exovision.

The ground exploded upwards.

Paula was flung high into the air above the villa, spinning out of control. For a second she thought she'd punctured the exotic energy generator. But the yellow spectres were still leaping around like flames in a hurricane. They lasted for a second before snuffing out.

Paula stabilized her tumbling flight fifty metres above the villa. When her sensors swept the scene below, she saw a huge crater had completely ruptured one side of the building. It was twenty metres wide, with walls of raw smouldering earth. The bottom was open, leading into some underground space. Twisted metallic wreckage lay everywhere.

'Get here now,' Paula ordered the *Alexis Denken*. She directed the three combatbots to attack the coordinate of the exotic energy generator. A lethal barrage of disruptor pulses and proton lasers lashed down, illuminating the broken villa with an incandescent nimbus far brighter than the lightning flaring overhead.

Paula was dropping fast now, anxious to escape any possible contact with the exotic energy. She'd been lucky before, but that generator was quite capable of caging her, suit and all. Someone was scrambling up out of the crater. Her field scan showed her a large person. Higher, with an integral force field that was barely functional.

'Troblum,' she broadcast.

He stumbled to a halt at the top of the crater. Head swinging round as if he were drunk.

The *Alexis Denken* broke surface and accelerated hard. Ten combatbots shot out of its forward hold to add their protective cover. And another craft was suddenly streaking in towards the villa at mach nine, slicing round the low surrounding hills in a cacophony of brutalized air.

Paula touched down on a patch of muddy soil that minutes before had been a pleasant herbaceous border. The first starship had reached the crater, its profile a classic rocketship cone with eight radial forward-swept tailfins. Its nose dipped down towards Troblum, an airlock irising open.

'Stop,' Paula told him. Then her field function showed her another figure emerging out of the ground into the ruins of Florac's villa. This one was glowing white, completely impervious to any field scan. Paula instinctively ignored Troblum, knowing she was now confronting the real threat. They faced each other across the steaming remains of the swimming pool.

The *Alexis Denken* came thundering through the monsoon surrounded by its entourage of combatbots. It halted behind Paula, hovering a couple of metres off the ground, and extended its force field to envelop her. Enough firepower to vaporize a medium-sized city focused on the lambent figure standing calmly inside the shattered walls. Troblum vanished inside his starship's airlock, and the craft swung through ninety degrees to point at the storm clouds. Then the third starship arrived. Paula expected it to fire on Troblum's ship. But instead it took up position behind the white figure, mirroring Paula and the *Alexis Denken*. Troblum's ship accelerated upwards at twenty-five gees. The *Alexis Denken* reported a great deal of powerful weapon systems in the interloper's starship were powered up.

'Marius, is that you?' Paula asked.

The white figure pointed. Somehow Stubsy Florac had survived the carnage. He was crawling over the smashed wooden floorboards, blood seeping from dozens of lacerations.

'Damn it,' Paula hissed. If she slugged it out with her opponent the outcome was uncertain. ANA had equipped her well, but the Faction whose representative she was obviously facing had a pretty formidable arsenal, too. If she won, she'd never know who was challenging her, and through her ANA, so brazenly. There would be nothing left of the vanquished except a dispersing ion swarm. And whoever won, it would mean the certain bodyloss of Stubsy Florac, and probably his death. There might even be more survivors hidden in the villa's wreckage; he did have several of the stupid Amazon bodyguards. Despite all the traits and qualities she had cast off over the centuries, her certainty of right and wrong remained absolute. She, Paula Myo, did not have the right to put civilians in danger, even civilians as repugnant as Florac. Her place in the universe was to uphold the law. However inconvenient Florac was at this moment, she could not risk allowing him to come in harm's way.

In any case, Florac would be a valuable witness. An opponent such as a Faction was best dealt with by ANA, not herself and a representative clashing in this fashion.

She stood still, staring at the cold glowing figure on the other side of the pool. Her field scan probed at the lustrous force field, but couldn't find a single flaw. One thing: it wasn't Marius – too short.

The white figure was drawn up into its starship. A hand was raised in a mocking wave. A silly wiggle of the hips and then the airlock closed, cutting off the shining aurora. The starship slid smoothly into the storm clouds, creating a dark whorl as it vanished into the stratosphere. Paula used the sensors on the *Alexis Denken* to track it as far as possible. The stealth effect came on when it was clear of the ionosphere. There was a minute quantum signature which the smartcore could just detect as it accelerated high above the equator, then it must have dropped into hyperspace. The finest sensors ANA could devise picked up a tiny disturbance among the quantum fields which indicated an ultradrive. Then there was nothing.

Paula put her lips together and whistled a long single note. The combatbots hovering above the villa showed her Stubsy Florac writhing in agony on his decimated wooden flooring. She hurried over in time to see strange grey growths blooming from his mouth and nose.

Her u-shadow opened a link directly to his macrocellular clusters. 'Florac? Can you receive this?'

The furry grey substance was emerging from his eyes.

'Who was it, Florac? Do you know who did this?'

The only reply that came down the link was a burst of white noise.

'Okay, I'm getting you into a medical chamber. My ship has the best in the Commonwealth. You'll be fine.' She picked him up and flew straight into the airlock, ordering the smartcore to initiate level one decontamination procedures. She *really* didn't like the look of the grey fungal stuff.

'Hang on in there, Florac, you'll be okay. You stay with me, understand?'

It only took her a few seconds to get to the cabin, but he was convulsing by the time she lowered him into the coffin-sized medical chamber. The steel-sheen malmetal top closed fluidly over him.

A scan revealed that the grey substance had invaded his entire body, consuming and corrupting every organ. It had twined itself round his nerves, not damaging them, but embracing them. Paula watched the read-outs in disgust and dismay as the intruder fed a continuous stream of impulses into every nerve fibre in Florac's body. Fronds inside his brain stimulated selected neural pathways to ensure his consciousness remained intact.

There wasn't enough of his original flesh left for the medical chamber to sustain. As Paula watched, Florac died in as much agony as it was possible for a human nervous system to conduct.

'Extract his memorycell,' she ordered the medical chamber. But even that wasn't possible, the grey fronds had gnawed away at the memorycell, breaking it apart. She reviewed the read-outs with growing alarm. The grey stuff seemed to be some kind of biononic viral, capable of breaking down both organic and inorganic compounds. It was already seeping into the instruments and manipulators interfaced with Florac's body, transforming them into more of itself, an effect inching into the casing of the medical chamber.

'Hell!' she grunted. The *Alexis Denken* shot out of the atmosphere to an altitude of five thousand kilometres, then ejected the entire medical chamber. It tumbled away from the starship, sunlight glinting off its bright metal and plastic surfaces. Paula swept a powerful gamma-ray laser through it several times, making sure every molecule of the viral was disassociated, then finished it off with a single disruptor pulse. The now white-hot slag of the medical chamber burst apart in a sparkling swarm of effervescence.

Several ground-based sensor systems locked on to the *Alexis Denken*. The smartcore received identification demands from every city on the planet. Paula simply ignored them, and flew back down to the villa again.

The combatbots were circling overhead as the monsoon continued to soak the rubble. Long rivulets gurgled along the cracked paving, thick with scum and powdery mud. Paula's armour boots splashed through them as she made her way cautiously to the crater. The torn earth walls were mildly radioactive. Spybots swooped down to scan the remnants of the underground chamber. The first thing they detected amidst all the charred plastic and warped metal was the burned body. It appeared to be another of Florac's bodyguards. Then they picked up the signature of the grey substance. There was a patch clinging to a chunk of fractured rock. Its edges rippled as it sought to grow.

'Damnit,' Paula swore. There was nothing for it. She called two of the combatbots down, and began a systematic sterilization of the site using gamma-lasers. That was when she called ANA. 'Things are getting a little crazy out here,' she confessed.

'The Accelerators must be desperate to keep Troblum silenced.'

'No. That's not what happened here.' Paula was standing in the remnants of the lounge, using her field scan on the broken fragments of the exotic matter generator. There wasn't much left, and she was fairly certain her own firepower hadn't been wholly responsible. It had self-destructed at some point during the fight. 'Whoever was here could have eliminated him the second he turned up. They didn't. They wanted to use him as bait for me. This exotic matter system was intended to capture me. It's an extremely elaborate trap. Someone went to a lot of trouble. I got lucky Troblum's ship arrived when it did, another second and I would have been engulfed.'

'You have acquired a great many enemies over the years.'

'Yes, but this one has the backing of a Faction. They had an ultradrive ship effectively equal to the *Alexis Denken*, they had this revolting viral, and they knew I was coming to meet with Troblum. Logically, they must be allied with the Accelerators, yet they didn't eliminate Troblum. Who would the Accelerators possibly turn to at this point, who then wouldn't do what they needed most and silence Troblum? It's not logical. This person certainly doesn't seem to have any moral qualms about killing anyone. And I was obviously intended for the torture chamber, or some variant.' Even as she said it, a really bad feeling was growing in her mind. She remembered that ridiculous wiggle which the glowing white figure had performed as it ascended into the starship. There was certainly one person who would fit the bill – but that wasn't possible. *She* was very definitely in suspension, and had been for over nine hundred years. Of course, if anyone had the ability to break her out, it would be a Faction . . . 'They wouldn't dare,' she whispered. But the Accelerators were becoming increasingly arrogant. And they had been planning their moves for decades.

'What do you intend next?' ANA asked.

Paula stared round at the rain-sodden area as the lightning flickered again. 'I need a full forensic examination here. It's a long shot, but if there's anything that will tell us where the exotic matter cage was built and by whom, I need to know.'

'I will dispatch a team immediately.'

'Thank you. I'm going to investigate Troblum a little closer. I need to work out where he's gone. There's nothing else I can do until Oscar snags the Second Dreamer for us.'

'As you wish.'

Paula looked up into the wild clouds, wishing she could see the stars. 'Any change on the devourment phase?'

'Not yet.'

'Will you be able to survive it?'

'I don't know. What will you do?'

'Ultimately? If it can't be stopped. I'm not sure. The *High Angel* will take me to another galaxy if I want. But right now we need to prevent our dear species from making things any worse.'

*

Araminta didn't sleep the whole night long. How could she?

No, she'd said.

No to the Skylord. No to the entity that was offering to guide a goodly portion of humanity to what they regarded as their nirvana.

No. Said because: *I'm the Second Dreamer.*

It's me. Me!

Oh, Ozzie, please help me. This simply cannot be.

Me, she kept turning that over and over. *How could it be me?* Because of some distant ancestor she'd never even heard of until the other day, this Mellanie and her friendship with the Silfen. All that, all those unknowns from centuries ago had come pressing down on her, had taken away her destiny, her self-determination. Fate had chosen her.

Me!

And now the millions, the billions, of Living Dream followers would look to her to help them join with the Skylord. And she'd said no.

The Skylord had been surprised. Shocked, even. She'd felt that wounded astonishment linger as she withdrew her mind from contact. That wasn't an answer which fitted its reality. She might just as well have said no to gravity for all the sense it made.

What she'd done terrified her. But it was instinctive. She didn't want to be the Second Dreamer. Just hours before the contact she'd decided her future after days of soul-searching and self-discovery. She was going to be Mrs Bovey(s). She was going to get herself more bodies and become multiple. And they'd live here in this grand house, or a new one she'd build, equally delightful. And half of their bodies would be in bed together the whole time. She would make him as happy as he made her. And the future would be bright and lovely and full of promise. There might be children. What kind of children did multiples have? Did he want them? They'd never talked about any of this yet. So much was waiting for her out there in the years to come, so many discoveries. So much joy.

Of course she'd said no. What else could she say?

I will not be a part of that. That is not me.

Billions wanted it to be. They were going to insist.

But they will never know who I am. I will never talk to the Skylord again.

That was the decision she'd made when dawn came to the sky outside the bedroom. She was wretchedly tired, and shaking. There were dried tears on her cheeks from the quiet sobbing in the lonely hours as gentle rain had pattered against the window. But she knew her mind now. She would stand firm.

47

On the big bed beside her the blond teenage Mr Bovey lay on his back with a slight frown, mouth twitching as he dealt with a sour dream.

Nothing as bad as mine, she told him silently. He too would never know, she decided, the burden would be too much. *This will end. Eventually. I will endure and ride it out.*

Araminta bent over and kissed the youthful body. Gently at first. On his brow. His cheek. His mouth.

He stirred. The frown eased away. She smiled at that, and kissed his throat. Her hands caressed the supple muscle on his chest as the melange program rose out of her lacunas. Her raging thoughts stilled as she breathed slowly and carefully, following her own deep rhythms to achieve the composure she sought. Now she could concentrate fully on the body beside her.

For the full hour which followed there were no distractions, no external thoughts and doubts. It was so good to forget Skylords and Second Dreamers and Living Dream, replacing them with good dirty human sex.

'Forgive me, especially after this morning, but you don't look so good,' Mr Bovey said.

Araminta nodded grudgingly as she finally climbed out of the big bath. It was such a luxury just lounging in oiled, scented water rather than snatching a quick minute in a spore shower. One her poor body deserved. 'Your fault,' she teased. She couldn't quite put the right emphasis behind it. Her thoughts were drifting back to the revelations of last night with the surety of a tide.

It was the young Celtic one who handed her a huge towel. 'Are you all right? You're not having second thoughts?'

'Ozzie, no! This is the only truly good decision I've made. Probably ever.'

He smiled proudly, but couldn't completely hide his worry. 'You seem . . . troubled. I'm concerned.'

She started to rub the water off her legs. 'It's been a big week.

I'm all right, just didn't sleep well, that's all. I'll take some kind of pep infuser when I get home.'

'Home?' he frowned.

'I've still got to get the apartments finished. We both know I need the money.'

'Right.' He scratched at his hair, looking perplexed. Araminta wasn't used to that. Whenever they had serious conversations Mr Bovey always preferred to use his middle-aged black-skinned body, the one she'd had their very first date with, who almost qualified as the father figure. She never had worked out if that was deliberate on his part.

'Look,' he said. 'I hate to be the one with the bad news, but you clearly haven't accessed the unisphere this morning.'

Just the way he said it made her heart sink. She had told her u-shadow to suspend any unisphere contact before they went to bed last night; now it reconnected her and began pulling out priority news items. 'Oh, great Ozzie,' she gasped. It was all there. The invasion by Ellezelin forces down by the docks. Paramilitary troops moving across the city. Large capsules patrolling the skies, halting any civilian traffic.

When she rushed over to the window she could make out several of the capsules floating passively above the River Cairns, insidious dark ovoids set against the dusky dawn-lit clouds. Colwyn's weather-protection force field was on, covering the entire city. It wasn't any storm the invaders were interested in, they were preventing any capsules from leaving.

And worse, much much worse, the message from Director Trachtenberg at Centurion Station about the Void starting to expand. A devourment phase all the commentators were calling it. And they were equally clear that it was the fault of the Second Dreamer for rejecting the Skylord. No such thing as coincidence was the phrase that kept reverberating round her head. Everyone was using it.

'I can't stay here,' Araminta moaned.

'You're not serious? It's dangerous out there. They're restricting the reports, but our fellow citizens are not taking this lightly. There's been several clashes already, and it's not even breakfast time yet.'

They're here for me, she realized. *A whole world invaded, violated because of me. Ozzie, forgive me.*

'I'll just go straight home,' she said stubbornly. 'I have to get to the apartments. They're all I've got, you can see that, can't you?' She felt shabby saying that, it was emotional bullying, but all she wanted to do was get away from him. It was completely wrong, this was the person she was planning to marry, hes should be trusted. She just couldn't risk trusting him with something of this magnitude. He'd agreed to marry a girl struggling to make it as a property developer, not some walking galactic catastrophe.

'I do understand,' he said, so very reluctantly. 'But they've shut down all the capsule traffic. Half of mes are stuck all across town.'

Araminta started to pull her clothes on. There was a whole closet in the bathroom which was hers, so at least she could dress practically with dark jeans and a blue sweater. 'My trike pod is in the garage. I left it here a couple of weeks back.' Her u-shadow was hurriedly checking travel restrictions in Colwyn City. The traffic management net carried a full proscription on non-official air vehicles, backed by the certificate of the Mayor's office and the Viotia Federal Transport Agency. However, ground vehicles were still permitted to operate in the city precincts, with an advisory caution that citizens should only use them for essential trips. There were a great many links to official Viotia government bulletins about their inclusion in the Free Trade Zone at core planet level, and how after a brief transition period everything would return to normal and a strong economic growth phase would begin, bringing a major upswing to everyone's lifestyle. Just for an instant she recalled Likan and his grand plans for the Free Trade Zone, but she dismissed those thoughts at once.

'Let some of mes go,' Mr Bovey said. 'I can check the place over for you.'

'I am not going to start our life together by being dependent on you,' she said, hating herself now.

He looked even more unhappy. 'All right. Ozzie, but you're obdurate.'

'Think of it as tenacious, and how that works in your favour in bed.'

'Ozzie help the paramilitaries if they get in your way.' But his sympathetic smile wasn't exactly wholehearted. 'I don't suppose one of mes can come with you?'

'Have you got a ground vehicle?' she asked.

'No.'

'You're really sweet. Still want to marry me?'

'Yes.'

'Even when there's going to be many mes?'

'Just take care.'

There was a whole team of hims assembled to wave goodbye to her when she clambered on to the trike pod. She was mildly surprised to find the power cell still had half a charge left. All his familiar faces wore the same mournful expression as she waved airily. Then she set off down the narrow gravel track which cut through the grounds to the road outside. There was a point when she'd just passed the last of hims when she thought her resolution might buckle and send her rushing back, confessing everything. It was coupled with a horror that she'd never see him again, that no matter her determination this was all too big for her to cope with.

If that's so, then I can't drag him down into it.

So she kept the trike steady and true, riding across the garden that retained its light coating of glistening moisture from last night's rain. The old iron gate at the end of the track creaked as its actuators swung it open for her. Then she was out on the empty road lined with tall lackfol trees whose reddish-green leaves were chittering in the gentle breeze that stirred under the city's force field dome.

The worst part of the trip was riding over the big single-arch bridge to the northern bank. She felt horribly exposed to the big capsules that slid through the air on either side of the bridge. It was so strange seeing the city without its normal capsule traffic zipping about, as if the metropolis was injured somehow. People on the bridge seemed to share the feeling. Many citizens had decided to walk to work, showing their defiance through an obstinate insistence on pursuing their normal day as best they could. Public cabs still hummed along the central rails, packed tight with commuters. And she'd never known so many people actually had trike pods; a great many of them clearly hadn't been outside their garages for years.

As she cleared the apex of the long bridge, Araminta allowed herself to dip into the local gaiafield, receiving the strident emotions of her fellow residents, the determination and anger they radiated and supported each other with. It was a buoyant kinship; though she didn't dare allow any of her own feelings to trickle out. She was all too conscious of people like Danal delving into the confluence nests, trying to locate any hint of her thoughts, her location, her identity. And how was that for irony, one of her hunters buying an apartment from her, actually living next door to his prey, neither of them knowing. She wondered if he'd be able to scent the guilt on her.

Ahead of her she could see three capsules hovering over the far end of the bridge. Dozens of the suited paramilitaries were clustered there, examining everyone coming over. She almost turned around there and then, but that would draw attention to her. And they'd be watching the whole bridge for such a reaction, she was sure of that. So she pressed on, wondering what that ancestor Mellanie would do: she who'd bequeathed so much trouble into Araminta's easy life. Was she some kind of tough government agent, a War hero; why was she a Silfen friend? Araminta promised herself that when she got back to the apartments the first thing she'd do was look up the woman whose fault this all was.

The paramilitaries were simply standing waiting in intimidating ranks, holding long rifles across their chests as everyone from the bridge walked or drove past them. The unisphere nodes at the end of the bridge were querying u-shadows. Araminta sent her identity certificate, looking nervously at the bulky figures, wondering what their faces looked like. They were sharing nothing with the gaiafield, which was strange for anyone affiliated with Living Dream must surely have gaiamotes. Were they nervous? They must know an entire planet hated them.

Whatever smartcore the Living Dream forces were using to try and identify the Second Dreamer didn't seem unduly interested in Araminta. None of the paramilitaries showed any interest in her as the trike trundled past them. Just on the other side, a group of local youths was gathering. Shouts echoed through the damp air, directed at the paramilitaries. Several marques of construction site bot waddled and rolled towards the dark ranks, waving power tools threateningly and leaking miscreant programs that blocked and distorted the cybersphere nodes.

By the time she was a hundred metres along Gathano Avenue past the bridge, the paramilitary squad commander finally took action against the taunts and belligerent bots. The shouting increased in volume and anger, interspaced with the unpleasant high-pitched *humm* of energy weapons directed at the bots. Araminta increased her speed as a pair of capsules swept overhead to reinforce their colleagues. The last thing she could afford now was to be taken into custody.

By the time she reached her apartments in the Bodant district forty minutes later, the number of people milling round in the park outside was disturbing. She knew she was being prejudiced, but most of them looked like the kind of gang members which the unisphere news always claimed had a stranglehold on the neighbouring Helie district. When she allowed their gaiafield emissions to register, she found an atmosphere of dark resentment swirling across the park, more frightening than the anger of the commuters. There was purpose here. Violence wasn't far away.

She steered the trike down into the underground garage, thankful for the dual gate security, then took the lift up. When the doors opened on the fourth floor Araminta prayed that Danal and Mareble were either out or wouldn't hear her crossing the vestibule – how good had she made the sound proofing? The Living Dream followers had only moved in two days ago, declaring they could no longer wait until the official completion date, which left her with a load of work to finish for them before the full price was deposited in her account. *Not today!*

The door of the apartment she was using closed behind her and she pressed her back up against it, as if reinforcing the charming old-fashioned brass lock. Breath hissed out of her in a sorrowful gasp, and she slowly slid down onto the parquet floor.

I can just stay here. I don't need to go out. I can get nutrient fluid for the culinary unit pumped in. I can work on getting the last two apartments finished. By the time that's done all this will have blown over.

Except for the Void expansion phase. But the Raiel will fight that, that's what the unisphere shows say.

It was a pitiful delusion, she knew.

Maybe thirty minutes later Cressida called. Just seeing her icon appear cheered Araminta up no end. If anyone knew what to do it would be Cressida. And maybe, just maybe, she could tell her cousin about being the Second Dreamer.

'Darling, how are you? Where are you?'

'I'm okay, thanks, I'm at the apartments.'

'Oh. I thought you were with Mr Bovey.'

'I was. I came home this morning.'

'You crossed the city yourself?'

'Yes. It wasn't any trouble. I used my trike pod.'

'Dear Ozzie, that was stupid, darling. You're not to do anything like that again, do you understand. I mean it. Life is about to get very ugly here. I've been talking with my contacts in City Hall and the state government house. These Living Dream bastards are not going to go home. Viotia has been royally screwed by our crap-for-brains Prime Minister.'

'Yes. I know,' she said weakly.

'And the worst place for anyone to be right now is Colwyn City. They think that dickhead the Second Dreamer is living here. And there's no way he'll escape. They've broken just about every single article of the Commonwealth constitution by invading us, they're not going to stop now. Do you know who've they've sent to oversee the search?'

'No.'

'Well don't tell anyone, but Cleric Phelim himself has come through the wormhole to take charge.'

'Who's that?'

'Oh, darling, keep up! He's Ethan's chief of staff, the enforcer himself. A greater turd you will not meet, and I include your old chum Likan in that list.'

'Oh, great Ozzie.' Araminta drew her knees up to her chin and hugged her legs tight.

'Sorry, darling, didn't mean to worry you excessively. We'll be all right, of course. Which is actually why I'm calling. There's a way out, if you're interested.'

'What way out? The weather dome is on, no one can get out.'

'Ha, that just deters capsules. After all the damn thing is only there to protect us from clouds and wind, not ward off Ocisen Empire warships or the Void boundary. There's actually a big gap, well twenty metres anyway, between the lower edge of the dome and the ground to allow normal air flow. We'd all suffocate in a week without that.'

'So we can get through?'

'We can just walk out until they seal that up with their troops, yes. Even then there are various tunnels available if you know the right people. My u-shadow will send the files over for you. Anyway, the point is: some friends and I are chartering a starship. We're leaving completely, not just Colwyn but Viotia itself. There's a seat on it for you if you want, I'm holding it as part of our family's block booking.'

'Um . . . but Mr Bovey?'

'Darling, you'd need five starships to get all of hims off. Be realistic. And be sensible. In times like this you have to think about your own arse.'

'But they're not letting anyone out of the city, let alone offplanet.'

'You leave that to us. Anybody who believes Living Dream is some kind of irresistible force has clearly forgotten about lawyers. We're chartering a foreign-owned starship with full diplomatic status. If Phelim tries restricting that he'll find himself staring down a Commonwealth Navy warship disruptor cannon. Let's see who blinks first then.'

'I see.'

'So are you in or out?'

'I . . . I don't know.'

'There's one thing, darling, which I'm going to have to bring up. It won't be cheap. Where do you stand on selling the apartments?'

'Oh. Not good. I still don't have deposits on the last two, and I haven't completed any of the others. Nobody's going to buy anything now.'

'Yes, that is a problem. You didn't find that offload sucker like I told you then? Never mind. You should never underestimate the market when it comes to making things happen for a profit. Give it a day and there'll be venture groups on half the External worlds offering Viotia citizens cash for their business and properties; it'll be way below yesterday's market rate, but they'll be thinking long term. Once Living Dream grabs the Second Dreamer things will start to stabilize. Give it twenty years and everything will be back to normal, and those properties will be five times the value.'

'If it's going to be normal again, why are you leaving?'

'Normal for a Free Trade Zone hagiocracy planet, darling. Which I have no intention of spending the rest of my lives on, thank you very much. I want a nice liberal market-based democracy with all the opportunities for misunderstanding and conflict that entails. Wherever there's an argument you'll find us lawyers offering to help. And help equals lots of money. On which subject; I've already transferred my cash accounts offworld.'

'Already?'

'Certainly, darling; the banks were keen to welcome me. And I wasn't exactly the first. There's enough money flying offplanet right now to leave our beloved Prime Minister a magnificent economic nightmare by lunchtime, never mind tomorrow. The only thing she has left to worry about is how painful her bodyloss is going to be when her previously loyal voters get their hands on her. So – do you want me to see if I can offload your apartments for you? I have some finance seeker semisentients I can assign the problem to.'

'Um, yes. Yes, I suppose so.'

'Great, so I'll reserve that ticket for you.'

'Yes. Do that.' Araminta just said it without thinking. She didn't want to leave, but Cressida had to be placated somehow, and anything else might be suspicious. *Ozzie, it didn't take me long to become a paranoid schemer, did it?*

'Don't worry,' Cressida said. 'Ten days from now we'll be sipping cocktails on the pool terrace of La Cinal on Etinna. It'll be fun, a new beginning.'

The call ended, and Araminta stared at the semi-decorated open-plan living room in a mild daze. She couldn't believe that even Cressida could abandon her whole life with such casual ease. But then that was Cressida for you, thinking faster and smarter than anyone else. She'd probably run through the whole shock, anger, assessment, calculation, and action stages in the first hour; while Araminta was still firmly mired in the shock segment. Certainly she'd never thought what life on Viotia would be like after things settled down; and of course Cressida was right, they would be part of the Free Trade Zone for ever now. Unless the Senate and Navy intervened, or Viotia's residents organized a rebellion.

Or the Void devours us.

Whatever the future outcome, Cressida was right about one thing, Araminta couldn't just wait around hoping to avoid detection. She started to think what it must cost politically and economically to invade a planet. Cleric Conservator Ethan and his sidekick Phelim wouldn't do that and then just hope they'd stumble across the Second Dreamer. They'd have a plan. And it would be a good one.

Araminta forced herself to get to her feet. She didn't know what she was going to do, but doing nothing was not an option.

*

It took two hours, and a stint in the ship's medical chamber, but Troblum eventually stopped shaking. When he emerged he could barely manage to cover the couple of metres from the chamber to his big chair. He sank into its padding, fearful he would start trembling again. The medical read-out in his exovision showed him just how many drugs were coursing through his bloodstream right now, working in conjunction with his biononics to suppress his body's animal reactions. He had been *terrified*.

He was also rather surprised that he was still alive. All he could remember of the neutron laser shot was a dazzling flash, and a noise that was so great his bones had felt it rather than his ears. His biononics were still repairing his retinas and inner ears. How he staggered into the ship's airlock was some kind of miracle; the smartcore had to give him directions, telling him how to move every limb.

But he was alive, and almost intact. The smartcore had used sensors to follow the Cat's starship flying away from the villa, then vanishing. Her stealth systems were as good as his own if not better. He hadn't waited around to find out how good Paula's ship was, he'd simply stealthed up and dropped into hyperdrive. Now he was sitting in transdimensional suspension ten lightyears out from Sholapur.

'You were lucky,' Catriona Saleeb said.

'I know.' He glanced at the single item of his collection to survive. Mellanie Rescorai's handheld array lay on the decking where he'd dropped it. The foxory casing was blackened round the edges, the outline of his hand clearly visible. He closed his eyes and turned his head, making sure he was looking up at the ceiling before he opened his eyelids again. All of it, gone. The entire collection. Destroyed by his own hand. Every unique significant piece. It was as if history itself had been weakened.

'You won't be again,' Trisha Halgarth said, twirling a strand of Catriona's hair round her index finger as she nestled up against her friend. 'I'm surprised the Cat didn't finish you off.'

'I'm not,' Catriona said. 'She's going to come after you, Troblum. She's going to catch you. And then you'll die. It'll probably take several years.'

'Shut up!' he yelled. 'Shut up. Support me.'

'Okay,' Catriona said, she cuddled Trisha. 'You're not safe as long as the Cat is around.'

'And Paula didn't kill her off,' Trisha said, sounding vaguely puzzled. 'So you've got two options left.'

'Two?' he queried.

'Go after her yourself, and finish the job.'

'No! That's not an option. Only Paula can do that. She's still the only one I trust. I can't believe ANA is so compromised. That's got to be down to flaws in the unisphere which a Faction can manipulate.'

'Think on it,' Catriona said earnestly. 'The Cat is allied with the Accelerators, they gave her everything she wanted, ship, weapons, the lot; and somehow she knew where you'd be. You can't trust ANA, not any more. I certainly don't,' she added haughtily.

'It has to be the unisphere,' he said, more to himself than the girls. 'They intercepted my message.'

'Which only makes your position worse,' Trisha said. 'That leaves option two. Run! Run far and run fast. We've got to make it to another galaxy. *Mellanie's Redemption* can do it. You'll be safe there.'

'What if Living Dream is right and the Void works for them?' he asked. 'What if the Cat gets inside? What if she can manipulate it the way the Waterwalker did?'

The girls exchanged a look. Both pouted. 'What are you thinking?' Catriona asked.

'I should warn them,' Troblum said. 'Paula at least. She understands about the Cat. Paula knows she has to be stopped. Paula wouldn't give up.'

'So give her a call, and let's get out of here,' Catriona said.

Troblum couldn't help it, his gaze had dropped to Mellanie's array again. 'My collection is gone because of her. The damage.' Just thinking about it was threatening to send his body back into shock again. Medical read-outs edged back towards amber alerts. 'It was all I ever had,' Troblum wailed. He began to curl up, as much as he ever could, his belly squashing out across his upper legs. 'It took me centuries to collect them all. They were safe with me, I was their guardian.' He was sobbing so hard the words were virtually unintelligible. 'They were so precious, so valuable. They helped make us what we are, they were a part of our evolution. Why did nobody ever understand how important they were?'

'Troblum,' Tricia crooned. 'Poor Troblum.'

'There are other pieces,' Catriona said. 'Remember you visited the Smithsonian, they actually let you touch the *Charybdis*, the curator was so impressed with your own preservation work. She knew you were an equal. You see, so much still remains. And its legacy is for ever.'

'Not with her still alive,' he muttered darkly. His hand came up to wipe the moisture from his eyes. 'She is the destroyer. She is death. She is the Void: her.'

'Call Paula,' Tricia said urgently. 'Do it.'

'I have to know,' he whispered. 'I have to know we're safe. That she's dead for good. I can't live thinking she might appear behind me. That she'll take me, and . . . And . . .'

Catriona sighed. 'You can never know that.'

'Yes, I can.' He pushed himself up out of the chair, and walked to the back of the cabin. A small doorway expanded, and he squeezed himself through. An equally small companionway let

60

him through into the starboard midsection hold. There wasn't quite enough room for him to stand, he had to crouch, and hunch his shoulders up. No matter how he twisted, his worn toga suit always brushed against the stolen cargo. The little space was crammed with machinery, piled up at random like a cybernetic dragon hoard. One thousand three hundred and seventy-two components, Troblum recalled. He frowned, and picked up the first one. A hyperfield power manifold, a curving sliver of some substance that seemed to alternate between being crystal and metal. He knew what each component was, but there was no structure to the piles; everything had been shoved in at random as his commandeered bots had pilfered it from the Accelerator station's replicators.

So all he had to do was assemble it, start with the central units and slowly create the new machine in the correct sequence, then integrate it with the starship's existing hyperdrive, and he'd have a fully functional ultradrive ship, quite capable of flying to Andromeda, or beyond.

'Can you do it?' Catriona asked. Her head was poking through the hatchway, a dubious expression in place.

'It'll work,' Troblum said. 'In theory.' He couldn't even see the central units.

'Then what?'

'We'll have a genuine escape route. But I'm still going to contact Paula.'

'Through the unisphere?'

'No. I'm too frightened of the Accelerators' capability. They were the ones who set the Cat on me. Next time it'll be Marius, or someone else who isn't going to be distracted by an old grudge.'

'Then how are you going to get in touch?'

Troblum picked up a carbon-black icosahedron, trying to index it. 'There is one other person left that I trust implicitly. He's connected to Paula, or at least he was back during the War. I'll tell him what I know about the Accelerators. He can carry

61

the message to Paula. Maybe once ANA knows about the swarm it will stop the Accelerators. The Cat will be on her own then. That's when Paula can finish her.'

'Who?' Catriona asked. 'Who do you trust?'

'Oscar the Martyr.'

Inigo's Eighth Dream

Edeard awoke to the marvel of soft fingers caressing his abdomen. It was a lovely sensation matched to the warmth of the supple mattress, the touch of fresh cotton sheets, the fading blossom scent of Jessile's perfume. He smiled, his eyes still closed as he sighed a delighted welcome to the new day. A kiss fell on his cheek. Her nose nuzzled his ear. His smile widened, and the possessive hand slipped along his skin, past his belly button, and further yet. Jessile giggled.

'Now that's what I call rising to greet the dawn,' she murmured lecherously.

The other girl giggled as well.

Edeard's eyes snapped open. Memories came flooding back. Just to confirm them, Kristiana was lying on his other side watching him and Jessile with covetous intent, her flimsy white negligee far too small to contain her full figure even if the lace bows down the front had been fastened. He recalled how enjoyable it had been undoing those bows last night.

A weak 'Haaaa' was all Edeard could manage.

'Me first,' Jessile insisted, her sharp teeth emphasizing the claim on his earlobe.

Kristiana produced a reproving pout. 'Don't forget me, Waterwalker.'

Edeard couldn't answer. Jessile's kiss had now engulfed his mouth. He folded his arms around her as she slithered on top of him. The memories of last night gained texture, and he remembered her delight and exactly how to cause it. His hands moved in the way which made her shudder helplessly, then he applied his third hand *just so*.

For the last three weeks, as autumn embraced Makkathran, Edeard had learned how to harness his telekinetic ability in the bedroom to the best possible advantage. Another arena of life in which poor old Ashwell lagged far behind the sophisticated decadence of the city. But he hadn't lacked for girls eager to teach him the most intimate secrets of this darkest art. His fame and strength had proved irresistible to the beautiful mischievous daughters of the nobility. They relished demonstrating their ill-gotten skill, almost as much as he enjoyed being the beneficiary. He never was sure exactly who was corrupting who.

'I've never seen steps into a bathing pool before,' Kristiana remarked as she walked down into the bubble-coated water. 'We have these awful wooden ladder things hanging on the side in all the pools in Great-grandfather's mansion.' Her hand stroked Edeard's face as she sat on the seat shelf beside him. 'This is much better.'

'There are quite a few pools in the constables' tenement that have steps like these,' Edeard assured her, confident she wouldn't be going in any to find out.

'Not fair you've got them and we haven't,' Jessile complained. She pouted. Jessile had a very pretty pout, Edeard decided. It certainly got her just about everything she wanted.

He relaxed between them, which spoke volumes about how his life had changed since that day in Birmingham Pool. On several evenings there had been fights in the theatres over who got to bed him – such reputable girls, too. He'd never really considered what kind of life popularity would bring. And he had enough of his dour Ashwell upbringing left to convince himself it wouldn't last. But in the meantime . . .

At his instruction, a ge-chimp brought two sponges and a

bottle of soap oil to the rim of the pool. 'Would you do my back?' he asked, and leaned forward.

Both girls took a sponge. Even with shielded thoughts, they clearly didn't have cleanliness in mind as they began to apply the liquid with languid movements.

'What are you doing tonight?' Jessile asked.

'Celebrating, I hope,' Edeard told her. It was the last day of Arminel's trial; his verdict was a formality. At least Edeard sincerely hoped so, but then he'd thought that last time. *That good old Ashwell optimism again.* The trial was the biggest event in Makkathran, and had been for the last four days as the opposing lawyers presented their respective cases. Only the grandest of the city's aristocracy managed to get into the public gallery; everyone else relied on sight and sound gifting from the official court recorder. 'How about you?'

'My fiancé will be back from patrol this afternoon,' she told him. 'Eustace is a lieutenant in the militia. Guarding our borders,' she added with a large dollop of irony.

'Ah,' Edeard said. He glanced at her left hand, seeing a slim silver band like twined vines. A single diamond was set in its crest.

She bent round to look at his expression. 'That doesn't bother you, does it? You're the Waterwalker.'

'No. Not worried.' He did wonder what kind of marriage it would be, a thought which must have shone through his shielding.

'I'm a third daughter,' Jessile said with a kindly smile. 'We're marrying because after twenty-three years I'll finally get out of the family mansion, and he gets a dowry to live off. Poor boy's a fifth son of the family Norrets' second son, which entitles him to a big slice of nothing. Daddy's promised me an estate in Walton province; they say it has a nice big house.'

'That's why you're marrying?'

'Of course.' She paused the sponge on the top of his spine. 'I know I'm going to miss Makkathran, but I suppose I'll get used to country life. I'll visit the city every season.'

65

'What about love?' he asked.

Both girls smiled delightedly, letting wistful admiration flow free from behind their own veiled thoughts.

'You're so sweet,' Jessile said. 'That's one of the things about you. I can sense it so easily. We all can. You're just endlessly fascinating. Is it true the first time the Pythia met you she said you'd be Mayor?'

'What? No! She said no such thing.' He struggled to remember what she had said.

'I'd like you to meet my friend Ranalee,' Kristiana said. 'She's a Gilmorn, they're a merchant family. Horribly rich. She's a second daughter, very marriageable; and she's expressed, in complete confidence to me, how strongly she'd enjoy knowing you.'

'Uh, right.'

Kristiana stood up in front of him, wiping long damp hair from her shoulders with deliberate slow movements. 'She's pretty, too; and young, in case you were wondering. If I introduce you, we could all celebrate together tonight.'

Edeard found himself short of breath.

Boyd was waiting outside Edeard's maisonette, wearing a long fur-lined coat over his smartest uniform. A slushy rain was dribbling out of an overcast sky, damping his hair. He started to say something, then stopped abruptly as Kristiana and Jessile emerged just behind Edeard. The girls were swathed in long woollen wraps, as were currently fashionable. They just about covered up their expensive theatre dresses.

'Ladies,' Edeard said courteously.

They both smiled demurely, and allowed him to kiss them on the cheek.

'Don't forget,' Kristiana said. 'Tonight. Me and Ranalee.'

Boyd watched in awe as the girls hurried along the walkway to the stairs. They were giggling after a few paces, arms linked, their heads leaning in together to not-quite-whisper.

'The Alrado theatre in Zelda district,' Kristiana's longtalk shot at him.

'I'll be there,' Edeard smiled happily at their departing backs.

'Two!' Boyd exclaimed once the girls were clattering down the stairs.

Edeard knew his smile was now boastful. Didn't care.

'Lady! How do you do it. Step aside Macsen, the new king is on his throne.'

'How was Saria?' Edeard countered. 'Wasn't last night your fifth?'

'Ninth, actually.' Boyd's grin turned sinful. 'She's a Matran, you know, sixth daughter of their next District Master.'

'Good for you,' Edeard said. He still didn't really know his way around Makkathran's aristocracy; though he'd certainly met an awful lot of the younger members recently.

'She let slip she'd be acceptable to a proposal. Can you imagine that? Me, the son of a baker marrying into the Matrans!'

'Is it so unusual?'

Boyd slapped Edeard's back. 'Oh you country boy!'

Edeard wondered what his friend would have to say on the subject of a second daughter in the Gilmorn family. Right from the beginning he'd thought the city's obsession with lineage and money to be unhealthy, as if such considerations were paramount. Of course, it might just be that Ranalee was a lovely person as well. *Only one way to find out.*

They made their way across the low bridge over the Outer Circle canal and into the Majate district. Arminel's trial was being conducted in the central chamber of the Courts of Justice, the largest there was. Outside, the walls of the big ante hall were punctured by a series of deep arrière-voussure arches leading to the offices of the judiciary and their clerks. A lot of people in fine robes were already gathered there waiting when Edeard and Boyd arrived. Edeard respectfully acknowledged the looks cast in his direction as they made their way over to the cluster of constables around Captain Ronark. He recognized several members of the Upper Council: Imilan, the Chemistry Guild's Grand Master; Dalceen, the District Master of Fiacre; Julan, District Master of Haxpen; and Finitan, of course, who at least seemed genuinely welcoming with the sly grin he shot at Edeard.

'About time,' Kanseen said as they joined the constables. 'We're about to go in.' There was the faintest hint of suspicion leaking through her guarded mind. Edeard reckoned that was deliberate, she usually had a very strong shield. She never voiced any dismay at the success he was having with girls right now, but he knew it bothered her. In any case, he knew she'd had numerous invitations from various Grand Family sons; though that would more likely be a cause of annoyance for her.

'They wouldn't start without him,' Macsen teased.

'I've given my testimony,' Edeard said with a straight face. 'I don't really need to be here.'

She pulled a face at him.

'And yet your ego delivered you here in time,' Macsen said, equally innocently. 'How fortunate we all are.'

'Any word on Dinlay?' Edeard asked, ignoring Macsen's taunt. He was slightly disappointed their squadmate wasn't at the Courts of Justice. When they'd all visited Dinlay last, just a couple of days ago, the doctors had said he was almost ready to leave the hospital. It would be light duties only for another month or so, but the bullet wound was healing well.

'Bit much to expect him to be here as soon as he's out,' Captain Ronark said. 'He'll probably start tomorrow.'

'Yes, sir,' Macsen said.

'Here we go,' Sergeant Chae said.

Master Solarin from the Guild of Lawyers emerged from the nearest archway, assisted as always by a couple of ge-monkeys. After the debacle of Arminel's previous trial, Edeard had asked Captain Ronark if the district station could retain their old legal tutor as prosecuting council this time. To his surprise, the captain had agreed. But then, as everyone in the whole city knew, this time Arminel and his cohorts were going to be found very *very* guilty. It was just that Edeard felt more comfortable with Solarin prosecuting. At least the ancient lawyer knew how to present a case, and wouldn't succumb to any procedural tricks employed by the defence.

'All waiting for me?' Master Solarin said cheerfully. 'How very flattering. Come along then, let us do battle one last time.'

The clerk of the court appeared at the big doors leading to the central chamber. 'The case of Makkathran versus Arminel, Gustape, Falor, Harri and Omasis is called to session,' he announced loudly.

Master Solarin made his painfully slow way to the central chamber, with everyone else falling into place behind him, as tradition dictated.

Once again Master Cherix had been retained as Arminel's defence council. He followed the constables in, accompanied by two junior lawyers, seemingly unperturbed by the stature of the case.

'Wish I could afford him,' Boyd whispered to Edeard and Kanseen as they made their way to their seats. 'In fact, if I ever do get arrested, I'm going to ask for him.'

'When you get arrested, you mean,' Kanseen smiled back.

Edeard grinned. But Boyd was right. Even with an open and shut case, Cherix had been flawless in his presentation, citing Edeard's provocation, the grudge between Arminel and Edeard, inflamed tension, the panic on the day; doing his best to mitigate the ultimate sentence.

'They had to have someone that good,' Chae said as the squad settled in their benches. 'It's politics. The trial must be seen as fair.'

When the central chamber was filled to capacity, the clerk called for silence, and the three judges walked in.

The day before the trial began, Solarin had told them that Owain, the Mayor himself, would take the role of chief judge of the proceedings. It was a very rare event for the Mayor to sit in court, even though his office was the head of the judiciary. Edeard somehow hadn't been surprised. Politics. Again. The city wanted to see the gang members punished. And there was an election in the spring. The nature of the case gave Owain the perfect justification to step in.

Owain and his two fellow judges called the court to order, and requested the closing statements from both councils.

Edeard listened with a growing sense of excitement, maybe even a sense of suspense. It was a foregone conclusion, Solarin's relentless speech made that perfectly clear, expertly demolishing the mitigating circumstances Cherix had so carefully built up. But even so, Cherix almost made Edeard feel sorry for Arminel: a life led astray through no fault of his own, dreadful childhood, abandoned by parents, fallen into crime because the city didn't care . . .

Surely they won't fall for this? As he looked at the faces of the judges, they were totally impassive, their minds perfectly shielded.

After the submissions, Owain announced a recess so the judges could consider their verdict. Edeard and the others found themselves back out in the ante hall again, trying not to let their feelings leak to everyone else.

Grand Master Finitan came over to talk to them. 'Any doubts about the outcome?' he asked quietly. 'You seem subdued.'

'No, sir,' Edeard said. 'But Cherix is good.'

'He has to be. The Grand Council can't afford any accusation of bias.'

'Politics.'

'You are becoming a proper citizen of Makkathran, aren't you?'

'I do my best, sir.'

'I know.' Finitan drew him away from the other constables. 'Then consider this; the offer you will be made after the case is over is not about ability, it is made to test you.'

'Sir?'

'If you accept, it will show you understand the city's politics, and indicate you play by the same rules as the rest of us. If you refuse, if you claim you're not worthy, or wish to demonstrate your humility before the Lady, or something along those lines, then you're telling everyone you're a dangerous idealist.'

'Yes, sir,' Edeard said blankly; he didn't have a clue what the Grand Master was talking about.

'You have my blessing either way. But it has to be your own choice. I would simply ask you to consider what you can accomplish on the outside looking in. Think about it.'

'I will, sir.'

Finitan patted Edeard on the shoulder, and went back to the group of Masters from the Grand Council.

'What was that about?' Macsen asked.

'I haven't got the faintest idea.'

The three judges took two hours to deliberate. When the court was recalled, Arminel and his four fellow accused were made to stand as Owain read out the findings.

On extortion all five accused were found guilty.

On conspiracy: guilty.

On the attempted murder of two constables, a charge levelled at Arminel alone, he was found guilty.

Arminel kept his face and mind composed the whole time. Edeard was expecting the man to at least glance in his direction, but his resolve never wavered.

Owain then put a square of scarlet drosilk on his head. Edeard finally saw Arminel tense up.

Gustape, Falor, Harri and Omasis were sentenced to twenty years in the Trampello mine. They were led away to the holding cells. Arminel stood alone, facing the three judges.

'The crimes you have been found guilty of are exceptional,' Owain declared. 'I don't believe that I have ever encountered such deliberate wickedness in my time on the Grand Council. To compound this, you have constantly refused to cooperate with the constables and tell them the names of other members in your vile criminal organization. While this might earn you their gratitude, it does nothing to encourage leniency on my part. We have never had the death penalty on Querencia. For this you can thank the Lady, who in her wisdom believes that there is no human soul which cannot be redeemed. However, I see no sign that your salvation is possible. As a consequence I find myself with no alternative but to sentence you to incarceration in the Trampello mines for the remainder of your life. May the Lady bless your soul upon its ascent into the radiant heavens, for no one else will.' He banged the gavel. 'This court is concluded.'

The spectators filed out of the central chamber while Edeard and his squadmates sat on their benches in a mild daze.

'Wow,' Macsen said.

'Life,' Boyd said.

'That's just about unheard of,' Kanseen said.

Master Solarin turned to face the constables. 'I believe the last case where a life sentence was issued was forty-two years ago: the Golden Park Ripper. A most unpleasant individual. Before your time, of course. For that you may consider yourselves lucky.'

'Wow,' Macsen said again.

'Congratulations, young man,' Master Solarin said, and put his hand out.

Edeard took the old man's grip gently. 'Thank you, sir. You got the verdict for us.'

'I didn't have much work to do, thanks to your extraordinary gift. I wish you luck in your future endeavours. It has been a privilege to be you legal instructor. But to use an ancient phrase, I think you have outgrown me now.'

'Oh no, sir. I'm hoping for a lot more cases.'

'And you'll get them, of that I'm in no doubt. And I'm not the only one, it would seem. Do you see the gentleman over there?' His gnarled finger pointed with only a slight tremor.

Edeard and the others glanced in the direction the old lawyer indicated. They saw a man in a flamboyant blue jacket and grey drosilk shirt making his way along the main aisle. He was probably approaching the end of his first century, yet still hale and healthy, with thick brown hair hanging over his collar, only a few strands of which were turning to silver. He had heavy gold rings on every finger, and loops of gold chain round his neck. His face was fattening, the result of many years of good living. Even so, he looked physically powerful. He was watching them with pale-green eyes that were overshadowed by a broad forehead. Some accident or fight long ago had left him with a jaw that was unable to close straight, giving him slightly lopsided features. His whole appearance was one of a successful, self-confident merchant. As if to confirm this, he was accompanied by two beautiful girls who wore expensive dresses and a lot of jewellery. They were several years younger than Kristiana, Edeard decided with a little burst of sympathy for them. Then he met the man's gaze. It was a scrutiny every bit as intense as the one the Pythia had given him all those months ago. Edeard instinctively knew there was an enmity between them, and returned the stare levelly even though he didn't know why.

'Who is that?' he asked quietly.

'That,' Master Solarin said with extreme distaste, 'is Captain Ivarl.'

'Has he some kind of ship?' Edeard asked. He was mildly put out by the way the others groaned disparagingly.

'No,' Chae said. 'He doesn't own a ship, though he makes out he used to captain a merchantman. Ivarl is the owner of the House of Blue Petals.'

Edeard had heard of that establishment; a bordello in the Myco district, next to Makkathran's port.

Captain Ronark had come forward to stand at Edeard's shoulder. 'If the gangs in this city can be said to have a leader,' Ronark said. 'it is Ivarl. He at least likes to style himself the master of our criminal fraternity. It was probably him who sent Arminel back to ambush you.'

'Ah,' Edeard said. He smiled politely, and inclined his head towards the villain.

Ivarl returned the gesture, tipping his gold-topped cane in

Edeard's direction. Master Cherix came up behind him, and murmured something in his ear. Ivarl smiled tightly, and came over to the constables.

'My congratulations on an exemplary case,' he said. His voice was rough and Edeard suspected the injury that left his jaw askew had caused some deeper damage.

'Thank you,' Edeard said with a heavy dose of irony.

'This city is so much better off without such people,' Ivarl continued. 'They are cheap vermin; they bring nothing to our lives. You, though, you are an exceptional man, Constable Edeard.'

'I do my best.' Edeard was uncomfortably aware of the way Macsen and one of Captain Ivarl's girls were smirking at each other. He wanted to smack his friend hard.

'As do we all,' Ivarl said. 'Everyone in their own small way contributes to the flow of life of this fine city. In this respect, I extend an invitation to you and your friends to enjoy the hospitality of my house.'

Edeard was very aware of everyone waiting for his response. *So this is what Finitan was warning me about. I've shown the gangs that not all constables are pushovers, that their usual violence doesn't work against me, so they want to see how far I'm going to take this. Politics!*

He allowed an old, deeply personal, image to leak from his mind: the smouldering ruins of Ashwell, with corpses protruding from them.

'I haven't been down to your district of the city yet,' Edeard said. 'But I'm planning on visiting soon.'

Ivarl's pudgy lips pressed together in a big display of disappointment. He shrugged elaborately. 'I look forward to meeting you there, young man.' He turned and walked away, a girl clinging possessively to each arm.

Only then did Edeard notice the looks the others were giving him. 'What?'

Captain Ronark smiled. 'Good man, Edeard. I knew you wouldn't betray yourself.'

Chae gave him an admiring grin, and walked out with the captain.

'Where was that place?' Boyd asked with trepidation.

'The village I grew up in,' Edeard told him.

'Lady, just seeing it frightened me.'

'I wanted some emphasis. I wanted to make sure Ivarl understood.'

'Oh, I think he got it. You don't have to worry on that score.'

'Shame, though,' Macsen said wistfully. 'Did you see the blonde one?'

'You peasant,' Kanseen hissed at him.

'Hey! I can make noble painful sacrifices, too, you know. You have to have *standards* to be a part of the Waterwalker's squad.'

'Don't call me that,' Edeard said wearily.

'Too late,' Boyd said. 'Far too late.'

It was mid-afternoon when they got back to the Jeavons constable station. They claimed their usual table in the hall, and the ge-monkeys brought over plates of sandwiches and mugs of tea. Of late, the station food had improved; local shopkeepers were keen to supply the constables with their better products at reasonable prices, grateful for the noticeable reduction in gang activity in the district.

Edeard appreciated the gesture, but it made him very aware of the expectations settling on his shoulders. *And now I've seen the real enemy. Arminel might be gone, but Ivarl can send a dozen more just like him on to the streets. A hundred.*

After the elation of the trial it was a sobering thought. He hadn't really changed anything, just made himself famous. *And ultimately, what use is that to people?*

'Result, or what?' Boyd said as he picked up one of the sandwiches, a malted roll containing ham and cheese with a strong tomato chutney. He bit in contentedly.

All the other constables in the station were making a point of coming over to congratulate them on the verdict. Edeard was finally getting embarrassed by the admiration.

'Yes. A result all right,' Kanseen said, picking through the rest of the sandwiches. 'But it's only one result.'

'Trust you to pour on the ice water,' Macsen said.

'She's right,' Edeard said. 'We're going to have to do a lot more than this before the gangs even start getting worried.'

'Not so. Ivarl is worried enough about the Waterwalker to crawl out from under his rock and get a firsthand look,' Boyd said.

'Will you please stop calling me that?'

'I thought Arminel would get thirty to forty years at least,' Macsen said. 'But for the rest of his life? He's only, what, thirty? That's at least a hundred and fifty years in Trampello. It's not exactly a pavilion on the Iguru. A hundred and fifty years! Owain must really want to be re-elected.'

'I'm not sorry for him,' Edeard said. 'He was going to kill me.'

'Because Ivarl told him to,' Kanseen said.

'You think so?'

'No way could he put together an ambush like that without a lot of help. He'd need permission. Ivarl must have agreed.'

'Oh Lady,' Macsen muttered in alarm. 'Look out.'

Edeard's farsight showed him Captain Ronark leading Chief Constable Walsfol into the hall. Everyone fell silent, benches were scraped across the floor as the constables stood up. Even the ge-chimps stopped moving.

Chief Constable Walsfol walked directly over to Edeard's table. He was in his full dress uniform, an immaculate black tunic with gold buttons and scarlet epaulettes with a diamond stud. Edeard had been introduced briefly the day after he arrested Arminel; he'd actually been quite impressed with the Chief Constable. The man was in his second century, and the fact he'd fought his way to the top of the constables was evident in his manner. Walsfol was a straight-talking man, secure since his position was achieved through the support of the stations.

Walsfol saluted smartly. Edeard hurriedly returned the salute.

'An excellent day, Constable,' Walsfol said in his clipped aristocratic accent. 'You have done this station proud.'

'Thank you, sir.'

Walsfol took a pair of epaulettes from his pocket. They had a single silver star on them. 'As a consequence of your bravery and actions in Birmingham Pool, I would like to offer you promotion to corporal.'

It might have been Edeard's imagination, but he was sure the word 'offer' was stressed. But he was so relieved that this was the test Finitan had spoken of rather than Ivarl's crude attempt at bribery he simply said, 'Yes, sir; thank you, sir, I'd be honoured to accept.'

Captain Ronark led the applause as the Chief Constable attached the epaulettes to Edeard's shoulders. *Of course Finitan wasn't talking about Ivarl*, Edeard chided himself, *the Grand Council want to know if I'm going to support their authority. Lady! Do they think I might be a challenge to them?*

Walsfol finished, and saluted again.

'Corporal Waterwalker,' Macsen said, holding up his beer and laughing.

Edeard had now completely surrendered to the ribbing he was getting. They'd all wound up in the Olovan's Eagle for a few celebratory drinks, claiming a small booth in the upstairs bar where they were relatively undisturbed.

'I wonder which squads will be under your command?' Kanseen mused. 'Corporals are normally in charge of three.'

'Please don't team us up with Droal's lot,' Boyd said. 'They're worthless crap artists, and everyone knows Vilby is on the take.'

'I didn't know that,' said Edeard.

'What, with all your psychic superpowers?' Macsen asked.

Edeard showed him the hand gesture Obron always used to employ, only to find it summoned up a mournful nostalgia that unexpectedly made his eyes water. *Obron, he would be twenty-three now . . .*

'You're going to have to think about this, Edeard,' Kanseen said. 'Seriously, they're all going to watch what you do with the promotion. It's an opportunity to put together a team of your own constables, people you know you can rely on.'

'Yeah, yeah.' Edeard didn't really want to think of all the responsibility which came with his new position. Unfortunately, his problem was that he couldn't stop worrying about what he should do next. Gangs and constables would both want to see what he was capable of: whether he was just some strong lad from the countryside happy with the attention of all the city girls, or someone who would stand up for the law and make a difference. *The Orchard Palace probably want to know as well.*

'I suppose I'll have to keep you lot,' he said with a grand show of reluctance.

It was Boyd's turn for the hand gesture.

'Even Dinlay?' Macsen said in such a soft voice only Edeard heard him.

'Yes,' Edeard said with a tiny directed longtalk. 'Even Dinlay.'

Macsen scowled into his beer glass.

'And what are you going to do with this team of yours?' Kanseen asked earnestly. 'It's only fifteen people, after all.'

'Two months ago it was just the five of us,' Edeard said calmly. 'We can shape ourselves into something useful, I'm sure. That's if Ronark will allow us. There are procedures, after all.'

'Not to start with,' Boyd said, uncharacteristically serious. 'You've got some momentum behind you, Waterwalker, and a great deal of goodwill. This is your chance to make something of it.'

'Dear Lady, give him a beer and listen to the politician sprout forth,' Edeard groaned.

'I know Makkathran,' Boyd insisted. 'There's a chance here for you.' He put his arms around Kanseen and Macsen. 'And we three native guides are going to make sure you don't blow that chance.'

'You three,' Edeard rolled his eyes. 'Great. How can we fail?'

'We stick together,' Macsen said. 'Always have, always will, no matter what.'

'No matter what!' They all drank to that.

Boyd pushed his empty glass across the table. 'And with your new corporal's pay, I believe you can afford the next round.'

'Sorry,' Edeard said, standing up and buttoning his tunic. 'I have an appointment at the Alrado theatre, and it's a long walk to the Zelda district.'

'An appointment?' Macsen inquired keenly.

'Someone from the Guild of Clerks, they're helping me with taxes.'

He left to the sounds of their derisive laughter. Just as he started down the awkward curving stairs he heard Kanseen exclaim: 'No! I bought the last round.'

It was cold on the streets outside Olovan's Eagle. Frost was clinging to the city's pavements, and there were flakes of snow drifting down past the bright orange lights shining out of the buildings. People wrapped in thick coats wove past Edeard as he made his way along Albie Lane towards Flight Canal. He'd thrown out a seclusion haze to ward off curious farsight, as did all Makkathran's citizens going about business they regarded as private. The effect was like a mild version of concealment.

Edeard was approaching the iron bridge over to the Haxpen district when his farsight swept over a figure for the third time. They'd been trailing him for some time, ignoring his obvious wish to be left alone. He focused on them to find it was: 'Salrana,' he exclaimed.

She scurried forwards, thoughts radiant with impish delight. Almost as tall as him now, he acknowledged. Her full length dark-grey poncho coat flapped as she moved, a big hood pulled well forward. 'You're so slow,' she admonished, giggling. 'I've been following you ever since you left the tavern. If I was an assassin, you'd be dead by now.' She pushed her hood back, allowing her auburn hair to flow free, and kissed him breathlessly. 'You know, I hardly recognized you with your hair so long. The city fashion suits you.'

Edeard grinned back, very aware that she was still pressed up against him. He studied her face with its sharp cheeks and lovely dark brown eyes that were wide and teasing. She was gorgeous now, and because of that he kept trying to avoid her. They still longtalked every day, but he kept using the trial as an excuse for not actually meeting up. Just being with her on a cold gloomy street made him embarrassed about all the girls he'd tumbled these last few weeks, so spending a pleasant afternoon together with her would be torture.

Why? he asked himself. *She's beautiful, and she wants me, and I'd adore having her in my bed and my life. We really would be the perfect couple. The only other who even comes close is Kanseen.*

His hesitation was born out of some stupid notion of duty. At least that was always the excuse he gave himself. He really did feel protective towards her – and that was hardly necessary any more. It wasn't as if they were alone against the world these days. Maybe he was just afraid to change the way things were; there had been so many upheavals, she was his constant in a very unsteady life. And how she'd hate being told that. She was young and vivacious, and wanted some fun. She deserved happiness. And they *would* be happy together . . .

'Gosh, seeing me really does cheer you up, doesn't it?' she mocked.

'Sorry,' he smiled, pushing his emotions down below any possible farsight perception. 'It's fantastic to see you, but that just reminds me what I've got to do tonight.'

'Really?' she asked brightly. Her arm tucked through his, and they started to walk over the iron bridge. 'You poor thing. It must be truly terrible having to entertain Kristiana *and* Ranalee in your bed.'

Edeard stopped in shock. 'How on Querencia did you know that?'

She giggled again, delighted to have flustered him. 'Oh,

Edeard, the whole city knows who's snagged the Waterwalker tonight. Kristiana has been bragging in half the saloons in town today. And you know what this city is for gossip.'

'Yes,' he said brokenly. Then, because he couldn't help it, he asked, 'Are people really talking about my love life?'

'Talking. Singing. Writing books on it. I think they're planning a play for the ox-roast on Golden Park this New Year.'

'Shut up.'

She pressed him against the railing and kissed him again. Her skin was warm, soft and silky. Her scent strong. 'Will the second act be us? And the third and the fourth?'

Edeard almost pushed her away. Instead, with a massive effort of will he smiled back ruefully, and turned round to lean on the rail. Then he put his arm round her. Her mind's flash of delighted surprise at the gesture was intoxicating. 'Have I been really stupid?' he asked.

'Only rejecting me. The rest of it, you're just like any Grand Family son on his fifteenth birthday. You've got the run of the city, Edeard. The difference between you and them is that you earned it. People are fascinated to learn what's going to happen next; if Arminel was just a fluke, or if you're truly going to be the Waterwalker.'

He sighed. 'I hate that name.'

'I hope . . . Edeard, I hope you live up to it. Did you know church attendance has gone up since Birmingham Pool? You displayed duty and honour that day, as well as courage. They're traits so sorely lacking in this city. It showed people what was absent from their own lives. It was a wonderful thing, Edeard.'

He stared down into the dark water with its surface crust of slush. There were ripples near the far bank where fil-rats were nesting. A couple of gondolas were edging their way towards them along from High Pool on the Grand Major Canal, their lamps glinting on their prows, their gondoliers harmonizing a gentle melody. 'I don't know what to do next,' he confessed. 'Actually, that's not true. I know what I should do. But if I go there, if I use my talent to take on the gangs, then there'll be no turning back. Right now I can do nothing, and all the fuss will die down. But . . .'

She hugged him back. It was a gesture more intimate than any of her flirting had ever kindled. 'You can't do that,' she whispered. 'You know you can't.'

'Yeah. I know that. Thank you.'

'I'm just passing on the Lady's teachings, Edeard. That's what I've given my life to.'

'You're such a good person, Salrana,'

She leaned in playfully. 'I don't want to be. Not with you. And those family girls, they say you're a good lover.'

Edeard shivered with mortification. *All Makkathran is discussing that?* Yet, at the same time . . . 'You don't want to believe everything you hear.'

'Don't I?' she said archly.

'Well, okay, I admit that bit's true.'

'Oh, listen to you!' She thumped him on the shoulder, then immediately pulled him in closer and kissed him again.

It was like that time back in the bottom of the well. He knew he shouldn't. But, actually, there wasn't any real reason why not. *For once let the heart rule, not the mind.*

A couple walked past them, farsight gently examining the young couple embracing with growing ardour. Heads turned.

'It *is* him,' the woman whispered. 'The Waterwalker.'

'And that's a Lady's Novice!'

A longtalk voice was directed at a number of acquaintances: 'You'll never guess—'

Edeard and Salrana broke apart smirking like scolded apprentices. They straightened their clothes and moved down the slope of the bridge to the Haxpen side.

'I'm going to get a reputation worse than Dybal,' Edeard decided.

'Good camouflage. The gangs will underestimate you if they think you're just a wicked womanizer.'

'Yeah,' he laughed. ''Tis a terrible price. Come on, I'll walk you back to Millical House. It's sort of on my route.'

'No, it isn't.'

'Actually, it is. I *am* going to try and achieve something. You and the Lady are right, it would be wrong not to try.'

'And that's tonight?'

'Yes. It's perfect. Nobody will expect me to do any kind of constable work tonight.'

'I certainly didn't.'

'I know. We really need to talk.'

'We've talked for three years, Edeard!'

'Yeah.' And he was hugely tempted. *As always. Perhaps dealing with Ivarl could wait one day.*

'Actually, I'm not being fair,' Salrana said.

'Oh?'

'My House Mother told me yesterday. I'm being assigned to the Lady's hospital in Ufford for the winter.'

'Where's that?'

'Capital town of Tralsher province, that's south of the Iguru.'

'What? No!'

'Yeah. Nursing is all part of our training.'

'But there are hospitals in Makkathran.'

'The Church doesn't work that way. It wants us to learn of life outside the crystal wall.'

'You know more of life outside than any city Mother does, or ever will,' he said with petulance.

'And telling them that would not be helpful.'

'I could ask Master Finitan if he could speak to your Mother.'

Salrana chuckled softly. 'Really? That ought to do it. A friend of his wants a Novice as a mistress, so could you please change her traditional training schedule to make that possible?'

'Ah. No, put like that, I suppose not.'

'You suppose right.'

'But you wouldn't be my mistress.'

'Wouldn't I?'

'No,' he shook his head firmly. 'No. Never. We would be equals. True lovers.'

'Oh, Edeard.' A tear emerged from her eye as she looked up at him. 'Say that again. Promise me! Promise we'll be lovers when I get back.'

Edeard took both her hands in his own. 'As the Lady is my witness, I promise.'

Edeard took the tall bridge beside High Pool, the one with the crystal apex. On this night the transparency made no difference, it looked like he was walking on some glossy black substance smeared by slush. It brought him out into the empty streets of Eyrie, which he hurried through on his way to the Zelda district. He hadn't planned on coming this far, but if everyone knew he was meeting the girls there, he should at least appear to be on his way in case he was being observed. Part of him was still aghast that the city knew about his love life, though he accepted he really only had himself to blame. It was strange that none of his friends had mentioned it. Did they assume he knew? That was the problem with not growing up in the city, everyone took it for granted he was familiar with the culture.

Once he was over Grove Canal the buildings changed to a warren of modest houses and shops and craft halls. The walls closed in as he deliberately chose a route that took him down the narrowest streets. In Polteral Alley he was completely alone. It was a tiny passageway between the backs of buildings, a zigzag that was barely one person wide. Indeed, there were alcoves in the walls to allow people to pass – given their slightly strange inward bulge a couple of feet above the ground he could only speculate what the city's original inhabitants had looked like. At night nobody used it, the thick walls prevented anyone from using farsight along its length, and it effectively blocked longtalk. If you were mugged in here, no one would know until morning. Edeard sent his farsight out ahead of him, checking the alcoves were all empty. When he was halfway along, he stopped under an overhanging section of wall and wove a concealment around himself. Once he was sure no one was following him, he asked Makkathran's somnolent mind to allow him passage once more. It was easier for him now; after that first time behind the shops in Sonral Street, he'd taken to practising in secluded spots like this one. There were many in the city.

The pavement under his feet *changed*, producing a subliminal swirl of coloured symbols. Edeard's feet sank through it as if it had no more substance than fog. Some force lowered him gently into the drain fissure running beneath the buildings. As always he felt as if he was plummeting from a great height.

Edeard walked for several minutes until the drain opened out halfway up the curving wall of the big tunnel which ran directly underneath the Grand Major Canal. He placed his feet tentatively on the little steps he'd asked the city to create down the wall. Even so, with the water gurgling over his boots, it was a treacherous descent. His previous explorations had revealed that Makkathran's entire canal network was duplicated down here in the city's hidden underworld, not that he'd ever walked their length. The crest of the main tunnel glowed with a faint tangerine light, showing him the stream which ran along the bottom. It was higher than usual tonight, indicating how much water was dripping out of the pavement slush and into the drains. A ledge allowed him to walk beside it, though he had to splash across the broad circular pools of the junctions. Water poured in over the tops of his boots. It was *freezing*. Not for the first time, he wondered if he could somehow bring a little boat down here. In the end he settled for using his third hand to hold the water back from his shins. He'd found that doing the whole Waterwalker trick and stabilizing the surface was too exhausting to maintain for any length of time.

Eventually, he turned off down the tunnel below the Upper Tail Canal. After a few hundred yards he scrambled his way up into another drain. He wasn't terribly familiar with the Myco district, but his farsight could easily penetrate the city's substance now. To his mind, it was as if the structure around him was built from nothing more than cloudy glass. He stopped below a secluded corner of a little square, and the city lifted him up, elevating him out into the thickening snowfall. By the time he emerged he'd cloaked himself in a concealment again.

A couple of sailors in their traditional magenta-coloured half-cloaks walked through the square, oblivious to him. He grinned at their backs, and set off in the opposite direction.

The House of Blue Petals fronted the Upper Tail Canal, looking directly across the warehouse domes of the port. A four-storey establishment with a vermiculated facade, the oval windows surrounded by onyx-like anthemion friezes. Protruding from the upper slope of its mansard roof were several hemispherical windows, as if it had grown giant eyes to peer up at the nebulas of Querencia's skies. Edeard frowned up at them, puzzled by the faint violet glow that emanated from within. It had been a long time since he'd seen anything other than Makkathran's ubiquitous orange glow at night.

The three tall doorways of the ground floor were all open. The sound of piano music was spilling out into the street, accompanied by laughter and loud voices. Doormen in black jackets similar to constable tunics stood on either side of each heavy wooden door. Edeard held his breath and slipped past them, watching anxiously to see if they could sense him. One of them frowned, looking round at some phantom disturbance, but didn't raise any challenge.

Half of the ground floor was a bar, with the piano in the middle hammering out a jolly tune. Smartly dressed stewards mixed cocktails behind a long polished counter, which groomed ge-monkeys delivered. Polished tables were accompanied by high-backed leather armchairs where the customers relaxed with a drink as they waited for the madam to come round. Two big black iron stoves on opposite sides threw out a comforting heat as coal blazed away behind their grilles. The room was a high one, taking up two floors, with a wooden gallery running round it. Girls with strangely stiff curly hair leaned over the railing, wearing low-cut, brightly coloured dresses; grinning at the men below as they made eye contact and blew kisses and made saucy longtalk calls.

Edeard watched the wide wooden stairs which had been fixed to the wall, seeing who was coming up and down. It wasn't just sailors who visited Ivarl's establishment; judging by the clothes a large proportion were men from the Guilds and families. He even saw a couple of militia officers in their sharp blue and scarlet uniforms. No constables, though. *Probably can't afford it.*

He waited, getting a feel for the routine, and probing about with his farsight. The madam would go from table to table, sharing a few pleasant words with the clientele. There would be a brief discussion about the girls, some requesting an old favourite, some taking their pick from the gallery. A fee was either handed over discreetly or for regulars an addition made to their account, and as soon as the man had finished his drink he'd go upstairs to be greeted by the courtesan he'd chosen.

After a couple of minutes standing near the foot of the stairs, Edeard followed a carpentry Guildsman up to the gallery. The selected courtesan flounced along to throw her arms round the Guildsman in welcome. They headed off down one of the side corridors. Edeard hurried past the other girls, startled by how strong their perfume was, which made him worry he might sneeze. Then he was wiggling through an archway shielded by curtains. That was the most difficult part, trying to disguise the motion of the thick red velvet.

On the other side was an unembellished corridor leading back to stairs which took him up to the third floor. He'd sensed the layout of the rooms up there, with over thirty people gathered in groups. Ivarl was easy enough to discern, Edeard wasn't going to forget his mind in a hurry.

Edeard didn't bother with the door, opening it unseen would be impossible. Instead he asked the city to change a section of the wall, and ghosted his way through. The gang master was holding court in a long room at the end of the building. Four of the grandiose oval windows looked out eastwards to the Lyot

Sea. Tonight they were covered by thick curtains. A green-enamel stove burnt hot in the corner, making Edeard wish he wasn't wearing his coat. Nobody else in the room was.

Ivarl's grey shirt was unbuttoned, showing off a thick mat of hair on his chest. His boots were off, resting against the side of the deep-cushioned leather settee he was lounging on. Seven other men were in attendance. Their fine clothes emphasized the illusion of them belonging to some Grand Family or merchant house. It was an image Edeard couldn't get rid of, as if they'd somehow established a Guild for their criminality, and enjoyed the same benefits as any of Makkathran's legitimate enterprises. When he'd first learned of the gangs, he'd assumed they'd consist of sour-faced men in shabby clothes meeting furtively in dark underground rooms – not this.

There was a table along one wall, with gold and silver platters laden with food every bit as delicious as that served in a Lillylight restaurant. It complemented a selection of wine from estates Edeard had never even heard of.

Three girls were walking round with bottles, filling up the cut crystal goblets held by the men. They were wearing long diaphanous skirts and simple suede slippers; nothing else. Edeard stared, feeling mildly guilty, as if he'd deliberately snuck into their bedroom. *Lady, you stupid country boy. What did you think girls would wear in a place like this?* Then he *really* looked at them. Two were the girls who'd accompanied Ivarl to the court this morning. The third . . .

Edeard couldn't help the little groan of dismay which escaped his throat. Luckily, the men didn't hear him over their own conversation. It was Nanitte, the dancer Macsen had brought back to his maisonette the night before the ambush at Birmingham Pool. Now that was scary. Ivarl clearly operated at a level which had completely eluded Edeard. This room was the right setting for the gang master after all; he was smart and sophisticated, with money and an unseen influence that extended a great deal further than Edeard liked to think about.

Edeard had come here in the hope of overhearing a few incriminating conversations. Now he knew that Ivarl wasn't going to be removed simply by a couple of well-planned arrests and some raids. If he was going to do this, to take out Ivarl and ruin the gangs, he was going to have to sharpen up his own act considerably. He would have to learn how Ivarl functioned, where his interests lay, who his friends were. With a depressing sensation, Edeard guessed that the gang master could never have grown to this stature without help from the city's establishment.

One thing at a time.

He strengthened his concealment, and settled down to listen.

*

It snowed the day after New Year. Big soft flakes sliding down out of a grey sky, deadening the sound of the city. Edeard bathed early, then ate a decent breakfast of scrambled eggs and grilled bacon, with some slices of Orkby black pudding thrown in the frying pan along with his mushrooms. He was pretty certain he wasn't going to get any lunch today. When he dressed he made sure his new, thickened drosilk waistcoat was fastened properly, then added a pair of drosilk undertrousers as well. There could well be a lot of resistance from the gang members during the raid, and he knew over half of them were armed with pistols.

He went out on to the walkway to finish his mug of tea, looking down on to the pool in the central oval courtyard. Snowflakes sank silently into the still surface as strands of vapour rose up. The water was too warm to freeze, but not warm enough for any of the kids to swim in. Edeard had thought about increasing the pool's temperature, as he'd done with his own maisonette, but once again he'd resisted for fear of drawing attention to his ability.

Boyd and Dinlay came along the walkway, their cheeks flushed by the cold air. Dinlay as always was immaculately turned out, with a regulation knee-length coat exactly the same colour as his tunic, even the silver buttons were the same size and shape.

Boyd had chosen a brown leather greatcoat, quilted on the inside. Edeard had admired it so much, he'd gone to the same shop in Cobara district to get himself one.

'Everything okay?' Dinlay asked anxiously. Since his return to duties two months ago, he'd been working hard to prove himself to his squadmates. Too keen, really; but they'd all gritted their teeth and waited until he lost his manic edge.

Edeard was praying to the Lady that this raid would make him feel like a full part of the team again; he had one last trick to make that a reality. 'No movement. The ge-eagles have been watching the street all night. Trukal and Harawold are still inside. Lian is with his girlfriend in Sampalok.'

'What about Ivarl?'

'Where he always is,' Edeard said. He was actually surprised by how little Ivarl ventured out of the House of Blue Petals; but then anyone he wanted to see responded quickly to his summons. There were Grand Council Masters who didn't command that much respect. On the plus side, that made it a lot easier for Edeard to keep watch on his opponent; by now he knew the House of Blue Petals better than any building in Makkathran except Jeavons station.

For the last two weeks he'd eavesdropped on the plans for their robbery in Vaji district. It was audacious and impressive, breaking in to the Chemistry Guild yard during New Year's Eve, and stealing their stockpile of platinum ingots. The planning was meticulous, using over twenty gang members and four gondolas. They'd gathered guard rosters, bribed a couple of Guild members to leave certain doors open, used girls to make sure other strategic people were away from their posts. They even staged a fight in a tavern to occupy constables from Vaji station – what could be more natural than a drunken brawl on New Year's Eve?

Once he'd learned all that, the real manoeuvring game began. Edeard told the squads under his command that he'd got a source in Ivarl's gang, and there was a robbery being arranged. That took less than a day to get back to the gang master, and the resulting friction and suspicion it unleashed among otherwise trusted lieutenants was a joy to behold. Then Edeard convinced Ronark to allow the robbery to go ahead, promising his 'source' had revealed the hideaway where the ingots were to be stashed. That was where the constables' raid should take place, he insisted, after they'd let the gang think they'd got away with it, and hopefully luring out senior gang members to the hideaway as they began to fence the platinum to unscrupulous merchants and loose-moralled jewellers.

After that, Ivarl called in Trukal and Lian to announce a slight change of plan that only the three of them would know about. Edeard almost laughed out loud as they quietly plotted their reverse deception. After all, the deceit and counter-trickery was starting to muddle his head, but this wasn't about the robbery anymore. This was him and Ivarl going head on. Watching Ivarl from within his concealment, he could see his adversary knew that, too.

Kanseen and Macsen arrived outside Edeard's maisonette. They looked eager.

'No hangover?' Edeard enquired lightly.

'Not from last night,' Macsen said. 'I have an example to set to the rest of your squads. I was in bed by nine o'clock with a cup of hot chocolate.' He winked at Boyd. 'Alisool knows how to make really good chocolate.'

Kanseen wrinkled up her nose. 'Lady preserve us from your ego.'

'Let's go,' Edeard told them.

When they got to the Jeavons station, the two other squads that were under Edeard's command were already waiting for them in the small hall. Everybody was sharing the same anticipatory glow. Droal and Urarl, the squad leaders, both saluted, which Edeard returned scrupulously. He was doing his best not to direct any attention towards Vilby.

'Everything all right?' Urarl asked. He was a couple of years older than Edeard, a third son from a smithy in the Cobara district. Strictly speaking he'd been due promotion, though he never showed any resentment towards Edeard for making corporal first.

'They haven't moved,' Edeard assured everyone in the hall. 'Chae's team has been observing them all night. The ingots are there waiting for us, and we've identified seventeen gang members involved. The courts are going to be very busy this afternoon.'

Captain Ronark led another three squads into the small hall. 'Ready to go?' he asked.

'Yes, sir,' Edeard said.

'Here's your weapons certificate,' the station commander said, handing over a small parchment with his official seal. 'I've just longtalked with the commanders of Neph and Bellis stations; they're reserving some squads to assist with the arrests. Good move, that. Don't want to put their noses out of joint.'

'Thank you, sir.' Edeard looked up as Probationary Constable Felax hurried into the room. The lad was only seventeen; he'd joined up just after Birmingham Pool, along with twenty others. Chae claimed his life was now a nightmare trying to train so many worthless screw-ups. Privately, of course, he was loving it.

'All the warrants signed, sir,' Felax said. 'Judge Salby says good luck.'

Edeard put the warrants into his pocket without looking at them. 'You can stay with us for today, we'll need runners.'

'Thank you, sir,' Felax said worshipfully.

'Okay, your attention please,' Edeard said, stepping up on a bench. 'The ingots taken from the Chemistry Guild are sitting underneath a house in Whitemire Street in Sampalok. They're being guarded by five or six armed gang members; however, we expect more gang members to arrive this morning to begin distributing them to dodgy merchants across the city. Keeping the ingots in one place is risky for them. So we need to move in after those carriers arrive and before they leave. That will give us the maximum amount of people to arrest. Once we have recovered the ingots, we'll also be arresting everyone involved in the crime; but I have to stress we need the ingots as evidence. The first time I was in court with Arminel taught me that.'

A ripple of laughter went round the room.

'We have three ge-eagles and ten ge-hounds from this station as back-up; and in addition we'll have a number of other squads from Bellis and Neph. We know some of the gang members are armed, which is why we're being issued with pistols; but please only use them as a last resort. I don't want any casualties. This is a big operation, and it's going to send a very loud New Year message from us constables to the gangs that this is going to be their last year in Makkathran.'

Macsen and Dinlay led the applause and whistles.

'It's going to be total chaos,' Macsen said as they made their way down the Grand Major Canal on a gondola, another four gondolas following them carrying the rest of the squads.

'Why?' Dinlay demanded irately. 'Edeard has done a great job organizing this.'

'Oh yeah? Who has responsibility when we arrive? The squads from Bellis and Neph are going to want to grab the credit, and they'll be led by sergeants. No disrespect, Edeard, but there are too many constables involved. The squads aren't used to working as a big team.'

'I know,' Edeard said. He sat back happily in the gondola, and smiled up at the sky. It had stopped snowing, with the clouds starting to clear. Strong fingers of winter sunlight were stabbing down to glare on the snow-clad buildings of the city. With people starting to return to work after the New Year holiday, Makkathran had an air of clean expectation. He liked that.

'What are you up to?' Kanseen asked suspiciously.

'Actually, it's a lot worse than Macsen says,' Edeard said cheerfully. He glanced back at the gondolier, who was trying not to show too much obvious interest, and leaned forward to whisper to his friends. 'The gang knows we're coming.'

'How?' Boyd asked.

'My source told me.' In fact the link was a simple one. Three nights each week Vilby paid a visit to a private room in the Black Horse tavern where Nanitte was waiting for him.

'Who in the Lady's name is this source?' Macsen demanded. 'Everything we've done these last weeks is governed by what they've told us – you!'

'Can't tell you.' Edeard hadn't quite summoned up the courage to tell Macsen – of course, Macsen probably wouldn't even remember Nanitte.

Macsen growled and slumped back.

'So what do we do?' Dinlay asked.

'Use their arrogance against them.'

The squads from Bellis and Neph were waiting on the bridge by Mid Pool. Edeard's gondola pulled in to a mooring platform, and he got off to consult with the two sergeants in charge. Macsen had been right, their eagerness was palpable; Edeard knew they wouldn't follow his polite requests to coordinate with him. It would end up in a rush to make the arrests. He took out a map and showed them where the suspect house was in Whitemire Street, and they agreed to a pincer movement with their squads going through Pholas Park while Edeard took his across Myco, so they could converge on the hideaway from opposite sides. If the gang members did sense them coming, they'd still be trapped.

Edeard's gondola carried on down Great Major Canal, with Bellis on one side and Sampalok on the other. The difference was pronounced. Along the canal, the cylindrical buildings of Bellis were roofed by long twisting spires, cup-like juliet balconies bulged out of the walls as if they'd sagged open.

Sampalok was made up from big tenements not dissimilar to the one Edeard lived in, except these were three or four times the size, and the maisonettes were smaller. Families here were packed in tight. The broad streets circling the tenements were cluttered with rubbish; the district's ge-monkey sanitation teams seemed unable to cope. It was worse than Ashwell had been. And that would be a good starting point, Edeard thought, improve basic living conditions, give people higher expectations. *So why doesn't the District Master do something?*

As if reflecting their surroundings, the residents close to the canal stared sullenly at the gondolas carrying the constables. They spat into the water and made obscene gestures. A few third hands nudged at the small craft. Gangs of kids jeered when they saw the uniforms.

'Little buggers,' Boyd grunted.

'They need to be shown a different way,' Edeard said. 'That's all.'

'Too late,' Macsen said. 'This is what they know, it's the way life is lived here. You can't change it.'

Edeard stared at the skyline of sturdy uninspiring buildings, thinking how he could improve them, the new forms and functions he could shape. 'Don't be too sure,' he whispered.

Kanseen gave him a curious look, but said nothing.

They all disembarked at First Pool and made their way into Myco. It was strange for Edeard seeing it in daylight for once. Nothing like as shabby as its neighbour, the small district was occupied predominately by the families of fishermen and ship-builders, with a large Guild presence. They had a much stronger sense of community; pride Macsen called it.

'News for you,' Chae's directed longtalk informed Edeard as they walked down Maley Street, not far from the House of Blue Petals.

'What?'

'You're not going to believe who's just turned up to examine the ingots.'

'Who?'

'The good Captain Ivarl, himself.'

The squad members close to Edeard started grinning, hungry with anticipation.

'That makes sense,' Edeard replied.

'Lady, we've got him,' Boyd told the others, giving them a broad thumbs up.

'What do you mean?' Chae asked.

'He's come to gloat,' Edeard told him. His own farsight showed him the squads from Bellis and Neph hurrying through Pholas Park. As expected, they had already crossed into Sampalok via the bridge over Trade Route Canal, which put them a lot closer to the hideaway than Edeard. They'd arrive a good ten minutes early.

'What are you thinking?' Kanseen asked shrewdly.

Edeard halted the squads, and beckoned Felax forward. He handed an envelope over to the young probationary constable. 'I want you to go directly to the house in Whitemire Street and deliver this to the sergeants from the other squads.'

The lad saluted. 'Yes, sir, Waterwalker.'

'Quick as you can now,' Edeard said. He instructed one of the ge-eagles to keep watch on the lad as he started running.

'What's happening?' Macsen demanded.

'Slight change of plan,' Edeard announced. 'Follow me, please.'

He turned off down Campden Avenue, which was lined with winter-flowering Jakral trees whose sky-blue puffball flowers were just budding. Water dripped of the encrustations of snow on their overhanging branches. There were a lot of whispers and longtalk queries behind him, which he ignored. They were heading away from Sampalok now; the avenue led straight to the Upper Tail Canal which bordered the Port district.

'Dinlay,' Edeard called. 'Take Urarl's squad, and split off down the next alley.' He held up the map so only his friend could see it. 'That's the building we want; you come at it from this side,' his finger indicated. 'Make sure no one leaves, remember to watch the windows, and the roof.'

'What's in there?' Dinlay asked.

Edeard leant forward so his lips were almost touching Dinlay's ear. 'The ingots.'

The switch had been made with considerable precision in the middle of the night. As the gondolas loaded with ingots made their way back from the Chemistry Guild yard to the safety of Sampalok they passed under several bridges along Roseway

Canal, including the broad stone and iron archway at the end of Abad's Royal Boulevard, which led over to Nighthouse district. It took precision timing, but Ivarl made sure that another gondola was going in the opposite direction at exactly the same time. For a few seconds the gondolas were out of direct view of the ge-eagles which the constables were using to observe them. The solid bridge structure made farsight difficult especially when the gondolas were surrounded by a seclusion haze. Identical boxes were thrown between the gondolas.

Edeard had to admire how smoothly they'd managed it. What Ivarl hadn't taken into account was for Edeard to know the plan in its entirety, and be using the sight of a ge-cat swimming idly under the bridge. Grand Master Finitan had been happy to help, loaning Edeard fifteen of the genistars so he could position several under each bridge. Once Edeard had confirmed the switch had been made, it was easy for him to track the new gondolas as they took a long route back round to Myco, where they landed the boxes at a slipway. Ivarl's men carried the boxes into a fisherman's warehouse.

'Oh dear,' Chae's sardonic longtalk reverberated round Edeard's squads. 'Captain Ivarl seems to be upset about something.' His gifted sight showed the gang master rushing out of the house in Sampalok, his face red, almost running. Several of his lieutenants were following, their expressions anxious.

Edeard grinned at the warehouse, twenty yards ahead now. The big doors were open, showing a gloomy interior filled with barrels. Several fishermen and women were sitting outside, mending nets. More nets were hung up in great loops inside, drying off.

'Seal it up,' Edeard told his squads.

The people working on the nets looked up in alarm as the constables appeared. Ge-eagles swooped low, keeping a keen eye on the slipway leading into the warehouse. Ge-hounds growled in warning.

'Please remain where you are,' Edeard announced. 'I have a warrant to search the premises.'

Dinlay and two constables blocked one of the fishermen who tried to sprint away.

'Kanseen, take Macsen and Droal inside, have a scan round for me, please. You might want to check the cellars.'

'You sneaky beast,' she muttered, grinning as she went into the warehouse.

Then Edeard's farsight caught someone running down the slipway on the other side of the warehouse. He jumped off the side of the canal, holding the surface of the water firm as he landed. It held his weight, with only a slight dint under each foot as he ran round to the slipway. People on the other side of the wide canal stooped and stared. Fingers were pointed. Cheers echoed across the icy water. Children called their friends to watch. It was the Waterwalker, they cried, he's doing it again.

Edeard arrived at the end of the slipway. Lian was there, trying to push a small dinghy into the water. 'Don't go,' Edeard asked nicely. 'We're only just getting started.'

Lian was longtalking frantically. One hand went to the coat pocket with his pistol.

Edeard gave him a warning look. 'It didn't do Arminel any good. Remember?'

Lian glared furiously, but backed away from the boat, raising his hands. Droal came down the slipway behind him and removed the pistol before slapping on the handcuffs.

'What is going on?' demanded the sergeant from Bellis station. Edeard's farsight observed them arriving at the house in Sampalok.

'We farsighted them moving the stolen items earlier,' Edeard replied, keeping his mental tone level as he examined the dinghy. 'Didn't have time to tell you. Sorry. My runner has a list for you. It has the names of everyone involved in the Chemistry Guild robbery. Most of them live in the tenements close to the hide-away. Would you arrest them, please?' He was aware of the callous humour shining out of Chae's mind as the Bellis sergeant snatched the envelope from Felax.

'Oh, Lady,' Kanseen exclaimed. 'Edeard, you've got to see this.'

'On my way,' he said.

The cellar under the warehouse was one of Ivarl's clandestine stores. Edeard had only taken a fast sweep with his farsight a couple of days earlier for fear of attracting attention. He'd noted the crates, bottles, and sacks piled up in the three vaulting cellars underneath. There were a lot of them.

Macsen and Urarl began opening crates, finding an astonishing array of expensive silverware. Smaller boxes contained jewellery. The sacks held bales of raw drosilk. There were bags of tea and spices from provinces hundreds of miles along the coast. Bottles of fortified wines were stacked to the arching ceilings.

'It's going to take a week to list all this,' Urarl said in astonishment. They'd only opened the first few boxes in one cellar.

'Help's on its way,' Edeard assured him.

By wonderful coincidence Ronark arrived at the same time as Ivarl. The Jeavons captain led three gondolas carrying accountants from the Guild of Clerks, who had followed Edeard down the Great Major Canal at a leisurely pace. They moored to the slipway at the same time Ivarl came hurtling out of Campden Avenue, out of breath and very *very* angry.

'I forgot you said you lived around here.' Edeard smiled at the gang master. 'How nice to see you again.'

Ivarl glared at Edeard, then at the impassive Captain Ronark. His gold-topped cane was raised. He hesitated.

'Is there something we can do for you?' Edeard asked as Dinlay and Kanseen carried the first boxes of ingots out of the warehouse. Ivarl's wild-eyed stare switched to the boxes with their precious contents.

'Would you like to retrieve something in here, perhaps?' Edeard continued. 'We'll need to see an invoice of course. There are a great many items stored in the cellars. Strangely, the Mayor's port inspectors have no record of them being landed at

Makkathran, and consequently no duty being paid. I'm sure the accountants will soon calculate how much is owed on them. Until then they'll be placed in a city store. Perhaps someone will come forward to claim them and pay the tax.'

A reluctant grin appeared on Ivarl's face. 'You're good, Waterwalker.'

'Just doing my duty.'

'But you have to be good the whole time. And good fortune is a fickle thing.'

'Yes. I'm sure Tanamin will agree with that.' It was two nights earlier when Edeard had listened to the sickening instructions Ivarl had issued to Harawold on the punishment to be given to Tanamin, who hadn't extorted enough money from his patch in Fiacre district.

Ivarl couldn't cover up the flash of surprise in his mind. When he did veil his emotions he was regarding Edeard with the kind of caution reserved for a cornered fastfox. 'Yes. Very good, I see that now. Are you sure you won't accept my hospitality? Together we can accomplish a great deal.'

'There's not much to be accomplished from inside the Trampello mine.'

'I see. That's a shame.'

'Was there anything else?'

'No. Not today.'

2

By midday the Ellezelin paramilitary capsules streaking across Colwyn City had all taken to using their sirens, producing a constant doppler-mangled cacophony as they rushed between burgeoning trouble spots. Scarlet and azure laser fans would often sweep through the open balcony doors of Araminta's apartment as another one flew across the park outside, accompanying the discordant sound. Araminta scowled as the dazzling light flared across the kitchen area of the living room once more. She'd been making herself a cup of tea from a kettle, while the old culinary unit strove to fabricate the components of a simple chicken sandwich. She cursed, and kicked the base of the stupid unit as another set of thermal error symbols flashed up on its screen. Perhaps the laser light was disturbing its internal systems?

She sighed and shook her head, annoyed with herself for thinking something so silly. The worst thing was just sitting around doing nothing. *Actually no, it's not knowing what to do.*

Another capsule screeched overhead. Araminta slammed down the kettle, and stomped over to the open balcony doorway. The capsule had vanished behind the apartment building by the time she got there, presumably harassing the people in the park, which seemed to have developed into quite a centre for disobedience against the invaders. She would have liked to slam the doorway shut as well, but the glass wall sheet was formflow, so she had to settle for the glass slowly curtaining together. At least when it had become a single sheet again the sound of the sirens did reduce considerably – as it should with the expensive sound-deadening layer she'd added. The doorway had been open all day to give her some sense of connection to the city. It was kind of stupid, yet comforting at the same time. In fact, all she'd been doing was avoiding thinking about the real events. She'd certainly not done any work on the apartment.

Her u-shadow had pulled a steady stream of news out of the unisphere, all relating to the Void expansion. There were very few hard facts, and far too much speculation and accusation. But her u-shadow was running an adequate filter, supplying her with the basics. Nothing much had changed. The observation team had evacuated Centurion Station. All the shows were playing the images of the base itself collapsing. Of more interest were the enigmatic DF spheres flying into orbit around the star. Commentators in the news studios were busy speculating on exactly what they were capable of; apparently they'd been copied by the Anomine who used them to imprison the Dyson Pair. Now everyone was hoping that they had more aggressive functions than simple force fields, no matter the gigantic scale.

Despite the loss of Centurion Station, a large number of sensor systems out amid the Wall stars were still operational and feeding their data back to the Commonwealth via the tenuous Navy relay. The Void boundary continued to expand, its surface rippling and distending to engulf the star clusters already falling in towards it. That voraciousness was cited by many as having purpose. Which came back squarely to the Second Dreamer and the Skylord.

After the balcony doors *clicked* shut she sank to her knees on the bare concrete floor. The tears she'd managed to contain all morning threatened to finally emerge. *It's too much. No one person can expect to deal with all of this. I can't have put the entire galaxy in peril. I can't.*

Her u-shadow reported a new file shotgunning into the unisphere, passed between each node without restriction by the management routines and given unlimited access to everybody's interface address. It was a live feed to an address code she didn't recognize, but had Earth as its node host.

'Only ANA can achieve this level of coverage,' the u-shadow told her.

'Access it,' she ordered. If ANA wanted to talk to everybody it must have some words of comfort.

Gore Burnelli was standing on some rocky cliffs, his back to the clear tropical sea beyond. He wore a simple white shirt, his fair hair tousled by the breeze. Grey eyes stared out of a handsome twenty-year-old face, with skin tanned to a dusky gold. He looked directly at Araminta, making her feel incredibly guilty for no reason she could define.

'I doubt anyone out there in the Greater Commonwealth will remember me,' he said. 'But I used to be one of the wealthy people who helped form the original Commonwealth. If you check my record you'll see I had a brief moment of fame in the Starflyer War. I hope that what I've done in the past will qualify me for a moment of your time here now; however, this is not about me. I'm speaking to one person alone: the Second Dreamer. I understand that you didn't realize the Skylord would kick off a devourment phase when you spoke to it. I don't blame you. I don't condemn you. And unlike everyone else I'm certainly not hunting you down. On which front, please be warned it's not just Living Dream that's coming for you, a number of other agents are searching, who represent various political factions both here in ANA and other Greater Commonwealth groups.'

'Oh, great Ozzie,' Araminta wailed. Now the tears really were flowing free.

'Everyone is making a lot of demands of you,' Gore said. 'I expect you're frightened and uncertain. I also expect you want to stay out of sight, certainly everything you've done so far indicates this. I appreciate that. You're coming to terms with what you are, and nobody can help with that. You have a lot of decisions to make, and I don't envy you any of them. If you want to get in touch with me, I'll help in any way I can, that goes without saying. Again, that's not why I am making this appeal. There is one thing that does not require a decision: the Void devourment phase must be stopped. As far as we are aware you are the only one who can *currently* do this. I say that because someone else is trying to help.' Gore took a breath and squared his shoulders, trying to be brave. 'My daughter, Justine, was at Centurion Station when the devourment kicked off. Unlike everyone else there, she didn't head back home. Against all my wishes, my pleas, my hopes, she's aimed her ship directly for the Void. It's one of the secret ultradrive ships you may have heard rumours of. Very fast. Which means that in another day or so she'll arrive at the boundary. Justine's not like me, she's sweet and kind, very much an optimist, all the things to be proud of in our species. She's been involved in diplomatic work for centuries. She's flying alone to the Void in the hope she can talk to the Skylord; she believes that reason will prevail. But first she has to get inside. Humans have done that once before. Inigo and the Waterwalker showed us that. I appeal to you, Second Dreamer, to contact the Skylord one last time, and ask it to let Justine in. That's all, just ask it that one thing, nothing else. You don't have to talk about the devourment phase, or the Pilgrimage. Just give my daughter a chance to try to negotiate with whatever passes for authority in there. Justine is going to fly into the boundary come what may; despite everything I've said to try to stop her, she believes in humanity, that our nature should be placed upon this alien altar and given a chance. She believes in us. I hope, I beg, you will do what you can to give her that chance. Don't let my girl die in vain, I beseech you. If there's anything you need or want, then contact me in complete safety at the code on this file. Please. One last time, help put a stop to what's happening out there. There's not much time left. Help her. Only you can.'

Araminta put her hands over her head as the message finished, wanting nothing more than to curl up in a ball and leave the universe altogether. 'Thanks for fucking nothing,' she told the haunting memory of Gore. At the same time she felt a tiny lifting of doubt. *Maybe this Justine woman can do something. Maybe it's not all down to me after all.*

That just left getting in touch with the Skylord without Living Dream and all the others tracking her down. *Yeah, that should be dead easy for someone who can't even get a culinary unit to make a sandwich.*

*

In the middle of a desert of dry mud was a house, an igloo of baked sand. It had a wooden door that years ago had been painted dark green. Harsh sunlight and dusty winds had abraded it down to the bare wood, though some flecks of green still persevered in the cracks between the oak boards.

He knew that door. Knew it well. Knew what lay behind.

The sun hung at the apex of the world's sapphire sky, bleaching all colour out of the desert. It was always thus.

He dismounted from the huge Charlemagne just short of the igloo, his plain white robes flowing around him. The deep hood protected his face from the sun's penetrating rays. Somehow, those few steps to the door took forever. His limbs were fighting an unknown force that resisted every movement. He kept asking himself if he wanted to do this because he eventually realized that the force fighting him was fear. Fear of what waited for him on the other side of the door. He carried on anyway, because in this, as always, he had no choice, no will, no independence. The effort left him trembling from exertion, but eventually the door was in front of him. He raised his hand, placing it palm down on the warm wood, feeling the familiar sand-smoothed grain. Pushed.

The door opened, and darkness spilled out, contaminating the sunlight. It built round him like a fog, and his dread spiked upwards. But the door was open. There was nothing now between him and the person living in the house. Something moved in the shadows, a presence that was reaching out.

'You and your father both had the courage to make the right choice in the end,' a voice told him. 'Not that my opinion counts for anything. But I'm glad. I figure I owe you this second chance.'

'My father?' He lurched forwards—

—the ground crawler lurched again as the front tracks cleared another ice ridge, and the wedge nose tipped down sharply. Aaron shook himself as the real world claimed him back from bedlam, gripping the chair arms, staring out of the slit windscreen. It was profoundly dark outside, midnight beneath clouds that towered five kilometres into the screaming hurricane sky. Headlight beams were clotted by driving snow. The small glimpse of the ground they did allow revealed ice boulders half the size of the ground crawler. Regular bursts of lightning showed the wicked, sharp-edged boulders scattered across the frozen land in all directions without end. Narrow gaps between them were becoming fewer, and had been for the last hour. It was a nightmare geography out there. Their progress was pitiful, and getting worse.

He checked the vehicle's inertial navigation system. In the last two hours they'd travelled a grand total of seven and a quarter kilometres, and very little of that was in a nice straight line forwards. Over a day now since the unknown starship fired a Hawking m-sink into Hanko. He was beginning to wish he had the math to work out an accurate timetable for how long it would take the weapon to digest the planet from within. But knowing the exact moment when the continents would implode wasn't going to make the ground crawler go any faster. His early rough estimate of three days was realistic enough.

The crawler's net slowed the tracks, which Aaron perceived first as a change in the constant vibration afflicting the cabin. When he asked it why he was shown a radar sweep. There was a rift in the ground ahead, a vertical drop of over ten metres.

'Lady!' Inigo exclaimed as he studied the radar profile; his face was gently shaded by the weak violet light emitted by the two polyphoto strips on the cabin roof. 'It's going to take half an hour to cut our way down that.'

'You're the expert,' Aaron muttered sourly.

Inigo gave him a tight smile. 'I certainly am.' He gripped the manual control stick, and backed up, then activated the forward power blades. They extended out of the nose and began rotating. The ground crawler edged forwards again, and the spinning blades touched the ice. A wide plume of dirty ice granules shot up into the snowstorm. The screech from the blades resonated round the cabin, and the whole vehicle began to shake as they started to dig themselves a track. Inigo steered them carefully, curving round to run parallel to the rift, always descending. The plume reduced visibility to zero. He was relying on the vehicle's sensors and his own field effect scan. The lost messiah must have had some sophisticated filter programs, Aaron decided; his own scan revealed little beyond the crawler's bodywork. The ice they were traversing showed up as a thick unified substance laced with rock and soil, like a haze of interference; yet Inigo was able to discern the structure, knowing when to back off and when to apply pressure.

The noise of the power blades set Aaron's teeth on edge. Its tone was constantly changing as they hit soil, then back into ice. Then the blades hit some kind of rock, and the rasping was so bad he wanted to hit something. When he glanced back at Corrie-Lyn she was pressing her hands over her ears, her teeth bared in a wild grimace of dismay. Inigo adjusted the stick fractionally, curving them away from the dense strata. Rock and ice gravel spewed out sideways, falling in a long arc down the side of the rift. Inigo drove them into the ice again, gouging a wider cut.

So they descended in a series of howling bumps and jolts, creating their own ramp. In the end it took over forty-five minutes to reach the base of the rift. The power blades retracted. Aaron gazed out in dismay at the field of ice boulders which the lightning flares revealed. They were larger than the ones at the top of the rift, and closer together.

'Crap,' he grunted. 'We're never going to get through this.

How far does it extend?' If they didn't clear the boulder field in the next couple of hours, they would never make it to the ship before the implosion.

'I don't know,' Inigo replied unperturbed. 'We don't exactly have survey maps.' He steered the crawler along the base of the rift, looking for an opening.

'You must do!'

'Not recent ones. They're all a thousand years out of date, and the surface ice does shift. Slowly, admittedly, but the movement throws up a fresh topography every century or so.'

'Shit!' Aaron finally did hit something, his fist thudding into the cabin wall. 'We have *got* to make better time than this.'

'I know.'

Corrie-Lyn came forward from her seat and slipped her arms around Inigo's neck. The low cabin lighting made her beautiful features deeply sensual. 'You're doing your best, ignore him.'

Aaron growled in frustration, and hit the wall again. Back at the Olhava camp, Inigo had finally admitted he did have a private starship hidden away, for emergencies. Aaron's elation at the escape route had quickly cooled as the ground crawler got underway. According to Inigo his ship was safe in a tunnelled-out cavern seven hundred kilometres south-east of the camp. Aaron had assumed they would make it with almost a couple of days to spare. Then they drove straight into the ice boulder field.

'We always trailblaze through this kind of thing,' Inigo told him as Corrie-Lyn rubbed her cheek adoringly against his. 'That's how I got to be so good with the power blades.'

'Get better or we die,' Aaron said bluntly.

Inigo flashed him a grin, then turned the ground crawler into a small gap. Razor-sharp shards of ice creaked and snapped against the bodywork as they scraped their way through. Aaron winced, convinced they'd wedge themselves in again. They'd done that once before a few hours back. He and Inigo had to go outside and use their biononic field effect to cut the vehicle free. It had felt good using his weapon functions, even on a minimum setting. He was accomplishing something.

The only benefit of the journey was that Corrie-Lyn hadn't touched a drop of alcohol since they started.

'So have you any idea who was in that starship?' Inigo asked.

'No. I didn't even realize we were being followed, which is disturbing enough. To track the *Artful Dodger* you'd need something as good if not better. That kind of hardware is mighty difficult to come by, so it was either ANA or a Faction. But ANA wouldn't use an m-sink like that, and I'm kind of surprised a Faction did.'

'No honour among thieves, eh?'

'None,' Aaron agreed. 'Using an m-sink has the sure taste of desperation to it.'

'Hold a mirror up,' Corrie-Lyn said. 'It was a ruthless despicable act, slaughtering all those people without warning or reason. The pilot must have been just like you.'

'There are people in this universe a lot worse than me.'

'That I don't believe.'

But it's true. He smiled privately.

'So where were you supposed to coerce me into going?' Inigo asked.

'I'll know when we're safe on the ship.'

'Really? That's . . . interesting.'

'It's depraved,' Corrie-Lyn said.

'Actually, it's a simple and safe security measure,' Aaron told them. 'If I don't know, I can't be forced to reveal it.'

'But you do know,' she said. 'It's buried somewhere in your subconscious.'

'Yes, but I can't get to it unless the circumstances are coming up straight aces.'

'You've damaged your own psyche with so much meddling.'

'I've told you often before, and I'll enjoy telling you many times again: I like what I am.'

'Oh Lady, now what!' Inigo exclaimed as the crawler's net halted them again. He glanced at the radar screen with its concentric orange bands swirling round like an accelerated orrery. 'That's weird.' His grey eyes narrowed as he squinted through the windscreen. The headlights revealed a white blur of snow, but no boulders. Lightning flashes turned the black night to a leaden smog. There were no discernible shapes ahead of them.

Aaron's field scan revealed the ice had flattened out in front of the crawler's tracks. Then it ended in another sharp-edged rift. He couldn't pick up anything beyond. 'There's nothing out there.'

'I think that's the problem.'

They both suited up to take a look. Inigo said he didn't want to get the crawler too close to the rift until they knew what they were dealing with. Aaron shrugged and went with it. He didn't like wearing the surface suit – his biononics could produce a good defence against Hanko's foul environment – but it added an extra layer of protection, which his instinct insisted was the right thing in a situation with so many unknowns.

The two of them kept close to the headlight beams, leaning into the wind. As they shuffled closer to the edge, Aaron's field scan still couldn't detect anything beyond.

'Where the hell's the ground gone?' he demanded. His field scan probed the ice beneath his feet. There were a few centimetres of crisp snow, then clear ice down as far as the scan could reach. It was as though they were on the top of some giant frozen wave.

'Must be a gully of some description,' Inigo replied. 'If the pressure is right the ice can fissure instead of throwing up a ridge.'

'Great.'

'It should close up soon. I've never seen an ice fissure over five hundred metres long. You check that way. And don't go too near the edge.'

'Right.' Aaron started to walk parallel to the edge, keeping a good three or four metres between him and the drop. He soon came to a flat triangular prominence jabbing out from the verge, which he shuffled along cautiously, feeling the slight stirrings of vertigo. If anywhere would allow him a decent look into the gulf below, it would be here.

He extended his field scan to its maximum, sweeping it through the heavy swirl of snow. Even at full resolution he couldn't detect the other side of the rough fissure. Nor was there any sign of a bottom. He was standing on the brink of some massive abyss. Instinct kicked in, firing up his misgivings. Something Nerina said back at the camp registered. 'Hey, are we—' His scan showed him Inigo's field function was switching, reformatting energy currents. His own biononics responded instantaneously, strengthening his integral force field, shielding him from any damage Inigo's outdated systems could possibly inflict. Accelerants rode his nerve paths ready to implement his response. Tactical routines rose out of macrocellular clusters, fusing effortlessly with his thoughts, analysing his situation. That was when he realized just how badly he'd screwed up by trusting Inigo. '*Shiiiit!*'

Inigo fired the biggest disruptor pulse his biononics could produce. It slammed into the ice a couple of metres short of Aaron's feet. For a moment, the whole prominence fluoresced an elegant jade. As the light faded, a single giant crack appeared with incredible speed, splitting the prominence off the edge of the Asiatic glacier.

Aaron stared in shock at the ruptured ice. Tactics programs rushed to find a counter—

'Sorry,' Inigo said simply. The thoughts leaking out of his gaiamotes even proved he meant it. 'But sometimes to do what's right . . .'

The entire prominence split away cleanly. To Aaron's accelerated nervous system it appeared to hang there for some terrible eternity. Then gravity pulled the colossal chunk of ice straight down with Aaron standing at the centre. It began to twist as the edges screeched down the cliff. His force field reconfigured, extending into a twin swept-petal shape – wings that could glide him away. Not good in the midst of this snowstorm, but better than anything else. That was when the vast cataract of avalanching snow triggered by Inigo's shot thundered into him, engulfing the tumbling prominence and him with it.

The whole mass continued to plummet down the mile-high cliff, taking a long time to reach the bottom.

Silverbird arrowed through the Gulf, the immense expanse of ruined stars and tattered ion storms which lay between the dense halo of ancient globular clusters that comprised the Wall stars and the boundary of the Void itself. Justine was receiving the hysradar and quantum scanner images direct, surrounding herself with the mass structure of the real universe translated into scarlet and turquoise mists. Tiny points of emerald light shone within the shifting cosmic oceans, showing her the supermassive stars which had so far retained their integrity during their long spiral into oblivion. Less than a hundred lightyears ahead of her was the frosty glow of the loop, an orbiting band of supercharged matter ten lightyears across which emitted a galaxy-spanning blaze of X-rays. Beyond that was the awesome black surface of the Void boundary. She watched its topology fluctuate, marvelling at how ocean-like the waves were, with peaks and troughs ripping about chaotically, stirred by incomprehensible internal storm-forces. Quite often she would see an undulation swell out to reach the elongated plume of a disintegrating star that was still lightmonths away. Phenomenal gravity sucked the matter down into the event horizon with a last devastating flare of ultra-hard radiation, the kind which had powered the loop for a billion years. Even that siren call would end soon. At its current expansion rate the Void would engulf the loop in another week. Then it would just be the Wall and the Raiel DF defences that stood between the boundary and the rest of the galaxy.

Justine felt her body shiver again. It was hard to comprehend the scale of the forces outside. She was feeling very small and alone.

'Dad?'

'Still here, darling. The relay is holding. Big Bronx cheer for the old Navy techs who put it together.'

'We left the last known sensor systems behind five minutes ago. The link might not last much longer.'

'Course it will, angel. This was meant to be.'

'Yeah, right.'

'I'm looking at the access figures for the unisphere. You've got over half of humanity looking over your shoulder right now.'

'Hi there, half of humanity,' she said brittley.

'You're doing fine. And I'm in deep shit with ANA for publically admitting there's such a thing as ultradrive.'

'Ha! You're always in trouble.'

'True. Without me, lawyers would just wither away and die. They think of me as their messiah. Remember when we got caught planting the Florida estate with alien vines?'

'Hell, yes. The UFN Environmental Commissioners went apeshit with us.'

'There are banks we own on the External worlds still paying off that fine.'

Justine barked a laugh. Drew down a juddering breath. She desperately wanted out of her ancient body with all its silly biochemical-derived fright. Anyone would think her personality was genuinely scared. 'Any sign the Second Dreamer accessed your appeal?'

'Not yet. I expect he'll be talking to the Skylord quite soon now. After all, he'll have to face me if he doesn't start getting his ass in gear. Isn't that right, Second Dreamer?'

'Now, Dad,' she chided.

'Yeah, yeah.'

'I think I'm going to skim round the loop. That radiation is strong enough to slice through the *Silverbird*'s force fields as if they were tissue paper. Can you believe the figures I'm getting.'

'You'll be quite safe in hyperspace.'

'I know, but . . .'

'Whatever makes you comfortable, angel.'

Justine instructed the smartcore to fly to galactic south of the loop. 'That's odd.' The sensors were picking up an artificial signature over forty lightyears behind her. She focused on the origin, which the smartcore displayed as two amber circles. 'Uh, Dad, are you getting this?'

Gore took a moment to answer. 'Yes.'

'Whatever they are, they're travelling ftl.'

'See that.'

'I didn't know there was anyone else flying round this part of the galaxy.' Tabulated data flowed up into her exovision. 'Christ, they're massive.' A wild thought surfaced. 'Do you think they're Skylords?' she asked eagerly.

'No, darling, I don't. They're bigger than that. And that's an interception course.'

'Oh.' Her mood dropped fast. 'The Raiel. And they're fast, too. Faster than *Silverbird*. Just.' It would be touch and go if she reached the boundary ahead of them. 'I don't suppose they're here to escort me in safely.'

'I'm calling Qatux right now. He'll sort this out.'

'Okay, Dad.'

The external sensor visualization flashed white for a microsecond, as if a lightning bolt had zipped through it. Once it cleared, there was an ominous translucent lavender shell emerging where the Raiel ships were, expanding rapidly. Secondary data streams showed her the anomaly was centred on a mass point the size of Earth's moon that had been curving in towards the Void on a ten-million-year journey to its death. *Had been.* It had vanished, converted directly to exotic energy which was now flowing through hyperspace.

'Oh FUCK,' Justine yelled. *Silverbird* strengthened every defensive system it had.

The hyperspace shockwave struck the little ultradrive ship with the force of a wayward dinosaur. Justine screamed as she was flung out of the couch, crashing into the forward bulkhead. Alarms shrieked back at her. A multitude of exovision schematics turned amber and red.

The crowd of anti-invasion protestors down in the park gasped in unison as the *Silverbird* juddered, then let out a long 'Ohooo,' of wonder and relief. Araminta couldn't help but join in, thankful Justine had survived the third shockwave propagated by the pursuing Raiel warships and was now picking herself up off the cabin floor again. It was a sound which was replicated right across Colwyn City and beyond. A long way beyond.

She slipped in through the apartment block's underground garage entrance. The door was still open a couple of metres, not wide enough to admit a capsule, but sufficient for her to take her trike out. She'd deactivated the mechanism as she left, opening up the little control box and physically disconnecting the wiring. Now she plugged the coloured cables back into their blocks. The door slid shut behind her, and she hurried through the near-deserted concrete cave to the lifts.

'You okay?' Gore asked.

'Bastards!' Justine replied shakily. 'What, this isn't hard enough already?'

Araminta sank back against the cool metal wall of the lift, feeling the way Justine looked. She'd driven round for an hour on the trike before parking it in a public bay at the Tala mall. Now there was nothing to prove she was at the apartment block – it was the best cover she could think of. The walk back to the Bodant district had taken forty minutes, during which the Raiel warships had started blowing up small moons to try and stop Justine. *Everyone* accessed that. It made her kind of conspicuous; she was just about the only person moving on Colwyn's streets.

'You're doing fine,' Gore assured his daughter. 'Just fine.'

Araminta used her old override code to unlock the door to Danal's apartment. Neither he nor Mareble were in. Presumably they were out partying with the occupying army, she thought resentfully. The bare structure of the place had just been finished when Araminta handed it over. Since then, Mareble had moved in a few basic furnishings. Araminta gave the cooker a critical glare, the big metal thing looked ridiculously primitive. It had taken Mr Bovey a long time to find it for her, and installing it had been a nightmare.

In Araminta's exovision, Justine was climbing back into her chair, which folded protectively around her. 'Main systems are functional. Drive units have reduced capacity. These energy bursts are stressing a lot of components. I guess they're trying to wear me down.'

Araminta crept over to the balcony windows, and peered out across the park. There were several Ellezelin capsules hanging above the encircling road. They were all stationary; like everyone else their occupants were captivated by the chase thirty thousand lightyears away. Below them, the crowd stared up into the heavens whose stars were smeared by the weather dome. She nodded in satisfaction.

'They're firing again,' Justine yelped. 'Oh Christ.'

The *Silverbird* shuddered violently. Araminta gritted her teeth, feeling the huge tremor of anticipation in the gaiafield. More sections of the ship reported overloads. The speed fell off as the drive reconfigured its energy manipulation functions around degraded components. Justine changed course, streaking into the loop, the shortest distance to the barrier. Both Raiel warships followed unerringly. Closing the gap.

Araminta pulled a big sky-blue cushion out of a nest pile and into the middle of the living room. She was annoyed to see the ebony-wood parquet had been stripped back to the bare wood. Didn't Mareble understand how difficult it was to get the varnish application correct? The work that had gone into cleaning the little wooden blocks!

She sat down on the cushion and crossed her legs, banishing such negative thoughts.

'Good strategy, darling,' Gore said. 'There aren't many planets inside the loop.'

Araminta retrieved Likan's program from her storage lacuna, feeling her mind finally settle. It was a risk using this apartment, but she wasn't sure how good Living Dream was at tracking people through the gaiafield. The day Danal had moved in he'd confided to her that he was helping with the search for the Second Dreamer, and how the confluence nests were being altered somehow to facilitate that. So she certainly didn't want to be in her own place when she did this, just in case they were accurate enough to fix the exact location. And they might just think Danal's apartment was some kind of false reading. She didn't know anywhere else she could go. Other than to Mr Bovey's house, but that would expose him to the paramilitaries, which she could never do.

The shadowy spectres of sensation that lurked within her subconscious expanded outwards. She let her attention swim across the myriad thoughts it contained. Drifting. Content in a way the program alone could never kindle.

Most of the thoughts she could ignore. Some were intriguing. One had a mental signature she knew, associated with a dark tone that almost made her shy away. Instead, she concentrated.

'My Lord,' Ethan was pleading. 'Hear us please.'

He was calling with all his mental strength, amplified by countless confluence nests, directing his appeal outwards into the infinite. *Wrong*, she mused from her lofty Olympian distance. *The Skylord is not beyond us, it is within.*

She drifted further, devoid of urgency.

'If you don't call them off I will personally rip your fucking arkship apart molecule by molecule with all of you in it,' Gore was yelling. 'You think the Void is a Bad Thing? Do you, huh? You believe that? Because let me tell you: it is your mommy with her titty out for you to suck on compared to me.'

Araminta couldn't help grinning. *Now that's the kind of father I would have liked.* Out in the park, people were cheering. A cry taken up across hundreds of planets. The gaiafield filled with determination and support, the raw emotion of billions, swelling the sense of unification to near ecstasy. Go Gore, humanity whooped. Araminta added her blessing, a whisper lost in the multitude.

'I can do nothing,' Qatux protested. 'They are warrior Raiel. Not our kind, not any longer.'

'Find a fucking way!'

Araminta lifted herself away from the turmoil, drifting towards a strand of familiar quiet thought. Opening herself in greeting. The nebulas of the Void emerged from darkness to glimmer spectacularly around her. Half of space was a gauzy splash of aquamarine with a few distant stars shining through. She recognized it as Odin's Sea where a Skylord coasted between two of the scarlet promontories, spikes of whorled gases light-years long, swelling to buds big enough to contain a globular cluster. And here, the thoughts of what once was mingled with more purposeful notions. An awareness wove through this space, not conscious, but knowing purpose.

Silverbird burst out of the loop and streaked towards the final implacable barrier. All around it, broken stars sleeted inwards, shedding the glowing husks of the planets they had once birthed as if they were an encumbrance during the final tumultuous plunge to extinction.

'Oh, God, here we go again,' Justine whimpered. Ten light-years behind her a gas-giant imploded. Hyperluminal quantum distortions burst out from its vanishing point.

The *Silverbird* dropped out of hyperspace, flying free in spacetime that no human would recognize. It was a dark universe inside the Wall stars. Thick braids of dust and gas shielded the light of the galactic core behind the starship. Ahead, few photons escaped the macrogravity cloak of the Void as suns sank through the event horizon. A lurid vermilion band shimmered across space, the swirl of ion clouds enraged by the loop's fatal discharge, illuminating the fuselage like the devil's own gaze. Radiation alarms howled in fright as the force field started to collapse. The fuselage blistered.

'One of us comes,' Araminta said. 'See?'

The distortion shockwave was almost unnoticeable in real space as it flashed past. Dead streamers of atoms were stirred briefly by the unquiet force leaking back out of the quantum interstices. *Silverbird* powered back into hyperspace, smouldering from radiation burns.

'You,' Ethan exclaimed.

The Skylord resonated with interest. 'I still search for you. The nucleus aches with longing.'

'I know. You must stop that. Please welcome our emissary. She approaches you.'

'Where? I sense you are so far away.'

'I am. She is close to you now. Feel for her. She bleeds emotion as do we all. Guide her as you should. Open your boundary.'

'The Heart will welcome you.'

The two Raiel warships were closing on the *Silverbird*. Justine's sensor display showed her another gas giant-sized mass barely five lightyears away. If they targeted that it would be the end. The *Silverbird*'s ultradrive was struggling to maintain acceleration now.

'Hurry. Please,' Araminta implored.

The Skylord radiated satisfaction as it receded.

'I thank you,' Gore said. 'Whoever you are.'

Justine sank back into the couch, her mind fully open to the gaiafield, letting every emotion pour fourth. Hopes. Fears. Everything she was.

Ahead of the *Silverbird*, the Void boundary changed. A vast circular wave rippled out, creating a crater ten lightyears across. From its centre a smooth cone of pure blackness rose up towards the starship.

Justine regarded the exovision images in surprise. She was gripping the couch arms tight, her skin slick with sweat. 'I'm not so sure—'

Behind her, the Raiel warships slowed, allowing the *Silverbird* to race onwards.

' – this is such – '

At fifteen lightyears high the cone stopped expanding.

' – a good – '

Its apex opened like a flower, petals of infinite night pealing back. Exquisite nebula-light shone out into the Gulf.

' – idea – '

Silverbird passed across the threshold, into the Void.

' – after all.'

The cone closed up. It sank back into the now quiescent boundary. *Silverbird*'s communication link to the Navy relay ended. Both Raiel warships executed tight curves and headed back towards the Wall.

'Please, talk to us,' Ethan appealed. 'The Skylord has anointed you as our Second Dreamer. We await you. We need you.'

He was given no reply.

Araminta slipped out of Danal's apartment, and tiptoed across the vestibule to her own. Outside, a brash dawn light was lapping against the weather dome. The crowd was cheering ecstatically. That felt good.

'Well, whadda you know, I saved the universe.' Araminta grinned wildly at the ridiculous knowledge, then yawned. Being a hero was actually quite exhausting. She sank down into the big old armchair with its strangely lumpy cushions. *Just five minutes' rest.*

*

Cheriton McOnna didn't like the 'in character' clothes Beckia had produced for him out of the replicator on board *Elvin's Payback*. Really didn't. Nothing wrong with the touch of them, a cotton shirt, wool-lined waistcoat with brass buttons, and trousers that were like suede but a great deal softer. No, it was the colours and style, the shirt's lace-up front, its grey-green colour which was more like a stain than a dye, and the odd tight cut of the black trousers. He plain refused to wear the felt hat with its flamboyant green and blue feathers; although he reluctantly agreed to carry it after Beckia got all stroppy. It wasn't good to get Beckia stroppy.

She'd been right, of course. As soon as he walked into the Confluence nest building on Daryad Avenue in the centre of town, he fitted in with the Ellezelin workforce. Security was strong around the building, an old brick cube with dark arching windows. Colwyn's three confluence nests were the first priority for the occupying forces. But Liatris McPeierl had done his job well, infiltrating a complete legend for Cheriton, including DNA. When he walked into the airy marble-floored lobby he was told to put his hand on a sensor pedestal while three armed and armoured guards watched him cautiously. The building's new net cleared him, and they waved him on. He gave them a cheery smile, backed up with a contented emanation into the gaiafield.

The nest itself was housed on the fourth floor in a sterile chamber which took up half of the available floorspace. He reported for duty to Dream Master Yenrol in the overseer's office, which looked out into the nest chamber through a glass partition. Normally, the office was only occupied a few hours each day when the overseer or their assistant ran a six-hourly assessment to ensure the nest was operating smoothly. Now there were seven technicians all struggling for elbow space as they installed banks of new hardware, while on the other side of the glass more technicians were blending fresh bioneural clusters with the original nest.

'What's your field?' Yenrol asked. He was both agitated and puzzled. Cheriton's late assignment coupled with the pressure to get the job done was making him very twitchy.

'Pattern definition,' Cheriton replied equitably. 'The routines I've developed will help isolate the Second Dreamer's thoughts within the gaiafield. It should give us a stronger source to trace.'

'Good,' Yenrol said. 'Okay, great. Start installing the routines.' He'd turned back to a half-completed hardware unit before Cheriton got a chance to reply.

'Okay then,' Cheriton mumbled, keeping his gaiafield emission a level flow of eagerness and enthusiasm. He found a free console seat, and nodded to the man in the next seat.

'Welcome to the eye,' his new colleage said. 'I'm Danal.'

'Glad to be here,' Cheriton said. 'What do you mean: eye?'

'Of the storm.'

Cheriton grinned. 'This is the quiet part?'

'Exactly!'

Danal, it turned out, had been on Viotia for some time now. He and Mareble had come in anticipation of being close to the Second Dreamer. 'We wanted to be here when he revealed himself,' Danal admitted. 'I've been upgrading nest sensitivity since we arrived in the hope our Dream Masters can locate him.' He gave Yenrol a guilty glance, stifling his gaiafield emissions for a moment. 'I wasn't expecting this,' he confided.

'I know what you mean,' Cheriton said, all sympathy. 'I was praying to the Lady that Ethan would be elected Cleric Conservator, but I didn't think anything like our presence here would be necessary.'

Danal gave an awkward shrug, and got back to work. Cheriton continued loading in the routines he'd concocted. They did perform the recognition function, but in reverse, so that the nest would develop a mild blind spot should it receive any thoughts originating from the Second Dreamer. It would inform Cheriton first before reverting to the advertised function.

The modification team's frantic work stalled as Justine's madcap flight swamped the unisphere.

'She's so close,' Danal said in awe as the *Silverbird*'s sensors revealed the undulating surface of the Void. Then everyone winced as the Raiel transformed the second moon into a hyperluminal quake.

'How are they doing that?' Cheriton murmured, fascinated by the level of extraordinarily sophisticated violence involved.

'Who cares?' Danal said. 'The Void can resist their devilry. It has for a million years. That's all that matters.'

Cheriton raised an eyebrow. It took a lot of self-control not to leak his dismay at the man's bigotry into the gaiafield. 'Let's hope Justine's ship can withstand it, too.'

'She's not a believer. She's an ANA creature.'

'She's human,' Cheriton said. 'That means she should be able to get inside. Somehow.'

'Ah. I hadn't thought of that.'

'Please,' Yenrol entreated the modification team. 'Keep working. If the Second Dreamer is going to show himself, it will be tonight.'

Danal flashed Cheriton a shamefaced smile.

Oscar hadn't expected things to happen quite this fast. He should have known better. If the Starflyer War had taught him nothing else, it was that events ruled people, not the other way round.

So here he was encased in a stiff paramilitary armour suit, sitting halfway down the passenger section of an Ellezelin police capsule, floating over the Cairns. Beckia was sitting on the bench next to him, while Tomansio was forward in the command seat. The capsules were designed to hold fifteen paramilitaries. However, its original occupants were now resting in a drug-induced coma back in the Bootel & Leicester warehouse, so at least he had plenty of room to stretch out.

Like the rest of the Commonwealth, they were accessing Justine's mad dash through the Gulf.

'The welcome team has just stepped up to active status,' Liatris reported: he had stayed behind in the *Elvin's Payback* to monitor the occupying forces and provide unisphere support. 'Everyone thinks that the Second Dreamer will intervene for Justine.'

'He didn't after Gore's appeal,' Oscar said.

'The Raiel should give things a degree of urgency,' Beckia said. 'I agree with Living Dream, if it's going to happen it'll happen tonight.'

Oscar shrugged, which didn't come off well in his armour.

'Did you know Gore and Justine?' Tomansio asked.

'I think I met her once, some senior officer function on *High Angel*. Everyone was trying to chat her up.'

'Including you?' Beckia teased.

'No, I was aiming for the ones she turned down. Rejection always leaves you vulnerable to a quick bout of cheap meaningless sex.'

'Ozzie, but you're dreadful.'

'Anything from Cheriton?' Tomansio asked.

'Nothing since his last check-in,' Liatris reported. 'Nobody questioned his appointment to Yenrol's staff. He's installed his routines in the nest.'

'Is he wearing his hat?' Beckia asked innocently.

Oscar couldn't help the smile creeping on to his mouth. That had been quite an argument.

'I'll find out next time,' Liatris promised.

'What have you got for us on the welcome team?' Tomansio asked.

'All deeply loyal Living Dream followers; it doesn't look like Phelim fancied contracting out for this job. They're on secondment from the Makkathran2 cabinet security office.'

'Ethan's private bodyguards,' Tomansio declared. 'What are their enrichments?'

'Very heavy duty weapons, and they're accelerated up to at least our standard. But I don't think they have biononics; there's no record in any file I can find.'

'Okay, thank you. Keep deep mining, I want everything you've got on them.'

'Will do. Files coming over.'

Oscar's u-shadow told him it had received the heavily encrypted files. When he scrutinized them he couldn't help a sharp intake of breath. The welcome team that Councillor Phelim had put together to interdict the Second Dreamer were carrying the kind of firepower he'd thought exclusive to members of the Knights Guardian. They were also extremely devout. Phelim had given them complete authority over all the invading forces to accomplish their goal. 'We need to be quick,' he murmured.

'That we do,' Tomansio agreed. 'I wouldn't want to be caught in the act by this lot.'

'I bet they have got biononics,' Beckia said. 'They'll justify it by saying it will help bring about the Dream. Their kind always does.'

'I didn't know Living Dream disapproved of biononics,' Oscar said.

'Oh yes. Nothing like the Protectorate, though; bionomics aren't quite a sacrilege, they simply don't have any place in the Void. Most people believe they won't work in there anyway.'

'Why?'

'Because there was never any functioning technology on Querencia. The most sophisticated thing the Waterwalker ever encountered was the machine gun. And that's purely mechanical. There was no electricity, no genetics, no bionomics. Given the humans who landed, their ship would have had access to the most advanced technology and information base the Commonwealth could provide, it is inconceivable that their new society couldn't even make a battery. They certainly know their chemistry and medicine, even astronomy. Something stopped them from following the electromechanical route.'

'The internal structure of the Void,' Oscar mused.

'Quite. Whatever the quantum structure is that permits true mental powers, it must also block electricity.'

'That's ridiculous. You can't stop current flowing, that implies a whole level of atomic reactions would cease to exist. There wouldn't be any stars.'

'The Silfen paths mess with human hardware-based technology,' Tomansio said.

'That's direct interference generated by their paths.'

'All I'm saying is that it appears there's something inimical to electronics in the Void.'

'The original colony ship survived to land on Querencia.'

'And the Living Dream is still arguing if it landed or crashed,' Beckia said. 'The interference with electronics could come directly from the Heart itself, like some kind of overlord making sure civilization doesn't rise above a certain level.'

'Why the hell would anyone go to so much trouble making the Void in the first place just so they can use it to keep sentient species as pets?'

'No idea,' she said merrily. 'The firstlife are alien, remember. They think differently.'

Oscar gave up with an irritable wave of his hand. 'All right, so thanks to the whole firstlife zookeeper theory, the welcome team are unlikely to have biononics.'

'That's about it, yeah,' Tomansio said.

'Either way,' Beckia said. 'We don't want to go head to head if we can help it.'

'Right.'

'Liatris, can you get us assigned to the welcome team back-up, please,' Tomansio asked.

'Way ahead of you. Your assignment should be coming through in a couple of minutes.'

'Thank you.'

Oscar drew a sharp breath as the Raiel warships obliterated a gas giant. 'Jesus H. Christ, give the poor girl a break.' The *Silverbird* dropped back into real space. Oscar grimaced at the radiation battering its force fields, his memory flipping back to the fight for Hanko when he'd captained the *Dublin*. There were a lot of parallels. MorningLightMountain's ships had used exotic energy blasts to smack the *Dublin* about. And at half a million kilometres above the surface, their force field had only just withstood the star's radiation. All that was nothing compared to the hell *Silverbird* was now enduring. Oscar couldn't help the burst of encouragement pouring out of his mind and into the gaiafield, as if prayer alone could make a difference.

Justine powered back into hyperspace.

'Good tactic,' Oscar said approvingly. Another part of his mind was dwelling on the fact that the *Elvin's Payback* was the same type of ship as *Silverbird*. *We could be out there doing that.*

'Stand by,' Cheriton said on the ultrasecure link. 'The Second Dreamer is making contact with the Skylord.'

'Where is he?' Tomansio growled out. 'Armour active, please. Oscar, do exactly as we tell you, clear?'

'Yes.' He just managed not to add 'sir'.

'Haven't got his position yet,' Cheriton said. 'My routines are still fudging the nest for us.'

Oscar opened his mind wide to the gaiafield.

'—close to you now. Feel for her,' the Second Dreamer was imploring.

'Here we go,' Cheriton said. 'First fix is the Bodant district.'

'En route,' Tomansio said, and pushed the capsule round in a hundred and eighty degree curve above the dark river. Viotia's dawn sun shone into the capsule through the forward section of the transparent fuselage.

'Ah, crap, the rest of the nests are focusing on the origin,' Cheriton said. 'I thought they'd take longer.'

Tomansio pushed their speed up. 'Ozzie! How long have we got?'

Thirty thousand lightyears away, the Void began to extend out towards the *Silverbird*.

'If it screws with technology is she going to be all right when she's inside?' Oscar asked.

'Let's just concentrate on the job you've given us, shall we?' Beckia chided. She was activating her armour. The helmet visor rippled shut.

'He's near the edge of the park,' Cheriton told them. 'The Dream Masters are pulling out some very precise coordinates. Damn, they're good. Sorry guys, you're not going to make it. The welcome team is being given his location.'

'Shit,' Tomansio reducing their speed. 'It'll look suspicious if we arrive a couple of seconds before them, and that's all the time we've got.'

'What's plan B?' Oscar asked.

'Snatch him away from the welcome team, but that's going to be difficult. This is all happening too fast. I wanted to be properly embedded in the occupation forces here before we moved to this phase.'

'Kill the wormhole,' Beckia said. 'We can use *Elvin's Payback* to intercept the welcome team in interstellar space when they ship the Second Dreamer back to Ellezelin.'

'That would give us a better chance,' Oscar said. 'That ship's a damn sight better than anything Living Dream will have.'

'We don't know that,' Tomansio said. 'And it would take a lot of aggression to take out the wormhole.'

'I could go through and do it,' Liatris insisted.

'They'd know exactly what happened, and why,' Tomansio said. 'This is looking like we'll have to switch operations to Ellezelin itself. Oh, here we go, deployment orders from the welcome team. It's an apartment building.'

'Something wrong here,' Cheriton said. 'One of my new colleagues, Danal, is having a fit. That apartment block is where he lives. As best we can determine the Second Dreamer is actually in his own apartment.'

'Ah hah, everybody might just be underestimating the Second Dreamer, after all,' Tomansio said. 'Good for him.'

'And for us,' Beckia agreed.

'He's going to have to get out of there quick,' Oscar said. He was viewing an exoimage map of Colwyn. Nine cruisers were converging on Bodant Park. Five had orders to establish a secure ground perimeter. Two were assigned to provide air cover. The rest, including theirs, were to back up the welcome team inside.

He glanced down as they passed over the bright illuminum buildings of a marina, then on across the park. There were thousands of people spread across the grass, still cheering and jumping up and down with glee as their all-night vigil was rewarded. A real party atmosphere had developed and the pull it exerted through the gaiafield was intoxicating.

The capsule carrying the welcome team roared overhead, barely subsonic and decelerating hard. Up ahead, the glass pillar corners of the target apartment block gleamed with a purple and blue iridescence, naively signalling its position. The welcome team capsule circled it possessively, trailing a thin vapour trail. Happy people down in the park frowned upwards at the boorish intrusion. Dismay and resentment appeared in the gaiafield like necrotic sunspots in an otherwise healthy corona.

'Oh great,' Oscar grunted as more and more celebrating citizens became indignant and aggrieved. 'That'll help.'

'They don't care,' Tomansio said. 'This whole planet doesn't matter to them. All they're interested in is finding the Second Dreamer.'

'I wonder what he's like,' Oscar said as they slowed to hover above the strip of well-maintained gardens in front of the block.

'Neurotic,' Beckia said. 'Got to be.'

'Smart and scared,' Tomansio said. 'Which makes him dangerous to Living Dream.'

The rest of the capsules assigned to support the welcome team arrived. 'This is Major Honilar,' the welcome team commander announced. 'Perimeter squad, establish yourselves immediately. No one in or out. Janglepulse anyone who attempts to cross your line. Custody support squad, seal off the ground floor and shut down the lifts. Use the stairwell to isolate each floor. Now listen up. I want to make very sure you all understand this: there is to be no lethal weapons usage at all. The Second Dreamer is in there, and he *must not* be harmed. If you encounter any problem, for example if he is using a force field and tries to break through, call us. We will deal with him. I don't want your dirty hands on him.'

'Yes, sir,' Tomansio replied as he directed their capsule down on to the garden. The welcome team's capsule was planting itself on the roof next to the golden crystal dome containing the spa.

'What do we do?' Oscar asked as the door expanded and he stepped out on to a border of fuchsia bushes, his boots crushing the white and scarlet flowers into the loam.

'Exactly as we were told,' Tomansio said. 'And remember, don't use your biononic field function. I know it's superior to anything in these armour suits, but the welcome team will detect it.'

'Okay.' They joined the rest of the custody support troops as they marched into the ground-floor lobby. Behind them, the perimeter squad started to push back the first batch of angry citizens who'd arrived from the park.

'Danal has just been arrested,' Cheriton told them. 'Two officers from cabinet security are hauling him off right now. He's not a happy man.'

'That must be a deliberate distraction,' Tomansio said.

'Yeah, but by who?' Beckia said. 'The Second Dreamer or another bunch like us?'

The lobby was filled with contractors' equipment and caskets piled high with rubbish. Bright temporary lighting on a metal frame cast strong shadows.

'The welcome team have taken command of the apartment block's net,' Cheriton said. 'Hang on, I'm assessing the results from their scrutineers.'

Tomansio led Beckia and Oscar into the concrete stairwell. More rubbish had been casually tipped off the floors above, forming a heap of dusty debris at the bottom of the stairs in the basement. A couple of paramilitaries went down to investigate the garage.

'According to the net there are about thirty people currently in residence,' Cheriton said. 'The whole damn place is being redeveloped. The fourth floor only has four people registered for two apartments. Danal and Mareble, and a married couple. Someone called Araminta is refurbishing the remaining three on that level. Mining her now.'

Oscar hurried up the concrete stairs. The long line of suited paramilitaries was making a lot of noise as they trooped up with him. Instructions relayed from Honilar assigned six of them to each floor. Oscar was seriously impressed with Liatris when he, Tomansio and Beckia were given the fourth floor.

They emerged into the vestibule to find all the apartment doors broken open and two of the welcome team standing guard in full military armour suits. Oscar could just see through the doorway into apartment three, where the terrified occupants were in the middle of the big living room. A man and woman: him in a pair of shorts, her in a long nightshirt. Standing side by side, their arms raised as another of the welcome team covered them with a large gun. She was shaking and crying, while her partner was trying to be resolute. The way his leg muscles were trembling betrayed him more than any gaiafield emission.

Major Honilar came out of Danal's apartment. 'No sign of

him. He couldn't have got out of the building, he didn't have time. I want every resident on every floor in custody and taken to our headquarters. Search and scan each apartment, make sure you have everyone.' He turned and went back into Danal's apartment.

'Pair up,' Tomansio said. 'Take an apartment each.'

Oscar accompanied Tomansio as they went into apartment number four. He scanned round with his suit's sensors, resenting how slow and restricted they were compared to a bionomic field scan. *You're spoilt*, he told himself. The suit didn't detect any body-size thermal signatures. The apartment was halfway through refurbishment. Several inactive bots were lined up in the living room. New cables and pipes were laid out along one wall. Junked utility fittings were stacked up by the door. Crates and boxes with BOVEY'S BUILDING SUPPLY MACROSTORE printed around them were waiting to be unpacked. Some furniture had been left, a coffee table that was now badly scuffed, with several mugs on top, waiting to be washed. An ancient couch with a matching armchair that had odd lumps in its cushioning.

His u-shadow was displaying the reports from the other squads, who were busy rounding up the residents on other floors. So far, their identities matched their files.

'In here,' Tomansio said, using their secure link. He was standing in the doorway to a bedroom. The bed itself was a bare mattress with a big sleeping bag crumpled on top. Four suitcases were lined up along a wall; one was open revealing a collection of woman's clothes. The small dresser was swamped by hair-styling tools and membrane scale cases.

'Not listed as lived in,' Oscar said.

'Depends what lists you check. Liatris, run another search on Araminta. Has she sold this apartment?'

'I'm on it.'

While Tomansio checked the other two bedrooms Oscar went into the main bathroom. The floor had been stripped back to the bare concrete, as had the walls. A brand new carved stone bath cuboid was sitting in the middle. Halfway up the wall behind it, the stub of the original cold water feed pipe jutted out of the concrete, its valve dripping into a plastic bucket beneath. The old toilet bowl was still plumbed in. A big hot water tank stood in one corner, already boxed in by the struts of a false wall, just awaiting the cover boards which were stacked in front of it. A maze of pipe work was strewn round its base. Components for a spore shower were lying ready for assembly.

'Nothing,' he told Tomansio.

'The other bedrooms are empty.'

Oscar found him behind the living room's kitchen bar. The old culinary unit had been removed to stand on the ground, though the nutrient feed pipes were still plumbed in. A kettle and a microwave were sitting on the scratched marble work surface. His thermal scan showed him the kettle's temperature was above ambient. 'This place has been used recently,' he muttered.

'We need to talk to her,' Tomansio said. 'If anyone can tell us who's been in and out of these apartments, it's her.'

'That shouldn't be too difficult,' Oscar said. 'We know who she is. Finding her will be easy for Liatris.'

'Yeah.' Tomansio's sensors swept round one last time. 'Grab something from her bedroom, just so we can run a DNA verification that she's the one living here. Then we'd better get back and help with rounding up the rest of the suspects.'

'Poor bastards,' Oscar said as he picked up a small scale applicator brush. 'What do you think Honilar will do with them?'

'Good question. How do you prove you're not the Second Dreamer? It's not as if there's physical evidence. I guess if he doesn't get a confession they'll use a memory read.'

Oscar shuddered. 'That isn't exactly going to endear them to the Second Dreamer. They need him to help them get into the Void.'

'Oscar, face it, with today's medical techniques you can make someone do just about anything you want.'

'Medical techniques?'

'That's what they started out as.'

'I suppose you know how to do that?'

'We all had training in that area, yes.'

Despite the heavy armour suit with its perfect insulation, Oscar suddenly felt cold.

*

Paula had rarely experienced a pang of déjà vu as strong as the one that hit her when the stained glass door opened and she walked into the entrance hall. And she hadn't even been to the old building before. She walked past the empty concierge desk and stared at the glass cage lift. It was the age of everything around her that was generating that weird sensation tickling the back of her mind. According to the Daroca City Council files the interior was perfectly authentic, exactly as it had been during the Starflyer War. She wasn't going to disagree, as someone who had lived through those times she could feel the décor was right.

The lift took her up to the fifth floor, and she walked into Troblum's penthouse apartment. On the trip over from the spaceport she'd accessed Lieutenant Renne Kampasa's ancient Directorate files on the one time she'd visited – ANA had to deep access the memory. With the file came a note that Troblum had requested access to that same file a hundred years ago, along with associated forensic reports.

His restoration work was excellent, Paula acknowledged as she walked into the huge open-plan lounge. The balcony had a magnificent view out over the Caspe River, with the rest of Daroca filling in the background.

It didn't take her long to establish there wasn't anything useful in the apartment, and all Troblum's personal files had been wiped from the building net. The only mild exception was in the bedrooms, each of which inexplicably had their closets full of girls' clothes. Troblum's own clothes, comprising three ageing toga suits and his unpleasant underwear, were stuffed into a chest of drawers in the master bedroom. For a moment Paula wondered if the dresses belonged to Troblum's girlfriend. She raised an eyebrow when she took out a designer leather miniskirt. It might be slightly prejudiced of her to think it, but what would a girl with a figure to wear such an item see in Troblum? Then she recognized the label, one she hadn't seen for over seven hundred years, and realized that the skirt was also Starflyer War vintage style. She let out a whistle of admiration; he'd even reproduced the girls' wardrobe as best he could.

Now that is true obsession.

Paula started going through the other apartments in the ancient converted factory while her u-shadow accessed the building's net to analyse the remaining files. It was the largest apartment on the third floor which drew her attention. The others were all relatively authentic reproductions, but this one had been modified again. All the internal walls had been removed, and the resulting chamber sealed against the outside atmosphere with a sustainer membrane and clinical-grade air filters. Rows of heavy benches ran the entire length, each one equipped with a series of data nodes and high voltage power sockets. She could see the outlines where objects had once rested. They must have been there for decades to make any kind of impression on the stainless steel surface. The net subsection for the apartment had also been thoroughly wiped.

'Three courier capsules were requisitioned to collect items from the building around the time Troblum disappeared,' her u-shadow reported.

'What items?'

'Unknown. They were stored in stabilized cases.'

'Ah,' Paula said. 'I bet it was a collection. Most likely Starflyer War memorabilia. Stubsy Florac often procured historic relics for clients. Where were the cases taken?'

'The capsules made three separate trips to the city spaceport, they were collected by different commercial ships registered in the External worlds. No record of their ultimate destination.'

'It was to Florac.' She knew it. *That's why Troblum was there, to pick it up. And it would have meant a great deal to him. That can only mean he was planning to leave the Commonwealth entirely.* She opened a link to ANA. 'Troblum was more scared than I realized.'

'Marius does that to people.'

'Yes. But there was something else. Remember what he told us when he first made contact. He had something that I would understand, and his mania is the Starflyer War. A time I am familiar with.'

'That hardly narrows it down.'

'Something else does,' Paula said. All she could see was that figure ascending into its ship amid the ruins of Florac's villa. A slight person. That wiggle of the hips, a taunt, a couldn't-care-less contempt. None of today's agents and representatives had that kind of attitude, not even the Knights Guardian. They all prided themselves on their steely professionalism. 'I have a bad feeling about this.'

'What feeling?'

'I have one last trip to make. I'll tell you after that.'

'Can't you tell me now?'

'No. Believe it or not, I'd be embarrassed if I'm wrong. You'll think I'm obsessive. I have to know for myself.'

'How intriguing. As you wish.'

'Are you making any progress on mining Troblum's life for me?'

'Yes. In many ways he is an odd person, especially for a Higher. I have a reasonably complete timeline for you. It has some suspicious gaps, and he even served on a scientific mission for the Navy.'

'Really.' Paula's u-shadow received the file. She scanned the contents list in her exovision; one of the more recent items attracted her. 'A presentation to the Navy about the Anomine and the Dyson Pair barrier generators? And Kazimir himself was there. I'd like a summary of that, please.'

'Of course.'

'Thanks, I'll review it on my way back to Earth.'

'You're coming here?'

'Yes, this little problem of mine will only take a moment to confirm. I'll be there in an hour.'

*

Major Honilar rounded up thirty-three people from the apartment block, and shipped them back to the security headquarters that were set up in Colwyn's docks. The cordon around the building was maintained, even in the face of growing hostility from the crowd in the park. Five paramilitaries from the support squad made one final sensor sweep after the transport capsules carted off the unfortunate residents, but they found nothing. Once they'd finished they left, reassigned to other more urgent duties. The occupying forces were having a hard time of it as more and more of Viotia's inhabitants joined the physical protests against their presence.

An hour and a half after the last of the suited figures clomped out of apartment four on the fourth floor, the muffled sound of a power tool resonated round the bathroom. One after the other, three fixing bolts around the top of the hot water tank spun round then dropped on to the floor. The hemispherical top of the tank tipped up a fraction. Fingers appeared in the gap, and pushed against the thick thermal insulation foam, shoving the top aside. It too fell on to the floor with a loud *clang*.

'Sweet Ozzie!' Araminta groaned.

She took a long time just to lever herself up to a standing position. The cylinder was only just big enough to hold her in a terrible crouch position. Every limb throbbed as she finally stretched them free. Cramp attacked her joint muscles, bringing tears to her eyes. She was close to sobbing when she eventually straightened her spine. It was another five minutes of simply standing and letting the pain subside before she attempted to climb out, using the false wall boxing as a ladder.

The only noise was the crowd outside jeering and taunting the paramilitaries on the cordon. Araminta peered cautiously into the living room. Nobody about. Her macrocellular clusters couldn't detect any individual data signals. She'd isolated herself from the unisphere, and knew she couldn't reconnect without being detected. She crossed the living room, feeling unnervingly exposed. The main door was ajar, its expensive brass lock broken, which drew a scowl. As far as she could determine, the whole fourth floor was deserted. She shut the door, and jammed a crate of kitchen fittings behind it.

'Okay then,' she said, and sat down in the ancient armchair. Got up again and went over to the kettle. She was just about to switch it on when she wondered if some tricky little monitor program would notice the power usage. Five minutes later she'd extracted the power cell from a bot, and wired it up to the kettle.

She sat back down in the armchair with a cup of wonderfully hot tea and some of the classy chocolate biscuits she always kept around.

So now what?

Inigo's Ninth Dream

Edeard hadn't visited the House of Blue Petals for nearly a month. Now, with the court case winding down, he stood on the street facing it as the sea breeze gusted along Upper Tail Canal. Finally, the winter was ending, with the onset of spring conjuring some much-needed warmth across the Lyot Sea. A light drizzle swept through Edeard's concealment to dampen his face. He continued to stare at the building with its long oval windows, frowning at the vague feeling of disquiet stirring in his mind. Men went in and out the same as they always did. The doormen stood like muscular statues on either side of its three tall doors. Even the piano music drifting out across the street was pleasingly familiar.

When he pushed his farsight through the sturdy walls, he detected nothing out of the ordinary. The bar was full of eager clients, with the stewards mixing their drinks which the ge-monkeys delivered. The madam made her rounds. All around the gallery, the girls pouted and batted their eyes, radiating faux longing. Up on the third floor, Ivarl's mind was its usual tight knot of suppressed thoughts. He was in his office as always, with several people in respectful attendance.

It was all perfectly normal.

So what's wrong?

One day he would really have to make sense of these sensations which occasionally haunted him. But this was hardly as bad as the night Ashwell was attacked. He would just have to be alert, that was all.

The two sailors walking up the steps never knew they were shadowed, putting any nerves down to the questing gaze of the uniformed doormen. They were waved through. Edeard followed them across the threshold.

The décor had changed slightly. Ivarl had bought some large coloured-glass globes over two feet in diameter, their swirling patterns of amber and aquamarine clashing in gentle curlicues. Ten of them stood on ornate wooden pedestals around the walls of the bar. Edeard gave them a mildly disapproving glance, and slipped further into the room.

A dog barked loudly.

Edeard froze. He hadn't realized the animal was there, its mind was similar to the ge-monkeys. It was a beagle, chained up to one of the big iron door hinges. Even as he reached for its mind to quieten it down, the doormen were slamming the doors shut. Huge metal bolts, three inches thick were rammed home, locking the doors tight.

He whispered: 'Oh crap,' as people started shouting. Several clients were in a panic, scurrying round to find some route out. He had to flatten himself back against the bar as one militia officer ran past demanding to know what was going on. A group of the uniformed doormen had clustered together around the bottom of the stairs. They were brandishing revolvers.

'Gentlemen, your attention please,' Ivarl shouted. 'Quiet!'

Edeard looked up as the room fell silent. Ivarl was standing on the gallery, both hands on the rail, looking down, his irregular lips open in a brutish smile. Edeard almost let out a cry of dismay. Tannarl was standing beside him, surveying the upturned faces with that superior leer of his. Edeard had met Ranalee's father only once before, at a fabulous ball the Gilmorn family had thrown in their mansion. As they'd shaken hands he'd seen where Ranalee got her hauteur from.

Lady, but I'm an idiot.

'I'd like to welcome my newest guest to this House,' Ivarl

announced loudly and smugly, he held up a pair of socks Edeard recognized – they'd been left behind in *that* lodge on the Iguru, that was what the beagle must have scented. 'And I extend the full use of the bar to you . . . Waterwalker.'

The clients gasped in consternation, looking round to spot Edeard.

'Everyone else is now entitled to a free night with my girls. Please make your way up the stairs. Quickly gentlemen, thank you.'

As the doubtful clients did as they were told, Tannarl produced a large pistol which he checked casually. Several of Ivarl's lieutenants had also appeared on the gallery, equally well armed. There was no way Edeard could get up the stairs unnoticed, the group of doormen at the bottom were pressed close together, and using their third hands to form a barrier. Every client was scrupulously checked over before they were allowed up.

When Edeard used his farsight to probe down, he couldn't find any tunnel directly underneath the House of Blue Petals. It would be easy enough for him to ghost through one of the walls, but he'd have to reach it first. He was very isolated here by the bar, and he wasn't sure about his hold on the beagle's mind.

Edeard looked at the pistols lining up around the gallery. Again, he could protect himself, but at the cost of concealment. He couldn't decide if he'd be safer standing under the gallery, or moving round when they started shooting.

The last of the clients scuttled up the stairs.

'I know you're here,' Ivarl called down. Tannarl aimed his pistol down into the bar, and fired. The noise was thunderous. Edeard flinched as the bullet smacked into a high-backed chair, blowing a big chunk of wood out of the back. He'd never seen a bullet that powerful before.

Ivarl laughed, and pointed his own pistol down. Edeard scuttled to the side of the bar and crouched down. The barrage of shots which followed sent splinters and clumps of cushioning feathers flying through the air. Some of the lieutenants had a grand time shooting abandoned glasses on the tables.

Ivarl held his hand up and the firing stopped. 'Ready to say hello yet, my young friend?'

Edeard looked across the floor. It was covered in debris now, and cushioning feathers were still fluttering through the air. He would never be able to walk across it without disturbing something. They'd see him instantly.

Ivarl began to reload his pistol, slotting unusually long bullets into the cylinder. 'They say you come from the country somewhere back west,' he said casually. 'That probably means you're unfamiliar with parts of our city and how it works. Everyday stuff the rest of us take completely for granted. For instance, did you know that if there's a fire the walls simply repair themselves? In a month, you'd never even know anything happened.'

Edeard eyed the back of the bar. He might be able to make it to the rear storeroom without making too much commotion.

One of the wooden pedestals began to tilt as a third hand pushed it. Then it fell over, sending the colourful globe crashing down. The glass smashed. Liquid splashed out. Edeard gave it an alarmed look, he hadn't known the globes contained anything. That was when he realized the liquid was actually Jamolar oil, used in lanterns everywhere on Querencia except Makkathran, where there was no need. The remainder of the globes were shoved over, smashing to flood oil out across the floor. He watched it spreading towards him with growing alarm. This was getting serious, he wasn't sure his shield could cope with fire and these bullets. The oil was getting very close to the nearest stove.

Ivarl finished loading his pistol, and snapped the chamber back. 'Come out, come out, wherever you are.'

Edeard looked above the gang lord. The ceiling which vaulted across the whole bar was inset with broad lighting rosettes whose tips extended down to the walls in a scribble of slender volutes. Their pale-orange radiance was at its strongest. He ordered them off, and to remain off. The bar was plunged into darkness, with the flickering coal flames behind the stove grilles shedding tenuous fans of light. He leapt up and started sprinting for the door.

A pale silver light flared above and behind him, revealing his splashing footprints.

'Huh?' Edeard twisted round to see both Ivarl and Tannarl encased in a glowing nimbus.

'You're not so special, Waterwalker,' Ivarl jeered. 'You can't even walk on fire.' He thrust his hand out. The glow brightened all along his arm, then tiny sparks were cascading from his fingertips, falling down from the gallery like a phosphorescent spray.

Edeard dropped his concealment. The oil ignited.

Flames soared up from the slick floor. A vicious blast of air knocked Edeard into the piano. The shield he'd flung round his body just managed to survive the impact, mitigating the blow. He didn't dare breathe as the flames surged round him, reaching far above his head.

Up on the gallery the girls were screaming as the fire licked up round the wooden railings. Thick smoke churned through the air.

'I see you!' Ivarl shouted victoriously. He started shooting.

Edeard dived for the floor, ploughing up a thin wave of flaming oil which sizzled across his shield, barely an inch from his clothes and face. He was managing to ward off the worst of the heat, but his skin felt as if he was immersed in acid. His leather coat was smouldering. Still he didn't dare draw a breath. Bullets punched into the floor beside him, scattering razor-sharp splinters. Up on the gallery, the squealing girls were fleeing down corridors. Terrified clients shoved them aside in their own haste to reach safety. Ivarl and his lieutenants remained steadfast, their shields protecting them from the worst of the flames. They fired away manically with their pistols.

Bullets started to strike Edeard as his attackers drilled through the fire with their farsight. They were like hammer blows on his back, sending pulses of agony along his spine to explode in his brain. He couldn't sustain his shield much longer. He desperately needed air.

His thoughts pushed down hard into the floor, willing escape, pleading *Help me!* and the floor miraculously *changed*. He started to fall. There was nothing below him. A bullet hit the shield at the back of his head. He screamed, and blacked out.

Edeard woke to a uniform pain that throbbed horribly. Even before he was fully conscious, he threw up. After that, he simply lay where he was in the hope the pain would fade. His hands and cheeks were sore where the heat from the flames had penetrated his shield. He could feel bruises all over his back. Bright light made him blink sticky tears from his eyes.

Slowly he began to shuffle round and sit up, wincing at every move. It was very quiet. He managed to focus. What he saw made little sense.

He was lying on the floor of a great tunnel. Not as wide as those which mirrored Makkathran's canals, but perfectly circular. Nor was there any water trickling along the bottom. The walls were as smooth as glass, which is what they could well have been made from. He couldn't be sure, for they glowed with a painful intensity. A proper white light, too, not Makkathran's usual orange. In fact this whiteness had a shade of purple blended in, which was why his eyes wouldn't stop watering. Up the curve of the wall was a line of scarlet points which shone with equal intensity. They stretched out on either side of him as far as he could see. And that was the problem, he couldn't see any kind of end to the tunnel, not in either direction.

Edeard clambered to his feet, wincing as he gingerly probed his back with his fingertips. His coat was ruined, the leather was hard and cracked, with some strips flaking off as if a knife had been slashing at him. His boots were also in a bad way, the drosilk resin soles had blackened and turned soft. Where he'd lain on the tunnel it was smeared with patches of oil. He eased himself out of his coat, and patted the drosilk waistcoat underneath. The weave had several loose dints. It had probably saved his life, he admitted. When he touched the back of his head he gasped at the pain from the lump.

'Thank you,' he said out loud to the city, and slowly sank back down again. He knew he was going to have to rest up for a while. His farsight couldn't reach further than a few inches through the tunnel wall. By now he'd decided he was in one of the very deep tunnels which lay a long way underneath the usual canal tunnels he used. If so, then he was really alone in a way he'd never been before. Nobody had been down here since the city was built, and he still didn't know what kind of creatures those might have been. Whoever they were, they'd certainly built very well, though why they would want to build a lighted tunnel like this was beyond his comprehension. But then, that was true of the whole city.

He tried to relax, though it was difficult. Without the city's usual background babble of longtalk, which he always ignored, the isolation was quite crushing. He was also angry at himself for what happened in the House of Blue Petals. Of course Ivarl would figure things out eventually. Concealment was not a secret in this city, not among the Masters, and quite a few others. And that ability Ivarl had, the glow that surrounded both him and Tannarl, the sparks, that was something Edeard had never heard of before. Now though, he wasn't entirely surprised, not since that final night he'd spent with Ranalee.

Like all the Grand Family daughters, Ranalee was a lovely-looking girl. She had raven hair which she (well, her maids, anyway) brushed straight every morning so that it would fall halfway down her back. Her face was also long, with narrow eyes, and a cute little nose. Again, all nice features, except in combination they gave the impression of coldness. That seemed to be another eternal feature of Makkathran's aristocracy, the richer or more powerful the family, the less laughter was to be found in their lives. However, she was fiendishly enjoyable in bed. And, truth be told, he was rather excited at the way she spent a couple of weeks manoeuvring Kristiana out of the picture. That single-minded possessiveness when focused on him alone made her even hotter.

He certainly didn't object when she announced they would be spending the weekend at a family-owned lodge out on the Iguru. Macsen and Boyd enviously wished him luck. He'd often wondered afterwards if they were being prophetic.

The lodge was a work of art, made from carved timbers and decorated with a tasteful excellence which only the Gilmorn money could provide. He enjoyed the very human architecture after the city's relentless non-human appearance. They took 'almost no one' with them, as Ranalee defined the five servants who were there to cater to her every whim. At night she dismissed the staff to their cottage. 'Outside their farsight range,' she explained with relish, 'because we won't be able to keep a seclusion haze going.' He was led into the main bedroom with its huge normal bed, one with a wooden frame and springs and a feather mattress; the first he'd slept on since Plax, he realized with a fond recollection of Franlee. Ranalee made him wait while she attired herself in some of the most expensive lingerie produced by the city's couturiers. Never before, Edeard thought, had so much money been so incredibly well spent. It must have been the wine and being graced with such a *vision* that left him so vigorously aroused. Ranalee exploited that state and her own sexuality quite ruthlessly. Sweet little Franlee would have been appalled by their behaviour.

'I like that you're so receptive,' Ranalee told him as they lay side by side on the lavender-scented sheets. Ranalee, he'd discovered, wasn't the kind of girl who wanted to cuddle afterwards. Candelabras in each corner of the room produced a mild yellow light, enabling him to see the expression of distant satisfaction on her face as she stared up at the bed's embroidered canopy. 'On every level,' she added.

'Yes,' he said, not quite sure what she was saying.

'I have a proposition for you. I'm sure Kristiana and others have made it, but I have the contacts and ability to make it work better than they ever could. And, in addition, you wouldn't be entirely dependent on Gilmorn money, which for someone like you would be quite important, I imagine.'

'Uh, what kind of proposition?' Edeard was still reliving the last couple of hours. He'd never been so ferocious before, it was an abandon she had demanded and responded to in kind. The exhilaration had been overwhelming, making him desperate for it never to end.

She turned her head to give him a shrewd stare. 'I marry you, and arrange for rewarding contacts with all those desperate third and fourth daughters.'

'Marry?' he blurted. They'd known each other for a few weeks.

'Yes. I am a second daughter, you know.'

'Er, yes. That's very flattering, Ranalee, but I'm not quite sure, er, what I want.'

'Well it's about time you seriously started thinking about it. You have value now, you should capitalize on it.'

Edeard wondered if he had misheard something. 'Capitalize?'

'Well, face it, for all you're popular and interesting, you'll never be Mayor.'

'Why not?' he asked indignantly.

Ranalee laughed. 'You're not one of us, are you? You don't belong to a Grand Family.'

'The Mayor is elected by the city.'

'Dear Lady, are you joking?'

'I can make it to Chief Constable. As a Grand Council member I'd be eligible to put my name forward.'

'With our family backing, you probably could get that far. But when did the Chief Constable ever make Mayor?'

'I don't know,' he admitted.

'Never.'

'Oh.'

'So don't be so silly. I'm talking about the future.'

'All right.' He was stung by the crack about him not being able to achieve much on merit. 'What's the proposition?'

'I told you. I'll be your gatekeeper.'

'I'm . . . sorry, I don't get any of this.'

She rolled on to her side, and reached down between his legs. 'Exploit your potential. That's what the families truly value. These, to be precise.' Long-nailed fingers closed around a very sensitive piece of anatomy.

'Potential?'

'Lady, you're ignorant. I just didn't realize how much. How do you think families like mine achieved our position?'

'Some of it was luck, being in the right place at the right time in history, some of it was down to hard work, your family especially. Your ancestors took huge risks exploring new markets with their ships.'

'Crap. It's breeding.'

'Right.'

'You doubt me? The one thing the families cherish more than anything is a strong psychic ability. That's what we use to maintain our position; farsight that can see what our rivals are up to inside a seclusion haze, a third hand strong enough to protect ourselves, and a few other useful little talents, too. We prize that trait above all others in a mate. That's what every family bloodline nurtures. And now you've walked out of the wilds and into the city, a simple country boy with more strength than a dozen family sons put together. We want you, Waterwalker. We want what these contain.' Her fingers closed tighter, nail tips sharp on his scrotum.

Edeard kept *very* still. His tongue licked round his lips as she held him on the threshold of pain. 'Okay, I get it now.'

'Good boy. So I marry you.' She smiled and stretched provocatively. Her voice purred, echoing round inside his skull. 'You get this magnificent body whenever you want and in whatever fashion you desire. And you've already discovered how fantastic that will be for you. I'm everything a man dreams of. Aren't I?' The way she spoke it was a taunt, a challenge.

'Yes.' He couldn't lie to her. That same husky voice had goaded him throughout the night. It spoke directly to some animal deep inside, awaking the most shameful desires. Yet she was the one suggesting them, rejoicing at how bad their bodies could behave. The notion of every night for the rest of his life spent like this one was igniting a fever inside him. He would fight every bandit on Querencia to make it happen.

'I will yield to you,' she promised meekly. 'You will father a host of lovely little girls in me. They will run round the mansion and live a life of luxury and make you so unbelievably happy while you clear the scum out of the city and ascend to the Chief Constable's office. That's by day,' she vowed tantalizingly.

'And by night?'

Ranalee's smile mellowed, she eased her grip a fraction. Her lips were now so close they brushed his ear. 'I will bring a multitude of the city's minor daughters to our bed.' Now her hand crept up to hold his stone-hard member. Edeard smiled in utter bliss as she directed his imagination to the satisfaction his masculinity could achieve for him. 'Each of them yearning for you to sire a daughter. They will pay to receive your fulfilment again and again.'

'Yes,' he groaned ecstatically.

'Beautiful girls. Young girls. Girls like Kristiana married off to equal nonentities out in the merchant classes or the militia – our country cousins. They'll have the daughters who'll go on to marry the next generation of first sons. Every family will be in a fervour for them.' She sucked in her cheeks thoughtfully, suddenly playful. 'Maybe I'll be able to negotiate a percentage of the dowry as part of your stud fee.'

Edeard was suddenly bedevilled by an image of Mistress Florrel, which he must have allowed to slip out.

Ranalee laughed delightedly. 'Her! Yes, that's why she was so sought after, she is an amazingly strong psychic; I'm four generations down from her myself. And don't forget Rah, either.'

'Rah!'

'Why do you think every Grand Family claims to be descended from him? We actually are. A third hand strong enough to cut through the city's crystal wall, who wouldn't want that?'

'I never knew any of this,' he said softly. It all made such perfect sense now she'd laid it out.

'Within three generations your descendants will rule Makkathran. That's less than a hundred years, Waterwalker. And then you will be king in all but name. Think what you can achieve with such power.'

'I will break them,' he said, eager now she had opened his eyes to so many opportunities. 'I will destroy the gangs. The city will regain all it has lost since Rah's time. The Skylords will come again to carry us off to Odin's Sea.'

'I will go there with you.'

'Yes, together!'

'As it is this night, it will always be for you. I pledge myself to that cause. Your pleasure will never end.' She rose above him, face gleaming triumphant in the tranquil candle light. 'Now you will celebrate our union,' she told him, her whisper filling the room in a crescendo.

Edeard's mind lost all focus as his flesh obeyed her demands. He was lost between ecstasy and delirium.

'You will give me our first daughter this night,' Ranalee decreed.

Edeard laughed ecstatically. 'Let's just hope it is a daughter.' Tears of joy were running from his eyes.

'It will be. They all will be. Every girl knows how.'

'How?'

'How to take care of an inconvenience like that. They must be girls.'

'But the boys . . .'

'There can be no boys. They have no value. The families practise primogeniture, apart for the odd embarrassment like the Culverits. So your daughters can marry directly into a family's main lineage.'

'What?' His thoughts were swirling as panic contaminated his physical delight. 'What?'

'The embryos are not people,' she crooned. 'Not at the stage where their gender becomes apparent. There isn't even any discomfort for me. Don't think of this any more.'

'What? No!'

'Relax, my beautiful strong Waterwalker. Do what you do best.'

'No,' Edeard shouted. He felt smothered, fighting for breath against a torrent of horror. 'No, no, no.' He pushed. Pushed hard. Pushed with his third hand. Pushed himself away from such evil.

Ranalee wailed in shock as she flew through the air. Edeard was panting hard, trying to shake the miasma from his thoughts. He felt as if he was shaking off a nightmare. His heart was yammering in his chest. He searched round frantically to see Ranalee sprawled across the rug at the foot of the bed. She looked dangerous, her hair wild, a snarl on her lips as she stood up and faced him.

'What happened?' he gasped, still fearful. He could barely resist the urge to continue, to bend her over the bed and take her – and from that to rule Makkathran through his offspring.

'I set you free,' she growled.

Her voice seemed to clang around the inside of his head. He groaned at the intensity, jamming his hands over his ears.

'I showed you your real desires. Follow them. Liberate yourself.'

'Stop it,' he begged. He was curling up, struggling against his own treachery, the yearning to follow her path into the future.

'Inhibitions aren't for people like us. You have strength in your blood, as do I. Think what we can achieve together. *Believe in us*—' That last she caterwauled at him.

The force behind the command almost sent Edeard tumbling from the mattress. Her mind was bright and hot. It finally made him realize it wasn't her voice he was battling. Somehow she was speaking directly into his mind. Insidiously potent longtalk had corrupted his own thoughts, forcing him to bend to her will as if he were no more than a genistar being ordered to clear up manure. He clenched his teeth, and *concentrated*, willing his third hand to contract around him, becoming hard enough to deflect longtalk. Pleading to the Lady to make him strong enough.

'Listen to me!' Ranalee demanded.

Edeard could see her lips still moving, as her voice faded away. Every trick he'd learned in the city about shielding his emotions was woven together and reinforced by his telekinesis. He crouched on the mattress, hearing nothing, sensing nothing. Isolated.

Ranalee glared at him. Once his nerves had steadied, he glared back. His hands were trembling from shock and fear.

'You,' he gulped down a breath. 'You tried . . . You wanted me to . . . Oh, sweet Lady.' The thought of what he'd only just managed to elude sent another shiver along his spine.

Ranalee regarded him contemptuously. She said something.

Edeard cautiously allowed her voice through the shield his third hand had created. But not her longtalk. Lady, no! That he kept perfectly blocked. 'What?'

'You stupid pitiful country peasant.'

'Bitch,' he spat back.

Her contempt matured into utter scorn. 'You think that isn't you? You believe you are noble and kind? Do you know how the dominance works? It plucks at the true strings of the heart. And I am a master of those passionate tunes; I play men for the simpletons they are. I recognize what lurks within, Waterwalker. You are all ruled by your ego and your lust, the *real* traits flowing in the blood. Everything I offered is a seed inside you. I simply give you the chance to let your true nature grow.'

'I am not like that.'

'How many family girls have you already bedded? You gave in to yourself on that quickly enough, didn't you? How many months have you and your pitiful squadmates spent in a lowlife tavern plotting and scheming to overthrow the gangs and make you Chief Constable? That is exactly what I offer you. Not in the way your childish daydreams imagine, I can give you all that for real. Grow up, Waterwalker. Your supposed virtue cannot bring you to power by itself, for that power is ultimately what you crave. The power to shape the city in your vision. That's right, is it not?'

'Yes,' he murmured. 'An honest city. One where people are not bred for advantage and profit.'

'Sometimes you have to do what's wrong in order to do what's right.'

He stared at her, stunned.

'Oh. A phrase even you've heard, then? Do you know who said it? Rah himself, as he forced his way through Makkathran's walls. He knew that only inside would his people have sanctuary from the chaos spilling out from the ships which brought us here. So he gave us the city. He *took* the city, and by doing so gave us order and stability that has stood for two thousand years.'

'No,' Edeard shook his head. 'I'm not ... children shouldn't be born for that. They should be loved for themselves.'

'They would be. And ours would be destined for greatness, too.'

'It's not right.'

'Really? And what if you only marry one girl, a nice sweet little thing who loves you dearly the way it is out in your backward villages? What do you think awaits those children of the Waterwalker? Me. That's what. Me, and all the others like me. The fewer children you have, the more valuable they become. The boys will be seduced by family daughters, the girls will be taken as trophy wives by our first sons. It will make most excellent sport. We will have the strength of your blood, one way or the other.'

'Not like that you won't.'

She tossed her head, regarding him with true aristocratic derision. 'You can achieve so much, Waterwalker. If Makkathran is to be remade as you would wish it, then it must change almost beyond recognition. I have no quarrel with that, for I would be atop that change. But radical change must come from within. You know how that has to happen now, your blood must spread wide, carrying with it your will.'

'I can change things from where I am.'

'No,' she said harshly. 'Change imposed by an outsider is an external threat, the one thing that would pull all of Makkathran together. The families, the common man, even the gangs; they would unite to defeat you.'

'Those groups, they want me to win, to get rid of the gangs and the corruption that allows them to thrive.'

'They want you to get rid of the gangs, that's all. You can't do that, not without help from the established order, they're woven too tightly into our streets and canals for you to root out. The Councils and the Guilds won't help you unless you're committed wholeheartedly to supporting them. You don't have a choice. Your subconscious knows that. I saw your every feeble thought tonight.'

'So you're the easy way?'

Ranalee ran her gaze lecherously along his naked body. 'Lust for power wasn't the only craving you exposed. All men are the same in the end. I enjoyed that part as much as you did.'

'I refuse to play this game with you.'

'Idiot,' she sighed in disgust, and held out an arm. Her third hand fished a long robe from the closet, which glided through the air to her. 'But then our children were never going to inherit their intelligence from you, were they?'

Edeard clambered off the bed, feeling intolerably weary. He was also disgusted with himself, because he knew that part of the night had been true. Her insidious power had unleashed what lay within him.

'It might already be too late for you,' she taunted.

He recovered his underwear. 'What do you mean?'

She patted her stomach. 'I'm at the right time in my cycle, and you certainly delivered adequately. I'll be such a good mother. I'll even keep it if it's a boy. He can start breeding in a little over a decade. A rival to you.' She smiled to deliver maximum hurt.

Edeard's heart fluttered. There was a phial of vinak juice in his luggage. He'd been so desperate to get her into the bedroom he'd never taken it. She hadn't given him time. All deliberate, he knew now.

Fool! She's right, you really are nothing but a backward peasant! Ranalee caught his distress and laughed.

Edeard's third hand gripped her and shoved her up into the canopy above the bed. Her eyes bulged with shock as she found she couldn't breathe. Below her, Edeard pulled on his shirt, taking his time, not looking up. 'I lack your skill in killing unborns,' he said calmly. 'So I'd have to eliminate you to make sure he was never born into the life you envisage for him, or her.' He eased off a fraction, and Ranalee sucked down precious air. 'You're too weak,' she hissed furiously.

'Sometimes you have to do what's wrong in order to do what's right.' He let go of her.

Ranalee crashed down on to the big bed, bouncing hard on the mattress. She scrambled round, and found Edeard leaning over her. She shrank back in trepidation from the expression on his face and the timbre of his thoughts.

'You should never talk so casually about death and killing,' he told her. 'Not to those of us who have killed, and will kill again.'

'You'll die alone with your dreams broken,' she cried defiantly.

'If you are pregnant you will inform me, and I will bring the child up myself.' He pulled his boots on, and went out into the night, leaving his luggage (including socks) behind.

It had been a long miserable walk back to Makkathran. With only himself for company he was forced to face aspects of his psyche that he didn't much admire. Again and again he considered Ranalee's proposal. He suspected she might be right about how impossible it would be to rip the gangs out of Makkathran. *Dear Lady, was this the proposal Finitan spoke of? It can't be. It can't.*

How he longed for Akeem's wisdom. Just one last question for his old Master. When he pictured Akeem's kindly ancient face, his old Master was shaking his head in that amused dismay of his which had greeted so many apprentice follies, as if to say: *you already know the answer.*

When dawn did eventually break and Edeard begged a lift off a farmer driving his cart to market, he was resolved. He would take on Ivarl and the gangs on his own terms. That way he gave himself a victory over the darker nature resting in his soul.

Now, looking along the brightly lit tunnel that seemed to go on for ever beneath the city, Edeard knew he had another long, lonely trek home.

'I really am going to have to get help to deal with these bastards,' he decided wearily. Neither the tunnel nor the city answered him. He shrugged and got to his feet again. It wasn't quite so painful as last time. He looked one way, then the other. There was absolutely no difference between them. Both ways saw the tunnel extend out to vanishing point. And the silence was starting to get to him. It was as profound as the time he'd used his third hand to defend himself against Ranalee's voice.

Talents, she'd said, *useful little talents.* Plural. Edeard had never heard of anything like the liquid light which Ivarl and Tannarl could manifest. And to think; when he'd hauled Arminel back to justice across the surface of Birmingham Pool he'd considered himself invincible. It made him wonder how many other nasty little surprises the aristocratic families kept among themselves.

He probed round with his farsight, trying to find exactly where he was. The tunnel was very deep. He examined the structure above him, searching for a clue of his fall, the direction he'd come from. Makkathran had altered itself again to let him through, but he couldn't detect any difference in the solid bulk overhead. When he focused, he thought he glimpsed something. His farsight swept back, and there he was. It was like an image of himself embedded in the city's substance. Falling, with his arms waving madly, his coat trailing smoke. As he studied the image, it moved slowly. If he focused on the substance above, it seemed to rise back, following his own point of concentration.

When he changed direction, so did the image. *Memory*, he realized in delight. *The city remembers me.*

Edeard tracked the image of himself to the place where it dropped out of the tunnel roof. It was kind of funny to see himself landing splat on the floor, but it still didn't tell him which way to walk, just where the House of Blue Petals stood above. He reached out for the city's peaceful thoughts, and projected an image of Transal Street in Jeavons where he always used a disused cellar to go down into the canal tunnels. *Do you have a memory of how to get there?* he queried.

There were no images, which he'd only half expected anyway. Then he began to scrabble round for his footing because the tunnel was somehow tilting. The floor shifted down alarmingly fast, and Edeard slipped on to his back. He started sliding along the smooth surface, picking up speed as the angle kept increasing. It was already way past forty-five degrees, and building. The infinite line of red lights was flashing past. He instinctively knew what was going to happen next, even though it was utterly impossible. *How can a tunnel possibly tilt?*

There was never any answer. The only sound in the tunnel was Edeard's scream as he began to fall down the now vertical shaft.

When he stopped to draw breath he didn't bother screaming again, after all this was how he dropped down into the canal tunnels. It was just that he never had such an impression of speed before. Maybe if he shut his eyes . . .

He opened them hurriedly. That was too much, he had to match up what he was seeing with what his body felt. The red lights were now a solid smear he was going so fast. This was the freedom of the ge-eagles! A side tunnel flashed past, and he gasped in shock. Before he could wonder where it led, another had come and gone. He managed a tentative laugh. No one had ever travelled like this. It was stupendous! This night crowned him king of the city, and Honious take Ranalee, Ivarl and all their kind. For they were the real ignorant ones.

There was only one truly frightening moment, when his body

was twisted by whatever guided him and kept him clear of the tunnel walls, and he abruptly flipped out of the main tunnel into one of the junctions. He drew a sharp breath, but his worry soon faded. If the city wanted him dead he would have joined Akeem in Odin's Sea a long time ago.

Eventually, his wayward flight ended as the tunnel shifted back to horizontal. Edeard wound up sliding for a long way on his arse until the tunnel floor was completely horizontal again. He looked up, and sent his farsight flowing through the bulk above. The top of the tunnel changed in that eerie and now thoroughly familiar way, and he fell up. Darkness engulfed him, and a minute later he popped up into the chill air and weak orange light of the Marble Canal tunnel.

The sight of it was immediately disheartening. Knowing he was going back up to the city streets brought his defeat into sharp focus. He couldn't tell anyone, couldn't turn to anyone. Worse, he didn't really know what to do next.

Maybe I should just leave. Ride away to Ufford, and Salrana and I will live happily out in the country where we belong.

It was so tempting. But if he didn't take a stand against the gangs, and the likes of Ranalee and her family, nothing would ever change. And ultimately the city's decay would bring the countryside down with it. The problem would belong to his children, and by then it would be even greater.

Edeard sighed, and started his trek home.

He spent the next day in his maisonette, longtalking Dinlay at the station, claiming he had a cold. Lian's trial was in its eighth day, but he'd already appeared in the witness stand. The prosecution didn't need him again. Dinlay wished him well.

One of his ge-monkeys was dispatched to the nearest doctor's house to fetch a soothing ointment, which he dabbed on his scorched skin. Then he apologized to Jessile and asked her not to come round for the evening, claiming he didn't want to pass on his cold. She commiserated, and got her family's cook to send round a hamper loaded with chicken soup and other treats.

What he wanted was to spend a couple of days resting up, thinking about his next move; certainly he needed to talk to Grand Master Finitan. Then at lunchtime on the second day Kanseen longtalked him.

The Cobara district had always delighted Edeard. It didn't have streets like the rest of the city. Instead, over a hundred great pillar towers rose out of the ground, all a uniform four storeys high, wide enough for each level to provide enough room for a family to live in. But it was above the towers where the architecture excelled. Each tower was the support column for a broad bridge spanning the gap to the next tower. Most towers provided the base for at least three such bridges, and many had more than that, webbing the district with an array of suspended polygon structures. That was where the district's true accommodation began, extending up to six storeys high from the low curve of each bridge platform. They formed triangles, squares, pentagons, hexagons and, right in the centre of the district, the bridges made up the famous Rafael's Fountain dodecagon which housed the Artist, Botany, and Cartography Guilds. The fountain itself roared up from a big pool in the middle of the dodecagon, its foaming white tip rising higher than the arching crystal roofs.

Edeard walked past the fierce jet of water, his third hand sweeping away the stingingly cold spray that splattered round the edges of the pool. He was well wrapped up in his fur-lined cloak, with a black ear-flap hat pulled down over his hair, and a maroon scarf covering his mouth. Nobody recognized him through his seclusion haze, though he was very conscious of the ge-eagle slipping through the dull grey sky that was keeping pace with him.

After the fountain he took a left, heading towards the Millagal tower, with its red and blue striped walls, covered by a leafless network of gurkvine branches. Teams of ge-monkeys were out in force, clearing the last of the slush on the plaza, which extended across the whole district beneath the thick shadows of the elevated buildings. Winter gave Cobara a strangely subterranean aspect, with only sallow slivers of sunlight reaching down through the elaborate structures above. In summer, the plaza was full of people and small markets and street artists and kids playing games. Today, they were all huddled next to their stoves in the rooms overhead, complaining about spring's late appearance.

Edeard was glad there were few people about, his mood was still down. He arrived at the base of the Yolon tower, and went through the wide archway. A massive set of stairs spiralled up the central lightwell. He grunted at the sight of them, each curving ledge spaced just wrong for human legs. One day, he reflected as he made his calf-aching way upwards, he would just throw caution away and reshape every Lady-damned staircase in the city.

Three bridge cloisters radiated out from the top of the stairs. He took the Kimvula one, and was immediately heartened by the bustling atmosphere so high above the ground. The cloister was narrow in relation to the height of the walls on either side, five storeys of ogee arches and oriel windows. Nevertheless, it was wide enough for stalls to be set up along both sides. He unwrapped his scarf as he walked past them, it was warm inside the cloister, the winter sunlight shaded with a faint pink tinge by the crystal roof. People flocked round the various stalls, haggling with the owners. The air was scented with spices, and very dry. Someone, somewhere, was roasting honeyplums.

A third of the way down the cloister he turned into a narrow side corridor which led to yet another spiral stair. Sighing, he trudged up a further three storeys. The hallway on this floor was illuminated by the city's orange light radiating from the circles positioned above each doorway. He found the red door, with its ivy hinges painted purple, and knocked politely even though he could sense the minds behind the wall.

Dybal opened it. The old musician wasn't his usual self, he still wore a vibrantly coloured shirt, and his hair was immaculately braided, but the forceful good humour was subdued. 'Thank you for coming,' he said. His eyes narrowed as he took in Edeard's blotchy pink face. 'Are you all right? You look like you've been burnt.'

'I'm okay. I had an accident, that's all.'

'Strange, that'll be the second accident I've heard of this week; there was a fire in the House of Blue Petals two nights ago. You shouldn't hang around that place, Edeard, it's been the ruin of many a poor boy.'

'I'll remember, thanks.'

Edeard was led into the parlour, which had a bulbous bay window looking out across the pentagonal space outside. Far below them, big nutpear trees grew in a series of troughs which curved out of the plaza floor. Their denuded branches shone bright white amid the shadows of the bridge buildings.

The rest of his squad were already there. Boyd and Dinlay standing close to a coal-burning iron stove, looking concerned and radiating worry. Kanseen was busying herself with a samovar of tea, her thoughts tightly shielded as always. Macsen knelt on the floor next to a chair where Bijulee was sitting, his arm on his mother's legs. She'd obviously been crying. Now she was dabbing at her face with a handkerchief, wearing a brave smile.

Edeard looked at the bruise that was darkening round her eye, and winced. His dismay suddenly turned to anger. 'Did you know them?' he blurted.

She directed a fond smile at Edeard. Even with the bruise, she was still beautiful. 'No. I told them not to call you. I don't want you worried by this.'

'Mother,' Macsen said. 'It's our fault this happened.'

'No,' she insisted.

'What did they do?' Edeard asked, almost afraid to know. He could see Macsen's hands clenching into fists.

'Nothing,' Bijulee said. She smiled up at Kanseen, who brought her a cup of steaming tea over. 'Thank you. They were just some thugs.'

'Four,' Macsen growled. 'Four thugs.' He gave Edeard a significant look.

'They told me that actions have consequences,' Bijulee said.

'And that Macsen should watch out.' One hand caressed her son's head. 'They said you should find a different job. Then . . .' She indicated her eye. 'I never saw it coming. Me! I used to think I was city-smart. Lady, how stupid of me.'

'Bastards!' Macsen exclaimed.

'Cowards,' Dinlay said.

'We've always known that,' Kanseen said.

'Do you remember what they looked like?' Edeard asked. 'Can you gift us?'

'I'm afraid I can't,' Bijulee said. 'It's all a bit of a blur. Maybe tomorrow when I've calmed down.'

'Of course. I'm so sorry this happened. I don't know what Ivarl thinks he can achieve. The trial is only going to last another couple of days. Lian and the others are going to get decades in Trampello. What does he think he's going to get me to do by this?'

'It's not your fault.'

Macsen's jaw muscles clamped down. He continued to gaze up at his mother full of concern and adoration.

'Did anyone see anything?' Edeard asked Dybal.

'No. It was the middle of the morning in the Bellis market. Hundreds of people were there, and nobody can remember anything. They do what they always do, and rush to help afterwards.'

'I'm sorry,' Edeard said again. He felt so useless. 'I'll do everything I can to make sure this doesn't happen again.'

Dybal gave him a sad smile. 'I know you will. You're a good lad, Edeard, I appreciate that. I appreciate what you're trying to achieve, too. People need hope, especially now. Shame there's only one of you. This is a big city.'

The squad got ready to leave. Edeard found Macsen's blatant hostility quite disconcerting; his friend was normally the most level headed of them all. 'Can I talk to you for a moment?' Edeard asked Dybal.

The musician ushered him into a small room which held over a dozen guitars as well as a drum set. A desk overflowed with sheet music. Normally Edeard would have been fascinated by the instruments, today he took a shaky breath. 'I know this isn't a terribly appropriate time.'

Dybal took off his blue glasses and polished them with his sleeve. 'I'll help you any way I can, lad. You know that. You're important. Not just because you're Macsen's friend.'

'Thank you. Er . . .'

'You'll find there's very little shocks me, if that's any help.'

'Okay. I just wondered if you knew anything about longtalk dominance?'

Dybal raised an eyebrow. 'The old lust slave serenade? You don't want to be messing with that kind of mischief, Edeard, no matter how pretty she is. Trust me, there can be repercussions. Anyway, from what I've heard, every mother and daughter in the city is forming a disorderly queue to drag you off to bed.'

'I don't want to use it. I want to stop it being used against me.'

'Ah. I see. Some of those family daughters not taking no for an answer, eh?'

'I wish it was that pleasant.'

Dybal studied his face closely. 'I'm sorry to hear that. First off, keep your mind tightly shielded. Which is a shame. You always seem a little more open than those of us born in the city, it helps make you so endearing.'

'Right.'

'This technique works through your own weakness. Parts of us should always stay buried, Edeard. Common decency is normally enough to keep those kind of thoughts suppressed, but once they've been kindled it's hard to put them aside again.'

'I know,' he said miserably.

Dybal's hand gripped his shoulder. 'Don't worry. Listen, there is no shame in possessing these thoughts, we all have them. If some little vixen managed to sneak through your defences and fired them up one night then that's a lesson learned, and a valuable one at that. The fact that it disturbed you this much is a pretty clear sign that it's not part of your natural personality, which is encouraging to me if not you. And I have faith enough in you to think you're strong enough to survive a crisis of conscience. But just in case: here's a recognition gift, it should help warn you if anyone tries that little trick again.'

Edeard examined the burst of thoughts Dybal shot at him, memorizing the technique. 'Thank you.'

'Now get yourself back on those streets, and generally kick the shit out of Ivarl and his cronies.'

Nobody in the squad said much as they all walked back across four districts to the constable station in Jeavons. Edeard just knew there was going to be a big argument when they got there. Macsen was going to pick a fight no matter what. Bijulee had been too much. Which meant Edeard was going to have to do something, and he was now starting to feel bad about not trusting them with the real enormity of everything he'd discovered. If the next couple of hours went wrong, then everything they'd achieved would all be over.

There were a couple of other constables in the small hall, who took a fast scan of the suppressed emotions seething through the squad and hurriedly made their exit. The thick wooden doors slammed shut. Edeard raised his eyebrow at that. Someone's third hand was adrenaline powered today.

He unbuttoned his cloak's neck clasp and sat at his customary bench at the top end of the hall.

'My mother!' Macsen said brutally.

'Yeah.'

'Yeah? That's all you can say? Yeah?'

'Did you really think Ivarl *wouldn't* try to apply some pressure?'

'Pressure! Lady-be-damned, that was my mother they used as a punchbag. My mother!'

'It's his way of trying to get to me,' Edeard said quietly, his hand went to his cheek of its own accord, stoking the tender flesh. 'You're the only friends I've got, my one vulnerability. He's bound to use that as hard as he can.'

'Yes,' Kanseen said so wistfully that Edeard shot her a curious glance. She shrugged. 'My sister was hassled last week. She was carrying Dium at the time.'

'Why didn't you tell me?' Edeard exclaimed bitterly.

'Trust, probably,' Macsen said viciously.

'Oh . . .' Edeard flung his hands up in dismay. 'In the Lady's name!'

'We thought we were in this together, Edeard. We were with you at Birmingham Pool remember? Does that mean nothing to you?'

'It means *everything*!' Edeard shouted. Finally he was too distraught to keep himself in check.

They all swayed back as his doubts and confusions blazed out. He made an effort, gritting his teeth and placing his hands palm-down on the old wood of the table. 'Sorry,' he told their shocked expressions.

'Edeard, in the Lady's name, what's wrong?' Boyd pleaded. 'What happened to you, to your face? And why won't you talk to us any more?'

'He didn't trust us with the Myco warehouse,' Macsen said harshly. 'Why should he trust us with anything else.'

'You're such an arse,' Kanseen snapped at Macsen.

'I do trust you,' Edeard said, even to him it sounded like a bored recital. 'I got burned when I was sneaking around the House of Blue Petals. That's all. It's not as bad as it looks.'

'You went there by yourself?' Kanseen asked disapprovingly.

'Yeah. It's how I've been keeping track of Ivarl.'

'That's dangerous,' Boyd said. 'Edeard, you can't do that on your own.'

Macsen let out a scornful grunt. 'He's the Waterwalker, he can do anything. He doesn't need us holding him back, do you?'

Edeard sighed, this was worse than he'd steeled himself for. 'The warehouse raid was the most public thing we'd ever attempted. Ivarl had laid a trap, he was going to make us – me! – a laughing stock. The whole thing was set up to destroy my credibility. I just used some misdirection. There were over a hundred constables involved, and we didn't know half of them. If everyone had known, it would never have worked.'

'We're not *everyone*,' Macsen barked. 'We're your friends, your squad. Or so I thought.'

'Hey, ease up,' Dinlay said. 'It was good procedure.'

'Yeah, well I expected you to take his side.'

'What's that supposed to mean?'

'Come on,' Edeard said. 'We can't do this. Ivarl will be laughing at us.'

'So his opinion is valuable to you, is it?' Macsen said. 'Whereas mine – no contest.'

'That's not—'

'Don't get upset,' Kanseen interjected. 'He's just angry.'

'No shit?' Macsen spat at her. 'Why do you think that is? I am a part of this fucking squad, this so-called team. I had faith in you, Edeard. Faith. Me, of all people, me! And how do you treat that? You just bloody use us to boost your own stature. The Waterwalker saves the day again. Well crap on that.'

'I didn't *use* anyone. We were all on that raid together. I made you a vital part of it. Did you know there was going to be a robbery? Did you know where they were going to stash the platinum? Did you know there was going to be a switch?'

'So what are you saying? I'm not worthy enough because I can't spy as well as you? Are any of us, because that's what this is about. Even Dinlay's pissed at the way you exclude us.'

'I am not,' Dinlay said, so quickly Edeard didn't even look at his friend's face.

'If all you want is a bunch of constables who'll run around and do your bidding, then fine,' Macsen said. 'There are dozens of them in this station alone. But if you want to work with me, then you come down off your tower and start trusting us again.'

'Screw you!' Edeard said. 'You have no idea what we're up against. Not the faintest clue. I'm protecting you.'

'I don't need your protection. And I know more about the gangs than you ever will, country boy. I grew up in Makkathran.'

'I grew up in Makkathran,' Kanseen said. 'Dinlay did, Boyd did. You had a nice cushy life on the Iguru.'

'I did what?' Macsen pushed his face out towards Kanseen.

'Stop it, now,' Edeard said. 'I didn't include you in certain things because I was frightened.'

They stopped arguing, and shot each other puzzled looks. Edeard rested his elbows on the table and put his head in his hands. He was worried there were tears leaking from his eyes he was so worked up. 'You're all I've got. I don't want us broken up. Not just because I depend on you. We have something here, and it's more than just kicking the crap out of Ivarl. We have hopes. I couldn't stand it if those were broken. I'd be left with nothing once more. I'd rather be dead.'

Kanseen came and sat on the bench next to him as the others started to radiate concern. 'What is it?' she asked, putting her arms round his shoulder. 'What's the matter, Edeard? We all trusted each other at the start. Nothing's changed, not really. Tell us.'

Edeard lifted his head and stared straight at Macsen, letting his friend see all his anguish. 'Do you want to do this?'

'Yes,' Macsen said, now looking really worried.

'Really?'

'Yes!'

'Everyone?'

Boyd and Dinlay nodded.

Kanseen squeezed his shoulder. 'Of course.'

'All right, then. But I want you to swear on the Lady that you won't shoot the messenger.'

'Hey, we're grown ups,' Macsen said.

'No, we're not,' Edeard said. 'Not really.'

'You're getting very depressing,' Boyd said with a nervous smile. 'Just what do you want to tell us?'

'What we're up against. The scale of the gangs. I want to make you understand.'

'We do know, Edeard,' Dinlay said sympathetically. 'They

166

even tried to intimidate my sister Carna last Wednesday. Lady, they won't do that again in a hurry.'

'Carna?' Macsen said. 'She's the, er . . .'

'My big sister,' Dinlay said with a contented smile. 'Very big.'

Edeard cocked his head at Boyd.

'Yeah,' Boyd nodded dismally. 'Isoix had some more trouble.'

'So?' Macsen insisted. 'What's your big secret?'

'I'll show you,' Edeard said slowly. 'Sometime in the next few days. I'm not sure when, but be ready. When I call for you go to the Flight Canal end of Golard Street.'

'You mean near the Black Horse?' Macsen asked.

'Yeah, but don't go in there for the Lady's sake. And make very sure you're not followed.'

'Easy.'

'Actually, it isn't. Ivarl uses ge-eagles to shadow all of us, but I'll take care of them. It'll be night, so that'll help you.'

'He does what?' Kanseen asked; just for a moment her mind betrayed real alarm.

'He watches us,' Edeard said quietly. 'He has for the last month. I've been messing with the ge-eagles he uses, but I can't manage to protect you the whole time.'

'Shit.'

Edeard climbed to his feet. He gave Macsen a sorrowful look. 'I am sorry about Bijulee.'

'I know.' Macsen stuck his hand out.

Edeard shook reluctantly, still dreading what was to come. 'Remember, the messenger is just that.'

'Got you.'

Edeard went back to the court the next day to watch the prosecution and defence councils deliver their closing statements. He was interested that Ivarl couldn't be bothered to turn up to hear Lian be found guilty, nor was he there the following day when a twenty-five-year sentence was handed out. After the judges left the chamber, the constables from Jeavons station crowded round Edeard to congratulate him. Then they had to make way for Grand Master Sparbil of the Chemistry Guild who had been in the court for every day of the trial.

'Thank you, young man,' Sparbil said, giving Edeard's healing face a close look. 'The loss of that material would have meant a considerable financial weakness for my Guild. I am in your debt.'

'I was doing my job, sir,' Edeard replied.

'I'm sure you were. But I remain grateful. If we can ever assist you, please just ask.'

'I will. Thank you, sir.'

'Finitan was right about you, I think you are of benefit to the city. A shame District Master Bise doesn't share that opinion, but don't worry, he is outnumbered in Council.'

'Bise?' Edeard knew the name, Bise was Sampalok's District Master. He'd never seen Bise turn up at the House of Blue Petals in person, but he knew the Master had extensive financial connections with Ivarl's organization.

'High politics, I'm afraid,' Sparbil said with a grin. 'Not that there is anything high about it, of course. Our little voting bloc in the Council is full square behind you. Unfortunately, our opponents take the opposite view. But that's the way it is in Council. If they had come down on your side, I'd probably be against you by now. Same with the weather; if they vote for sun, I'll vote for rain.'

'Uh, I see.'

'Take my advice, don't put yourself forward as a candidate for Chief Constable for at least another two hundred years. That way you can remain out in the city where you'll still be in a position to accomplish something.'

'Yes, sir.' Edeard gave the Grand Master a formal bow, frowning at the man's back. *The Grand Council is taking sides over me?*

'A drink tonight?' Chae asked. 'This victory is probably more significant for you than Arminel's was. It shows the gangs you're not going away. That needs to be celebrated properly.'

'No, thank you, I have a date.'

'Ah, good for you, lad. Enjoy it while you can, while you're young. They turn sour when they get older.'

'Who?'

'Women. All of them.'

'Is everyone in this city a cynic?' Edeard asked that evening.

Jessile pulled a beer bottle out of the wicker hamper she'd brought. 'Who's cynical?'

'Everybody, so it seems. Or maybe I'm just paranoid.'

She smiled sweetly. 'You probably are.'

'Thanks.' Edeard took the bottle and flopped down on to the maisonette's heavy old couch. He felt exhausted, even though all he'd done was sit around in court all day. Victory should have perked him up, yet all it seemed to have done was raise another bout of questions and doubt. How he longed for things to be as they were before Birmingham Pool. Life had been so much simpler then.

'Put your feet on the stool, I'll pull your boots off.'

He leant back and did as he was told. It was nice having Jessile around. After that final night with Ranalee he'd almost sworn off family girls for life. Except he remembered how genuinely nice Jessile was, almost the opposite of Ranalee. She was undemanding. Enthusiastic in bed. And discreet. At least she was now. Which was a good thing, he reflected. He was desperate to recover some of his public dignity after those months of excess following Birmingham Pool.

Her fiancé hadn't been in the city for three days before he was sent back out again, much to her dismay. They hadn't even managed to set a day for the wedding. So in the meantime, she was happy to carry on seeing him – just not so visibly.

Two lonely people, basically, he thought. There were few mornings when he didn't look out of the window, searching the brighter skies which would signal Salrana's return.

He glanced guiltily at the letter propped up in one of the maisonette's alcoves. It had arrived yesterday. Salrana had written it three weeks earlier. That was how long a letter took to reach

Makkathran from Tralsher province. In it she explained how she might have to stay on for a few more weeks. The Mothers were desperate for help, she said, and she couldn't let them down. There were so many people who looked to the Church for help in Ufford.

'Lian got twenty-five years,' Edeard said as they sat down to supper. His ge-monkeys had been busy preparing the food the chefs in her mansion had packed in the hamper. 'The others got between three and eleven years.'

'That's good,' she said.

'Really? Have you noticed a drop in crime?'

'Did you mention something about cynicism?'

'Sorry.'

'He's going to be another six weeks at least.'

'Who? Oh. Right.'

'I got a letter this morning. They're staying on in Reutte province to help another town. Eriach, I think.'

'Yeah, it's on the western side of the Ulfsen Mountains.'

'You know it?'

'I passed it on my way here.'

'Well, they've got bandit trouble now.'

Edeard looked up from the asparagus and kafish quiche. 'What sort of trouble?'

'Raids on hamlets, and the roads aren't safe. Honestly, the militia pushed them out of the estates around Tetuan and they just popped up again a few miles away.'

'They have a habit of doing that. Frightening them away isn't good enough. They'll just come back later. If you want to be rid of them, you've got to push them back and back until they've nowhere to run to any more. Don't give them anywhere to hide. Then you can go in for the kill.' He stopped. 'That might work.'

'What?'

'Nothing, just an idea.'

'There's not even any certainty that Eustace will come back after Eriach. Suppose the bandits appear somewhere else?' She started turning her silver vine ring, unconsciously rubbing the diamond.

He put his hand on hers, squeezing lightly. 'He'll be back.'

'Thanks. I know.'

'Did he mention if they have guns?'

'Guns? No. He hasn't said. Do you think it's likely? He might get shot!'

'Some bandits have guns. Not many,' Edeard lied quickly, allowing her to sense a calm confidence in his thoughts. 'They just get hold of the odd pistol from farms, that kind of thing. To be honest, pistols have a very limited range anyway.'

'Oh.' She gave him a nervous smile. 'Don't scare me like that.'

'Sorry. No sane bandit is going to tangle with a mounted militia squad. He'll be perfectly safe. You'll be married off by midsummer.'

'I hate that he had to go. It's all politics. Mayor Owain only sent the militia so he can look strong and benevolent at the same time. That's what Daddy said. And I'll bet Owain's Guild merchants are there following the militia around, selling guns to the locals.'

'See? Everyone's a cynic.'

She grinned at him. 'I guess we are.'

'Owain might have sent the militia for political gain, but it's been beneficial. Reutte needed help. The local sheriffs couldn't cope. Quite a few farming families have arrived in the city since New Year. I spoke with some of them; they were forced off their land.'

'I know.'

'He will come back.'

'Thank you, Edeard. You're a lovely man.'

After the meal they settled down to read a book Jessile had brought. *Kadril's Voyage*, which told of the legendary merchantmen captain who'd opened up the trade route to the south, finding a navigable route through the Straits of Gathsawal. Edeard enjoyed the tales of ocean life and fights against pirates, even though he suspected the author had enlivened the tales somewhat. They took it in turns to read to each other, slowly sipping red wine as the coal in the stove hissed and snapped. Edeard felt the tensions drain away from him. This was what he wanted his life to be like. Success in the courts, pushing the gangs from the streets, then home. Not back to the maisonette, but a true home, one with Salrana, maybe. He'd even seen a few vacant buildings in Cobara and Igadi that were possibles. They would need the room eventually, he hoped, for the children. Children who would know a city without the shadow of crime and the excesses of the families; playing in streets and parks where they were safe. And it could be done, his idea had been growing since supper, expanding in that lazy way that certainties possessed.

'You look a lot happier,' Jessile murmured. She closed the book and leaned in against him.

'You have a soothing voice,' he told her.

Her nose rubbed against his cheek. 'My voice, is it?'

'Yes.'

'I wish you had a piano in here. I'm quite an accomplished player, you know. Music would be extra soothing.'

It was that casual grumble which made him smile so merrily. She really had no idea how little a constable earned; on his pay it would take months for him to buy a piano. 'We'd never get it up the stairs.'

'Never mind.' She kissed him, her thick hair brushing his face and neck. 'I bought a new satin chemise today. It's not very big, I'm afraid. Would you like to see me wearing it? Well . . . trying to wear it.'

'Yes.'

'Say please.'

'Please,' he croaked hoarsely.

She got up, showing him a truly immoral smile. 'Back in a minute.' She picked up the hamper and disappeared into the bathroom.

Edeard took a breath to recover. He was beaming in anticipation as he rolled off the couch and ordered the light down to a cosy glimmer. At which point he became aware of Vilby walking over the bridge into Silvarum. 'Oh Lady, no!' he groaned.

'What's the matter?' Jessile called out.

'Er, I'm really sorry about this, but—'

The squad was waiting where Edeard had told them, huddled together under an overhanging wall on Golard Street, where the pavement was only four feet wide. It was dark, with the nearest light coming from behind the undulations of a nebuly moulding on the wall two houses down.

'Saria was furious with me,' Boyd was saying. 'It was her great-aunt's annual ball, half the District Master families were there.' He was dressed in a splendid cerise frock coat, with a white shirt that was all lace frills. Silver buckles gleamed on his knee-length boots.

'Sounds like you're making social progress,' Kanseen said. Her face wore a faint frown, she was glancing along the street as if searching for something.

'I didn't know he was going to call us away so suddenly.'

'He was really worried about this,' Macsen said. 'That's not like our *great* Waterwalker.'

'Well you didn't help,' Dinlay said. 'Not the way you were shouting at Edeard the other day. All those wild accusations . . .'

'Hey, I'm entitled,' Macsen said, raising a finger for emphasis and waving it right in front of Dinlay's face. 'That was my mother they attacked. And it's his fault.'

'No, it's not.'

'Oh yeah, if he knows so much like he claims, then he should have warned us. If I'd known what was happening I could have stopped those thugs attacking my mother.'

'We didn't tell him what was happening to us,' Kanseen said. 'We're all to blame.'

'He doesn't trust us. He couldn't even be arsed telling us about the ge-eagles. We're his decoys, that's all.'

Edeard dissolved his concealment, appearing beside Macsen's shoulder. 'No, you're not.'

'Ho Lady!' Macsen jumped back in shock.

'Where in Honious did you come from?' Dinlay demanded.

'I've been here all the time.'

'You heard . . . ' Dinlay's thin face blushed hotly.

'Now do you understand? This is not a game. I want to change this city. I want your help to do that.'

'And you think that's the way to get it?' Macsen asked.

'If a couple of insults and a bad temper can put an end to this squad, then we were never going to achieve anything. We were just some kids thrown together with nothing special holding us. I'm hoping that's not true. I'm not pretending I don't have a weakness. I made an arse of myself chasing girls. I'm too frightened to tell you everything I know about Ivarl. I didn't know how to handle the warehouse raid so I went along with Ronark's suggestion. And I'm certainly not sure where we go from here, although I've got an idea.' He shrugged. 'That's it.'

Macsen glanced round the others, unhappiness shining though his shielded mind. 'All right, that's honest enough. Crap on inspiration, mind. But I'm willing to see what you want to show us.'

'Me too,' Kanseen said.

'Yeah,' Dinlay said.

Boyd gave a soft chuckle. 'Count me in.'

'Thank you,' Edeard said.

'Do we get to learn the concealment trick?' Boyd asked eagerly. 'I always thought it was a city myth.'

'Oh, you get to know it,' Edeard said. 'You're going to need it. Ready for the gift?'

'Yeah!' the squad chorused.

After half an hour practising along the street, Edeard led them into the Black Horse tavern. They weren't perfect. Boyd's concentration kept slipping; Macsen's farsight wasn't half as good as he always claimed, which meant he couldn't combine the ability with his third hand in a way that was truly effective. But Kanseen and Dinlay were surprisingly adept. Apart from the occasional lapse from Boyd and Macsen, when their ghost-like shape would flare out of nowhere, they remained invisible, certainly from casual scrutiny. The only way they knew where each other was standing was by a tiny direct longtalk, the kind of thing they'd practised a hundred times out on the streets. Edeard helped by dimming the tavern's lights around them, producing long deep shadows. They crept between them, passing unseen through the back rooms.

Edeard's nerves built with every step up to the second floor where the private rooms were. Macsen was playing along for now, but how he'd react to this . . . Without Macsen, the squad would be seriously weakened, and he was going to need their full strength if he was to have any hope of success over the gangs.

'Ready?' Edeard asked outside the door.

'Yeah,' Dinlay whispered.

Then Edeard heard a metallic click – a pistol's safety catch pulled back. 'Is one of you armed?'

'Yes,' Boyd said.

'Well, actually, all of us are,' Dinlay said defensively. 'We thought we were going to be raiding a gang hideout.'

'Oh Lady, no, no, this isn't a raid. It's not actually dangerous, we just have to catch them in the act. So put the pistols away, please.'

Several grumbles rolled along the apparently empty corridor. Fumbling sounds followed.

'Ready?' Edeard asked again, reflecting on the impossibility of acting as a team when you couldn't actually see each other. 'Go!'

As one they dissolved their concealment. Edeard used his third hand to smash the lock, and flung the door open. The squad charged in.

Vilby's face was a mask of astonishment and fright; his head lifted off the pillows to stare at the squad. He couldn't move any further, his own handcuffs fastened his wrists to the odd metal hoops driven into the wall above the bed. Nanitte, who was straddling his chest holding a jar of honey in one hand, turned round and let out a soft gasp of shock. Then she saw one of the intruders was Macsen, and her face registered real concern. 'Ladycrapit.'

Edeard could sense the longtalk yell she was directing out towards the other end of the city. It wasn't much: 'They've caught me with Vilby. I never sensed them coming, they were bloody invisible.' His own face was part of the accompanying gift she sent. No one replied to her.

'Don't come back to the station,' Edeard told Vilby. 'And get you and your family out of the tenement by tomorrow evening. Only constables live there.'

'But—'

Edeard closed his third hand round the man's chest. Honey squelched out around the edges of his grip. 'Don't,' he growled in warning.

Vilby sagged in defeat.

Kanseen lifted an eyebrow as she gazed at the tacky mess covering the man's groin. 'Well, thanks a whole lot, Vilby, I'll never be able eat a meringue again.'

Boyd sneered down. 'You know, you really need to leave them in the oven longer, a proper meringue is never that sticky in the middle.'

'Is that right?' an interested Dinlay asked as they turned and walked out of the door.

'Oh yes. Any half-wit baker's apprentice knows that.'

Macsen hadn't said a word. He was staring at Nanitte, who returned the look unflinchingly.

'Come on,' Kanseen said. She put her hand on Macsen's shoulder, and gently propelled him out of the room.

Edeard gave Vilby a derisory wink and closed the door as he left.

The waitress in the Olovan's Eagle was puzzled by the squad's lack of good humour as they clustered together in the corner booth. Edeard tipped her a brass farthing, and scooped the beer glasses off her tray with his third hand. He put the first one down in front of Macsen. 'Sorry,' he said cautiously.

Macsen shook his head and put his hand round the glass. He stared intensely into the dark amber liquid with its thick head.

'It's a war of who knows most,' Edeard said.

'Lady,' Kanseen grunted heavily. 'I think we get that now, Edeard.' She took a long drink of beer. 'Was anyone I've . . . ?'

'No.'

'That's lucky. For them. I would have ripped their balls off and stuffed them where the sun doesn't shine.'

'Um,' Boyd ventured. 'About Saria?'

'A lovely girl. Don't worry.'

'So it's just me then, is it?' Macsen said bitterly. He was still glaring at his beer. He hadn't managed to look at Dinlay since they'd left the Black Horse.

'Not exactly,' Edeard cringed as he gave Dinlay an awkward glance. 'Chiaran.'

'No!' Dinlay squawked in horror. 'She's a constable.'

Boyd turned his head slowly to give Dinlay a fascinated look. 'Who's Chiaran?'

'Her father is in debt to one of Ivarl's lieutenants in Fiacre. She's helping to pay it off.'

'She can't be.'

'You never said anything about a Chiaran to me,' Boyd said with a rising smile. 'You sly old thing.'

'Sorry,' Edeard said.

'Oh Lady!'

'Well, aren't you the clever one?' Macsen said, still not looking up.

'Actually, no,' Edeard said. He took a breath. 'I'm sure you all remember Ranalee.'

Kanseen actually spilt some of her beer. 'What?'

Edeard's shoulders slumped. 'The Gilmorn family has strong ties with Ivarl. It's all part of the way the port works – I discovered afterwards. Too late afterwards, unfortunately. I think that's how Ivarl found out I knew about Vilby.' He couldn't quite bring himself to tell them about *that* night.

'Wait, he knows you knew?'

'Yes.'

'But . . . Oh, Lady be damned.' She took another gulp of beer.

'So,' Boyd said with a frown. 'If he knew that you knew he . . . I don't get it. Why would he go ahead with the Chemistry Guild robbery if you both knew what was happening?'

'I told you it's a war of who knows the most, and then how you apply it.'

Macsen finally looked up, fixing Boyd with an icy glare. 'Get it now? All of this is a giant pissing contest between Ivarl and Edeard, which of them can outsmart the other.'

'Which is why you have to understand,' Edeard said firmly. 'Fully understand.'

'Well I understand now,' Macsen said bitterly. He faced up to Dinlay. 'I'm the idiot who got you shot. Me!'

'Hardly,' Dinlay said with a nervous guffaw.

'I told her. I said we were going to do undercover work after we talked about watching Boltan Street.'

'When did we say that?' Edeard asked.

'Day we caught Arminel in the store room,' Kanseen supplied.

'Oh yeah.'

'Arminel used it, didn't he?' Macsen said. 'He used that to mount the ambush at Birmingham Pool.'

'We don't know anything for certain,' Edeard said. 'What I was trying to show you tonight is just how smart and organized Ivarl is. Not only that, his organization is big, it reaches right across the city.'

'You've made your point,' Kanseen said. 'We were naive. That'll stop now.'

'I'm sorry,' Macsen said. He was pleading with Dinlay now.

'You didn't shoot me.'

'It was my fault.'

'No it wasn't,' Edeard said. 'You all know Arminel, what he's like. If they hadn't come after us that day, it would've been another. You don't send people like Nanitte to spy on us unless you're making a real effort to eliminate us.'

'And Chiaran,' Dinlay said forlornly.

'And Chiaran,' Edeard conceded. 'That means he's still out to get us, even more since the warehouse. It's going to get ugly.'

'She was beautiful,' Dinlay said. He took off his glasses and polished the lenses intently.

'We're all good, though, aren't we, Waterwalker?' Boyd said cautiously. 'Tell us that at least. Tell us nobody here tonight belongs to Ivarl.'

'We're all good,' Edeard promised them.

'Nanitte,' Macsen moaned, and slumped back into his seat. 'What about the others? Have any more girls belonged to Ivarl?'

Edeard grinned. 'I don't have the time to keep track of that list.'

'Nor your own, it would seem,' Kanseen observed archly.

'Nor mine,' he conceded.

'Lady, this is wonderful,' she muttered. 'We have to seek your consent for our lovers now. It's like I'm living at home again and getting my mother's approval.'

'What were her criteria?' Boyd asked eagerly.

'Well, she wouldn't have let you through the front door, that's for sure.'

Edeard laughed. 'It's not that bad.'

Kanseen gave him a level gaze. 'Yes, it is.'

'You don't have to tell me who you're with every night. And as of now, I'm not going to farsight. Just . . .'

'Be paranoid?'

'I was going to say cautious. If you want me to check out a new acquaintance, I will.'

'Paranoid is good,' Boyd said. 'Unlike all of you, I, of course, chose very well.'

'You had no choice at all,' Kanseen said. 'Saria chose you. She makes all the decisions for you.'

'She does not! I am my own master.'

Kanseen reached forward and plucked the sleeve of his remarkable frock coat. 'Did you choose this? Did you even pay for it?'

Boyd turned red as the others laughed.

'So what do we do now?' Dinlay asked.

'And he does mean "we",' Macsen said. 'That's right isn't it?'

'Yes,' Dinlay stumbled. 'It's just . . . Chiaran.'

'Get rid of her,' Macsen said harshly. 'She's not your girl-friend, she's his whore. Do it with longtalk, that's nice and insulting. In fact, I'll be happy to do it for you.'

'Would you?'

Macsen turned to Edeard. 'Do you want to use her first?'

'No,' he said. 'No, it's tempting. But if we're going to do this I don't want us stooping to his methods.'

'It's not going to be that clean,' Kanseen warned.

'I know.' He smiled round at his squad. His friends. 'But we'll manage.'

'So what exactly do we do now?' Boyd asked.

'I've been thinking about this,' Edeard told them. 'The biggest part of Ivarl's income comes from the protection rackets. He has teams in every district intimidating shopkeepers and stallholders. I want to push them out. I want to start by making Jeavons clean, then keep going, force them to retreat across the city until we've got them penned up in Sampalok.'

'Then what?' Kanseen said. 'And how would you make them retreat there? Do we intimidate them? They'll fight back.'

'I don't know the details. We need to consult with Grand Master Finitan about how to begin such a scheme, and the politics behind it. We'd certainly need Grand Council support, maybe even a new law.'

'All right,' she said. 'Even if you get him to support you in council, and we get all the station captains to play along, and a hundred other crappy impossible details sorted out, how do we find them? There must be hundreds of gang members working this racket. Are we all going snooping round the House of Blue Petals?'

'Ah.' Edeard gave them a rather smug grin, and reached into his tunic to produce a thick black notebook. He put it down between all the beer glasses. 'You must be talking about this list I made of all the names I overheard.'

*

'A grand alliance against gang-related crime,' Grand Master Finitan said. 'Nice idea.' He turned in his high-backed chair to stare out through his office window.

Edeard and the squad sat in smaller chairs in front of the big desk, all of them trying not to gape at the remarkable view offered by the office's vantage point.

'Do you think the Council would support it, sir?' Edeard asked. If it hadn't been for the tea and biscuits served to them by the ge-chimps, Edeard could well imagine himself as part of some lowly apprentice class being lectured by the Grand Master.

'If you went up to individual Masters and Representatives to ask them for help expelling the gangs, each and every one would look you straight in the eye and pledge their full and unswerving support, save Bise, of course. Privately, any new law to banish suspected gang members wouldn't even get read out in Council, never mind voted on.'

'Why not?' Dinlay asked.

'Expense. Legally proving a man is a gang member would consume a lot of time in court, and an even greater amount of lawyer's time, which never comes cheap. And what would you effectively be accusing them of? If you can prove membership you can prove felony, which can get them carted off to the mines anyway. No, you need some other way.'

Edeard groaned. It had seemed like such a good idea.

Finitan swung back to face them. 'Don't give up, Edeard. You're the Waterwalker. We all expect great things of you now.' He produced an enigmatic smile. 'More than creeping around bordellos at night, anyway.'

Edeard blushed.

'So what would you advise to get rid of them?' Kanseen asked.

'If you want anything done, you need to make it to everyone's advantage. Support is essential, the wider the support, the better chance you have of succeeding.'

'But the Council must have been trying to get rid of the gangs for years,' Edeard protested. 'Why has there been no progress?'

'I'm going to sound boring on the subject, but: expense. Not just in financial terms. Consider how Ivarl's lieutenants control the dockers. The merchant families have a nice quiet arrangement with Ivarl, they pay him to keep the dockers in line. Take that control away, and the dockers will demand decent pay, and quite right too. It's a skill controlling teams of ge-monkeys to remove the contents of a ship's hold, or fill it. So they get more money, which has to come from the ship owner and warehouse merchant and shopkeeper. That cost will be passed on to the customer. The price of everything goes up. Admittedly not by much, but it's the start of an uncontrollable reaction, a destabilization if you like. Why shift the balance of power in an arrangement that works? And the dockers are just the tip of the iceberg. So many things would change.'

Once more, Edeard remembered what Ranalee had said. *External change is revolution.* 'But the gangs are wrong,' he insisted. 'The law must prevail.'

'Yes, indeed. But you of all people should know by now how entrenched they are in the city.'

'There must be a way.'

'Find a method of gathering a broad spectrum of support,' Finitan said. 'From there you can go forward.'

'I need the support of the Council.'

'Ultimately, yes. But you must start at the other end, down on the street where the gangs are felt every day. Tell me, before you decided to mount your crusade, what was happening out there? I don't mean among the rich and worthless of my class, but people who were directly affected by the gangs and their violence? People who had given up looking to the constables for aid?'

'They were forming street associations,' Boyd said.

'Yes. Vigilantism, which the Council also frowned upon, not least because such associations circumvented the law.'

Edeard tried to understand what Finitan was hinting at. 'We support the street associations?'

'No. The station captains don't approve, for the simple reason that street associations undercut their authority, and that of the courts.'

'Then what?' he asked, confused.

'You can't support them, but there's nothing to stop you sharing a drink in the tavern after duty, now is there?'

'Ah,' Macsen said. 'And we might just discuss who is going round traders to extort money and what they look like and where they live.'

'Indeed you might.'

'And those private citizens are within their right to call for assistance when the gangs do come calling,' Kanseen said.

'If they knew for sure that a constable squad would come, they would be more inclined to cooperate,' Finitan agreed.

'And if cooperation at that level were subsequently seen to work,' Edeard mused.

'It would be supported,' Finitan concluded. 'A support among people who are not easily bought off by political horse trading. Pressure would grow on the District Representatives to continue and expand the campaign.'

'But we're still back to the original problem,' Edeard said. 'Arresting them and hauling them into court. Each case takes weeks and costs a fortune. Not to mention tying us up as we sit around for days waiting to be called as a witness. If we remove one of them, Ivarl will send ten to replace him. I need to push the whole lot of them out of Jeavons.'

Finitan eyed the genistar egg sitting on his desk. 'What you need is a legal option. Have you consulted a lawyer?'

'This is the joy of a constitution that has reigned supreme for an unbroken two thousand years,' Master Solarin said contentedly. He was sitting behind his desk, which was piled with folders that strove to mimic the towers of Eyrie. Edeard had trouble seeing him they were so high. 'You can find a law to cover every eventuality. Politicians love to pass laws. It shows the people they are working hard on their behalf.' He coughed, and reached for a lozenge in the little brown paper bag under a skewed tower of green and blue folders.

'Then it can be done?' Dinlay asked eagerly.

Edeard had brought Dinlay with him, while Macsen and Kanseen went to meet Setersis. Not that he didn't trust Dinlay with anything, it was just that Macsen would be better suited to deal with the chief of the Silvarum stallholders association. Boyd, of course, was with Isoix, discussing their notion with the Jeavons chamber of trade.

'Such impatience,' Master Solarin muttered disapprovingly. One of his ge-monkeys brought a thick leather-bound tome over to his desk, and placed it gently on the huge square of blotting paper in front of the ancient lawyer.

When he'd been shown in by a legal apprentice, Edeard had thought the whole office had been built from books. Each of the five walls was covered from floor to ceiling in shelving, holding thousands of volumes of law. There might have been a window, but it had long since been blocked over. The ceiling had three blunt stalactites that shone orange, giving the books a dingy brown hue.

Master Solarin opened the book. He licked the tip of his forefinger, and began to turn the pages. Edeard wanted to volunteer to help. It was all so painfully slow. He deliberately didn't turn to look at Dinlay.

'Ah ha,' Master Solarin said happily. 'I thought I remembered this one.'

'Sir?' Edeard asked.

'I believe I may have found what it is you are looking for.'

Edeard leaned forward. The page the book was open at had greyed over the decades, but the ink was still firm and black.

'Here we jolly well go,' Master Solarin said. His shaky hand traced a line of the print, his mouth working silently.

'What does it say?' Dinlay pleaded.

Edeard shot him a warning glance.

'It says, Constable Dinlay, that nine hundred and thirty-two years ago, the Grand Council passed the by-law of district exclusions. This is an edict which allows the District Master or District Representative to declare the right of admittance revoked for any person deemed detrimental to the sanctity of the locale. Issuance of such warrant may be duly authorized by the District Master or District Representative on their own authority, without supervision by a judge or magistrate.' He looked up from the book. 'I believe it was proposed in Council by the District Master of Cobara so that he might prevent an over-amorous suitor from wooing his only daughter. If you remember your history, Constable Dinlay, the two young lovers in question were Henaly and Gistella.'

'Really?' Dinlay said with a happy smile. He turned to Edeard. 'They cloped on the *Oxmaine*, and founded Love's Haven, and planted the vineyards there. That province still produces some of the best wines on Querencia.'

'Wonderful,' Edeard said, resisting the impulse to use his third hand to give Dinlay a good smack. 'So we can use this law to ban gang members from coming in to Jeavons and Silvarum, without having to legally prove they're gang members?'

'Any person for any reason, provided their name is on the warrant and signed by the District Master or Dist—'

'Yes! The District Representative. How do I get them to sign?'

'Oh Dear Lady, were my lectures completely in vain?'

'You petition them,' Dinlay said proudly.

'Indeed, Constable Dinlay. I am glad not all of my words fell on deaf ears. As a resident of Makkathran you have under most ancient law the right to make a petition of enactment. Such that a District Master, or – ' Master Solarin paused for emphasis, 'a District Representative, can require the constable station commander of their district to enforce whatever law the supplicant believes has been violated. Now, as the assistance of the citizenry is implicitly required, as stipulated in the articles of formalization of the constabulary six hundred and twenty-two years ago, this elder right of petition has subsequently fallen into disuse. However, it has never been retired.'

'You mean we can use this loop hole to get the District Master to sign the warrants?' Edeard asked.

The skin of Master Solarin's ancient face produced even more creases as he frowned in disapproval. 'You will never become a lawyer, Constable Edeard, for which blessing my Guild will doubtless be most relieved. There is no such thing as a loop hole. Lawyers merely advise our clients on how to apply laws and the precedents they establish.'

'Thank you, sir.' Edeard rose from his chair.

'A word of caution, my young friend.'

'Sir?'

'You can petition them to enact a law, but you cannot force them to undertake said enactment. To obtain those signatures, you will need their cooperation.'

'I understand, sir. My colleagues are working on that.'

It was a big petition. Edeard had to back up the initial street association meetings personally, persuading the stallholders and shopkeepers and tavern owners and merchants, and a dozen other tradespeople that his idea was worth trying. With his small base of political allies like Setersis, Ronark, and Finitan, and his own reputation, he began to gain the backing he needed. A week after the meeting with Solarin, the Jeavons chamber of trade and the Silvarum chamber of trade simultaneously laid down a formal request to see their respective District Masters and Representatives.

They convened in the library of District Master Vologral's mansion. Edeard had only met the Jeavons Master twice before, at formal events. There they'd made small talk, trying to weigh each other up. He was heartened by the fact Vologral was an ally of Finitan on the Grand Council.

Vologral and the other three Masters stood behind a long table, listening to the official request as made by the speakers of the chambers of trade, then he turned to Edeard. 'Can this work?'

'I believe so, sir,' Edeard said. 'We know probably seven out of ten involved in the protection rackets, certainly in our districts. Those are the ones we already have warrants for. If the gangs send in new faces to collect their money, we'll know who they are straight away, and we can add them to the list.'

'But keeping them out . . .' Vologral looked apprehensive.

'In total there are fifteen bridges into the two districts. Each one will have a pair of constables on duty from now on to enforce the exclusion. We just need the legal basis.'

'And the mooring platforms? How many of them? You can't guard them all.'

'There will be three permanent patrols inspecting the mooring platforms at random; in addition our ge-eagles will be scouting constantly. I'd point out that a court can levy a considerable fine to any gondolier who violates a city by-law. We'll need to make an example of the first few cases, possibly with confiscation of their craft. After that, they won't be so keen to help the gangs.'

'I can imagine the Gondolier Guild's reaction to that,' Deveron, the Silvarum Representative muttered.

'The Waterwalker is making an effort to help us,' Setersis said quietly. 'I for one am happy to cooperate.' Deveron looked at him, and said no more.

'Very well,' Vologral said. 'I am provisionally inclined to grant your petition. I will sign the warrants. However, I give you notice, Waterwalker, that I will review the situation in three weeks' time, after the Festival of Guidance. If I am not satisfied that racketeering has subsided, or you are not holding the line against the gangs, they will be revoked. Do you understand?'

'Yes, sir. Thank you, sir.'

'Do you have the warrants here?'

Edeard beckoned Felax and the other three probationary constables who were waiting at the back of the delegation. Each of them came forward carrying a tall stack of paper.

'Great Lady,' Vologral grunted when he saw how many

warrants the young constables had brought. 'I didn't know I was excluding half the city.'

'Seventy-three people to start with, sir,' Edeard said.

'Gentlemen,' Vologral said to his fellow Masters, 'let's hope we don't get writer's cramp.' He sat down at the long table.

'What happens to the rest of the city?' Deveron asked. 'Aren't we just exporting the problem?'

'They'll wait to see if it works,' Setersis said. 'If it does, they'll join in quickly enough. Decent people have had enough.'

Vologral signed the first warrant. 'So suppose you do succeed? Exclude them from everywhere but Sampalok, for I know damn well that Bise will never sign one of these. What then?'

'I imagine that will be up to the Grand Council, sir.'

'Ha!' Vologral gave Edeard a sly smile of approval as he reached for another warrant. 'Not such a country boy after all, eh?'

It began the very next morning. Ronark changed the squad shifts, which in itself was fairly historic; dispatching five constables to each of the bridges leading into Jeavons from Drupe, Tycho and Majate. Silvarum's station captain did the same with bridges to Haxpen and Padua.

As dawn broke, the constables took up position. News of the exclusion had spread in that lightning-fast way any novelty did in Makkathran, especially one concerning the Waterwalker. A lot of people turned up to see if it was actually going to happen. At some bridges they applauded when the constables appeared. Sandwiches and hot tea and coffee were produced and offered to the new guard squads. Then everyone settled down to see what the gangs would do.

At midday, eight men walked across Golden Park. They were young and tough, knew how to handle themselves in a fight, and had a strong third hand. By the time they reached the district's southern point adjoining Birmingham Pool there were five ge-eagles orbiting high above them. Only two of which belonged to the constables.

'Getting a real burst of nostalgia here,' Macsen sang out as Edeard's squad jogged along Macoun Street.

'Nostalgia is a happy sensation,' Kanseen grunted. 'This isn't.'

Edeard tended to agree with her. He glanced at Isoix's bakery as they sped past. 'You all right?' he asked Dinlay with a direct longtalk whisper.

'Oh Lady, yeah.' Dinlay's thoughts were aflame with expectation. They'd spent the morning walking round the two districts on a random route, making themselves visible, knowing there would be a showdown at some time. It should have been a time of high excitement for Edeard, but he'd got another letter from Salrana; she'd been delayed again.

He ran out of Macoun Street on to the broad sweep of the alameda. The weeping hasfol trees were just budding, a multitude of blue and yellow striped leaves expanding out of their whorls to greet the warmer skies. Right ahead of them was the blue and silver bridge which looped high over the waters of the Great Major Canal to Golden Park. Sergeant Chae was standing at the foot of it, giving Edeard's slightly out-of-breath squad a nonchalant look. 'I'm insulted,' he said loftily. 'You don't trust me?'

'Procedure, sir,' Macsen puffed. 'We're the reinforcements.'

'But I haven't called for you, yet.'

Edeard gestured at the bridge. 'All yours, sir.'

'Thank you.' Chae glanced round at the eager crowd that was building. 'This is nostalgic, eh?' He turned and led the four constables of his squad up on to the bridge.

'Have any of them got guns?' Boyd asked.

'I can't sense any,' Kanseen said. 'Edeard?'

'No. Nothing. Ivarl will want it to appear like they're just ordinary citizens. He needs to make us the bad guys.'

'Hey, Waterwalker,' a young boy yelled out cheekily. 'Are you going to do it again?'

'Not today.'

'Oww, go on, please. Run over the pool. I didn't see it before.'

The eight men had reached the other end of the bridge. Chae

and his squad were standing on the apex, arms folded. Waiting patiently.

'This is a different day,' Edeard said out loud. The crowd were dividing their attention between him and the gang members over on Golden Park. 'This day we banish the gangs from your streets and lives.'

The gang men stepped onto the bridge.

'You!' Chae bellowed. 'Pocklan, we know you and your friends. Come no further.'

The eight men kept walking forward.

'I have a warrant signed by the District Master of Jeavons excluding you from this district.'

'I have done nothing wrong,' Pocklan shouted back. 'I am a free man. I may go where I please in this city. That is the law.'

'Halt and turn around. Go back where you scum came from.'

Boyd nudged Edeard. 'Look who's here,' he growled.

Edeard glanced over where Boyd indicated. Master Cherix was standing at the front of the crowd, watching intently.

'We knew they'd try to quash the warrants in the courts,' Dinlay said.

'Please don't let this come down to lawyers,' Kanseen moaned.

'I'm visiting my mother who lives in Jeavons,' Pocklan said, appealing reasonably to the silent spellbound crowd. 'She has only a few days to live. Would you deny me that right?'

'What a load of bollocks,' Dinlay said under his breath.

'Piss off,' Chae said, jabbing his finger forcefully back down the bridge. 'Now.'

'Sergeant,' Master Cherix said. It wasn't a particularly loud voice, but the authority behind it carried a long way.

Chae turned round, an expression of utter disgust on his face, backed up by some very strong thoughts escaping past his shield. 'Yes? Sir?'

'I am this fine gentleman's legal counsel. May I see this so-called exclusion warrant, please?'

'It's back at the station.'

'Then until you produce it, and let him see it, as is his right, my client is free to go about his business in whatever district of this city he chooses. As do his equally innocent colleagues.'

'All right then,' Chae said, and jabbed his finger at Pocklan again. 'Wait here. I'll send a runner.'

'No, Sergeant,' Cherix said. 'You cannot detain my client without just cause. It is your responsibility to bring the warrant to him. Until it is read to him, he is free to go as he pleases.'

'I can't run around the district after him and the others,' Chae said.

'That is not my client's problem,' Master Cherix said affably.

Pocklan's smirk was indecent. 'Step aside,' he told Chae.

Edeard walked forward. 'Master Cherix.'

'Corporal Edeard. How nice to see you. I believe you can be of some help in this unfortunate matter. Your colleague here was about to act unlawfully. As a constable of this city, I am asking you to see the law is enforced equally and fairly.'

'My pleasure.'

Master Cherix beckoned Pocklan. 'Come on across the bridge now, please, my dear chap. You are quite safe with the Waterwalker himself guaranteeing your legal rights.'

'Were you referring to a warrant like this?' Edeard asked innocently. He pulled a roll of parchment out of his tunic.

Master Cherix's unctuous smile flattened as he started to read. 'But this warrant names—'

'You.' Edeard smiled. 'Yes. And as such, I am required – by law – to assist you out of Jeavons as quickly as possible.' He reached out with his third hand.

Master Cherix yelled in consternation as his feet left the ground. The cry turned to pure panic as he kept on rising. The crowd on the alameda gasped as the lawyer soared away over the bridge, continuing to gain height.

'Put me down!' Cherix screamed with his voice and longtalk. He was higher than the buildings behind the alameda; higher than the white metal pillars lining Golden Park. Still ascending. The watching ge-eagles had to curve sharply to avoid him.

'Did you hear something?' Edeard asked.

'He told you to put him down,' Kanseen pronounced solemnly.

'Oh, fair enough,' Edeard said. He let go.

Cherix fell out of the sky with an incoherent shriek of fright. He landed in the middle of Birmingham Pool, producing a tremendous splash. The crowd cheered wildly.

Chae turned back to Pocklan. 'Now where were we?'

Pocklan gave the sergeant a furious look; then glanced over his shoulder to where an impassive Edeard was waiting. He turned and led his companions back into Golden Park.

Macsen put his arm round Edeard's shoulder, squeezing strongly. 'Now why is it, do you suppose, people you don't like always wind up getting dunked in Birmingham Pool?'

'Nostalgia.'

*

Edeard had been looking forward to the Lady's Festival of Guidance for what seemed like most of the winter. His friends, and the girls he'd encountered, were always speaking of it in enthusiastic tones. Firstly, it signalled the onset of summer, which, as far as he was concerned, couldn't arrive fast enough. But the main reason was to celebrate those who had passed away in the previous year. Everybody who had lost someone made a small memorial boat out of flowers – of any and every colour except white. Mainly it was the children of a family who made them, producing elaborate and colourful boats up to a yard long. They represented the soul of the departed one.

At midday, the Pythia conducted a service of memorial in the Lady's church in Eyrie. When that ended all the flower boats would be placed in the city's canals. The gondoliers, bedecked in white flowers, guided them down to the port singing hymns of commemoration. Gondolas represented the Skylords, who the Lady promised would come to Querencia once again to guide the souls of humans into the welcome embrace of Odin's Sea. At the port, the gondolas would stop, and the flower boats would carry on, drifting out across the waves.

It sounded delightful; especially the evening, which was one giant party. Now the day was here, and Edeard dozed fitfully as the dawn came to a clear sky, promising good weather for the festival. Chief Constable Walsfol's longtalk intruded sharply into his thoughts. 'Ugh, sir? he responded groggily as the dregs of yet another bizarre dream drained away. He hadn't known the man had such a powerful longtalk. It made sense, though. After Ranalee, a lot of things about the city hierarchy were clearer to him.

'I need you to report to the Culverit family mansion in Haxpen,' Walsfol told him. 'Come at once.'

'Yes, sir,' Edeard said sleepily. 'Er, why?'

'I will meet you there and explain the situation. You'd better bring the rest of your squad, too.'

Edeard rubbed his eyes. He hadn't got to bed until well after midnight. Late last evening, the Lillylight Street association had spotted a gondola with three known gang members making their way along Victoria Canal. Edeard and a couple of Silvarum constables had intercepted them at a mooring platform on Flight Canal. No resistance had been offered when the men were told to leave, but he'd still kept watch on the gondola as it made its way back down the Great Major Canal.

That was the way of his days now. Constantly alert for attempts to infiltrate racketeers into Jeavons and Silvarum. Called to shops and other businesses when unknown gang members did get through. Two days wasted in court on charges of aggravated psychic assault filed by Master Cherix, who, thankfully, in law was no match for Master Solarin.

He groaned and pushed his feet out from under the nice warm sheets. Jessile shifted round on the springy mattress. 'What?' she mumbled.

'Have to go,' he said softly, and kissed her forehead.

She moaned again, and curled up tighter. 'I won't be here tonight, have to be with family for the party. See you tomorrow.'

'Right.' But she was already asleep again. He ordered a ge-chimp to bring a fresh set of clothes. While he was struggling into them in the dim light he started to call the others. It was rather satisfying spreading the misery.

Edeard pulled his boots on beside the door, and gave his own flower boat a wistful glance. It wasn't much, a simple frame of card a foot long, over which he'd stuck a dozen red and yellow roses. His friends assured him it was just right, exactly what everyone else constructed. For him it was a belated memorial to Akeem, and all the others of Ashwell village.

He met up with Boyd and Kanseen on the tenement walkway outside. They weren't in the best of moods at being hauled from their beds so early. Edeard couldn't bring himself to look at Kanseen. She hadn't been alone.

'Are we waiting for Dinlay?' Boyd asked as they made their way down the stairs.

'He'll join us there.'

A smile spread across Boyd's face. 'You mean he was with someone?'

'Not our concern,' Edeard said, a fraction too sharply. Now he really couldn't look at Kanseen.

'Any idea what this is about?' she asked.

'None. But if we're being summoned to the Culverit family by Walsfol himself on this day, you can bet it isn't going to be trivial.'

'Julan is the Haxpen District Master,' Boyd said. 'He's one of the waverers, isn't he?'

'I think so,' Edeard said, rubbing his hand over his brow. In truth, he'd lost track of which Master was for them. Their allegiances were very fluid. Lately he'd given up trying to follow the Grand Council machinations, and just prayed Finitan would prevail tomorrow.

Boyd opened the big wrought iron gate at the entrance to the tenement. Macsen was waiting outside. He raised an arm in greeting.

'Dinlay's still not over Chiaran, you know,' Boyd said cheerfully.

'We all got a nasty shock over Ivarl's methods,' Edeard told him as they went out into the street. 'Let's just forget about that and move on, shall we?'

Boyd was clearly going to make some other snide comment, he'd even started to open his mouth when a voice cut across the empty street: 'Waterwalker,' a woman cried.

She had been sitting up in the doorway of a tailor's shop opposite the tenement. Edcard's farsight had sensed her as they were on the last flight of stairs, but she hadn't been carrying any weapons. She did have three children with her, which was mildly unusual at this time of day, but not anything to concern himself over. He'd assumed she was simply bright and early for the festival. Now she came striding across the street, pulling the sleepy miserable children with her. The eldest was no more than five, while the youngest, a girl, was barely old enough to walk.

'Where do I go, Waterwalker?' she demanded belligerently. 'Tell me that, eh? Where?'

'What?' Edeard asked, very confused. Macsen was hurrying over to them.

'How will my children eat? Ask him, Dannil, go on, ask the great Waterwalker where your next meal is coming from.' The middle child, a boy in a ragged green pullover and worn grey trousers, was thrust forward. He looked up at Edeard and his lip began to quake. He burst into tears. 'I want me da!' he wailed.

'What?' Edeard asked again.

'Eddis, my husband,' the woman barked. 'You exiled him. Threw him out of his own house. We live in Fonscale Street. Now you bastards come along and tell him he's banned from Silvarum, where we've lived for seven years. He can't come home. Can't come to the house my family has lived in for three centuries. What kind of a law is that, eh? So you tell me, where do I go? How do I feed the children without their father. Eh? Answer me, you backward country shite.'

Edeard just stared at her, his mind a shocked blank. Boyd groaned, and rolled his eyes up, appealing to the Lady. 'Oh crapit,' he groaned.

Kanseen was having none of it. 'How did he feed them before?' she asked. 'What job did your husband have?'

'Go to Honious, bitch. You've done this to us. You've ruined our lives.'

'What job?'

'He's a good man. He put food on the table for us. He loved his kiddies.'

'Yours maybe,' Kanseen said. 'But he hurt other children, didn't he? Threatened them, hit them, made their parents hand over money they'd worked hard for.'

'He never did.' She covered the eldest boy's ears. 'Lies. That's what you speak: lies! You'll all go to Honious. Eddis worked in the abattoir on Crompton Alley. Dirty work, hard work that no genistar can do.'

'You knew what he did,' Kanseen snarled. 'If you miss him, then go to him, follow him to his new home. But remember this, we will wipe the city clean of his kind. After this year, there'll be no more of him.'

The woman spat at Kanseen, who swatted it away with her third hand. All three children were crying now.

'I want you to tell Eddis something from me,' Edeard said. 'Tell him that if he leaves the gang behind, if he finds himself a proper job – and there's plenty to be had – he'll be welcome back in Fonscale Street. I'll cancel the warrant myself. That's all he's got to do.'

'Screw you!' She pulled at her children. 'You know nothing about life. Ivarl will dance on your ashes yet. And no Skylord will ever rescue your soul.'

Macsen touched the brim of his hat as she stomped off down the street. 'Thank you, madam, always a pleasure to help the citizenry,' but he didn't say it very loud.

'You okay?' Kanseen asked.

'Yeah.' Edeard gave her a shaky nod. 'Yeah, I suppose so. Lady, how many families have been split up like that?'

'Are you serious?' an incredulous Kanseen asked. 'What about the families of Eddis's victims? The people you're supposed to be helping? Isoix and his children? Don't they deserve some consideration?'

'Yes, sorry,' he hung his head. 'I just wasn't expecting this to be so hard.'

'Cheer up,' Boyd said, and put his arm round Edeard. 'It can only get worse.'

Edeard was about to remonstrate, then saw Boyd's mocking expression, and he managed a weak smile. 'Much worse.'

'Far, far worse,' Macsen promised.

'Let's go and see what misery and torment Walsfol has in store for us then.'

As he set off with his friends, Edeard chastised himself for not expecting such an ambush. The only real surprise was that it hadn't happened earlier. Although they'd managed to add another fifty warrants to the original batch, fifteen had been cancelled. There had been a few genuine cases of mistaken identity, but more than one person in the associations had used the scheme to settle an old grudge. Then there were some traders who'd taken advantage in order to get commercial rivals banned from the district, reducing competition. Each reported case of abuse had to be properly reviewed and sorted out, which took a great deal of time for the constables – but not as long as a court case, as Edeard had to keep pointing out to the grumbling Masters and station captains.

But even with the troubles and abuse and legal challenges and the racketeers' unrelenting attempts to get past, he considered it a success. And in that he wasn't alone. The gangs had made hardly any collections in Jeavons and Silvarum, and only two traders had been assaulted before the constables arrived. Makkathran's remaining districts had watched the results keenly. Under continuing pressure the Masters of Haxpen, Lillylight, Drupe, Ilongo, and Padua were drawing up their own warrants and talking to the station captains about enforcement. In another couple of days, they could well be signed. Tomorrow was the last day of Vologral's three-week trial. Not that the District Master and Representatives would have the final say. Not any more. The

Grand Council was due to convene to debate the 'disturbance' to city life caused by the reintroduction of the exclusion warrants. Finitan was leading the bloc of Councillors arguing their benefit. If they lost, the warrants would be revoked; and as Finitan had told him, Bise was preparing an act to rescind the original law. He had a lot of tacit support, Finitan said, because no one was sure where the whole thing would end. Was it the Waterwalker's intention to turn Sampalok into a criminal ghetto, cut off from the rest of the city? And exactly how did such a young inexperienced constable come to lead such a campaign in the first place? Politically, the Masters were becoming very nervous of Edeard. Finitan was coming under increasing pressure from his fellow Masters to produce a valid conclusion to the campaign.

Edeard didn't actually have one. When he did think that far ahead, to a time every district had issued warrants, he'd assumed the Grand Council would step in with a final solution. Expulsion was his preferred option, though he wasn't sure how that would be achieved, nor where the gang members would be banished to. He'd just wanted to start the ball rolling, to give people hope. Only now were the true consequences becoming apparent.

Though even he had to laugh when on the day after Cherix received his ducking in Birmingham Pool, District Master Bise very publically signed an exclusion warrant preventing Edeard from entering Sampalok. Less amusing was the dignified announcement from the Pythia saying that she would never prohibit anyone from entering Eyrie to attend the Lady's church. Owain also declared no warrants would apply to Anemone and Majate, so that all citizens would be able to reach the seat of government, a right which Rah himself had laid down. And as for the protestations from the Gondoliers Guild about restricting their trade ... There had never been a gondola strike in Makkathran before. Even though it had only lasted a day, it shocked everyone. There were threats that more would be called, especially if the vote in the Grand Council tomorrow didn't go the way the gondoliers wanted. The Dockers Guild had also pitched in with a promise to support the gondoliers.

Thankfully, Edeard was getting a lot of support and encouragement from various traders and merchants. Ordinary people, too, were grateful, if their reaction to the constable squads on bridge duty were anything to go by.

Edeard just wanted tomorrow's Council debate to be over, one way or the other. The weight of expectation that had fallen on him was awesome.

Dinlay was waiting outside the main entrance of the Culverit family mansion. The first rays of sunlight had already reached the highest level of the ten-storey ziggurat, to glint on the huge horseshoe arch windows. Five pistol-carrying guards with the family's insignia on their coats opened the grand iron-bound front gate. The squad walked in through the giant archway to find themselves in a broad courtyard. Vivid topaz climbing roses smothered the pillars on every side, while tall granite statues of past Culverit Masters and Mistresses gazed down sternly. An equerry greeted them and ushered them inside. Edeard sighed when confronted with a spiral stair.

'I suppose the family live on the top floor,' he muttered to Boyd.

'The Master's family do, of course.'

The summit of the mansion was a house larger than the Jeavons constable station, surrounded on each side by a strip of hortus garden. It was the traditional residence of the District Master, with the lower floors occupied by dozens of relatives and household staff and clerks who administered his estates.

As they ascended, Edeard became very conscious of the mood swirling round him. There was anger, predominant in the men, and a great deal of fright and sorrow.

'Something bad has happened here,' he said quietly. Macsen gave a short uncomfortable nod of agreement.

Walsfol and Julan were waiting for them on the upper hortus garden that faced the Grand Major Canal. Even so early, the Chief Constable was wearing a pristine tunic, his gold buttons shining brightly in the rising sun. Julan, by contrast, was one of the few aristocrats who showed his age. A hundred and fifty three years made his shoulders sag, and his grey hair thin. He wore a rumpled house robe over his nightshirt. His eyes were red rimmed, and sunken with abject despair.

The squad had brought Edeard up to date with Culverit family gossip on the way over. Now, as never before, they were the subject of intense speculation and discussion within the rest of Makkathran's aristocracy. Master Julan had married very late in life. In itself that wasn't too unusual among his class. It was a truly romantic marriage. Apparently he fell completely in love with his wife (a hundred and eight years his junior) as soon as they were introduced, and was utterly devoted to her until her tragic, untimely death six years ago. Though what scandalized everyone was that the first child she produced had been a daughter, Kristabel, as was their second child, during whose birth she'd died. There was no son to inherit. It was almost without precedent in the city. But to the dismay of Lorin, Julan's younger brother, there was a clause in the Culvert family's legally registered claim to the Haxpen District to allow the lineage continuation through a daughter if there were no sons. The situation had occurred only twice before in Makkathran's two-thousand-year history.

Consequently, Julan was estranged from a good percentage of his relatives; meanwhile Kristabel was the most desired girl in the city, with every noble son desperate for an introduction. Any party she was due to attend was besieged by potential suitors. 'And Lady, wouldn't you just know it, she's an exceptionally pretty thing, too,' Macsen had finished wistfully.

'We have a problem,' Walsfol announced as soon as the squad was ushered on to the high terrace. 'No doubt the entire city will know by breakfast, but Mirnatha has been abducted.'

Edeard risked a sideways glance at Dinlay.

'The second daughter,' Dinlay explained with direct longtalk.

'I'm terribly sorry, sir,' Edeard said to Julan. 'Obviously, if I can do anything to help, I will.'

Julan's distress abated long enough for him to give Edeard a fierce judgmental stare. He held up a small square of paper. 'You can start by explaining this.'

Edeard gave him a puzzled look, and appealed to Walsfol. The Chief Constable gently extracted the paper from Julan and handed it to Edeard. 'A ge-eagle delivered it not quite an hour ago.'

With a sinking heart, Edeard read the note.

Mirnatha is very sweet. The price of her return alive and still sweet is eight thousand gold guineas. If you agree to our price, fly a yellow and green flag from the Orchard Palace this noon.

The Waterwalker is to deliver our coinage by himself. He will go to Jacob's Hall tavern in Owestorn at midnight. Further instructions will be given to him there. If anyone is with him, or if he tries to snatch her back without paying she will be killed.

'Oh, Lady, no,' Edeard groaned.

'I can't order you to deliver the money,' Walsfol said.

'You don't have to, sir, I'll take it of course. Er . . . do you have the money?' he asked Julan. With that much coinage you could buy Rulan province and still have enough left over for a fleet of the fastest merchant vessels.

'It can be found, yes.'

'Where's Owestorn?'

'It's a village out on the Iguru,' Dinlay said. 'Maybe two hours' ride from South Gate.'

A long way from any possible help, Edeard realized, and even I can't longtalk that far. 'The note was delivered after Mirnatha was taken,' he said delicately. 'Is there any proof that it came from those who hold her?'

Julan held up his hand. His fingers clenched a blue ribbon with a long tuft of gold-brown hair. 'This was attached.'

'I understand.'

Tears were running down the old man's cheeks. 'The ribbon was from her nightdress. I know it was. I kissed her goodnight.

201

I kiss my Mirnatha every night. She is so precious—' He began to cry, sobbing helplessly. Walsfol moved to comfort him. 'We'll have her back for you, my friend, be assured. Every effort will be made. The constabulary will not rest until she is in your arms again.'

'She is but a child,' Julan wailed. 'Six years old! Who could do such a thing? Why?' He stared wildly at Edeard. 'Why have they done this? What is your part in this? Why you? Why can't I go? She's my baby.'

'I don't know, sir.' Somehow, just having so much anguish directed at him made Edeard feel shamed.

'Of course you do,' a thin voice snapped.

Edeard's farsight identified her being helped though the doorway behind him out on to the hortus, but he didn't want to turn round.

'It is your fault,' Mistress Florrel insisted. 'And yours alone. You caused this with your ridiculous crusade against the gangs. Why couldn't you just leave things well alone? Nobody was being harmed. This city worked perfectly well before you arrived.'

Edeard took a deep breath, trying to keep a shield around the growing anger in his mind. Mistress Florrel was in one of her usual archaic black dresses, wearing a tall hat that seemed to have purple fruit growing out of it. A man in fine aristocratic robes was holding her arm as she made her way slowly towards Edeard.

'Lorin,' Macsen murmured. 'Julan's younger brother.'

Mistress Florrel stood directly in front of Edeard, her shoulders all hunched up as if in sorrow; but still managed to fix him with a merciless stare. 'Well?'

'Mistress Florrel.'

'What have you got to say for yourself?'

'I will bring the girl back and deal with those responsible.'

'You will do no such thing. You will hand the money over as you're told. Nothing more. I don't want this made any worse by your wretched stupidity. Officers from the militia will take full charge of things from now on. Gentlemen of good character and family, that's what we need. Not some country buffoon.'

Edeard felt his teeth grinding together.

Boyd put his hand on Edeard's arm, smiling politely. 'We will cooperate in any way we can, Mistress Florrel.'

Her eyes narrowed. 'I know you. Saria has taken a shine to you.'

'Yes, Mistress.'

'Ha,' she dismissed him with a flutter of her hand. Her voice took on a tragic tone. 'My dear, dear boy,' her arms rose up in sympathetic greeting as she shuffled over to Julan. 'How are you coping? This is all too, too terrible.'

'She'll come back,' Julan managed to stammer.

'We'll make sure of it, brother,' Lorin said effusively. 'What has passed between us is nothing now. I am resolute in helping you endure this ordeal.'

Julan bobbed his head. 'Thank you,' he whispered.

'Come along,' Mistress Florrel said. 'Sit down my dear Julan. You family is here to comfort you now. That is what you need. You are no longer alone or surrounded by fools. Go and get him some tea,' she told Walsfol imperiously. 'Now my boy, have you enough money to pay the ransom? I will help if not. We simply must get her back to her home and loving family.'

Walsfol inclined his head respectfully to Julan as he left the hortus, and signalled the squad to follow. They hurried after him.

'Now what?' Edeard asked.

'I hate to concede the point, but Mistress Florrel is right in one respect,' Walsfol said. 'This is about you.'

'Yes, sir,' Edeard said miserably.

'Stay here for now in case they get in touch again; and for the Lady's sake keep out of *her* way,' Walsfol said, pointing back through the horseshoe arch in considerable irritation. 'I'm going to convene the station captains. Somebody out there must know where that poor girl is. One of them will talk.'

Edeard was looking round the magnificent lounge with its clutter of fabulous artwork and gilded furniture. 'How did they get up here?' he asked in bewilderment. 'And then how did they get out again, carrying Mirnatha? In the Lady's name, there are hundreds of people in the mansion, and this is the tenth floor.'

'A valid question,' Walsfol said in a low voice. 'The captain of the house guard here is called Homelt. Talk to him. The kidnappers must have had some inside help. Take a look round the girl's room. There must be some clue, some evidence we can use to uncover the kidnapper.'

'Do you think she's still alive sir?'

Walsfol took another guilty look out on to the pleasant hortus. 'Very few kidnapping victims are ever returned. Just enough to make the families and merchants pay out in the hope that their loved one will be the exception.'

'So she might still be alive?'

'Yes. She might. We have to carry on in the belief that Mirnatha is going to be handed over safe and well in return for the money.'

Edeard wasn't much encouraged by his tone. They found Homelt waiting for them in the central corridor. He was in his fifties, thickset but still fit. The kidnapping had left him angry and distressed; it was taking up a lot of self-control just to clamp down on his emotions. He'd spent twenty years in the constables, he told them, serving out of Bellis station. 'I was a good constable,' he insisted. 'Not like some of them, who were just in it for the pay-off. I did my duty and earned this post.'

'So how did they get her?' Edeard asked.

For an instant it looked like Homelt might strike out. He stood quite still and took a long breath. 'I don't know. And that's the Lady's honest truth. It was the middle of the night. All our gates are locked and guarded. There are more guards on random patrol inside. There's always someone on the stairs. I just don't understand.'

'What about new guards?'

'Yesterday, I thought I could trust every one of them. Today

I'm not sure of anything any more. We don't take in just anyone, they have to be known and sponsored; and like you we've got a pretty good idea who's in with the gangs.'

'All right, so tell us what happened.'

'The kid's nursery maid raised the alarm really early on. The first thing we did was double the gate guards, then we searched the whole mansion, every room I promise you. Not just farsight, we physically inspected everywhere. Then that bloody ge-eagle flapped down on to the tenth-floor hortus. The Master . . . I've never seen him so broken. She was a lovely little thing, she really was. Nothing like you'd expect a family child, none of the airs half of them have.'

'Can I see the room please?'

'What do you think?' Dinlay asked as Homelt led them along the corridors. Dispirited staff hung their heads as the squad walked past. Edeard couldn't detect the faintest flash of guilt, they all shared the same numb horror. The three nursery maids were in their parlour next to the family rooms, all weeping openly. Even the ge-monkeys were subdued, caught up in the emotions saturating the mansion.

'The same as you,' Edeard said. 'Somebody with a concealment ability. There's no other way.'

'The gangs have that?' Kanseen asked in alarm.

'Not the street soldiers we normally deal with, but I found out the hard way that Ivarl has a considerable psychic power.'

Mirnatha's nursery room was the same size as the whole of Edeard's maisonette. The walls were draped in pink tapestries depicting colourful fairies and nikasprites and birds. Dressers and chairs were lined in streamers of fluffy pink feathers. There were two big dolls houses whose elaborately dressed inhabitants were strewn everywhere. A wooden rocking horse stood in one corner. The wardrobes were full of sweet little frocks.

Edeard found it painful just standing on the pink carpet looking round. He sniffed the air. 'Do you smell that? Something tangy?' Walking round, the smell was strongest by the bed with its twee lace canopy.

'Chloroform,' Homelt said. 'That's how they kept her quiet.'

'What's chloroform?' Edeard asked. The squad was regarding him with an expression he was starting to tire of.

'It's a chemical,' Dinlay said. 'If it's inhaled it puts you to sleep. Nearly every kidnapper uses it. You soak it into a cloth and hold it over your victim's face.'

'Chemicals?' Edeard said. 'They used chemicals on a six-year-old girl.'

'Yes,' Homelt was giving him a strange look.

Edeard took a final look round the nursery and pushed the glass doors open. The section of the hortus directly outside was mainly laid with grass, with some ornate yew trees in urns standing along the silver-grey balustrade. He stood with his hands pressing down on the rail and looked down. Each of the terraces in the ziggurat was laid out below him, forming a series of horticultural steps down to the ground. Now spring had truly arrived, the plants formed a blaze of colour as their flowers opened to greet the warm days. Mirnatha's hortus faced east. Away to his left, the Great Major Canal stretched out in a perfectly straight line to the Lyot sea in the distance. People were just starting to appear along its side, claiming their position in readiness for the festival. He let his farsight expand along it, past Forest Pool and Mid Pool down to First Pool, which formed the base of Myco. There was the House of Blue Petals, its interior impressively restored after the fire.

Ivarl stood in front of his office's oval window, stretching his farsight towards Edeard. Just for a second, Edeard was back in his room at the Ashwell Eggshaper Guild, searching the towers of the village gate for any sign of the guards, with the bandit chief watching him.

'I wouldn't have believed even you would stoop to this,' Edeard informed his adversary coldly. 'She's six years old, for the Lady's sake. Six!'

'I'm sorry about the girl,' Ivarl replied. 'But it wasn't me.'

'You're a bad liar.'

'You and your activities have started to dismay some very

important people in this city. And that stunt you pulled vanishing in the fire, that was impressive, even to me. They're starting to work out what you are and what you're capable of. I have a feeling myself that even you don't know your full potential yet. Not that it matters, because that potential has already made them fearful. You won't be allowed to reach it, they'll make sure of that. That's what today is about, not the girl. She's just a means to an end, but you know that already don't you?'

'Where is she?'

'I don't know. Nor do I know who does. If you want her you'll have to deliver the ransom.'

'Is she still alive?'

'I would imagine so. They need to entice you out of the city by yourself, away from any possible help. If she's dead, they lose their advantage and their ability to manipulate you. Just an observation; from someone who has a lot more experience than you in such matters.'

'Who? Who has done this?'

'Oh, please, Waterwalker.'

'I hold you responsible.'

'Really? Is the truth too great a burden for you? This is your war, and you should have considered the consequences before you began it. It's far too late now to act outraged when it goes against you. And you can't back out now. You're the only one who can save her.'

'Will you negotiate for me? I'll go to them in Owestorn if they let her go.'

'You really are that stupidly noble, aren't you. Dear Lady: youth and its virtue. This city will be doomed if you ever sit in the Mayor's chair at Council.'

'Will you talk to them?'

'They don't want a martyr, Waterwalker. Your death alone is not enough. It is how you die that is important.'

'She's only *six years old*!'

'There is nobody left for me to talk to; my oldest and dearest friends no longer hear me. You should have chosen your opponent with more care. As you are to the constables and the shopkeepers and merchants, so I am to my people. And I'm losing the battle. It's not just money you've cost me, it's my authority; and out of the two that is going to prove deadly.'

'If she dies, I swear you will too.'

'You don't really think either of us will see tomorrow's dawn, do you?' Ivarl shook his head and raised a hand in farewell before going back into his study.

Edeard snarled in frustration, and slammed his hand down on the rail.

'You're the Waterwalker, aren't you?'

'Huh?' He turned round to see Kristabel standing underneath a pergola entwined with a thick emerald vine. First impression, which he always felt dishonoured by, was big wild hair and stick insect legs. Equally shaming was the accompanying thought. *She's nothing like as pretty as Macsen made out.*

Kristabel was tall with a long thin face that with her current mood made her appear incredibly melancholic. A slender body was wrapped in a loose white cotton nightdress. Like her father, she'd been crying. Her hair, which was actually gold-brown like her sister's, was threaded with lighter streaks. She'd been rubbing it or raking her hands through it, twining it into stringy strands which stuck out badly.

Edeard remembered his manners and bowed. 'Yes, Mistress, that's me.'

'Mistress!' She smiled, which turned into a grimace as she fought back tears. 'I'm mistress of nothing. Our family is a giant curse, a joke. How could the Lady allow this to happen?'

'Please don't give up hope. I will do everything I can to ensure your sister's return.'

'Everything you can. And what's that?' She winced. 'I'm sorry. She's my sister. I love her so much. Why didn't they take me? Why?'

'I don't know.' Edeard desperately wanted to put his arms round her, to offer some comfort. She was younger than him by a year or so, he decided. And her pain, swirling out of an unshielded mind, was humbling.

'If you talk to them,' she said. 'The beasts who did this, offer them me instead. I want to take her place. Please. They can do whatever they like to me, I don't care. I just want my Mirnatha home. Tell them that. Make them understand. I'm more valuable anyway, I'm the first daughter. I will be Mistress of this district.'

'Your task, Mistress Kristabel, is to stay here and be strong for your father.' He let conviction fill his voice. 'I will bring your sister back to you.'

'Words, that's all. Promises, I have heard the like a thousand times from the lips of Masters. They are worth nothing.'

'Let me try. I am not a Master. Do not give up hope yet. Please.'

She wrung her hands together in anguish. 'Do you really think there is hope?'

'Always,' he told her gravely.

'Are you going to deliver the ransom?'

'If that is what's needed, then yes.'

'I overheard our family guards. They say it's a trap.'

'It is.'

'You don't even know Mirnatha.'

'I don't have to.'

'You really are a good man, aren't you? Is that why the gangs hate you so much?'

'I expect so.'

She straightened up, smoothing her nightdress, then gave him a questing glance. 'Did you really turn down Ranalee?'

He bowed again. 'Yes, Mistress.'

'Don't call me that.' She smiled bravely, then darted forward.

Edeard felt her lips upon his cheek. He was too surprised to pull back.

'The Lady bless you, Waterwalker.' She turned and scurried away down the hortus.

He walked back into Mirnatha's nursery with his thoughts in complete turmoil.

'What's the matter with you?' Dinlay asked.

'Why are they doing this?' Edeard asked, gazing round the room. He'd never actually seen so much pink in one place before.

'To screw you over,' Boyd said.

'It was a rhetorical question. They want me out in Owestorn because they think if I'm all by myself they can kill me, right?'

'It's what I'd do,' Macsen said, ignoring the exasperated glare Kanseen gave him. 'They'll have a small army out there. Even if we're only ten minutes away, it'll all be over by the time we can reach you. They'll probably pick us off as well for good measure.'

'But that turns us into martyrs like he said. That gives our cause strength. Possibly even enough strength to carry tomorrow's vote.'

'Who said?' Dinlay queried.

'That's not so good then,' Macsen admitted. 'Mirnatha won't be coming back either.'

'That way you get the blame,' Boyd said. 'With no surviving witnesses they'll arrange it to seem like you tried something reckless. The city will believe you're responsible for her death; after all you had the ransom money. No criminal in their right mind would jeopardize that much coinage, especially after such a well-executed kidnap.'

'And the exclusion warrants end along with us,' Edeard concluded. 'Clever.'

'So what do we do?' Kanseen asked.

Edeard turned to the small wooden bed, exquisitely crafted to resemble a swan, picturing a small sleeping child curled up daintily under the mauve sheets. 'Find her.'

'Yeah,' Macsen said. 'That would be good. Word of the kidnap is already spreading through the city. People are getting upset, you can sense that. Everyone is going to be looking for her; it's a double sacrilege on this day. The gangs will have no sympathy on this. She'll be hidden deep, that's if she's even still alive.'

'She's alive,' Edeard said, taking a slow step towards the bed. 'They need her until midnight. That's how they control me.'

'Snatch Ivarl,' Dinlay said excitedly. 'Fight fire with fire, they'll never expect that. They'll have to exchange her for him.'

Macsen gave Dinlay an astonished look. 'Well I certainly never expected to hear that from your lips. I'm impressed; it has the advantage of complete surprise. Edeard?'

'No. Anyway, Ivarl had no part in this.'

'How do you know that?' Boyd asked.

'He just told me.' Edeard stroked the bed's canopy, still trying to imagine Mirnatha.

'He told you—' the rest of the squad were giving each other amazed glances.

'Yes. Do me a favour, guard the doors, stop anyone from coming in here. I need to be alone for a while.

'Okay,' Macsen said reasonably. 'Do you want to tell us why?'

'I want to remember,' Edeard said.

They were good. They didn't question him further. They had strong doubts, he could tell that, but they went out and stood beside the doors, and started talking among themselves.

Edeard pressed himself to the wall behind the bed, and slipped his farsight into the unyielding substance of which the mansion was fabricated. 'I need to know,' he told it. 'I need to see what you remember.'

Down at the very threshold of perception, attuned with the city's slumbering thoughts, images shimmered like the recollections of a dream. People moved inside the nursery. Himself and the squad. He followed the memory back. Julan was in the room, shouting in fury. Kristabel, crying as you would at a funeral. Further back, the frantic guards and nurses. Beyond that, the nurse coming in to find no sign of Mirnatha. And then there she was in the dead of night, a delightful little girl clutching her fluffy bear as she slept, untroubled by dreams.

Edeard slowed his quest through the stream of memory, and moved forward again. It was long after midnight when the figure materialized in the near-lightless nursery. A man wrapped in a dark coat, dissolving his concealment to stand above the bed. Edeard didn't know him, but the features were vaguely familiar; if pressed he would say the kidnapper was related to Tannarl – one of Ranalee's army of cousins, perhaps. And his cloak was expensive, as were the boots. This was no ordinary gang lieutenant. The man took a pad of cloth from his pocket, and splashed some liquid on it from a small brown bottle. The pad was pressed hard over Mirnatha's face. She struggled briefly. Edeard clenched his fists, wanting to pound the kidnapper, to make him suffer before he died.

A deeply unconscious Mirnatha was lifted from her bed. The fluffy bear was dropped to the floor. And the man's concealment enveloped both of them. A second later, the door opened and shut as if by its own accord.

'Oh Lady,' Edeard exclaimed in dismay. No matter how many times he immersed himself in the memory, the mansion couldn't see the kidnapper inside his concealment. He held the moment the kidnapper lifted the child from her bed, seeing it as plain as if he were standing right beside them.

There must be some other way the mansion can remember him. Though Edeard didn't have much confidence. He and the squad had experimented for weeks to see if concealment had a weakness, a way they could sense through it. They hadn't found one yet. Akeem's final gift appeared to be without a single flaw.

Now, studying the kidnapper, Edeard desperately tried to think what might betray the man's position. The beagle had caught his scent in the House of Blue Petals, but the city didn't smell. The air that moved as he walked back down the stairs? There was no memory of anything so slight.

He looked at Mirnatha's face as she was lifted up, so pale, her hair dangling limply. The kidnapper's face drawn slightly as he struggled to accept the child's weight.

'Weight!' Edeard shouted happily. And he was right. The floor remembered the weight; each and every footfall. Now, shifting through the vast pool of memories stored within the substance of the mansion he concentrated on the sensation of weight alone. In his mind he could visualize the corridor outside the nursery, its floor a simple white strip, blue dints along the edge where expensive antique tables and chairs rested. A leaden maroon imprint appeared outside Mirnatha's nursery door, another followed, the imprints pattered their way along the corridor and into the main stairwell. The kidnapper spiralled his way down—

The squad gave Edeard a curious look as he came out of the nursery. It wasn't right that he should be smiling.

'What in Honious's name have you been doing in there?' Dinlay asked. 'We've had our hands full keeping the family out. And Julan says the ransom is ready. The flag is flying over the Orchard Palace. A militia escort is saddling up to escort you clear of the city. You're going to need a couple of ge-horses to carry so much gold.'

Edeard glanced up at the corridor's crystal roof to see the sun was almost directly overhead. Outside, the usual longtalk babble was subdued; Makkathran's citizens were incensed by the kidnapping, their fear and hatred combined to a sullen resentment. This was not the happy Festival of Guidance they wanted.

He had no idea it had taken so long to filter through the mansion's memories. It didn't matter, nor did the ransom. 'I know where she is,' he announced.

'Where?' Dinlay demanded.

'No, how?' Macsen asked shrewdly.

Edeard gave him a level stare. 'The city remembered.'

'The city remembered?'

'Yes.'

Macsen gave Kanseen and Boyd a very dubious look. 'Uh huh.'

'She's underneath a fish smoking business on Layne Street in

Fiacre. The family use two levels of cellars under the building to smoke their fish, but there's another level beneath that. Four chambers. They've taken it over.'

'They?'

'Ten of them, maybe more. Even I can't farsight that accurately from here.'

Boyd clapped his hands delightedly. 'Brilliant. We've got her.'

'Not quite. You don't need over ten people to stop one six-year-old from escaping an underground prison. And they know we can work a concealment.'

'They'll kill her,' Dinlay said forlornly. 'There's too many to take them by surprise.'

'I think you're right,' Edeard said.

'So what do we do?' Kanseen asked.

Edeard smiled. 'Take them by surprise.' He longtalked Ronark back at the station, and asked for some weapons to be brought over.

'You're sure she's still alive?' Macsen asked.

Edeard smiled. 'Yeah. She's alive.'

'Finally, some good news. The city isn't happy, Edeard. Today was supposed to be a festival. Everyone knows now, and there's a lot of agitators out there blaming you.'

'Charming.'

'The Pythia is going to begin the service of Guidance with a plea to release Mirnatha,' Dinlay said. 'That's at midday, in ten minutes. Do you want to tell her before she begins?'

'Lady, no. We haven't got Mirnatha yet.'

Kanseen shook her head as she broke off trying to farsight. 'Lady, I can barely sense the smoking business from in here. I can't tell what's underneath.'

'They're there,' Edeard assured them.

'So what's the plan?' Dinlay asked. 'We could surround the building. Once everyone knows Mirnatha is in there, the gangs won't be able to do anything. They'll have to let her go.'

'Come on,' Edeard said. He led them down the corridor, retracing the kidnapper's footsteps. 'They're not going to let her go just because people don't like it. These men were chosen because they'll fight to the very end. They're the ones we've already broken, people like Eddis who have nothing to lose. This is not about the girl, it never was. It's about tomorrow's vote and how to get the outcome they need.'

Mistress Florrel stepped out of the lounge doorway just as they reached the main stairwell

'Where do you think you're going?' she snapped at Edeard. 'Running away, I suppose. Well, good riddance to you.'

'We're going to get her back, actually,' Dinlay said hotly.

Edeard winced.

'You're doing *what*?' she was trembling with outrage.

Edeard cleared his throat, and looked calmly at his most persistent foe. 'I might know where she is. I'm going to do my duty and bring her home. That's what we all want, isn't it?'

'You'll do no such thing. If you know where she is you'll inform the Mayor immediately. A regiment of the militia will bring back my poor dear Mirnatha. They know exactly how to deal with anyone who dares to attack one of my descendants.'

'With respect, Mistress Florrel, they don't. I will bring her back unharmed. You have my word.' Edeard turned to the top of the curving stairs.

'Come back here, young man,' Mistress Florrel said with quiet insistence.

Edeard couldn't believe it. Thanks to Dybal's recognition gift, his mind perceived her longtalk trying to insinuate itself into his consciousness, a soothing compulsion for him to come to her just as she had suggested. She was trying to dominate him.

He raised an eyebrow disdainfully as his mental shield closed. 'Naughty,' he said, and wagged a forefinger at her.

She blanched, her hand pressing theatrically against her throat.

A smiling Edeard led the way down the stairs.

'Bet we never make it out of the mansion,' Macsen said cheerfully as they reached the ninth floor.

'Outside?' Boyd said. 'That's ambitious. We'll never make it to the bottom of the stairs.'

'Do you know who took the girl?' Kanseen asked.

'No.' Edeard gifted them the vision of the kidnapper. 'Do any of you?'

'He's a Gilmorn,' Macsen said. 'Or sired by a Gilmorn at any rate. Look at that nose.'

'Maybe we should tell Julan we've found his daughter,' Dinlay said, with a hint of anxiety. 'I mean, surely he deserves to know? If we're going to put her at risk he must have the final say.'

'I'm not telling him what I can do,' Edeard said flatly. 'I don't know where his allegiance is.'

'Well, he's hardly going to be on their side,' Boyd said.

'Not today, no. But, let's face it, we don't even know who *they* really are, do we?'

The squad had reached the third floor when Grand Master Finitan longtalked Edeard. His telepathic voice was directed so skilfully it was as though the Master was standing beside him on the stairs whispering into his ear. 'Edeard, whatever have you done to my least favourite aunt?'

'What did she say I'd done?'

'Well arrogance and incompetence were the mildest complaints. I'm supposed to be longtalking you out of rescuing Mirnatha. Apparently she thinks I have "influence" over you.'

'Are you going to?'

'Certainly not. Do you know where the poor girl is?'

'I think so.'

'Edeard, I hate to be unpleasantly harsh on poor little Mirnatha, but you do understand what's at stake, don't you?'

'Tomorrow's vote.'

'There is another tactic I could use in Council. I've hesitated before now because it looked like we could win a straight challenge.'

'What tactic?'

'A plebiscite. There will be enough Masters to support that motion. Many of them are troubled. They see the progress you've made in Jeavons and Silvarum, and there is enormous pressure from the general population to continue your campaign. But Mirnatha's death would give them the option to vote down the warrants. If we were left in uncertainty for the Council meeting tomorrow then they would jump at the chance to defer the decision and be able to place blame elsewhere.'

Edeard paused on the stairs. 'You mean do nothing?'

'It's a long way to Owestorn. You might be able to ensure news took a equally long time to come back.'

'Sir, I cannot do that. More than anyone I want the gangs out of this city. But I cannot play politics with the life of a six-year-old innocent. I know where she is, and I know what has to be done to bring her back to her family. Right now that's all that matters.'

'Of course. You'll have my support no matter what. May the Lady be with you this day.'

'Thank you, sir.'

They were on the last flight of stairs when Julan's voice echoed down from above. 'Stop! Stop, I forbid this. You must not do anything rash. I have the ransom. Waterwalker! Come back. The flag flies above Orchard Palace as they asked.' His longtalk was added to the plea. 'You promised me. You said you would bring her back.'

Edeard looked up to see the broken Master leaning over the rail far above. 'I will bring her back to you, sir. Trust me.'

'No, no. There is to be no fighting. Pay the ransom. That is the only way she will come back unharmed.'

'I give you my word I will not endanger her. If it takes the ransom to release her, I will carry it to them for you.'

'Wait. You know where she is, don't you?'

'I'm not sure.'

'My aunt says you do. Wait, I will come with you.'

'Oh Lady,' Edeard groaned.

'We can be there before he even gets down here,' Boyd urged.

'No, we can't,' Macsen said through gritted teeth.

Edeard looked down. Homelt and a number of guards were

standing at the foot of the stairs. 'Does nobody want this girl to live?' he growled.

'We do, Edeard,' Kanseen assured him.

'Right then.' He took the last flight of stairs at a run.

'I have my orders,' Homelt said as the squad confronted him. His hand rested on his pistol holster.

'What are they?' Edeard asked reasonably.

'Not to let you leave the mansion. It's not just Master Julan. I could maybe ignore that on this day. But Lorin backed him up, and he does have his wits about him. I'll say naught about Mistress Florrel.' The guard captain glanced up, several people were on the eighth flight of stairs, making a commotion as they wound their way inexorably down.

'Fair enough,' Edeard said. 'Don't let us out.'

Homelt flashed him a hugely relieved look. 'You'll wait for the Master?'

'Not quite.' Edeard leaned forwards. 'She is alive. I know where she is.'

'I will come with you, Waterwalker,' Homelt said softly.

'No. This is not the help she needs. Already the news is spreading. We have to be quick. You know they'll kill her, and you know why.'

Homelt's anguish was visible for all to see. 'What do you want me to do?'

'Take us down to your deepest cellar. The one on the north-western corner of the mansion. And we'll need your pistols, too. Hurry man, or it'll be too late.'

Homelt glanced up the stairwell. Julan was on the seventh flight of stairs. 'Quickly then.'

The cellar door was ancient wood, long since blackened so that no grain showed. Nails holding the hinges against the city's original open arch were in need of re-inserting; the city's substance had rejected over half of their length. That looseness made the heavy door swing about unsteadily as Homelt drew the bolts back and opened it. Barrels and crates cluttered the small room, caked in decades of dust and fil-rat droppings.

'I don't understand,' the guard captain said, peering into the gloomy space. 'What's in here?'

'Us,' Edeard told him. 'Lock us in here. That way you will have obeyed your orders to the letter.'

'What about Mirnatha?'

'Trust me.'

For a moment Edeard thought he might refuse and march them all upstairs for Julan and Lorin to sort out. But after a moment of hesitation while his mind showed a huge amount of uncertainty, Homelt ushered them all into the cellar, gave them a pistol each, and shut the door.

'Far be it for my humble self to criticize,' Macsen said as the bolts were slammed back into place with some force. 'But I don't understand either.'

'If we are to rescue Mirnatha alive, it means we won't be able to take prisoners,' Edeard told them gravely. He brandished a pistol, examining its mechanism with his farsight. 'Are you still with me?'

'We're with you,' Kanseen said. 'But will you please tell us what in all of Honious is going on. I thought we'd got past this whole trust thing.'

Edeard grinned broadly. 'This'll test your trust as nothing else. Step where I do, one at a time. You will feel like you're falling, but I promise you're not. If you can't do this, I'll think no less of you.' He asked a circle of floor to let him though. It *changed*. Edeard stepped on it, and fell through the blackness into the Great Major Canal tunnel. Once he'd landed on the ledge above the water he moved to one side and waited.

It was Boyd who came through first, yelling in shock the whole way until his feet touched the ledge. 'Fuck the Lady!' he bellowed in fright-driven excitement.

Still grinning, Edeard grabbed his friend's shoulder and dragged him aside as Kanseen came through; little whimpering sounds burping out of her throat as her arms windmilled furiously. She looked round in astonishment. 'This is incredible. It's . . . I had no idea this existed.'

Edeard caught her arm and just managed to pull her out of the way of Dinlay's feet. Dinlay's eyes were screwed up shut behind his glasses.

'Waaaahoooo,' Macsen yelled wildly as he dropped through the roof of the tunnel.

Edeard faced his friends, still unable to wipe the grin off his face. He'd rarely sensed their minds so unguarded; but surprise had left them too jittery to veil their emotions as usual. 'So,' he drawled. 'You must have been keeping these tunnels from me, what with you city natives knowing everything there is to know about your own home.'

'You bastard,' Macsen said happily. 'What is this?'

'This is the tunnel under the Great Major Canal, every canal has one.'

'But how . . . ?' Dinlay was blinking up at the roof of the tunnel, his farsight probing the substance to try and find where they'd come through.

'I'm the Waterwalker,' Edeard told them. 'Remember?'

'Seriously,' Kanseen asked with a noticeable edge in her voice. 'How did we get here?'

'I'm not sure, exactly. I just ask the city, and it lets me through.'

'You. Just. Ask. The. City.'

'Yep,' he said, faintly apologetic.

'After today, you have a lot more explaining to do.'

Edeard sobered up. 'Then let's get today over with.'

Their mood followed his down to a more sombre level. He started to walk along the tunnel towards Forest Pool. 'The fish smoking business is only one street back from Pink Canal.'

'So you do have a plan then?' Macsen said.

'Yes. The way we come down reverses. The five of us will slide up into the cellars close to where Mirnatha is being held.'

'You said there's ten of them?'

'At least. I'm worried the kidnapper is there as well. He can conceal himself, so we'll never know for sure until we're there. The first thing they'll do at any sign of rescue is kill Mirnatha.

It won't matter how clever I've been finding her, or how good we are at sneaking up on them, if she's dead at the end of it all.'

'Why go up there at all?' Kanseen asked. 'Just ask the city to let her fall down here.'

'First off, she's shackled to the wall. We'd have to break the chains, and even I can't do that from down here. Secondly, there's no tunnel directly underneath her cellar, not even a drain. We're going to have to come up in the one next to hers.'

'Crap,' Boyd muttered.

'We go up concealed,' Edeard said. 'If I can get into the cellar where they're keeping her, my third hand should be able to protect her from bullets. It's going to be up to you to cover my back.'

They splashed across the shallow basin that emulated Forest Pool high above. Edeard could just farsight people gathering along the sides of the canals. Children with their flower boats, eager to launch them. Adults still seething over Mirnatha.

'How many in her cellar?' Kanseen asked.

'Two that I can sense.' He still wasn't sure about the kidnapper. The cellar had many old crates and lengths of wood as well as a couple of small benches. If anyone with a concealment was sitting on them he couldn't tell. Certainly the cellar floor had no current memory of anyone else standing on it. It would take a long time to filter through the day's memories.

'How are you going to get to her, then?'

'Brute force. As soon as we're all up there, I make a run for the door. I can smash through it and get in front of her, where I can protect her. Then I just hang on while you take the others out.'

'And if it goes wrong?'

'Then we're all dead, and Makkathran has to find someone else to campaign against the gangs.'

Kanseen gave him a disapproving grin. 'You're going to make a terrible Chief Constable. Grand Councillors are supposed to be smooth and subtle.'

'You can teach me. You'll have a hundred years, after all.'

'No,' she said. 'You move quicker than that.'

Edeard led them along Pink Canal tunnel, then off into the drain fissure until they were standing underneath the cellar closest to where Mirnatha was being held captive.

'I can sense her,' Kanseen said excitedly. 'The poor thing's terrified.'

'Everyone ready?' Edeard asked.

When they assured him they were, he said: 'I think I can do this so we all go up together. Remember, keep yourself concealed until they know I'm there, then take them out. And for the Lady's sake don't call out. You're not actually falling, it only feels like it.'

'Wait,' Boyd said. 'It feels like we're falling when we're going *up*?'

'Yes. And no; I don't know why.'

Macsen clicked the safety catch off his pistol. 'Let's just go. See you all up there.'

'All right,' Edeard said. He concealed himself, and waited until the others had vanished from his sight, then told the city to take them up.

The cellar he slid up into was barely high enough for him to stand upright. It was a simple oblong box of a room, with dark walls inset with narrow alcoves, and a shallow vaulted ceiling of lierne ribs. Ancient fishing nets and tishcrab cages were piled up along one wall. One doorway opened on to a spiral stair up to the smoking caverns above. The kidnappers were sitting at two wooden tables in front of it, slowly consuming a quantity of food. There was no beer or wine, just water, Edeard saw. Whoever had organized this had chosen well. These men had a ruthless discipline; they'd use the pistols resting on the table without a qualm. Just standing among them made him worry for the squad.

One of them started to look round the room, frowning. 'Did you hear something?'

Edeard made for the half-open door. He wiggled his way

round through the gap, not daring to breathe. Behind him, the kidnappers were picking their pistols off the table. Powerful longtalk voices were directing questions at the guards upstairs.

Edeard looked along the low corridor. The smell of fish and oak-smoke was heavy in the air. Directly opposite him was a door to the cellar where Mirnatha was being held. It was made from tyewood planks three inches thick, with iron hinges that had recently been re-set in the walls. There were heavy bolts on either side, and both sets were drawn shut. He braced himself against the wall, summoned up the full strength of his third hand, then leapt forwards.

His concealment dropped as he was halfway across the corridor. The door burst apart as he smashed it with his third hand, putting up no more resistance than if it had been made of glass.

A shout in the cellar behind: 'Hey!' as their farsight caught him. Then he was through the smashed door, and folding his third hand protectively round the dazed little girl.

Three pistol shots boomed out behind him, appallingly loud in the confines of the underground chambers. His farsight caught Kanseen flicker into view behind one of the kidnappers sitting at the table. He was rising to his feet. Kanseen's pistol was aimed at the back of his skull. She pulled the trigger, and his face exploded outwards in a spray of gore. Kanseen vanished again. Dinlay was firing into the side of another kidnapper; his mind ablaze with rage and fear. He vanished. Macsen appeared on the other side of the cellar.

Edeard's pistol was swinging round to line up on one of the two men guarding Mirnatha as he charged across the cellar. It was hardly a perfect aim, but he fired anyway, getting off four shots. More pistol shots echoed round him. Shouts and longtalk howls behind him created a bedlam of white-noise. The guard he'd shot at grunted in shock, and stared down at his tunic to see a huge stain of blood spreading across his chest. Two bullets punched Edeard, knocking him to one side. One bullet hit his third hand directly above Mirnatha's head. Then he was squashed up against her, closing his arms round her shaking shoulders as she screamed a soprano wail that never ended. More pistol shots. One slammed into his neck – fired by the uninjured guard. Edeard reached out with his third hand, his strength shoving through the man's own shield. He ripped at the man's brain. The skull cracked, blood pulsed out of his ears as he crumpled to the ground.

Another bullet smacked into Edeard. He shifted his farsight focus to see the injured guard slumped against a wall; holding his pistol up, arm wavering about. He was drawing breath in feeble gulps as his blood spilled onto the floor. Edeard's third hand wrenched the gun from his numb fingers. Rotated it a hundred and eighty degrees. Pulled the trigger.

Three more shots from outside, and the shouting cut off.

'Edeard?' Macsen shouted.

'All right! In here.'

'Are you okay?'

'Wait,' he ordered, tightening his physical hold around the girl, keeping his shield as hard as rock. Mirnatha had fainted. He instinctively knew something was wrong. After the first guard had gone down, the second one had fired. Two shots had struck him, and a third was aimed at Mirnatha. They couldn't possibly have come from just one pistol.

The squad were tumbling out of the cellar opposite.

'Wait,' he called again. 'Don't come in.'

'What's happening?' Boyd demanded.

Edeard knew he should have been delighted that all his friends were alive. Instead he scanned round and round the room, looking for the slightest telltale sign. The cellar floor revealed nothing. There were no human feet standing on it. Edeard used his third hand to shatter the bench the guards had been using. Nothing. He crunched the second bench and all the chairs. 'Lady!'

He lifted up a length of splintered wood, and sent it scything round the room. Kanseen and Dinlay were crouched halfway down the corridor, pistols held ready, their faces registering bewilderment as their farsight followed his actions. Edeard swung the wood through three orbits of the cellar without connecting to anything. He scraped it along the wall at waist-height, jabbing it viciously into every alcove as he performed a complete circuit. Again, nothing.

'You're good,' he acknowledged, and reached out with his farsight to feel what the cellar floor and walls were feeling, hunting for that elusive pressure of human feet. His perception swept back and forth. Then, finally, the kidnapper was revealed.

'Very clever,' Edeard said, and meant it. He turned round, still keeping Mirnatha centred within his protective telekinesis. He aimed his pistol up at the ceiling to one side of the door, and fired the remaining two shots in quick succession.

The kidnapper's concealment fizzled out as the bullets struck, revealing him clinging to the small lierne ribs like some human spider. He fell inertly to the floor, landing with a dull crack. It was the same man who'd snatched Mirnatha from her room.

Edeard walked over to him and stared down. 'She is six years old, and you used her,' he exclaimed in disgust.

The man's mouth opened. Blood spilled out. He somehow managed a small sneer. 'Rot in Honious,' a weak longtalk sputtered. Then his thoughts were dimming. Edeard kept his farsight on those final flutters of emotion, searching for the slightest hint of regret. Some explanation of why a person could be so cold.

More blood bubbled out of the kidnapper's mouth as he exhaled for the last time. Yet Edeard could still sense his thoughts, enfeebled wisps of their original strength and pattern. The body had died, but they persisted. Then they moved.

Edeard gulped in shock, and took a step back as the kidnapper's soul diffused gracefully out of his body. The spectral entity hovered over the corpse for a few moments, then ascended into the ceiling and was lost to Edeard's farsight.

'Did you sense that?' he asked the squad in astonishment.

'Edeard?' Kanseen asked. 'Is it safe?'

'Uh, yeah. That was his soul, wasn't it?'

'His soul?' She edged cautiously across the remnants of the door. Any curiosity was instantly forgotten as she saw Mirnatha.

'Whose soul?' Macsen asked brashly as he followed Kanseen in.

Edeard couldn't take his eyes off the ceiling where the soul had vanished. 'The kidnapper's.'

'Did you get shot?' Macsen asked in concern.

'No.'

A moan from Mirnatha succeeded in drawing Edeard's attention back down. 'Don't let her see this,' he blurted. There was blood and gore all over the cellar. And the bodies. A scene that was even worse in the cellar at the bottom of the stairs. 'Are all of you okay?'

'Oh, *now* you ask,' Boyd joshed.

'I think I'm going to be sick,' Dinlay said. His constable tunic was covered in blood.

Edeard's third hand snapped the iron shackles round Mirnatha's wrists. Kanseen blinked at the nonchalant show of strength. 'You carry her,' she said, stroking the girl's brow, gentle with concern. Her hand and sleeve was speckled with arterial blood.

'But—'

'This is your victory,' Kanseen insisted.

Edeard nodded. 'Thank you. All of you.'

Boyd's solemn face broke into a wild smile. 'By the Lady: we *got her*! We bloody did it.'

They were all laughing in shaky relief as Edeard scooped up the small child, and carried her out of the cellar. People were crowding round the top of the stairs as he made his way out of the smoking chambers. Workers and family members with worried faces and probing farsight. That worry changed to consternation as the Waterwalker himself emerged into their midst. They backed off fast.

'No good trying to hide,' Boyd said as they made their way out through the shop at the front of the building. 'The local constables will be calling.' He paused. 'That's if the Culverit family guards don't pay you a visit first.'

Edeard stepped out into the midday sun, blinking at how bright it was. It seemed as if he hadn't been outside in the light for a week, yet it was less than an hour since Homelt had taken them to the mansion's cellar. He got his bearings swiftly enough, and started walking down Layne Street.

Mirnatha stirred as they turned into Arnold Avenue, heading for Pink Canal. She started suddenly, looking round frantically.

'It's all right,' Edeard told her. 'We're taking you home to your family. Your father and sister are worried about you.'

She gave him a wide-eyed stare. 'You're the Waterwalker.'

'Yes. I am.'

'They took—' she cried. 'I was in a dark room. I couldn't farsee anything. They were horrible— I— I—'

'It's over. Look. It's a bright sunny day. We should be back at your home in time for you to see the flower boats.'

She clung to him. 'What happened to the bad men?'

'You won't see them again, I promise.'

There were a lot of people lined up along the side of the canal, standing at least six deep as they waited for the end of the ceremony in the Lady's grand church. It was mostly excited children at the front, clutching their flower boats; with parents standing behind, pleading and warning not to put their craft into the water until the Pythia was finished. Edeard actually smiled as he finally saw the multitude of flower boats being held ready. They were spectacularly beautiful; from endearing little paper craft with a couple of daisies clutched by toddlers, to elaborate vessels with a rainbow of blooms crafted by proud older children. Their happy faces were wonderfully uplifting.

He started to make his way through the crowd. Heads swivelled in his direction. Surprise turned to shock when they saw the squad; uniforms covered in blood, tired yet cheerful, with the Waterwalker himself carrying the kidnapped girl who smiled up at him with shy adulation. Silence fell. The crowd parted, giving him a clear path to the mooring platform at the end of the avenue.

Someone started clapping. Whispers of amazement turned to exultant longtalk and shouts of approval. More people were joining the applause.

'It's the Waterwalker.'

'They've rescued the girl!'

'Mirnatha is alive.'

'Dear Lady, look at the blood.'

'It's his whole squad.'

'They did it, they saved her.'

Three gondolas were secured to the platform, each of them garlanded with hundreds of snow-white flowers. Edeard stepped on to the first boat as the gondolier took his hat off and held it to his chest, staring at Mirnatha. 'Get us to her mansion,' Edeard told him.

'But the festival . . .'

'The Pythia's ceremony isn't over yet. And I think Mirnatha deserves to go home, don't you?'

'Yes, sir. Of course.' He picked up his punt.

By now everyone was packed right up to the edge of the canal. The applause and cheering put Edeard right back to that day in Birmingham Pool. 'Let's see how quick you are,' he told the gondolier as they pushed off.

It wasn't far. They went down to Forest Pool, then up the Grand Major Canal to the Culverit mansion's private mooring platform at the edge of High Pool. Mirnatha sat up on the prow, looking from side to side in utter bliss as waves of applause and cheering followed her progress home.

'Do you think they'll even bother with the vote tomorrow?' Macsen said quietly as he waved at the enthusiastic onlookers crammed along the canal. Flower boats were being held aloft and waved in heartfelt greeting for the little girl. The whole canal rippled with dramatic colours.

'Not a lot of point,' Boyd replied.

'Can you boys just enjoy the moment,' Kanseen said. 'I mean, come on, we're getting some adulation this time, too.'

'I'm going to be sick,' Dinlay said, dabbing at the congealing blood on his uniform.

'Don't you dare,' she told him crossly.

Mirnatha gripped Edeard's arm. Her other hand pointed ahead to the mansion's mooring platform. 'I see Daddy,' she squealed. 'And Krissy. They're both there.' She started to wave frantically, longtalking for all she was worth.

'And Mistress Florrel isn't,' Boyd muttered contentedly.

The gondolier steered them smoothly into the side of the platform. Julan snatched his daughter out of the craft, hugging her and weeping uncontrollably. Kristabel joined in. Mirnatha began to chatter at an incredible speed, telling them what had befallen her. One last final *hurrah* broke out among the crowds, running the whole length of Grand Major Canal.

Edeard and the squad stepped on to the platform. Homelt stood in front of him, and bowed his head. 'Thank you,' he said. 'Though the Lady knows how you pulled off that stunt. There is *no way* out of that cellar.'

Edeard gave him a knowing grin. Then Julan grabbed him roughly by both shoulders and pulled him close. 'I thank you, Waterwalker, I thank you from the very bottom of my heart! My baby, my baby is saved.'

'I'm sorry we didn't take you with us, sir,' Edeard said. 'But my squad is a good team, we work best by ourselves.'

Julan couldn't stop crying. He clutched Mirnatha tighter. 'I understand. Thank you all. You were right. I was wrong. Please, I was crazed with worry . . .'

'Nobody was wrong, sir. Mirnatha is back home. That's all that matters.'

'Yes, yes.' He lifted his daughter up again. She giggled and kissed him. 'Whatever you desire in this world, it is yours, and still it will never be enough to express my gratitude to you all. Say it, and I will see it is done.'

Macsen put on a wholly reasonable expression and opened his mouth. Kanseen's third hand poked him in the ribs. He looked pained, but didn't say anything.

'We really are just doing our duty, sir,' Edeard claimed.

'What nonsense. I will start my payment by welcoming you to our family's celebration feast tonight.'

'That's very kind of you, sir,' Boyd said hurriedly, before Edeard could say no. 'We'd be honoured.'

'Thank you, Waterwalker,' Mirnatha giggled. She leaned forward in her father's embrace and gave Edeard a messy kiss.

'Yes,' Kristabel said, appearing directly in front of Edeard as her father made his way up the steps at the back of the platform. 'Thank you indeed.'

He didn't quite know what to say, so settled for a modest shrug. She was still in her flimsy white cotton nightdress, though a grey-green woollen shawl was wrapped round her shoulders. Her hair wasn't quite so wild now. The squad edged closer.

'You kept your word,' she said.

'Er, yes. Actually, it was a pretty stupid thing to—'

Her finger touched his lips. 'No. It was the greatest thing you could possibly do. No wonder the gangs and Masters are so frightened of you. I have faith in you, Waterwalker.'

'Mistress.' He made a real hash of a formal bow, producing something more like a nervous twitch. Kristabel all serene like this was quite impressive. Imposing, actually.

'Ah yes, Mistress,' she said teasingly. 'Well, as future Mistress of Haxpen, I shall require the first dance with you at our family party tonight. And the last. And, I think, every one between.'

'Oh.' Edeard paled. He was a rotten dancer. 'My pleasure.'

Kristabel's smile widened to include all the squad. 'Please, today my house is yours. And every day to come. The view from the upper hortus is the best in the city from which to watch the flower boats on their way to the sea. And you must bathe and freshen up. I'll see that the staff find some clothes that fit, ready for the party.'

Edeard watched her start up the wooden stairs to the fabulous ziggurat mansion towering above them. The hem of her night-dress flapped around her knees. *I must not look at her legs. I must not.*

Kanseen's head slipped sinuously over his left shoulder. 'You do know, don't you,' she said quietly, 'that you can't actually sleep with every girl in this city?'

Edeard looked at Kristabel's legs. Slim, yes; but rather shapely, too. 'I know,' he said wistfully.

Kanseen kissed his ear playfully. 'But you could do a lot worse than Kristabel.'

3

The night was as black as only Hanko's thick curtains of storm-cloud could make it. Wind howled around the ice boulders, creating strange antagonistic harmonics. While overhead occasional forks of lightning turned the tragic landscape into a monochrome silhouette.

Right at the edge of the Asiatic glacier a flare of tangerine light burst into existence, creating an eerie aural blaze around the top of the titanic cliff. It vanished in an instant. The ice trembled in reaction. After a while, the spray of tangerine light gushed up again. Brighter this time. Larger ice fragments jumped and juddered at the vibrations hammering through the surface.

A pause filled by the eternal yowl of the blizzard.

The light appeared once more. This time splinters of ice erupted from the top of the cliff, swirling away into the mile-high abyss. A hand wearing a thick grey gauntlet crept up and patted the surface, scrabbling for a firm purchase.

Aaron heaved himself up, and rolled on to the top of the glacier. After a moment he clambered to his feet. He swept the surrounding area with his biononic field scan function, seeking traces of the ground crawler. The trail it had taken was plain enough, retracing its original route through the boulder field.

He started to run after it.

He was very VERY angry.

*

The Clippsby cafe on Daryad Avenue served exactly the kind of breakfast Oscar loved. Industrial strength coffee, bacon baguettes, and almond croissants with a dip pot of agal syrup. Despite the three of them wearing the Ellezelin police uniform the owner served them readily enough. The only other customers were also Ellezelin troopers grabbing a late breakfast between alerts. This morning should have been so different. Everyone in the city had stayed up, accessing Justine's heroic dash for the Void. Unisphere and gaiafield alike were enraptured by the appearance of the Second Dreamer, rumour and speculation were currently the foremost indulgence of billions. Yet here in Colwyn the atmosphere of wonder had been ripped to pieces by the welcome team's raid. There had been a lot of people in the park outside the apartment block. They'd reacted predictably enough to such a brash act, taunting the paramilitary troops on the cordon. It was touch and go if a full riot would erupt. As a result, the city seemed even more paralysed than yesterday. Very few citizens were going in to work. They were either too fearful of getting caught up in disturbances, or they were heading out to join the crowd in Bodant and other hot spots where they might get lucky and give some hapless foreign trooper a good kicking. Either way, not much was open in the centre of town.

Oscar accepted another refill from the waitress, smiling in gratitude. The cafe owner might have cajoled her to serve him, but she certainly didn't have to smile back as she was pouring. 'So what now?' he asked Tomansio as the woman stomped off and the privacy shield shimmered on around their table.

'Information is the key, as always,' Tomansio replied, trying not to frown at the food piled up in front of Oscar. For himself he'd ordered a smoked gruslet and cream cheese sandwich to go with his green tea. 'We know without any doubt that the Second Dreamer was in that apartment block. Which means either the welcome team have him, and major Honilar will find that out for sure in the next six hours, or he escaped before we got there.'

'We were there fast,' Beckia said. 'I don't think I could have got out, not without a lot of fuss.'

'This man is smart,' Tomansio said. 'Using Danal's apartment was a superb misdirection.'

'But how could he have got out?' Oscar asked. 'They would have seen any capsule lifting from the apartments.'

'Stealth?' Beckia suggested. She wrinkled her nose in dissatis-faction. 'But if he's got a stealth capsule why would he actually commune with the gaiafield from Danal's apartment? That doesn't make any sense.'

'The only practical escape route would be some kind of tunnel not on the city plans,' Tomansio said. 'And the apartments are being refurbished by a whole load of different developers. That would give him plenty of scope for such an activity.'

'That presupposes he knew he'd need an escape tunnel,' Oscar said. 'How would he know Ethan was going to annex the whole planet and flood the city with paramilitaries?'

'Connections in Living Dream,' Beckia said with a baffled tone. She shook her head. 'That doesn't make any sense either. If you have those kind of connections, why go on the lam like this?'

'You don't suppose this is Inigo, do you?' Oscar suggested.

Tomansio pulled a breath through clenched teeth. 'I'd hate to rule it out, but this simply isn't Inigo's way of doing things. He doesn't need to sneak around. For a start, his word alone is the only thing which could stop Ethan's insane Pilgrimage.'

'Not so insane,' Beckia muttered. 'And not so easily stopped. Not any more. The whole of the Greater Commonwealth just watched Justine's ship go through the barrier. The Second Dreamer *can* get the Pilgrimage inside. That's a phenomenal boost to Living Dream's credibility.'

'It also secures Ethan's leadership,' Tomansio said. 'Even if Inigo did turn up now, he might not have the authority to pull it off.'

'Wouldn't be the first time a religion outgrows its messiah,' Oscar said.

'No, indeed. So . . . we're left with the same problem everyone else has: finding this extremely slippery Second Dreamer.'

'I don't believe in secret tunnels,' Oscar said. He drank some of his coffee, enjoying the bitter liquid burning its way down his throat. It had been a long time since he'd got some sleep. 'There's something about this which isn't right.'

'Care to elaborate?'

'I can't, unfortunately. I'm just not convinced that the Second Dreamer is some kind of supersmart covert operative. Living Dream had to out him in the first place, now he's communing with a Skylord, which is something Inigo never managed. That doesn't come over as someone who's thought out the consequences of their actions.'

'He managed to elude us,' Tomansio said reasonably. 'That takes a lot of talent and thought.'

'Does it? No offence, but we were rushed, as was the welcome team.'

'The welcome team has spent months training for this.'

Oscar gave the bottom of his coffee mug a miserable glance. 'I don't know. I just don't get what his long plan is. Everything he's done says to me that he's reacting to events, not controlling them. What we have is a normal bloke caught up in monstrous events and doing his best to keep afloat.'

'He could be getting help from some Faction,' Beckia said.

'From what my source tells me, he hasn't,' Oscar said. 'But we can't rule it out.'

'Okay, enough,' Tomansio said. 'It's pointless to argue this. Once we find him, we can ask him. In the meantime, we have ourselves the mother of all shadow operations here.' He opened a secure link to Liatris. 'Have you located Araminta for me yet?'

'No. Sorry, boss. She's disconnected her u-shadow from the unisphere. Hardly surprising after the apartment raid. I've got monitor programs loaded into every node in the city ready for when she comes back on line. Interestingly, so do a number of other people. And I'm also watching her credit account, but until she comes back out of the Stone Age she's invisible to me.'

'All right, what about her history? Anything there to clue us in? Boyfriend? Girlfriend? Someone she'll turn to?'

'She's an interesting girl. Recently divorced.'

'Husband's location?'

'On Oaktier, and migrating inwards.'

'Ozzie! Okay, give me something in the city, even if it's just which salon she uses.'

'She doesn't have a regular salon.'

'Liatris!'

'Don't panic, I've got some nuggets for you. And trust me, this took some serious reference matching on her data patterns.'

'Go.'

'Her cousin, who handled the divorce, is Cressida, a very senior partner in the best law firm in town – extremely well connected locally. And, incidentally, she and a whole group of friends are just about to mug Ethan. Get this, they've hired a passenger ship from Dunbavand lines, one with full diplomatic status to evacuate themselves.'

'Really?' Tomansio's mind popped a burst of mischievous delight into the gaiafield.

'Relevant?' Oscar asked.

'The Dunbavand family is a major Far Away political force. God help Living Dream if they try and interfere with their ship's flight schedule. Forget diplomats squabbling in the Senate; the original Dunbavand patriarch was a Starflyer War hero, which gives his descendants a certain kind of very stubborn mindset. They really would consider dispatching a warship into Viotia orbit to enforce their right of passage. Smart lady, this Cressida.'

'One of the tickets she booked is for Araminta,' Liatris told them. 'She's also trying to find an offworld investment consortium to buy Araminta's apartment development project.'

'Then we watch Cressida.'

'Already set up. I've got more scrutineers and monitors surrounding her than Living Dream have followers.'

'Excellent. Until Araminta makes contact with Cressida we concentrate on our original objective, riding the welcome team's data wave. Anything from Cheriton?'

'No. He's gone down to the docks with Mareble to try and get Danal out of Major Honilar's clutches. Once he's done that we'll have us a very strong ally among the confluence nest technicians.'

It might have been the lack of sleep this morning, or the really very strong coffee numbing his synapses, but Oscar was slow mulling over their discussion. *Why is she hiding? The welcome team raid was scary, sure, but that wouldn't make her do this, unless she was in the apartment block. And if she was there . . .*

'Araminta also spent a weekend with Likan,' Liatris said.

'No shit?' Tomansio said.

'I'm not sure it's significant. Likan normally works his way through two or three women a week in addition to his harem, and Araminta seems to have been playing the field since her divorce.'

'I used to work for Nigel Sheldon,' Oscar said. 'I even met him a couple of times when Wilson and I were building up the Navy. He'd be horrified about this modern ideology that's hijacked his name.'

'And the relevance is?' an exasperated Tomansio asked.

Oscar gave him an apologetic shrug. 'Sorry. Just thinking.'

'Is she seeing anyone special?' Tomansio asked Liatris.

'Not that I've found yet. I'm running traffic analysis on her capsule, but it's got to be slow and discreet, there are another three similar investigations that I spotted, and that's in addition to Living Dream, which is now officially interested in her. But the local police have found her trike. It was parked at the Tala mall yesterday afternoon. Her last confirmed sighting. Major Honilar has ordered the records from every city sensor to be shoved through visual recognition filters to work out where she went. That should keep them busy for the rest of the day.'

'Thanks, Liatris.'

'She has to be able to tell us something,' Beckia said. 'She had to be badly frightened to vanish like this. I guess that's what Major Honilar does to people.'

'Agreed.'

Oscar grinned at the two of them. Beckia had said it without even realizing, but then it would take someone with his background to make that particular connection. If anyone in the Commonwealth knew all about vanishing, and staying vanished, it was Oscar Monroe. Which just left motivation . . .

Tomansio caught the grin and frowned. 'What?'

'Don't you get it?' Oscar was delighted with himself. *Well, how about that, the old relic has still got it.*

'Get what?' Beckia asked.

'I spent decades living a lie, hiding my actual self from everyone I knew and loved and worked with. It's actually a lot easier than you'd think. So I guess it takes one to know one.'

Tomansio's square jaw dropped. 'Oh, great Ozzie . . . you think?'

'I think it's highly likely.'

Beckia hunched forwards, giving Oscar an astonished look. '*She's* the Second Dreamer?'

'Give me a better candidate.'

'Bloody hell.'

'It won't take Honilar long to work it out.'

'And when he does, she'll be in deep shit,' Tomansio said urgently. 'No local girl will able to stay ahead of the welcome team.'

'She's done pretty well so far,' Oscar protested.

'You can only get so far on luck, and she's used up her quota. We need to supply some help. Liatris, start laying a false data trail for the good major.'

'Give me ten minutes, I'll have him running all over town.'

'She was there, wasn't she?' Beckia said with growing admiration. 'Somehow. In the apartment when we were looking.'

'Unless she spent last month digging a tunnel, yes,' Oscar said.

Tomansio gave him a certain look. 'It's still cordoned off.'

'Let's go.'

Their borrowed capsule was parked on the pad outside. Oscar

raced past the waitress, feeling only mildly guilty for not leaving a tip.

It took Araminta two cups of tea and half the packet of biscuits to work up enough nerve to shove the crate to one side and open the door a fraction. There was no one in the vestibule. No sound from anywhere inside the building as far as she could tell. Outside, it was different. The angry shouting was loud. There were thuds as lumps of stone and concrete landed around the paramilitary troops; glass was being smashed constantly. The distinct humming of capsules ebbed and flowed. She strapped on her tool belt, shrugged into a thick fleece jacket to cover it, and headed for the stairwell.

The cordon included a shield reinforcing the broad garage door, which buzzed as if a high voltage current was running through it. In the dim lighting which pervaded the ramp, Araminta could just see a dull sparkle shimmering off the door's surface. There was no way she could get out, it would take a good quantity of enhanced explosives to break through. She turned and headed to the other side of the garage which contained the utilities support area. It was dark inside the first room. Still reluctant to use any power, she fished a torch out of her belt, and walked between two rows of big tanks. At the far end was a smaller door into the waste handling room. She'd only been in here a couple of times before, to make sure the interface with her new units was compatible.

Bulky, quite primitive-looking, machinery filled most of the space; big metal spheres with lots of piping snaking about between them. Araminta wiggled between a couple of water sanitizer cisterns. Behind them, the side wall was a sheer surface of reinforced enzyme-bonded concrete. Just above her head was a rectangular hole where six feed pipes went outside to connect with the main civic water supply. The gap between the top of the pipes and the edge of the concrete was about half a metre. She clambered up one of the sanitizer cisterns, wincing every time she gripped a hot pipe by mistake. That put her level with the hole. A metal grid covered the far end. Grass and soil was pressed up against it.

Gritting her teeth in determination, she dropped her thick fleece and wormed her head and shoulders into the hole. She still had to stretch to apply the power socket against the grille's locking bolts. They were stiff from disuse, and she was scared of making too much noise with the power socket; but after several minutes cursing and blinking sweat from her eyes, the grille came loose. Then it took another five minutes pushing and shoving before the grass and soil gave way. The tool belt had to be discarded before she could claw her way through the uncomfortably claustrophobic gap.

Araminta crawled out onto the narrow strip of grass between the apartment wall and the wooden fence. Blouse torn on snags, skin scratched and bleeding, trouser knees muddy, hair a tangled mess, hot, flushed, and sweaty. She glared back at the little hole. *I can't have put on that much weight!*

The noise of the crowd was a lot louder. Amplified voices were constantly warning them to back off. A capsule slid over the band of sky above her. She quickly pulled her tool belt out of the hole, and started using the screwdriver on the fence boards. With three of them unfastened she could slip through the triangular opening and into an almost identical strip of ground on the other side. The neighbouring building was a combination of retail and office units; half of which were unoccupied and available for a low rent. She crept along the side of the building to the waste casket bay at the back. The gates beyond opened on to a thin alley of badly cracked concrete. Someone had left an old jacket on the ledge running along the bay. She pulled it on over her torn blouse, and slung the tool belt over her shoulder. Then taking a breath she sauntered out into the alley.

Two of Ellezelin's armour-suited paramilitaries were standing on cordon duty outside the back gate to the apartment block. Araminta ignored them, and walked off down the alley. Every second she expected a challenge, but it never came. After twenty metres she made a sharp left turn down another alley, taking her out of their view. Then she just kept walking.

*

After forever he strode through a white jungle. Trees of translucent crystal towered above him, refracting a soft shimmer of pure sunlight, sprouting long white leaves. The undergrowth was thick, creepers and bushes mangled into dense tangles of silver hues that were impossible to push through. White clouds scudded overhead. A cloying mist wove long swirling streamers round the shiny tree trunks, reducing visibility. White birds darted about, triangles of feathers fluttering fast. White rodents scampered round his booted feet. His boots were clotted with white mud from the steaming loam.

'I know it's difficult,' said the voice behind the trees. 'But you have to choose.'

He longed for colour. Darkness, even. But all the jungle offered was faint shadows. Shapes were starting to blur together. Losing cohesion. The blazing universe was absorbing him. When he lifted up his hands they were hard to see. White on white. Just looking at them was dizzying.

'You can lose yourself. Lose what is. Lose what you have done. Your life will never have existed. Sometimes I wish I could offer that to myself.'

Then the enemy started to close in. He saw them all around, little flickers of motion darting through the undergrowth. They were waiting for him. He knew it. It was an ambush.

He yelled defiance at them. His biononics unleashed a terrible burst of energy. Clumps of undergrowth disintegrated into kinetic maelstroms. He was thrown from side to side by the sharp leaf and stone fragments swatting against him. Vision reduced, but still it was all white: in front, on both sides, above, below. White. White. White.

Through it all crept the enemy – malicious, determined, lethal. He blasted away at them. Seeing them burn. Powerful white flame consumed them, sending torrents of white smoke into the sky.

Shot after shot was fired into the suffocating uniform whiteness. It began to constrict about him. No matter how violent his energy discharges they couldn't penetrate it.

'Help me,' he cried out to the voice. 'Take me out of this. I choose. I choose! I remember I chose. I wanted not to happen.'

He could no longer tell which way was up, and tumbled through the whiteness. His own screams were loud in his ears as the whiteness slipped and banged against his suit visor. Then he hit something which stopped his headlong rush with a suddenness that knocked the wind from him. There at last was another colour, red sparkles of pain danced across his vision as he drew a desperate breath. He closed his eyes, squeezing the lids shut then blinking them open.

Shards of grey-black rock lay sizzling against the ice, slowly sinking in through the puddles they were creating.

'Shit,' Aaron groaned gloomily. He forced himself on to all fours, then slowly staggered upright.

The whiteout had got to him, providing an insidious outlet for the demons churning around his subconscious.

What the hell is inside me? What did I try and cast away?

He shook his head, running a full status check through his biononic systems, and reviewed the routines in his macrocellular clusters as well. Cooler air blew into his helmet, allowing him to take some sobering breaths. Looking around he saw he'd left the field of ice boulders behind. The wind had dropped, leaving just a few flurries of snow skipping through the air. Steam was pushing up out of a dozen craters where his energy shots had vaporized the ice. He could see the serrated crystalline boulders lining the horizon behind him. Exovision superimposed his route, sketching it with simple lines of glowing orange. The ground crawler had been easy to follow through the field, scraping past boulders to leave crumbled shards on the ground, or where Inigo had simply carved his way through the smaller gaps. Now they were out on the open top of the glacier it was hard to tell.

Aaron trotted away from the area he'd devastated, circling round. There was no indication of the ground crawler at all. The thin dusting of ice shifted continually, completely eradicating any sign of the tracks. As he stood and watched, his own footprints were smeared away behind him almost as soon as he made them. There was no residual heat signature. It had been at least six hours since Inigo and Corrie-Lyn had driven out of the boulder field. On this frozen world, their infrared traces would have vanished within twenty minutes.

He had absolutely no way of telling which way they'd gone.

'Fuck it.' There were no options left. His inertial guidance mapped a route back to Jajaani, via the Olhava camp, the only route he was sure didn't have glacier cliffs or other obstacles. Not that he'd ever get there before the planet imploded, he reflected; but if any rescue attempt was going to happen, that would be where the starship landed. It was all he had left. Simply lying down and waiting for the end wasn't him. *Whoever me is.*

He started to run again. His biononic energy currents reconfigured to scream a distress signal into the eternal storm.

*

The local star's azure spectrum shone brightly on the hull of *Mellanie's Redemption* as it dropped out of hyperspace five hundred kilometres above Orakum. Troblum accessed the external sensors, seeing a planet that was essentially the same as every human-settled world in the Greater Commonwealth. Blue oceans swathed in puffy white cloud, brown land masses with a fuzz of green. Its electromagnetic emissions were a lot lower than a Central world, reflecting the relatively small population of Advancers and naturals. The kind of world that provided an ideal quiet life. Knowing what he did about Oscar Monroe, Troblum wasn't at all surprised that the old War hero had chosen this place to settle.

He ordered the starship's smartcore to enter the atmosphere in full stealth mode. His muscles ached from the crouch position he'd been compressed into for the last ten hours. Even now that he'd finally made some headway into cataloguing and arranging the components into distinct piles, the starboard midsection hold was still badly cramped. He was beginning to worry about the assembly process, which was going to require a decent volume to work in. Not that he was anywhere close to starting that yet.

When *Mellanie's Redemption* passed through the ionosphere he went back into the cabin and took a quick spore shower. There were still sore patches on his skin where the medical module had repaired the damage he'd received at Florac's villa.

'You should put some cream on those,' Catriona told him. The beautiful girl's curly hair bobbed about as she tilted her head to one side, registering deep concern.

'It doesn't matter,' he grunted back.

'It matters to us,' Trisha cooed.

Troblum pulled his shabby purple toga suit on, somehow strangely concerned about his dignity in front of the two girls. Having them see him naked was oddly disquieting. Back at the Arevalo apartment they never did, the daily routines were all perfectly established. He was comfortable with those. But here in the starship's cabin there was little privacy, and the projectors could throw the images just about everywhere. 'Thank you,' he said, hoping it would shut them up – he didn't want to load in program restrictions, not now he'd constructed their personalities so perfectly. 'I'm all right.' The last seam on the suit fastened up, and he straightened himself without wincing.

'What are you going to ask him?' Tricia asked as the starship sank down through the clouds. Far below the fuselage the sensors had already picked out the white circle of the house set in its rambling grounds on the edge of a vast prairie of native vegetation.

'I just want five minutes of his time, that's all. Then this will all be over.'

Troblum switched the stealth effect off when they were below five hundred metres. The starship settled on the big patch of level grass where two capsules were already parked in the shade of tall reddish-brown trees. He walked down the airlock stairs, sniffing the faint alien pollen in the air. Two figures were already hurrying down the spiral stair that was wrapped round the house's central pillar. Although he normally hated the country-side, Troblum had to admit the raised house in this bucolic setting was fabulous.

His u-shadow reported pings being aimed at him by the men walking towards him. He responded courteously enough with his identity certificate, praying they wouldn't send too many queries about him into the unisphere. The Accelerators would be waiting for any giveaway, though even if they confirmed his location he should be relatively safe from Marius here.

'I'm Dushiku,' the first man said. 'Can we help you?'

'Is that really your starship?' the second one asked. He was younger, definitely a first lifer, everything about him leaked eagerness and an endearing naivety, not just his gaiafield pres-ence. 'It looks fantastic.'

'Thank you.'

'Are those wings?'

'Heat radiators.'

'Oh.'

'Jesaral, enough,' Dushiku chided.

'Sorry.'

'I'd like to speak to Oscar, please,' Troblum said.

Their attitude changed immediately. Dushiku chopped off his gaiafield emissions as his face hardened. While Jesaral pouted and allowed a wave of upset and worry to spill out of his mind.

'Oscar is not here,' Dushiku said stiffly.

'Have I said something wrong?'

'No,' Jesaral said, his handsome face frowned in misery. 'It's just that Oscar isn't very popular round here right now. He left us in a hurry a few days ago. Apparently we don't mean nearly as much to him as he does to us. That's always good to know, isn't it? Poor old Anja is still crying her eyes out.'

Dushiku's arm went round the younger man's shoulder, squeezing in comfort. 'It's okay, he'll be back.'

'Who cares?' Jesaral said with sudden contempt.

'Do you know when he'll be back?' Troblum asked.

'No.' Dushiku gave him a sharp look. 'Do you know him?'

'We have a mutual friend. It is rather important I contact him.'

'His u-shadow is blocking our calls,' Jesaral said. 'But don't let that put you off, you might have better luck.'

'I'll try that, thank you.'

'Really?' Dushiku said. 'Why didn't you do that originally instead of coming here?'

'I, er . . .' Troblum's social program reported that Dushiku was becoming irate and curious, and he should say something soothing. It didn't say what. 'It's complicated. Where's he gone?'

'Ask her,' Jesaral said with a effusive glower.

'Who?'

'That Paula Myo character. She was the last of his *old friends* to turn up here unannounced. I didn't know there were so many of you.'

Troblum stood perfectly still, staring at the now-wary men. *That's a big coincidence. Very big. Why would Paula visit Oscar? And what is he doing now? Could they be working together? I didn't see him at Florac's villa.*

'Do you know her?' Dushiku asked.

'I know of her. I have to go now.' Troblum turned, and made for the airlock ramp.

'Hey!'

'Sorry to have bothered you.'

'What the hell did you want from him?'

'Nothing. Nothing at all.'

'Who in Ozzie's universe are you people?'

With the ramp under his feet, Troblum felt a lot safer. He was already ordering the smartcore to power up the drive.

'Give him back to us,' Jesaral yelled. 'I want Oscar back. I want my Oscar. You bastard.'

The airlock closed. *Mellanie's Redemption* lifted immediately, accelerating hard, only just keeping subsonic. Troblum knew that was ridiculous, Oscar's lovers didn't present the remotest threat. Yet he wanted to get away from them fast. The stealth effect shrouded the fuselage in a refractive smear as they reached the cloud level. Troblum checked, but there were no sensors probing the sky hunting for him.

'Well they were terrifying,' Tricia said contemptuously. She and Catriona were snuggled up together on the cabin's long couch.

'Worse than the Cat.'

'You were lucky to get out of there alive.'

'Shut up,' Troblum snapped.

Both girls pouted, then turned to each other, pawing and stroking like kittens. Troblum ignored them and slumped into a big chair. He was still shocked by the revelation. Paula Myo had visited Oscar! It was the last thing he'd expected. He let out a small grunt of admiration. That was it. Of course, those two working together would be the last thing anyone would expect. *So what's he doing for her?*

The starship reached four hundred kilometres altitude. Troblum told it to go ftl, and fly ten lightyears clear from Orakum.

Oscar's unisphere code hung in his storage cluster. Immensely tempting. But since Sholapur he simply didn't trust the unisphere. Knowing Oscar and Paula were in contact surely gave him some kind of advantage. He just couldn't think what.

Catriona raised her head and gave him an affectionate look. 'So where are we going?'

'Nowhere,' he said, coming to a decision. 'I'm going to assemble the ultradrive. After that I'll do what I can to warn Paula and ANA. At least if it all goes wrong then, I can run.'

*

Paula hadn't visited Paris for decades. The city had reduced considerably since its heyday of the First Commonwealth era. ANA had been as ruthless here as it had everywhere on Earth, pruning away buildings it considered irrelevant. Residual national nostalgia didn't carry much weight in its hard-nosed analysis. However, the truly historic remained. The Eiffel Tower, of course. Arc de Triomphe. Notre Dame. The Palais de la Concorde. Most of the original buildings along the Seine.

She teleported in from Sky Pier station above Bordeaux, materializing outside the ancient five-storey building where she'd spent so many centuries working before the days of ANA and Higher culture. Beside the door, the original brass sign still gleamed against the dull stonework.

INTERSOLAR COMMONWEALTH
SERIOUS CRIMES DIRECTORATE

Paula gave it a melancholy smile, and walked into the marbled entrance hall. So many memories haunted this place. Embedded in the structure, they sprang to life everywhere she looked. Images and sounds stronger than the gaiafield could ever produce, and far more meaningful. All those colleagues she'd worked with over the centuries, the cases they'd solved, the battles against innumerable chiefs and political appointees and lawyers. They all echoed round her, welcoming her back.

An ANAdroid was waiting for her at the lift door, a human simulacrum with featureless gold-brown skin. It wore a simple blue and green suit uniform identical to all its kind. There were tens of thousands of them in the city, performing the maintenance and support functions which the antique buildings and their priceless contents needed. Stabilizer generators alone couldn't preserve the city's fabric, not when it was still in use by nearly eighty thousand humans.

'Welcome back, Investigator Myo,' it said as the lift doors opened. The voice was as genderless as the body.

'Thank you.' Paula put her hand on the security pad, allowing the management system to confirm her DNA. Her u-shadow then had to go through a further lengthy authorization procedure before the lift would descend. They passed through at least two force fields on their way down to the vault. There was also an exotic energy scrambler field around the three sub-levels, preventing anyone from teleporting in, or opening a wormhole inside.

The lift opened into a long hall. It reminded Paula of the ANA reception facilities, where thousands of recently downloaded bodies waited to see if their minds would adapt to the expansion and freedom inside ANA itself. Only here, instead of the glowing violet spheres, the floor supported long rows of dark sarcophagi.

'This way,' the ANAdroid said, and gestured politely.

Paula accompanied it, their footsteps echoing round the vault. 'How many are stored here?' she asked.

'We currently provide suspension for eighteen hundred and forty-three people.'

She wondered how many she was responsible for entombing down here. *A good percentage, I'll guess.*

'Most still have several hundred years to serve on their sentence,' the ANAdroid said. 'Some exceptional cases will remain down here a great deal longer. A few are even scheduled to remain for longer than the city has already existed.'

'Yes,' Paula said as they stopped beside one of the bulky suspension cases. *And this is one of them.* 'I'd like to see her, please.'

'You may use a field scan. It will not interfere with the suspension systems, they are quite robust.'

'Open it.'

'As you wish.'

The suspension case's malmetal lid flowed apart. Paula looked down at the body inside. The Cat lay there, her body webbed with the silver threads used to provide long-term suspension, ensuring her cells remained intact throughout the sluggish centuries as she lay poised on the cusp between life and death. 'All hail Schrödinger,' Paula muttered. Her field scan swept through the Cat, confirming the small scars and burn patches that she'd acquired in that last ferocious firefight which resulted in her capture. The hospital had healed her for the trial. At the time, several senior members of the Directorate, and indeed the President's office itself, had questioned why Paula had allowed her to survive. Political types to whom the rule of law was an irksome guideline to be bent or broken with impunity at every convenience.

Paula nodded in satisfaction. This was definitely her old adversary. *The original one at least.* Not that originality stood for much any more.

'How many people have visited her?'

The ANAdroid wasn't designed for surprise, but it somehow managed to convey that impression. 'Your inspection three hundred and eighty years ago is the only one, Investigator.'

'Thank you,' she told the ANAdroid. That was the time when a political group on Far Away had boasted that they'd managed to extract their idol from purgatory. They hadn't of course, it was just a bid to gain more influence.

The lid flowed back into place, sealing the Cat back into a darkness that was due to last for another four thousand years.

'Are you satisfied now?' ANA:Governance asked as Paula emerged out into the mellow Parisian daylight.

'Not entirely, no.'

'It is not possible to break into the Directorate vault.'

'I know. But there are a few other possibilities. Resurrecting her is something I've given a lot of thought to over the centuries. There are still plenty of fanatics out there.'

'The Knights Guardian don't actually want her alive and walking round. It is politically convenient to have a leader who will return in the far future. That gives them plenty of leeway.'

'Now where have I heard that before.'

'This is a strange weakness of yours, Paula.'

'We're all entitled to one.'

'So do you still believe it was her on Sholapur?'

'I think it's a strong possibility that I encountered a full clone version.'

'Her DNA is probably easy to obtain. But where would they get a copy of her memory? We know she never had a secure store, she was too worried your Directorate would gain access to it.'

'Her weakness,' Paula said flatly. 'However, there is one copy that I know of. I'll check it out.'

'I'm not being critical, but there are other matters that require attention. Quite urgent attention. If the respite Justine has bought us is to have any value, I must know what the Accelerators are planning.'

'Are you trying to guilt me into chasing round after Marius and his cronies?'

'I have to use guilt?'

'If the Cat has been brought back in some form by the Accelerators, they clearly want her for some very dirty deniable work. But, as I suspect they're discovering, she's not easy to control. Her personal agenda will always come first. I can use that to catch her. Once she's in custody, she can be fully interrogated.'

'An interesting application of logic.'

'But logical nonetheless.'

'Assuming you're correct about Sholapur.'

'I believe a great deal of my usefulness to you comes from my instinct, a facet of personality you have yet to acquire.'

'Correct.'

'Thank you. However, you are right about following other leads. I reviewed Troblum's file on my way here. That presentation he made to Kazimir was very interesting.'

'Yes. I considered it to be well argued, and highly plausible.'

'That's not what I mean. It implies he has a very strong knowledge of the Dark Fortress itself.'

'The Navy maintains an effective force around the Dyson Pair, it would not be possible for him to gain access to either of them.'

'It would if he was part of the Navy science team. There aren't many people, especially Highers, who have his physical profile. Please review all the Navy personnel to have served at the Dyson Pair since the Starflyer War.'

There wasn't even a moment of hesitation. 'That was an excellent deduction. I have the file.'

Paula examined it. The identity was recorded as one Kent Vernon, a physicist from Salto. Exoimage showed her a face similar to Troblum's, but with ebony skin. 'He darkened his pigmentation considerably, though that face is definitely recognizable. Oh, of course, that name. He is descended from Mark Vernon.' She smiled at the memory of Mark, a man really out of his depth, but a thoroughly decent human being. 'And Mark was married to Liz, who was Afro-American. Very neat,' she complimented. 'If lacking in imagination. I'm surprised his Accelerator controller allowed that.'

'He served a six-month tour duty on the Navy Exploration Division science ship *Poix* fifty-six years ago,' ANA reported. 'That particular research mission was concentrating on the inner two lattice spheres. They made some progress mapping the integral quantum function. Though the Navy project is still ongoing; we still don't quite understand the mechanism behind the Dark Fortress.'

'Even you?'

'Even me.'

'And according to his file "Kent Vernon" subsequently downloaded into you,' Paula said as she scanned the exoimage. 'That ties up any loose ends as far as an inconvenient outside investigation is concerned. So let's see what real facts we can find.' Her u-shadow called up the records from Troblum's apartment, and Daroca's utilities. Those for the period fifty-six years ago were already deep cached, but they were soon accessed with her authority rating. 'Look at that power consumption rate,' she said.

'Nominal, for ten years. Implying Troblum wasn't there. Whatever he was doing took him off Arevalo for a decade.'

'What kind of device takes a decade to build?'

'That was what Troblum wanted to tell you.'

'Why didn't he just come straight out with it?' she said in annoyance.

'He is a genuine paranoid. Understandably, given the clandestine projects he's been associated with, and under the supervision of Marius. A paranoia which was fully vindicated by events on Sholapur. He has probably left the Commonwealth altogether now. His starship seems quite capable of such a flight, even without ultradrive.'

'I'd certainly like to leave, so I can believe that,' Paula admitted. 'Unfortunately, wishful thinking is a luxury right now. List everyone who served with Troblum, and mine their history, please; start with his captain.'

'The captain of the *Poix* was Donald Chatfield. A Higher, currently resident on Ganthia.'

'All right, I concede this is more pertinent than the lead I have on the Cat. I'll go and interview Chatfield.'

'As you wish.'

'And you really can't guess what the Accelerators might have built?'

'No. According to Gore, they wish to duplicate me and fuse this replica with the Void to initiate post-physical evolution. The systems to initialize another such as myself would be complex, but they wouldn't require any input from the Dark Fortress technology.'

'Will that fusion work?'

'Who knows?'

'Very well, I'll call in as soon as I have something.' Paula activated her field interface function, designating her exit co-ordinate. Earth's T-sphere immediately translated her back up to Sky Pier. As she crossed the reception centre to the station terminus her u-shadow told her Kazimir was calling.

'Bad news,' he said.

Paula's heart performed a little flutter. There weren't many people left in the galaxy she cared about, but Justine was one of them. 'Justine?'

'No. I have no further information on mother, which as far

as I'm concerned is good news . . . But I am in contact with the *Lindau.*'

'I don't know the ship.'

'It's the Navy scout I dispatched to Hanko to monitor the whole Aaron situation for you.'

'And?'

'They don't have the best sensors in the fleet, but there's something wrong with the planet.'

'Wrong in what way?'

'Its gravity. We believe someone has fired a Hawking m-sink into it.'

'Oh Christ. No! Why would they do that? It's a dead planet anyway.'

'The Restoration project base at Jajaani has stopped broadcasting. *Lindau* is still picking up some of the project's surface beacons, so it looks as if the base itself was targeted.'

'But an m-sink? That's a monstrous overkill. We know those ships were ultradrive, they'll be equipped with weapons powerful enough to take out an undefended civilian base.'

'I don't know the reason, I'm just reporting the results. Naturally, there's no sign of either ultradrive ship.'

'Naturally.'

'However—'

'Ah! Yes?'

'The *Lindau* has also picked up a very powerful distress signal from the surface. It's a standard biononic emission. Nobody listed as a member of the Restoration team was Higher.'

'So it's either Aaron, or Inigo himself.'

'Yes. Which leaves me with a rather painful decision. With an m-sink eating away at its core, that planet isn't going to last much longer. The *Lindau* estimates a few hours more at best before the mantle starts to readjust prior to implosion, at which point nothing is going to survive. So, do they land at Jajaani and see if there are any survivors?'

'No,' she said immediately. 'They have to recover whoever is sending that signal with biononics.'

'One person.'

'If the m-sink hit at Jajaani, there will be nothing to recover from there, not even bodies, and certainly not any secure memory stores. Everyone working in Restoration projects knows there are risks, they all have back-up memories and DNA samples on their homeworld. They will be re-lifed. If there is the slightest chance that survivor is Inigo, or can tell us where Inigo is, then you have to rescue them.'

'I was thinking along those lines myself, but it's always satisfying to receive your endorsement. I'll speak with the captain, and keep you updated.'

'Kazimir.'

'Yes?'

'Warn them to take extreme precautions. If it is Aaron down on the surface, there's no telling what he'll do.'

'I know. I'll emphasize the need for caution.'

Paula drew a deep breath, and gazed down through the transparent hull section of Sky Pier's reception centre. Bordeaux was spread out below the station, lush and beautiful in the lazy sunlight. She'd visited a few times when the vineyards were still producing their renowned wine, and the remaining citizens stubbornly resisted the advances which the Commonwealth provided. Something about the area and its culture had made her feel comfortable and welcome, satisfying that deep human yearning for a simple life, a fundamental which had never been sequenced out of her psyche by her creators. She wondered what its long-departed people would make of today's life with all its associated bizarre problems. Somehow she suspected they'd be less than impressed.

Looking down on the region again, a small part of her wanted to just teleport down there and settle in one of the remaining homes. Cut off communication, deactivate her biononics; leaving her far away from Kazimir and Aaron and Marius and the Cat, and all the rest of it. Supposedly, there were several primitive groups on Earth, living as their ancestors had two thousand years ago. ANA always denied it, but rumours persisted.

Not this time, though, she decided. So she walked into the terminus with its glowing Cherenkov light from the wormhole which led back to Orleans. From there another wormhole connected directly to Arevalo. By the time she got back to Daroca spaceport, the *Alexis Denken* would have been resupplied, and the medical chamber replaced. The starship would be ready to fly her onwards. *Again.*

*

It had been over a year since Araminta had visited the house. At the time, she'd looked on the compact drycoral building as a development project, seeing costs and returns in everything, ignoring the family which had welcomed her in and given her a lovely Sunday dinner. Now, when the door opened, and Tandra's face peered out, Araminta couldn't help herself, she burst into tears. Life hadn't been so bad back when she was waiting tables in Nik's. It really hadn't: she'd been part of a larger collective family, Tandra and the other waitresses had included her in their gossip and lives, they'd hung out together between shifts, and some evenings they'd gone out in a big group having a good time even though she'd been flat broke. The very same people she'd ignored and left behind once Laril's money had come through. Tandra's immediate unqualified concern and graciousness at the stray appearing unannounced on her doorstep simply made Araminta feel even more wretched.

'There, there,' Tandra crooned and gave her a motherly hug. 'It's all right.' Martyn, her husband, was also attentive, clearing the kids' toys from the settee in the living room. Mixal and Freddy, their five-year-old twins, were given fruit smoothies to hush them up while Araminta blew into tissues and tried to get her sobbing under control. 'I'm sorry,' she wailed. 'I shouldn't have come. I've nowhere else to go.' And at the back of her mind was the worry that just by being here she was putting Tandra's family in danger.

'You're more than welcome, and you know that,' her old

friend told her. 'Did you have a fight? Have you left him?' She was giving Araminta's roughed-up clothes a highly suspicious examination.

'No. Nothing like that. There's a whole bunch of people in the park outside my apartment. They're very angry. The invader soldiers are there as well. I was frightened.'

'Those bastards,' Martyn grunted.

Tandra shot him a warning look, her gaze darting pointedly to the twins, who were watching intently over the back of a chair they were sharing. 'Yes, they are unpleasant people who have behaved wrongly,' she said with parental formality. 'However, the law will prevail, and they will be expelled from our world.'

Martyn rolled his eyes. 'Yes. They will.'

'And until they are, you can sleep on the couch,' Tandra assured her.

'Just for one night,' Araminta promised. 'That's all. I need to get myself back together.'

'No boyfriend?' Martyn asked.

'Not right now,' Araminta lied.

He didn't say anything, but his tight little smile triggered a fresh wave of Araminta's guilt. She didn't dare delve into the gaiafield to learn his emotional state.

'We're staying here at home for the rest of the afternoon,' Tandra said. 'The twins are having the day off school as a treat, aren't you?'

'Yes!' they yelled gleefully.

Martyn was looking out of the window. 'How did you get here?'

'Walked.'

'From where?'

'Bodant.'

'That's miles!'

'They won't allow capsules to fly, and my trike pod is being fixed.'

Tandra and Martyn exchanged a look. 'You sit there and rest,' Tandra said. 'I'll give those clothes a wash. Martyn, some tea.'

'Coming right up.'

'Thank you,' Araminta said meekly.

Tandra waited until he'd vanished into the galley kitchen. 'Anything else you need to tell me?'

Araminta shook her head. 'I really will go in the morning. I've already got an idea what to do. There's someone I need to talk to. I'll call him tomorrow.' *When I've worked out how to.*

'Okay. I'd better go get a robe for you. Martyn will have a heart attack if he sees you walking round the place in your underwear.' She patted her own legs. 'He's only used to women a size or ten bigger than a youngster like you.'

Araminta grinned. 'I missed you.'

'Sure you did. Out there enjoying yourself every night, I bet you thought of me the whole time.' She gave the twins a critical look. 'I swore I'd never have any kids again this life around, this one would be for me, but what the hell . . . A girl doesn't stand a chance with a Love God like Marty.'

Araminta started laughing. Then stopped, casting a guilty look at the kitchen archway.

'That's better,' Tandra said. 'You have the world's greatest smile, honey, that's why the rest of us always insisted on pooling the tips on your shifts.' She ruffled both of the children as she went past. They gave her an adoring look. 'I just love the sleepless nights, the worry, losing my figure, no money, and lack of sex. It's character building.'

'I'm going to find out myself one day.'

'Sure you will. And your introduction starts today.' Her voice rose a couple of levels. 'Guess what, Aunty Araminta is on dinner duty tonight. Then she's going to give you both a bath and wash your hair.'

'Yes!' the twins yelled jubilantly.

'Still want to stay?'

'Oh yes,' Araminta said. This house, Tandra, the twins: it

felt like an oasis of decency amid the madness raging outside. After the last two days, she badly needed to remind herself what normal was. *Then I might be able to work out how to get back there myself.*

*

Seven hundred years ago, Wilson Kime had officially handed over control of the Commonwealth Navy to Kazimir. It was the fifth time Wilson had held the role of Supreme Commander, on that occasion it was essentially a ceremonial appointment, lasting a single year before he downloaded into ANA. His final farewell to the physical.

After the formal hand over for the benefit of the President, senior Senators, and unisphere reporters, the two of them had gone up to the Admiral's office on the top floor of the thirty-storey Pentagon II tower. Wilson had given Kazimir two pieces of advice as they stood looking across the agreeable parkland of the Babuyan Atoll dome.

'Don't ever give in to political pressure,' Wilson had said. 'I've been President myself, so I know the convenience of a military who'll snap to and say yes to every dark instruction you issue. Resist them. Stick to the fundamentals. We have two roles as ordained by the Senate in more honourable times: protecting the human race in all its forms against alien aggressors, and peaceful scientific exploration of the galaxy. That's all. Don't let the Executive wear that down. The general population must have faith in us.'

'I can hold the line,' Kazimir assured him.

'And second, feel free to change this goddamn office. I always hated it; never got round to redecorating, so now every crappy white molecule qualifies as tradition because this is the way it was when we gained our victory over MorningLightMountain. Every other admiral from Rafael onwards just rolled over and accepted that. I want you to give the conservation fascists a good kicking and bring in your own furniture.'

Kazimir smiled at the man's strange passion. They shook hands. 'I will,' he promised.

To date, he'd proudly held that line through some extraordinary difficult political events. The second promise hadn't been broken, exactly. Like Wilson, he just hadn't got round to changing things yet.

Today he looked out of the office to see a circular habitat that also hadn't changed that much in the last seven centuries. Pentagon II was still the same (which was more than could be said of the original back on Earth that ANA had decided wasn't significant enough to maintain); several buildings had been reshaped, *High Angel* adapting their growing-stone material in accordance to each new set of human requirements. It was the living parkland itself which had seen the most alteration, the average level of the tree canopy had risen by over fifty metres since the day Kazimir had assumed command. Under the protective dome of the Raiel arkship, the organic environment was perfect. Every species of tree prospered in a way they could never do on a planet with variable seasons and winds and fires and earthquakes and diseases and parasites and bark-eating creatures. Here there was no real reason for them to die, so they just kept on growing, nurtured by their flawless climate. There were some monster arboreals out there, twenty or so had even reached the same height as Pentagon II, their osmosis now assisted by *High Angel*, which had reduced the gravity field around them, allowing nutrients to flow unhindered all the way to the topmost branches. It was a forest which could never exist on a planet, and all the more alluring because of it.

When he glanced up, Kazimir saw Icalanise was a slim tawny crescent overhead. The New Storm seemed to bulge out of the Great Northern cloudband. He'd been watching the moon-sized storm growing for two centuries now, absorbing all the smaller storms it clashed with to become the largest of all the gas giant's cyclonic swirls. Human starships flittered around the orbital cluster of stations and micro-gee factories like a metallic shoal, mostly Navy craft, with a few commercial freighters and passenger ships. *High Angel* was still the largest Navy port in the Greater Commonwealth. Its residents took a lot of pride in that, supplying a disproportionate amount of officers.

Kazimir gathered his thoughts and returned to his big white desk. The office's ancient tragwood furniture really was aesthetically awful, made worse by the clinical glowing walls and ceiling. But he did concede it was comfortable as he sank back into the cushioning.

'Convene the ExoProtectorate Council,' he told his u-shadow. The office dissolved from his natural vision, leaving him in the perceptual conference room with its white and orange furniture (not much of an improvement on his own, he reflected sadly) looking out over the tempestuous furore of the Millavian plains.

Gore and Ilanthe appeared first, sitting next to each other. The Accelerator faction representative had changed her appearance since the last meeting, allowing her dark hair to hang down to her waist in a single tail wrapped with red leather bands; she wore a stylish black dress of horizontal pleats. She nodded politely to Gore, who was in his golden incarnation, dressed in a perfectly tailored tuxedo.

'Any news of Justine?' Ilanthe asked.

Gore's gaze flicked to the chair Justine had occupied last time the Council convened. 'Nothing. I guess we'll have to wait to see if the Second Dreamer deigns to reveal anything to us.'

Crispin Goldreich arrived. The ancient Senator gave Justine's chair a look. 'Gore. Kazimir,' he said formally. 'My sympathies to both of you.'

'Yeah, thanks,' Gore said.

'I prefer to consider her successfully positioned to assist us further,' Kazimir said. 'She has achieved something remarkable, after all.'

'Yes,' Crispin said sheepishly.

Creewan materialized in his chair, to the left of Kazimir. The Custodian faction member gave the Admiral a formal bow. He hadn't completed the motion when the Darwinist faction representative, John Thelwell, arrived in a seat on the opposite side of the table. The two of them always seemed to appear at the same time. Kazimir wondered idly if there was some kind of alliance involved, though how such diverse factions could find any common ground was a mystery.

'Aren't you going to activate Justine's ANA personality?' John Thelwell asked in some surprise.

'Why?' Gore asked. 'Her actual is still alive. Duplication is still our biggest anathema, isn't it? Or have you converted to that pervert multiple philosophy.'

Thelwell threw up his hands. 'Fine. If that's how you want to play it.'

'If you're ready,' Kazimir said. 'I have the secure link to the *Yenisey* available.'

'All right,' Gore said. 'Let's take a look and see what the Ocisens have come up with.'

Captain Lucian was proud of his small crew. For nine days the *Yenisey* had flown in pursuit of the greatest fleet of warships the Ocisens had ever assembled. If intelligence summaries about the Starslayer-class ships was correct, then not even MorningLightMountain had enjoyed this level of firepower to deploy against the Commonwealth. Unsurprisingly, then, tension on board had been building as they closed on the fleet. Yet he considered they'd coped remarkably well. This mission wasn't anything they'd expected or trained for; however, as one they had risen to the challenge. Toi, the systems officer, actually relished the chance to confront the Ocisens.

'They've learned nothing in five hundred years,' she said. 'They genuinely believe we're just a bunch of decadent animals who got lucky on the technology front. We are the classical immovable object in their way, and all they do is crack what passes for a head against us. They don't try to learn or adapt.'

'This fleet is proof they have tried to think round the problem,' Kylee, the first tactical officer argued. 'They saw what they needed to overcome us, and they set out to obtain it. That's adaptive.'

'They set out to steal it,' Toi said.

'Negotiating an allegiance is hardly stealing.'

'I don't believe they could do that. They found the leftovers of a post-physical, and bootstrapped themselves up a whole weapons-level.'

'Even that's pretty adaptive.'

The argument had been just about continuous. The four of them had completely different positions, not that it interfered with their tasks. Although Lucian was slightly concerned about Gieovan, the second tactical officer, whose solution to the whole Ocisen problem was unpleasantly crude. He would be allying himself directly to the Accelerators at download, Lucian decided, if not the Isolationists or possibly the more radical Darwinists. For a moment, he did worry about confronting the fleet with Gieovan's hand on the trigger of their formidable arsenal. But none of them ever allowed their personal views to affect their professionalism. He was confident they'd deliver the result Admiral Kazimir had tasked them with.

For eighteen hours they'd flown beside the Ocisen fleet in stealth mode, and monitored the alien warships. To Lucian's huge relief, they were all Ocisen.

'Unless they've got stealth,' Kylee pointed out after the first hour.

'You can't stealth a continuous wormhole drive,' Gieovan countered. 'In any case, you can only minimalize the hyperdrive emission and damp down its distortion effect. You're never truly stealthed to a top-level sensor array. Detection and concealment technology are a constant race for superiority.'

'But we're not registering anything?' Lucian asked.

'No, captain,' Gieovan. 'We could use more active scanning, of course, but that would give us away.'

'Let's not make this any more difficult. Continue monitoring their communications. We need to identify the command ship.'

The Ocisen fleet hierarchy was of course a replica of their imperial structure, with the Emperor's nest having ultimate authority. Individual captains had very little leeway. Consequently the communication traffic reflected that, with one ship issuing orders to everyone else. There was no cross-ship chatter.

Once they'd identified the command ship beyond any doubt, Lucian called Admiral Kazimir and received authorization for the interception.

'Knock them out of ftl,' Kazimir said, 'and deliver our warning. They are to turn around or every ship will be disabled.'

'I'm not quite sure we can achieve that,' Lucian said. 'The *Yenisey* packs a hell of a punch, but there's over two and a half thousand ships out there, including nine hundred Starslayers. If even twenty of them combine, they can get through our shields.'

'Lucian, I could never countenance disabling the fleet in deep space, not when they're already so far past the Empire's boundary. They simply don't have the ships nor resources to mount a viable rescue operation. The crews would perish. That is not something I wish to have on my conscience, nor that of any of my officers. No, today is simply a reminder of our technological superiority. I suspect it will have to be repeated several times until they realize they cannot physically achieve their goal.'

'Understood, sir,' Lucian said with some relief.

The four of them settled on their couches in the main cabin, and merged with the smartcore. It gave them a perceptual viewpoint from the front of the fuselage. *Yenisey* curved away beneath them, the main hull was a fat cylinder eighty metres long, with a conical nose section. Midships sprouted three radial fins supporting bulbous weapons nacelles, each of which curved down to a sharp point. A uniform luminous blue representation of hyperspace flowed around them, as though they were some yacht sailing an ocean.

Lucian was fed senses that revealed flaws in the blueness, a constellation of dark splinters surrounded by a green haze of exotic energy: the Ocisen warships. He directed the *Yenisey* until it was holding station a kilometre away from the command ship.

'Are we ready?' he asked quietly.

'Yes, sir,' Kylee replied.

'Excellent. Gieovan, you have fire authority as of now. Keep scanning for any anomalous activity – just in case. Toi, I want total systems availability, high-status.' He scanned the Ocisen ship. It was two hundred and fifty metres long, a fat ovoid shape, with thin edges like curving wings. The hull was rough, strewn with irregular lumps, as if it had somehow become encrusted with barnacles during its flight. Although the scan couldn't perceive its colour, he knew it would be a dull metallic shade, dappled by furry green patches. All Ocisen starships were like that after they developed their semi-organic extrusion technology.

'Pull it out,' he told Kylee.

The *Yenisey*'s energy manipulators produced wildly fluctuating waveforms that intersected the exotic energy cascading fluidly around the Starslayer. Instabilities immediately started to skitter along its wormhole. Kylee analysed the modifier effects which the warship's drive exerted in an attempt to regain control, and simply overwhelmed them with the raw power available to the *Yenisey*'s systems. The rest of the fleet shot away from them as the wormhole's pseudofabric broke down. Within a second they had vanished into the blueness.

Spacetime reasserted itself, swamping the blueness with infinite black. Stars shone with unwavering intensity. Eight hundred metres away, the massive Ocisen warship started a laborious tumble. Its protective force fields flickered dangerously as uncontained energy pulses swept out from the ruined drive.

'Attention Ocisen ship,' Lucian broadcast. 'This is the Greater Commonwealth Navy ship *Yenisey*. You are hereby ordered to turn your fleet around and return to—'

'Oh, shit,' Gieovan gulped.

A smooth spherical starship appeared from nowhere a kilometre ahead of the Starslayer. Its force fields were impenetrable. The *Yenisey* couldn't even get an accurate quantum signature scan to determine what kind of drive it used.

'Admiral,' Lucian called urgently. 'We can't—'

The unknown ship fired.

*

'What the fuck was that!' Gore yelled as the secure link abruptly vanished.

Kazimir took a second to review the TD link data, he was so surprised. His tactical staff had produced a number of scenarios, mostly incorporating the Ocisens utilizing weapons technology they'd procured from a more advanced species. *This* hadn't been a remote consideration.

'I don't recognize that design at all,' Ilanthe said. 'Do we have any spherical ship on the Navy's intelligence registry?'

'There are some species that utilize a sphere,' Kazimir said slowly as his u-shadow supplied their most highly classified data. 'But we don't list anything that can disable the River-class starships quite that quickly.'

'Disable?' Gore snapped. 'What is that, the new politically correct term for blowing it to shit?'

'All we know so far is that the *Yenisey*'s TD link has failed—' Kazimir began.

'Come on!'

'I'm afraid I agree with Gore,' Ilanthe said. 'That was not a warning shot. *Yenisey* is a warship, one of the best we've got, and designed to operate at long distances. The last thing that fails is the communication. After all, we kept in touch with Justine until the Void swallowed her. '

'My staff will run a full analysis,' Kazimir said. 'It should help define the nature of the attack.'

'The weapon, you mean,' Crispin said. 'I'm with Gore on this, Admiral, you can't start hiding behind language. All of us here today are long past that.'

'You are correct,' Kazimir said, knowing that they were right, the *Yenisey* was lost with all hands. It was hard, he hadn't lost a starship in combat in six hundred years, not since the last Ocisen expansion wave. The crew would be re-lifed, of course, but still he had to endure the fact that he'd sent them out there into a hostile environment, while they were woefully under-equipped. It was a classic command failure, deploying your people on the basis of bad information under political pressure. *The wonder of hindsight.*

'In the light of this catastrophe, I propose we send our deterrent fleet to intercept the Ocisen Empire ships,' Ilanthe said. 'I don't believe we have any choice. Following the loss of the *Yenisey*, we are seeing a very real and credible threat to the entire Commonwealth. Who knows what that unknown ship is capable of.'

'They are still a long way off,' Kazimir said. 'We can use that interval to discover what their full potential is.'

'You're playing God with our future,' Creewan said. 'I for one won't tolerate that.'

Kazimir gave him a withering look. 'I hardly think one unknown warship constitutes an end to our civilization.'

'You don't know it's just one,' Ilanthe said. 'You don't know if that was their best weapon, or their equivalent of a bow and arrow. Kazimir, what is wrong with you? You are charged with defending our entire species. Will you please act as if you care?'

'I care very much indeed. I continue to maintain we need intelligence on the ally which the Ocisens have found themselves. I would like to propose that we send at least one more scout mission to determine what we can of the threat level. We do have time, and I am reluctant to formulate a final response without greater intelligence.'

Ilanthe glanced round the table. 'I will support that on the condition you at least mobilize the deterrent fleet. If the next interception is destroyed, then the deterrent fleet must be deployed against the Ocisens.'

'I second that,' Gore said.

The other three gave their assent.

'I will dispatch four Capital-class ships,' Kazimir said. 'They should be there within five days.'

'I'm not familiar with Capital-class ships,' John Thelwell said. 'Are they part of the deterrent fleet?'

'No. They are a grade below that. But I am confident they

will be able to hold their own, at least until we know more about the Ocisen's allies.'

Gore and Kazimir remained in the perceptual reality after the others left. Outside the window, the ice meteorites fell in silent splendour, triggering vast electron webs across the dark sky.

'You know, in all my time, and for all my clout with ANA, I've never managed to get a single hint out of it concerning the deterrent fleet,' Gore said.

'I would hope not,' Kazimir told him. 'It is our ultimate defence. Its nature should not be available for scrutiny and discussion, however well intentioned. It is enough that we have it.'

'Now there's the thing, see. Down at my most basic level, I'm an old-fashioned boy, rooted in the physical and distrusting of politicians. I'd hate to think our entire survival prospects are based on a cosmic-sized poker bluff.' His golden face looked straight at Kazimir. 'Do we actually have a deterrence fleet, son? Is it real?'

'It is real, Grandfather. And if the Ocisen allies prove stronger than our Capital-class, I will personally lead it into battle against the Empire's fleet.'

'All right then. Forgive an old man his quirks.'

'Of course.'

'So what do we do about your mother?'

'Wait until she contacts us.'

'You think she will?'

'I think she's probably Mayoress of Makkathran by now.'

'Yeah,' Gore grunted. 'You're probably right. But how will we ever know?'

'Ask the Second Dreamer.'

*

Aaron was making good time. He'd already retraced the entire route back to the Olhava camp. Now it was just a simple jog across nine hundred kilometres of a dead planet's broken, frozen, radioactive ground, and he'd be back at Jajaani. Which the impact would have reduced to a fractured nightmare of geology where the few survivors from the outlying camps would be mounting futile rescue attempts. Still, it was his only chance. Not that cheating death meant anything to him. This way was the only possible way to salvage his mission. He was still furious at himself for being so gullible. Inigo must have been playing him from the moment he walked into the excavation chamber. Leaking weak thoughts and meek emotions into the gaiafield, lulling him to a level of trust.

Stupid. I would never have let it happen if I was thinking straight.

But too late for self-recrimination now. If he did get out of this, he'd have to maintain a keen watch on his own motivations and responses, make sure they hadn't degraded further under the assault of the unknowns in his subconscious.

The land he was jogging through was an ancient undulating volcanic plain, scoured of vegetation and crisped over by a thick skin of ice; residue of the deluge that had swept down from the highlands to the south during the last burst of weather before the temperature plummeted. Odd splinters of rock stuck up through the dull grey crust, torn out of the bedrock by the final inundation of water. Ice particles swirled constantly, as patchy as any summer morning fog. Dense clouds zephyred round in the windshadow of the outcrops, drumming hard on his suit as he moved through them.

His macrocellular clusters were still picking up the beacon line back to Jajaani. There was no communication traffic – other than his own distress call. The beacons simply stood there, tiny glows of virtual light across the forlorn world. The next one was eight kilometres ahead.

Aaron's u-shadow reported someone sweeping a communication beam across him. He shook his head in disbelief, momentarily suspicious this was another attempt by his subconscious to subvert him. Exovision displays started to show solid data. The broadcast point was directly overhead, and using the same emergency band as his own distress call.

'This is the Navy scout ship *Lindau*, are you receiving us?'

Aaron stopped dead, and lifted his head to the dreadful tumble of grey clouds. 'Hello?'

The signal beam immediately strengthened and focused. 'Ozzie be damned, who the hell are you?'

'Cyrial,' he said, picking a name at random from the Restoration staff they'd interviewed back at Jajaani.

'Well, Cyrial, this is the luckiest day of your lives. Stay put, we're coming down to pick you up.'

'Have you found anyone else?'

'No, sorry, you're the first.'

Aaron stood and waited as the scoutship fought its way through the clouds in a burst of violent lightning. Ingrav units strained against the wind, lowering it metre by metre. The ship was a broad cylinder, thirty-eight metres long, its comprehensive sensor clusters retracted into stumpy fins around its midsection. Two thermal dissipater rings around the rear fuselage glowed a bright ruby red, indicating how much power it was drawing on to hold steady against the fierce atmosphere. Snow hammered against its force field, kicking out a blue sparkle.

Malmetal landing struts swelled out fore and aft, and it came to rest ten metres in front of him.

'You will never believe how good you look to me,' Aaron told his rescuers.

'We got us a pretty good idea.' The airlock expanded open, and a short ramp slid out. 'Sorry about this, but we've been told we have to take precautions. Nobody knows who attacked the Restoration project base. We have to hold you in isolation while we scan you and confirm your identity.'

'Man, you can shack up with every daughter I ever fathered for all I care. I'll even give you their unisphere codes. Pretty things they are, too.' Aaron brought every weapons insert he had to full power, adjusted his biononic energy currents for extreme combat, and walked up the ramp.

Justine

The moment after Justine realized she wasn't dead was the most tranquil point in her entire life. What, as a five-year-old, she'd imagined walking into biblical heaven would be like, just lacking the angels. Once she acknowledged she actually was still alive, she checked round while the feeling shrank back down, as if wounded by her practicality. She could hear her heart beating. She was breathing. Exoimages revealed other body functions were nominal, including the macrocellular clusters and biononics. The cabin lighting remained on. Gravity field held steady.

'Status?' she asked the *Silverbird*'s smartcore.

'Life support operational. Secondary systems performing at optimal post-damage level. Hyperdrive inoperative.'

'What's wrong with it?'

The smartcore didn't respond at once, which sent a chill down her spine. If it was taking this long to diagnose the failure, the damage must be significant. She stood up, and walked over to the galley alcove. The bruising on her legs and back from getting thrown around made her draw a breath.

'Quantum state of this location does not correspond to external universe parameters.'

'Wow,' Justine replied. She stared at the section of bulkhead nearest to the smartcore. *Well, we knew it was different inside the Void.* 'Okay, show me where here is, please.'

Her exoimage wrapped her in the view gathered by the hull

sensors. Justine gasped in delight as the glowing nebulas of the Void shimmered softly all around her. As she watched, she could see movement amid some of the far-flung patches of luminescence – just as they had when the Waterwalker gazed up at them from Querencia. Stars glinted through the exotic ragged veils, lightyears distant.

Wait . . . distant? In every direction?

'Where's the Void's boundary?'

'Unknown,' the smartcore replied.

'But we came through it less than a minute ago.'

'Yes.'

Oh crap. 'What about nearby objects? Can you sense anything?' *Like the Skylord?*

'No radar return inside five million kilometres. No visual acquisition of any large mass. Hysradar inoperative. No local gravity field registering.'

'Hell.' *It's dumped me in the middle of nowhere.* Justine slumped down in the chair, at a loss what do to, or feel. Then she remembered one of the marvels of the Void. *I wonder.* She smiled tentatively, and looked at the glass of chilled white wine the culinary unit had just produced for her. Closed her eyes, and tried to let her mind find it. Strange shadows swept through the darkness, a lot duller than anything she'd ever perceived in the gaiafield. Justine snapped her eyes open. *Farsight!* 'Okay then, now we're cooking.' She smirked at the wine glass, and imagined reaching out for it, lifting it high. The surface of the pale white liquid trembled, producing a tiny ripple. Then the base of the glass tilted up a fraction. 'Yes!' she laughed exultantly. Another ten minutes saw the glass shift a couple of inches.

All right, not exactly the Waterwalker's strength, but I've only just got here. And it's all real. Every single one of Inigo's dreams is real. Holy shit.

'Start cataloguing the constellations,' she told the smartcore. 'See if you can find any which match the ones that are visible from Querencia. Also, locate the nearest star.'

Once it had begun that task she stripped off and went for a

good long shower. A real one, with water and gel – no modern spore rubbish. Her flight through the Gulf had lasted for what seemed like an eternity, leaving her stressed, aching, and exhausted. The tiny TD link back to her father had revealed the support and encouragement of a good proportion of her species, which had buoyed her along at the time. Now the residue of that emotion had fallen on her as an awesome feeling of responsibility. She was the ambassador for an entire universe to a whole different universe. It was all getting a bit much for her poor old biological brain to cope with.

After the shower she ate a decent salmon *en croûte* and mint-buttered jersey potatoes, washed down with some champagne. The smartcore still hadn't recognized any nebulas by the time she'd finished her raspberry Pavlova. She was asleep less than a minute after lying down on the bed which the cabin extruded for her.

Ten hours later she woke. Rested and almost immediately impatient. The smartcore still couldn't find a recognizable nebula, not even with meticulous three-dimensional projection of the ones it could map. Whatever angle it examined them from, they simply didn't match. Either she had emerged a *very* long way from Querencia. Or so much time had passed inside the Void that they had simply changed beyond recognition. Neither option was good.

The nearest star was three lightyears away. There was no detectable mass point between her and it.

Justine ate a light lunch, and told herself it was never going to be easy. Perhaps the Skylords were sailing towards her in their fabulously serene fashion. They were all slower than light creatures after all.

That afternoon, she rubbed medicating salves on her bruises, and ordered the gym to extrude for an hour's workout. She went to sleep with music playing quietly in the background, feeling not a little annoyed with the Skylords. And perhaps just a tinge claustrophobic. Or maybe that was agoraphobic. Would being completely alone in a universe bring a sensation of closing limitations or infinitely expanding horizons with associated loneliness?

On the second morning she had a light breakfast of eggs and toast. The (lightweight plastic) cup containing her freshly squeezed qurange juice drifted across the cabin from the culinary unit and nestled into her open waiting (physical) hand.

'Yes!'

Bandits and Ranalee watch out! There's a badass new girl in town.

Two days later every nebula had been thoroughly analysed. Justine had to face up to the simple fact: she was completely lost.

She ran a review of the ship's capability. The direct mass converter could power her almost indefinitely. Her small level-seven replicator could produce most of the ship's components. The few bots on board were capable of high-level maintenance. And best, or worst, of all, the medical cabinet could hold her in stasis for over a century without serious damage to her current body. It could also grow a clone and download her stored memories into it if her situation became extreme.

All in all, it was a pretty crappy way of whiling away your immortality.

However, the smartcore did report a few disturbing irregularities; not everything functioned perfectly the whole time. She saw unexplained glitches in the log of some systems. They'd always gone when she ordered a real-time review, and the analysis never gave any reason why they'd occurred in the first place. The only constant was that the more sophisticated the system, the more susceptible it seemed to be to the odd malaise.

She took another day to make her decision, or rather nerve herself up for what she knew had to be done. The ships which had brought the Waterwalker's ancestors to Querencia had fallen from the sky, or crashed. The legends were never clear on that. However, they had certainly never flown again.

Something in the Void was inimical to technology – presumably the different quantum structure underpinning what passed for spacetime in here. Though she was uneasy at the whole mental supremacy concept which the Void sustained, having the mind as king opened up some disturbing potentials. It could well be that the collective Heart was wishing the *Silverbird* to fail.

She did have confidence that the *Silverbird* was a lot tougher at every level than the old colony ships which had somehow blundered in here all those centuries ago. Her first instruction was for the smartcore to run a comprehensive analysis of the quantum structure, and from that to determine any conceivable reconfiguration which would make the ftl drive function again. Secondly, she used the small on-board confluence nest to amplify her own thoughts as she composed a message of greeting to the Skylords, asking them to find her, asking them to fly to her. A message it repeated ceaselessly.

After that the ingrav started to accelerate the little starship to point seven lightspeed towards the nearest star, a velocity which would take her there in a little over four years. The force fields could cope with a dust cloud impact at that velocity.

Justine ordered the smartcore to revive her at regular intervals, or in case of emergency. She reviewed the sensor images one last time. Nothing had changed outside. With that, she stepped into the medical chamber, and began the suspension process.

Inigo's Tenth Dream

The Poilus theatre was halfway along Doulon Lane, in the Cobara district. There was no sign outside, it occupied the cellars underneath the toyshop whose windows were full of brightly coloured wooden dolls and puppets. Entry was through a narrow doorway in a recess formed by the angle between the toyshop and the neighbouring tanner's. Two doormen in long dark coats stood outside, stamping their feet on the pavement to keep warm in the chilly midnight air.

Edeard and Kristabel arrived as the clock in Renan Plaza chimed quarter past the hour. When Edeard pushed his cloak's hood back the doorman gave a start, then smiled.

'They told us you'd be coming,' he said. 'Welcome to the Poilus, Waterwalker. Mistress.'

The door was opened, revealing curving stairs leading downwards. Warm air spilled up, accompanying a loud grumble of conversation and someone playing a guitar.

'He's about to start,' the doorman added as Edeard led Kristabel down.

It grew warmer with each step. Edeard could sense the excitement growing in Kristabel's mind. She gave him a tentative smile as they reached the theatre itself. It was a broad vaulting chamber, with side alcoves converted to bars. Iron-caged oil-lamps on the walls complemented the small lighting strip at the apex of the ceiling. Edeard gave the glass bulbs a wary gaze. The far end of the cellar had a wooden stage, where the guitarist was struggling against the hearty voices of everyone crammed together on the main floor.

Kristabel took her coat off. Those nearest to her cast curious glances as they saw the pearl-encrusted blue silk gown she wore. Then Edeard shrugged out of his cloak, showing off his black and scarlet dress jacket with silver brocade and snow-white ruff shirt. There were a great many surprised grins.

'Hey-ho, the dandies have arrived,' Macsen called out loudly.

Kristabel grinned, and hugged Macsen. Then Dinlay appeared, shoving a drink at Edeard. Boyd was laughing delightedly in greeting. Saria embraced Kristabel. A merrily drunk Kanseen gave Edeard a big kiss.

'What kept you?' Dinlay demanded. He had his arm around the shoulders of a strapping girl whose flaming red hair reached down to her waist. Edeard struggled to make no comment; Dinlay always seemed to wind up with girls at least as big as himself.

'It was a good party,' Edeard said loyally.

Kristabel laughed, and stroked his cheek. 'My poor boy,' she said. 'He was so brave,' she explained to the squad. 'All of Daddy's friends simply had to talk to him during dinner, and they're all as old and dull as him; then all their daughters wanted a dance afterwards.'

Edeard gave Boyd a helpless shrug. 'This whole price of fame thing.'

'Never mind,' Macsen said eagerly. 'It will only ever be temporary. In ten years you'll be a fading memory, just some trivia question in a parlour game on New Year's Eve.'

Edeard kissed Kristabel. 'You see, my loyalty training is finally working.' She laughed and hugged him back. It was so easy, so natural. They both smiled happily at each other. Perfectly at ease. Edeard knew it wouldn't be long now, and the anticipation was a soothing warmth right in his heart. Nothing like the other girls he'd taken to bed where it was like he was in some kind of competition, nor even the cosy comfort of Jessile. Kristabel and him was going to be as perfect as two people could be together.

'Here he is,' Dinlay yelled.

Up on stage Dybal ambled into view. A huge cheer went up from the audience as he waved. The rest of the band made their way on stage, three drummers, a saxophonist, a pianist, and two more guitarists. It might have been the haze of the Jamolar oil, or the quantity of very good wine Edeard had consumed back at the party, but Dybal and his band seemed to glow in bright colours. Their clothes were truly outrageous, and for that alone Edeard joined in the rapturous greeting.

The songs were fast and loud, the complete opposite of the tunes the musicians had played during the party. Lyrics spoke of love and loss, treachery and corruption, derided and mocked the Council. They were angry. They were sad. Music pounded Dybal's words home. Edeard and Kristabel danced wildly. They drank. He even took a drag on a couple of kestric pipes that were passed round. So did Kristabel, her mind radiating impious delight as she inhaled.

Dybal played for over an hour. Long enough for Edeard to be drenched in sweat. The theatre walls were running with condensation by the time he finished his second encore.

'That was fabulous,' Kristabel said as she hugged Edeard. 'I can't believe the Council is still in power. Viva the revolution!' She punched her fist in the air.

He hugged her back, and touched his nose to hers. 'That's your own father you're talking about.'

'Who cares!' She twirled around. 'Thank you for bringing me.'

'I've been wanting to hear Dybal for a long time.'

'Why didn't you?'

Edeard shrugged. Around them, people were heading for the steps back up to the street, all of them tired and happy.

'I didn't want to come alone,' he said.

The smile she answered with made the risk of such honesty worthwhile.

*

As soon as they came back out on to Doulon Lane, the squad went their various ways, calling goodnight to each other. There were very few people on the street at this late hour. Edeard buttoned up his cloak again before putting his arm around Kristabel. She leant in against him, her mind showing him complete contentment. They walked back towards the pool at the end of Garden Canal with the nebulas painting pale colours against the night sky. It might have been the residue of kestric but they seemed to have a lustrous sparkle as Edeard gazed up at them. Honious particularly tonight was beset by internal shimmering.

'You often do that,' Kristabel said.

'What?'

'Look at the nebulas.'

'Do I? I suppose I just wonder how much we really do know about them.'

'I can name most of them.'

'Ah yes, but that's not knowing, is it? What are they really? Do you think our souls are destined to drift among them?'

'The Lady says that's what befalls us if we don't lead a life that holds us true to ourselves.'

'Yeah,' he said grumpily as he thought back to those interminable Sunday mornings as a small boy at the back of Ashwell's church, with Mother Lorellan reading from the Lady's scriptures in a drab monotone. *And who decides what true is?*

Kristabel just pressed harder against him, humouring the strange doubts flecking his thoughts.

Her private gondola was moored at a platform on the edge of the pool, with a lamp swinging from the frame of the little canvas cabin. There wasn't much room inside. Edeard and Kristabel had to snuggle up close on the bench. She pulled a fur rug up round their legs. As the gondolier set off up Garden Canal, they began to kiss. He ran his hand through her abundant hair, tasting her lips, then her cheeks, her neck, returning to her mouth. She moaned excitably, her mind enraptured. Even their thoughts seemed to merge.

Eventually she pulled back, giving him the most tender smile he'd ever seen on her delicate face.

'What?' he asked. There was no way he could possibly have misunderstood her feelings. Few of the girls he'd know had ever been as open as Kristabel.

'I'm ready for this,' she murmured sensually. 'And I know you are.'

'Oh yes,' he assured her.

'It's just—'

'Your father?'

'No, Daddy actually approves of you. He's not quite as traditional as he comes across.'

Edeard couldn't help the grin of disbelief creeping across his face. 'I know.'

'I think we both know this isn't going to be some casual affair.'

'Yes.' There was some echo of what she said that tickled at his subconscious, which he dismissed.

'So I want this to be right.'

'It will be.'

She kissed him lightly. 'It's very late. We've both been partying. You have patrol duty at seven tomorrow. None of that is good.'

'Okay?'

'I know you had a bad experience with Ranalee, but the family has a beach lodge outside the city. It's really lovely. I would like us to go there. Just you and me. For a week.'

He was incredibly sensitive to the feel of her pressed up against him. Her whispered yearnings and the candid desire in her mind were affecting him with the same potency as any of the illicit fires Ranalee's dominance had kindled. 'Yes,' he breathed harshly.

'Would you like that?'

'Yes.' His throat was so tight he could barely get the word out. 'Yes, I would like that.'

'I don't want to pressure you into a week with me. I will go back to your maisonette with you now if you'd prefer.'

'No. The beach lodge sounds wonderful.'

'Really?' Her cheek rubbed up against him. 'Thank you. Thank you for giving us this chance.'

The gondola turned along Flight Canal, and headed down towards High Pool. They didn't even kiss any more. Their faces rested against each other while they smiled. Edeard looked straight into her eyes and mind, relishing everything he saw. The eagerness, the physical yearning, the excitement that twinned anticipation. The adoration. It was all mirrored, he knew; exactly what she could sense in his own mind. The openness was . . . *sweet*.

Homelt was standing on the ziggurat mansion's landing platform. He grinned as Kristabel climbed out of the gondola.

'Good morning, Mistress. Did you have a nice time?'

She flashed him a warm smile. 'Yes, thank you, a very nice time.'

Homelt looked down at Edeard, who tried to keep a straight face and failed dismally. He nodded briskly.

'Is my father still up?'

'No, Mistress, he went to bed several hours ago. There's only myself and the night-guards awake now.'

'I see. Well, good night, Waterwalker.'

'Goodnight, Mistress.'

Homelt gave them a surprised look, then escorted Kristabel up the wooden stairs into the mansion.

'Can you be ready for next Tuesday?' Kristabel's longtalk asked.

Edeard didn't even think of the mountain of work and schedules he'd have to reorganize. And a week from Tuesday was the graduation ceremony, which he *could not* miss. It would be tight. 'I will be. Whatever it takes.'

'I'll hold you to that.'

He caught one last glimpse of her atop the stairs. Smiling in expectation. It was, he reflected, an enchanting smile. Macsen had been right about her beauty after all.

The gondolier simply took him over to the other side of Flight Canal where he could walk home through Silvarum into Jeavons. There were two exceptionally bored and sleepy constables standing guard on the bridge over Arrival Canal. Both were startled to see Edeard at that time in the morning, but he stopped for a moment to speak with them. The correct thing to do politically, as Finitan had drilled him, create goodwill and support at every opportunity for you never know when you might need it.

Politics, as he had learned, could never be ignored in Makkathran, not at any level. It was Finitan's clever play which had exploited the kidnapping to get the result they needed in the Grand Council following the Festival of Guidance. It was also politics which had prevented the Gondoliers from going on strike as they'd threatened, for that would have made it look as if they were siding with the kidnappers. For now, the city remained on his side. He knew it wouldn't last, that there would be other attempts to subvert the Council, to turn his supporters away from the exclusion warrants. In all probability, those efforts would never end. He had to remain vigilant, which he was trying his hardest to do.

Kristabel, though, seemed to be filling his mind these days. He thought of her when he should be concentrating on duty rotas or meetings with District Masters or sniffing out the gang masters. He thought of her when he got up. He thought of her when he was out on patrol, remembering her laugh, the way she looked, her scent, the trivial things of which they spoke. And when he finally did get a few free hours at the end of each day and could be with her, she simply filled his whole world.

Now this. They were finally to become lovers in the truest sense.

When he eventually got back to his maisonette and lay on the bed there were only a few hours until dawn when he was supposed to lead a patrol through Jeavons and round Tycho.

Rather than sleeping as he should, his mind was awhirl with how to rearrange duty periods so he could spend next week away. That and how she'd felt pressed against him in the gondola. Her smile. The promise. It would be difficult for the squad to cover for him; though he no longer cared. Makkathran could fall into oblivion now. He and Kristabel were to be lovers. It was hard to believe; he'd never been so happy before.

In one respect, Kristabel and Ranalee were very similar; their notion of 'just us' was one which could only ever apply to a daughter from a Grand Family. Admittedly, Kristabel only brought three of her personal staff, not five, but the wagon which accompanied their carriage was heavily laden with luggage cases and hampers of food. And of course there was the team of coachmen, and the wagon drivers, each with their own apprentices. In addition there were the ge-wolf handlers, which Homelt had assigned to them for the road.

He wouldn't have minded that so much if they'd simply been able to go. But first there were all her (rather too giggly, he felt) girl friends they simply had to say goodbye to as they left the Culverit mansion. Poor Mirnatha was distraught that her sister and the Waterwalker were leaving her behind, acting as if the separation was forever – so she had to be promised presents and treats on their return. He also had to shake hands with her father and swear no harm would befall his precious daughter; and that was while Lorin was watching impassively from a balcony above.

Edeard had arrived at the mansion with his one bag shortly after breakfast. The coach didn't pull out of the family stables in Tycho until just before midday. Kristabel sat straight-backed on the cushioned bench opposite him, her hair woven into a broad beret with little corkscrew curls dangling down. Simply sitting quietly she carried herself with the kind of imperious nature that Ranalee forever sought yet would never be able to achieve.

'You were impatient,' she said loftily. 'I had to rush my leave-taking, it was almost rude. Was there some reason you wished to hurry?'

He just managed to maintain his composure. 'No, Mistress.'

'Really? I will enjoy testing the limit of your anticipation this evening.'

'Even your cruelty is a joy, Mistress.'

Kristabel managed to keep a straight face for another few seconds, then she was laughing wildly. 'Oh Lady, I thought they were never going to let us get away!' She launched herself at him, and they spent the rest of the journey cuddled together.

The south road out of the city was as well maintained as all the roads across the Iguru. Twice they passed militia patrols, which had recently been increased to compensate for the growing numbers of highwaymen waylaying travellers. Edeard suspected such incidents were due to the way his own exclusion campaign was squeezing the gangs out of city districts. A number of those named in the warrants had simply left. Apart from that, their trip along the coastal route was without incident. The tall palms lining the road had survived the winter, and were now shedding their scarlet fronds to make way for the new season's emerald growth. Fields on either side were being readied for the summer crops, with large teams of ge-monkeys preparing the vines and citrus groves and fruit gardens, while ge-horses pulled heavy ploughs. This time of year always cheered Edeard up, reminding him of more carefree times during his childhood. Everyone's mood improved with the onset of spring.

He hadn't known what to expect when they reached the beach lodge. Best guess was a pavilion like the one Ranalee's family owned. He only started to suspect something different when Kristabel opened the carriage windows, and watched him with mischievous intent. They were no longer riding through fields. The land outside had transformed to gritty hummocks smothered by long reedy grass with shrivelled wind-bowed trees huddled in the lees. Ahead of them the track wound down into a modest cove, with promontories of dark rock. A small stream gurgled alongside. Then he saw it, standing back from the white beach, just behind the crumbling sandy bluff.

'Oh, my Lady,' he gasped in delight. Kristabel squeezed his

hand in shared glee. 'I always loved this place,' she sighed wistfully.

The lodge was a half-living sculpture. Five ancient muroaks had been planted in a circle, then pruned and guided for decades. Their first boughs were three yards above the ground, woven into a platform and reinforced with sturdy planks to form a level floor. But it was the wall which fascinated Edeard. Above the floor, the trunks had been allowed to fork, then fork again. As they'd done so, master gardeners had trained them into tall arches, before bending them back towards the apex when they'd all been twisted together into a final whorl of bark and branches that opened out to shade the lodge from the summer sun. It would need that shade, he realized, for the wall arches were filled with glass. A slender open deck encircled the entire lodge.

The coach stopped outside, and Kristabel led Edeard up the curving wooden stairs to the door where the lodge keeper was waiting for them. The old man bowed deeply, welcoming Kristabel as if she were his own family.

Edeard examined the wall's thick archway pillars, marvelling at the buds of green leaves that were starting to open amid the wrinkles of grey bark, seeing how the stubby twigs were meticulously pruned every autumn. In another month, the entire lodge would appear to be lead-framed panes of glass supported by lines of verdant leaves.

'It's astonishing,' he said. 'I didn't know people could create something like this.' He couldn't imagine anything like it in Ashwell, nor any of the towns he'd passed through on his way to the city.

'Two hundred and eighty years in the growing,' the lodge keeper said proudly. 'It was my great-grandfather who originally planted the trees. Our family have tended them for the Culverits ever since; and my son will take over when I pass on.'

'Two hundred and eighty years to grow,' Edeard repeated, impressed.

'Makkathran makes us lazy,' Kristabel said. 'It provides us with so much. We can get things right by ourselves.'

Inside, the lodge was divided up into seven rooms by ancient wooden panelling. The central room, under the knot of trunks, was the bedroom, with a big circular bed in the middle. An ingenious array of pulleys and twine allowed slatted blinds to be opened or closed against the overhead windows. A thick slab of stone in the living room acted as a hearth for a tall brazier. It already had a fire crackling away, its smoke slithering up through an iron chimney cone.

Edeard and Kristabel sat on the long settee, staring out at the sea a couple of hundred yards away. He wished it was slightly later in the year, when it would be warm enough to swim. A big twin-masted trading ship sailed slowly past, en route to the ports in the south. The servants and ge-monkeys bustled round, setting out their luggage while the lodge keeper lit the iron stove in the kitchen to boil some tea. Kristabel's fingers laced through Edeard's. 'Don't worry,' she said dryly. 'They'll all stay in the cottages behind the bluff. Out of farsight range. I wouldn't want to shock them tonight; some have been with the family for decades.'

Edeard grinned, remembering Ranalee saying more or less the same thing. He turned back to the sea.

By coincidence, the Culverit family's beach lodge was only a couple of miles south of the cove where Ivarl's body had washed up. Edeard remembered that morning quite clearly. A week after the Festival of Guidance he'd received the message from the coastal warden asking him to identify the body. He borrowed a terrestrial horse from the militia stables, and rode out through the south gate.

The sea and the rocks had not been kind to Ivarl. Edeard had never seen what water did to a corpse before. The bloating surprised him, as did the sallow colour of the skin. Even so, there was no doubt it was the gang lord.

'Never seen anything like this,' the old coastal warden said.

Edeard's farsight probed at the cords which still bound Ivarl's wrists and ankles. There was something appallingly elegant about the perfectly wound cords, the complicated knots – so inconsistent with the ugliness of death, especially this one. He'd counted nine deep puncture wounds before giving up. Ivarl had not been allowed to die quickly or peacefully.

His adversary's killing bothered Edeard a great deal more than the kidnapping did. If for no other reason than it demonstrated there was some kind of organization stirring in the city of which he had no clear understanding. Despite investigating Ivarl's closest lieutenants, they'd never managed to determine who'd killed him. Then again, Edeard found himself wondering about Ivarl's soul. Had it fled the body in the same fashion he'd sensed down in the cellar when Mirnatha's kidnapper had died? That souls were real disturbed him more than he cared to consciously admit.

That night Kristabel banished all his doubts and concerns.

The family servants might have been outside farsight range, but he was convinced they'd be woken by his cries of joy.

In the morning they dressed in plain white robes and ate breakfast on the little deck which ringed the main lodge. A warm breeze swirled around them, making Kristabel's wild hair sway about. After she'd finished her bluegrape segments, she called her maid over to brush the tangles out and arrange it for the day. Edeard settled back as the girl began her task, and told the ge-chimps to clear his plates. Out to sea, three sets of sails were passing between the rock wings of the cove. He envied the sailors their freedom. 'I'd like to do that one day,' he declared. 'When the gangs are no more, and the bandits have vanished back into the wilderness, we should take a ship and sail around the world.'

'Nobody has ever found a way through the southern ice flows.'

'Then we go north.'

'Through the atolls of the Auguste Sea? Lady, Edeard, they have reefs which stretch for hundreds of miles. The whole sea is a treacherous maze that can rip the hull off any unfortunate ship that drifts too close to the coral.'

'Then we use a strong third hand to break the reef; or farsight and ge-eagles to find a way out of the maze. That's my point, no one has ever really tried. We don't know what else is on this world other than bandits. What if other ships fell here on a different continent or island? What if they kept the science which built those ships?'

'Then they would have probably found us by now,' she said as her maid finished applying jewelled clips.

'Oh. Yes. But still, what fun it would be to explore properly.'

'I suppose it would be. I never really have time to think such things.'

'I can't believe no one in Makkathran has attempted to do this. The families have such money as could build the most wonderful ships, and there are so many bored sons. Don't any of them look beyond the horizon?'

'Many do, but all they're looking for are girls with suitable dowries. Nobody thinks in those terms, Edeard, not any more. The last person to attempt such a voyage was Captain Allard, and that was over a thousand years ago. He was the Havane family's second son, who built exactly the kind of ship you talk about, the *Majestic Marie*. Makkathran had never seen its like before, nor have we since. It was a real galleon, over two hundred feet long, and had three masts. Eighty men set sail on her, all of them experienced sailors, with the best equipment Makkathran's Guilds could produce. They never came back. Allard's wife went on to live past her two hundredth birthday; every day she went down to the docks to ask the newly arrived ships if they'd seen her husband. The watching widow, they called her. They say her soul still haunts the docks even today.'

Edeard gave the sea another longing look. 'I never got to know history like that when I grew up, not real history. It was all about who built which farmhouse or Guild centre, and when their families arrived in the province. Lady, it was so dull.'

'You poor thing.' She reached out and gripped his arm. 'So where did you learn to sail?'

Edeard flushed slightly. 'I haven't. Not yet.'

Kristabel burst out laughing. 'You can't sail, and you want to voyage around the world? Oh Edeard, this is why I love you so. You have such wild visions. You make it sound like anything can happen.'

He grinned sheepishly. 'I have to deal with the gangs first. Then when I've time, I'll learn to sail.'

'Well, be careful of pirates,' she eyed the ships offshore suspiciously. 'Our captains are reporting more sightings. They don't pick on the larger ships yet, but small vessels have started to disappear.'

'At least no one can blame me for that.'

'Why should they?'

'The highwaymen are mostly gang members driven out of the city by the exclusion warrants. They're very difficult to catch.'

'Let the town sheriffs and the militia deal with them. It's about time other people started to help deal with criminals instead of looking to Makkathran to do everything for them. That's one attitude I'd like to see changed.'

Edeard gave her a proud smile. 'The Grand Council won't know what hit it when you arrive.'

'And that's another thing. Why should the families practise primogeniture? In this day and age! Do they think I'm not good enough?'

'They're fools,' Edeard said promptly.

'You have your ambitions,' she said primly. 'I have mine.'

'Time will see us triumph.'

'Lady, you're even beginning to sound like Finitan. We need to get your mind off such things.' She stood up and held a hand out. 'Come on.'

Edeard let her lead him down on to the sand. The grains surged round his bare feet in a pleasant shifting sensation.

'I won't ask you to do *that* by the way,' Kristabel said. 'I imagine you get tired of people pestering you for it.'

'What?'

She gestured at the low waves rolling ashore. 'Walk over it.'

'Oh. Thank you.'

They carried on towards the sea. Kristabel undid the belt

holding her robe, allowing it to flow free from her shoulders. The sight of her trim body in the daylight was very arousing. She kept on walking.

'Uh, isn't it a bit cold to go swimming?' he asked lightly.

She gave him a curious frown. 'Not here. The water around the city is always several degrees warmer that the rest of the sea in these parts. It's something to do with heat seeping through the bedrock, which makes the water nutrient-rich. That's why Makkathran and the coastal villages have so many shellfish boats.'

'And of course everybody knows that,' he said with rising exasperation.

'Well, yes.' She put her hands on her hips. It might have been intended as a taunt, but all she achieved was an extremely erotic pose as her robe fluttered behind her. 'Why?'

'One day, I would like to dump you and my squadmates into the middle of Rulan province. Then it would be my turn to laugh while you all ate poison berries and fell into drakken pits and failed to light a campfire or get your fingers stuck picking gache fungi. Just once. So you all know what it's like.'

Kristabel straightened her neck, and sucked in her cheeks. 'You came to live in the city. I have no intention of ever going to live in the countryside.'

'Oh really?' He took a step towards her.

'Dreadful place. No culture and very smelly.' She held fast for a moment as Edeard stared in outrage, then turned and ran giggling into the water. Edeard flung his robe aside on to the sands and charged after her.

Kristabel was right, the water was slightly warmer than he'd been dreading. That didn't exactly make it warm enough to enjoy a good leisurely swim. But he managed to catch up and grab her. They both tumbled over into the waves, laughing exuberantly.

'This would be a good time to teach me how to make a fire outdoors,' Kristabel said through chattering teeth.

Edeard had given her his robe after they came out of the sea; but it didn't help warm her much. His own skin was covered in goosebumps as they walked up the sands towards the bluff.

'Very well,' he said with dignity. He reached out with his third hand and gathered broken branches and chunks of driftwood. Kristabel clapped merrily as they whirled through the air and began to pile up in a hollow at the base of the bluff. 'Now, see, we need some dry leaves at the centre,' he explained meticulously as his third hand bunched some fragile brown gorelow leaves together. 'And these trinpine spines are really useful, too, they catch easily.' He squatted down beside the wood to make sure the tinder was positioned just right. Kristabel knelt down beside him, her mind shielded, but wearing an expression of deadly earnest. 'So now I just need some flints.' Two suitable stones leapt up out of the sand and flew towards him. 'You have to spark them fast, and direct the sparks with your third hand so they always hit the same spot. At the same time you stir a gentle flow of air where they hit. But not too much, because that will blow it out. Learning to use just the right amount is tricky.' He twisted round to take hold of the stones with his flesh and blood hands. There was a peculiar silver glimmer of light behind him. 'Huh?' he turned back to see the tinder burning brightly.

'Oooh,' Kristabel cooed. 'That was so impressive, Waterwalker. A girl knows she'll always be provided for when you go hunter-gathering in the wild.'

'How did you . . . ?'

There was a diabolical gleam in her eyes and mind. She held up her hand. Cold white flame scintillated along her fingers and arched across into the base of the wood.

'Oh.' Despite the chill, he was blushing hotly.

Kristabel nearly fell over she was laughing so hard. Her words had to be forced out. 'You are so easy to tease. Really.'

'Obviously.'

'Darling Edeard,' she stroked his cheek. 'I'm sorry.' Then she swayed forward, unable to stop laughing.

It was no use, he couldn't stay angry with her. His petulance gave way to a rueful grin. 'Yeah, but that trick won't help you with gache fungi,' he informed her.

She swarmed into his lap, and twined her hands round his neck. Her smile rivalled the noonday sun. 'If I ever get attacked by legions of gache fungi, I promise in the Lady's name I will do everything you tell me from that day onwards, and I'll never laugh at you again.'

'Okay. Now show me how you do the fire trick.'

'I'm not supposed to; the families like it kept quiet.'

'Think of it as the start of the revolution.'

She kissed him. 'All right.' Her mind gifted him the technique.

It was actually quite simple, he thought, as he examined the knowledge. Squeezing a little stream of air, and spinning it very fast at the same time to create a big static charge. 'Easy!' He lifted his arm up, and let his telekinetic strength agitate the air around it. A blinding flash spat out, fanning wide to punch into the loose pile of wood. A ball of flame bloomed around the branches with a severe *thud*. Several flaming sticks twirled though the air, trailing smoke. Edeard and Kristabel ducked.

'By the Lady, Edeard!' she exclaimed. Her mouth gaped in surprise.

The bonfire was now blazing furiously. Kristabel laughed again.

'That's better,' he said as the flames shot even higher. 'I'm starting to warm up now.'

Kristabel still had her hands behind his neck; she arched her spine, falling backwards to pull him down on top of her. 'Me too.'

Edeard gave the beach lodge a mildly guilty glance, then grinned lewdly. 'I always heard sex on the beach is the absolute best.' His third hand unfastened her belt.

The legend, he discovered, was quite right; sex on the beach was spectacular.

As soon as the night fell on the second day they went back to the bed in the middle of the lodge. Long after the candles had spluttered and died, Edeard lay on the bed watching the nebulas twinkle and sway across the night sky. He smiled languidly, yet sleep refused to claim him. 'How far away are they?'

Kristabel peeked up at the ceiling. 'Are you still watching the nebulas? I don't know. A long, long way.'

'Do our souls reach them without guidance from the Skylords?'

'I can't remember exactly what the Lady's teachings say. I think it's difficult for souls once they've been cast adrift from their old bodies. They just sort of float away through space.'

'Lost. That's why we need the Skylords.'

'Yes,' she grinned and cuddled closer. 'You see, you know more than I do. You must be very devout.'

'Hardly. I can barely remember that much. But how did the Lady know?'

'Because the Firstlifes told her, or the Skylords told her what the Firstlifes said. I can't remember which. Though the Firstlifes would know, they're the ones who created the universe.'

'This Void. The ships that brought us here came from outside.'

'They certainly came from somewhere else.'

'If they fell here from the other side of the sky, then they must have passed through the nebulas.'

'I suppose so.'

'Then they would have known exactly what they were like. Why didn't they stay there, in Odin's Sea? The Lady says it is the doorway to the Heart, where souls live for ever in unity and bliss.'

'The ships were falling. They couldn't stay.'

'They fell onto Querencia. While they are in the sky, ships fly. The people inside them control where they go, just as captains set course in our traders.'

Kristabel propped herself up. He could only see the darkest outline of her, while her soft hair brushed against his chest.

'Why are you asking these questions?'

'We have souls, Kristabel. I've sensed them. When I shot Mirnatha's kidnapper, my farsight watched his soul take flight.'

'On its way to Honious,' she growled.

'Not if it just drifts around the sky.'

'Edeard,' she asked tentatively, 'are you mocking me?'

'No!' he promised. 'Never. I just don't understand why the Skylords have abandoned us. What do we do to call them back?'

'The Lady says we have to be true to ourselves.'

'Most people are, aren't they? I know so many who were. Decent honest folk who died. Are their souls all lost?' *Is Akeem alone and astray somewhere in the sky? Is Melzar? Obron?* For some reason he didn't want to examine, he suddenly thought of Salrana. Salrana who was working conscientiously in Ufford's hospital, waiting for the day she returned to Makkathran – and him. She'd devoted her life to the Lady, and she was decent. *Certainly more than I am. Would her soul be lost in the Void?* Such thoughts made him very uncomfortable, and for more than one reason. *I really ought to write to her, explain I have found Kristabel. But I would never want to hear such news from a letter. Lady!*

'I don't know, Edeard,' Kristabel said, 'and that's the truth. If you want answers to such notions you'll have to ask a Mother. I can get you an appointment with the Pythia herself if you like. We're related, distantly.'

'No. I'm sorry. My thoughts are wondering tonight, that's all.' He tried to put the memories of Salrana away. *I'll deal with that in an honourable way when she returns.*

He felt her hair shift across him. Her fingers stroked his cheek. 'I thought I'd managed to calm you.'

'You did. I am so completely exhausted my mind is in a daze, that's why I'm being so stupid.'

'Do you want to make love to me again?'

He smiled up into the darkness where he knew her face to be. 'I can't actually move right now, let alone do that.'

'You'd better recover by tomorrow.'

'I'll go to sleep now, I promise. I'll be ready for you again tomorrow night.'

'Tomorrow morning,' she said sharply.

'Yes, Mistress.'

Kristabel, he discovered as she woke him at daybreak, wasn't joking.

During the days they walked along the coast, exploring neighbouring coves and beaches. Sometimes they'd take a swim, then warm themselves afterwards making love in the dunes. Kristabel especially took a delicious thrill at the prospect of being discovered by some estate worker or housekeeper. Obliging her wasn't exactly difficult for him.

On the fourth afternoon they walked back along the lodge's track, surveying the fields and groves that spread back from the small strip of wild ground that ran behind the shore. The coast line was a series of rugged coves reaching almost the entire way back to the city. Many of the larger ones were dominated by villages that had extended or adapted the curving cliffs to make harbours for their fishing fleets. The rest had been incorporated into the estates of Makkathran's Grand Families, who had built pavilions or lodges where their younger generations could idle away the summer.

Further south, the land dipped to become a saltwater swamp before rising again at the end of the Iguru. Then the Bruneau Mountains stood up to fence off the arid southern plains. Towns and farmland continued to cling to the coast as it curved eastwards all the way down to Charyau, Querencia's southernmost city, just past the equator.

'They say you have to wear long clothes all year round there,' Kristabel said as they stood on top of a tall hummock, gazing southwards. On the horizon they could just make out the snow-tipped peaks of the Bruneau range. 'The sun is so strong it shrivels your skin, especially if you're not used to it.'

'Do they have stories of anyone else sharing our world?' Edeard asked. 'Perhaps strange ships that they've sighted at a distance out at sea?'

'No. Our ships trade with them all the time, and their schooners regularly make port in Makkathran. If there were any stories like that, we'd hear them.' She tilted her head to one side. 'You're so interested in what lies beyond our reach. Why?'

'I'm just curious about the world, that's all.' He didn't want to tell her his main interest was discovering where the rapid-firing guns were produced. 'Doesn't it even bother you that we don't actually have a complete map of Querencia? The ships that brought Rah and the Lady must have seen what it looked like before they landed. Why didn't any survive?'

'There you go again, thinking differently. What you said makes perfect sense, but no one else ever makes that kind of connection.'

'Is that so bad?'

'No, but it does mark you out. I'd love to understand why you think the way you do.'

'Just the way I am, I suppose.' *And the things I see in my dreams.*

'I wish I'd met your parents. I'm sorry if that sounds selfish, but they must have been very special people. Do you remember anything of them?'

'Very little,' he sighed. 'Akeem told me my mother arrived in Ashwell from another province. He said she was beautiful, and smart. All the men vied for her hand, but she only ever wanted my father. Actually, he'd only been there twenty years himself, so I don't suppose he counted as a local. He had a farm outside the village. It was a big place, or at least I thought so; I remember it having furniture that was very grand compared to the other houses. I don't know why. We couldn't have earned more than the other farmers. Akeem said Father didn't get involved very much with Ashwell. I can't say I blame him for that.'

'I didn't want to stir up anything that would hurt you.'

'It doesn't. They died a long time ago, I stopped grieving years ago. I hate the bandits who killed them, but Akeem was a true father to me. I was lucky to know him.'

Kristabel put her arm through his, and they made their way down the hillock. 'There are bandits everywhere,' she said. 'In many forms. People who prey on the bounty that others have worked hard for. The gangs are no different.'

'I know. That's what angers me about them, just that they exist. And worse, that people accept their existence.'

'I think our gangs are smarter than your bandits; they've managed to ingrain themselves in our lives.'

'City and country again?'

'Almost. Though they seem to share the same brutality and hatred. They're broken people, Edeard. That's why they do what they do.'

'Are you saying we should show them sympathy?'

'I don't know what must be done.' She stroked his face, gazing sympathetically at him. 'You do understand everyone is expecting you to provide that answer, don't you?'

'I don't have an answer. That's the Grand Council's job.'

'They will blame you if no solution comes forward. Can't you hear their voices: you began this, you came to the District Masters with this notion. You excluded gang members from some districts, and forced them into others. Why should those districts suffer at the expense of others? What will you do to get rid of the threat you highlighted, and you went to war against?'

'Oh, Lady,' he groaned.

'You have to find something, Edeard, some way out.'

'There isn't one.'

'There is at least one, and you know it. Banishment. Permanent banishment from the crystal walls. Exclude them from the whole city.'

'That'll never happen, Master Bise won't allow that to happen in Sampalok for a start.'

'Honious take Bise. You've got a huge political momentum growing behind you. Exclusion has been seen to work. You have to carry it forward. If you hesitate now, you'll lose that momentum.'

'Banishment? You're not serious?' His mind went back to the

morning of the kidnapping, and how he'd been berated by Eddis's wife. 'Where would they all go?'

'I can see how much this troubles you, but I think you're wrong to worry so. This is one time that imagination of yours is leading you astray. You're visualizing whole city districts being forced out at gunpoint. Edeard, the real trouble is caused by a couple of hundred people at best. I remember the night Daddy signed the exclusion warrants for Haxpen; you gave him four hundred and eighteen. That's everybody, Edeard, every gang member you can find. That number is nothing compared to our total population, they're so small they're not even a minority. Get rid of the gang masters and their lieutenants, and the rest will be lost. They'll rejoin society. They won't love you, but at least they won't be causing the kind of trouble they do today.'

'I suppose so. But where will the masters go? That's just giving someone else our problem.'

'Look,' Kristabel said forcefully, and held her arms out, twirling round to gesture at the entirety of the landscape. 'I'll make Daddy loan you the biggest ship in our fleet, and you can take them to the furthest atoll we can navigate to; or we'll buy them fifty wagons and lead their caravan into the wilds beyond Rulan. Let them build their own houses and grow their own food. Edeard! You're not responsible for them, not afterwards. You are a city constable, a position that was regarded with utter scorn before you arrived. You made us all feel safe again, you gave us hope. Don't falter now. Makkathran cannot afford your doubts.'

He stared at her in awe.

She shifted round discomfited. 'What?'

'You are so incredible. I can't believe you even notice someone like me.'

Kristabel looked at the ground. 'But I do.'

'Makkathran is lucky to have you.'

'I won't be a figurehead for the family, a mere caretaker between Daddy and my firstborn, someone who just votes for

whatever the Mayor says. I will make a difference,' she said
fiercely.

'I know you will.'

Their last night in the beach lodge together was one Edeard
never wanted to end. Again, when the candles had long died
Edeard sprawled over the bed staring upwards as his thoughts
slowly came together in realization. Not least, what Kristabel had
said to him throughout the week, in so many ways, none of
which had really registered before. She lay beside him now, her
arm across his chest, head nuzzled into the crook of his neck,
one leg over his. It was where she belonged. For eternity.

'I love you,' he said in wonder

Edeard was dreading his return to Makkathran. Some part of
his brain enacted the beautiful fantasy of them staying in the
beach lodge forever. It wasn't just their physical union, though
Kristabel was all he had ever imagined a lover could ever be. He
didn't want anything to break the perfection of the week they'd
spent together.

'I don't want to leave either,' she said at breakfast on their
last day.

'I suppose we have to go back,' he said grouchily.

'We do, and don't sulk.'

'I wasn't – sorry.'

'You say that too much, as well.'

'Thanks.'

'I have a present for you,' she said, and instructed a ge-
monkey to bring in one of her cases.

Edeard hadn't noticed it among all the other cases. For
someone who'd spent most of the week naked or clad in wisps
of silk and lace, she seemed to require a vast wardrobe. Now he
leaned over with interest as she opened it, and held up the jacket
inside.

'A proper uniform for you,' Kristabel said. 'I can't have my man looking ordinary at the ceremony, now can I? Not on this day. The day.'

Edeard took the jacket from her, admiring the cut and the seriously black fabric. It was a standard constable's dress tunic, but at the same time so much more stylish. Kristabel produced some matching trousers from the case, and a white shirt, belt, tie.

'Thank you so much,' he said, then his mood dropped. 'I don't have anything for you.'

She gave him a strange look, almost as if he'd said something hurtful. 'That's because you don't have any money. And that's good, because that's not what I'm looking for in a man.'

'You're wonderful.' He kissed her.

'We don't have time, we have to be back in the city by midday. Go and put it on.'

'We could spare a few minutes,' he suggested hopefully.

Her finger pointed to the bedroom door. 'Go and put it on.'

Edeard did as he was told. It fitted perfectly, and as he studied himself in the mirror he couldn't help the very self-satisfied smile splashed across his face. He did look great.

'Oh, Lady,' Kristabel murmured huskily from the doorway. 'There really is something about men in uniform.'

'The tailor got my size just right, was he spying on me?'

Kristabel's eyebrow raised a fraction. 'I know your exact size,' she purred. 'Now come on, we need to get going.'

Strangely enough, when they did get back to the city he was cheered by the sight of it. The raucous babble of thoughts and longtalk spilling out from the human minds was a reassuring presence. Then there was the familiarity of the buildings and streets and canals. The way no one paid any attention to them as they walked back from the stables, not even bothering with a seclusion haze.

'I'm home,' he decided as the gondola took them along Grand Central Canal to the Orchard Palace.

His squadmates were waiting for him in the Malfit Hall, and gave him a hearty greeting.

'Look at this!' Macsen exclaimed, tugging at Edeard's splendid new uniform. He glanced at Kristabel, who was chatting away to Kanseen. 'Anything to *announce*?'

Edeard frowned. 'No. We had a lovely time. And I'm certainly not giving you lot any details.'

Macsen and Boyd both shook their heads in despair.

'Still the country boy,' Macsen said sadly.

'What?'

'And have we got some news for you!' Dinlay said proudly.

'What?' Edeard repeated dumbly.

'After the ceremony,' Kanseen taunted. 'It needs time to explain.'

'Come on,' Macsen said. 'We'd better grab our seats while we still can.'

At Edeard's graduation ceremony the block of seats had taken up less than a fifth of the available floorspace. Today, some families who'd come to watch their sons and daughters graduate had to stand around the walls.

As before, Mayor Owain appeared at the top of the grand stairs, flanked by the District Masters and the Guild Masters. As they descended to the floor, the giant roof above displayed Querencia's sister planets drifting through another exquisite dawn of wispy gold-tinged clouds.

Owain began his little speech on the makeshift platform. Edeard, who was near the back of the hall, looked along the line of Masters behind the Mayor. This time they all looked attentive, as if gauging the mood of the audience. Their tenseness was a contrast to the excitement and satisfaction of the new constables and their families. Then he saw Bise, whose long face was rigid with animosity; he was staring directly back at Edeard. For a second Edeard was taken aback by the loathing he saw and sensed. He composed himself, and matched the Master's hostility with cool indifference.

Loud applause broke out as the first probationer stepped up to the platform, and Owain awarded him his epaulettes. Edeard applauded politely throughout the ceremony, which lasted a long time. The only time he clapped with genuine enthusiasm was when the probationers from Jeavons station received their epaulettes. Young Felax glowed with pride as he hurried back down the steps, holding the small bronze buttons aloft so his parents could see.

Edeard and Dinlay shared a grin at that.

'Oh, Lady,' Dinlay groaned. 'Was I like that?'

'I don't know. I was too busy trying not to trip down the stairs.'

On the row behind them, Chae leaned forwards. 'You were both an embarrassment,' he assured them.

Edeard knew he was expected to participate in the reception that followed. Not so many months ago, the very idea would have filled him with dread. Now, after all he'd been through, he didn't care any more. Besides, Kristabel was on his arm the whole time, smiling and impressing people a lot more than he did. So he took a wine glass from a ge-chimp, refused the canapés, put on his best smile, sealed up his mind, and started to tell parents how wonderful their newly qualified constables were, and how glad he was that they'd be helping him, and yes he did think the gangs would ultimately be defeated, and no he couldn't give a time scale, it was confidential, and yes they did have a way to finish the exclusion campaign, and please urge your District Master and Representative to support the warrants.

'We're splitting into political groups,' Kristabel whispered into his ear an hour into the party. 'How very Makkathran of us.'

Edeard scanned round with his farsight. She was right. Three distinct groups of Masters had collected on the Malfit Hall's black floor. One led by Finitan, who was all smiles and enthusiasm, with District Masters who'd joined the exclusion campaign. Most vociferous among them was Julan, who was almost unrecognizable as the broken man of the Festival of Guidance. His enthusiasm was sweeping people along as he greeted families to congratulate them; they weren't used to talking to District Masters, let alone ones so effusive and pleasant.

'Your father is a talented politician,' Edeard observed.

'Try and say that as if it was a good thing.' Her third hand pinched him sharply on his buttock.

Edeard resisted the impulse to return the jab. Finitan caught his eye and smiled approvingly at Kristabel before turning back to the head of the Fiacre pottery association whose third daughter had just received her epaulettes. There were another eight District Masters in their group, representing Jeavons, Silvarum, Zelda, Drupe, Tosella, Lillylight, Ilongo, and Padua. Finitan also had the Masters for Vaji, Cobara, and Myco in his orbit, where they were being assiduously courted for their support.

The biggest group, clustering together in the middle of the hall, were the undecided. Still the majority of districts.

Then there were those who formed a picket around Owain. The most traditional families, Edeard noted, with Bise at their centre. They too were glad-handing, chatting happily with the new constables. He was rather perturbed to see the Pythia was among them. Surely she could see the exclusion warrants needed to be extended? Then he remembered she had gently refused to prohibit anyone from entering Eyrie. It had been reasonable enough, people should be allowed to attend the Lady's church.

'This division isn't good,' he said to Kristabel as the guests started to leave. 'Makkathran needs to be united if we're to defeat the gangs.'

'Quite.' She led him over to Finitan and her father.

'Welcome back,' Julan said. He embraced his daughter, then shook hands with Edeard. There was a slight pause when he looked at Edeard, as if expecting something. Finitan, too, seemed to be waiting. Edeard wasn't sure what to say.

'Right then,' Finitan said. 'This is as good a time as any. Edeard, while you and Kristabel were away, we've been pressuring the remaining District Masters and Representatives to join the exclusion warrants scheme, sadly to little avail. The Mayor has been equally effusive in opposition to it.'

'But why?' Edeard asked.

'Because, as he rightly points out, we have no conclusion, no final answer as to what to do with these people.'

'I do,' Edeard said, feeling confident after everything he and Kristabel had talked about.

'You do?' Finitan asked.

'Yes, sir. The only thing we can do. Banishment.'

'Ah. That's a bold statement, young Edeard.'

He grinned sheepishly at Kristabel. 'It was pointed out to me that, although it sounds drastic, the actual numbers of people we need to get rid of are tiny in relation to the city's overall population.'

Finitan and Julan exchanged a look. 'That makes this easier then,' Finitan said. 'It's quite plain that Owain is going to steer this into another clash in Council, and delaying tactics will work in his favour. We need to grab the initiative back from him, and proposing banishment is exactly the kind of prospect that will galvanize people into supporting us.'

Edeard glanced over at the Masters gathered around Owain. 'I don't understand, I expected it would make things worse in Council.'

'It will,' Finitan said with a smile. 'And we can capitalize on that division.'

'Ah,' Kristabel said, she nodded in understanding. 'Of course.'

'Of course, what?' Edeard said.

'I am going to announce my candidature for Mayor,' Finitan said. 'And banishing the gangs will by my campaign pledge to the people of Makkathran.'

'What did he say?' Boyd asked as the squad made its way back to Jeavons station after the ceremony.

'That he's going to run for Mayor,' Edeard told them all. He was still taken aback by the notion, though the excitement was growing. *With Finitan in charge, so many things can change.* 'There'll be a party in the Blue Tower tonight so he can make a public announcement.'

'Not Finitan, you arse,' Macsen snapped. 'Master Julan?'

'Julan? He didn't say anything. But with his support, Finitan stands a real chance.'

'All right,' Kanseen said. 'Forget that. What did you say?'

'I said that I'd support him in any way I could.'

They all gave each other puzzled looks. Edeard could sense their minds closing against him, but not before several traces of irritation and disappointment were manifested. He guessed taking a week off had annoyed them more than he'd realized at the time.

'Okay then, at least we've been busy,' Dinlay said as they passed through the station's main gate. 'Unfortunately, so have the gangs. The gondoliers pulled another body from the canal last Thursday. The second son of a cloth merchant from Igadi district.'

'Lady!' Edeard groaned. 'It didn't take them long to regain their courage.'

They settled in the small hall. Dinlay's third hand shut the doors behind them. Kanseen sat down on one of the tables, her boots resting on a bench. Macsen directed a ge-chimp to fetch some water. 'That was very cheap wine at the party,' he complained as he gulped down several mouthfuls from a glass tankard.

Dinlay pulled a bench over to sit opposite Edeard. His face was exhibiting a great deal of contentment. Boyd sat next to him, trying not to show too much amusement at his squadmate's attitude.

'So what did the second son do to annoy the gangs?' Edeard asked.

'Nothing,' Dinlay said. 'They're using a variant on the old extortion racket.'

'A clever one,' Macsen said, finishing his second tankard of water.

'They're not bothering with small shops and stalls any more,' Dinlay explained. 'They've moved up a social class to target the smaller merchants. And they don't ask for money, they want a share of the business itself.'

'It's a route to legitimacy,' Kanseen said.

'If you've got a warehouse full of stock, someone comes along and asks if they can buy a share in your venture. But the thing is, they want to defer payment for that percentage.'

'It'll come out of increased profits, is what they usually say,' Boyd said. 'So far, nothing criminal. Certainly nothing you can use to complain to the constables or courts.'

'Except you know who it is and what they're asking,' Dinlay continued. 'They make that very clear. If you don't comply, then a family member gets hurt.'

'Or in some cases, murdered,' Macsen said. 'As with the cloth merchant's son. Which is extreme, but those are the cases we get to hear about.'

'So we don't know how widespread it is,' Edeard said.

'No. But everyone is complaining about how prices are creeping up, and there's no reason. There's no shortage of anything; the port is crowded with ships delivering cargo, and the city's warehouses are full.'

'The lower and middle level of merchants don't have the kind of protective associations which shops and small traders have,' Kanseen said. 'Their commercial rivalry precludes almost all cooperation.'

'But they have personal guards,' Edeard said.

'No, they don't,' Dinlay said. 'Oh, the patriarch will have some toughs with him when he collects large payments from clients, or pays a ship's captain, but we're not talking about the kind of small army which the Grand Families employ here. These merchants have large families who are completely unprotected, and they're a vital part of Makkathran's economy.'

'I see,' Edeard said. He had hoped for a brief respite after he got back, but he should have known better. 'So we need to identify who—'

'No, we don't,' Dinlay said merrily.

'We don't?'

'Already done it.'

'Ah.' Now a lot of the squad's attitude became clearer to

Edeard. He looked round, seeing their smug faces. 'So what do you need me for?'

'To provide us with brute strength back-up during the arrest,' Macsen said with an innocent tone.

Edeard laughed. 'Tell me.'

'First the bad news,' Boyd said. 'The House of Blue Petals has a new owner.'

'Who?' Edeard asked sharply.

Boyd gave Dinlay a sly glance, as if seeking approval. 'Buate.'

'Never heard of him.'

'Nobody had,' Boyd said. 'Turns out he's Ivarl's half-brother.'

'Oh, great.'

'Would you like the bad news now?' Macsen asked.

Edeard gave him a brusque stare.

'Rumour has it that Buate has a partner.'

'Go on.'

'Ranalee.'

Edeard dropped his face into his hands, and chuckled softly. *I should have seen that coming, especially after Tannarl teamed up with Ivarl that night.*

'Edeard?' Kanseen queried.

'Actually, that's good news,' he told them.

'It is?'

'We finally have a link between the gangs and a Grand Family. Can we prove she's the partner?'

'The Occupancy Deed is filed at the city Registry,' Dinlay said, taking off his glasses to give them a polish. 'It's considered privileged unless a crime has been committed either on the premises or by the owner. We could lodge a request in the lower court to view it. But all it tells us is who's claimed residence rights to the structure, and as we know Buate is family it won't tell us anything new. And the articles of corporation governing the Blue Petal's business will be held by the Guild of Tax Clerks. However, the nature of the business means the arrangement with Ranalee isn't likely to be written down anywhere.'

'So it's just hearsay?'

Dinlay shrugged. 'Yes.'

'And this is what you managed to discover while I was away?'

'As my soon-to-be-father says, everyone's a critic,' Macsen said with mock dismay. 'No, actually, we have been doing difficult observation work under dangerous conditions for little pay and scant thanks from our corporal and station captain.'

'For the love of the Lady, will you tell me what is going on?'

'We followed several gang members who are covered by exclusion warrants – with good reason. One of them was a member of an enforcer crew,' Dinlay said, grinning broadly. 'They've just told a merchant called Charyau in Neph that they want a third of his business. He imports salsponge.'

'What the heck is salsponge?' Edeard demanded. 'And I swear on the Lady if just one of you gives me that *pitying* look over this I will dump the lot of you headfirst in Birmingham Pool and hold you under.'

Boyd opened his mouth ready to explain. A frown creased his forehead, and he turned to Macsen. Macsen pursed his lips and gave Kanseen inquisitive stare.

'Well don't ask me,' she said. 'I've never heard of it before.'

'It must be valuable,' Dinlay mused. 'Charyau has a big family, who dress in fine clothes and carouse all over the city; and there's also two mistresses he covers in jewellery.'

'Did he agree to their terms?' Edeard asked.

'No,' Boyd said. 'The Lady blessed him with a backbone and a lot of pompous bluster. He refused.'

'So we followed the enforcer crew home to Sampalok.'

'You went into Sampalok?' Edeard asked in surprise.

'Like I said: difficult and dangerous,' Macsen announced portentously. 'Which is why we know that they're going to kick the crap out of Rapsail, Charyau's firstborn, as the first warning. And they're going to do it tonight.'

'Where?' Edeard asked eagerly.

*

Riorn Street was a sinuous pathway on the northernmost corner of Abad, linking the Roseway Canal to the Great Major Canal. The buildings which made up its walls were all tall and imposing, though one of them did incline outwards, allowing broad strands of unkempt gurkvine to dangle down from the eves like a living partition along the street. It was the building next to the overhanging vegetation which housed the Reckless Colonel, a restaurant and theatre of good repute, where the wealthier sons of the city's gentlemen congregated for a pleasurable night among their own.

Good, expensive food was to be found on the starched white linen cloths of its hexagonal tables; the cellar was stocked with an enviable selection of vintage wines from across Querencia. The lounge area offered deep and cosy chairs and settees, while the dancers who graced the stage performed their elegant moves with amazing agility to the pitch-perfect house band. Five large doormen stood outside the glossy wooden doors, physically and telekinetically strong, their presence alone enough to deter anyone foolish enough to be born beneath a certain status in life.

It was after two o'clock in the morning when one of them tipped his tall peaked hat to Rapsail, who tottered unsteadily down the three awkward steps to the pavement. A heavy rain was lashing the street, dimming the orange lights shining down from the building walls. Rapsail tightened his leather cloak around his long blue and scarlet jacket as he grunted his inebriated 'goodnight' to the doormen, and began to weave an unsteady route towards the Great Major Canal.

Alcohol suppressed his farsight as much as it did his optical focus. He had no awareness of the five men lurking in the deeper shadows and alleys off Riorn Street. Nor did he notice as they emerged from their secluded refuges to walk both behind and alongside him. It was only as they started to close in that he frowned with intoxicated confusion.

'I say, hello you fellows,' he slurred.

A third hand closed around his ankles. For a moment his legs moved sluggishly, then he peered down at his immobile feet. Rapsail blinked down at his polished leather shoes with their fashionable brass and silver buckles. They didn't seem to be doing what he wanted, which was to get him far, far away from this place.

'I say, that's off.'

One of his assailants laughed. They circled him now, dark spectres with hoods pulled over their heads, faces shadowed and wreathed with a seclusion haze. Rain pattered heavily on their oilskin cloaks to form quick rivulets over the fabric.

'What do you want?' Rapsail's instinctive self-preservation was starting to get through his alcohol-saturated brain. He tried to longshout, but that required too much concentration.

A hand tugged his hood away from his head.

'I warn you, I have friends in this city. Powerful friends.'

'This is a message for your father,' Medath, the enforcer crew's leader said.

'What message?' Rapsail asked as the rain slicked down his hair.

'He'll understand.'

A fist slammed into Rapsail's podgy stomach. The young man doubled up immediately, falling to his knees. Tears of pain mingled with the rain on his cheeks. 'Oh sweet Lady, no. I have money. Please.'

'It's not your cash we want,' Medath explained patiently. 'It's your inheritance.'

Two of the men pulled leather-weighted coshes from under their cloaks, while two more used their third hands to pinion Rapsail in his cowed position.

'After all,' Medath said reasonably. 'You won't be needing it. Cripples don't have anything to spend it on.'

Rapsail whimpered piteously.

'Damage him,' Medath ordered. 'Badly.'

Two coshes were raised into the air, slick with water. They kept on rising, pulled out of grasping fingers to whirl away into the night. Both men grunted in surprise. Medath fell into a crouch, long blades sliding into his hands. He scanned round with his farsight, probing every doorway and alcove along the street as his telekinetic shield hardened. One of the other enforcers aimed a kick at Rapsail's head. His boot was yanked backwards, sending him crashing down. There was a sickening *slap* as his face smacked flat on to the pavement. He yelled 'Help me' through the blood pouring out of his mouth and nose. Then froze in terror as he was tugged violently across the pavement. He slid away from his comrades at frightening speed, hands scrabbling at the wet surface to no effect. His shrieks were cut off as he vanished round the corner.

'Dear Lady!' another gasped. He started to run. His feet left the ground, and he was propelled through the air to crash into the nearest wall. He crumpled to the ground, stunned.

The remaining three enforcers closed together. Medath kept his blades held ready; the others drew pistols. Laughter echoed down the street. It was too much for one. He fired at a clutch of shadows. The bullet stopped a mere couple of feet from the pistol muzzle, hanging in mid-air. Raindrops curved neatly around it.

'Waterwalker,' Medath breathed.

'Good evening.' Edeard walked forward, his body becoming visible amid the wavering shadows and unceasing rain as he reached the middle of the street. The rain avoided him, parting above his head to leave his splendid new tunic perfectly dry. Behind him, Kanseen and Dinlay emerged from nowhere.

'You're under arrest,' Edeard said. He extended a hand, and the two pistols were wrenched out of their owners' fingers. 'Cuff them,' he told Dinlay. He turned to Kanseen. 'Get the knives.'

Medath watched her approach. He rotated the blades skilfully, and proffered the handles towards her. Edeard was walking towards the enforcer who'd been flung against the wall, bending over as the man groaned weakly.

'I'll take those,' Kanseen said, and held out a hand for the knives.

It was Medath's one chance, he sent them flying towards her

with a vigorous flick of his wrists. At the same time he shoved his third hand against Edeard with his full strength. 'Fight them,' he bellowed at his two accomplices. Kanseen stumbled as she warded off the knives, tumbling on to the pavement. Dinlay was grappling with one of the enforcers, while Edeard came to his aid, swiftly restraining the second with a resolute telekinetic grip. By the time they'd got them both subdued and cuffed, Medath had sprinted away. Edeard's farsight followed him charging over the iron bridge just above Mid Pool.

Macsen and Boyd cast off their concealment. Boyd had the unconscious first enforcer slung over his shoulder. Macsen hurried over to Kanseen and helped her to her feet.

'Well, that was humiliating,' she said as she tried to brush water off her uniform trousers.

'He believed it,' Edeard said. His farsight showed him Medath was over the bridge and into Pholas Park.

'For a real tough guy, he can run very fast,' Boyd observed in amusement.

Edeard turned to the man he'd cuffed. 'Hold your arms out, Sentan.'

'You know my name.'

'Of course I know your name. I know your house, I know what you ate for lunch, your girlfriend, your three children who've got themselves proper jobs. Now hold your arms out.'

'What are you going to do?'

Edeard used his third hand to pull Sentan's arms up. The man flinched at the force.

'Please,' he implored. 'I . . . I'll stop this. By the Lady I will.'

'No, you won't,' Edeard said. He slipped the key into the cuffs and unlocked them. Sentan gave him a frightened look.

'I'm not arresting you,' Edeard said. 'Any of you.'

'Please, Waterwalker, oh please, no. Don't kill me.'

'Shut up. I'm tired of wasting my time in court with people like you. So this is what you're going to do: leave.'

'I . . . what?' Sentan gasped.

'You and your friends are going to leave Makkathran.

Tonight. Now. My squad will escort you to the South Gate. You will walk through it and you will not come back.'

'Where will I go?'

Edeard leaned forward, putting his face an inch from Sentan. 'What do your victims do after you've beaten them, after you've snapped their bones and made their blood run over the floor of their homes while their children are made to watch, after they've been carried off screaming in pain to the hospital? They get on with their lives as best they can. Do you understand me now?'

'Yes.'

'If you come back. If you set foot in my city again. I will know. Do you believe that? Do you believe me?'

'Yes. Yes, sir.'

'Then go.'

Sentan bowed his head in defeat. Edeard went over to Rapsail, who was still kneeling on the ground. He was a mess, his trousers soaking wet, hair plastered against his head, cloak in disarray. 'Thank you,' he sobbed. 'Thank you, Waterwalker.'

'Get up,' Edeard told him without sympathy. Behind him, Dinlay and Macsen were sorting out the cowed enforcer crew; moving them down the street on the start of their journey out of the city.

Rapsail managed to clamber to his feet, and stood swaying as the rain continued to lash against him. Edeard made an effort to calm down; he was sworn to protect Makkathran's ordinary citizens, but people like Rapsail made it difficult to feel any empathy for his kind.

'There's a reason you were picked on tonight,' Edeard said coldly. 'Your father didn't come to us, to me, when Medath's friends gave him their ultimatum. If I don't know what the gangs are up to, I cannot protect you from them. Tonight you were lucky, and for that you are in debt to my squad.'

'Of course,' Rapsail said. 'Father will pay you handsomely for your services. We are gentlemen of honour.'

'I do not want money,' Edeard ground out.

Rapsail was sobering fast, even in his befuddled state he could sense Edeard's anger. 'Of course not, I apologize profusely, Waterwalker. Er, what do you want?'

'Information. Your family is not the only one they have come visiting. Tomorrow, when you have sobered up, I will visit you and your father, and we will discuss how the constables can remove the gangs' influence from your fellow merchants.'

'Yes, yes of course.'

Edeard beckoned Kanseen over. 'Get him back home in one piece. Tell his father I'll be there in the morning.'

'I've really got the good duties tonight, haven't I?'

Edeard grinned awkwardly. 'You did well, I know that wasn't easy for you. Thank you.'

'Huh!' But she couldn't help a small flash of gratification from leaking out. 'Come on, sir,' she said, and took a grip on Rapsail's shoulder.

'I say, a girl constable.'

'Yes. Sir.'

'And a jolly pretty one, too.'

Edeard and Boyd drew in a sharp breath together, wincing. But Kanseen allowed Rapsail to continue living.

'Let me come with you, Edeard,' Boyd said as the unlikely pair walked away. 'Please.'

'I can handle this.'

'They nearly killed you last time.'

'I was trying not to cause a fuss, then. I think we all know those days are behind us now.'

Boyd gave him a very sceptical stare. 'All right.'

'I need you to go back to the Reckless Colonel. Somebody there was longtalking directly to the enforcer crew. Make it clear to the owner he's now on my shitlist; I want his full cooperation from now on. And see if you can turn the informer as well.'

'Lady, is that all?'

'We all have different abilities; that's what makes us good as a team.'

'All right, but just be careful.'

'All I'm going to do is introduce myself.'

'What if Ranalee's there?'

'The Lady isn't that cruel. Is she?'

Edeard had stayed out of Myco ever since the night of the fire. He knew he was physically capable of protecting himself from anything Ivarl and his lieutenants could throw at him. What he lacked was motivation. He hadn't quite lost his nerve as far as confronting Ivarl – or his replacement – was concerned. It was just that he needed time to restore his confidence. The kidnapping and Kristabel had done that.

Edeard slid up smoothly and silently, up through the city-altered floor into the lounge of the House of Blue Petals to find it nearly deserted. The doors were closed and locked. Two drunks were snoring on couches, with blankets thrown over them by considerate staff. Three ge-monkeys and a couple of tired stewards were busy in the room at the back, washing the last of the glasses. The fires in the iron stoves had sunk to a cosy red glimmer.

He took a good look round. The furniture was similar to last time, though it was all new of course. Even the piano looked the same. There were no globes full of oil, or any other container for that matter. No beagle, either.

Edeard shed his concealment, and walked up the stairs to the gallery. Several of the rooms were still occupied by girls and their clients. The madam and two doormen were sitting in a small parlour, eating a very late supper as they waited for the girls to finish.

It felt strange to be visible as he walked along the corridors and up stairs where before he had always crept about like a nervous ghost. As he approached the long room on the third floor which Ivarl used to hold court in, the doors swung open for him, pulled by someone's third hand. Edeard walked through.

'I wondered when you'd pay me a visit,' Buate said.

That he and Ivarl shared a parent wasn't in question. Edeard guessed it must be their father. He had the same broad forehead and strange green eyes. But where Ivarl's powerful frame had started to inflate, Buate was slim and muscled, as if he'd spent his life doing hard physical work. He was also younger than his half-brother, probably no more than seventy, with luxuriant black hair arranged in trim ringlets that hung below his collar – a fashion that was current amid the Grand Families in the city's northern districts. As was the expensive gold-embroidered leather waistcoat that he'd left unbuttoned to reveal a vivid scarlet shirt. His jewellery was more discreet than Ivarl's, a couple of gold bands on his fingers, and one diamond stud earring. A very large diamond, Edeard noted.

Buate was sitting behind the desk, gazing at his visitor with aristocratic contempt. Unlike Ivarl, who had always kept the office tidy, there were papers and legal scrolls scattered everywhere. As if to counter the difference, Nanitte was there as before, sitting on a broad velvet-covered couch to one side of the desk; above her gauzy skirt she wore a strange narrow corset of leather straps that looked uncomfortably tight. She gave Edeard a blank stare, her mind perfectly shielded.

Edeard used his third hand to close the door. 'It will only be the one visit,' he said, deliberately ignoring Nanitte – though there might have been a bruise on her cheek, the light was too poor for him to be sure. 'This kind of visit, anyway.'

Buate picked up a silver stiletto, playing with it absently. 'And what is this kind of visit, Waterwalker?'

'A friendly one.'

'Indeed? What kind of friendship do you imagine we could have?'

'Brief.'

Buate laughed. 'I see why my dear brother enjoyed you as his sparring partner.'

'I don't remember seeing you at the funeral.'

'I was busy in the provinces. I only returned to Makkathran after I heard the sad news.'

'Do you know who killed him?'

'I thought he drowned.'

'No. He was dead long before he hit the water. Torture tends to do that.'

'That's awful. I trust you're busy finding the criminals who did this.'

'That's one of the reasons I'm here.'

'Ah. How interesting.'

'Did you hear Grand Master Finitan has declared his candidacy for Mayor?'

'It was the talk of the house tonight.'

'His campaign will be centred on banishment.'

'Yes, so I heard. I'm afraid he won't be getting my vote. Too many of my friends would suffer under such a policy.'

'That's why you need to lead them away.'

Buate's detached amusement faltered. 'Excuse me?'

'I want you to go now. Leave the city. Take your colleagues and your business associates and your lieutenants with you. This way you'll be able to leave with most of your money; you can live a good life in exile.'

'Normally I'd just laugh at something so preposterous. But I can see you're actually being serious.'

'A lot of people are going to get hurt over the next few months. There will be deaths. You can avoid that. Think of this as an appeal to your better nature.'

'You believe I have one?'

'I think you're smarter than your dead brother. He was a jumped-up thug, using equally stupid muscle against small fry. But now you're here, and I see things are already changing. The gangs are targeting merchants and larger businesses now. You're trying to integrate yourself deeper within the city's economy, and submerge yourself from legal challenge. That takes a more methodical mind.' He reached out with his third hand, and aggravated a whole ream of paperwork on the desk, sending the sheets fluttering across the floor. Nanitte scrambled to pick up those that fell across her and the couch. 'The mind of someone who appreciates paperwork.'

Buate dropped the stiletto, and watched the swarm of paper with disapproval. 'Please don't do that.'

Edeard sent a last flurry of papers chasing up towards the high ceiling. 'A smart legal mind. And I've grown to dislike lawyers.'

'I have no idea what you're talking about. I am not acquiring businesses, nor have I any desire to. The House of Blue Petals provides a more than adequate income.'

Edeard heard loud footsteps pounding along the corridor outside. He cocked his head to one side and gave Buate an expectant look.

'Boss!' a man yelled.

The doors burst open. A very out-of-breath Medath came charging in, his oilskin cloak scattering water on the polished floor behind him. 'Boss! Boss! The Waterwalker was there, he caught us with Rapsail and – AAARGH!' Medath nearly fell over backwards in fright. He clutched at his heart, eyes bugging as he drew a juddering breath. Buate was actually trembling in anger as he glared at his enforcer.

Edeard smiled contentedly. 'T-t-t timing is everything in our line of work, don't you find?'

'You can't be here,' Medath cried. 'You're back there.' His finger pointed madly out towards the city. 'I ran . . . Boss?'

'SHUT UP.'

Edeard made his smile vanish. 'Leave the city. Take this cretin and all the others like him with you. You cannot win. Not against me.'

Buate rose from the chair, his hands pressed palms-down on the desk. 'You understand nothing. Go back to your countryside, boy, before you and everyone you love gets hurt. This city is not for you.'

They stared at each other as Medath continued to pant loudly behind them.

'Makkathran is already mine,' Edeard said. 'You have no idea what I'm capable of.' He turned and started to walk for the door.

'You're as weak as my brother,' Buate spat after him. 'Next time it won't be Mirnatha who gets taken.'

Edeard spun round, flinging an arm out. Buate was torn from his seat to smash against the wall between two of the oval windows. He squirmed impotently seven feet above the floor. Thin worms of dazzling static crackled in the air around him, jabbing down at his clothes. Buate wailed in dread as tiny puffs of smoke squirted out of each strike point.

'If anything ever happens to her or any of my friends, you will join your brother in a manner that will make his passing seem a delight.' Edeard abruptly withdrew his third hand. Buate fell to the floor, landing badly on his shoulder. He grunted savagely at the pain.

'You keep bad company,' Edeard told Nanitte, and closed the doors behind him.

*

Edeard woke alone in his maisonette. His ge-chimps bustled round getting breakfast ready as he walked down the steps into his pool. For all the fun Kristabel and he had sponging each other down in the beach house, he'd missed the sheer luxury of the bathing pool with its perfect temperature. At first he thought that might account for his melancholia, then he acknowledged he just missed not waking up with Kristabel.

As he munched his way through the mix of nuts and fruit which the ge-chimps had prepared he wondered if he should longtalk her. It would be nice to find out when they could actually meet up next; yesterday had been so ridiculously busy. He was sure that she would expect him to go to the Culverit mansion and be with her to spend a night together, even though they'd be a lot comfier in the maisonette with his modified bed and the other simple comforts he'd created. Then he paused with a glass of apple and mango juice halfway to his mouth. Of all the family girls he'd been with, every one had been brought back to the maisonette – excepting the occasional night spent in an inn's room or that nightmare weekend with Ranalee. Not once had he been taken back to their bedroom at the family residence.

Has Boyd ever gone back to Saria's mansion for a night? I can't remember. Lady, I wish I understood these kind of customs better.

The Grand Families could get quite stuffy about formalities.

I'll ask Kanseen, she'll tell me.

Until then, he foreswore off longtalking Kristabel. Of course, if she were to call to him . . .

Macsen was waiting by the gates at the tenement's entrance. 'How did it go last night?' he asked.

'Not too good. Buate wasn't inclined to leave Makkathran.'

'I could have told you that.'

'I knew it myself, but I had to put it to him.'

Macsen grinned. 'Your conscience . . . It'll be the death of us.'

'Most likely. But you should have seen Medath's face. It was worth ten times the risk just for that. So how did your part go?'

'Sentan and the rest of them trudged off down the south road. Quite a picture, it was. We stayed by the gate for over an hour, and sent a ge-eagle out to watch, but they never came back.'

'Ah well, four down, four hundred to go.'

'We can't do this four at a time. Besides, it took us five days hard work just to uncover this one scheme.'

'I know. We just have to hold the line until Finitan gets elected.'

'You really think he will?'

'He has to,' Edeard said earnestly. 'Most people in the city want the gangs expelled. Owain doesn't stand a chance.'

'You don't know that. He could pull out a policy that will be even more popular.'

'If he wanted to be that popular, he'd enact banishment right now, and stop trying to wreck our exclusion warrants campaign.'

'The politicians in this city are a lot smarter and devious than you give them credit for. You'll see.'

Edeard didn't believe him, he knew Finitan would win. They

reached Arrival Canal and went along to the first mooring platform to hail a gondola.

'At least we get to see Rapsail's hangover,' Macsen said.

The meeting with Rapsail and Charyau was awkward and stilted. Charyau was torn between gratitude to the constables, and fury at himself and Rapsail. Rapsail especially came off badly. *Waster. Parasite. Worthless.* Were some of the more frequently used words. But Edeard was now quite accomplished at talking round reluctant citizens, especially important ones – or those who considered themselves important.

It wasn't Charyau's self-directed fury Edeard manipulated. It was the anger and fear the merchant felt towards the gangs who had come so close to taking his life's accomplishments away from him. In the end there wasn't that much to exploit. The whole experience meant that Charyau had undergone an almost evangelical conversion. Neph was going to get its first merchants association, of that he swore on the Lady's life. He was going to compel his friends and rivals; there were old favours he would call in, he promised, social ties he could use, even financial debts. Together Neph's merchants would stand against the gangs and this insidious new strategy. Everything he learned would immediately be delivered to the constables – by Rapsail.

Edeard walked into the small hall at the Jeavons station in an exceptionally fine mood. Several probationary constables had delivered names that their station captains wanted adding to the exclusion lists, which he passed on to Urarl's team for checking. They did that as a matter of course now, making sure the names were genuine. Several traders and shopkeepers had also forwarded people they suspected. Edeard sent runners to the relevant constable stations, asking that the new suspects be observed. Three new warrants needed drawing up by the Lawyers Guild, producing nine copies each. Which he'd then have to humbly ask the District Masters and Representatives to sign.

'I wish we could just have one warrant to cover all the districts,' Boyd complained.

'After Finitan gets elected,' Edeard promised. 'But I did have one idea after I saw Buate last night. If the gangs are taking shares in legitimate businesses, it'll entail a lot of paperwork. Droal, how do we get the Guild of Tax Clerks to investigate someone we suspect of cheating on taxes?'

'Get an inspector appointed to review the case.'

'Dinlay, can you organize that?'

Dinlay smiled. 'My pleasure.'

'Talk to the Myco station captain as well. The inspector should be given a constables escort while he's in Buate's office, I don't want them intimidated.'

'Leave it with me.'

'That should leave Buate with a large annoyance,' Edeard said in satisfaction.

'If he's as smart as you say, he'll have accountants who can face up to a tax inspector,' Macsen said.

'Yes, but it will cost him time and money. I want to open up as many angles of attack as we can.'

Edeard turned to his own paperwork that was piled up on a couple of the benches. There were actually more sheets and scrolls than he'd seen in Buate's office. He hadn't realized how clerk-like this battle was going to become. All he truly wanted was to be out on the streets arresting criminals.

'Any gang activities we can smack down today?' he asked hopefully.

'Some interesting talk coming out of the Ilongo stallholders association,' Macsen said. 'I'm going to follow that up this afternoon.'

'Good,' Edeard said. He wondered if Kristabel was having lunch right now. If so, it would be on the hortus on their mansion's tenth level. A long table with a white awning fluttering idly overhead. Family and friends gathered to chatter and laugh with Makkathran as their backdrop, wine to drink, tasty food to eat. Then an afternoon spent shopping, or at a spa bath, where they would prepare for this evening's parties.

He picked up a piece of paper from the newest pile. It was a report from the Lillylight station about attempts by gang members named in the exclusion warrants to infiltrate the district and menace their old haunts again. Their methods were becoming quite sophisticated, distracting bridge guards, disguising themselves . . .

The small hall's doors shut as the squad went out to lunch. Edeard looked up, realizing just he and Kanseen were left. She was giving him a concerned look, which worried him.

'Do you want to talk about it?' she asked.

'Er, look, I asked you to tackle Medath because he'd believe he could overcome you. I know he can't.'

Her lips came together reproachfully. 'I'm talking about your week with Kristabel.'

'What about it?' He suddenly realized that being here alone with her wasn't an accident.

'Edeard, please, the two of us . . .' She gave him a compassionate smile. 'There's a way we are closer than the others. I still almost think it's a shame you and I didn't happen, but well, now—'

'I know. And I'm happy for the two of you. He needs someone like you. It's a perfect match, and I haven't told anyone.'

'Edeard! This isn't about me. I'm here as a friend asking if I can help. Why didn't it work out? I mean, be honest, it's not that you lack experience as a lover, now is it? There have been enough girls these last months.'

'I—' he knew he was blushing. Yes, Kanseen was a friend, a very good one, especially after . . . well, anyway, he wasn't used to talking about such things with her. The others, yes. That was boys' talk. Not that they ever went into real detail. 'Nothing was wrong. Thank you,' he said stiffly. 'Not in *any* way.'

Kanseen stared at him, as if she was trying to figure out a

major puzzle. It was almost as if she was angry with him. Then her expression suddenly changed to one of surprise, then dismay. Her hand went to her mouth. 'Oh no. No!' It was as if she was beseeching him to say anything else.

'What?' he asked apprehensively.

'Edeard,' she stood in front of him, and took both his hands in hers. 'You do understand what last week was, don't you?'

'Yes. If you must know, I had the most wonderful time of my life. It was a miracle I ever came back to Makkathran. Satisfied now.'

'A week and the day,' she said it as if it were some kind of test.

'Which day?'

'Oh Lady, you really don't know.'

'Er . . .'

Kanseen tightened her grip. 'Edeard, a Makkathran girl of good family, *particularly* one in Kristabel's position, invites a man to spend one week outside the city with her for one reason, so they can both find out if they are compatible in bed. If you are going to spend the next two hundred years together you really, seriously, need to know that before you start.'

'Two hundred years?' Edeard's legs were somehow unsteady. The feeling of dread that was creeping over his entire body was horrifyingly similar to that time when he'd woken in Ashwell to discover the bandits. 'What two hundred years?'

'Marriage! You nincompoop. Oh, Edeard,' Kanseen was mortified. She let go of him and crammed her hands against her forehead. 'If your week worked out *that way* you are supposed to ask her father for her hand in marriage *the day* you return. That's the custom. A week and the day.'

'Oh dear Lady, this isn't happening.'

'There was nothing wrong, was there? You just didn't know.'

'Kristabel thinks we're getting married?' He sat down heavily.

'She was expecting you to ask. Everyone was. We were all worried for you that it had gone wrong.'

'Oh Lady. Wait! Who else knows?' *Because this is Makkathran, and everything is in public.*

Now Kanseen looked really upset. 'Well, there have been a few people speculating who was the one with the problem.'

'A few?' He knew all too well what that meant. *The whole Lady-damned city is talking about it.*

'She must hate me,' he said in an aghast whisper. *Not Kristabel; not her angry with me. I can't stand that.*

'No. Um, look, I'd better go over to Haxpen and explain—'

'No!' Edeard sent his farsight surging into the Culverit ziggurat. He found her easily enough, in her grandiose bedroom, curled up on the bed, her mind a low glimmer of pure misery. Little Mirnatha was in there too, not saying anything, just miserable on behalf of her beloved elder sister. In the corridors outside, servants mooched about, sullen and trepidatious. Julan sat in one of the day lounges, trying to radiate a composed persona, but he couldn't help the distress he felt inside from leaking through, the concern for his daughter.

'Oh Lady,' Edeard groaned in disbelief. 'I am such an idiot.'

'You didn't know,' Kanseen repeated.

He shook his head, banishing the small hall from his mind. 'Kristabel?' his directed longtalk asked gently.

On the bed, she tensed then curled up tighter. Her mind's strongest shield tightened round her thoughts.

'Kristabel, please, I'm so sorry.'

It was no use, she was completely closed to him.

'Fuck!' He smashed his fist down on the bench, unconsciously putting his telekinetic strength behind it. The ancient wood splintered with an almighty *crack*. Both halves of the bench hit the ground. A small sea of paperwork skidded down on to the floor. He stood up. 'I'm going to see her.'

'I'm not sure that's a good—'

'My mistake,' he was almost shouting now. 'I will put this right. I have to.'

'Edeard.'

The gentleness of her tone caught him by surprise. She put her arms round him, and kissed his brow. 'The Lady's luck be with you, Waterwalker. You deserve her.'

'Thanks,' he said, shamefaced. 'Er, any other customs I should know about? Before I . . . you know.'

'Only that it's a custom, not a law. Go get her.'

He perceived the two ge-eagles as soon as he stormed out of the station. They watched him carefully as he made his way over Arrival Canal into Silvarum. Someone was very interested in his movements. And he recognized at least one of the ge-eagles from the aviary at the ziggurat. His farsight skipped on ahead. Homelt was standing outside the main gates, marshalling several family guards. Armed guards – in the daytime, no less. The gate itself was closed and locked; as were all the other entrances into the mansion. It was Lorin who was organizing everyone, striding around the main courtyard issuing orders.

'You little shit,' Edeard muttered under his breath. Lorin was making no effort to conceal his eagerness at sealing up the vast ziggurat mansion.

The constable guards on the bridge between Silvarum and Haxpen gave Edeard a respectful salute as he hurried over. He returned it casually. His longtalk whispered into several ge-monkeys in the Culverit mansion, stirring long-dormant amorous thoughts that were wickedly misdirected. Five of them began to scamper across the courtyard behind the main gate, their affection for Lorin unbound.

Citizens strolling along the streets outside the ziggurat heard peculiar squeaks of desire mingling with Lorin's outraged and downright fearful yells. Agitated, frightened thoughts were broadcast wildly as clothes got torn. Servants and guards came hurrying over, adding to the physical and emotional commotion. It took several minutes for the ge-monkeys to be calmed and led away. There was so much noise, that even Homelt peered in to watch in bemusement as Lorin's unwelcome new suitors were coaxed back to their nests. He looked round the courtyard thoughtfully, then closed the big main gate again, trying to suppress a smile.

When Lorin recovered his dignity, and a servant handed him a new cloak to cover his ripped sleeves, he cast his farsight out beyond the walls again – to no avail. The family's ge-eagles were now circling aimlessly above Birmingham Pool.

'Where is the Waterwalker?' he demanded. No one could tell him.

It wasn't quite the grand gesture entrance Edeard had hoped for. Even though he'd slipped through the ground-level walls with no problem, he still had ten flights of those ever-damned Makkathran-style stairs to climb. And he was in a hurry, fearful that every second of delay would act against him.

When he finally passed through the wall into Kristabel's bedroom he was nearly breathless from all the exertion. Kristabel was still on the bed, sitting at one end, shoulders slumped, head in her hands, with her thick mane of hair hanging down over her knees. The broad glass doors to the hortus were open; Mirnatha was outside, bending over the vine-clad wall to look down on the western districts. Edeard abandoned his concealment and closed the glass doors.

Mirnatha spun round, her little mouth open in shock. Her fright vanished when she saw it was Edeard who'd materialized in the room, replaced with immediate indignation. Her hands jabbed into her sides as she glared at him in affront.

'It's all right,' Kristabel told her with a croaky voice and unsteady longtalk. 'Walk round the hortus, for me, please.'

Mirnatha gave Edeard a final glare, then stomped off.

Edeard went down on his knees in front of Kristabel, and laced his fingers together as if in prayer. 'I am so sorry,' he said. 'Please, marry me. I didn't know before.'

Kristabel combed some of her hair away from her face. Her eyes were red and puffy, while by contrast her cheeks had paled as if she was ill. 'Marry you?'

'Please?'

Confusion clouded her gaze. 'You didn't know?'

'This week and a day thing. I had no idea, I swear. Please believe me, I would never try to deceive you in any way, let alone this. I love you, Kristabel.'

'You didn't know?' Her voice had risen in hope.

'No. By all the Lady holds precious, I did not know.'

Her tears began to flow again, but now her mouth had lifted in a smile. 'You didn't know?' It was nearly a wail.

Edeard bowed his head in suffering. 'Gache fungi,' he pleaded.

Kristabel started to laugh, it swiftly turned to sobbing. She swatted his head, then somehow they were clutching desperately at each other.

'I thought . . .' She wept. 'I thought you'd . . . I don't know what I thought. I didn't understand. After that week – everything we did, everything we shared – I didn't know why.'

'Shush,' he urged her, and held her tighter. 'Shush. It was a stupid mistake, and all my fault. And I will spend the rest of my life making it up to you. I promise. Now I'm going to go to your father right this second, and ask his permission. I know I've only got a day. That's . . .' he paused. Gulped. 'If you'll have me.'

'No,' she said.

'What?' he demanded, stricken.

'Yes,' she said quickly. 'Sorry, yes, of course I want to marry you. Look at the state I'm in at the thought of not. But no, I don't want you to go to Father.'

'Why?'

'Because this is guilt talking.'

'No, it's not. I want to marry you. I can't believe you actually want me, but if you think I'm going to be stupid again then I—'

'Listen,' she said, and grasped his hands, forcing them to be still. 'Look at me.'

Edeard did as he was told. Even with tears all over her face she was bewitchingly beautiful.

'When I asked you to spend the week with me, I knew what I was asking,' she said. 'I gave you what I thought was a choice, the traditional *a week and the day*, or just become lovers that night there and then, with no obligation. You went for the week, which in itself tells me a lot about you, that you'd respect me rather than settle for a quick tumble. But you didn't know what that was supposed to be, what it meant. You weren't thinking of marriage. And that applies now as much as it did then. You haven't thought this through. Believe me I have, and I know what I want. But Edeard, you've known for about . . . how long?'

'Kanseen just explained to me,' he admitted.

'An hour, then.'

'No! Not that long, I came straight away, I promise.'

'All right, half an hour. Edeard, you don't make a decision like this in half an hour. You're doing it because of a huge misunderstanding, and you very gallantly don't want to upset me. Which only makes you more adorable, but it still doesn't make this the right thing for you.'

'That's all wrong. I want to marry you. I do.'

'Fine. Did Kanseen explain why we have this custom?'

'To see if we're okay physically.' He cleared his throat self-consciously. 'I think we passed that test, didn't we.'

'We did. Very much so. But did she say why we needed to find that out first?'

'Because if we marry we'll spend a long time together, centuries probably. Everything has to be right.'

'Yes, and even that's no guarantee; especially if we marry as young as we are. A hundred years is a long time to sustain love, let alone two hundred. So do you see now? I'd thought about this from the moment we met, and I knew it was the right thing to do for me to ask you. But you hadn't thought about it. You still haven't, except for this wild impulse. Edeard, I need you to think clearly what you're asking. I need that from you. Please.'

'Oh.' He sat back on his ankles. 'Of course,' he said formally.

She grinned, and peered closely at him. 'And that doesn't mean you spend a week trying to work out how long you have to wait to make it seem like you've considered everything properly. Understand?'

'Yes.' Edeard could actually feel the warmth of the blush rise up his cheeks. 'Lady, what is life going to be like with you?'

She smiled back, and kissed his nose. 'As difficult as I can make it.'

'That's fair.' He held her head so he could kiss her properly.

They spent a long time in a soft embrace before finally moving apart. Edeard's farsight revealed a highly agitated Lorin urging Homelt and four armed guards up the third flight of stairs. Fit though they all were, it was hard going.

'Your uncle's on his way,' Edeard murmured.

'And Mirnatha is back,' she said spryly.

Edeard turned round to see the little girl pressed against the glass, peering through. Then his farsight caught Julan approaching down the central corridor.

'Oh Lady,' he groaned.

'I'll deal with Daddy,' she said, and directed her longtalk to him.

Edeard allowed the glass doors to open again.

'Are you sorry?' Mirnatha asked.

'Very sorry,' Edeard assured her. 'Your sister and I have made up now.'

'I knew you would.'

'I wish I'd known.'

She tilted her head up to scrutinize him. As he squirmed under the gaze, Edeard finally understood the phrase, *six going on sixty*.

'If I was older, I'd have you for my husband,' Mirnatha decided.

'Er . . . that's good.'

Kristabel kissed her sister on the top of her head. 'Once more round the hortus.'

'Krissy!'

'Go. Now.'

Mirnatha gave her a sullen glare, and pranced out.

Kristabel smiled after her. 'I already feel sorry for her husband.'

'Your father?' Edeard queried.

'Placated. For the moment. We're both going to have to talk to him.'

Edeard tried to smile supportively.

'He'll understand. More than anyone.' She went over to study herself in a full-length mirror. 'Oh my sweet Lady. Look at me.'

'You look fabulous.'

'That's very loyal. If not very realistic.' Kristabel directed a longtalk summons to her maid. 'I'm going to get ready to face people again. I will be some time.' She started teasing strands of hair out of the tangle.

'Okay.' Now he started looking round the bedroom properly, he saw that what Mirnatha was to pink so Kristabel was to frilly lace trimmings. It was slightly unnerving.

'You can wait if you'd like,' she said.

'I would. Yes.'

'Edeard, not in here.'

'Ah, right.'

Kristabel found a set of clips on a dresser. 'And Edeard.'

'Yes?'

'What exactly did happen to poor Uncle Lorin down there in the courtyard?'

'I've no idea,' he said innocently, and hurriedly closed the door behind him.

Captain Larose was waiting outside the Jeavons station entrance. Just seeing him in his ceremonial blue and scarlet jacket, with his sword and pistol hanging from his white leather belt, his back held perfectly straight, took Edeard back to the day he'd first encountered a militia officer on the road to Makkathran. Larose had the same aristocratic arrogance as that patrol officer, as well. Five ordinary soldiers accompanied him.

'Waterwalker,' Larose said as Edeard approached.

'Captain?'

'Mayor Owain requests that you attend him.'

Edeard didn't know what to make of that at all. 'I see.'

'Excellent.' Larose turned to his soldiers. 'Fall in, chaps.'

'Why the escort?' Edeard asked.

Captain Larose smiled thinly. 'The Mayor does rather enjoy the trappings of office. He says it helps remind people of the order of things.'

'Oh.'

'Personally, I find all this pomp and ceremony a real pain in the arse. My mess staff spend half the night getting my uniforms ready.'

Edeard resisted the impulse to look down and check his own tunic. Apart from the new one Kristabel had got for him, he was still wearing the ones he'd bought during his probationary period. They were starting to show signs of wear and tear.

'Where are we going?' Edeard asked as they started to walk along Chates Street towards the Brotherhood Canal. He'd assumed they'd be going to the Orchard Palace.

'The militia stables,' Larose said. 'The Pholas and Zelda regiment is leaving for Talence province today, and it's customary for the Mayor to see the troops off.'

'I didn't know that.'

'It's happening a lot now. I'm probably going to get deployment orders myself soon.' He gave Edeard a rueful grin. 'Not exactly what I signed up for, but one has a duty, yes?'

'Yes,' Edeard agreed promptly.

'Good man. You've been quite an inspiration to people lately. It's about time someone brought the gangs to heel. Things simply cannot go on as they are.'

Edeard was mildly surprised. He'd assumed the captain wouldn't really approve of him; he'd met so many arrogant useless family sons that these days he simply classed them all together as beneath contempt. But for all his airs, at least Larose seemed to have some awareness of what was going on in the world.

The wooden stables in the middle of Tycho's wide meadowland were bustling with activity. At one end, the regiment themselves were mounting up and forming ranks. Two hundred officers and soldiers on horseback, dressed in their full uniforms and regalia. Edeard had to admit it was a rousing sight. The purple and green insignia of the regiment was prominent, never more so than on the elaborately feathered headgear of the Colonel, who sat astride his midnight-black terrestrial horse with two groomed ge-wolves keeping flank.

Down at the other end of the stables, Edeard's farsight observed the mess staff and ge-monkeys getting ready in an altogether less structured manner. Nearly forty wagons were loaded with supplies, with the final bales and boxes being hurriedly piled on board under the cursing of the quartermaster and his aides. Two smaller covered wagons contained arms and munitions, each guarded by five soldiers and their own pack of ge-wolves. A small flock of livestock was being herded by ge-dogs, while chickens and geese squawked from inside their cages. It looked like a much more difficult operation than getting the soldiers ready.

Mayor Owain was standing on a wooden platform at the end of the stables, surrounded by a gaggle of advisers and three other Masters. He wore his maroon and sapphire robes with a start-lingly white fur trim, the hood loose over his shoulder. As always, Owain's mind was perfectly shielded, while his facial expression radiated interest in the vista before him.

'Not long,' Larose muttered to Edeard as they waited at the foot of the stairs of the platform.

The regimental bugler sounded formation, and the horses quickly arranged themselves in front of the Mayor's platform. Ten ge-eagles settled on the stable roofs. The colonel saluted from his saddle.

'I wish you good fortune on your endeavour,' Mayor Owain said to the assembled regiment. 'I am confident you will restore order to Talence province. Whilst bandits may find it easy to elude local farmers and sheriffs, they will soon discover it is altogether different to run and hide from a stalwart man of the regiment riding after them. It is with pride that I see you leave today, knowing that our city is the symbol of hope that all on

Querencia turn to in their moment of deepest need. I know that above all, the militia can be relied on to complete their task with honour.'

The colonel led his troops in a hearty three cheers for the Mayor, who applauded them back. Then the bugler sounded slow advance, and the regiment began its ride to the City Gate, and its undertaking beyond. Their ge eagles took flight, soaring out towards the crystal wall.

Owain stood on the platform, his face perfectly composed until the last man rode past. It was only when the first of the wagons began to roll out that he turned and made his way down the steps.

'Your honour,' Edeard said courteously as the Mayor reached the ground.

'Waterwalker, thank you for coming. I hope it's not too inconvenient.'

'No, sir.'

Owain actually smiled. 'Ah, polite as well as effective. How long before you're our Chief Constable, eh?'

'I don't think Walsfol has anything to worry about, your honour.'

'We shall see. Walk with me, please.' He waved a hand at the gaggle of advisers, who fell back discreetly; Captain Larose and the soldiers took up position just behind them. Owain chose a narrow track which led back towards the Outer Circle Canal around Majate. The meadowland on either side was just about deserted.

'I regret that we seem to have started off on the wrong foot, young Waterwalker. I blame myself, you are Finitan's protégé, after all.'

'He supports banishment, your honour.'

'Yes. So do I.'

'I didn't know that, your honour.'

'Still polite even in the face of provocation. You are too kind, Waterwalker. You see me as someone who has opposed your clever exclusion warrants, and who of course will fight Finitan and his proposal.'

'It does seem that way your honour, yes.'

'I'm sure it does. That is because you are young, and your pardon – can as yet only visualize short-term benefits. Do you really think, do you believe in your own heart, that I do not want this city rid of crime?'

'No.'

'Precisely. Well I thank you for that courtesy. I actually rather like the idea of the exclusion warrants. You are to be congratulated on implementing them, and against such strong political opposition.'

'Given what I understand of this city's politics, a policy which you opposed would always gain support from other quarters.'

Owain grinned smoothly. 'Which brings us to today. What did you think of the regiment?'

Edeard glanced back towards the stables. The last of the wagons had now left the wooden buildings. Animals bleated as they were herded along behind. 'I think the bandits will be in a lot of trouble.' The Jeavons station's ge-eagle was spiralling lazily above City Gate, showing Edeard five new wagons belonging to the Weapons Guild. They were parked to one side of the road, waiting. He knew they would follow the regiment all the way to Talence province, where they would sell pistols to the frightened farmers and villagers, profiting Owain's Guild still further just as Jessile said. It wasn't a crime, he acknowledged, but that didn't make it right, either.

'Yes,' Owain said. 'But why are they there in the first place?'

'They are everywhere.'

'Indeed they are. The bandits and the gangs are symptomatic of our society's failings, Waterwalker. That is what I am truly opposed to.'

'I'm not sure I understand, your honour.'

'If you banish the gang leadership from the city, where will they go?'

'Beyond the borders of the furthest province, or some distant island, that's what I had in mind.'

'Of course. It would seem humane, I'd expect nothing less from a man of principle like you. We're all guilty of listening to the city's tittle tattle about you, Waterwalker; but not once have I heard it said you lack integrity, and for that I thank the Lady. But have you considered what will occur a year, or even ten, after they begin their banishment? The resentment? The lure of returning? If they didn't come back here they would surely join with the bandits.'

'So what is your proposal? I assume that's what we are discussing.'

'We are. My proposal, as you put it, is that we do not treat the gangs and the bandits in isolation. We all live on one world. We must become one nation. Our problems must be dealt with in unison. The militia regiments out in the countryside, the constables here in the city. When we have rounded up all of the miscreants, then we can exile them in perpetuity. I like your idea of a remote island – that would certainly make them containable.'

'So what's the difference between you and Finitan?'

'Finitan thinks only of the city, of short-term solutions. Don't tell me you haven't worried about what happens to people after banishment.'

'I've considered it, your honour,' Edeard admitted. 'We seem to be making things worse on the Iguru, what with all the highwaymen; that's why I wanted banishment.'

'But do you see we can't treat these problems in isolation?'

'I understand both problems have to be confronted, yes.'

'I am happy to hear that. Unfortunately, the easy one is the city. You have shown us how it can be achieved, Waterwalker. Nobody doubts you will ultimately succeed, not even poor old Buate.'

'I'd settle for Bise capitulating.'

Owain laughed. 'Don't worry. When the time comes, I will

stand over Master Bise personally, and ensure he signs the exclusion warrants for Sampalok.'

'Your honour?'

'It is simple politics. Master Bise believes he can gain more influence by supporting me. In Council it pays me to encourage such support. Ultimately, Bise will accept the inevitable, and his nefarious allies will be purged from our streets.'

'That's . . . a relief to know.'

'I thought it would be. So, whilst not asking you to switch your support – for Finitan is your patron, and I would not want to foster such disloyalty – do you at least agree with some of my objectives?'

'Yes, your honour, I do.'

'Thank you.'

'Why can you not reach a concord with Master Finitan?'

'Sadly, we have been adversaries for too long. Neither of us trusts the other. And I have to say, I will campaign long and hard to retain my office no matter what we agree or disagree in private. Such is the nature of humanity, worst of all flawed specimens like us ancient conservative Masters. Do you think it likely that Finitan will back down?'

'No.'

'Precisely. I wanted to reassure you of my own goals, because whoever wins this election, it is you who will be fighting the gangs on the streets.'

'Thank you, your honour.'

'I admit, knowing you will be working for the city is of considerable relief to me. The constables have performed little short of a miracle since the day you walked on water. And that resounding victory over dear little Mirnatha's captors was extraordinary. I admit to joining the cheers of joy along Grand Major Canal that day. I ask the Lady that she will be equally generous granting the militia victory. Theirs will be the more difficult task, and the one bogged down in politics.'

'How is that?' Edeard asked. They'd nearly reached the Outer

Circle Canal, up ahead he could see the bronze and jade bridge which Rah himself had commissioned.

'The countryside wishes to enjoy the benefits of the city without having to pay the cost,' Owain said. 'Five times since last summer I have dispatched our regiments to aid desperate provincial governors. And what payment have we received? A grudgingly given reimbursement for our basic costs. To what avail? The regiments ultimately have to come home, leaving the lands open once again to infiltration by the bandits. It is a nonsense, a gesture which achieves nothing in the long term. If we are to achieve stability and an end to this dreadful felony, then the provinces will have to pay taxes to Makkathran for organizing their defence. Militias will have to be stationed permanently and strategically across the countryside. Such achievement will require tremendous organization, one province cannot be favoured above another. All costs – and they will be considerable – must be borne equally. The rule of law available to all without prejudice. Both the Master in his mansion and the farmer in his cottage will have to answer to the same authority.'

'One nation,' Edeard said.

'Precisely. At the moment city and provinces are naught but a loose affiliate. And look where it has taken us, to the verge of anarchy. To face this new threat, we have to consolidate the forces of civilization, to strengthen our boundary and enforce our justice. Only in a nation where equality reigns can this happen.'

They walked over the bridge together. Edeard's mind was awhirl trying to take in all the Mayor had said. Standing in the shade thrown by the sprawling conglomeration of Parliament House's buildings, Owain faced Edeard.

'I hope you no longer consider me an enemy, Waterwalker.'

'I never really did, your honour.'

'That gladdens me. Maybe one day, when your generation has risen to high office, you will extinguish the vanity and foolishness of petty politics that so bedevils us today. I wish you luck in that.' He inclined his head, and walked into the tower housing the Guild Of Clerks. His entourage went with him; Captain Larose smiled knowingly as he passed Edeard.

'Ho Lady,' Edeard exhaled. He turned and made his way slowly round the base of Parliament House, towards the bridge which would take him back into Jeavons. *So whoever wins, they'll support me against the gangs.*

Despite everything the Mayor had said, he still hoped it would be Finitan. Though the idea of a penal colony on a remote island was an intriguing one.

Of all the people in Makkathran, Nanitte was the one Edeard would never have expected to see waiting for him in the street outside the tenement. But there she was when he made his way home that evening.

'Can I talk to you?' she asked as he reached the tenement's entrance.

Edeard's farsight swept round. He wasn't just searching for people he knew (this wouldn't look good to Macsen, for a start), but to see who Buate had got watching. 'You've got one minute,' he said, after confirming there was nothing immediately suspicious.

'Not out here, this is too important.' Nanitte's voice was brittle; her old self-confidence had gone.

Edeard took a good look. Beneath her dark-blue cloak, she wore a low-cut green and white dress, with her hair arranged in long waves. Now, out here in the sunlight, he could see the heavy makeup on her face. Even that didn't completely cover up the bruise. Her lip had recently been split as well.

'All right,' Edeard said reluctantly. 'Five minutes.'

Nanitte looked round the inside of the maisonette with interest. Her hand slid over the cold alcove, fingers touching the milk jug and fruit. 'It is all different in here, just like they said it was,' she said as she walked over to the bed. A hand tested the firmness of the spongy substance.

'Who said?'

'Girls I've talked to. On Ivarl's behalf, of course. They talk freely to me rather than him.'

Edeard grunted. 'Right.'

'He was obsessed with you.'

'And his brother?'

Nanitte slumped. 'I hate him.'

Edeard indicated her face. 'He hits you.'

'Among other things, yes.'

'Leave him.'

She laughed bitterly. 'You said that with a straight face. You really do come from another place, don't you?'

'Probably.'

'I want to leave him,' she said. 'Those things you said to him the other night. That's all going to happen, isn't it?'

'Yes. Even if Owain gets elected; I was talking to him today.'

'So I'd be thrown out of the city.'

'That depends how deep your involvement is.'

'I was surprised I'm not on your warrants already.'

'We're concentrating on the violent ones for now.'

'It wouldn't be much of a life for me out there, not like that, not the whore of an exile.'

'Why are you here, Nanitte? What have you got to tell me?'

'He's going to buy guns, a lot of guns.'

'Who from?'

She gave him a thin smile. 'If I left now, by myself, I thought perhaps I could go to one of the big towns beyond the Iguru Plain, somewhere no one would know me or what I am. I could buy a small house, or some land. If I had that, I could find a husband, a nice provincial man. I'd be able to make sure he loved me; whores make the best wives, did you know that? I'm not quite sure I could do the whole housemistress and children thing for him, but we'd be happy, and all this, my life, would be gone.'

'I wish Buate thought like that.'

'No, you don't. You're enjoying this, it makes you *live*. You need to see him defeated, you want Makkathran liberated from the gangs he controls. You need an ending, Waterwalker. Throwing them out just so they can drift back into the city over months and years won't be good enough for you. The Waterwalker requires finality. I don't know what you'll do to achieve it, but I know I don't want to be here when you do. Out of you and Buate, I think I'm actually more afraid of you.'

'That's a very nice summary of me. Shame it's not particularly accurate.'

Nanitte glanced through the archway into the bathroom, her eyebrows rising at the sight of the perfectly flat steps leading down into the bathing pool. 'It's not just Mothers who can see the future, you know.'

'Why don't you just tell me what you know of the guns? I'll take you to the City Gate myself. He'll never be able to stop you.'

'And how would I get my house and my land?'

'I thought . . . You must have money.'

'I was a dancer once. A long time ago. That's all I ever really wanted to be. Then one day Ivarl visited the show I was in. That was it. He knew the theatre owner, of course, and I was young and stupid, stupid enough to believe his promises. After I'd been with him for a while I realized that was it, I'd become a part of that life, there was no way back. No theatre owner would ever hire me unless he told them to. I gave up.'

'I'm sorry.'

'So there you are, Waterwalker, I'm not just some girl working at the House of Blue Petals; I'm *his*. Do you know what it is to be owned like that? To be less than some genistar?'

'I won't patronize you by saying yes.'

'Thank you. So now you know. If you want me to tell you when and where he's getting the guns, you have to pay me. That's what all men do, they pay me for what I've got.'

'I'll have to ask my station captain, or maybe Finitan.'

She came to stand in front of him, as self-assured as any Master. 'You don't have that much time. I need the money today. I want to be gone by morning.'

'There's a reason these things take time to arrange.'

'I told you of my dream, nothing more. We both know I can survive anywhere. Is that what you want for me, to keep on doing what I do? I thought you were going to save us all, Waterwalker.'

'I haven't got that kind of coinage.'

'Kristabel does.'

'I can't ask her.'

'Why not? Actually, why aren't the two of you engaged? All of Makkathran wants to know that. You can tell me. I'm leaving, remember.'

'Stop this.'

Nanitte discarded her cloak as she went over to the bed and bent across it, her hands slid over the sheets. 'If you really want her, I can show you how to make your next week and the day work perfectly.'

'Get off the bed.'

'You know I'm good. Who do you think showed Ranalee the physical side of her ability?'

Edeard nearly reached out to grab her with his third hand, only just managing to keep his temper in check.

Nanitte straightened up. 'You see what I am, Waterwalker. How low I am? They made me like this. And now I can't go back, not after talking to you. You saw what happened to Ivarl, and he wasn't even turning on them like I am. So now you have to ask yourself how badly do you want them? Bad enough to ask Kristabel for the kind of coinage she would spend on shoes to match one of her party dresses? Or are you just going to let this opportunity slip away because it's all turned too personal for you?'

'This is not personal.'

'Good. Then I'll just wait here while you go and get my money.'

'We can't trust her,' Macsen said the next morning when Edeard called them into the small hall.

'Why not?' Edeard asked, trying to be the reasonable one. He'd felt terrible going to Kristabel for money. She of course had made light of it; saying how much she wanted to help. Her understanding didn't make him feel any better.

Nanitte had counted the coins in the bag he brought back to the maisonette, unable to disguise her surprise by how much there was. 'I should have done this a long time ago,' she said.

'Just tell me about the guns,' he said. And she did: about the meeting in Buate's office which she'd been excluded from; the men she'd never seen before, with accents that didn't come from any city district; how Buate had started talking about constable-killer pistols, and levelling up the score.

'Because she's Nanitte,' Macsen said, not understanding why that wasn't enough.

'I could sense she was telling the truth about the guns,' Edeard said.

'I'd be more concerned about the rest of it,' Boyd said. 'Your pardon, Edeard, but you don't have the greatest instinct when it comes to honesty. You always want to find the best in people.'

Edeard gave his tall friend a surprised glance. 'All right, so what could she have been lying about? The worst case is she made an arse of me and ran off with a lot of coinage, how does that put us in trouble at the exchange?'

'What was that phrase you used?' Dinlay said mildly. 'Oh yes: the constable-killer gun.'

Edeard scratched the back of his head, wishing that part hadn't existed. 'Yes,' he conceded. *Could that mean repeat-fire guns? Nanitte said they talked with a foreign accent.*

Part of him wished it were true, that he could finally prove Ashwell's destruction had come at the hands of an unknown clan from somewhere else in the world. 'But if that part of her story is genuine,' he said immediately, 'then we really need to intercept the handover before these weapons get distributed to the ordinary gang members on the street. If they get their hands on them we'll be facing a bloodbath.'

'Good point,' Macsen said grudgingly.

'They know we can conceal ourselves,' Boyd said. 'I noticed a lot more dogs in Sampalok when we were following up the Charyau thing. Most of the gang members have one these days.'

'I can protect us from a lot of bullets,' Edeard said. 'And you know we can escape in ways they could never dream of.'

The rest of the squad looked at each other.

'Okay,' Kanseen said. 'But if these pistols are anything like Nanitte claims, we're going to need some reliable back-up.'

'I'll talk to Chae and Ronark,' Edeard said.

Two nights later Edeard was wishing he had a little more confidence in the five squads of constables who were patrolling the Padua and Zelda districts. It was supposed to look like the patrols were purely random, following the whim of their corporals and sergeants. To anyone with a mistrustful mind they were highly suspicious.

Or am I being too paranoid?

Whatever, he and the squad had concealed themselves inside the base of a skewed tower in Eyrie, not too far from the Lady's central church. The tower next to them was supposed to be where the exchange would take place. Edeard didn't feel confident enough to wait there, no matter how good his concealment talent.

People were wending their way round the lofty twisted towers on their way to the huge church for the evening service. It was good cover for the gun exchange, he admitted, especially as the Pythia had refused to employ exclusion warrants for Eyrie.

'That's the third time,' Kanseen's directed longtalk whispered. She gifted them the image of the ge-eagle that swooped silently round the tower outside. Then it darted in through a high curving entrance and did a fast circuit of the huge empty space inside.

The tower chosen for the exchange was one of the tallest in Eyrie, a monstrous kinked spire whose jutting vertical ribs changed from smoky grey at the foot, through a gentle amethyst to a sullen carmine at the top, where eight tapering spikes curved up around the edges of its slanted platform. The open chamber at the bottom actually had three entrances where most towers only had one. Several lengthy stalagmites and stalactites of mauve-tinted crystal cluttered the interior, while at the centre a broad smooth shaft connected the black floor to the apex of the cave-like ceiling fifty feet above; a single narrow opening led to the spiral stair, which wound the entire height of the tower.

'Get a load of this,' Boyd said. He'd sensed someone outside with a terrestrial dog on a lead. The dog was sniffing the ground as it was slowly walked around the tower.

'Isn't that Paral?' Macsen queried. 'He's got an exclusion warrant against him.'

Whoever it was, the man with the dog walked away towards the bridge back to Fiacre. A couple of constables in ordinary clothes sauntered casually after him.

Orange light was beginning to shine out of cracks in the bark-like tower walls as the sun slid below the horizon. Another ge-eagle made a swift pass through the tower's chamber

Edeard kept his farsight focused on a gondola that had pulled up at a nearby mooring platform. Four men with a strong seclusion haze stepped off it, carrying large iron-bound wooden chests between them. His farsight could just perceive the shadowy shapes of solid metal inside. Another gondola moored, the men on that one carried smaller boxes. 'The ammunition,' he muttered.

The church shut its wide doors as the evening service began; bright orange light shone out of its roof dome and hundreds of windows along the three wings. A quire began to sing softly. Nearly a dozen people left wandering round outside began to make their way towards the tall tower.

'Oh, great,' Dinlay moaned. One of the people stepping through the swathes of orange illumination cast by the towers was a very cocky Medath.

Edeard grinned unseen. 'He'll die of fright when we appear.'

The men from the gondolas made their way into the tower, coming together to face Medath's group.

'I make that fifteen of them,' Macsen said.

Edeard was trying to resolve the shapes inside the chests. They were definitely pistols, and not complex enough to be the repeat-fire types that had been used at Ashwell. *Thank the Lady.* Then he recognized them. 'Okay, I've seen these pistols before. They're the ones Ivarl and his people used against me on the night of the fire. They have very large calibre bullets, but I can definitely ward them off.'

'Then we'd better stop them opening the chests,' Boyd said.

'Move out,' Edeard said. As he hurried silently out of their hiding place and towards the tower ahead he called Chae. 'Move in now. There's fifteen here, but they'll have watchers.'

'Already spotted three,' Chae reassured him. 'We're coming.'

Their deployment plan was simple enough. Dinlay and Boyd would take one tower entrance, Kanseen and Macsen another, while Edeard would go in through the third.

'They're coming.'

Edeard paused, frowning at the clear longtalk. He couldn't tell where it had come from; it certainly wasn't any of the squad. Up ahead, the minds of the gang members were now radiating alarm. Their farsight scoured round.

He strode up to the threshold, listening to the low anxious voices echoing off the mauve stalagmites and curious crannies in the chamber walls. The two groups were huddled together near the central shaft, with sentries positioned near each entrance.

'Ready,' Kanseen's longtalk announced.

The sentry nearest Edeard swung round, sending his farsight prying at the entrance Kanseen was blocking.

Edeard stepped into the tower, and dropped his concealment. His shield hardened around his body.

The sentry gaped in dismay. 'Waterwalker,' he yelled with voice and mind.

Edeard's third hand reached out as he ran forward, yanking the two cases of pistols away from the gang members. They tried to prise them back, but lacked the strength.

Medath and his colleagues drew their own pistols. Of course, Medath already had one of the long-barrelled weapons. Edeard snarled in consternation. Two of the gang members started firing. Edeard dropped the cases on the ground outside the tower and concentrated on protecting himself. Men were running for the two open entrances. The first one to reach the opening covered by Kanseen and Macsen yelled in shock as Kanseen appeared abruptly barely a yard in front of him. Her third hand punched directly against his temple, felling him instantly. She vanished. More shots were fired at the air she had occupied a second before. Edeard deflected a whole swarm of bullets, then people were playing chase around the stalagmites.

'Stop this,' Edeard bellowed, his voice reverberating loudly round the chamber. 'We know who you are. Several squads of constables are closing in. Our ge-eagles are flying outside; you cannot escape.'

A whole volley of bullets lashed at him. He shook his head in dismay. Dinlay rushed past, half visible as he pursued two men. Someone went sprawling, their inertia assisted by telekinesis so their head smacked into a stalagmite. Edeard snatched up two gang members and crashed them together. They fell limply on to the floor. Two more found themselves leaving the ground, and screamed wildly.

'Get up here.'

It was the same longtalk voice as before, cutting cleanly though the shouts and mental babble inside the chamber. Edeard looked round zealously, trying to see who it was. His farsight caught Medath rushing into the opening at the foot of the central pillar.

Four of the gang were now standing together, their hands held high in surrender, pistols abandoned at their feet. Boyd appeared directly in front of them, his pistol raised ready. More pistol shots echoed round the chamber. Then there was a pain-wracked howl, overriding all the other voices. Macsen flicked into visibility behind a man who was clutching at his shoulder;

blood poured through his fingers. Macsen pulled his pistol away from the wound. 'Next time it will be a head shot,' he announced loudly. 'Now stop this, you are under arrest.' He vanished again.

Edeard raced over to the central pillar. On the way his third hand picked up three gang members, who immediately stopped struggling. He dropped them beside Dinlay. The sound of footsteps reverberated out of the pillar's opening. When Edeard looked inside he saw the spiral stair winding upwards.

'Oh come on,' he yelled up at Medath. 'There's nowhere to go.' *But who told him to go up there? Could they really see though our concealment?* With a growl of anger, he started running up the steps. Almost immediately, he slipped on a cumbersome curve, banging his knee badly. The burst of pain was enough to stretch a mist of red sparkles across his vision. Medath's footsteps were becoming fainter as Edeard scrambled upright again. 'If that's how you want to do it,' he muttered, and set off again.

'Edeard?' Kanseen's voice echoed up the stairs.

'Medath went up here. I'll get him. You hang on down there.'

The pillar walls were incredibly thick, restricting his farsight more than he liked. He could just make out the constable squads swarming towards the tower. In the chamber below, his squad-mates surrounded the defeated gang members. Above him, there was a moving glimmer which he knew was Medath's mind.

Round and round the pair of them went. A tiny thread of orange light twinkled out of the narrow vault of the roof above Edeard. Just enough to illuminate the horrible curving stairs. He had to stretch his legs at each semi-jump upwards. How Medath kept up such a pace was beyond understanding. Edeard's heart was hammering loudly, while he could feel his lungs burning inside his chest. Sweat was pouring down his back and legs. When he was two thirds of the way up he simply had to slow, which only increased his anger. Medath started to pull ahead.

By the time Edeard reached the last spiral he was practically walking. Each breath had to be hauled down into his lungs with a big heave of his chest. Hair was glued against his forehead by sweat. Concentration was difficult. Nonetheless, he managed to send his farsight out on to the circular platform which topped the tower. The eight spikes that rose from the edge stabbed up into the sky, their slightly crooked tips peaking at another forty feet above the platform floor.

Medath was out there. Standing ten feet in front of the central cone where the stair exited. He was already aiming the pistol at the opening, waiting for Edeard to emerge.

'Oh Lady,' Edeard wheezed in dismay. The anger which had carried him so far was now diluted by fatigue. *I should have just waited at the bottom, hunger would bring him down eventually.* He started up the last few steps. It would be easy enough to deal with Medath. But then, Medath would know that. *And I still don't know who that longtalker was. Or where they are.*

As if to reinforce his concern, a clammy feeling of trepidation began to manifest. It was so strong he had to pause again. Something was badly wrong, he knew that without knowing why. He took a more cautious step upwards, and began a thorough survey of the platform. He froze. Medath wasn't alone out there on the platform. The floor was feeling the weight of four more pairs of feet, yet Edeard's farsight could find nothing.

'Nanitte,' he spat as his anger rose again. *Oh, crap; Macsen will never let this one drop.*

When he was almost up to the exit, Edeard concealed himself again, and asked the city to let him through the wall. He emerged out on to the platform five feet to the side of the exit. The first thing which surprised him was the wind. Down on the ground, it was perfectly calm, up here it pushed against him. He leaned into it. His four concealed foes were standing together over by one of the spikes. Edeard could see nothing against the pale wash of nebula light that shimmered across the heavens above Makkathran.

As quietly as he could, he made his way over to them. He passed within a couple of yards of Medath, who was still staring at the stair exit, his long-barrel pistol held steady. Once Edeard was past the comically alert gang man he realized the platform floor actually slanted down towards the edge. A tinge of what must be vertigo produced a shiver along his legs. He refused to let it get the better of him, and crept forwards.

The feet began to shift. At first, the two foes at the front took a step backwards; then they all began to move closer to the spike. Edeard grinned savagely, and carried on after them.

He was only five yards away when something struck him with colossal force, impacting on his left side, just below the bottom of his rib cage. Edeard cried out as much from surprise as pain. His concealment faltered as he fought for breath. Medath swung round. Another blow slammed into Edeard, knocking him to the floor.

'Shoot him,' a longtalk whisper ordered.

How did they see me?

Medath fired. The bullet almost got through Edeard's shield. A powerful telekinetic shove sent him skidding down the slight incline. He had a terrible flashback to the day by Birmingham Pool when Arminel had pushed him over the edge. *Lady help!*

'Again.'

The bullet struck him, as did a further telekinetic blow. Edeard was shunted over the edge of the platform. His arms flailed wildly, but straining fingers missed anything solid.

'Can you fly, Waterwalker?'

Edeard plummeted downwards, screaming all the way. He instinctively tried to grip the tower with his third hand. He could even feel the force lock into the grainy structure of the wall. It didn't stop his descent.

His thoughts arrowed down to the city's slumbering mind as the air roared around him. *Can you help?* he pleaded to the slow, giant thoughts.

It was useless. He was falling. Falling.

Kristabel!

Somewhere on the edge of perception he heard her scream wildly. He directed one last thought – *I love you.* Content she would know. It made death more bearable. Falling.

Beneath him a vivid wave of alarm gushed from the minds of the constables scurrying round the base of the tower. Falling.

Any second now.

He braced himself for the terrible burst of pain which would strike for an instant before death.

Falling.

'How the Ladyfuck are you doing that?' Chae's dazed voice asked.

Something slapped Edeard's arse. It was the ground.

'Huh?' Edeard grunted dumbly. He looked up to see a circle of about ten faces peering down at him, all of them wearing utterly incredulous expressions. His hands patted the ground in disbelief. He was down. Intact. 'I fell . . .' he blurted. But of course, it always felt like he was falling when the city lowered him down to its tunnels. It must be the same out here.

There was a near-hysterical laugh threatening to bubble out of his throat. Tears were already leaking from his eyes as the shock kicked in.

Some of the constables staring down were shoved aside. Kanseen and Boyd lunged into the gaps.

'Edeard!' Kanseen squealed. 'Oh Lady, what happened?'

'Trap,' he said weakly. He pointed up at the dark shape of the tower looming above them, surprised by how much effort it was just to raise his arm.

'Medath?' she asked in surprise.

Edeard nodded. It was hard to breathe, his body was tingling everywhere, and now he was starting to shake. His farsight could just discern a pulse of animal terror from somewhere. It was growing fast. 'What's happening?' he rasped. 'What?'

'Edeard?' Boyd was sounding very faint. Chae was frowning, glancing round.

Edeard didn't have the strength to speak. 'Can you sense that?' he longtalked.

'What?' Kanseen asked.

Then Chae was broadcasting pure alarm. 'Move!' The old sergeant pushed at Kanseen with his third arm. At the same time he tried to jump backwards.

Edeard saw it then. Directly above him. A black human

silhouette against the green-glowing beauty of the Ku nebula. Edeard tried to roll away, what was left of his telekinetic strength roused feebly to ward off the plunging body.

Medath hit the ground two feet away from where Edeard was lying. Chae was only half clear. The collision produced a vile *crunch* as a multitude of bones snapped.

Edeard stared vacantly at the tangle of broken flesh beside him. Blood dribbled out of Chae's slack open mouth. The sergeant's eyes moved very slowly to meet Edeard's gaze.

Far away someone was wailing. It sounded like Kanseen.

'Sergeant?' Edeard asked.

'Oh, by the Lady,' Chae longtalked. 'For a moment there, that really hurt.'

'No,' Edeard said. 'Oh no.'

Chae let out his final rattling breath. Edeard tried to hang on to the man's mind, his farsight following the thoughts as they diminished. As they dwindled towards their extinction they disconnected from the body. Edeard perceived the spectral shape of Chae rising up to stand over his own corpse.

'Sergeant?' Edeard sent in desperation.

'Oh, my Lady,' the spectre sent back.

'Sergeant!'

'Edeard?' It was Dinlay kneeling beside him: frightened, shouting.

'Can you see him?' Edeard whispered.

'Edeard, you're going into shock. Try to focus on me.'

'This isn't shock.' Edeard gifted them his perception. There was a collective intake of breath as the constables gathered round saw their sergeant's spirit smiling gently.

'I can feel it, Edeard,' Chae explained. He was looking up, searching the heavens. 'So beautiful. They're calling to me. The nebulas are singing. Can you hear them?'

'No,' Edeard wept. 'No, I can't.'

A gaggle of Mothers from the central church was arriving to investigate the furore, their anxious voices stilled as they received the gift of Edeard's perception. Then the Pythia herself was standing next to Chae's broken body, an expression of serene joy on her face. One hand reached out tentatively, trying to touch his spirit.

'I want to go,' Chae told his enraptured audience. 'I have to. There's nothing left for me here.'

'You'll be lost up there,' Edeard told him. 'Stay with us, stay until the Skylords return to guide you.'

'The songs, Edeard, oh the songs. What a welcome awaits us.'

'Wait. Please.'

Chae smiled down. It was as though he was giving a blessing. 'Don't worry about me. I'll follow the songs.'

'May the Lady bring you safe to the Heart,' the Pythia said.

'Thank you, Dear Mother,' Chae replied. He reached up to the sky as if it were a physical thing he could hold and own. His shape began to waver. As he looked down for the last time the slightest frown appeared on his phantom features. 'Who are you?' Then his outline swirled away with astonishing speed as it rose towards the nebulas he sought.

Edeard fell back with a last sob. Darkness claimed him.

*

Consciousness returned with a slow flush of warmth. Edeard felt perfectly content lying wherever he was, with his eyes closed and his mind at rest. He was breathing normally. Not particularly hungry. A light sheet lay across him. What more could anyone ask?

'Kristabel,' he said, knowing she was there. He didn't use farsight, he just knew.

'You're awake.' Her fingers stroked his face.

He opened his eyes to see her smiling down at him. It was the most wonderful sight.

'Don't you ever do that again,' she chided.

'I won't.'

She kissed him. 'People have been worried,' she said.

'I'll bet.' Edeard looked round. He was in some grand room, high ceilings, walls covered in tapestries and oil paintings.

Familiar wood-framed glass doors opened on to a hortus; bright sunlight shone through. 'Is it midday already?'

'Um, Edeard, you fell two days ago.'

'Oh.'

'Our doctor said you were suffering a combination of exhaustion and shock. She gave you something to keep you asleep, she said you needed time to recover.'

Edeard pulled a face as he licked his tongue round inside his mouth. Something tasted bad.

Kristabel handed him a tall glass of water.

'Thanks,' he lifted himself up gingerly as she pushed some pillows behind his back to support him.

'You're the talk of Makkathran. Again,' she told him with a sly grin.

Edeard gave a feeble shrug.

'I thought you were going to die when you called me.' Her eyes began to fill with tears.

'I'm sorry.' He reached for her, holding her close for a long time. When she'd calmed she said, 'And now you can fly, too.'

'I can't, actually. That's something else altogether. The city, Kristabel, it helps me.'

'The city. You mean Makkathran?'

'Yes.' He could sense the puzzlement in her mind. 'I'll try and explain, it's quite complicated. Perhaps I should explain to everyone. I don't know.'

She rested her hand on his chest. 'You just wait. There's an awful lot you need to say to a great many people. But you need to be very careful exactly what you tell them, and you're not in any condition to make those decisions right now.'

'Okay.' He knew she was right about that.

'You also saw poor Sergeant Chae's soul. If you thought you were famous before, you won't believe what you are now.'

'I thought I hallucinated that part.'

'Thanks to your gifting, the Pythia herself spoke with his soul as it departed. You don't get a more believable witness than that.

She's been waiting to talk to you about what she's calling your "Lady-blessed connection to the spirit world". We're to inform her immediately you've recovered,' Kristabel said significantly.

Edeard instinctively gripped the sheet tighter, drawing it up a couple of inches. He was only wearing a baggy nightshirt underneath. *So who undressed me?*

Kristabel gave him a lofty glance. 'I sent my maids in to prepare you for your rest.'

'What!'

She burst into giggles. 'The doctor and the Novices attended you.'

'Oh.' Not that it made the idea much more tolerable. Novices!

Kristabel hugged him. 'Thank the Lady, you're still my silly Edeard.'

'What about my friends?'

'Waiting outside. Very impatiently. Causing a lot of trouble for the staff. And they're all fine. Before you ask: the gang members are under arrest and awaiting trial in the cells under Parliament House. Their "constable-killer" guns were recovered; and you'll never guess where they came from.'

'Where?' he asked eagerly.

'The Weapons Guild.'

'No.'

'Yes. Apparently they're a secret type the Guild holds safe in case the city is ever attacked. The design dates back centuries. Owain is furious. He's ordered a full inquiry into how they were taken out of storage. Nobody was supposed to know about them apart from the Guild's most senior Masters.'

'That's got to be damaging to Owain in council.'

'I expect so. Daddy was really cheerful when he told me.'

'Thank you,' he said softly.

She gave him a breezy smile. 'What for?'

'Being here.'

'You're welcome, Waterwalker.' She kissed him again. A more sultry embrace this time, containing a great deal of promise. 'I'll call them in. I know you want to see them. Don't worry, the doctor already instructed them to be quick, and not to stress you.'

They came in as one group: Kanseen anxious until she actually saw him awake and sitting up in bed, then she became quite emotional; Boyd nervous, almost shy; Dinlay boyishly eager, holding a big basket of sugared fruits. Macsen however had a huge grin on his face. 'Nanitte,' he whooped gleefully, finger jabbing at Edeard for emphasis. 'I told you so!'

4

Despite its size, there were few people in the Malfit Hall as the junior Cleric escorted Marius across the jet-black floor. Those who were there gave the Higher mistrustful glances as he glided along effortlessly. It was nothing personal, they simply didn't enjoy non-believers being in this hallowed place.

He passed into Liliala Hall, whose ceaseless storm played out across the ceiling. As he walked beneath the apex, lightning bolts arched between billowing clouds, searing narrow gaps in the vapour to reveal the bland Mars Twins. At the far end an arching door let them into the Mayor's suite of chambers. Ethan was waiting in the oval sanctum. It had been restored to its original state, the way the Waterwalker had arranged it while he was Mayor. Chairs and the desk were carved from muroak, and polished with natural wax, giving off a faint lavender scent. The three high diocletian windows on the wall behind the desk provided its occupant a splendid view out across Outer Circle Canal and the western corner of Golden Park, with the lazy green undulations of Low Moat filling the gulf to the crystal wall beyond.

'Thank you for coming,' the Cleric Conservator said genially. He was sitting behind the desk, the hood of his white robe pulled forward. Even with the loose folds of fabric concealing the side of his head, the semi-organic modules were visible adhering to his skin.

Marius bowed respectfully. 'Thank you for seeing me, Conservator.'

Ethan's hand fluttered in dismissal to the assistant Cleric.

'I trust you are almost recovered,' Marius said as he stood in front of the desk. The air in his wake was tainted by wispy shadows from his shimmering black toga suit.

'Almost,' Ethan smiled thinly. His hand rose to indicate the nodules. 'Only three remain, and my doctors tell me they will be removed before the end of the week. It is amazing how the human body's powers of recuperation can be bolstered by good news.'

'Good news?'

Ethan hesitated, wondering if the representative was trying to taunt him. 'A human has passed into the Void, with the help of the Second Dreamer.'

'In an attempt to negotiate a rejection of your Pilgrimage.'

'I doubt any ANA representative will comprehend the most basic tenet of the Void. It exists to embrace life, to elevate us to the highest pinnacle our poor spirits can aspire to.'

'Indeed,' Marius said, with a deliberate irony.

Ethan caught the implication, and smiled gracefully. 'With respect, I hardly consider you comparable to Justine Burnelli. From what I've seen, you remain firmly rooted in the physical aspects of the universe.'

'I will accept that in the spirit I believe it was intended.'

'Thank you,' Ethan sank back in his chair, eyeing the representative curiously. At the start of his campaign to become Conservator he had been cautious about accepting the man's help. Like every aspirant for high office in history, he had used his aide to make the first exploratory contacts. Phelim had returned animated by the possibilities available. Ethan had agreed to listen. Politically, the assistance Marius provided was subtle and invaluable, allowing Ethan to build alliances within the Council and among the Clerics of the Orchard Palace, propelling him to a position where he could put himself forward for election with a great deal of confidence. Included with that was the offer of ultradrives for the Pilgrimage ships, a gift that would generate a near-certain success. All of this had been given freely because their 'objectives' were complementary. And in all that time, Marius had never hinted what his Faction's objective actually was. Ethan knew it wouldn't be long now; it would be interesting to see what the price could possibly be.

'However, hasn't the Void itself demonstrated Justine's essential humanity by its response to her thoughts?' Marius asked the question as if it was some easily dismissed oddity.

'One small dream,' Ethan said. 'A fast glimpse of her predicament. She certainly hasn't found the Heart, or even a Skylord. As her eagerness to reach that star shows, she is concerned only with the physical.'

'Yet she demonstrated the mental abilities available to the Waterwalker.'

'She hardly has his strength.'

'She was only awake for a few days of the Void's timescale, and she appeared to be acclimatizing comfortably.'

'This too serves to reinforce our doctrine. The Void will become our salvation. The Second Dreamer will lead us to our destiny as the Dreamer Inigo always intended.'

'I think we both know it wasn't the Second Dreamer who provided this latest glimpse from within the Void.'

'Yes,' Ethan conceded.

'Does Living Dream know who received Justine's thoughts and vision?'

'No.'

Marius smiled; on his round face with its thin nose, the gesture was unpleasant. 'Yet another Dreamer, Conservator? They seem to be coming quite commonplace.'

'Three Dreamers in two hundred and seventy years is hardly "commonplace". But I do consider it significant that two have appeared so close together at this particular time. Events are coming to a climax, in accordance with the Dreamer Inigo's vision.'

'Of course. I am gladdened that the Second Dreamer has proved it is physically possible to enter the Void, it must be inspirational to your movement.'

'It is.'

'And I don't have to emphasize how important the Second Dreamer is to you. How close are you to acquiring him?'

Ethan smiled back into that barely human face with its steady green eyes and humourless thoughts. 'Her. Actually.'

'Really?'

'Yes. We believe we have identified a possible candidate. Given that the welcome team on Viotia now have her identity, it is impossible for her to elude us for any significant time.'

'Congratulations, Conservator. It must be gratifying having your goal so close to realization.'

'It is.'

'How are you progressing with construction of the Pilgrimage ships?'

'Again we are blessed by good fortune. The construction is on schedule. Would you like me to arrange a tour for you?'

'Time, alas, is tight. In more ways than one.'

'What do you mean?'

'This isn't yet common knowledge, but the Commonwealth Navy sent a River-class warship to intercept the Ocisen Empire fleet. They were supposed to disable the command ship and deliver a warning.'

'Supposed to?'

'The Navy ship was destroyed. It would appear the Ocisens are stronger than Admiral Kazimir expected.'

'Sweet Lady.'

'Unless they are stopped, they will be here before your ships are completed. There will be no Pilgrimage.'

'The principal justification behind ANA was to give the Commonwealth an unassailable defence against alien aggression following the Starflyer War. It was supposed to ensure complete technological superiority.'

'Don't be too upset. It was, after all, just one ship. A stronger navy force should be sufficient to deter the Ocisen fleet. Even we concur with that prognosis.'

'But there are no guarantees.'

'There never are in life.'

'There are in the Void,' Ethan said reflectively. 'Unfortunately, we can't build the ships any faster.'

'I know. We are all dependent on ANA.'

'A wing and a prayer.'

'Quite. On a happier note, now we are so close to success my sponsors have a request.'

'Ah,' Ethan widened his smile. He almost relished this. Would it be a preposterous heretical demand, or some simple require-ment that would trigger a political avalanche in the wake of the Pilgrimage's departure? Was he going to welcome the stipulation, or fight it to his dying breath?

'We would like to send some observers with you.'

'Observers? That implies they will remain aloof, which I sincerely doubt is possible within the Void.'

'Nonetheless, we would be grateful if you would take them with you.'

'We welcome all those who would reach for the Void, what-ever their initial reasons. How many?'

'Two or three on each ship. We don't wish to burden you.'

'I see.' Though in truth Ethan didn't. He knew this must be momentous to whatever Faction Marius represented, yet even he was surprised by how eminently reasonable the request was. 'I will make sure enough suspension chambers are reserved.'

'They will not be travelling in suspension.'

'Is there a reason for that?'

'They don't wish to.'

Ethan considered that, wondering if this was where he should make his stand. Of course, there was no reasonable argument he could put forward against it. Only instinct. 'Will they be antag-onistic to our Pilgrimage in any way?'

'Your pardon, but they care nothing for your doctrine. They are merely scientists who wish to study the Void.'

'And if I refuse?'

Marius adopted an amused tone. 'You are trying to determine how honourable I am, if I will be *awkward*.'

'Will you?'

'More than most I have facilitated your rise to your current position. The gift of the ultradrive engines is phenomenally generous even by Higher standards. And when you accepted this, you knew we would ask a small favour in return.'

'I did. And you know I will allow your colleagues to travel with us, I'm just trying to understand the motivation behind this, how badly you want it.'

'Very badly indeed. The Void is a magnificent scientific enigma. My sponsors believe it should be solved.'

'Why would you want to "solve" something you can become a part of at any time?'

'It is greater than us.'

'And it will share itself with you.'

'On its terms. To accept that is not in our nature.'

'It is in mine.'

'Shall I move to the threat now?'

'Please do,' Ethan said smoothly.

'Even with ultradrive, the Raiel present a problem. Clearly this previously unknown warrior caste will not let you approach the Void boundary. Allowing a lone human in a small ship to slip past is one thing, but the Pilgrimage ships with their millions of hopeful dreamers? You will either turn back or die. The resources they have available are phenomenal; I suspect even a full Commonwealth Navy escort would struggle to protect you, and Governance has quite clearly stated it will do no such thing.'

'It is the last obstacle,' Ethan admitted. The one downside to Justine's triumph, and shocking in its magnitude. He'd always known the Raiel opposed Pilgrimage, but no one had known they had such ships, or the resolution to prevent entry into the Void. The unisphere commentators had been very keen to point this out over the last few hours. Pilgrimage to Certain Death, the less savoury ones had named it.

'In addition to the ultradrive, we can equip your ships with force fields which the Raiel cannot penetrate,' Marius said.

'I find that claim difficult to believe.'

'Nonetheless, we have such systems available.'

'Your passengers.'

'Yes.'

'The Lady moves in mysterious ways. But . . . She would want your scientists granted the opportunity to achieve their destiny along with the rest of us.'

Marius cocked his head to one side. 'I'm sure she would.'

'I will have the cabins set aside for you.'

'Thank you.' Marius bowed, and rotated effortlessly. He moved towards the door. Just as he reached it he stopped. 'Oh yes,' he said, still not facing Ethan. 'And we'll need a cargo hold in each ship for the equipment.'

'Equipment?'

'They will need instruments to study the Void, obviously. I will send details to your office.'

The door opened, and Marius slipped through in a swirl of silent shadow.

Balmy sea air gusted across Golden Park, stirring the long branches of the cherry trees that were planted along the side of the giant plaza. A cloudless sky helped magnify the heat. In his cotton shirt and thick denim trousers, the Delivery Man was getting uncomfortably warm; and he didn't want to use his biononic functions to cool down for fear of attracting attention to himself. Inigo had supposedly chosen this spot to build Makkathran2 because the climate was almost identical to the original on Querencia. So because of that quest for perfection, he had to make do with a ridiculous wide-brimmed leather ranger hat, because that's what the natives back in the real Makkathran apparently used to wear to keep the midsummer sun from frying their brains. At least it left him indistinguishable from the rest of the crowd occupying the plaza.

Golden Park was full every day now. The usual crowd had

swollen considerably when the Second Dreamer rejected the Skylord as the faithful had sought guidance from their new Cleric Conservator; and from that day on they had flocked here to witness the monumental events elsewhere in the galaxy. The Delivery Man could appreciate that, feeling the kind of comfort that only ever came from being immersed in a multitude who shared beliefs and emotions. The most basic human need to belong, amplified by the gaiafield.

On a very minor level he was experiencing that himself, the longing to be back home, playing with the girls as night fell across London. Bath time. Stories at bedtime. A leisurely meal with Lizzie.

He didn't want to be here. It was that simple. This kind of observation was the kind of active operation the Faction had assured him he'd never be involved with. All he ever agreed to do for them was deliver essential items of equipment to the people who would use them. Inevitably, as the years progressed he'd allowed himself to be cajoled into assignments that entailed a great deal more than mere delivery. But this . . .

Once again he was keeping tabs on Marius. He'd done it before without protesting, though Marius always gave him the creeps. Which wasn't the kind of emotional nonsense a Higher should be infected with. It was just that his opposite number was a lot more *professional* at all this than he was. Nor did the unfolding events help his equilibrium; Justine's flight into the Void, the destruction of the *Yenisey*, the Viotia invasion; he couldn't imagine what the end effect on Commonwealth society would be. He just knew his place was at home, caring for his family in the face of such uncertainty. Instead, here he was wandering about with the crowds, making sure he was oozing the same emotional wonder and trepidation into the gaiafield as everyone else, wearing medieval clothes – generally blending in. He could see the Outer Circle Canal through the throng, with several gondolas sailing along sedately, backdropped by the Orchard Palace with its roof that resembled merging waves.

All the time he kept his eye on the wire and wood bridge

which led over to the Palace's main entrance. It was the one Marius had walked over not an hour before. Remote sensors secreted around the canal watched the other bridges for him. Infiltrating systems inside the Palace itself was difficult. Living Dream employed some extremely sophisticated shielding and counter-intruder systems, though a number of stealthed micro-bots were currently inching their way inwards. Even if they managed to get past the great halls and into the Mayor's suite of chambers, they'd be too late.

The Delivery Man's biononic field scan function detected a familiar biononic signature ten metres away. He let out a resigned sigh, and turned to see Marius standing waiting. He was getting a lot of disapproving stares as his dark toga suit refracted the bright sunlight in abnormal undulations. But his implacable demeanour was enough to keep them away.

'Gotcha,' Marius said.

The Delivery Man nodded. 'Yes. Congratulations.'

'Fancy a drink?'

'Why not?'

Marius glide-walked his way across Golden Park, and over the ginger sandstone bridge into Ysidro. The Delivery Man narrowed his eyes as he took in the circular three-storey building with an improbable hexagonal rustication pattern on the walls. Tall lancet windows gave the appearance of some ancient human castle tower.

'Isn't this the one where—' he began.

'Yes,' Marius said.

They went into the tavern, and managed to find a quiet table by one of the windows. A waitress took their order, and quickly returned with a hot orange chocolate with marshmallows for the Delivery Man and a peppermint tea for Marius. Once she'd gone, they wove their screening shields together, creating an almost invisible yet secure bubble around the table.

'The game is changing,' Marius said.

'The game is the same, the stakes are rising,' The Delivery Man countered.

'Fair enough. I don't like you because you symbolize what we're attempting to leave behind. But I respect you; you play by the rules. There are some people in our line of work who no longer do that.'

'We didn't wreck Hanko.'

'Hanko?'

'Please! One of you fired a Hawking m-sink into it.'

'Did we?'

'Yes.'

'Are you sure about that?'

'Don't do that. Don't call me in for a drink and play the subversion recruiting routine. I chose my Faction because of my beliefs, just like you.'

Marius raised his cup in salute. 'My apologies. My point is that you and I are both nearing the end of our usefulness to our respective Factions.'

'No. If *we* hold things together you and I will continue in our current form. Only if you get to enact your particular Armageddon does everything alter.'

'You don't have a clue what we're doing.'

'Fusion is not a pretty concept. It assumes elevation to perpetual godhood. The conflict here at this table is enough to convince me that should not be allowed to happen; and we both know there are Factions a lot more radical than us.'

'My apologies again. You have all the answers.'

'Of course, you could choose to come over to us. That would undoubtedly mean the end of your Faction. Problem solved for everyone.'

'I don't think so.'

'I had to ask.'

'I know.'

The Delivery Man tried to sip his chocolate through the cap of semi-molten marshmallows. 'So now what?'

'As I said, the game is changing. We are entering the last stages of an operation which has been centuries in the planning.

As such, it is no longer a game. Please do not think we will tolerate any interference.'

'The human race for all our facets and our institutional stupidity is something I believe in. I admire our diversity, our stubbornness. The dynamic of conflict is one of our greatest traits.'

'Please don't give me the "we're at our greatest when our backs are against the wall" speech.'

'I can't because you seem to want to eliminate our conflict, our differences, to rebuild us in your image. I will not allow that to happen. My Faction will not permit that.'

'Which is my point. You no longer have that luxury of choice, it was taken from you decades ago when we succeeded. This, today, this is just the result of our actions.'

'You cannot believe that morally you have the right to elevate everyone to post-physical status whether they want that or not.'

'We won't be taking everyone.'

'Then stop trying to manipulate everyone.'

'You seem determined to remain in the past. Is that your wife's influence?'

The Delivery Man placed the chocolate cup on the table, it was all he could do not to shatter the china his grip had tightened so. 'Be very careful.'

'We have the right to evolve.'

'You do. You do not have the right to evolve the rest of us, nor ruin what we have built in the process.'

'Much good your ANA:Governance has done you. It is the most conservative Faction of all.'

'It made you possible.'

'Exactly. And now, like an enfeebled parent jealous of our youth and vision, it strives to hold us back.'

'It neither encourages nor refuses your ambitions, it is neutral as always. We, on the other hand, are not. Find a way of doing what you want without harming others, without endangering the entire galaxy.'

'We do neither. You cannot stop us elevating ourselves into

something glorious. Do not try. That is what I am saying to you. We have come to the end of this tedious routine, you and I. Next time we meet it will not be sitting in a tavern over a friendly drink.'

'If that's the way it is, then that's the way it is.' The Delivery Man watched Marius give him a sad little smile, then glide out of the tavern. Only then did he exhale a very shaky breath. 'Oh dear Ozzie,' he hissed. 'I can't do this any more.'

✳

The storm had been rising steadily for three hours now. A continual cloud of miniature ice daggers were hurtling horizontally through the air, smashing into the ground crawler at close to a hundred miles an hour. The noise was astonishing, as if they were buffeting their way forwards through a jungle of glass.

As before, the land shifted without warning, sending the ground crawler rocking violently. Corrie-Lyn gripped her seat tighter. It was the fifth mini-quake in the last hour. And they were coming closer together.

'I'm sorry,' Corrie-Lyn said. She was sitting beside Inigo as he attempted to steer them across hilly land locked into shape by the permafrost. All the loose snow that had accumulated in dunes and crevices was slowly and methodically being swept up by the wind, hardening further as it took to the air to join the atmospheric bedlam. They could see nothing through the narrow windscreen now, even the powerful headlight beams created little more than a dusky glow in the merciless blizzard. The ground-crawler's sensors could only scan a derisory fifteen to twenty yards ahead. His biononic field scan function merely supplemented the perception.

'Nothing to be sorry for,' Inigo told her. He reached out and gripped her hand. Corrie-Lyn leaned in towards him.

'If I hadn't come, none of this would have happened. The restoration team would still be alive. You could have carried on rescuing people.'

'The universe doesn't work like that. They would have found me, one way or another. I'm glad it was you.'

'I've killed you.' The tears were running freely down her freckled cheeks.

Inigo stopped the ground crawler and put his arms round her. 'That's just fright you're feeling. You must not blame anyone, least of all yourself.'

'How can you be so calm?'

'All I have seen, all Edeard showed me, it gives me hope. Hope doesn't die just because a life is lost, nor even a million lives. The human race carries on. We have before, many times, we will again.'

'As stupid as ever,' she grumbled, wiping at the tears.

He caught her hand, and brought it to his own face, then slowly licked the moisture from her fingers. 'That's my Corrie-Lyn.'

She nestled up against him. 'I still think it's my fault. I should never have let that psychopath talk me into this.'

'From what you've told me you didn't have a lot of choice.'

'I could have been bolder. I could have thrown him off a cliff like you did.'

'Well, in the end that hasn't made a lot of difference, has it?'

'I'd prefer not to spend my last moments with him, thank you.'

'We're not dead yet.' Inigo let go of her, and turned back to the console. 'Only another two hundred kilometres to my starship.'

'You really have one?'

'I really have one. Smart man, that Aaron, working that out.'

The ground crawler lurched forwards again. Corrie-Lyn came over from her seat to stand behind Inigo. Her hands massaged his shoulders.

'How far have we come?'

'About eighty kilometres in the last seventeen hours.' He nodded at the windscreen. 'It's getting worse out there. I'm guessing the quakes are the start of the implosion. No wonder the atmosphere is kicking up.'

'We're not going to make it, are we?'

'No.'

She bent down and nipped his ear. 'Hey, you're a messiah. You're supposed to inspire your flock.'

'Would the flock settle for certainty?'

'I thought there were no absolutes.'

'I can see you're going to be a difficult convert.'

The ground crawler juddered alarmingly as the landscape outside heaved. Corrie-Lyn's grip tightened as she struggled against being thrown to the metal decking.

'Lady,' Inigo grunted. The portal projecting the sensor images showed a crack in the ground running almost parallel to the ground crawler, in some places it was over two metres wide. It hadn't been there before the quake.

Inigo upped the speed of the tracks, sending them wobbling away from the crack.

'Why did you leave us?' Corrie-Lyn asked.

'No great revelation,' he said. 'I was tired. Tired of the expectations. Tired of the Council. Tired of the adulation.'

'And me?'

'No, never you. I wouldn't have stayed as long as I did if it hadn't been for you.'

'I don't believe you.'

Inigo laughed. 'If you're not an absolute, you're definitely a constant. Why don't you believe me?'

'Because I know you, or I did back then. You believed in the dreams, in the life the Waterwalker showed us, the life we could live in the Void. You never tired, not of that, not of being our Dreamer. What happened?'

'Maybe I shouldn't have left. Lady, look what's happened because I did. Ethan as Conservator! He was never elevated to Council for a reason, you know. Why did the conclave vote for him? What were you thinking of?'

'Change,' she snapped at him. 'Pilgrimage. The Second Dreamer made it possible, or at least believable. But that's not relevant, that's today, not seventy years ago. Why, Inigo? Don't you at least owe me that?'

'There was a dream,' he whispered. His mind released a deluge of sadness through his gaiamotes, strong enough to make her shudder in dismay.

'The Last Dream?' she gasped. 'It's real?'

'Not in the way rumour had it.'

'But the Waterwalker died. That was his victory, he'd finally lived every life. The Skylords guided his soul to Odin's Sea. I was there,' she growled. 'I lived that dream, the dream you gave us. I lay back on the pyre atop the tallest tower in Eyrie and watched the Skylords return to fill the sky above Makkathran. I rose with him while the whole city sang their hymn of farewell. I received his final gifting to the world. He went to the Heart of the Void! It was so beautiful, and I believed it. I believed in *you*.' Corrie-Lyn shoved her way along the side of Inigo's chair, and knelt down, putting her face inches from his. 'That is the dream I recall so few times because it is so powerful I weep each time at what those of us trapped outside the Void never had. That is the dream that counts. That is the reason I am a member of Living Dream, *your* movement. And it is why I always will be no matter who is in charge or what ridiculous petty politics affect the Clerics. You gave us that. You made *us* dream.'

Inigo stared at the sensor projection of the treacherous ground, refusing to meet her eye. His gaiamotes closed up, shutting off his emotions.

'Tell me,' she demanded, so frightened she was trembling. 'Tell me what dream you had.'

'It's just me,' he said. 'That's all. It was just my reaction. There's nothing to stop the Pilgrimage, nothing to prevent the faithful from achieving their perfect lives. It just affected me.'

'What is it? *Please*, Inigo?'

'I had one more dream,' he said, still watching the display. 'I saw what happened to Querencia afterwards. After the Water-walker died. It was the life of one of his descendants living in Makkathran.'

'What did they do?' she asked. 'Did they misuse the gift?'

The ground quaked again.

'No,' Inigo said, with a faint smile. 'They used it perfectly.'

Corrie-Lyn grimaced in annoyance as the quake got worse. She clutched at the back of Inigo's seat. Both of them looked at each other as the crawler began to tip over. The sensor display showed the ground lifting and splitting.

Inigo loaded a quick sequence into the ground crawler's small smartnet. Anchors fired out of the lower fuselage, drilling long spikes deep into the frigid soil. Superstrength cables rewound, the tension tightening the heavy machine's grip on the anchors.

'Inigo,' Corrie-Lyn wailed.

He gripped her hand. 'We're together,' he promised, and opened his mind to her again.

The ground beneath the crawler heaved with a profound roaring. All six anchor spikes came flying back out of the disintegrating soil, crashing into the side of the vehicle with an almighty *clang*.

'Together.'

The ground crawler started to roll. Corrie-Lyn yelled in panic as she was thrown into the side of the cabin, then the walls carried on moving. Inigo was hanging upside down in his seat as the safety webbing held him in place. Corrie-Lyn tumbled down towards the back of the cabin as the angle shifted. The ground crawler was skidding along on its roof. Another judder from the ground pushed it up on its nose and twisted. Several storage locker doors popped open, releasing a clutch of clothes and crockery and food packets that pelted through the interior, bounding about dangerously.

Corrie-Lyn lost her hold on the galley section to be tossed about. She felt her arm break as she hit the external door. The pain was awful, dulling her mind, even the cabin dipped into grey. She actually thought: *This is the end*.

A couple of miserable breaths later and she was still whimpering where she'd fallen. The ground crawler had stopped moving.

'Hang on,' Inigo called above the constant clamour of the blizzard. 'I'm coming.'

She watched him through a haze as her stomach grew very queasy. He had to climb up the side of the forward cabin, twisting round the front chairs with a contortionist's agility. Somehow the ground crawler had finished up standing on its nose, with the deck inclined.

Inigo wound up sitting on the back of the driver's chair, cradling her. She stared up at the bulkhead above with its small storage locker doors swinging open.

'My arm,' she cried. The dull pain was rising to hot agony. Her exovision medical displays were flashing up tissue damage summaries.

Inigo looked round the cabin. 'These crawlers always have medic packs; there'll be one around somewhere. Get your nerves to shut down the pain.'

She nodded, which nearly made her squeal. Concentrating on the physiological icons was difficult, but eventually her secondary routines were closing off nerves to her arm. Her ankle was damaged, too, though that was minor compared to the arm. She let out a huge sigh as the pain faded. Nothing she could do about the queasiness, however.

Inigo left her to rummage through all the junk that was cluttered round them. He found a first aid pack. The case started to analyse the data her macrocellular clusters gave it, and opened up various plyplastic appendages which wiggled across her shoulder. Inigo cut away her sleeve to give it access to her skin.

'Now what?' she asked.

He glanced at the portal display, which remained resolutely blank. 'We're wedged into a fissure, with our arse sticking up into the air. How's that for dignity.'

'Can your field functions get us out?'

'Not easily. I suppose I can give it a go, though.'

'That's good. I was almost worried there.'

He chuckled, and stroked her face. 'We'll just wait a minute. I want to be certain you're all right before I leave you.'

'I don't want you to leave right away,' she said shakily.

'Then I'll stay. We're not in any hurry. Not today.'

*

The *Alexis Denken* was only ninety minutes out from Arevalo when Kazimir called.

'We just lost our communication link with the *Lindau*,' he said.

Paula, who was sitting at her piano trying to master 'Für Elise' yet again, let her shoulders slump. 'Oh, crap. I thought you were going to warn them to be careful.'

'I did. Evidently I wasn't clear enough.'

'So now Aaron has a Navy ship?'

'A scout ship. And it might be Inigo.'

'Or the Waterwalker himself. Or Nigel's come back. Or maybe . . .' But she didn't finish that one.

'There's no need to be cruel.'

'We're getting stretched very thin, Kazimir.'

'I know. But there is some good news. The *Lindau* might not be communicating, but I can still keep track of it.'

'How?'

'There's a secondary transdimensional channel generated by all Navy ship drives. It's used for one thing only, to supply us with their location for precisely this reason.'

'I never knew that. So where is it now?'

'Still on Hanko.'

'Interesting. If you're Aaron and you've got yourself a lifeboat, why wait around on a planet that's about to implode?'

'To find what you originally came for.'

'Exactly. Keep me updated.'

'Of course.'

'Are you going to send another ship?'

'The *Yangtze* is already on its way; I doubt it will get there in time.'

'A River-class no less? You are taking this seriously now. Let us hope it has better luck than the *Yenisey*.'

'And the *Lindau*.'

*

It was raining outside Colwyn City, turbid clouds drizzling the fields and hills with a slick of cold water. A morose day whose lack of wind condemned it to suffer under mist which stifled the land and obscured the upper skies with their pink cirro-stratus clouds. However, inside the force fields, it was dry and sunny as the gloom was diverted round the curving protective barriers.

The woman was making the most of the artificial climate, walking in a leisurely way up Daryad Avenue's pronounced slope to window shop. Almost half of the stores along the avenue were open, though most of the bars and restaurants were shut. Supply deliveries were non-existent in Colwyn now that the invaders had shut down all capsule flights.

Most people in the city centre that morning were heading down the slope towards the river. It was the day the Senate delegation was due to arrive. The residents wanted to give them a welcome they couldn't ignore as their starship touched down at the docks. Already, the crowds were swelling round the sealed-up perimeter.

The woman either didn't care or didn't know. She was young, and attractive, wearing a fashionable grey-blue dress whose skirt showed off long legs. Men making their way down the slope cast admiring glances and pinged her. She smiled loftily, ignoring the attention. She also somehow managed to ignore the Ellezelin paramilitary capsules racing low overhead, their sirens screeching and dousing the pavement with strobing lasers.

Ignoring them to a degree that she was unaware of three larger capsules prowling the sky above the avenue's rooftops. Unaware as they suddenly stopped their circling to powerdive. She was still unaware right up to the moment when their seven-gee deceleration smacked them down beside her with such force their pressure waves burst the glass window she was looking

375

through. She screamed as she was shoved painfully to her knees amid the glittering shards, her arms folded round her head to try to protect her. The big capsules halted, floating ten centimetres above the concrete. Their malmetal doors opened fast, and Major Honilar jumped out, leading his welcome team into a surround and secure formation, putting the woman at the centre of a circle produced by the nozzles of fifteen high calibre energy weapons. She was screaming incoherently as they encircled her, blood running from a hundred tiny glass nicks, her dress all but shredded.

'Shut the fuck up,' Major Honilar bellowed at her.

Everyone on the outside of the three capsules who had flung themselves flat, lifted their heads to see what in Ozzie's name was going on. They saw an armour-suited figure grab the woman's hair and lift her brutally to her feet. Saw the agony on her mutilated face. Saw the horrific amount of blood saturating her clothes, dripping liberally on to the pavement. Several of the more astute ones delivered what they were seeing directly to unisphere news stations.

'Araminta, you are now in the protective custody of the Intermediate Ellezelin forces.' The suited figure pushed her towards the nearest capsule.

'Hey!' someone on the street protested.

One of the welcome team fired a small enhanced explosive projectile over their heads. The detonation forced everyone to cower on the floor again.

'If anyone attempts to interfere with our operation they will be shot,' Major Honilar announced loudly. He pushed the bloody, sobbing woman into his capsule, which lifted immediately, its malmetal door still closing as it reached rooftop height. The remainder of the welcome team retreated back into their capsules, covering the prone bystanders in a classic hostile withdrawal protocol.

Sitting drinking their morning tea on the balcony of the cafe opposite the drama, Oscar and his team watched the last capsule lift hurriedly into the city's artificially clear sky.

'Good deployment,' Beckia said with grudging admiration. She was wearing a silver-edged beret in the local style, helping to make her look even more beguiling.

'As subtle as a kick in the balls,' Tomansio retorted dismissively. 'Look at them.' He waved a hand towards the stunned citizens who were slowly picking themselves up. There was a lot of anger on their faces.

Oscar watched several of them shaking their fists at the sky, shouting obscenities. He was glad he was back wearing civilian clothes. It wasn't going to be pleasant for any of the Ellezelin troops caught alone after today.

'I think Major Honilar is getting somewhat aggrieved,' Beckia said. 'What's that, the fifth Araminta the recognition programs have found for him this morning?'

'Liatris is doing well,' Tomansio said.

'I doubt the latest victim thinks that,' Oscar said. He couldn't drink his cinnamon-flavoured espresso now. The callousness he'd just witnessed was triggering a lot of guilt. The poor woman was perfectly innocent, her only crime to have roughly the same dimensions and features as the real Araminta. That way the whole incident could be blamed on the recognition software that had plucked her image from one of the streetwatch sensors along Daryad Avenue, alerting the welcome team to her location.

'This is your operation, Oscar,' Tomansio rebuked. 'You knew what would have to be done. Don't go soft on us now.'

'Of all the people in the galaxy, I am the one who *really* understands the concept of collateral damage best of all,' Oscar announced.

'So you are. Then you know she was a necessary casualty.'

'That doesn't make it right.'

'Oscar, Ellezelin invading Viotia isn't right. Hunting Araminta isn't right, but we're all doing it because we all know she has to be found.'

'What was her name?' Oscar asked, staring down on the broad avenue. More people were heading down the slope now, marching to the docks to make their demands heard by the Senate delegation. It was all futile, he knew. Living Dream didn't care for their opinion, nor that of the Senate. The delegation and talks with Phelim and the Prime Minister were just buying the welcome team more time to find their target.

'Does it matter?' Beckia asked.

'Yes, actually, it does,' Oscar said. 'We used her.'

'I'll have Liatris check it out when he has a moment,' Tomansio said.

'Thank you.'

Tomansio and Beckia finished their drinks. Oscar still couldn't bring himself to touch what was left of his. People were getting hurt, and he was the cause. He knew it was stupid, but he really hadn't considered that aspect of the operation when he agreed to help Paula. Dushiku's unisphere interface code hung in his exovision, so very, very tempting. Talking things through with his calm, rational partner would make things feel so much better. It was also a sign of weakness which the Knights Guardian wouldn't take too kindly. So he sighed when Tomansio and Beckia rose from the table and gave him an enquiring glance.

'Coming,' he said.

They took a public cab from outside the cafe. It rode quickly and smoothly along the metro track that ran down the middle of Daryad Avenue, taking them up the slope into the grid of taller modern buildings. Ten minutes later it dropped them off in the Palliser precinct, where they walked into a bar that was several social levels below the cafe they'd just left. It was wedged in between a trike repair garage and a wholesale packaging store. A cheap framework of composite which was supposed to have aircoral grown over it, only someone had messed up the pruning hormones leaving one corner and half the roof misshapen, with lumps and cracks. Plastic sheeting had been epoxied over most of the splits decades ago, sealing it against the elements, but they didn't look good. A lot of the patches were peeling away. The current owner had pushed them back and held them down with thick black tape. Sallow fungal weeds were growing out of the pocks on the roof, parasiting the aircoral's paltry nutrients.

Oscar glanced down to the far end of the street where the Colwyn City's big confluence nest building stood at the intersection, squat and aloof, looking fortress-like compared to the shabbiness of the structures around it.

Inside, the bar was little better, with the windows obscured by ancient hologram adverts, and fading overhead lighting strips adding little to the illumination. Tables were scattered about on the ancient wood floor, interspaced with pool tables and tri-gamer stations. Only the counter had decent lighting, with suspended white globes projecting a monochrome glow across the beer pumps.

There were less than ten customers in total. Two hardcore barflies up on stools lining up shot glasses and aerosols, one loner sitting at a tri-game feeding it with his cash coin, and the others huddled round tables. They all ignored the newcomers.

Tomansio gave the bartender an order for four beers and they claimed a corner table. A service bot trundled over with their glasses. Two minutes later Cheriton sauntered in. He did draw some glances, with a big grey coat buttoned up tight so he didn't show off his 'native' Ellezelin clothes. Nothing he could do to disguise the hat, though, which he held in one hand.

'So?' Tomansio asked as Cheriton sat down.

The gaiafield expert raised his glass as they used their bionomics to establish a screening field. 'Paranoia reigns supreme. They've got the building net scanning and logging all calls. If I'd encrypted anything I sent they would have dropped a cage over me.'

'Are they suspicious?'

'Not of us, but they know someone is messing with the welcome team's search. We're not the only covert team here.'

'Liatris has spotted at least two other infiltrations,' Beckia said.

'Well between us we're certainly stirring up a yarsnapper nest of distrust. The Third Dreamer hasn't helped.'

'I would have thought they'd enjoy that,' Tomansio said. 'A near real-time connection into the Void that shows we can get inside, and we have psychic powers when we do get there.'

'Living Dream certainly welcomes that, but it does raise questions about why our dear Cleric Conservator hasn't been chosen for any communing, nor the rest of the Cleric Council for that matter.'

'Are they chasing after the Third Dreamer now as well?' Oscar asked.

'No. Best guess is that it's someone with a strong natural connection to Justine.'

'What do you mean, natural connection?'

'It was always assumed Inigo was related to Edeard somehow, some distant family connection. As we don't know which colony ship wound up inside the Void, the link could never be proven. So Living Dream is assuming the same for Justine.'

'There can't be many left,' Oscar said thoughtfully. 'She's been inside ANA for centuries. All her contemporaries are in there, too, that or they're real-dead.'

'Apart from Admiral Kazimir,' Cheriton said.

'No!'

'Probably not,' Cheriton admitted. 'But we'll never be able to trace it anyway. Justine's dream emanated from the Central worlds' gaiafield; where the Confluence nests are all built and maintained by Highers. Living Dream can't touch them.'

'Thank Ozzie for that,' Beckia said.

'Hang on,' Oscar said. 'Araminta can hardly have a family connection to a Starflyer.'

Cheriton grinned. 'It's not exactly a perfect theory.'

'So Living Dream's emphasis is still on the Second Dreamer?' Tomansio asked.

'Very much so.' Cheriton took another drink of the beer. 'You need to get Liatris into my building's net and subvert their monitors to establish a secure channel for me. If he doesn't I'll have to go aggressive to get out if I send you a warning again.'

'I'll tell him.'

'What progress are you making with Danal and Mareble?' Oscar asked.

'Some, though I'm not sure it's going to help much. Danal was given a memory read.'

Everyone round the table winced.

'Yeah,' Cheriton said. 'As were all the others they rounded up at the apartment raid. I took Mareble down to their headquarters in the docks. She got to see him, but he's still in custody, and she had a restriction order placed on her. As far as Major Honilar is now concerned, just knowing Araminta is a crime.'

'So they're no use, then?'

'I wouldn't say that, exactly.'

Beckia gave Cheriton a knowing glance. 'You didn't?'

'What could I do? The whole merry widow syndrome really kicked into overdrive for a while there. She was very upset when I got her back to her hotel room.'

'Dear Ozzie,' Oscar chuckled into his beer.

'It establishes me as a genuine supportive friend,' Cheriton said, a shade too defensively. 'That could be useful. A lot of followers are having their faith shaken by the way Phelim is acting. This wasn't what they signed up for.'

'Okay, good work,' Tomansio said.

Cheriton put his beer back on the table. 'Have you got any idea where Araminta might be?'

'Not one. Liatris is running a hundred analysis routines trying to figure out where she could have taken refuge. Honilar won't be far behind him; even he is eventually going to work out he's being deliberately distracted.'

'Great. Then the paranoia will really kick in.'

'They'll go for her family next,' Oscar said miserably. 'Make a big splash of arresting them to flush her out.'

'Do you want to warn them?' Tomansio asked.

'If they believe us, and it's a big if, that might make it harder for Honilar to round them up. Worst case scenario it'll take him an extra half hour. You keep telling me every minute is precious.'

'Sounds like a plan. I'll start calling them.'

'I'd better get back,' Cheriton said. He stood up and slipped through the privacy screen.

'Nothing from the monitors we've got on Cressida,' Beckia said as they waited for Tomansio to complete his anonymous calls to Araminta's family. 'We'll go to Nik's next, see if any of her old colleagues can give us a hint where she might be.'

'Sure,' he said. His u-shadow told him Paula was calling on a secure channel.

'Any progress?' she asked.

'The Second Dreamer is Araminta, a Viotia native. So far she's managed to give everyone the slip. We're chasing up what leads we've got, but we're not the only ones here.'

'You're sure it's Araminta?'

'Oh yes.' Oscar smiled fondly as he recalled their second visit to the apartments. He'd actually laughed out loud when he saw the top of the water tank lying on the bathroom floor. And from what they could determine, she'd stopped for a cup of tea and some biscuits before scooting out of there. That was real class – or total insanity. Either way, he was rather looking forward to the time when he finally got to meet her. 'Living Dream knows it, too.'

'Can you get her first?'

'We'll do our best.'

'I have something to tell you,' Paula said.

'This doesn't sound good.'

'There is a Faction agent in a very powerful starship, equivalent to yours. They just fired a black hole weapon into Hanko. The planet is currently imploding.'

Oscar's skin turned chilly. He stared at the bar's colourful hologram adverts without seeing them. 'Hanko?'

'Yes. I'm sorry, Oscar.'

'But I captained the *Dublin* there during the Prime attack,' he protested weakly. 'We went through hell protecting Hanko.'

'I know. This is a new and very dangerous type of weapon. No one expected it to be used like this. I'm telling you so you understand the Factions are becoming desperate. Be very careful acquiring this Araminta. It is not a game.'

'I understand. Why was Hanko so important to them?'

'Inigo may have been on it.'

'Wow. I see. Did he escape?'

'We don't know. There's no communication link to the planet any more.'

'Shit.'

'Oscar. There's something else. I'm telling you in case I vanish. I suspect there's a good chance the agent was the Cat.'

'Oh no. No, no, no. Not her. She's in suspension. You put here there for fuck's sake. That was the one thing I made very sure of after they re-lifed me.'

'I don't know for certain yet. And it'll only be a clone if it is her.'

'*Only* a clone? Oh Jesus. Where is she?'

'I don't know. But if she turns up on Viotia, your Knights Guardian might be tempted to jump ship.'

'Oh fuck!' he said that out loud, very loud. Beckia and Tomansio gave him a curious glance.

'Now you know,' Paula said. 'You can take precautions.'

'Precautions? Against the Cat, in an ultradrive ship, with a superweapon? What kind of deranged moron let her have these things in the first place?'

'As I said, the Factions are getting desperate.'

'Wait. Why would you vanish?'

'She, or someone like her, tried to kill me. She'll probably try again. You know what she's like.'

'I want to go home.'

'And you will. Not long now.'

'Damn, I hate you.'

'Hate is good. It helps keep you focused.'

'It's not good,' he protested irritably. 'It makes you irrational.'

'Which makes you unpredictable. Which gives your enemies a difficult time determining your actions. It will be harder for her to set a trap for you.'

'I didn't have any goddamn enemies before you dragged me into this.'

'If you genuinely need back-up, I will come to Viotia. I simply prefer not to unless there is no alternative. Do you want me there?'

Oscar took a long breath and glared up at the ceiling. 'No. I have everything perfectly under control.' He told his u-shadow to end the call.

'Everything all right?' Tomansio asked.

'Blissfully wonderful. Come on, let's get over to Nik's.' *While Viotia's still here.*

*

The winds on Hanko had always presented a problem to starships, or any flying machine, whether they used ingrav or regrav. The pressure which the unpredictable turbulence produced on the hull pushed the vessels about as they neared the ground. At high altitude it didn't really matter, precision wasn't necessary above the cloud level. But close to the ground it became more of a problem. Squalls and microbursts could shove the whole ship down unexpectedly, bringing it perilously close to a crash. As a consequence, nothing flew below eight hundred metres unless they were landing at Jajaani. That was in ordinary conditions.

As the planet's frozen surface began to quake and buckle prior to its final, fatal implosion, the storms accelerated relentlessly with windspeeds rising to over two hundred kilometres an hour. Aaron found there was only one way to fly through such an environment: using the kind of speed and power that no wind could ever affect.

The *Lindau* hit mach twelve as he took it down to an altitude of five hundred metres. At that velocity, through a dense typhoon of hail, it didn't so much fly as rip out a vacuum contrail. Supersonic annular blast waves radiated out from the force field, blasting the ice and soil below to granulated ruin. A thick column

384

of lightning blazed along its roiling wake before discharging into sheets that spread over hundreds of square kilometres. Far above the starship, the upper cloud level bulged and seethed as if some massive creature was clawing at the planetary blanket.

Aaron reached the end of his run, and an eight-gee acceleration vector lifted the *Lindau* vertical. Seconds later he was out of the clouds and curving sharply at ten gees through the ionosphere to bring the nose down again. The starship's on-board compensators managed to relieve four gees, leaving him exposed to a full six gee force. Biononics braced his body again as he was shoved back into the pilot's acceleration couch. The *Lindau* plunged back into the lower atmosphere. It immediately began to vibrate with a frequency and intensity that threatened to shake the whole structure apart. Even with btrononic protection, Aaron could feel his bones and organs quiver as his flesh was squeezed. Alarms filled the cabin with a panicked howl. Red strobes drowned out the ordinary illumination, immersing him in hell's own lighting scheme. He heard overstressed metal tearing. Somewhere behind him high pressure gas roared out of a fracture. Toxic alarms added their unique note to the clamour. Aaron strengthened his integral force field.

Solar-bright lightning overwhelmed the hull's visual sensors as the starship began its new run five hundred metres from the ground. The vibration grew progressively more violent. Aaron ignored it all, scrutinizing every byte of data from the external sensors. Within the chaos of the terminal blizzard, the ship's instruments could only scan a few hundred metres with any accuracy. His search area was a huge zone that stretched from the Asiatic glacier back to the Olhava camp, which he was forced to cover in strips eight hundred metres wide – with a fifty-metre overlap to be certain of complete coverage.

The *Lindau* completed its manic run, and punched upwards. A fuselage stress strut snapped, tearing through cables and pipes. Sparks sprayed into the cabin as half the polyphoto light panels failed. Smartcore schematics revealed a deeper problem of primary power loss to several drive support systems. Aaron shunted the display into a peripheral icon, and powerdived the starship back into the clouds at eleven gees.

*

The Delivery Man teleported directly into the hallway to hear Elsie and Tilly squabbling over who could play with the grav-ball. Elsie had it, and was running round the front lounge victoriously, holding the toy aloft and shouting: 'My turn, my turn.'

Tilly was chasing after her sister trying to grab the ball back. 'Is not!' she yelled in frustration. The paediatric housebot was floating after the two of them, maintaining the safety-regulated one point seven metres away, chiding melodiously: 'Children to stop climbing on furniture. There is danger in this activity. Please calm down. Share your toys. It is rewarding.'

'Ratbag,' Elsie shouted at the bot. She threw the grav-ball. It hit the upper surface of the bot, and rebounded in a cloud of blue holographic light to hit the ceiling, where it flattened out for five seconds, quivering, before launching itself at the wall amid another photonic fizz. Tilly and Elsie sprinted for it, little faces grim with determination. Both missed as it shot upwards again, making a ridiculous *boiiing* noise. Another bounce off the ceiling and it was heading straight for Lizzie's favourite vase, a fifteen-hundred-year-old Rebecca Lewis from her Bryn-Bella period.

The Delivery Man hated the flowery monstrosity, but managed to snatch the grav-ball from the air just before it hit.

'Daddy!' Both girls immediately forgot their squabble and ran over for hugs.

'I've told you a hundred times you're not to play with this in the adult rooms,' he scolded.

'Yes, yes!' They wrapped their arms around him, tugging as they jumped up and down in happy excitement.

'Where've you been?'

'Did you bring presents?'

He handed the grav-ball to the housebot. 'All over, and no.'

'Awwww!'

'I was too busy, sorry.' *Staying alive.*

The three of them walked into the kitchen where Lizzie and a general housebot were preparing supper on the iron range cooker. Various pans were bubbling away, producing a melange of scents. It was dark outside, turning the windows into sheets of blackness coated in condensation.

Lizzie smiled and gave him a quick kiss. 'Glad you're back,' she whispered.

'Me too.'

Rosa tottered in from the conservatory, dressed in a red and black skirt with green stockings. 'Daa da.'

'Hello, poppet.' He scooped her up, and tidied some of her dark red curls.

'She said bot today,' Lizzie said.

'Did you?' the Delivery Man asked. Rosa smiled back, saying nothing.

'It could have been boot,' Lizzie admitted. 'Can you three do something useful and lay the table, please?'

The Delivery Man put Rosa down, and helped Tilly and Elsie arrange the knives and forks in the right places.

'I think I might cut down on investigations,' the Delivery Man said as he found some wine glasses for himself and Lizzie.

'That's good,' she said.

'At least the cases furthest away from the Central worlds. That should cut down on my away time considerably.'

She rewarded the decision with a kiss. 'Thank you.'

They all sat down together for supper. The housebot put a big casserole pot in the middle of the table, and lifted the lid off.

The Delivery Man poked the serving spoon in, and lifted out some steaming— 'What is this?' he asked dubiously.

'Sausage stew,' Tilly announced proudly. 'I made the sausages at school. We programmed the culinary cabinet down to level three for the ingredients.'

'I made the tomatoes,' Elsie said.

'It all looks lovely,' the Delivery Man assured them. He tipped the stew on to the plate, and added some vegetables and potatoes. Lizzie sipped at the wine, and grinned at him over the rim of the glass.

When they finally got the children to bed, the Delivery Man lit the fire in the lounge. The Georgian townhouse was perfectly insulated against the wintry night, but as Lizzie had educated him, a real fire gave them a *reassuring* warmth inside. They snuggled up together on the big settee with the rest of the wine.

'I heard a rumour today,' Lizzie said. 'You know what Jen's husband does?'

'Er, not sure, really.' For the first time in a long time he was actually relaxing rather than putting on a show of tranquillity.

'Something to do with the Navy. Anyway, she was telling me the Ocisen fleet might be more powerful than anyone is owning up to.'

'Really?' He knew it was only ever a matter of time before news of the *Yenisey* got out.

'Did you hear anything?'

'No.' But he did remember Marius's reaction to the news of Hanko. It was odd, as though the Accelerator Faction representative didn't know about the Hawking m-sink being used. *Why would he try to bluff on that?*

'And the news from Viotia was horrible. The unisphere showed some poor woman being grabbed by the paramilitaries. They'd attacked her in the street for no reason.'

'Terrible.' *Unless he genuinely didn't know. And if that's the case, who else would be able to get hold of one?*

'I can see you're really bothered by it.'

'Sorry.'

'It's okay.' She wiggled up closer. 'I am glad you're cutting back. You don't mind?'

'I can pick it up again in twenty years. I just don't want to miss out on the kids growing up. It's a unique time.'

Lizzie patted his leg as she tipped back some more wine. 'Good man.'

While the Delivery Man was getting ready for bed that night the Conservative Faction called. 'We need you to deliver a starship to Pulap tomorrow.'

'No,' he told them. A quick guilty glance through the bathroom door showed Lizzie moving round in the bedroom. He shut the door. 'Not any more.'

'This will be an entirely passive role for you, exactly as we originally promised. To the best of our knowledge there are no agents of any Faction on Pulap.'

'If he catches me, you'll need to re-life me. I don't want that.'

'There is someone else we will be using to monitor Marius from now on. An operative who takes a more active role than you.'

'Oh.'

'To reassure you further, Marius has just arrived on Ganthia.'

'What's on Ganthia?' He immediately cursed himself for asking.

'We're not sure. However, it is over two hundred lightyears from Pulap. We would not ask you to make this delivery unless it was urgent.'

'I don't know.'

'It will take us time to replace you. There was bound to be some overlap before your successor can be fully initiated.'

'I didn't say I was going to stop helping you.' He gave his image in the mirror an angry stare, then broke away and stuffed his clothes into the laundry basket. 'All right, I'll deliver the starship; but after this I want at least three days' notice of any assignment.'

'Thank you.'

*

Araminta didn't sleep much. The bed which the couch expanded into was fine, its ageing mattress accommodating and the duvet warm. The twins next door made no noise to bother her. It was all due to worry. Worry that any second the door would come crashing down and the Ellezelin paramilitaries would rampage through the little house to grab her, hurting Tandra and the children in the process.

I had no right to come here and put them in danger.

Worry, also, about what to do next. She knew who she wanted to talk to, but the how of it was difficult. In the hours she wasn't actively fretting she went through all the communication technology files stored in her lacuna. There were more than she realized; accumulated so she could hardwire her properties for unisphere access and integrate domestic systems with the house net. They gave her quite a good base of practical knowledge. All she had to do then was work out how to apply it.

She kept examining the whole problem like some particularly stupid program. If A doesn't work, try B, then C. She was on Z for about the eighth time when morning light finally started to glow through the cheap paper blinds over the window. But that eighth Z was certainly possible, maybe even quite clever. It also had the big advantage that no one would be able to predict it. That was the crucial part. She wasn't under any illusions now about how desperate Living Dream was to catch her. Every aspect of her life would be analysed for clues. And every one would be pursued.

Araminta sat up as Tandra tried to tiptoe through the living room to the galley kitchen.

'Sorry,' Tandra said. 'Did I wake you?'

'No.'

Tandra pulled the blinds up. 'Wow, you look terrible.'

'Didn't sleep much,' Araminta admitted.

Martyn emerged from the bathroom, dressed in a worn t-shirt and blue shorts. 'Morning,' he mumbled, scratching his hair then moving on to his armpit.

'Still glad you came?' Tandra asked lightly. She and Araminta started giggling as Martyn frowned at the pair of them. He walked through the archway to the kitchen.

'Can I steal some of your makeup?' Araminta asked when she heard him banging cups and bowls about.

'Hell yes, honey,' Tandra said. 'Half the membrane scales are way past their expiry date, but that's all a big con anyway. You use them, I sure don't get much chance to doll up.'

'Thanks.'

'You going to see a guy?'

'Not quite, no.'

'Okay. You want some coffee?'

Araminta smiled. The coffee Martyn had produced from the galley kitchen last night had been terrible. 'Lovely, thank you.'

Breakfast was a messy affair, with the five of them squeezed round the little table in the living room. The twins were playing up, taking forever to scoop down their cereal. Araminta munched on her toast, trying not to laugh as an increasingly exasperated Tandra threatened and pleaded with the children.

Afterwards, she sat on the bed in Tandra's room, and started applying the makeup scales. Tandra had a surprising number of cosmetic cases from various companies; some had been heavily used, while others were still untouched. Over half an hour Araminta managed to change the appearance of her features, disguising her rounded cheeks in favour of a more angular quality, careful shadowing under her jaw made it appear more prominent and square. Simple lenses changed her eye colour to a deep blue. She sprayed her hair, darkening it to near-raven; then plaited it in a way she hadn't done since high school.

Tandra bought her clothes in. 'Clean, and fixed as best as our poor old bot can manage. I must find a better stitching program.' She dropped them on the mattress next to Araminta. 'Now that's different. I barely recognize you.'

Araminta flashed her friend a grateful smile. 'Thanks.'

'Don't want to worry you,' Tandra said closing the door. 'But Matthew just called. There have been people in Nik's this morning asking after you. Three lots of people.'

'Oh, Ozzie.' All the fear and panic from yesterday came storming back into her mind.

Tandra sat beside her. 'Is it bad?'

'About as bad as it can get. I'm going to leave right now. I should never have come.'

'That's all right, honey, I could do with my life shaking up a bit.'

Araminta shook off her borrowed robe, and began pulling her patched trousers on. 'Not like this. Listen, if anyone comes asking for me, you tell them the complete truth. All of it.'

'What's to tell?'

'That I was here. Don't deny anything. Don't hold back.'

'Gee, if you're sure?'

She pulled on her blouse, marvelling that Tandra's cleaner had managed to get the grass stains out of the elbows. 'Never more so.'

With the toolbelt round her waist again, and the fleece covering it up she was ready to leave.

'Thank you again,' she said at the door. Martyn's uncertain grin only made her feel more ashamed.

'You take care now,' Tandra said, and kissed her goodbye.

Araminta walked fast for the first twenty minutes, close to a jog, putting as much distance as she could between her and Tandra's family. After that, with sweat soaking into her blouse she slowed a little, puffing away, hoping her flushed cheeks wouldn't dislodge the cosmetic membranes. She couldn't open the fleece to cool off, that would expose her toolbelt.

It was a long way to her destination, an office over in the Salisbury district, which was on the other side of town from Tandra's place. Quickest route would be straight through the centre, but she avoided that, anxious not to encounter too many people. Besides, there were more street sensors in the centre. So she walked in a long curve away from the river, then back down the slope to the north of the docks.

Three hours after she started she was in Salisbury. The buildings here were nearly all commercial, interspaced with a few estates of cheaper housing that had been shipped in from the Suvorov continent, prefab aluminium brick rooms locked together into bungalows in whatever configuration suited the landlord. Their gardens were marked off with chain link fencing, containing straggly lawns or big areas of gravel chip, with several parked ground vehicles and the odd broken capsule.

The metro line cut through the centre of the district, with a small number of branch lines splitting off. A few cabs hummed past. Trike pods were the preferred transport, though there weren't many zipping about today. Bicycles outnumbered them nearly two to one. There were enough pedestrians that she didn't feel too conspicuous. Even the Ellezelin capsules didn't use the skies above Salisbury.

Araminta had never been to the district before, so it took her another hour walking down the main roads checking the signs before she found Harrogate Street. A deserted stub of concrete ending five hundred metres from the intersection in a big field of rubble from some stalled redevelopment project. Amazingly, a metro line ran all the way up to the barrier round the waste ground. The buildings on either side were a mix of offices and industrial units and storage barns.

Now she was conspicuous, the only person on the pavement where weeds had started to lift the cracked concrete, and compacted rubbish clogged the gutters. A third of the way towards the redevelopment site she found the building she wanted, a medium-sized warehouse of composite panels and cheap solar roofing. The front had a single storey lean-to built on, housing the company offices. The company in question being Genuine Spanish Crêpes, as advertised by a small orange sign on the security-caged front door. The windows were all boarded up with sheets of armoured carbotanium, and the side walls covered in graffiti scrawls so old their glow had decayed to near invisibility.

Araminta walked down the side of the warehouse. Right at the end of the wall there was a small door. She pulled her cutter out, and removed the lock with a neat incision.

Inside the big enclosed space, light shone in through a row of misted glass along the roof's apex. There were five loosely piled pyramids of boxes on the bare concrete floor, all with the Spanish Crêpes logo on the side. She ignored them and hurried back to the offices at the front. Getting inside was easy enough. The door was locked but not alarmed. Laril was too cheap for that.

There were three offices, with budget furniture and fittings, looking as if the staff had just left for the day. Araminta hurriedly pulled down the blinds and began to search the offices one by one.

Spanish Crêpes had been another of Laril's rotten companies. It was supposed to be a franchise supplying Colwyn City's larger entertainment venues; with dozens of stalls and swarms of eager staff supplying quality food at reasonable prices, and paying Laril for the privilege. As always, it had limped along as he battled with licensing authorities, while buying stock from the cheapest suppliers he could find. Then there were subsidiaries dealing in the stalls and culinary units themselves; financed with a buyback scheme based offworld. More interlinked yet unregistered companies provided uniforms and transport. None of it had been declared to the Revenue Service.

Araminta knew about it all because he'd left a file open one day on their apartment's network. She'd never told him she knew about it; she'd even kept it from Cressida. It was to be her very last bargaining point if all legal means failed.

A thorough inventory of every desk and cupboard produced very little. Useless hardcopy of confusing receipts and agreements. Sample boxes of exotic crêpe fillings. Dead pot plants. Worn culinary unit components. Electronic modules – function unknown. Three cybersphere nodes. Kubes in neat storage cassettes. A box of company aprons in trial colours. A mid-capacity management array with out-of-date software.

However, as she sat at what must have been Laril's desk with its ancient console and three portals, she found five cash coins in the bottom drawer, underneath some carry-capsule manuals. Difficult to find, but not necessarily suspicious, so they weren't there by accident. Like everything Laril did.

She held one of the coins up, and smiled at it. Good old Laril, dependably unreliable.

Thirty minutes spent opening up one of the nodes, using a handheld interface to adapt the software configuration, registering a new company unisphere account with money from the cash coin, and she had a very basic communication link through the management array that didn't involve her u-shadow or include her identity. No tracer program or scrutineer would be able to place her at the Spanish Crêpes office.

In theory.

She laboriously typed in the Oaktier code stored in her lacuna. The tiny array screen printed up icons showing the channel being established.

Please, she prayed, *be curious enough to accept the call.*

The portal projected Laril's puzzled face into the air in front of her. She surprised herself by her reaction. But the sight of that awfully familiar thin brown hair, rotund cheeks and excessive stubble brought tears to her eyes. It was just so unbelievably reassuring that he remained exactly the same as always.

'Araminta? Is that you? Have you reprofiled your face?'

'Don't go,' she blurted. 'I need help.'

'Ah. I didn't know you knew about the, er, crêpes company.'

'Forget about that. Can you run a check to see if anyone is eavesdropping this link?'

His eyes widened in amused surprise. 'Okay. U-shadow analysing the connection route. Ah hah. The channel seems clean, but I'm not a true expert on these things. Are you all right? I've tried to call a couple of times. I was worried when your u-shadow didn't respond.'

Araminta took a deep breath. 'Laril, it's me they're after.'

'You?'

'I'm the Second Dreamer.'

'You know the Second Dreamer?'

'No. I *am* the Second Dreamer.'

'You can't be.'

Araminta scowled at the screen. This was Laril true enough, always the same, and never giving her credit. 'Why not?'

'For a start, you don't have gaiamotes.'

'Don't need them.' She explained about her previously unknown ancestry.

'You're related to Mellanie Rescorai?' was all he asked when she'd finished.

'You know of her?'

'Who doesn't? Especially here on Oaktier, this was her birthworld.'

Definitely Laril, no one else ever irritated her at this level. 'I . . .' she shut her eyes, drew a breath, and looked directly at his projection. 'I don't know who else to go to.'

He grinned, a hand reaching up to scratch the top of his right ear. 'Wow. I'm flattered.'

'You said if there was ever anything . . .'

'Yeah. Wasn't quite thinking along these lines, though.'

'I see.' *You can always rely on Laril to let you down.* She reached for the keyboard, ready to cut the channel.

'That doesn't mean I won't help,' he said in that soft caring voice he hadn't used since their first week together.

'Really?'

'I loved you then, and I guess I always will.'

'Thank you.'

'Sorry, but— You're really the Second Dreamer?'

She smirked. 'Yeah.'

'And you told the Skylord to get lost?'

'I don't want to go into the Void, especially not leading some crazy Pilgrimage for a bunch of religious nutters.'

'Succinctly put. Unfortunately there are bigger issues to consider.'

'I know. For a start, I've got half of Ellezelin's police force in the city looking for me. And Gore said there are others, too.'

'What can I do?'

'I don't know. It's just sort of instinct coming to you.'

'Again: flattering, in a weird kind of way. But let's face it, if anyone can advise you how to stay ahead of officialdom, it's me.'

'I'm not sure even you can help me on that score. Laril, the whole city is sliding into anarchy. Ellezelin is the only authority here. I don't think I can hide forever.'

'Okay, let me think for a moment here.' He patted at his forehead theatrically.

'Have you got someone now?' she asked quietly.

'Yes. At least, there's someone I've started to see regularly. She's just arrived on Oaktier, for the same reason as me.'

'That's good. I'm pleased.'

'Thanks. And you?'

'Yes. You'd probably be surprised by him, but yes.'

'So I have to ask, why isn't he helping you out?'

'I don't want to involve him. It's a bit much.'

'Okay, that tells me what I need to know.'

'What?'

'Now don't take this the wrong way, but you're thinking about this is all wrong.'

'How?'

'Too small. Basically what I'm saying is that it's not about you.'

'It's very much about me.'

'No. This is about the evolution of entire cultures and species. It might even be about the fate of the galaxy if you believe the Raiel. You play a part in that, a very minor part given the nature of the events playing out here.'

She started to argue, but he held up a hand.

'However,' he said, 'it is pivotal, and that's where your importance lies. You have a choice, Araminta, you can either be the small person, maybe try to run and hide. Then someone will catch up with you, and depending on who they are your role will be subsumed into their agenda. Don't make the mistake of thinking any of them will leave you alone to carry on as you see best. They won't.'

'And my other choice?' she asked waspishly.

'Try and beat them at their own game. Turn round, stop running, face them down, and use the power you've acquired to bring about your own tenets.'

'What are they?'

Laril laughed quietly. 'When you work that out you'll make the second choice automatically. Then: universe watch out.'

Araminta slumped in the chair, and gave his image a dirty look. 'Oh why did I call you?'

'Practicality. Listen. You'll either get there or they'll catch you first, so don't worry about it. In the meantime, I'll give you my advice, which you can ignore as always; but at least my conscience will be clean knowing I did my very best to help you.'

She pouted. 'I didn't always ignore what you said.'

'Excuse me, I must have missed the one time you said yes.'

'Go on then. I called you after all, so let's hear it.'

'Just let me take a moment. The galaxy's future poised on what I have to say, this is a real moment to savour.'

'Get on with it.'

His expression turned serious. 'Are you supplying Justine's dream?'

'Justine is dreaming?'

'Okay, well that answers that. Yes, she is, but she's gone into suspension, so that removes her from the outcome for a while. Which brings us back to you and your proven influence on the Skylord. If that is to mean anything you have to use it. Talk to the Skylord again.'

'I can't. They have some way of tracking me through the gaiafield. I only just got out of my apartment the last time, and that was mostly luck.'

'Ozzie! All right, you have to try and find a way, you need to talk to it.'

'What do I say?'

'Try to explain how many people want to come to the Void, try to make it understand how catastrophic that would be for the rest of the galaxy. If you don't want to be taken over by

Living Dream or a Faction as their unwitting figurehead, then you have to bring this to an end.'

'Yeah,' she said, exhaling heavily. 'I suppose I see that. I'll try using the gaiafield again, try to see if I can find a way round them finding me.'

'That's a good start. It sounds like you have a different ability to everyone else, so there's a chance it'll work in your favour. Here's an idea, if you can use the gaiafield without them realizing, you might want to check out Inigo's dreams. At least you'll have a better understanding what you're up against. Failing that, you're supposed to be able to commune with the Silfen Motherholm. Who knows what they'll say?'

'Thank you. That's actually—'

'Useful?'

'Very.'

'All right then. Now what about you? Where are you staying?'

'I haven't got anywhere.'

'You're in the Spanish Crêpes office, right?'

'Yes.'

'Bottom drawer of my desk you'll find a bunch of old manuals. Underneath them are some cash coins. Untraceable.'

She held them up, trying not to smirk.

'Ozzie,' he muttered. 'I never did fool you, did I?'

'Not much.'

'All right, there's a couple of thousand Viotia pounds loaded in. That'll help. Do you know about Wurung Transport?'

'No.'

'Okay, I'm not totally useless then. It's another company I ran. A garage unit in the building two down from where you are now. There's a fully licensed cab inside, just one, that's all the company owns. I can load the activation code in from here, so it'll be ready when you get to it. Now listen, there's some interesting software in its management system which allows you to avoid being tracked by the City control network.'

'Why?' she asked.

He gave an embarrassed shrug. 'It might be useful if there

were *things* you wanted to move round town without drawing too much attention to yourself.'

'Oh, Laril!' There was concern as well as exasperation in her tone.

'Those days are over,' he said. 'It also has a unisphere node. I'll remote switch it to stand-by, you can use it any time to call me. No one else will be able to access it.'

'Thank you.'

'Araminta.'

'Yes?'

'I'm glad it was me you called. I'm glad I can help.'

She stared at his image for a long moment. 'Why did you pick me?' she asked quietly.

'Oldest reason for a man to have: you're gorgeous.'

Ridiculously, she knew she was almost blushing. 'Don't change too much to become Higher.'

'You know me. Good luck. Call me when you need to.'

'Bye, Laril.' She switched off the management array and the cybersphere node, then went out to check on Wurung Transport.

*

The *Purus* and the *Congo* slid unnoticed among the awesome Ocisen Empire fleet as it raced towards the Commonwealth at four and a half lightyears per hour. A detailed scan revealed no craft other than the Starslayers plunging onward through their wormholes; whoever the Ocisen Empire's allies were they had a drive technology at least equal to the Commonwealth Navy ships.

They took up position a kilometre behind the new command vessel, and began to interfere with its continuous wormhole. After a sharp tussle of exotic energy the big Starslayer vessel was torn back into normal spacetime, its reaction control rockets firing continually to kill the errant rotation it picked up during the abrupt transition. Random flares of light slithered over its dark ovoid hull as the force field generators tried to regain equilibrium while the ftl drive's death throes spun out residual energy fluctuations. Both the *Purus* and the *Congo* dropped out of hyperdrive.

A featureless spherical starship appeared beside the wrecked Starslayer.

The *Huron*, the *Nyasa*, and the *Baykal* shed their stealth effect. The three Capital-class starships were almost as large as the Starslayer, and infinitely more potent. A second spherical starship materialized five kilometres from the first. The *Onega* and the *Torrens* revealed themselves.

For three seconds nothing happened. The humans held their breath.

Both the alien vessels opened fire.

It was ninety seconds before the ultra secure TD link to Pentagon II was re-established. The energy storm unleashed by the hellish firefight had strained the local structure of spacetime to a degree which even affected the underlying quantum fields, severing the link. Admiral Kazimir reviewed the updated situation fast. Both of the unknown ships had been destroyed, as had the *Congo*, while the *Torrens* had suffered so much damage it was unable to fight, though the crew survived. Most of the Starslayer's hull had evaporated from the titanic energy bursts, even though no one had aimed at it. What was left of the outer structure was glowing cherry-red, and bubbling furiously around the edges.

'Not completely invincible, then,' Ilanthe said in a relieved tone.

'So it would appear,' the Admiral agreed. They were all waiting to see if any more of the allies accompanying the fleet would turn back to assist their colleagues. The Capital-class ships had managed to detect fifty stealthed hyperdrives secreted amid the Starslayers. A truly formidable force.

'Maybe not invincible, but just about unstoppable,' Crispin said. 'Do we have an equal number of Capital-class warships, Admiral?'

'We have thirty-nine within deployment range,' Kazimir told

the depleted ExoProtectorate Council. He was dismayed that it was his own family that was missing. Whoever it was who had released his mother's dream into the gaiafield wasn't coming forward. Not that knowing their identity would be of any use – she would remain in suspension for some time. But it irked him to know that someone could reach her.

Even more dismaying was Gore's non-appearance. When Kazimir convened the ExoProtectorate Council, Gore's u-shadow reported him as unavailable. Kazimir couldn't imagine what would keep his grandfather from attending, especially as his absence would allow Ilanthe to dominate the Council. Not, he admitted to himself, that the outcome was going to be anything other than the one he really didn't want.

'The remaining unknowns are staying with the fleet,' reported Sorex, the *Onega*'s captain.

'Excellent,' Kazimir replied. 'Could you get in close for a scan of the wreckage, please.'

'So the fleet can be eliminated?' Creewan asked urgently.

'Numerically it would be difficult,' Kazimir said as the *Onega* dispatched a swarm of sensor drones towards the largest chunk of wreckage from the second spherical ship. 'As well as the unknowns, there are also nine hundred Starslayers to consider. Our combined River- and Capital-class ships would probably defeat them, but the cost would be severe. We'd be left with very few vessels.'

'Then we know what needs to be done,' Ilanthe said. 'I believe there is one class of ship more powerful than the Capital-class.'

'Yes,' Kazimir said with extreme reluctance.

'Admiral,' Sorex called. 'High resolution sensors are combining. Oh, great Ozzie—'

Kazimir and the rest of the ExoProtectorate Council stared silently at the sensor results which appeared above the big table. The little drones were flitting through the broken compartments and passageways of the spherical warship, contributing their separate scans to a cohesive image. The battered chunk of hardware was texture perfect, right down to individual structural components. Metal around the outside was still hot enough to glow. It was also terribly radioactive. Odd pieces of charred biological matter drifted around the compartments, torn from alien bodies as explosions and energy pulses ripped through the ship. Right in the middle, the bodies were larger. Intact. The drones concentrated on one.

Kazimir stared at the terribly familiar pear-shaped torso, with four gristly ridges running its length. Four stubby legs protruded from the curving base, while arms branched out of the body just above the legs, each one ending in an efficient quad-pincer arrangement. At the top of the body four small mouth trunks were open, drifting in zero-gee like seaweed in a slow current. Between them were the sensory stalks, rigid in death, each one fused to a neat electronic module.

'That can't be,' Crispin exclaimed. 'It can't! We contained them all twelve hundred years ago. All of them.'

'It is,' Ilanthe said emotionlessly.

'Yes,' Kazimir said, fighting both shock and a tinge of fear. 'An immotile. The Ocisen Empire has acquired Primes as its allies.'

*

The noise of ice crystals smashing themselves to sparkling dust on the ground crawler's metal shell was making conversation difficult inside. Even under the constant barrage by the wild elements, the vehicle hadn't moved. It was wedged fast in the fissure, with its narrow front windows covered by dirty granules which had filled the gaps around it. Minor quakes continued to shake it about, but they only seemed to tighten the fissure's grip. Several times, the thick metal bodywork had groaned in protest.

Corrie-Lyn sat awkwardly on top of the two forward seats, a blanket wrapped round her shoulders. Inigo was using an auxiliary console to squat beside her.

'Why did you never dream again?' Corrie-Lyn asked.

'The Waterwalker's era was over,' Inigo said. 'You know that. There were no more dreams to be had.'

'But if you had one following his ascent to the nebulas, there must have been others. You said it came from a descendant. He had many children.'

'I . . .' Inigo shook his head. His eyes glinted in the console's moiré radiance as he gazed at his old lover. 'We witnessed everything we needed to. I sustained hope in billions of people for centuries. That's enough.'

Corrie-Lyn studied the face looming above her. So familiar, yet the darkened skin and bad brown hair made him seem colder somehow. This wasn't quite the old Inigo she'd known and loved. *After all, it's been seventy years. Dreams don't always end like the Waterwalker's did. And I dreamed so hard about this moment.* 'Please,' she began.

The atmosphere howled at a volume which was painful on her ears. She gripped the chair, fearful that this was the final quake, the one that would send them falling into the planet's imploding core.

'It's all right,' Inigo's soft voice reassured her. 'Just the storm.'

She grinned uncomfortably. That voice hadn't changed, and the reassurance she gained from it was immeasurable. So often she had heard his strident messages to the devout gathered in Golden Park, and equally the tenderness when they were alone. Every time it contained total conviction. If he said it was just the storm, then it was so.

'Can you dream again?' she asked.

The cabin lights flickered. Red warnings appeared on the console as the tortured air outside wailed stridently. Inigo's fingers stroked her cheek. 'What is it you want?' he asked, his mind lustrous with compassion.

'I want to go to Querencia one last time,' she told him. 'I want to walk through Lillylight's arcades, I want to take a gondola ride down the Great Major Canal, I want to stand on Kristabel's hortus as dawn comes up over the city.' She gripped his hand. 'Just us. Is that such a terrible thing to ask?'

'No,' he said. 'It's a beautiful thing to desire.'

'Take us there. Until the end.'

The tears were full-formed now, rolling down his cheeks. 'I can't, my love. I'm so sorry.'

'No,' she cried. 'Inigo, please.'

'We can dream any of the Waterwalker's dreams together. Any. Just pick one.'

'No. I know them all. Even his last one. I want to know what happened after. If you won't take me there as it is now, then show me that final dream you had.'

'Corrie-Lyn, do you still trust me?'

'Of course.'

'Then don't ask this. Let us visit Edeard when he drops Master Cherix into Birmingham Pool, or as he confronts Bise and the regiment in Sampalok. They are such wonderful times. He shows people their future can be different to the one they thought they were condemned to.'

'Why?' she pleaded. 'Tell me why.'

The storm noise ended. It cut off so fast that Corrie-Lyn thought she had suddenly gone deaf. *This is it. No regrets. Well, not many.*

'Oh shit,' Inigo was looking up towards the rear of the cabin.

'It's all right,' she said valiantly. 'We're together.'

'Uh huh.' He shook his head, straightening up.

Corrie-Lyn wriggled into a precarious near-sitting position. 'What?'

'The Lady must hate us; she's guided us to a genuine fate worse than death.'

'Inigo, what are you—'

A blinding green flash filled the cabin. Corrie-Lyn squeezed her eyes shut in reflex. Her optic nerves were shining a blazing white and scarlet afterimage into her brain. She yelled in panic as some potent force slammed her sideways, sending her tumbling painfully down the side of the chairs to jam herself into the narrow space below. Her good arm waved round frantically. 'Inigo!' Then she was abruptly aware of a fearsomely cold air flowing across her. She drew a shocked breath, feeling it freeze-burning down her mouth and throat. Her vision was slowly recovering. She blinked to see Inigo braced on the console above her, clad in a shimmering force field. He was still looking up. Almost dreading what she'd see, Corrie-Lyn followed his gaze.

The rear two thirds of the ground crawler's cabin had completely vanished. Where it had been, grey ice particles were drifting slowly downwards through a funereal sky. Behind them, slivers of purple static writhed across the broad force field dome that now encased them in a bubble of serenity. A human figure was silhouetted against the curtailed storm, an integral force field providing additional protection from the wicked elements. Corrie-Lyn blinked again, trying to gain some focus through the sharp scintillations of her bruised retinas. Secondary thought routines in her macrocellular clusters managed to resolve the man's features.

'Oh Lady, fuck it,' she groaned, and slumped back down.

'Well, well,' Aaron said cheerfully. 'Fancy meeting you two here.'

Inigo's Eleventh Dream

At night Makkathran's grandiose rooftops shimmered like moiré silk as gentle nebula-light burned through the skies above them. Amid that soft sheen, the streets themselves were sharp orange threads of radiance forming an intricate filigree across the circular metropolis poised beside the sea. Floating high above the crystal walls it was possible to see a new radiance complementing the city's nocturnal lustre. If you knew how to look.

Far, far down at the limit of perception the faint light was just available. Small wisps of darkling iridescence emerging from the apex of buildings into the balmy night air. They trailed gauzy tails as they drifted upwards. It was as though Makkathran was exhaling a phosphorescent rain into the heavens.

The souls of the dead called out in joy and wonder as they began their flight into the awesome abyss of night. He could hear their voices as they passed him; the relief at being free of the body, of pain and misery, the regret for those they left behind, the thrill at the song which summoned them ever upwards. They called out to each other, eager to share the adventure of their newfound freedom. Some formed packs, twisting together into brighter nimbi to soar above the clouds in an exuberant celebration of liberty, others remained alone, revelling in their independence.

Occasionally, as he cast his sorrowful gaze downwards, he could see some souls linger. Distraught at their death, they yearned to remain among their loved ones. Unseen, unheard, the frail spectres grew wretched and dissolute as those they adored above all remained ignorant of their presence; the single comfort of knowing lost to false hope. Their grief was overwhelming, threatening to drown him if he immersed himself among them for any time. So he looked up again, at those who cast themselves longingly into the sky, wishing beyond reason that he could catch the faintest hint of the song sung from the heart of this universe. If he just strained, reached out . . .

Edeard woke with a start, sitting up in bed, his skin slick with sweat, heart pounding, gulping for breath.

Beside him, Kristabel rose to put her arms around him. 'It's all right, my love,' she cooed. 'Just a dream.'

'Every night,' he moaned, for that was what he'd dreamed or been shown since his fall from the Eyrie tower. 'Will this plague ever leave me? I'd willingly rejoin my old dreams in exchange for this curse.'

'Old dreams?' Kristabel ordered the ceiling to brighten. Perfect white light revealed the maisonette around them.

The sight of it, the normality, immediately made Edeard feel foolish. 'I'm sorry. I always had dreams. But these!'

'The souls again?'

'Yes,' he said weakly. 'I see them rising, and I can't hear the song they're following. So I try and listen, and . . .' He shook his head in annoyance. 'Sorry.'

'Stop apologizing. I'm just worried for you, that's all.'

'I'll be all right,' he flopped down, and glanced at the narrow window. 'What time is it?'

'Hours before dawn.'

'Huh! It might not be a dream then. I always visualize the city at night.'

Kristabel rolled on to her side, where she gave him a concerned look. 'Can you farsight any souls right now?'

'Not sure.' He closed his eyes, and stretched out his farsight. The dark shadows of city buildings slipped through his perception, fizzing with the sparkle of slumbering minds. Makkathran's all-encompassing thoughts were easy to discern, pervading the structure of everything, but strongest beneath the streets and canals, down amid the levels where pipes and tunnels and strange threads of energy wove around each other. They were faint, elusive even, but tangible enough. Of the souls which he knew must be there, he could find no trace. 'Nothing,' he said in defeat.

'It's not a contest. You haven't lost anything.'

'But I've sensed them twice.' Edeard stopped to think. 'I was close to the body each time, very close.'

'What are you saying? You want to go to a hospice?'

'No,' he lied.

Kristabel gave him a suspicious glance. 'Humm.'

'I wonder if I should see the Pythia again.' He didn't like the idea. Their last meeting hadn't been particularly pleasant for him. During the gentle questioning that had gone on for what seemed like hours, he'd felt awkward and defensive. The authority she possessed made him feel like a small child who'd committed some transgression then been hauled up before a loving but stern parent.

'What would she be able to teach you?' Kristabel asked, with more than a touch of scorn.

'Nothing, I suppose.' After that unsatisfactory meeting, he'd carefully read the Lady's scriptures again. It was the first time he'd read them properly since Sunday lessons at the Ashwell Church with Mother Lorellan. All he'd ever done then was learn passages by rote, never knowing their meaning.

Re-reading the scriptures was something of a revelation. They were hardly a religious text, rather an imprecise diary written in a very flowery prose, followed by what amounted to her thoughts on how to lead a better, more fulfilling life. Only the Skylords bound the two sections together. Vast airborne creatures who sailed sedately between Querencia and the nebulas; a migration whose purpose was unknown, but served to guide human souls to the Heart. However, according to the Lady, only souls that had achieved what she termed 'fulfilment' would be taken.

Reading through her homilies, he couldn't help but think of an elderly spinster aunt telling her relatives about how to be a good family. Be polite, be nice, be considerate, be charitable. Or maybe life was just very different back then – though he suspected not, judging by the diary part. At least that was interesting, though it only began as Rah caught his first glimpse of Makkathran from the mountains. All the Lady ever said of the ship that brought them to this universe was that Rah was leading people away from the turmoil which followed their landing. Beyond that, the past was never mentioned. She was admiring of Rah's perseverance as he broke through the crystal wall, making the three city gates. The wonder they all experienced that first time they sailed into the port seeing a fully built, yet deserted, city where they could make their home. How, as they floated along Great Major Canal that day, a Skylord was soaring above the towers in Eyrie. How it agreed to guide the soul of a dying friend to the Heart which lay beyond Odin's Sea.

The Lady went on to describe the founding of the city Councils, and the emergence of the Guilds, and how other refugees from the fallen ships sought them out, while others remained outside the walls and grew jealous. The petty and bitter disputes between city and country over whose law should prevail. She never saw the end of those quarrels, the final treaty to enshrine the rights of both provinces and city; and her disappointment in the seemingly interminable squabbling was reflected in her later writing; the years when the Skylord visits became less frequent. When she asked them why they were abandoning humans they told her it was because people were incomplete, their souls too immature to be taken to the Heart. The Lady felt shame for her species. Humbled that they would wither and die before the Heart accepted them, she devoted the remainder of her life to elevating humanity, to installing a sense of purpose and dignity into life through her teachings. Along with a now-ailing Rah and the last few Skylords to visit Makkathran she cajoled the city into creating the central Church in Eyrie.

When it was done, when she saw the embryonic Church swelling up out of the ground, she joined Rah on the top of Eyrie's highest tower, and let her soul slip from her body, so they could both embrace the guidance of the Skylord and travel into the Heart together.

No Skylord had been seen above Querencia ever since.

'That's good,' Kristabel said. 'I don't want you to turn to people like her for answers. They're the past. If you're the person I think you are, the one I believe in, you make your own decisions.'

'Wow.' Edeard stared at her, almost intimidated by her impassioned expression. 'I'll do my best,' he promised.

'I know you will. That's why I love you.' With that she cuddled up against him, ordering the illumination down low again. 'And don't think I haven't noticed what you've done to this maisonette, either,' she added.

'Er . . .'

'It's all right. I haven't told anyone. This is Makkathran, even you should know by now never to reveal your full abilities.'

'I do.'

'Until you have to, of course.'

'Right.'

She grinned in the darkness. Rather surprisingly, Edeard fell asleep again. This time, with her beside him, it was untroubled by dreams or visions of any kind.

In the morning, Kristabel got up as dawn began to produce a glow in the sky over the Donsori Mountains. She dressed quickly, and kissed Edeard goodbye as he lay drowsily on the bed.

'I'll see you in a little while,' she said quietly, and slipped out. Edeard followed her with his farsight as she walked off down the street. Her gondola was waiting in the pool that formed the top end of Flight Canal and the bottom of Arrival Canal. A ge-eagle from Jeavons station circled overhead, watching carefully, as she was taken to her family mansion. She would be let in to the ziggurat by a small side door, and appear at her family's breakfast table pretending she'd spent the night in her room, and every relative would maintain the pretence.

Stupid etiquette, Edeard grumbled to himself as he started to dress. His mauve cotton shirt had sleeves which barely came over his shoulders, while the trousers were the short ones he used for playing football in the park, ending well above his knees. The cobbler had shaken his head in dismay at the shoes Edeard commissioned; complaining they were little more than lace-up slippers with thick soles. But the strange clothing was perfect for Edeard's now-daily run, as he'd known it would be.

This morning he threw on a light sleeveless sweater to counter the early chill air, and jogged steadily away from the tenement. With so few people on the street he made good time to Brotherhood Canal, then ran along the path on the Ogden side until he was level with the militia stables where he cut across the meadows to the crystal wall itself. Golden morning light streamed through the crystal, creating a glowing barrier which curved slightly above him.

As he pounded onwards he felt strands of farsight wash over him, tenuous at best, his observers were trying to avoid being noticed. There were a few blatant scrutinies, accompanied by mental snickering. His routine had attracted a great deal of interest when he started it. The first couple of weeks had even seen kids running alongside as he left the tenement every morning. That casual amusement and mimicry had ended as he kept faithfully to his routine. On those early days after finishing his mild post-fall convalescence, he'd barely been able to last half a mile before having to stop, red faced and heart pounding. Now he could do forty-five minutes with ease.

Acena, the Culverit family doctor, had approved, commenting that she wished more people would take their health seriously. Others in the city had been less charitable. Edeard didn't care. Never again would he be so pathetically out of condition that he couldn't chase someone up a tower in Eyrie.

Once he was back level with Arrival Canal, Edeard headed

back across the grass as the stable hands began leading the remaining militia horses on their morning walk. He crossed at the green and yellow slab bridge back into Jeavons as the district started to come to life, with shops and traders busy preparing for the day's commerce. As always, he stopped at the bakery on the corner of Pharo Street to pick up some fresh croissants before heading back to the tenement.

Inside the maisonette he stripped off and handed the sweaty clothes to his ge-chimps for laundry. Beside the pool was a shallow oval-shaped recess in the floor, with a sheet of crystal curving round two thirds of it. Edeard stood inside, and told the room to let the water out. A thick spray gushed down on him from holes in the ceiling. He rubbed some soap on then ordered the water to cool slightly so he could rinse himself clean.

These days he actually preferred the novel mini-rainfall arrangement to bathing in the traditional pool. It was a lot quicker, and left him feeling refreshed even after the run. After the comment Kristabel made last night, he was wondering if he should extend the crystal sheet to make it big enough for two. Sharing might be a lot of fun.

He met Kristabel outside her mansion as arranged. The two of them took a family gondola across the city to Ilongo district, disembarking on the North Curve Canal, opposite the North Gate.

'You're happy,' Kristabel said as they started walking. She was wearing a modest azure dress with a simple white lace hem, and a broad green hat to shade against the warming sun. Her thick hair hung down her back in a single fluffy tail.

'The caravan families are very good old friends,' he replied, 'and I really don't have a lot of those.'

They picked their way carefully along the tracks that wound across High Moat heading for the caravan pens. There was a lot of traffic that morning, with carts laden with produce, herds of farm beasts driven along, and terrestrial horses cantering in and out of the various wooden stable blocks. They had to step aside smartly for carriages carrying nobility out into the Iguru Plain at considerable speed.

'That's bad driving,' Kristabel said indignantly as the third one sped past, cloaked in a mild seclusion haze. 'I recognize the crest, it belongs to the Ivesol family. I bet it's Corille off to their pavilion on Korbal Mount. She's started seeing Jamis on the sly, the third son of Upral; you know, the head of the Tarmorl family. And she's the eldest daughter; there's quite a dowry involved. I've heard her father say he wished his family copied ours, for she'd make a better District Mistress than her brother will ever do as Master.'

'Really?'

Kristabel's eyes narrowed in suspicion. She rapped her knuckles on his arm. 'Don't be a beast. These things are important. Those two families haven't been allied for over a century and a half.'

'I'll try and remember. Remind me, which district belongs to the Ivestols?'

'Lisieux Park.'

'Okay.' As he recalled, the Park's Master was a waverer in Council, leaning towards the current Mayor. He wondered if a family alliance with the ship-owning Tarmorls would tilt the Master towards Finitan.

'It helps,' Kristabel said slyly.

'What does?'

'That the Tarmorls support Finitan.'

'Ah.' Edeard grinned sheepishly. *What would I do without her?*

He wondered yet again if it was the right time to propose. It had been weeks since their break at the beach lodge, and he'd done his utmost to make time for himself and Kristabel at every opportunity. Yet his terror was now that she'd just think his only concern was time. It wasn't. There wasn't a minute of the day that went past without him thinking of what a life they could have together as man and wife.

He sighed as he scooted round a cart piled dangerously high with cages of geese. There must be some event or action that would convince her of how genuine he was, how much he'd thought it over, and still couldn't see a life without her. *Maybe if I just say that?*

But then what if it's not good enough? Oh Lady, why do you do this to me?

Not that her scriptures were any help. The closest she ever came on matters of the human heart were: To look into each other's souls and see yourself reflected there is the true sign of a blessed union.

The only trouble was, with the Lady being so old, every time he recalled a scripture he heard it in Mistress Florrel's voice.

Talk about a passion killer.

The pens along High Moat summoned up a real wave of nostalgia. This was the first part of Makkathran Edeard had ever experienced, he remembered being overwhelmed by the sheer quantity of people and animals sauntering along the tracks. The noise and dust were exactly the same as that day; if anything the traffic was thicker now. Three caravans were on their way out of the North Gate, hustled along by the Travel Master's apprentices who were trying to keep everyone moving at a decent rate and avoid jams at junctions between the various tracks. Instructions were shouted and longtalked, adding to the good-natured commotion.

Two caravans had arrived first thing that day. Stragglers were still lumbering along in their big wagons, drawn by bulky, stolid ge-horses. Edeard and Kristabel fell in behind one as they approached the pens. Assessors from several merchant houses were already walking alongside them, small ge-chimps curled up on their shoulders. Edeard remembered the little creatures with a fond smile. How the caravan families hated them; scampering up the crates and cages, examining produce with their oversize eyes and exceptionally sensitive noses, hunting for blemishes that had been strategically positioned out of sight.

Edeard and Kristabel arrived at the three pens which Barkus had been allocated, and stood for a moment looking at the wagons. Five were new, but Edeard recognized every one of the remainder. O'lrany's cart with pigs peering over the rear; as pungent as ever, though the O'lranys themselves always claimed they could smell nothing. The wagon of dark jarash, with its intricate inlays of claret-coloured wood that Golthor chiselled in each winter. Olcus, inspecting the axle of his wagon, while his three young children ran about in gleeful pursuit of a whistling loop. Olcus who gave Edeard a strange look, then craned forward as if not quite believing the tall young man in a jet-black constable's uniform.

'Edeard!' the man laughed joyfully, and flung his arms wide. 'You backward village boy. By the Lady, look at you!'

Edeard grinned and foolishly stepped into the embrace, only to have the man's powerful arms almost crush him in welcome. He'd been slightly apprehensive at how they'd greet him, but Olcus immediately dispelled all his apprehension. The rest of the families were hurrying forward now, calling out salutations. He was hugged, kissed, had his hand shaken and his back slapped.

'My boy!' Barkus exclaimed.

Everyone cleared away, and Edeard put his arms around the old man. For once he was glad of the skill he'd acquired in the city at shielding his thoughts. Barkus had aged, disturbingly so. His white whiskers were thinner than before, the thickset body appeared almost frail. He walked with the aid of a stick, necessitated by a pronounced shaking in his knees. But his waistcoat was still a colourful extravaganza of scarlet and topaz, with thin silver piping.

'Good to see you, sir,' Edeard said.

'We have heard so much about you,' Barkus said. 'I couldn't believe it at first. Rumours of the Waterwalker travelled far and wide among the provinces, but we never connected them to you. And now look at you.' His hands plucked at Edeard's jacket. 'Wearing a corporal's epaulettes, no less. Congratulations.'

'Thank you, sir. And yourself, how fares the caravan?'

'Pha!' Barkus raised his stick in disgust. 'Look at this wretched thing. A stupid fall in the snow last winter, and my leg snaps like glass. Our doctor has forbidden me from riding, I must sit passively on the wagon's seat while my sons lead us through the mountains. The Lady tests me sorely with so much indignity.'

'You look well.'

'Ha. Liar! But I forgive you. Now then, there is someone with us who is eager to meet you.' The old man grinned mischievously as he turned towards his splendid covered wagon, calling eagerly with longtalk. Edeard took the moment to turn and beckon Kristabel forwards. She walked timidly through the caravan families, unused to being completely ignored – but of course none of them knew who she was. Edeard had been waiting for this moment for a long time, for some reason he couldn't quite fathom it was important to him that Barkus and Kristabel approved of each other. He held her hand and turned back to Barkus, not really seeing the blue and white clad figure stepping out of the wagon. His smile was proud as he opened his mouth to begin the introductions.

'Edeard!' Salrana cried, and sprinted past Barkus to fling her arms around him, and land an effusive kiss on his mouth. 'Oh, my darling, it's been so long.'

'Look who we found in Ufford,' Barkus said happily. 'She's the one who's been busy telling us of all you've achieved.'

'Take me to bed right now,' Salrana whispered in his ear with a hot breath. 'I don't want to wait another minute.'

Every muscle in Edeard's body had frozen in shock. And misery. Shame was inflicting a fair share of the terrible immobility as well.

Salrana swayed back, puzzlement registering on her vibrant face and seeping into her mind. 'Edeard?'

'Uh,' he groaned. His gaze went automatically to Kristabel, who was also standing rigidly, her composure chilling down to a emotionless stare. He had never realized before how similar they both were; tall, slim, bright, lovely . . . But then he hadn't thought about Salrana for a long time now; his mind had conveniently pushed her aside. It was all too complicated. Something he'd have to deal with later, when the time was right.

Everyone around them turned amazingly silent as they

watched the reunion. They watched Salrana look at Kristabel. And no mental shield was strong enough to cover up the dawning realization in her mind. Her shoulders straightened. For a moment the two girls simply stared at each other. Salrana put her hand out. 'I'm Salrana; Edeard and I grew up together.'

'Kristabel.' The hand was shaken gracefully. 'He neglected to mention that.'

As one the caravan families turned to Edeard; except for Barkus, who sighed softly and raised his eyes to the clear blue sky above.

Edeard's farsight revealed a small city tunnel five yards below the pen. He really could make the ground open up and swallow him, as if he was some frightened drakken burrowing away from peril. It was *hugely* tempting. Except that such cowardice would lose Kristabel forever.

He dipped his head in penance to his love. 'I'm sorry. I should have told you that Novice Salrana and I survived Ashwell together. Salrana, I should have sent word that I am about to become engaged. I apologize, my behaviour is inexcusable.'

Kristabel's lips pouted as she gave him a curious look, but she said nothing. Her thoughts were none too steady.

'I see,' Salrana said, sounding as though she'd expected it all along. 'Congratulations to you both.'

'Come along my dear,' Barkus said, putting his free arm around Salrana's shoulders. 'I'll see you later, Edeard. That's if you can spare us an ounce of your valuable time.'

'Yes, sir,' Edeard mumbled meekly.

The rest of the families abruptly discovered something else that they had to be getting on with. Olcus gave Edeard a scolding glance as he turned away, propelling his children ahead of him. The eldest O'lrany lad produced a mischievous thumbs up before he mother shoved him along.

'I'd like to go home now,' Kristabel said with fragile dignity.

'Of course.'

They walked out of the pens together, receiving curious looks from the assessors who were still arriving. Edeard didn't dare say anything to her. He couldn't believe he'd allowed such a mess to happen. Putting off dealing with Salrana was probably the single most stupid thing he'd ever done, aside from not telling Kristabel about her, of course.

When they passed the end of a stable block he suddenly grabbed Kristabel's hand and pulled her off the track. She was too surprised to complain. Edeard conjured up his concealment around the pair of them as he stopped in the shadow of the stable's rear wall. A seclusion haze simply wasn't good enough for this. He wanted absolute privacy.

Kristabel frowned as her farsight probed the psychic baffle. 'You're not supposed to know how to use that—' Then she drew a sharp breath as Edeard dropped to one knee.

'Mistress Kristabel, I love you more than I know how to say, and I cannot imagine a life without you. Would you please consent to marrying me? I know this isn't the correct way, but I don't care, I just want you. I will fight the Skylords themselves if that's what it takes to prove my love.'

'Edeard?'

'I know I always mess up, but I don't mean to, really I don't—'

'Yes.'

'I just didn't know what to do about Salrana, so I kept on ignoring the problem—'

'I said yes.'

'I don't know what I was . . . What?'

Kristabel knelt down beside him, grasping his hands in hers, and smiling. 'I said yes, I'll marry you.'

Edeard's concealment faltered as he stared at her beautiful face. 'Oh, Lady. You did, didn't you?'

She inclined her head slightly, proffering herself for a kiss. He touched his lips to hers, and nothing else mattered any more. After the kiss, they just grinned at each other. Edeard slowly realized a couple of giggling stable hands were peering round the corner, goggling at them. Longtalk calls were pouring out to their friends, as they gifted everyone the sight of the Waterwalker and the future Mistress of Haxpen kneeling in the mud whilst snogging.

'Er, yes,' Edeard said, hurriedly rising to his feet. He held out a hand to Kristabel. She stood and gave the dark dripping stain down the front of her skirt a peevish look. Now Edeard was concentrating on his surroundings, there was quite a pungent smell of manure. A horrified examination of the ground revealed it wasn't just mud they were standing in. A mortified groan started up at the back of his throat.

Kristabel giggled wildly.

'Get about your business,' Edeard snapped at the youngsters, and put on a fierce expression. They fled, laughing all the way.

Kristabel hugged him delightedly. 'You are going to be the one who explains to our children how you proposed.'

'Yes,' he said meekly.

She kissed him properly. 'There's no need to fight a Skylord. You know how I feel about you.'

'Yes.' He glanced at the worn grey planks that made up the back of the stable. 'Can we, er . . . ?'

'Yes.' She held out her arm, and Edeard led her away from the stable back to the path.

'I appreciate the sentiment, though,' Kristabel said. 'Actually, I'm quite intrigued how you would fight a Skylord.'

Edeard blushed. 'Me too. Do I ask your father now?'

'Yes.' She gathered her composure, and looked straight ahead. 'And if he approves, he will put the motion before the Upper Council for a vote.'

'Right . . . *What?*'

'The direct heir of a District Master or Mistress has to get Council approval for their marriage. It's a formality. It dates back to the Nighthouse inheritance crisis eleven hundred years ago when the Master forbade his eldest son to marry a woman from Myco – he'd fallen out with her father, some dispute about unpaid cargo. He threatened to disinherit him, which the son challenged in court, so the Master had the law changed. After that the families used it to make sure the *right people* produce heirs. Nobody bothers with that any more, the really important marriages are quietly arranged between houses. Law simply becomes tradition. But it actually is still law.'

'Oh, dear Lady. When I am Mayor, I'm going to repeal every stupid law this city has and replace them all with something simple.'

'*When* you're Mayor?'

Edeard cleared his throat. 'If.'

'You're serious about that, aren't you?'

'Do you really think in this day and age I should have to ask Bise or even Owain's permission to marry you?'

'I suppose it is unpleasant if you think about it closely. But I've grown up with all this, so I just know the way things work. It hasn't bothered me before.'

'So was your father arranging a fiancé for you?'

'No. Daddy wouldn't do that. Not that it stopped other families from petitioning him, mind you. There were a lot of suitors.'

'Oh.' The idea of someone as beautiful and spirited as Kristabel being married off to some dismal second son for the sake of dynastic status quo was repulsive. It sent him thinking about everything Ranalee had said about bloodlines. *Yes, that law will definitely have to be removed.* Though he suspected it would take more than that to loosen the nobility's stranglehold on Makkathran's society.

'Why now?' Kristabel asked softly as they neared the North Curve Canal.

'Excuse me?'

'Why did you propose now? I mean, I know Salrana made it happen, but I'm curious why she did.'

'It wasn't guilt,' he said quickly. 'Salrana and I were so comfortable with each other. We'd been through so much together, I've known her all my life. We were going to be lovers when she got back from Ufford, which would have led to us getting married I suppose, at least I always thought it would. Then I met you.'

'You agreed you were going to be lovers?'

'Er, yes.'

'Sounds like the country town version of our family arrangements.'

'I'm not explaining this well. The point is, when I saw her today I felt just terrible at what I was doing to her, I really have broken her heart, which is about as unpleasant as you can get. She doesn't deserve that, she's such a nice person, the best our village ever produced. But despite that, there was no choice. I was never torn between the two of you. It was you, and only you.'

She stopped and kissed him again. 'That's lovely, and very flattering. I think.'

'I love you, Kristabel,' he said simply.

'And I love you too. So the first thing we have to do is go and tell daddy the good news.'

And dear old Uncle Lorin the bad. 'Right!' He straightened his shoulders and took a breath. 'I can do that. We'll go and do it now.'

'You understand, don't you, that after he says yes, we have absolutely no say in anything. If you thought you'd encountered tradition in this city before, it's nothing compared to what's about to happen. The formalities of marriage for the direct heir of a District Master were scripted a thousand years ago, and it *does not* change, not even for Haxpen and the odd Mistress like me.'

'Er, okay,' he said apprehensively.

'Ah, you say that now . . .'

'As long as you and I are together at the end of it, the city can do its worst. I mean, how bad can it be?'

*

Edeard arrived at the base of the Blue Tower in mid-afternoon, and looked up at the tall structure looming over the Tosella district. Its azure walls almost matched the bright cloudless sky above, as if it were attempting its own variant of concealment.

As he walked forward the shadows thrown by its huge buttresses fell across him. There was something about the Eggshaper Guild headquarters which always slightly intimidated him, and he was never sure why.

He walked into the grand entrance hall with its dark red flooring, standing in the angled grid of thick sunbeams shining down through the lancet windows far above. A Guild guard approached, wearing his plain white tunic under a pale drosilk jacket. Edeard gave him a wary glance, it was the same sergeant who had intercepted him on his first visit here.

'Waterwalker,' the sergeant said.

'Sergeant Eachal, Grand Master Finitan asked to see me.'

A reserved smile crept onto the sergeant's face. 'I know. It's always best to turn up here with an appointment.'

'Yes. I've learned that.'

Please,' Eachal gestured at the stairs. 'He is expecting you.'

Edeard's constant running was definitely beginning to pay off. The long, winding stairs were annoying, but nothing more. His breathing was constant the whole time they walked up.

'They say you saw Chae's soul after he died,' Eachal said.

'I did.'

'Was he happy?'

Edeard frowned. He was used to being questioned about seeing souls, but not quite like this. 'Not that he'd died. But he was content with what awaited him.'

'I'm glad he found peace at the end. There was a lot of hardship in his life.'

'You knew him?'

'The same way you did. I trained at Jeavons station.'

'You did?' Edeard couldn't help the surprise in his voice.

Eachal gave Edeard a furtive glance. 'I didn't turn out quite like you, but yes, that's where I served my probation, and eight years on the streets.'

'I didn't know.'

'You're not going to let us down, are you?'

'Let you down?'

'People have a lot of expectations now.'

'I'm aware of that.'

'Yet you're going to marry into the nobility.'

Edeard stopped and faced the sergeant. 'I'm marrying the girl I love. The gangs will not benefit from that. This city will see the full restoration of law and order, and it will apply to all equally.'

Eachal pursed his lips and nodded in apparent understanding. 'I'm glad to hear it.'

Edeard knew the man was still sceptical, yet didn't know how to convince him, nor why he should make a special effort.

As always, the view from Finitan's office was a huge distraction. Edeard managed to greet the Master formally while Eachal bowed and backed out. He'd been worried that the height of the office would somehow remind him of his fall from the tower in Eyrie, yet his nerves were calm as he gazed out across the rooftops.

'My boy,' Finitan said happily, rising from behind his desk to shake Edeard's hand. 'So glad to see you. And you don't have to ask, I will be delighted to be your nominee in the Upper Council when Julan introduces the Marriage Consent bill.'

'Ah, thank you sir.' He'd said he didn't care about the ludicrous formalities of the marriage, yet ... As soon as a delighted Julan granted his permission, the household's senior equerry had been summoned to inaugurate the preparations. There were the legal requirements, Julan had to ask the Mayor for a ruling to introduce the Consent bill before the Upper Council – which would be a week yet, the current session's legislative schedule was very busy. The Pythia was informed, and her blessing requested for the engagement; then her staff had to find a time when the main church in Eyrie was free for such a ceremony, which wasn't going to be until autumn at least. Letters of notification issued to the other District Masters, and by custom the Guild Masters as well. The official engagement party planned for the evening following the vote in Council – which was usually hosted by the groom's family, but would now have to be at the Culverit mansion.

Edeard had sat through the two days (two entire days!) of talks with Julan's household staff arranging such things. Given his profound ignorance in such matters his input was minimal, but still he had to be in the room where a dizzily happy Kristabel chattered endlessly with her housekeeper and stylists of the merits of various fabrics. For, given how important these events were, you had to dress *correctly* for them. In Kristabel's case it meant an entire new collection of evening gowns and a whole 'engagement wardrobe'; while the rest of her family started commissioning new robes and fashionable suits. Edeard was taken to one of the rooms on the seventh floor, where a tailor who specialized in dressing militia officers was summoned to produce a set of constable uniforms made from cloth more fitting to someone of his new 'status' – he was already dreading the day they'd arrive and he'd have to wear them at Jeavons station.

Once the engagement party was over, preparations for the actual marriage ceremony could legitimately begin. Between then and now, the happy couple would be receiving invitations to parties and civic galas which they would have to attend. A lot of invitations. And Uncle Lorin was to be their official chaperone at such events.

Finitan laughed at Edeard's broken expression. 'So thought of eloping yet?'

'Certainly not,' Edeard said loyally.

Finitan just laughed louder. 'Now you know how I feel about all the speeches I have to deliver. I'm addressing the Chemistry Guild apprentices this evening in the hope of a few votes cast my way. Will you be attending?'

'Kristabel's expecting me; I have to help her select the music for our engagement party.'

'That's nice. Do you know many songs?'

'Only Dybal's,' he confessed.

Finitan laughed again. A couple of ge-chimps scurried in through their little doorways in the bookshelf walls, bringing trays laden with tea and biscuits. Edeard eyed the brandysnaps and chocolate chip shortbreads keenly. He'd never found the bakery which supplied the Blue Tower, but Finitan always had the best biscuits in Makkathran. The main door opened behind him.

'I'm sure you remember Master Topar?' Finitan said lightly.

Edeard couldn't recall meeting Topar since his first day in the city which, now he thought about it, was odd since Topar was Finitan's deputy. And looking at the figure walking across the office, he was surprised by the Master's appearance. Gone was the overweight frame. He looked a lot leaner, but not necessarily healthy with it. His face was haggard, the full chubby cheeks had given way to deep worry creases in loose flesh, while his eyes seemed bruised. He still wore expensive clothes, a silk shirt and suede trousers, high black boots, and the traditional Master's cloak, but even they couldn't cover the fact that he'd undergone a time of considerable hardship.

'Master,' Edeard bowed.

'You've been making quite a name for yourself while I was away, so I'm told,' Topar said in his powerful baritone – that at least remained the same.

Edeard shrugged.

'How little any of us knew the day we arranged for you to join the constables,' Topar continued.

'Sir?'

'I apologize, Waterwalker, I'm blaming the messenger. It's not been a pleasant time for me.'

The three of them sat down as the ge-chimps handed out the elegant china cups.

'Partly my fault,' Finitan said. 'But you did come to us with an incredible story, Edeard. Ordinarily, I confess, I would have paid little heed to it: a lad from the provinces exaggerating a few brawls, seeking sympathy to gain entrance to the Guild. However, I found you pleasingly guileless, and Akeem chose you as his apprentice which really told me all I needed to know.'

'I don't understand,' Edeard said.

'The weapon,' Finitan said softly. His third hand opened a

drawer on his desk, and lifted out a package of leather wrapping. It drifted through the air to finish on the desktop.

Edeard froze as his farsight probed the contents. 'Oh my Lady,' he moaned. It was a repeat-fire gun.

Finitan's third hand unwrapped the package gingerly. Edeard gazed at the *thing* with utter loathing. The metal was tarnished, with ingrained rust corroding several areas, and the magazine had received several dents, but he would recognize the evil device to his dying day. 'Where did you get it?'

'Where you left it,' Topar said. 'At the bottom of the new well in Ashwell.'

'Huh?'

'That's where I've been, and as you know it's not an easy journey at the best of times. I only returned last night.'

'You've been to Ashwell?' Edeard thought he was over his life in the village with all its lost inhabitants, he really did, but staring at someone else who'd seen those forlorn ruins was triggering an avalanche of memories.

'I sent Master Topar to try and confirm your story,' Finitan said. 'Which, I'm afraid, he has done in no uncertain terms.'

'It was all as you described it,' Topar said. 'The weeds and moss have grown over the rubble, of course; but I knew Ashwell as soon as I saw it. The cliffs, the old rampart wall around. Even the well shaft you hid in was easy to locate; though it was mostly full of mud. How you moved that capping stone is a mystery to me. It took us a day to break it up and move the pieces away; then it was another week excavating the mud before we could recover the gun.' He gave the weapon on the desk a scowl.

'So now what?' Edeard asked.

'Now we've established the gun is real we need to know about those bandits,' Finitan said. 'If that's what they truly are. What can you tell us about their leader? You said you spoke with him.'

'All I can tell you is his anger. He hated me because I'd killed his kindred in their ambush.'

'Is that what he said?'

Edeard struggled to remember. It wasn't easy; for so long now he'd been trying to banish this very memory. 'Friends. That's what it was, he called them: our friends. I was to die because of what I'd done to our friends. Yes.'

'Interesting,' Finitan said. 'And how long between the ambush in the wood and the raid on your village?'

'Not quite a year.'

'So it wasn't an instinctive hot-headed response, then? They'd planned it out.'

Edeard nodded, hanging on to the memory no matter the pain. 'They knew us. They knew Salrana. The one from the church, that's what he said. I suppose they must have been watching us. I never considered that before.'

'Then they were organized?'

'Yes.'

'Hardly the kind of raid I would credit ordinary bandits with.'

'Their clothes,' Edeard exclaimed. 'The ones in the wood were wild, savages; they daubed themselves with mud, and they didn't even have shoes. But the ones who came to the village wore proper clothes, with boots.'

'And they had the repeat-fire gun,' Finitan concluded.

'They're not bandits, are they?'

'No, not the kind who have always lived around the edge of our society,' Finitan agreed. 'Though I suspect they are allied. These are the emissaries of something else entirely.'

'What?' Edeard asked.

'I don't know. But they are relentless.' Finitan gave Topar a small nod.

'There were five in my travelling party,' Topar said. 'Only two of us made it back to Makkathran. Edeard, I'm sorry, but the province is all but lost. Eight villages have been overrun, and that was when I left just before New Year. The capital is fortified and afraid, with families leaving every day. Farmers are deserting their land and heading to the eastern provinces. None of the caravans visit any more. Their economy is failing. The neighbouring provinces no longer offer help in any fashion; they are too worried about their own bandit incursions.'

Edeard's head sank into his hands. 'Witham?' he asked.

'Yes,' Topar said. 'It fell not six months after Ashwell. Since then, the raids have increased. It's the same every time, they wipe out the entire village, no one is left alive, the buildings are torched. The senselessness of it all is shocking, they're not doing it for anything other than the pleasure of killing. There's no reason for it.'

Tears were threatening to flow as Edeard thought of the pretty leatherworker apprentice he'd met at the Witham market. He'd never even managed to get her name, gauche boy that he'd been. And now she was dead, every garment or saddle or harness she'd laboured over was gone. Her family murdered.

'It's not your fault,' Finitan said gently. 'Stop punishing yourself.'

'I should go back,' Edeard said. 'I should go with the city's militia and burn them out of the land they've contaminated, every last one of them. He feared me before, and by the Lady he was right to do so. I will bring him and his kind to an end, one way or another.'

'Just calm down,' Finitan said. 'There will be a time when we confront the bandits, and you may well lead that battle. But there are many things we have to do before that day arrives.'

'Why?' Edeard snapped. 'If you and Owain combine in Council, you could send every militia brigade we have, and order the provinces to raise their militias with us. An *army* could descend on Rulan province. These new bandits would be wiped from Querencia forever.'

'Where do they come from?' Finitan asked. 'They're not barbarians, they wore clothes.' His third hand lifted the repeat-fire gun again. 'More importantly, where do they manufacture this? Do they have a city like Makkathran behind them? Two cities? A continent? We still don't know what lies beyond Rulan, not with any surety. All these things we need to establish beyond

429

any doubt before we embark on some massive campaign to tame the wilds. Such a venture will be deeply unpopular both here in the city, and out in the country.'

'And if you don't do it, these invaders will be standing in front of the City Gate within five years.'

'That they will,' Finitan conceded. 'This is the greatest threat we have faced since Rah led us here two thousand years ago. I am deeply worried, Edeard. Something is out there, some society, moving with a malign purpose. A society inimical to ours, bent on destroying us for no reason we know. More important, they have these Lady-damned repeat-firing guns. You with your strength could ward off the bullets fired at you by one of these guns, maybe even two or three. But I doubt I could withstand such an onslaught; nor could many people. You talk of marching our militia against them. One man armed with this weapon could wipe out an entire cavalry troop. And they have concealment, too. We cannot send our Militia soldiers against them, it would be slaughter on an unbelievable scale. Edeard, I am frightened by this, do you understand? I do not know what will happen.'

'Yes, sir. I understand.'

'They're not settling,' Topar said. 'That's the strangest thing. The lands they have driven us from in Rulan are reverting to wilds; weeds and grass flourish in the fields, animals roam free; the ruins of villages are choked in vines and creepers. Nobody lives there, these strangers are not clearing us out so their own kind can dwell in our place. When we arrived at Ashwell, we had seen no one for over a week, and that was a week of hard riding. It was only coming back we clashed with them. Our luck was foul that day; some lone patrol or spy saw us, and we ran away as soon as we realized they were after us. It was as though Honious himself was tracking us. They were unrelenting. So now I've seen these guns used in anger, Edeard, I know what horror you faced. The Lady performed a miracle when she guided you to safety that night. All we could ever do was flee, and three times even that was not enough.'

'Then what are they doing?' Edeard asked. 'What do they want?'

'I don't know,' Finitan said. 'But it is imperative we find out.' He stared at the broken gun, abhorrence glowing in his mind. 'If we fail to stop them out in the provinces, then we will have to make similar guns just to survive. Can you imagine the carnage that will unleash on this world? The damage one man can wreak with such a gun, multiplied a thousandfold. For once such a thing is made, it cannot be unmade.'

'It's already been made,' Topar said bitterly. 'We are not the ones at fault here.'

Edeard reached out his third hand, and grasped the gun. He brought it over to hang in the air before his face, probing the complicated mechanism inside with his farsight. In fact, there weren't so many components. 'Have you examined it?' he asked Topar.

'I have done nothing less for months,' the Master said. 'The whole way home I have studied it.'

'Is there some secret part, something that must have come from the ships that brought us to Querencia, or could any metalsmith build it?'

'The mechanism is ingenious, but that is all. There is nothing out of the ordinary about it, no magic or impossible contraption. A competent weapons Guild Master would be able to fabricate such components. Even a journeyman should be capable, I suspect.'

That caused Edeard to give the Grand Master a sharp glance. 'The long-barrelled pistols came from the Weapons Guild. An ancient design, Owain said.'

'Yes,' Finitan said significantly, though his mind was tightly shielded. 'It could be they already have this or something similar in their deep vaults. Knowledge or artefacts left over from the ships.'

'Is that where the invaders got theirs from, do you think?'

Finitan allowed dismay to ease through his mental shielding.

'I find it incredible that after two thousand years, we have never heard even a whisper of another civilization on Querencia.'

'Nobody has ever successfully circumnavigated the planet,' Edeard said. 'Or so I was given to understand. Maybe that's why. Maybe it isn't geographically impossible, it's just that nobody ever gets past this other settlement.'

'If they were that big and powerful, we would know of them,' Finitan said.

'Perhaps we should ask the watching widow,' Topar said mordantly, then he gave Edeard a keen look. 'Actually . . .'

'I haven't seen any souls since Chae,' Edeard countered. 'In any case, wondering where they are doesn't help us, it's what they're doing which is the problem.'

'If only we could find where they come from, we might be able to know their full intention,' Finitan said. He sighed. 'We're arguing in circles. It is my response we should be determining.'

'Perhaps a truce with Owain,' Edeard suggested. 'Makkathran needs to send scouts out into the wild beyond Rulan and track down the origin of the guns. I'd go . . .' he began uncertainly.

'No, you will not,' Finitan said firmly. 'We need you here to complete your victory over the gangs. Once the city is consolidated, we can start to make more detailed alliances with the provinces. That's what Owain never understands, we can hardly command unity with the countryside if we're unable to instil universal law here at home. Yet that unity must come in the face of these incursions. That makes you vital to my campaign, Waterwalker.'

Edeard nodded reluctantly. 'After that?'

'When the gangs are banished, and if I become Mayor, then it might be appropriate for you to track down your nemesis. Though the Lady knows how you will explain such an absence to your new wife.'

Edeard flinched, he hadn't thought of that. 'Sometimes you have to do what's wrong in order to do what's right,' he murmured quietly.

'Indeed,' Finitan said. 'In the meantime, I will focus on winning this damn election. That way I can lay the groundwork for the inevitable struggle which is to come.'

'It might come sooner than you think,' Topar said. 'The provinces around Rulan have already raised their militias. Their appeals to the Grand Council for help will arrive before long, people will come to understand what is happening out on our western borders.'

'Not just on the borders,' Edeard said. 'Ordinary bandits are everywhere in the countryside, and growing bold. You will have to move decisively once you're Mayor.'

'If, my boy, and it's still a big if. Owain is no fool and he has a lot of support in the city. People like his One Nation call.'

'But what we are talking about is the same.'

'Essentially, yes, but I will instigate it differently. Securing the City must come first, without that all will be lost. Owain is using unification to rally the city behind him, the city as it is. Ultimately, that will fail.'

'We're making progress,' Edeard said. 'I have a new tactic which we're almost ready to deploy. It's a bit of a gamble, but it might help resolve the current stand-off.'

'Then let us pray to the Lady that it does.'

Edeard stood, almost ready to go. 'Master?'

'Oh dear,' Finitan said with a kindly smile. 'This doesn't sound good.'

'I need a small genistar to scout round without drawing attention to itself.'

'An interesting challenge, I will see what I can sculpt for you.'

'And I was also wondering if you know how to see through a concealment. I'm convinced the people who set the trap for me in Eyrie were able to perceive me.'

Finitan gave Topar a fast bemused glance. 'As there is absolutely no such thing as concealment, then there could be no way to penetrate it.'

'Yes, sir,' Edeard said in disappointment.

'Certainly no such thing as this.'

Finitan's gifting rushed into Edeard's mind, a hugely complex methodology he could barely comprehend.

'I'll be sure I remember to not use it, then, sir.'

'We'll make a true Makkathran citizen out of you yet, my boy.'

*

The uniforms that arrived from the tailor were amazingly comfortable, made from some weave of cotton and drosilk that was as soft as it was strong. Edeard hadn't expected that. Unlike the dress uniform which Kristabel had given him, these were all for everyday use. They lacked the sheer gaudiness of militia uniforms, but the tailor had somehow contrived to make them a lot more glamorous than the ones Edeard had bought from the regular constable supplier. Platinum buttons shone brighter than Dinlay's ageing over-polished silver ones. The cut was subtly different, making him look sharp and smart, the kind of tunic a member of the nobility would wear if they could ever lower themselves to sign on at a station. And the shirts made mountaintop snow look grey by comparison. The tailor even supplied a special mix of soap flakes for the ge-chimps to use, so as not to sully that purity. And, as for the knee-high boots, space between the nebulas wasn't that black nor did it possess such lustre.

The first morning he put one on Edeard stood nervously in front of his maisonette's mirror and looked at the figure he cut. No way could he stop the prideful smile from lifting his lips.

Dashing, he decided, *yes, very dashing*.

The long weather-cloak helped, held by an emerald-encrusted brooch round his neck which he was trying to pin into place one-handed. His third hand ruffled it, and he admired the swirl it made around him. *Nice touch.* He practised the ruffle again, making the fabric flare out and undulate in slow motion. Perhaps it could become his signature; at night he would brighten the city's orange lights to silhouette himself as he emerged from nowhere to bear down formidably on criminals, cloak swirling like angry smoke behind him. At such an impressive sight the fight would go out of them, and they'd abandon their wrong doing, sinking to their knees in contrition. *Okay then!*

'Yow!' The brooch pin jabbed into his fumbling thumb. Edeard shook it, then sucked the drop of blood away. 'Lady-damn.' *All right, so the image needs a bit of work.*

He fixed the brooch in place, settled the hat on his head, and ran a finger along the rim, ending in a salute to himself. 'Now that's what I call an officer of the city.'

Macsen called it something else entirely as Edeard strode purposefully into their small hall at Jeavons station. Young Felax dropped his jaw in astonishment as Edeard walked past the bench he was sitting at. A cheeky chorus of wolf-whistles echoed round the small hall.

'Happy to see you're not abandoning your roots,' Kanseen sniped.

Edeard unclipped the brooch and removed his weather-cloak with a flourish. 'Anyone else jealous?'

'I'm so glad you taught us concealment,' Boyd grunted. 'Because there's no way I'm walking down a street next to *that*.'

Dinlay glared at him for the indiscretion. 'You look very smart,' he said. 'People have expectations from us now, it's right that you should look the part.'

'Thank you,' Edeard acknowledged. He looked round the hall. There were ten constables sitting at the tables now, men he trusted implicitly, reading through reports. The way files were building up they'd soon have to contract the Guild of Clerks to keep track of it all, Edeard thought ruefully.

'Seventy-two of them now,' Doral said.

'That's good,' Edeard acknowledged. Most of the files in the hall were those on the excluded, which were still being added to. But his team had been going through them, and assessing the reports from stations across the city, along with the priceless information coming in through Charyau and his network of merchants and traders. Edeard's old notes from his days spying on the House of Blue Petals were also examined keenly. Slowly and surely, they were identifying the senior echelons of the gangs. The leadership rarely met in person, so there was no hard evidence actually tying them together in any criminal act. But the way they collaborated and respected each other's territories meant that they knew each other, that they were organized along formal lines. In fact, it was intriguingly like a mirror to the way in which the interests of the established nobility locked together. Edeard was still a little irked that they hadn't proved a connection between the gangs and the more disreputable aristocratic families – such as the Gilmorns, for example.

'Can't we just go and arrest them?' Boyd whined. 'Surely seventy-two is enough? And Buate is still having to appear in the financial court each day.'

Edeard pulled a face. 'I'd like it to be a hundred,' he said. There was something about the number which was impressive. It would show Makkathran's citizens how they were making huge inroads against the gangs. That it wasn't just exclusion warrants and the promises of the Mayoral candidates they were deploying.

The idea wasn't to get convictions, Edeard knew he didn't have enough evidence for that. But a little known clause in the articles of arrest meant that if a constable swore there were grounds for suspicion that the detainee was involved in illegal activity they could be held for twenty-two days without charges being filed. The twenty-two days was supposed to allow the constables enough time to gather evidence and interview all concerned.

Edeard reasoned that with the entire leadership, or as many as he could reasonably identify, taken off the streets and held incommunicado for half a month, the gangs' ordinary street soldiers would be completely lost. 'A body without a head,' as Macsen had summed it up.

If gang resistance crumbled as Edeard hoped, liberating people from their tyranny, the prospect of it all coming back at the end of the twenty-two days would be a colossal argument in Finitan's favour to bring about the banishment. Finitan was also planning to introduce emergency legislation to the Grand Council as soon as the arrests began, extending the detention period to a full month. Forty-four days would take them past the election. It was slightly underhand, Edeard thought, but then this was Makkathran – he wasn't about to change it overnight.

He sat down at the table he used, and gave the neat grey cardboard folders a dispirited look. No matter how hard they worked, or how much he delegated, the paperwork never got any smaller.

'Something more for you to read,' Dinlay said.

Edeard looked up to see his friends clustered together, smiling as Dinlay held out a small red book.

'A gift from all of us,' Kanseen said.

Edeard took the book. It was very slim. Small gold-leaf lettering on the front read: *A Gentleman's Guide to Marriage*.

'Thank you,' he said, genuinely grateful.

'What does it say about the stag night?' Macsen asked. Caught himself, threw Kanseen a panicked look. 'I mean, friends' night,' he corrected.

She just groaned wearily.

Edeard flicked through the pages. 'An evening may justifiably be set aside for a fellow to bid his male acquaintances farewell, in the full knowledge that his bachelor ways are about to end. This should be a tasteful evening, revisiting those places retaining fond memories, and sampling their delights for the last time.'

'I don't want another night at Olovan's Eagle,' Dinlay protested. 'This is supposed to be special.'

'We could start at the Rakas restaurant in Abad, the one we went to after graduation,' Kanseen said.

Edeard was about to agree, but Salrana had been with them that day. 'Maybe a different one,' he said.

'There's a theatre in Fiacre I know of,' Boyd said breathlessly. 'The dancers take their clothes off as they dance.'

'Do they?' Edeard asked.

Kanseen deliberately focused on a point just above Edeard's head, her jaw set firm.

'That's not reliving the past,' Edeard conceded.

'We'll start off at the dog track in Andromeda, then make our way through some of the classy taverns in Lillylight,' Macsen said. 'There are plenty of good restaurants and theatres there, so we can make our choices on the night.'

'Excellent idea,' Kanseen said.

'Julan has to get the vote through Council first,' Edeard complained.

'It's considered *bad form* to vote against a Consent bill,' Dinlay said. 'There hasn't been a nay vote for over three hundred years.'

'Really? I didn't know that.'

'We know,' they said in union.

Edeard was supposed to spend the evening choosing the suit to wear at the charity ball thrown by the District Master of Nighthouse. Due in a fortnight's time, it was given every year to raise funds for city hospitals. Kristabel had accepted his excuse that there was just some constable work which had to be done at night. 'Be careful,' she told him, which almost made him feel guilty. Almost.

It was certainly the first time Edeard had ever been grateful to Buate; but the gang lord had arranged a meeting with several others on their One Hundred list. A get-together of that magnitude couldn't be ignored.

As dusk fell he led the squad out of the station. All of them were immediately aware of the three ge-eagles overhead, and a couple of small ge-dogs loitering down the street. It had been a while since the gangs had used actual people to spy on their comings and goings from the constable station.

'I want to try something,' he told the others. 'We're not going to use the tunnels for a while.'

They followed him over Marble Canal bridge into Drupe,

where the streets grew narrow, and the buildings tall. The ge-eagles kept level with them, drifting and soaring on the night air.

'I've been reading your book,' Edeard said. 'Apparently, after marriage, I shouldn't complain to Kristabel about events relating to managing my estate if they go poorly.'

'Yeah, I always avoid that when I'm with Saria,' Boyd said. 'It's for the best.'

'Nor should I be querulous about the proportion of the household budget spent on her wardrobe. Apparently it's her duty to always look her best for me, and support me in public.'

'Quite right,' Kanseen said.

'And I must not feel inadequate if I cede an argument to her.'

'That has to have been written by a woman,' Dinlay pronounced.

It was already dark at the foot of the buildings when they walked into Moslet Avenue, little more than a deep crevice between walls six storeys high. Small vaulting tube bridges linked the two sets of buildings, with slender orange light slits on their underside shining a weak glow down on to the pavement. The alley was a series of sharp corners, which restricted farsight, while its narrow width made anyone following them highly conspicuous. Precisely the kind of place that usually provided Edeard with excellent cover while he vanished down into the tunnels below.

He ordered the orange light strips on the bridges to dim down, turning the darkness to a claustrophobic force. A sweep round with his farsight showed him they were alone as they went round the first corner. Then he followed that up with a more subtle look, using the technique Finitan had gifted him. Someone was sneaking into the alley; registering in his mind as a grey swirl, like a small bubble of fog. At the core was the outline of a man.

'Keep going,' he told his friends. 'We need to hurry.'

They started to jog forwards. Edeard observed the figure behind them quicken his pace.

'Okay, stop here.' he ordered as they went round the second

corner. They were directly under one of the small bridges, invisible to the ge-eagles above. The concealed pursuer hurried round the corner, to see the squad huddled together as if performing some illegal act. Edeard's arm came up, pointing at him, cloak swirling to follow the move.

The narrow alley was suddenly drenched in brilliant white light. A terrific *bang* ricocheted off the confining walls.

Edeard's miniature thunderbolt struck the figure square in his chest. He was flung backwards to sprawl on the ground, concealment vanishing in the blink of an eye.

'Great Lady,' Dinlay gulped.

Edeard was watching the figure keenly; the man was twitching but making no attempt to get up. Farsight revealed he was still alive, his thoughts chasing an agitated sleep pattern. The thunderbolt must have knocked him unconscious, though his heart was still pumping wildly, and not entirely regularly. His thick leather jacket was smoking from a burn spot where the discharge had struck.

'Take care of the ge-eagles,' Edeard told Kanseen as his third hand lifted the inert figure, and drew him towards the squad. The birds would have witnessed the flash, he couldn't help that. But they would have been dazzled. Their owners still wouldn't know what was going on in the alley.

Once Kanseen had confused the already flustered genistars overhead, Edeard asked the city to let him into the drain tunnel below the street. The squad sank down, taking their captive with them.

Once they were safe below the surface, Edeard examined the man his third hand was still holding above the trickle of water. He was plain enough, probably in his late forties, with dark curly hair and a small, neatly trimmed beard. 'Anyone know him?' Edeard asked.

'I don't remember him from any of our lists,' Dinlay said.

Macsen let out a pained sigh. 'He won't be, look at how he's dressed.'

Edeard gave the unconscious man a closer look. The clothes

were simple, a black leather jacket worn over an indigo shirt, and beige suede trousers. Ankle length boots with discreet silver hooks for the laces. The kind of garb that could be worn anywhere in Makkathran without drawing undue attention. However, these days Edeard was familiar enough with the city's tailors to know quality when he saw it. 'Expensive,' he said.

'Certainly not cheap,' Macsen said. 'So we know he's not from the gangs, not directly.'

'The families?'

Macsen's face produced a pained expression. 'Again, nothing you could ever prove, not that he'll tell us anything.'

'What then?' Boyd asked. 'Come on, you obviously know something.'

'Look exactly where we are and how we got here,' Macsen said with the kind of serious, level voice that was unusual for him. 'And that blast of light you knocked him out with, Edeard, that's something new. There's rumours that your maisonette is different. A fall off a tower can't kill you. Small wonder the families are extremely interested in you.'

'The families can throw light like that,' Edeard said defensively. 'I just have greater strength.'

'No, it's more than just strength. Can anyone else see souls? Can they talk to the city itself? Nobody can. You stand above us, Waterwalker. A long way above.'

'So?' Dinlay said. 'We've always known Edeard is far more talented than the rest of us put together.'

'This goes way beyond psychic talent.' Macsen gave Edeard a level stare. 'You frighten people, Waterwalker. Even I'm nervous of you, and I know you better than most in this city. I don't think you'll abuse the power you have. But, face it, what's to stop you? That's why you're drawing this kind of attention.'

'I would never . . .' Edeard broke off, appealing to his friends. 'I want the city to work, to be a home we can all depend on, a place where everyone can be safe. You know that, that's why you're helping me. Isn't it?' he asked, aghast that they might not share his ambition.

'Yes,' Kanseen assured him. 'But you have to admit, Macsen has a point. Not only have you got your talent, but you're popular as well. I bet if you stood for Mayor, you'd get a sizeable amount of the votes.'

'I don't want to, I support Finitan.'

'I know that,' she told him. 'The point is, the Grand Families see how much support you have, and they know you want to instigate change. Change for them, a return to more democratic rule, the introduction of accountability, will diminish their power, and Lady help them, their wealth, too. That's what the city's entire political structure is geared around: preserving and expanding their estates. If you wipe out the gangs, you'll go after them next, and the way they've distorted and abused Rah's constitution. That's inevitable.'

'Some people say you are Rah,' Boyd said. He shrugged. 'It's true. I'm often asked. They think you've come back from the Heart to restore the city to the haven it was in the beginning. The gangs and the bandits we're plagued with right now, that's the kind of chaos Rah led his followers away from.'

'Oh, dear Lady.' Edeard gave Dinlay a desperate look.

'People have asked me, too,' Dinlay said apologetically. 'But I know you're not going to declare yourself emperor. That's stupid. They'd never say that if they knew you properly.'

Edeard felt incredibly weary. After everything he'd done, all he'd endured, to find he had created a huge source of mistrust and suspicion was a hideous revelation. 'I just want people to be safe,' he cried. 'I want the killing to stop. I want the fear to end. I want people to know their leaders and constables will protect them.'

Kanseen put her arm around his shoulder. 'I think that's what disturbs the families most of all; they can't believe someone with your strength can be honest. But you are, and I will stand by you to the end because of that.'

'Me too,' Dinlay said.

'I trust you, Edeard,' Boyd said.

They all turned to Macsen.

'Hey! Goes without saying.'

'Say it anyway,' Kanseen said.

'I'm with you.'

'Thank you.'

'But you've got to admit, everything you can do, it's way beyond anything Querencia has seen before, and I include Rah in that. Blasphemy or not.'

'Yeah,' Edeard admitted sheepishly.

'So . . .' Dinlay queried. 'Are you Rah?'

'No!'

'So why you?' Macsen asked. 'You must be something special.'

'Really, I'm not.'

'You were chosen,' Kanseen said. 'We know everything the Lady says in her Scriptures is true. You showed us Chae's soul — and haven't you got to love the irony in that? Him of all people. So if we have souls, and Odin's Sea is the path to the Heart, there's a lot more to this universe that we know.'

'Chosen?' Edeard repeated dumbly.

'I don't know by who, or by what, but there's no way you with all your abilities came forth at a time like this purely by chance. The Heart, or our ancestors, are speaking to us through you.'

'Maybe not them,' Edeard said, thinking of his dreams. 'But I can hardly deny what I can do, whoever gave me the gift. And I promise you, I'll do what I think is right with it. And if any of you disagree, then for the Lady's sake tell me.' He looked down at their unconscious captive. 'Which brings us back to him. Who is he?'

'The families have their own methods of maintaining order in the city,' Macsen said. 'After all, they could hardly rely on the constables, now could they? Not before the Waterwalker came along.'

Dinlay bridled. 'The constables have always brought law and order to Makkathran. We were established by Rah himself.'

'Rah allowed District Masters to police their districts,' Macsen replied equitably. 'Independent citywide constables weren't introduced until a lot later.'

Edeard held a hand up to silence a glowering Dinlay. 'You're saying there's another police force in Makkathran?'

Macsen shook his head. 'That's too strong a word. The true Grand Families are as old as the city; as soon as they established themselves they sought methods of consolidating their interests. Families have their own guards, for instance, they also have clerks, lawyers, doctors; a long list of employees to cover every requirement. Well there are also people who look after *political* interests, too, which is a very broad-ranging term. You've seen the grandest families are not subject to intimidation by the gangs. Their estates are immune. Why is that?'

'Because they work with them?' Edeard asked.

'No, no, you're thinking too literally. There is an *understanding*, nothing formal, nobody ever sat round a table and thrashed out boundaries. But the families take care of themselves at every level. If a gang was ever stupid or arrogant enough to overstep the mark, then certain members of the family would put a stop to the violation straight away, and in a fashion the gangs would comprehend.'

'But . . . Mirnatha,' Edeard said.

'Yeah. The biggest shock to hit this city since our day at Birmingham Pool. I hate to say it, but: cause and effect.'

'Are you one of them?' Dinlay asked. 'One of these family agents?'

'No.'

'You seem to know a lot about them.'

'Actually, I don't. One of my father's cousins hinted a couple of times that there was a group of relatives that might be interested in welcoming me as an associate. That was as far as it ever got. Father died, and well, you all know how my family treated mother and myself after that.'

'It makes a lot of sense,' Edeard said. 'Except I think it's more than a vague accord as far as some families are concerned. I know from personal experience that the Gilmorns are heavily involved with Buate's organization.'

Macsen nodded down at the man Edeard's third hand was still holding. 'There have been two well-executed attempts to get rid of you. They won't stop now, especially as your abilities still seem to be growing.'

Edeard thought back to that last conversation with Ivarl. 'You may be right. In which case we're not leading events the way we thought we were.'

'Welcome to Makkathran,' Macsen said.

'Where it's always about politics.'

'Good, you're starting to understand.'

Edeard inhaled through his nostrils. 'So what do we do about our friend here?'

'The ge-eagles have shown the family agents that you possess their lightning trick,' Kanseen said. 'And you can plainly see through concealment now. The next time they come after you, it's going to be with everything they've got.'

'That didn't answer my question.'

'Why, what were you planning on doing with him?'

'I don't know. I just disabled him because I had to.'

'He won't crack under interrogation,' Macsen said. 'He has too much faith in his own kind. That doesn't leave us with a lot of options.'

'There's a place I can put him where there is no way out,' Edeard said, wondering if Macsen was testing him. 'That will serve until we can decide what to do.'

'Sounds good.'

When Edeard rejected Finitan's offer of an apprenticeship with the city's Eggshaper's Guild, he'd done so in the conviction that his skill was a match for any of the practitioners in the Blue Tower. Now, looking at the tiny ge-mouse nestling in his hand, he knew how conceited he'd been that day when he'd made his life-changing decision. The little creature was no bigger than the length of his fingers, its dark pelt as soft as any terrestrial kitten, and the three curving talons extended from each twig-like leg were sharp and hard, enabling it to scamper vertically up most of the walls in the city. But it's head was the true marvel, sprouting long ears that could hear a pin drop within thirty yards, while the eyes were miniatures of those indigo-tinged orbs belonging to ge eagles, allowing it to see clearly in the dead of night.

Finitan had handed it over with a little smirk of satisfaction. 'At least you'll appreciate my efforts. Kindly look after my creation with care.'

'Yes, sir,' Edeard had said reverentially as he gingerly held the ge-mouse up, automatically soothing its agitated mind with balmy thoughts. Little eyes regarded him passively, and a sliver of trust manifested behind them. Edeard smiled back.

'Ah, what an apprentice you would have made,' Finitan said wistfully.

'What's its lifetime?'

'Sadly, no more than a week.'

Edeard felt a pang of sympathy, but he understood how that was so. He'd never seen a genistar this small before; and their lifespan was always proportional to size.

His admiration for the Grand Master's ability rose considerably. He had no idea how to go about sculpting such a thing. For a start, it was almost smaller than a two-week ge-dog embryo, which led to some interesting hatching questions. Akeem had always said that a standard ge-cat was the smallest possible genistar.

When Edeard and the squad arrived underneath the house in Sampalok that Buate was holding court in, he'd taken the little thing from his pocket and held it aloft. The city lifted it up from the tunnel to the lower cellar. Edeard longtalked into its mind, carefully directing it under the cellar door, and up the stairs to the mid-cellar. Its claws had to scrape at the hard city substance, finding minute crinkles to grip as it hauled itself up every curving shelf. There were two guards standing in the short, gloomy corridor above the stairs, both of them with pistols tucked into their belts. Neither of them noticed the ge-mouse scurrying past. Nor the man who was wrapped in concealment that Edeard perceived standing just inside the door.

Buate was already in the room with eight other gang lords. They sat around a big old table, with bottles of wine and beer opened before them. The ge-mouse squeezed behind a tall cupboard in the corner, and scaled the ancient wood silently, emerging on to the top where someone had left a set of aged china crockery. From there it gifted Edeard its sharp sight and accompanying sound of the angry voices.

Edeard shared the perception with the squad as they leaned against the tunnel wall far below the cellar floor.

'That's Gormat and Edsing,' Dinlay said. 'And that's Joarwel; he's shaved his beard off, look.'

'Are you sure?' Kanseen asked.

'Yes.'

'He's right,' Boyd said. 'No one has reported seeing him for a couple of weeks, that's why. He's a smart one, that.'

'I know Hallwith and Coyce,' Macsen said. 'But I don't recognize the others.'

Two more men arrived, giving Buate and the others a curt greeting.

'So why are we here?' Joarwel asked.

'Because we're hurting,' Buate said. 'For all we tell our men how everything is all right, that bastard Waterwalker is shutting us down one street at a time.'

'I don't need to be told that,' one of the unknowns said. 'Thirty years I lived in my house, then some child constable comes along waving that Lady-fucking exclusion warrant in my face. It was all I could do not to shoot the smug little shit on sight. Thirty years!'

'It's going to get worse,' Buate said. 'He's planning to arrest us all.'

'There aren't that many jails.'

'Not the men, just us. He's making a list; there's going to be a hundred of us on it.'

'Shit,' Macsen grunted. 'How did he find that out?'

Edeard shrugged. He wasn't surprised.

'Arrest us for what?' Coyce demanded. 'I've barely made enough to feed myself this year. Three of my boys have gone and got themselves jobs in theatres for the Lady's sake.'

'For nothing,' Buate said. 'He's not going to charge us, just hold us.'

'What's the fucking point?'

'Because he can hold us for twenty-two days. That's the law.'

'Twenty-two days!'

'Leading up to the election,' Buate said significantly. 'Without us, he thinks our men will fall apart.'

'Scumfucking bastard, we should slit his throat.'

'No. Slit his girl's throat and make him watch, then burn him alive. That's what we did to that grocer in Zelda. Didn't have no trouble from the shopkeepers after that.'

'Waterwalker's right,' Edsing said. 'Without us to hold it together, we'll be left with nothing.'

'Less than that,' Buate told them. 'If Finitan wins, we'll be thrown out of Makkathran.'

'Then what are we going to do about it?' Hallwith shouted. 'He can't win, this is Makkathran.'

'There have been several attempts to kill and ruin him. Yet he still walks the streets unharmed. He has powers we don't.'

'Are you saying he *is* Rah?' Edsing asked. 'That's the talk wherever I go.'

'Stupid superstition. He is an orphan from Rulan province, nothing more. I know this is true. His strength, though, is formidable.'

'They say the Pythia favours him.'

'I don't give a fuck what the Pythia favours. Our problem is not spiritual, it's very real. We are going to jail, and then we are going to be exiled to some Lady-forsaken island for the rest of our lives.'

Hallwith's fist smashed down on the table. 'We get it! Now tell us what we have to do?'

'Fight him, every one of us. That's all we have left. When they come to carry us off to the cells, we fight, because if we don't our life is over. We shoot every constable, burn every warehouse, sink the gondolas and the ships in the port. We show Makkathran that we are just as strong as the Waterwalker, and far more deadly.'

'But we cannot stand against him,' Coyce said. 'They threw him off the top of a tower, and he flew. Bullets are useless. I was there that night in the House of Blue Petals when your brother ambushed him. He's immortal. Lady! Maybe he is Rah.'

'The next one of you who says that, I will slit your throat,' Buate said. 'This is part of his strength, to cast doubt among us. Yes, he is strong, but he is one. One! While he comes for me, a thousand of us will rampage across the city. He cannot stop us all. That is *our* strength. And when they see what their precious Waterwalker has kindled, the people of this city will howl for his blood. It is he who will suffer banishment, and we will party in the Culverit mansion that night. Now you will go home, and you will arm yourselves, and you will select targets, and when him and that squad of his knocks on our door, you *will* open the gates of Honious to them.'

The squad took their usual table in Olovan's Eagle. They sat staring at their beer glasses, saying nothing; morose thoughts leaking through impoverished shields.

'Do you think they'll do it?' Dinlay asked.

'Most likely,' Kanseen said. 'We've pushed them back and back. Hurt them just like Buate said. What have they got to lose?'

'We just have to snatch them quickly and quietly,' Boyd said.

'A hundred separate arrests?' Kanseen said. 'Remember our raid on the fisherman's warehouse? Most of the city knew about it half a day early. Buate has been clever, he's priming them ready. It'll take one arrest to kick the whole thing off.'

'Then we do it tomorrow at first light,' Dinlay said. 'They're not organized yet. There were only ten of them there, Buate's orders won't have got any further tonight. We grab him first, then get the other district stations to pull in the rest of the list.'

'We're not ready either,' Edeard said. Rushing into the arrests was the first thing he'd thought of. 'It'll take us at least a couple of days to organize things with the station captains.'

'I think it's safe to assume Buate's riot and destruction scheme won't have the support of the Grand Families,' Boyd said. 'Maybe their agents would like to help us?'

'Not a chance,' Macsen said in a disgusted tone. 'To them, we remain the problem; without us Buate wouldn't be planning this. We are the source.'

Edeard took a deep drink of his beer. 'They know what we're planning, and we know what they're planning. But they don't know we know.'

Dinlay growled in dismay, clasping his hands to his head. 'Don't start that again.'

'It's our only advantage,' Edeard said. 'We have to think how to use it.'

'How?' Kanseen asked.

'I don't know,' Edeard said miserably.

'Buate doesn't have a plan,' Macsen said. 'Not really. This is instinct kicking in. And it's a good instinct, I'll admit that. If we don't make the arrests, he'll still try to wreck the city and kill the constables when the Council passes the banishment edict. He's got nothing left. Mass confrontation is his last shot to stay in the city. It's the only way he can make the Upper Council back off.'

'How do we turn a riot to our advantage?' Boyd asked. 'I don't see it, I really don't.'

Edeard wished he knew how to answer, to show his friends some leadership. He'd settle for a single strategy. Instead all he could do was stare into his beer and pray to the Lady for some kind of inspiration. And she was going to have to be quick about it.

*

The room was a simple cube measuring ten yards to a side, with a single light circle on the ceiling. One corner had a high bed, with the same stiff spongy mattress found on every Makkathran bed. A second corner had a small washing pool, where water circulated constantly. The third had a simple pedestal that served as a toilet. The fourth was empty. There was no door. Slits near the ceiling let fresh air flow through.

Farsight couldn't penetrate through the walls or floor or ceiling, they were all too thick. No sound carried in. The light circle did not respond to any command to dim or brighten, it remained constant.

The room's single occupant had spent the first day walking about, examining every square inch with his farsight, sliding his fingertips over the walls, looking for cracks, some hint of the way in – and out. He found nothing. Nor could he longshout for help, the thickness of the walls prevented that.

When he woke up to find himself in his not-too-unpleasant cell there were three plates on the floor in the centre of the room. They had bread and butter and two types of cheese, some slices of cold beef, fruit, and a rather nice apricot tart. He munched his way through the food during the day. On occasion he did a series of press-ups, then sit-ups. Several times he tried shouting to his captors. Pleas or insults it made no difference, there was no reply.

Eventually, the light circle dimmed down to the faintest orange glow. He waited for a while, then gave in and lay on the bed. It took a long time for him to go to sleep.

Eight hours later, the light strengthened. It revealed three new plates of food on the floor. Of the old ones there was no sign.

So began his second uneventful day.

At midday, Edeard slid up through the floor. The man was sitting on the bed at the time, eating some sweet green grapes. He stared in fascination at the way the floor around Edeard seemed to remain solid, his farsight examining it keenly.

'Now that really is impressive, Waterwalker,' he said with a rueful grin, and popped another grape in his mouth.

'Thank you,' Edeard said. 'And you are?'

'Who I am doesn't matter.'

'It might to your wife, or children.'

'Not married. Thankfully. Too quick on my feet. But congratulations on your engagement. Quite a catch, young Kristabel.'

'Why were you following us?'

The man glanced at his chest, fingering the scorch mark on his indigo shirt. 'Just going about my business, officer. I wasn't following anyone. Someone assaulted me and I woke up in here.'

'Yes. That was me. Sorry about the shirt. It's a nice one. Where would I get one like that?'

'A coastal town called Chelston. It's north of here. Several days' sailing in a strong wind.'

'You do understand that I won't let you out of here until I get some answers?'

'What happens when you don't get them? Do you try and beat them out of me?'

'No, of course not. You just stay here until you answer to my satisfaction. Apparently isolation is quite an effective method of encouraging cooperation.' Edeard glanced round the underground chamber which the city had converted for him. 'I'm not sure isolation is supposed to be quite as comfortable as this, but I'm a bit vague on the method. Sorry about that.'

'Asking tough questions in Makkathran is usually a little different,' the man admitted too casually. 'It normally involves blades and fire and heartsqueeze and lungsqueeze. Only the Waterwalker could come up with an interrogation as *strange* as this one.'

'But you know it's going to work. You're already getting disturbed by the confinement, I can tell. So why don't you skip the whole unpleasant part and tell me what I need to know, then I can let you out of here.'

'Where exactly is here, Waterwalker?'

'The constable station in Jeavons.'

'You're a poor liar.'

'I know. Everyone tells me I can't shield my thoughts the way you cityborn can. I leave too much emotion visible.'

The man popped down another grape and grinned. 'You're getting better.'

'Really? Have we met before?'

'Everyone knows you, Waterwalker.'

'But not everyone is frightened of me.'

'I'm not frightened.'

'Your family is, otherwise you wouldn't be following me round.'

'I told you, I have no family. Wrong place, wrong time, that's me.'

'Why do they fear me?'

'I know nothing of such things.'

'But if you had to guess?'

'That voyage I took up to Chelston, it's a standard run for the captain. He knows the route, knows what to look out for. He's sailed it all his life, as did his father before him, and his father before that, and so on back to the day the ship fell from the sky. It's a route that keeps him and his family clothed and fed and comfortable; it is their life. It's a route that works. How do you think he would feel if one day a reef suddenly appeared in the water ahead of him and threatened to rip the keel off his ship?'

'A smart captain would know how to steer round it.'

'His ship is very large, and extremely heavily laden. It doesn't turn easily.'

'I don't suppose it does, not with people like you holding it on course. But you never know, those waters on the other side of the reef, they might be easy to sail in.'

The man shook his head and sighed. 'How can anyone so naive get so far in this city? It is a mystery I doubt even the Lady can fathom.'

'Some say the Lady has chosen me to repeat her message to this world.'

'How wonderful, are you really going to claim that you are Rah reincarnated?'

'No. Because we both know I'm not.'

'Ah well, at least you're not declaring you have a divine right to wreck a society that's worked for two thousand years. That's some comfort to me, I suppose.'

'I'm marrying Kristabel, who is a greater part of this city than a dozen minor families like yours. Do you really think I will destroy everything her family has built? It is to be my family.'

'Minor families? You think attempting to anger me will cause me to slip my guard?'

'Does it anger you? The really great families will hardly be bothered by the return to law and order. But you, you're what? Something like a fifth son of a fourth son of a third son? Your branch of the family must have been kicked out of that fabulous mansion a long time ago. Do you look at it enviously every time you walk past? Do you hear the laughter coming over the wall? And now your father is what? Some market trader with delusions of grandeur? I bet he doesn't pay all his taxes. Is that the only way you can keep paying the bills in your new little house? Is that why you only have enough coinage to dress as pretty as one of Kristabel's foot servants? Is that why you joined this woeful little association of thugs, so you could fool yourself you're part of the Grand Families again?'

'Really, Waterwalker, I expected better. But you are very young, aren't you? I remain to be convinced you have what it takes to see this to the bitter end. For it will be very bitter indeed.'

'As far as you are concerned, the end has already passed you by. When banishment is enacted, you will be escorted from the city. You will not return. Ever.'

'Unless you're claiming a timesense greater than our beloved Pythia, you cannot speak of the future. So I'll just wait here to see how it plays out, thank you.'

Edeard tilted his head on one side to regard his unnervingly suave opponent curiously. He hadn't been expecting anything quite this difficult. 'Were you one of the four on the tower?' Edeard had returned to the base of the tower three times since he fell, examining the city's memories of that day. He'd felt the footsteps of his four assailants on the staircase winding up the centre three hours before the pistol exchange, but try as he might he simply couldn't backtrack them successfully. They came from a large crowd of worshippers attending the afternoon service at the church, several hundred people milling around together. It was too confusing to single out one set of feet. And, of course, after he fell no one knew what actually happened on the top of the tower until he regained consciousness. Even then he'd only told his friends. So no attempt had been made to apprehend the mysterious foursome when they scurried back down in the middle of the confusion and panic that raged around the base of the tower for well over an hour.

The man smiled. It was a harsh expression. 'When you fell, you thought it would be to your death. You didn't know you were going to live. That is our greatest concern. Who helps you, Waterwalker, and why?'

'The universe helps those who lead a good life. It says so right there in the Lady's scriptures.'

'Answer me that one question, and I will answer all of yours.'

Edeard gave a weary shake of his head. 'You will stay in here until you cooperate. I don't imagine it will take long. Isolation is an evil foe. And you are as isolated as it is possible to be on this world.'

'Do you truly believe you have time on your side?'

'We will see whose ally time really is. I'll be back. Eventually.' He told the floor to let him through, and sank away.

*

The financial courts were situated in the middle of Parliament House, running along the south side of First Canal. The nine horseshoe arch bridges connecting the buildings on both sides of the water were so thick, containing whole suites of rooms, that they essentially formed a tunnel over the little canal. Because of that, light inside the courts was supplied almost entirely from the concave octagons decorating the vaulted ceilings. They might as well have been underground for all the difference the high slit windows made, looking out into the shadowed cavity beneath the bridges. The dusky lighting certainly added to the general sense of gloom pervading the eighth court when Edeard crept in quietly at the back of the semicircular chamber. It wasn't laid out like a law court. Instead, long tables were arranged in tiers, with the tax investigator at a round table at their centre. Lamps were lit on the ends of each table, Jamolar oil producing pools of yellow light across the untidy stacks of paper and files. To Edeard's first glance it was as though paper had come alive to breed faster than drakkens. There *couldn't* be so many accounts relating to the House of Blue Petals. But each table had at least two clerks sitting at it. They were all dressed the same, in shirts and waistcoats. Most seemed to be wearing spectacles. None were under fifty.

The tax inspector's waistcoat was lined with silver, otherwise there was no way of distinguishing between him and his fellow Guild members. He would consult a page from a very large ledger, and ask a question relating to income or expenditure. Then Buate's team of clerks would mutter among themselves and go through files and books before producing receipts or affidavits, and offering an explanation as to how the money was spent or received. At which point the clerks retained by the Mayor's Inspector General would counter the claim, producing different bits of paper, or an entry in the ledger of the business concerned that was different to Buate's contention.

After listening to the evidence, the inspector would write laboriously in his ledger, and move on to the next question.

Three years' worth of records were subject to investigation. Every day's purchase of drinks had to be accounted for. Three years of the House of Blue Petals buying and cleaning bedlinen. Three years of genistar husbandry. Three years of replacement mats behind the bar. Three years of crockery, acquisitions and breakages and depreciation and amortization. Three years of the girls' cosmetics and hair styling. Three years of hairclip acquisition, each batch meticulously recorded and queried.

Buate sat at a table at the far side of the court. His shoulders slumped, eyes glazed, his skin paler than the drab lighting could shade. He looked up as Edeard walked in. His expression of misery slowly changed, as if his facial muscles were regaining strength, hardening his cheeks and jaw into a look of pure fury.

Edeard met it without flinching as the inspector demanded to know about higher than normal expenditure on smoked toco nuts on the sixth Thursday of June two years ago. Buate never shifted his gaze from Edeard while his clerks struggled to produce receipts for the jars.

In the end, it was Edeard who looked away first. He could barely believe it, but he was close to feeling sorry for Buate. Theirs was an epic struggle for the soul of an entire city, it should be fought out there on the streets and along the canals, followers slugging it out with fists and third hands, while their political masters plotted and schemed in Council. Not this. This was inhuman.

And I did it to him.

Edeard bowed his head to look at his boots; every inch the little boy at the back of the class struggling not to giggle. He hurried out of the finance court, then stopped in the cloister and laughed out loud. Clerks in their drab claret and olive-green waistcoats stared at him disapprovingly.

'Sorry,' Edeard said to them and their Guild in general. He made an effort to compose himself, then walked on towards Centre Circle Canal. He could do that. He could leave the court after a good laugh. *Good gloat, if I'm honest.* Buate couldn't. Buate had to stay there for six hours every day, as he had done for ten days now. And the investigation was likely to last another eight days at least, Edeard had been told.

If only we could do this to each of the hundred. We'd have broken them by now. We wouldn't need banishment, they'd have fled screaming through the city gates long ago.

But this kind of financial scrutiny was reserved for the larger city businesses that were constantly cheating taxes. The Chief Constable had to press hard with the Inspector General for an inspector to launch his formal examination of Buate's accounts. It had used up a great deal or time, and cost far more than it would ever produce in fines. Worst of all, the clerks still hadn't found any tangible link between Buate and Ranalee's family. Of course, that didn't really matter; he was just using the tax investigation as a major irritant against Buate while the Jeavons constables built up the One Hundred list. But a proven link would have been nice.

Edeard left the merged domes of the Parliament Building behind and crossed over the delicate white-wire bridge of Centre Circle Canal. The patch of land ringed by the little canal was too small to rate as a district, people just called it Rah's garden. A small green oasis in the middle of government's commotion. He walked along simple paths lined by tall perfectly shaped flameyews. Roses were throwing out their first blossoms of the season, releasing a gentle scent into the still air. Several fresh-water ponds were joined together by small streams, crossed by small brick humpback bridges. As he went across them he could see big emerald and scarlet fish gliding around smoothly; they seemed to regard him slyly as he went by.

On the other side of Rah's garden the rear of the Orchard Palace rose before him, higher than any of the domes behind. Captain Larose was waiting for him at the bottom of the broad symmetrical perron that led up into the palace. Edeard straightened his dress jacket, though it was something of a lost cause beside the captain's ceremonial uniform.

'Waterwalker.'

'Just you today, Captain?'

''Fraid so, old chap. Inside the palace I'm naught but a humble guide.'

'Then guide me in, please.'

They ascended the three levels of the perron and went in through a high arching door. Five long cloisters led away from the hallway.

'Congratulations, by the way,' Larose said. 'Kristabel's a fine catch.'

'Thank you.'

'I met her myself a few times. Obviously I didn't make much of an impression.'

Edeard thought it best to let that one slide past.

'Did you really farsight Sergeant Chae's soul?'

'Yes.' Edeard had finally learned to stop sighing as he answered that question twenty times a day. It was disrespectful.

'That must put life into perspective, eh?'

'Death isn't quite so frightening, but that doesn't mean that life shouldn't be celebrated.'

'You are an extraordinary fellow,' the captain declared as they emerged into the Malfit Hall. Edeard could well imagine the captain reading *A Gentleman's Guide to Marriage* and hanging off every word.

They passed into the Liliala Hall, where Edeard stopped to regard the ceiling with the same astonishment as the first time he'd seen the images in Malfit Hall. The storm swirled silently above him; light flickered all around, casting strange-angled shadows as lightning bolts zipped through the clouds. Then Alakkad slipped through a breach in the scudding clouds. A smooth black ball of a world, threaded with hundreds of glowing red lines as vast rivers of lava surged along the surface.

'I never knew this was here,' an enchanted Edeard said, craning his neck as he tried to see the entire ceiling at once. 'Can you see all of Gicon's bracelet?'

'You know your astronomy.'

'Some of it. We had a very old telescope in the Guild hall where I grew up. My Master enjoyed watching the skies. He always said he was trying to see if another ship was on its way to Querencia. I think he was actually watching for Skylords.'

'Indeed. Well, if you wait long enough you'll see all the worlds in the bracelet.'

Clouds surged back across Alakkad. Edeard would have loved

to linger. The bracelet was always his favourite feature in the night sky, five small planets rotating around each other, orbiting further out from the sun than Querencia itself. The ancient telescope had never shown him Alakkad in such detail. He wondered how Vili would look in here, or the Mars Twins.

Larose led him through into the series of splendid chambers that made up the Mayor's private rooms. Owain was waiting in the oval sanctum, sitting behind the largest desk Edeard had ever seen. He wondered what on Querencia could be in all the drawers, but held back from probing with his farsight.

'Waterwalker,' Owain said with a genuine smile. 'My full and sincere congratulations on this day. You're a very lucky man.'

'Thank you, sir.' It appeared the whole city was pleased for him and Kristabel.

Owain waited until Larose left. 'First off, allow me to apologize profusely for the episode in Eyrie.'

'Sir?'

'Those Lady-damned pistols. My Guild has held them in safekeeping for over a thousand years. They are perhaps our most closely guarded secret. How they came to be removed is still a mystery. Even if you managed to get them out of the vault, there are guards, locks ... It should be impossible. It *has* been impossible, until now.'

'Do you know who was responsible?' Ronark and Doral had interrogated all the gang members they'd apprehended that night, but they were nothing more than couriers; no one knew the actual source of the guns, the man who was offering them for sale.

'We think we've identified the principal thief,' Owain said. 'Though he has, of course, conveniently vanished. I'm ashamed to say he was one of my Guild's senior journeyman, a man called Argian.'

'I don't recall the name.'

'Studious man, destined to be a Master, though perhaps not to sit on the Guild council itself. Here,' Owain gifted his image.

Edeard was quite proud of the way he held his composure,

shield firm, no sense of surprise leaking out. 'Argian' was the man he was currently holding in the underground cell. 'I'll let the constable stations know, the patrols can watch for him.'

'Good man. Though I suspect he's left the city. Betraying us in such a despicable fashion carries a heavy penalty. He must have known that. I hope they paid him well.'

'Yes, sir.' Edeard was desperately trying to work out connections. It was inevitable that the family agents would have someone inside the Weapons Guild, and probably every other Guild come to that. It would be easy now to find Argian's family – who would never acknowledge any association, especially as they would know he was being held by the Waterwalker.

'But let us ignore that today,' Owain said. 'This is your day, yes. A time to be joyful.'

Edeard forced a grin.

'Don't worry, Waterwalker. This next part is just a formality. You know it's considered bad form to vote against a Consent act. We're long past such barbarity.'

'Thank you, sir.'

'It will be my pleasure to allow Julan to introduce it. So, are you ready?'

'I think so.'

'Well, I am. You and Kristabel will make a fine couple. And don't repeat this, but it never hurts to shake things up a bit. If you ask me the Grand Families are becoming somewhat jaded these days. Someone like you in their ranks is just what they need.'

*

Edeard slid smoothly through the floor of the cell to find Argian pacing round and round the room. The man was getting jittery. He was starting to talk to himself. It had started with little mutters on the morning of the third day, progressing to full sentences. The cell walls relayed both the images and the sound to Edeard. It wasn't very revealing.

'Well, we knew it wasn't going to be simple.'

'That much support, it's difficult to break.'

'Should we actually let him do it?'

'If he marries her, he might pull back. Lorin's said before that he's besotted. Pity Ranalee didn't succeed, that would have been the answer to everything. Stupid bitch.'

As he was eating his egg sandwiches for lunch: 'Poison. Not a fast one, something that would take weeks. Months. Yes, yes. Months. No one would suspect then.'

'Faster, faster. The election might be the killer. Riots will make them think twice. Kristabel. It all rests on Kristabel. She's young. Foolish. But she understands family. She might. She might.'

'We're right. We're right, though. Yes, we are. His blood will pass to all of us.'

'How does he do it? How?'

Argian was gnawing on his thumb as Edeard emerged. He stopped immediately, shoving his hand behind his back with a guilty expression.

'Your clothes are getting a little creased,' Edeard said pleasantly. 'I thought you might like some clean ones.' He held out the bundle of neatly folded shirts and socks he'd brought, with a jar of soap flakes and a flannel on top.

'Thank—' Argian broke off, staring at them.

'Found them in your room,' Edeard said.

Argian made a polite bow of defeat. 'Very clever.'

'Not really, Argian. I'm afraid it was Owain himself who gave me your name. Would you believe, you're the only official suspect for the theft of special pistols from the Weapons Guild?'

'Owain?'

'Yes.'

'No.'

'Yes. They've thrown you to the fastfoxes. I visited your mother. She's quite distressed by the allegations. I told her I thought you'd left the city. Best not to give her too much hope when it comes to ever seeing you again.'

'I find all this highly dubious.'

'Really, I thought they were being quite clever. Your friends obviously know I'm holding you, so they simply make sure I can charge you with a crime that involves the death of a constable. And there we are: suddenly you're no longer a problem. Was that part of the agreement when you signed up? Sacrifice yourself if you get caught? But then I don't suppose your kind ever did get caught before I came along, did you?'

Argian sat on the side of the bed, and gave Edeard a brittle grin. 'I'm not telling you anything.'

'You know, I'd made journeyman by the time I was seventeen,' Edeard said. 'You're what? Forty-eight isn't it? And still only a journeyman. No wonder you had to steal those pistols from a vault. I'd hate to use one you'd made.'

'I believe we've already established that provoking me doesn't work.'

'Yes. Actually, I don't think you ever were a journeyman, not really. I think it's just a tenure that gives you a facade of respectability.'

'Oh, well done. You actually worked something out for yourself. Or did your friend Macsen the bastard have to explain it to you?'

'Provoking me is not a good idea. I don't have your restraint.'

Argian held his hands wide. 'Do your worst. Oh yes, this is your worst, isn't it?'

'Not by any means. But I'm not in any rush.'

'I wouldn't count on that, Waterwalker.'

'Care to elaborate?'

'No.'

'I see,' Edeard sighed. 'Well, I can't stay, I have to get ready for my engagement party. And Kristabel needs calming down.'

'Why?'

'There was one Master who didn't sign the Consent bill.'

'Bise,' Argian said quickly.

'Yes. Apparently he hates me enough to commit the sin of *bad form*.'

'Shocking.'

'Well, it's not me he has to worry about. As I've discovered today, Honious has no fury like a woman upset during her wedding arrangements.'

'Poor Bise.'

'I'm not sure when I'll be back. We have a lot of parties to attend.'

Argian's self-control faltered. He gave Edeard a disconcerted look. 'You're really going to leave me in here?'

'Not quite. This isn't working as well as I'd hoped. And I need it to work. I have to know exactly who I'm up against. You're the key to that.'

Just for a moment a flicker of hope crossed Argian's face. Then Edeard dropped away through the floor.

'Lady damn you!' Argian shouted after him. His clenched fists rose to the ceiling. He froze as a tiny motion caught his eye. The walls were moving. 'No,' he breathed. The cell was shrinking. He put his hands against the nearest wall, and started to push, adding his third hand to his efforts. 'No.' There was nothing he could do to prevent the inexorable motion. 'No! No, no. Stop it.' He realized the ceiling was lowering as well.

'NOOO!'

*

Makkathran's opera house formed the heart of Lillylight district. A vast palatial sprawl which merged into the Manor of Octaves, where the Guild of Musicians was housed. When humans first moved into Makkathran they'd found a vast indoor amphitheatre, whose giant tiered ledges had a curvature impossible for humans to sit on comfortably. The lower half of the encircling wall comprised huge mullion windows of rectilinear tracery, and unusually for the city their crystal was coloured, sending out great rainbow beams to intersect the central stage. Above that, a thousand long white and violet stalactites hung from the domed ceiling, as if it was the inside of some massive geode. As night fell, the spires fluoresced with the city's ubiquitous orange light.

Grand Families had long ago staked their claim on various sections of the tiered ledges, and commissioned carpenters to construct elaborate benches. Over time, the benches had been walled off with carved panelling, producing snug private boxes.

They also steadily expanded back over the ledges, as Edeard discovered when he had to worm his way behind the boxes that cluttered the second tier to reach the Culverit family enclave. Kristabel, whose magenta satin gown had a wide flaring skirt, struggled to keep the obligatory smile on her face as she followed him along.

'I always forget how cramped it is back here,' she complained.

'We could always walk along the top of the boxes,' Edeard said cheerfully.

Her smile vanished. He kept quiet until they reached the Culverit box.

Inside, it was decorated in velvet and lace, with eight luxurious leather-cushioned chairs along the front. Three servants were already there, preparing wine and fruit in their small panelled-off section at the back. One of them took Kristabel's silk wool wrap. Edeard gave him his cloak, very self-conscious of the gilded turquoise jacket and smoke-grey trousers he was wearing. Then he realized that no one could actually see into the box, and relaxed.

'That's better,' Kristabel declared, as she settled in the central chair with a relieved sigh.

Edeard sat next to her. It was like being on a throne, with an excellent view of the flat circular stage across the top of the boxes on the ledge below. Seclusion hazes protected several boxes as their occupants gossiped before the show began, or entertained people they shouldn't. When he peered over the little balcony rail, Edeard saw the ancient Master of Cobara with his teenage mistress in tow, shuffling along the gap directly underneath.

'Don't you dare,' Kristabel said.

'What?' an injured Edeard asked.

'Ever do that to me,' she responded, her index finger lined up on the Master's bad wig.

He leant over to kiss her, and realized the chairs were actually too far apart, so he had to get out and move over to her, which sort of wrecked the spontaneity. 'You are far too fabulously energetic in bed for me ever to even think of anyone else,' he murmured into her ear.

'Behave.' But there was a demure smile on her lips that he recognized all too well.

'You know,' he said licking her ear lobe, 'no one can actually see in here.'

'The musicians can.'

'Ah.' Edeard turned and faced the stage. The first musicians were starting to emerge from the staircase well in the centre, carrying their instruments with them. 'Spoilsports.' His third hand hauled his chair right up next to hers, and he sat down again. 'You feeling better?'

She nodded. 'Yes.'

He'd never seen Kristabel so furious as that afternoon when Bise had contemptuously ignored the parchment as it passed along the long table in the Upper Council chamber for the signature of each Master. His refusal to sign the Consent bill had even appalled Owain, but he was immune to all remonstration. The Pythia herself couldn't get him to change his mind. So for the first time in three hundred and nineteen years a Consent to Marry bill was not approved unanimously.

It meant nothing to Edeard of course. But Kristabel was outraged. It was a slur on the entire Culverit family, not to mention her personally. After Owain had formally announced the Upper Council's majority approval, she'd stormed out of the Council chamber swearing revenge.

'He's an idiot,' Edeard said as the musicians began to take their places. 'And he's on his way out.'

'He's barely ninety,' Kristabel said. 'He'll be sitting in Council for another century at least. And I'll be sitting in there with him.'

'No, you won't. I'll have him sentenced to the Trampello mine, you'll see. I'm working on a way to prove his connection to the gangs.'

'Edeard, I love you dearly, but please, you really have to read up on the city's traditions and laws. Bise is a District Master, he can never stand trial in the law courts.'

'What? Why not?'

'Only the Masters of the Upper Council can try one of their own, for any crime. The exemption accountability law was supposed to stop frivolous litigation brought by anyone with a grudge.'

'Oh.' He tipped his head to one side and regarded her intently. 'How come you know that?' As soon as he said it, he knew it had come out wrong.

'For your information,' she said icily, 'between the ages of fourteen and nineteen I used to spend ten hours a week studying law under Master Ravail of the Lawyers Guild. I could pass your constables' probation exams in my sleep.'

'Right.'

'Did you think me unschooled and ignorant?'

'No.'

'I am to be Mistress of an entire District. Do you have any idea of the responsibilities involved?'

He took her hand, squeezing for emphasis. 'Yes, Kristabel.'

'Sorry.' She gave him a contrite smile.

'It's normally me that's saying that.'

'I know. I'm just so cross with him.'

'This is a battle fought at many levels.'

'But at least with your level you get to see some results.'

'Not really,' he admitted, as the first discordant notes of the musicians warming up began to reverberate around the huge auditorium. He was surprised by how loud they were. It must be something to do with the spiky roof, he decided.

'I thought you'd just about got your Hundred,' she said.

'We have.' He started to tell her about Buate's strategy to fight back, to inflict so much damage on the city that the Councils would call for Edeard to end his campaign.

'Clever,' she said when he finished. 'But inevitable. You've been very effective at curtailing his activities. This is what happens when you back people into a corner, they lash out.'

'You think I shouldn't arrest the Hundred?'

'The thing about elections is they're unpredictable. Your idea to crush the gang leadership beforehand is excellent. You show people what life would be like if Finitan gets to pass his banishment act. But if you don't arrest them, things stay as they are, or worse Buate starts a rumour that you're too afraid to act, and the vote could well go Owain's way.'

'Owain will support me; he told me himself.'

'Yes, but only as it applies through his One Nation manifesto. And for what it's worth, I think Finitan is right, we need to consolidate the city before we try to help the provinces.'

'So what do I do?'

'You can't allow a city-wide riot. That goes against everything you are as a constable. It has to be stopped.'

'Easily said. How?'

'Sometimes you have to do what's wrong in order to do what's right.'

'I know that. I even considered snatching the top gang lords and holding them in isolation, but it always comes down to the same thing: there aren't enough of us, not for that kind of work. I could only ever get two or three of them before the word would get out, and that's the trigger for the riot. I just don't see how it can be stopped.'

'You're probably right, so you have to try and contain it, and I know just the place.'

'Where?'

'Sampalok.'

'Oh, Lady.'

'No. He's the one who champions the gangs. He provides them with sanctuary, he even excluded you from the district. Well, it's about time he realized there's a price to pay for collaboration.'

'How in the Lady's name do I confine the riot to Sampalok?'

'If that's where the rioters are, that's where the riot will be. Push them in there, Edeard. Use their own tactics to defeat them.'

'But . . .'

'That's wrong?' she asked archly. 'Edeard, if you want to win you have to play to win. You're the Waterwalker. There's no one else going to do this.'

'Yes,' he said meekly as the conductor appeared on stage. Applause began to ripple round the auditorium. 'I know.'

*

'The pistols were easy to obtain. A key was provided, the guards that night were ones who knew not to ask questions.'

'A key? You mean for the vault?'

'Yes. Actually, you need five keys to get through three doors, and the combination numbers. The locks are impossible to pick with telekinesis, there are too many parts to manipulate simultaneously.'

'Who gave you the keys?'

'Warpal told me where a set would be left. The combinations were with them.'

'So Warpal is your leader?'

'There is no leader. We are simply people who agree on what must be done to maintain a basic level of order in the city.'

'Sons of Grand Families?'

'People who share a background of good family and breeding, who have the same understanding of life. It is nothing like as formal as you think.'

'But somebody must organize it.'

'Not really. We support each other and the final rule of law.'

'You protect the families from the gangs?'

'Precisely. And any other threats.'

'So why haven't you got rid of the gangs?'

'A criminal underclass is somewhat inevitable. As you're finding out, they're well organized. To defeat them we would first have to match them, and that's not what we do. We look after our own. If the lower classes want something done to stop the gangs, then that's up to them to do something.'

'And yet when I came along and started to do exactly that, you tried to eliminate me. Why?'

'You are more than a constable, a lot more. You have some power in this city which no one understands. And you have your own vision of law and order, a very rigid intolerant one. If you were to enforce that you would do untold harm to the families.'

'I don't want to destroy anything.'

'The road to Honious is paved with good intentions. Makkathran works perfectly well as it is.'

'For the nobility perhaps. The gangs have grown too big and powerful under your lax rule. You let that happen. Makkathran doesn't work for everyone, and it must.'

'We do what we can.'

'Were you one of those who pushed me off the tower?'

'Yes.'

'Who else was there?'

'Warpal, Merid, and Pitier.'

'Who organized it?'

'Warpal.'

'And who told him to do that?'

'That's not how we work.'

'Nobody suddenly decides to do such a thing. There has to be someone in charge of you.'

'Our older members offer guidance, that's all. They smooth the way into Guilds, provide us with additional funds, that kind of thing. They have ties to the family councils, so they're aware of problems emerging before the rest of the city. That way we can be informed of such instances and deal with them discreetly. Our work is quiet and infrequent. Some of us are never called upon.'

'So these older members control you?'

'They guide and advise. We each have a mentor, they are the ones who initiate us in the Families' confidential arts.'

'Like concealment?'

'That is one of them, yes.'

'Who is Warpal's mentor?'

'Motluk is mentor to both Warpal and myself.'

'Motluk?'

'He's a junior Master in the Leatherworkers Guild.'

'And which family does he come from?'

'He is Altal's son. The fourth, I think.'

'Altal?'

'Altal is the third son of Carallo, who is a Diroal, the fifth son of the previous Master. Carallo is married to Karalee, third sister of Tannarl.'

'A Diroal? Lady! You mean Diroal as in the District Masters of Sampalok?'

'Yes.'

*

The barrels were stored in a large Gilmorn warehouse on the edge of the Port District. Edeard enjoyed the irony in that as he got the city to change the floor they were stacked on. One by one the barrels fell into the tunnel beneath Tail Canal. Edeard's third hand scooped up eight of them, and they bobbed along through the air behind him as he walked the short distance along the curving tunnels under Myco's streets to stand beneath the House of Blue Petals.

With only a couple of hours left until dawn, it was still very dark inside the lounge as he and the barrels rose through the floor. His farsight found several people sleeping upstairs, including Buate, who was sharing his bed with two of the house's girls. A more detailed scan couldn't find anyone using concealment lurking within the building.

Edeard sent three of the barrels drifting through the doorways leading off the wooden gallery. His third hand broke open their tops, and the thick Jamolar oil inside spilled out along the corridors. Two more barrels were hoisted up to the top floor, drenching carpets and furniture in Buate's big study. Oil ran out under the door, washing down the corridors and stairs.

His longtalk prodded the minds of the slumbering ge-chimps in their little pen behind the kitchen. 'Go outside,' he ordered them as he walked upstairs. They obediently shuffled silently out into the street.

His third hand broke open two of the barrels downstairs,

leaving an intact one standing on top of the bar. Jamolar oil sluiced across the floor.

'Nostalgia,' he muttered as he started up the stairs to the upper floor. He stood in front of the door to Buate's bedroom. His third hand plucked an ember from one of the stoves in the lounge, and dropped it.

Flame *whooshed* across the room. The furniture caught alight immediately, long flames licking round the bar. Within seconds, oil dripping down the stairs had ignited, sending flames ripping across the first floor. The fire followed the damp trail up the next flight of stairs, and blazed into the study.

Edeard smashed the bedroom door down, and strode into the room as flames leapt and danced behind him. Buate's sleep-befuddled head came up from the pillows. The girls cried out as they saw the black figure silhouetted in the doorway, his cloak rippling in the air like some living appendage. They clung to each other in fear.

'What the Ladyfuck—' Buate gasped. His farsight was probing the building, finding fire everywhere.

'This establishment appears very accident prone,' Edeard observed.

The barrel on the bar exploded. Doors shattered, letting in a huge squall of fresh air. Flames roared up to the roof of the lounge.

'If I was you I wouldn't come back here, not ever,' Edeard said. 'In fact, I doubt there's anywhere in this city where you'll be safe.'

Flames trickled into the bedroom, flowing round Edeard's feet as they consumed the carpeting. His cloak flapped in agitation. Both girls whimpered, pressing themselves to the headrest. Smoke began to layer the air.

'You're dead, Waterwalker,' Buate shouted.

'Warpal tried and failed. What chance have you got?'

Buate stiffened at the mention of that name, causing Edeard to grin in amusement.

'Now get out of my city, take your people with you; and if

you ever try to start your riot you will join your brother in the manner I mentioned during my previous visit. Final warning.' He nodded politely to the girls. 'Ladies.'

They screamed as his third hand lifted them into the air. Then the bedroom windows disintegrated, and they found themselves floating through the gap to descend gently on to the street below, where the house's ge-chimps were scampering about in considerable apprehension.

Buate watched their flight in astonishment. 'What about me?' he yelled. But when he looked round, Edeard had gone. Flames licked hungrily at the base of the bed.

*

Edeard chose the middle of Golden Park at midnight. The huge plaza was empty, with nebula-light flickering off the tips of the white metal pillars that surrounded it. Only the faintest of shadows fell across the glossy cobbles as two dark figures appeared from nowhere.

'You are free to go,' Edeard said with an expansive gesture.

'Go where, exactly? I am a wanted man. How long do you think I would last out there?'

'Nobody will know you in the provinces.'

'You believe I should join Nanitte?' Argian asked with a show of bitter amusement. 'You are crueller than I thought, Waterwalker.'

'I am more desperate than you know.'

'Excuse me if I don't offer my undying sympathy.'

'I need your help.'

'I have given you everything I can. There is nothing left of me.'

'I ask only that you do what you were trained to do. I ask that you keep your loyalty to this city.'

'My time here is over. I have you to thank for that.'

'Keep watch for me, see what your people are doing.'

'That is not loyalty, that is betrayal.'

'Not to the city. You are an honourable man at heart. You

know something has to be done to rid us of the gangs, and pull back the excesses of the families. Things cannot carry on as they are, that will doom us all. Help me. If nothing else, be a moderating voice. If you truly fear I am too uncompromising, then stay and exert what influence you can on me.'

'Me, influence you?'

'You understand the true way things work. I would listen to your advice if it were to be given in good faith. Tell me how to achieve justice without alienating and ruining the best of that which is. Smooth the way. Do not let this city become divided by my blundering. Isn't that your calling?'

'You seem to have missed your vocation.'

'Was that a yes?'

Argian sighed as if in great pain. 'After all you have done to me, you expect me to help you?'

'I left you alone. That's all. If there were any demons in there with you, I didn't send them.'

'It will take me a while to gather my things together. If I see anything detrimental before I leave, I may tell you.'

'Thank you.'

*

Felax raced into the small hall at the back of Jeavons constable station, very flustered and out of breath. 'Waterwalker, Master Gachet from the Guild of Lawyers is here! He's talking to the captain. He says he has a warrant for your arrest.'

'Really?' Edeard asked with interest.

'Honestly,' the young constable assured him. 'I'm not joking.'

'I'm sure you're not.' His farsight caught a thoroughly disgusted Boyd handing over coinage to a smug Macsen. 'I'll be right there.'

The squad stood up to leave.

'Everyone keep going,' Edeard urged the other constables working at the benches. 'We're really close to a hundred now. I don't expect this nonsense to take more than a day.'

He left the small hall with his friends. 'Ready?'

Macsen grinned as the hall door closed behind them. 'Oh, Lady, yes.'

Edeard hurriedly pulled off his distinctive jacket. Macsen was already wearing Edeard's glossy boots, even though his feet were too large.

'Remember,' Dinlay said pleadingly. 'Just don't say anything.'

'Who me?' Macsen asked as he buttoned up the jacket.

'Let's see it,' Boyd said.

Macsen nodded, his mind betraying a brief flutter of nerves, then he concentrated. Shadows thickened around his face, turning him a malaised grey. Then they stretched and blurred.

Edeard held his breath while Dinlay grimaced in anticipation. The squad had practised this for a day, helping each other with ideas and techniques as they slowly developed the notion, refining and improving the original blanket concealment method. Surprisingly, it was Macsen who was the most capable. Edeard had assumed it would be Dinlay, who was always the studious one.

The shadows faded away from Macsen's face. Kanseen let out a little gasp of appreciation. Edeard shook his head in disbelief; he was staring at himself. His own face gave him an evil smile. 'How do I look? Actually, how do you look?'

Dinlay let out a hiss of exasperation. 'Stop talking! It ruins it.'

'Go!' Boyd urged. 'We'll take it from here.'

'Good luck,' Edeard told them. The floor changed beneath him, and he sank into the tunnel below. His farsight tracked Macsen, Dinlay and Kanseen as they carried on to Captain Ronark's office.

Master Gachet was waiting there, along with two court officials.

'Waterwalker,' Master Gachet said. 'I convey the compliments of my colleague Master Cherix, who says he will enjoy seeing you at the Courts of Justice where he will prosecute this case. He would be here himself, but there is the matter of an exclusion warrant against him.'

'What's going on?' Kanseen demanded.

'Master Gachet has a civil warrant,' Captain Ronark said in disgust. 'It is genuine.'

'Say nothing,' Dinlay instructed. Macsen shrugged, keeping his counterfeit face perfectly composed.

'I'd like to see it, please.' Dinlay held his hand out.

'You?' Gachet asked in surprise.

'I am considering a career in law,' Dinlay said. 'I will serve as Corporal Edeard's adviser until a registered lawyer can be appointed.'

A hugely amused Gachet handed the warrant over.

'You've been named by Buate as an assailant,' Dinlay read. 'You are also accused of arson against the House of Blue Petals.'

'And are required to pay compensation to its owners for loss of business,' Gachet mocked. 'Here's hoping your fiancée is understanding, else you will be handing over your pay for the next hundred years.'

'We'll get Master Solarin to deal with this,' Dinlay said. 'He'll have the warrant invalidated within five minutes.'

'Perhaps,' Master Gachet said. 'Until then: officers,' he gestured at the two court officials who looked dreadfully uncomfortable, 'attend to your duties.'

'Go with them,' Dinlay said.

The court officers stood nervously on either side of the Waterwalker, and escorted him out of the station, with Dinlay, Kanseen and Master Gachet accompanying them. Constables appeared along the corridor, to glower at the procession. Master Gachet did his best to ignore them, but the anger directed at him was intense.

It was a long walk across Jeavons to the Outer Circle Canal. Word was soon out that the Waterwalker had been arrested on Buate's connivance. People hurried out into the streets to see Edeard being taken to the Courts of Justice. He smiled in that way he always did, but never spoke.

Edeard slid up through the floor of the house in Padua and cast off his concealment. His third hand was only holding one barrel of Jamolar oil. It wasn't a big house. Edsing gasped in surprise as he appeared. Mirayse, his wife, stiffened, rushing to their three children and clutching them protectively.

Edeard crushed the barrel. Oil sprayed out, streamers looping across the room to soak furniture. A long cascade rushed out of the door and split into three, with each strand washing through a bedroom.

Edeard stared unflinchingly at Edsing, hardening himself against the distressed whimpering of the children. 'You will leave this place,' Edeard ordered. 'You will take those you command with you, or I will burn them out of their homes. Tell them that. Now go. The fire will start in half a minute.'

Edsing lined a finger up on Edeard, his features wound up in a snarl. 'You—'

'Twenty seconds.'

'This is our life!' Mirayse shouted.

'And it is now over,' Edeard informed her. 'Fifteen seconds.' He glanced pointedly at the children.

'Out out,' she shrieked, and jostled them along.

Edsing let out a howl of frustration and anger before running after his family.

Edeard held his hand above his head, and sank away. Just before his fingers disappeared beneath the floor, a single spark spat out.

'There is a twofold error here my lords,' Master Solarin said to the three judges hearing the application to dismiss. 'Firstly, I draw your attention to the malicious suit bill, with reference to its application for those employed by the city authority. The Waterwalker, as we know, is most prominent in the effort of ridding the city of actively violent criminals. Now, this campaign has caused a great deal of personal conflict between the Waterwalker and Buate, which my learned colleague knows full well.'

'Objection!' Master Cherix shouted.

Master Solarin chortled. 'Dear me, I hope I don't have to

mention a recently dismissed case of aggravated psychic assault between my client and the prosecution.'

'Objection!'

Edeard flew along the brightly lit deep tunnel, his arms held wide as if they were wings. Air drove against his face, whipping his hair about. His mouth was open to whoop ecstatically.

'Furthermore, in the case of Barclay versus Pollo it was deemed that nominated evidence must be independently verified in order for a warrant to be validated.'

'My lords I must protest that the defence is procrastinating,' Master Cherix said. 'The evidence is fully verified. I gathered the confirming testimony myself.'

'I have no doubt of that my lords. However, as my learned council is also fully aware, and has chosen to overlook, the testimony in this case is invalid.' Master Solarin bowed benevolently at the two girls from the House of Blue Petals who were sitting behind the prosecution bench. They giggled back at him. 'These quite delightful ladies upon whose testimony the prosecution's entire case is based are themselves employed by the establishment owned by the plaintiff. Impartiality in these circumstances must be discounted, as established by Rupart versus Vaxill, and with it, validation. I would ask for your immediate ruling on this.'

Hallwith's home was on the fifth floor of a bridge in Cobara. Two barrels hung in the air beside Edeard as he fixed the glowering gang lord with a relentless stare.

'Leave this place,' the Waterwalker commanded.

Oil poured out horizontally as the barrels splintered, forming a sheet of glistening liquid poised halfway between floor and ceiling.

'They were not employed by the House of Blue Petals,' Master Cherix said, radiating great weariness, as if he were sad to point out such an obvious flaw. 'They are free agents who pay a percentage of their earnings to the house. As such, Rupart versus Vaxill does not apply.'

Side tunnels flashed past at bewildering speed. Edeard had his hands gripped together in front of him, as if he were diving off a bridge into a deep pool of water. He rolled exuberantly as he hurtled onwards, wondering idly where all the branches led to.

'Which leads us to positive identification. Buate's testimony clearly states that the intruder was illuminated from behind. Contention is that, under such circumstances, a visual identification is impossible.'

'My lords, the honourable gentleman is making a poor joke. The Waterwalker is perhaps the most readily identifiable man in all of Makkathran.' Master Cherix frowned in annoyance as several people at the back of the court began whispering. A mental bustle of excitement spilled out. 'Edeard', Kanseen and Dinlay did their best not to smile and turn round. Boyd crept in at the rear of the chamber, carrying a canvas bag. He sat behind his squadmates and leant forward to whisper to Dinlay. Everyone sitting on the prosecution bench did their best to ignore him. The murmurs of surprise at the back of the chamber were getting louder.

The senior judge banged his gavel for order.

'I believe my learned colleague has just answered his own question, my lords,' Master Solarin said. 'Yes, the Waterwalker is renowned, which makes such allegations all the easier to perpetrate. Which I believe brings us right back to the malicious suit bill.'

Dinlay rose to whisper into Master Solarin's ear. On the other side of the judges, Master Cherix was receiving an equally urgent message from a junior lawyer on his team.

'My lords, I beg your indulgence for a slight recess,' Master Solarin said. 'It would appear there is some evidence forthcoming that will completely exonerate my client.'

The senior judge nodded agreement, and banged the gavel.

'Court will reconvene in one hour. The defendant is not to leave the building.'

Edeard concealed himself as he stepped nimbly through the cloisters that wove through the Courts of Justice. The squad was waiting in a lawyer's preparation room just off the court chamber where the hearing was being conducted. They turned round in surprise when the door opened seemingly by its own accord. It shut, and Edeard materialized in front of it.

Kanseen ran over and gave him a quick kiss.

'How did it go?' Dinlay asked.

'I visited seven of them in person,' Edeard said. 'And I managed to longtalk warnings to another twelve.'

'That ought to do it,' Macsen said, taking off the splendid jacket.

'It wasn't easy,' Edeard said as he shrugged into the jacket. 'Three of them had children.'

'We've been through this,' Kanseen said forcefully. 'Nearly all their victims have families, and they get hurt very badly.'

'I know.'

Macsen sighed in relief as he pulled off Edeard's boots. He wriggled his toes, smiling. Boyd opened the canvas bag and took out Macsen's boots. The old pair Edeard had worn were placed inside.

Boyd inspected the pair of them. 'Good to go,' he decided.

'My lords,' Master Solarin said with a formal bow. 'As you are probably aware by now, there have been several regrettable incidents of arson throughout the city this afternoon. To be precise, during this very annulment hearing. In each instance, the people concerned emerged from their homes claiming it was the Waterwalker who had threatened them and ignited the fire. People who by strange coincidence are named in exclusion warrants. Clearly, this is a serious criminal conspiracy mounted by undesirable elements of the city, deliberately aimed at wrecking my client's reputation.'

'Objection,' Master Cherix said. 'Hearsay. I believe we were earlier indulged in a lengthy legal argument over verification. I resent the hypocrisy now being practised by opposing counsel.'

'My lords, I lodged no motion. I am simply informing you of a sequence of events. It is for your lordships to weigh the particulars of the case and decide if the court's time and expense are to be wasted on trivia that will not last the first hour of a trial.'

The senior judge motioned both lawyers to sit. He conferred briefly with his two fellow judges.

'Application for the dismissal of the warrant is approved. Waterwalker, you are free to go.' The gavel was banged to end the session.

The dome on the eastern side of the Parliament House was one of the highest. It had a gallery running round the outside with a bulbous white balustrade that only came up to the knee of a grown man. The squad stood back from the railing, looking out across the city to the Port District. It was late in the afternoon, with the sun already starting to dip behind the rest of the Parliament House domes behind them.

Edeard's eyes were closed as he scoured the city with his farsight. He was focusing on Edsing and his family, who were trudging across the centre of Pholas Park on their way to Sampalok. They carried a couple of small bundles – all they'd salvaged from the fire. Mirayse hadn't stopped berating Edsing the whole way. Judging by his mental hue, Edsing was on the verge of striking her. 'They're moving,' Edeard informed the others. 'I make that over sixty are on their way to Sampalok.'

'Is that enough?' Kanseen asked.

'No,' Edeard said. 'I want the majority in there. I'll longtalk the others this evening, deliver the same warning. In two days' time we'll arrest the Hundred.'

'I sensed Buate as we left the court,' Boyd said. 'His shield was loose for a moment. He was very confused.'

Macsen grinned at the vast city before them. 'Another legend of the Waterwalker safely established. You can be in many places at once.'

'About that,' Dinlay said. 'Edsing lives in Padua.'

'Yes,' Edeard said, guessing what was coming.

'But Hallwith lives in Cobara, while Coyce is in Ilongo; the others are equally spread out. Yet you visited seven of them.'

Macsen was frowning now.

'We were only in the court for an hour and a half at best,' Dinlay said, 'How did you get round all of them in that time?'

'That running I do each morning, it keeps me in good shape. You should join me.'

'Nobody runs that fast.'

Edeard withdrew his farsight, and smiled at the four inquisitive faces looking at him. 'I'm the Waterwalker,' he told them mysteriously. His cloak flowed dramatically around him.

*

What was about to happen was no secret. The city's gossip-mongers had been busy the evening before reporting on how the constables in every district station were being called in and told to prepare. All of Makkathran knew this was the day.

Edeard sensed more people than he could number farsighting him as he walked out of the tenement that morning. He was taking a break from his running. It was going to be a long day.

'Be careful,' Kristabel had said as she kissed him goodnight after the party in Zelda the previous evening.

'I will be,' he assured her.

'No, Edeard,' she said, and placed her hand on his arm, grey-blue eyes beseeching him. 'No light-hearted pledges. Please. Be careful. What you are proposing tomorrow is dangerous. This is the crucial point in your fight, and everyone in Makkathran knows it. So I'm asking you, be on your guard. Warpal and his people must know that Argian has confessed all to you. If they see an opening they will strike like a fastfox.'

He took her hands. 'I know. I make light of it because I don't want you to worry. Now remember what you promised me?'

She sighed and rolled her eyes. 'I will stay at home, on the top floor, and I will suffer the extra guards Homelt assigns.'

'No matter what.'

'No matter what,' she agreed.

As he closed the tenement gate behind him, Edeard checked the Culverit ziggurat with his farsight. Sure enough, Kristabel was there having breakfast on the hortus with Mirnatha and their father; all three of them anxiously casting their farsight towards Sampalok.

His squad were waiting for him on the street outside. He tried to remember that first morning they'd stumbled down into the Jeavons station small hall to be shouted at by Chae. A bunch of stupid, semi-idealistic kids, none of whom really knew what they were letting themselves in for.

Now he could barely recognize those nervous eager youths in his friends. Macsen, who was dressed almost as smartly as Edeard, still the most self-confident of the group. Boyd, whose height no longer made him appear gangly, wearing his uniform with complete authority. If he told you to stop these days, you'd do it out of respect for the office he represented. Dinlay, who still couldn't quite be considered well turned-out, despite the new uniforms he wore these days, but who'd gained self-reliance and a realistic understanding of human nature. But then getting shot would do that for most people. And Kanseen, who smiled a whole lot more these days; as always the most solid and reliable of them all.

Edeard grinned round at them, knowing he could depend on them no matter what. Guessing he'd probably have to before the day was out. 'Let's go.'

There was a gondola waiting for them on Arrival Canal. It took them down to High Pool and turned on to the Great Major Canal. Edeard deliberately didn't look at the big ziggurat as they passed by, his attention was all on Sampalok up ahead.

Buate was already awake and up. After the fire at the House of Blue Petals he'd moved into an unclaimed building on Zulmal Street, halfway between the mansion of the Sampalok District

Master and Mid Pool. It had five rooms with strange convex curving ceilings. Two rooms made up the ground floor, then the remainder were stacked one on top of the other, making the whole edifice resemble a bulbous chimney with the stairs spiralling up a narrow cylinder along one side. The triangular roof terrace was besieged by the shaggy vines which carpeted the entire outside. A carpenter had installed a front door for him, and a few pieces of furniture had been assembled downstairs. Clothes and other essentials were still in the boxes they'd been delivered in. A lone ge-monkey performed domestic duties for him. Buate had tried to get the poor creature to climb the vines and prune them away from the windows, with little success. It was something of a come-down from the luxury and service he was used to at the House of Blue Petals. Edeard suspected that was deliberate.

Boyd nudged him as they passed through Forest Pool. 'Looks like everyone is up early today.'

Following Boyd's mental directions, Edeard's farsight observed Master Cherix walking over the central wire and wood bridge between Golden Park and Anemone. It was the route the lawyer had to take every day to reach his Guild offices in Parliament House now he was excluded from Jeavons.

'Even he can't get a law revoked,' Edeard said. He'd consulted Master Solarin about the articles of arrest, who assured him the twenty-two days holding period remained legally applicable, provided they had a deposition of suspicion from the arresting constable. It was an aspect he'd emphasized repeatedly when he met with the station captains yesterday to organize the arrests.

As he swept his farsight back from Anemone to Sampalok he saw the constables making their way across Pholas Park and Tosella. There were hundreds of them marching in from every station in the city, divided into arrest teams and bridge re-inforcement squads. Dozens of ge-dogs trotted alongside, while ge-eagles swarmed the clear sky overhead.

As they passed through Mid Pool Edeard felt a familiar farsight focus on the gondola.

'Salrana?' They hadn't spoken since that day in the caravan pens. His few attempts to longtalk her had been met by an icy mental shield.

Now, her directed longtalk spoke to him alone in the gondola. 'Edeard, people are afraid. Many families have come to the church this morning. What you are doing is scaring them.'

'I know. But once today is over, their fear will be gone.'

'You can't know that.'

Such doubt wasn't like her. Salrana used to be the one cheering him on the whole time. 'I can hope that, can't I? Where are we without hope?'

'You are becoming a politican, Edeard.'

'I will be Mayor, and you will be Pythia,' he replied warmly.

'We are not children any more. Your pride has pushed you into this ridiculous showdown.'

'It has not!' he told her irately. 'You know full well we cannot live with the gangs casting such a blight over everyone's lives. You see the suffering as much as I do, if not more. I am trying, Salrana. This might not be a perfect way for us to be rid of them, but it is something. The Lady will sympathize with that; as much as She would despise me for standing by and doing nothing.'

'Don't tell me what the Lady will think.' Her farsight abruptly withdrew.

Edeard turned to stare with exasperation in the direction of Ysidro. He refused to send his own farsight towards the Lady's church in that district, where Salrana was assigned.

She'll see, he told himself. *After today, she'll see I am right.*

Their gondola pulled in at a mooring platform on the edge of Mid Pool. Edeard and the squad went up the wooden stairs to the broad concourse surrounding the pool. It was eerily deserted. The buildings that formed the far side were four or five storeys high, all of them independent from each other, tall and narrow as were most of the structures in the district, with irregular bulges on their sides. Windows protruded out of them like insect eyes. More than anywhere in the city, Sampalok's structures seemed based on some organic formation.

Edeard could see entire families lined up behind the bubbles of crystal, staring at them. Trepidation filled the air like a noxious fume.

'He's this way,' Edeard said, and headed off towards the top of Zulmal Street. His farsight observed the constables gathering at every bridge into Sampalok, ready to prevent anyone from coming out into the city, especially rioters. There were almost no gondolas moving on the canals around the district.

He walked on for almost ten minutes along the twisty litter-strewn street. Always in the shade of the dark plant-swathed houses. The few people abroad gave him and the squad sullen glances before they hurried off down side alleys. A couple of them spat contemptuously. Edeard kept watching Bise's mansion, a lofty stepped tower surrounded by a thick rectangular wall with only three gates. There were a lot of people inside, but none were coming out. The big iron-bound gates were all firmly closed. He wasn't quite sure if any of the Hundred were inside. If they were, getting them out would be the task from Honious. *Probably not worth it.*

Edeard directed his longtalk to a single figure skulking down one of the side alleys they passed. 'Have you seen anything?'

'Eight of my people walk Sampalok today,' Argian replied. 'They're not using concealment, not yet. That would draw your attention to them.'

'Why are they here?'

'I spoke to Pitier. Of all of us, he holds views most similar to my own. He said they have been told to observe, but to hold themselves ready.'

'I see. Thank you.'

Buate was sitting calmly on one of his two chairs when the squad arrived outside. Edeard knocked loudly on the door. His farsight examined the man closely as he came to the door, but he carried no pistol or blade.

'Waterwalker,' Buate said in a jaded voice. 'Have you come to escort me to the financial court?'

'Nothing that pleasant. You are under arrest.'

'On what charge?'

'Suspicion of extortion. We intend to hold you while we gather corroborating evidence.'

'Are you sure you want to do this?'

'Yes.'

'Very well.' He closed his eyes, and longtalked strongly. 'This is it my friends. Go forward!'

Edeard quietly asked the city to bring the remaining Jamolar barrels up from the tunnel running under Zulmal Street. They slithered up quietly in the gaps between the swollen knobbly buildings, sitting unnoticed in the shade of the creepers and trees, displacing some of the rubbish cluttering the gutters.

The squad moved back out of the house, surrounding Buate. Doors were starting to open all along Zulmal Street. Men emerged, carrying long clubs or knives, hammers, pokers, broken bottles. Edeard ignored them, concentrating on the five barrels that had emerged at the side of Buate's house. His third hand detached the tops of each one.

'You won't make it ten yards,' Buate gloated.

On either side of the street, the men began to edge their way forward. They were giving Edeard and the squad nervous glances, but slowly and surely they kept moving. There was a great deal of longtalk slithering among them.

'Go on, go on,' was the most common phrase. 'Keep going. There's hundreds of us.'

'Stand back,' Edeard instructed loudly. A rock came whirling out of the sky, thrown by someone at the rear of the swelling mob. Macsen's third hand swatted it away easily.

Buate started to laugh. 'Not quite the people's champion you thought you were, eh, Waterwalker?'

Edeard's third hand sucked the oil out of all five barrels, consolidating it into a giant globe. He sent it streaking forwards. As it flew a couple of yards over his head he held up a hand. A single thread of light crackled out from his extended index finger.

The oil ignited with a loud roar, spitting out fat globules of flame. Edeard guided it down to a yard above the street then sent it racing on ahead of him. The men lining the route yelled in fear and dived aside. Great droplets of flaming oil splattered onto the street, hissing and fizzing in its wake.

'This way,' Edeard told a startled Buate politely. They began to walk back down Zulmal Street. The would-be mob were keeping their distance now, watching the fireball anxiously as Edeard began to draw it back. 'I never got to thank your dear brother for this idea,' he said to Buate. 'It was a good one.'

'It's a long way to Parliament House,' Buate growled. 'And we're not there yet.' He was using his longtalk to issue a fast stream of instructions.

Edeard's farsight showed him people taking to the streets all across Sampalok. He was ready for that. The constables had been instructed that under no account was anyone from the district to get across a bridge and spread their brand of disturbance into the rest of the city. From what he could perceive, the bridge reinforcement teams were holding well. None of the rapidly forming crowds were getting close to the end of a bridge. He picked out several of the Hundred directing people, goading them onwards. Stones and bottles were starting to be thrown and telekinetically guided on to the constables. Blade discs were also skimming through the air.

The arrest teams weren't fairing as well as he hoped. The most able farsighted constables were assigned to tracking those on the list, and guiding the teams towards them. They were having trouble pushing through the hostile crowds thronging the streets.

'The thing about fire, Waterwalker, is that you can never really control how it burns,' Buate said.

Edeard was very conscious of how quickly the fireball's oil was being used up. The street behind them was now jammed with angry people, yelling insults and abuse. More of the mob were starting to mill around in the alleys on the way back to Mid Pool. As soon as the squad passed, they came out to join the main press behind them.

'Edeard,' Boyd growled under his breath.

'You know that we can dodge anything they throw at us,' Edeard said with quiet reassurance to his friends. 'Our only real concern is to get this bastard into a cell.'

'Once ignited, a flame will burn until there is no more fuel,' Buate said. His hand waved at the mob following them. 'They don't need ringleaders any more. They're burning on their hatred for you.'

The barrels secreted down the alleys had been discovered. They were tipped over and smashed. Jamolar oil rippled down the street ahead of the squad. Edeard sent the fireball soaring high above the rooftops, then burst it apart in a vivid halo of flame. The mob below flinched.

Edeard just caught a flash of white light. The oil on the street burst into flame. People screamed and ran. A wall of flame raced towards the squad.

'Shit,' Edeard grunted. He asked the city to change the street, and the oil vanished, soaked away by the suddenly porous pavement. Puffs of smoke floated between the buildings, dissipating in the breeze.

Buate's jaw dropped. 'What—'

Edeard winked at him. 'Keep going.'

The crowd along Zulmal Street kept a respectful distance as the squad walked the rest of the way to the Mid Pool concourse. There were over a hundred constables on the broad semicircle around the pool, with more behind the bridges over to Bellis and Pholas Park. Livid crowds were boiling round the entrance to each street that led into Sampalok.

Macsen and Boyd handed a sullen Buate over to one of the arrest teams, with instructions to take him to the cells underneath Parliament House.

'Now what?' Kanseen asked, looking at the jeering crowd blocking the end of Amtol Street.

'I don't know,' Edeard said. He was longtalking with the senior sergeants at each of the bridges, checking up on the progress of the other arrest teams. 'We've managed to nab eight of the Hundred, including Buate. That's not going to have the effect

I wanted.' He gave the street mobs a worried glance. 'I don't want to send anyone in there again. That really will kick things off.'

'If we stand out here, we've lost,' Macsen said. 'You'll be admitting they're in charge of Sampalok, and there's nothing you can do about it.'

'I thought we didn't mind if they rioted in Sampalok,' Boyd said.

'There are a lot of decent folk who live here,' Edeard said. 'And this is a very big crowd. It's the same at every bridge. I didn't realize Buate still had this much control.'

'We could go in with concealment,' Dinlay said. 'Snatch the closest one on the list and bring him out quickly. That Hundred are the key to this, they're the ones stirring people up. Take them out one at a time.'

'You might be right,' Edeard said. He wasn't sure. The size and animosity of the response had caught him off guard. But then Sampalok residents always had a chip on their shoulder, it wouldn't take much to rile them.

He went over to the watcher crew at the end of the concourse next to Trade Route Canal to find out which of the Hundred was nearby. Before he'd even spoken to anyone the sergeant at the middle bridge into High Moat was longtalking that the crowd was rampaging along the streets, breaking into shops and businesses. Looting had begun. Edeard's farsight flicked over to the area, sensing a deluge of anger and glee. Not a good combination, he thought as his farsight found a ge-eagle overhead. The genistar's acute sight revealed flames and smoke pouring out of five or six buildings. When it swooped lower he could see dense congregations pressed up against commercial premises. Goods were being hauled out of shattered doors to be passed around the eager crowd. Scores of kids were running away, each clutching at some piece of loot.

The ge-eagle's thoughts filled with agitation. Something was pulling at it, forcing it down towards the curving, angled rooftops of Sampalok. Its powerful wings flapped madly as its distress mounted.

Edeard found that extremely alarming. Few people had the telekinetic strength to reach all the way up to a ge-eagle, and fewer still had the inclination to attack a defenceless creature.

It was inordinately difficult to farsight telekinesis, but Edeard could just make out the tenuous band of force stretching up from the ground. He focused on the origin, a youth no more than fifteen, standing in Entfall Avenue while the crowd surged around him.

'Stop that,' Edeard commanded.

The lad started. His telekinesis abandoned the ge-eagle, and he ran into the nearest building.

The sound of wood splintering reverberated across the Mid Pool concourse. Edeard looked round to see a group of people had battered down the door to a baker's shop in Mislore Avenue. Cheers rang out as the crowd swarmed in to help themselves to fresh loaves and cakes. Sharp cries from the baker and his family vanished swiftly. Then the grocer's next door was breached. A clothing shop. A tavern – to the accompaniment of much cheering. An ironmonger's. Cafe. A cobbler.

'What do we do, Waterwalker?' the senior sergeant on the concourse demanded.

Edeard looked at him, not knowing the answer. Then there came the sound of doors being broken on Zulmal Street.

'Lady!' He turned to the sergeant. 'Drive them back, get them out of those premises.'

The sergeant, who was from Vaji station, gave him a dubious stare. 'Yes, sir.'

A squad of over fifty constables formed up, with Edeard at the head. He led them into Mislore Avenue. As soon as the crowd saw him coming, they turned and ran. A sleet of projectiles hurtled through the air at the advancing constables. Edeard battered all of them away, sending them tumbling to the ground ahead of him. When he looked down the first side alley he could see directly into Zulmal Street; the riot and looting was worse there. Further up Mislore Avenue the crowd was breaking into a fresh set of shops.

'You did this!' a woman screamed at him. She'd run out of a splintered doorway, wearing a long yellow dress that was smeared with blood. Her hand clutched at a long knife which she waved extravagantly. 'You, Waterwalker, you ruined us. Two hundred years my family has lived here, two hundred years our shop has thrived, now we've lost everything. Rot in Honious, you bastard.'

Edeard stopped advancing down Mislore Avenue. All he was accomplishing was to push people into areas that were undamaged, providing them with further targets. 'Lady, help me,' he muttered.

Three more sergeants reported riots starting. Six sections of Sampalok were in chaos now.

'Trouble here,' Dinlay's longtalk reported. Edeard could tell his friend was trying not to panic.

'Back to the concourse,' he told the constables he was leading.

When he got there, he found the rioters in Zulmal Street had been emboldened by his absence. They'd spilled out into the concourse to confront the constables defending the bridge over to Bellis. Behind them, the looting was multiplying. Violence spilled on to the street at the beleaguered business owners did their best to defend their livelihoods. He saw clubs swing brutally. Third hands clashed. Then his worst fear was realized: a pistol shot rang out.

Everyone on the concourse froze, trying to see where the shot had come from. Out of the corner of his eye Edeard saw Kanseen fall. She was on the front rank of the constables (of course); now she crumpled to her knees, hands clutching her chest, breathing with difficulty.

'Kanseen!' Macsen bellowed. He shoved his way through the silent constables to reach her side. His arms went round her.

'All right,' she gasped. 'I'm all right. Lady! I'll never complain about these drosilk waistcoats again.' She was rubbing her chest where the bullet had struck. Macsen let out a sob of relief, and kissed her.

A furious Edeard strode out into the empty zone between the constables and the rioters. The nearest members of the mob shuffled backwards.

'Break this up!' Edeard roared. 'Go back to your homes. This is over.'

For a moment the silence held. Then someone unseen yelled, 'Fuck the Waterwalker.'

Two more pistol shots rang out. Edeard was ready for them. The bullets hung in the air a couple of feet in front of him. He was going to make a show of examining them and sneering contemptuously. Slap it into the rioters that he was invincible, that their moment of rebellion was over. But it was a signal for a renewed round of jeering.

'One of mine fired the shots,' Argian longtalked directly to Edeard.

Edeard's gaze flicked up to the roof of the building at the start of Zulmal Street. Argian was there, crouched down amid the profusion of flowering vines. 'Who? Where?' Edeard asked.

'Junlie. He's already retreating.'

The hail of missiles was starting again.

'All right,' Edeard snarled at the rioters. 'I warned you.'

Those in the front rank faltered, their taunts and abuse fading as they saw his determination.

Edeard's cloak billowed wide, freeing his arms. He brought them up in a wide curving motion, his eyes closed. Concentrating hard. He'd never really exerted his full telekinetic strength before, not like this. Not aggressively. Behind him, the surface of Mid Pool shivered. Twin plumes of water exploded high into the air. Their crests warped round to streak over the concourse, merging directly above Edeard. The constables underneath the giant airborne streams gasped, crouching down fearfully.

Edeard grinned mercilessly. He flung the water directly at the rioters as a single wavefront. It hit the ground in front of Zulmal

Street, throwing up a huge cloud of spume. The main bulk of water surged onwards into the street, knocking everybody off their feet. Third hands formed desperate body shields, warding the thundering foam away from mouths and noses. Edeard kept it coming, standing immobile as the vast torrent churned above him. Captured fil-rats squawked in terror as they were propelled overhead within the unnatural flood. The leading wave rushed fifty yards down the street – seventy – a hundred. Its force and size reduced gradually as smaller streams poured away down the side alleys.

The surface of Mid Pool sank down drastically as Edeard continued to siphon water out. Water along the connecting canals began to dip and race in to fill the depression.

Edeard took a deep calming breath, and slowly lowered his arms. Above him, the final swell of water splattered down into the street.

There was no more rioting. Water churned away down alleys and drains. Edeard looked at the hundreds of soaking bodies left clinging to the buildings and each other, flopping about like beached fish. A multitude of coughing and harsh gasps echoed along the walls of dripping vines. Sunlight shining through the placid stripes of alto-cumulus created a strangely beautiful sheen across the glistening surfaces.

'I told you,' Edeard announced impassively. 'Go home.'

Constables moved down Zulmal Street, helping people to their feet, making sure they were all right. Broken limbs were a common injury. Over two dozen were carried to the concourse where doctors had been summoned. Two arrests were made when they found a couple of the people on Edeard's Hundred list. Other than that there were no recriminations. The rioters slunk away, shivering in their sodden clothes. Mislore Avenue was equally quiet.

'What in the Lady's name is going on?' Chief Constable Walsfol demanded with a directed longtalk.

Soft and precise though the telepathy was, Edeard could sense the man's anger and fear. 'I had to do something, sir. The rioters were destroying the whole street.'

'You might have calmed your area, but the rest of Sampalok is falling into Ladydamned anarchy.'

'I know,' Edeard replied miserably. His farsight could see the mobs rampaging through the streets and alleys across the rest of Sampalok. Smoke was churning into the morning air, muting the bright sunlight across the district. Instead of giving them pause for thought, his actions had actually acted like some kind of spur to the mobs. 'I'll go over to Galsard Street next, it's closest. Then I'll move on to—'

'You will do no such thing,' Walsfol said. 'We're worried your actions are just inflaming the whole situation. You stand down, Waterwalker, I want you back in Jeavons by midday. I am ordering all constables to fall back behind the bridges.'

'But people are being hurt,' Edeard protested.

'Perhaps you should have thought about that before you began this action. You assured me that the disturbance would be minimal. I don't know who it was that forced the gang leaders into Sampalok, but all that's done is magnified this whole Lady-damned disaster.'

It would have been worse. Every district would be burning like this by now. Probably. Dear Lady, what have I done?

'Yes, sir.'

'The Mayor feels more direct action will be required to support the citizens currently under threat.'

'What sort of action?'

'We're not sure. The Upper Council has been in emergency session for the last twenty minutes, nothing has been decided.'

Edeard gazed round the concourse. A wide flow of shallow water was rippling back out of Zulmal Street to gurgle over the rim into Mid Pool. A couple of doctors had responded to the calls of the sergeants, and were moving along the row of injured. Lady's Novices in their blue and white robes were scurrying round, assisting the doctors and comforting the dazed patients.

A shot rang out. Every constable flinched, automatically

looking towards Zulmal Street. Edeard's farsight was unconsciously aware of his squadmates – just as Chae had taught them so long ago. Boyd's thoughts vanished from perception.

Somewhere close by, Kanseen screamed.

Edeard's farsight flashed out to where Boyd had been an instant before; one of the shops along Zulmal Street. A mind in the front room glowed with unrepentant satisfaction. There was a lifeless body in there, but farsight couldn't help Edeard identify who it was. He could however pick out the kind of kit every constable wore. 'Lady, no,' he whispered.

Then he was running across the concourse and into Zulmal Street. It was a baker's shop, of course. The deluge of water had poured in through the broken door, creating havoc inside. Shelving and counters had flipped over as the powerful current raced through into the rear. It struck the ovens in the kitchens, releasing dangerous clouds of steam as it quenched their fires. One of the heavy cabinets in the front had toppled on to a teenage lad, pinning him to the ground. That was how Boyd found him, whimpering in agony, coughing water, blood seeping into his clothes from where broken hip bones had punctured his skin. A son of the baker or a rioter, Boyd didn't care. The lad was suffering and needed help. Boyd helped. Using his third hand and a post of wood, he was crouched down beside the cabinet, levering it free.

When Edeard rushed in, Mirayse was still standing over Boyd's corpse, the pistol in her hand. Her clothes were splattered with blood, as well they might be. She'd put the pistol muzzle an inch from the back of Boyd's head to shoot. The front of Boyd's face had blown off, spewing gore across the cabinet and the poor lad underneath it, who was now weeping hysterically.

Mirayse giggled at the constables piling into the shop. 'I got you,' she said in a peculiar sing song voice. 'I got you. You killed my life. We're equal now.'

Dinlay lunged forward, face contorted in fury, his third hand reaching to heartsqueeze the demented woman. Edeard's shield protected her.

'No. She will stand trial.' His third hand plucked the pistol from her. 'Take her out,' he told Urarl. He lifted the cabinet effortlessly from the lad. 'And get a doctor in here.'

Urarl and two constables took Mirayse out of the shop. As they left, Argian slipped in.

Macsen dropped to his knees next to Boyd's corpse. He reached out tentatively, as if his friend were merely pretending. Blood mingled with the water soaking into his uniform trousers. Kanseen was gripping a sobbing Dinlay, tears leaking silently from her eyes.

'Why?' she whispered.

Argian held up the pistol. 'This model is the kind we favour. They would know her state of mind. It would be a simple thing to give her this and whisper where one of the Waterwalker's squad was.'

Macsen turned to snarl at Argian.

'Wait,' Edeard said. He found it strange he was so calm. Shock seemed to be slowing his thoughts, taking him a long way away. It was as though the events inside the baker's shop were taking place on some remote stage.

'What?' Macsen moaned. 'He's dead!'

Edeard stood perfectly still, reaching out with his farsight. His friends faded away, as did the walls of the bakery. Droplets from the drenched walls and furniture struck the puddled floor, tinkling like bells. Slowing. Greyness eclipsed the world he walked through.

Amidst this sombre silent universe a single figure glimmered. Edeard smiled. 'You stayed.'

'I haven't said goodbye,' Boyd's soul told him. 'I'd like to say goodbye. But it's difficult, Edeard. They can't hear me.'

'Take whatever you need,' Edeard told him, and held his arms out. The phantom Boyd touched him.

It was as though a spike of ice was being driven through his heart. Edeard's mouth opened to a shocked O, his own life was flowing out through the contact. The real universe rushed back in to engulf him.

Kanseen gasped as Boyd's spectral shape materialized above his own corpse. Edeard staggered, forcing himself to draw down a breath. The cold was spreading through him. Numbing.

'Boyd?' Dinlay said.

'My friends,' Boyd gazed round them magnanimously.

'Don't go,' Kanseen said.

'I have to. I can hear the nebulas calling. It's quite beautiful. I only waited for Edeard to notice me.'

'We need you, too.'

'Dinlay, tell Saria for me. Be kind, she will need a lot of comfort.'

'I promise.'

'Kanseen, Macsen; don't hide, not like this. Life is too precious for a single moment of happiness to be lost.'

'I . . .' Kanseen gave Macsen a forlorn look. 'Yes. Yes, you're right.'

Boyd regarded Argian. 'You, the doubter. Have faith in Edeard, he is stronger than all of us. I can see that. I can see the way he affects this universe, it flows to his will.'

Edeard grimaced, his knees sagging. The cold was becoming unbearable.

'I'm sorry, Edeard,' Boyd said. 'I weary you. I am one pattern you cannot sustain.'

'Pattern?' Edeard gasped.

'Why yes. That is what this universe is, a beautiful memory. There are so many patterns folded within its structure, they stretch back for ever.' He let go of Edeard's hand, and immediately began to diminish. As he did so, he gave a knowing grin. 'I never realized the city was alive like this, Waterwalker. But you know, don't you? You can feel its dreams. Get it to help you, today of all days. Stop being so timid. This needs more than water to finish it. Have courage and be bold.'

Edeard couldn't stop shivering. 'I will,' he pledged.

'You must think I'm so weak to leave,' Boyd said as his spectre lifted towards the sky, thinning out.

Edeard's perception followed it. 'No,' he said. Then he heard, 'We have to stay, he is all we have.'

'What?' he asked.

The sensation of a smile emerged from Boyd's essence. 'I understand.' And he was gone, ascending to the nebulas.

Kanseen was crying openly as they stepped back out on to Zulmal Street. 'I'm sorry,' she blubbed, wiping the back of her hand over here eyes. 'I'll be all right.'

'You do see souls,' Argian said in astonishment.

'Yes,' Edeard said. He was incredibly tired. It would be so easy to sit down and just close his eyes, chasing a moment's rest. After all, Walsfol had ordered him back to Jeavons. None of this was his problem any more.

Yeah, right.

'What do you want to do?' Macsen asked.

Edeard gave him a desperate look. 'I don't know.'

'My people,' Bise's longtalk voice called.

As one the squad turned to face the District Master's mansion at the heart of Sampalok. Bise stood on the roof, dressed in his flowing violet robes, the fur-lined hood thrown over his left shoulder. He held his arms out in benediction to his vast audience. 'I speak to all of us within Sampalok, those whose families have been here for generations and those newly arrived, seeking safe haven from the Waterwalker's persecution.'

Edeard immediately bridled.

'Don't say anything,' Kanseen ordered sternly. 'Arguing in public will make you seem petty.'

'Do not fight among yourselves,' Bise said softly. 'Your enemy is outside, and this conflict only strengthens him. Even now the forces who fear your freedoms are gathering in High Moat. I urge you to stand firm against them. Resist their occupation of your home, the last place in the city where you are independent men as Rah promised. I offer your families sanctuary within the walls of my mansion. Here they will be safe while you fight to establish your liberty against the oppression brought upon all of us by the Waterwalker.

'We have little time now. Listen to those who walk among you speaking with my authority. Resist the invasion of those who seek to banish you from this city which is your birthright.' Bise gifted a humble smile, and stepped down into the tower.

'What in Honious was that?' Dinlay asked. 'Some kind of election stunt?'

'I have no idea,' an equally confused Edeard grunted. He gave Argian a questioning glance. 'Could he really be the top gang lord?'

'No,' Argian said. 'It isn't like that. The Diroals have strong links with the gangs. They profit from having business rivals weakened, but Bise is smart enough to keep his distance. This is something else entirely.'

'Oh, Lady,' Kanseen groaned. She was facing north, her eyes closed as her farsight ranged out. 'The militia's coming.'

'What?' Edeard gasped.

'The militia. A whole regiment, by the look of it. They're coming across High Moat.'

It took a second for Edeard's own farsight to find the long rank of men marching past the caravan pens. 'What are they doing? The constables are holding the rioters in Sampalok, they can't get over the bridges.'

'There is a complete breakdown of law and order inside Makkathran,' Macsen said tonelessly. 'If you're the Mayor, how would you feel about that? The militia aren't going to reinforce the bridges, they're coming in to stop the riots.'

'How?' Edeard asked. 'This isn't a militia job. The constables are much better trained to break up mobs.'

'They're armed,' Kanseen said quietly.

The chill akin to that Edeard had experienced at Boyd's touch returned; of all the constables he'd organized to help today only the sergeants and corporals were authorized to carry revolvers. 'But the people on the streets . . .'

'And Bise has just told them to resist the invaders,' Dinlay said.

'They have to be stopped,' Edeard said. 'The militia can't shoot at civilians, even if they are breaking the law.'

'People in the mob are armed,' Argian said. 'It may be that the militia will be shot at first. That would be . . . convenient.'

'Will your people listen to you? Can you get them to stop this?'

'There is little to be done on the streets,' Argian said. 'Though I will try and speak to those of my fellowship walking Sampalok today. But it is Motluk and his kind who ultimately hold sway.'

'Talk to him,' Edeard said. 'This cannot be allowed to happen.'

'I will do what I can.' Argian turned and headed off along the street.

'With me,' Edeard told the others. 'We have to get to High Moat and stop this.' He started running back to the concourse, his farsight ranging out. 'Lady curse it, where are all the gondolas, why are they never about when you need one?'

'You planning to give the militia a good soaking?' Dinlay asked keenly.

'Whatever it takes.' The nearest gondola Edeard could sense was in Lilac Canal, heading away from Great Major Canal. It would take far too long. He stood in the middle of the Mid Pool concourse, twisting about, wracked by indecision. His support of Boyd had left him aching and enervated, he knew he didn't have the strength to pull many more stunts like the water cascade, especially not if he had to first run the entire length of Sampalok to reach the High Moat bridge. 'Lady damn it.' He sent his farsight straight into the Orchard Palace, finding the Mayor in the Upper Council chamber. 'Sir, please, I have to talk to you.'

'Waterwalker,' the Mayor's timbre was frigid. 'The only reason you're still in this city is so you can give evidence before the commission I'm setting up to examine today's events and determine who is to blame. After that I have no doubt the Grand

Council will pass a very specific act of banishment, with you as the sole name listed.'

'Sir, please, you have to call back the militia.'

'What Lady-damned choice have you left me? Makkathran has not seen the like of this disorder for over a thousand years. And it was all your idea. Arresting these Hundred trouble makers was supposed to put an end to chaos. All you have done is provoked outrage and horror. People, decent people in Sampalok – and there are many, contrary to your propaganda – are suffering untold brutality at the hands of a wild mob. A mob you provoked. I am the Mayor, and I will not let that stand. It must be stopped.'

'Let me stop it, sir. I can use water on them again; however many times it takes, a dozen if I have to. Please, you cannot let the militia shoot people.'

'Since you are so obviously very hard of understanding I will say this in simple terms. You are to leave Sampalok at once. The officers of the militia are not savages, they will deal with this in a fast and professional manner. Do you understand? If you do not comply this instant, I will have Walsfol issue an order for your arrest. Not even you can withstand a hundred constables at once.'

'Yes, sir,' Edeard said. His throat was strangely hard, making it difficult to swallow.

'So what are we doing?' Dinlay asked.

Edeard stared round. The squad were still waiting for his word. *And look where my ideas have got us. But I know what I am doing is right. I know it is. The politicians and families are twisting everything.* He smiled grimly at his friends. 'We're doing exactly what Boyd told me: being bold. Are you with me?'

Macsen put on a pained expression. 'Why are you asking that?'

Several constables were heading towards them, led by a very uncomfortable-looking sergeant. Edeard waved insolently at them. 'I think we just stopped being constables.'

'Oh, Honious,' Kanseen groaned.

'You'll really need to hold my hands for this,' Edeard said, suddenly relishing what he was about to do. His friends sensed his new mood, and grinned. So they held hands, the four of them standing together in the middle of the concourse. In broad daylight, with a hundred constables looking on, and thousands of farsight gazes playing over them, they sank down through the solid surface laughing defiantly all the way.

It was Macsen who screamed the loudest while they tore through the bright tunnel as if they were falling to Querencia from the very nebulas themselves.

'Edeard, what are you doing?' Finitan's longtalk asked when they surfaced in a deserted alley not far from the central bridge over Cloud Canal.

'I have to stop the militia, sir,' Edeard replied, impressed by how fast the Grand Master had found them. Then he saw a ge-dog at the other end of the alley.

'Listen to me, Edeard, do not use force against the militia. You do not have universal approval among their officers. And Owain has given them a free hand to deal with the rioters.'

'Why?' Edeard asked. 'Why is he doing this?'

'As the city sees it, he is clearing up the mess you have created,' Finitan said with infinite weariness. 'In doing so he usurps you as the force of law and order within Makkathran, and breaks the gangs at the same time. When people are killed in any number, this city will blame you. And because of that, they'll vote for him at every election for the next hundred years.'

'All this is about *votes*?'

'No, Edeard, as I told you right at the beginning, it is about politics. Always. Those in power are not easily dislodged. Certainly not by good intentions.'

'But what about Bise? He's offering people sanctuary in his mansion while the rioters defy the militia. He's making things worse.'

'Bise is a sacrifice Owain is prepared to make. They were allies

503

in Council until this morning. Each wanted to claim credit for defeating you. Bise underestimated Owain's resolve. It is a split which Owain has played perfectly. He is already talking of the Council putting Bise on trial for complicity, and there are enough of Bise's relatives who will leap at the chance of taking his District Mastership should he be disbarred. All Bise can do is make his gesture of resistance in the hope it makes things worse for Owain.'

'Do you think it will?'

'I have no idea. They may yet reach an accord before the point of no return is reached. Whether they do or not, nobody is going to vote for me, not after today, probably not even me. I'm seriously considering offering Owain my allegiance, that way I might salvage some of my political influence. Possibly, if I work with him, I can be a moderating voice.'

'No, you can't do that.'

'We all have to face reality, Edeard; he is consolidating the city behind him just as we hoped to do.'

'By causing people to die! There are family agents positioned among the crowd ready to escalate this conflict with the militia.'

'Then we will need the Lady to grant us a miracle, for I see no other way out of this. We are pressured on every side. And you, my brave friend, you will have lost all you have achieved.'

'This can't happen.'

'It already has. I will protect you as best I can, but I doubt that will be of much use tomorrow.'

Edeard bowed his head as he ended his longtalk with the Grand Master.

'What's the matter?' Dinlay asked.

'We're completely on our own,' Edeard told them. 'Owain has won. He's just swept the rest of us aside as if we didn't exist.'

'But we do exist,' Macsen said urgently. 'I am here with you to help stop the militia killing people. Let us go and do that.'

Edeard's farsight observed the first rank of the militia marching over the bridge from High Moat. 'All right,' he said with no real conviction. 'One last try.'

They were spotted as soon as they started walking towards the bridge. Thousands of farsight glances settled on them. More and more people became attuned to their position as the word spread across every district. The weight of attention was like the muggy air of a summer's day pressing down on the four friends as they walked onward. Nothing else was happening in the city, everyone was watching the events in Sampalok. A vast barrage of long-talked jeers and remarks fell on them. Edeard blocked them all out, trying to think what to do.

A miracle from the Lady, that's what Finitan said we needed. And he's right. But the Lady only ever performed one real miracle here in the city: her church. I wonder . . . That would be bold beyond even Boyd's imaginings.

The central bridge across Cloud Canal from High Moat was a low curve of the city's substance, lined by stubby emerald pillars with tangerine grooves spiralling up the outside. It led over into a small plaza where tall espaliered fruit trees grew up the sides of every building, covering the bowed walls with thick lines of blossom. The mild scents of peach and plum were now overwhelmed by the acrid smoke that chuffed out of the barricades. Both Burfol Street and Jankal Lane which led back into the heart of Sampalok had been blocked by piles of furniture that the crowds had set alight. Behind them the shops and businesses had all been looted. Edeard and the squad saw several named on the Hundred list moving among the confident crowd, congratulating friends, muttering instructions. He picked out a lot of pistols being carried openly. Inside the buildings it was a sorry story. Injured shopkeepers and traders nursed their wounds, while their families watched the triumphalist carnival outside with mournful thoughts and a great deal of suppressed rage.

Edeard reached out to Kristabel. 'Can you sense all this?' he asked.

'Yes, my love. Everyone in the city is watching Sampalok now. No one can believe the militia has been brought in; father fears the worst but there are so few voices in Council that will dare oppose the Mayor. Oh Edeard, what a mess, and it's my fault.'

'No.'

'Yes,' she insisted. 'It was my idea to drive them all into Sampalok, and look how many decent people have suffered already.'

'It was a good idea; imagine this replicated in every district. That's what would have happened.'

'Would it? I don't know any more.'

'The responsibility is mine alone. Kristabel, I'll probably have to leave the city soon. That's if I don't end up in the Trampello mine.'

'I'll be with you, you know that. Wherever you go.'

'No, darling, you're to be Mistress of Haxpen.'

'I don't think I want to be, not if it is to be a Haxpen under Owain's One Nation rule.'

'Let's not make any decisions until tomorrow, certainly not in heat.'

'Whatever you say. Is there nothing I can do to help you? Please. I want to be there with you.'

'No. But there are a lot of people hurt already. They need doctors.'

'I'll organize that; I'll talk to the Medical Guild's Grand Master. At least he's no Owain ally.'

'All right then.'

The alley came out on the Cloud Canal path just short of the bridge. Constables were standing on either side, watching helplessly as the militia regiment marched over. Soldiers were still arriving from High Moat, forming into neat ranks on the plaza. Except for one platoon which had lined up four deep across the path. Twenty-eight revolvers were aimed on Edeard as he approached.

'I would talk to your lieutenant,' he said.

The front rank parted to let their lieutenant through. He was tall, in his late-thirties, with blond hair curling out from under his black cap. Every brass button gleamed brightly on his green and sapphire tunic. A long sabre was strapped to his white belt.

Edeard kept his mind tightly shielded as his spirits sank

further. The lieutenant was like every clothead officer in the militia, a young aristocrat who qualified for a commission because of his infinite arrogance. Just for once he'd wished for one with a spark of intelligence and independence.

'Waterwalker,' the lieutenant inclined his head. 'I'm Lieutenant Eustace, I'm in charge here, and I have comprehensive orders from my colonel not to let you pass.'

The name was somehow familiar to Edeard, but he was sure he'd never seen the man before. 'If your orders are to stop the rioters, then I can do just that. I already have over at Mid Pool.'

'Which agitated the crowds elsewhere,' Lieutenant Eustace said. 'You're a menace, Waterwalker, the sooner you're out of this city the better.'

'People are going to get badly hurt,' Edeard said. 'Surely you can see that. I cannot allow this situation to rise to a point where the militia fires upon the crowd. The constables are enough to handle this.'

'Your sudden concern for the criminal element is touching. Who has spent the past year provoking them, eh?'

'Please, let me try. I'm asking you man to man, what have you got to lose? If I do quiet them down your colonel will be full of praise for you taking the initiative. If I fail, then you just carry on.'

'Man to man, eh?'

Edeard nodded. There was something wrong here, the lieutenant's face was completely expressionless.

'We have a saying here in Makkathran,' Eustace said. 'Something a boy from the countryside probably isn't aware of. Don't piss in the canals, you never know when you'll need to drink from them.' He waved his left hand in dismissal. It was a languid movement. Edeard saw the silver ring on his third finger and couldn't help the groan of dismay that escaped his lips. It was shaped as a vine with a single ruby in the crest.

Jessile's fiancé.

'Quite,' Lieutenant Eustace said thinly as he turned away. 'Take one more step towards the bridge, Waterwalker, and we'll find out just how many bullets you can shield yourself and your squad against. Now fuck off back to whatever diseased cowpat you came from.'

'Forget him,' Dinlay sneered as the platoon closed ranks again. 'Just go round them, use concealment. He's not a problem. We can get to the plaza easily.'

Edeard stared past the hard-faced platoon aiming at him, watching their comrades who were still filing into the plaza. A gentle drizzle of ripe blossom was drifting down around them like dry pink snow. 'I can't fight both sides,' he said.

'Just blast the lot of them with the water,' Macsen said. 'Anything that'll stop the shooting.'

'I'm not sure there's enough here,' Edeard said, giving Cloud Canal a miserable look.

'Air then,' Kanseen said. 'Can you use air? Hit them with a hurricane?'

'Well, probably—'

A pistol shot rang out. All four of them instinctively recoiled from the terrible distinctive noise. The platoon were glancing over their shoulders, becoming dangerously stressed.

'Oh, screw this lot,' Edeard growled. 'We don't have time.' Another shot sounded.

Edeard pulled an enormous column of water out of the canal beside the platoon. In the distance he heard, 'Militiamen, take aim.'

Lieutenant Eustace shrank down from the water as it began to curve over the canal path. His platoon started to combine their third hands to ward it off. Edeard let the enormous weight fall free.

'Fire!'

The air thundered with the power of two hundred and fifty revolvers fired together down Burfol Street and Jankal Lane.

'No,' Edeard yelled in horror.

His churning waterfall sent a dozen platoon members skidding off the path, scrabbling for a hold as they went over the edge into the canal.

'Fire!'

A second volley crashed out.

'Keep them off me,' Edeard told his friends. Macsen and Dinlay immediately started hammering the struggling, drenched platoon soldiers into Cloud Canal. Kanseen's third hand snatched revolvers from those who had the presence of mind to take aim on the Waterwalker.

High above Burfol Street, a wide cylinder of air started to spin. Tales of twisters had always been one of Edeard's childhood bedtime favourites. He always regretted never having actually seen the phenomena. Now, he squeezed for all he was worth.

The air thickened, turning dark as it let out a tortured screech. A gyrating finger wormed its way out of the bottom, heading down towards the plaza.

One of the sodden platoon members managed to fire a shot at Edeard. Dinlay saw it coming, his third hand pushing the soldier's gun arm aside. The bullet went wide, and Dinlay physically punched the man to the ground. Lieutenant Eustace jumped on Dinlay, and all three slipped on the wet path, going down in a thrashing heap. Another soldier leapt on.

Every petal of blossom in the plaza took to the air, a solid pink cloud that mushroomed over the nearby rooftops. The twister touched the pile of blazing furniture blocking Burfol Street. Flaming wreckage lifted effortlessly into the sky, swirling round and round the howling column. Two hundred feet above the city the chunks broke free, slung out sideways from the expanding wind. Militiamen and rioters alike ran for their lives as heavy burning chairs and benches and tables began their fast drop back to the ground.

Two soldiers jumped on Kanseen. She pivoted as they carried her along, sending herself and one of them over the edge of the canal to plunge beneath the water.

Edeard shifted the tip of the twister along the ground and steered it into the barricade at the bottom of Jankal Lane. As one collection of burning debris descended, so another fountained upwards.

Lieutenant Eustace scrambled up out of the scrum that had Dinlay pinned down. Macsen faced him, his smile turning feral. 'Don't know what you're so upset over. Our whole dormitory agreed she's crap in bed.'

Eustace roared in fury as he rushed Macsen.

Edeard let go of the air he'd shaped just before his strength gave out. In front of him, the three remaining soldiers from the platoon were gathering together as Macsen and Eustace grappled like wrestling serpents on the slippery path.

'Go,' Macsen yelled.

Edeard walked forward, his cloak undulating behind him. The trembling soldiers got off a couple of shots, which the Waterwalker never even seemed to notice. They flattened themselves against the wall of the canalside houses as he passed them, rigid in fearful expectation.

When Edeard reached the plaza the regiment was starting to regroup. Several officers yelled a challenge to him, which he ignored. Orders were shouted and longtalked, trying to get the ranks reformed and take aim on the figure in the black billowing cloak. A shower of tiny petals fell softly back to earth.

Edeard stood at the head of Burfol Street, seeing people peer timidly out of the doorways and alleys where they'd dodged the rain of furniture. 'Move!' he bellowed at them. 'If you stay here the militia will kill you, and if I catch you it'll go even worse on your soul.'

They started to run. Just a few at first. Then the Waterwalker advanced down the street. He raised his arm and lightning streamed from his fingers to claw at the denuded espalier trees. The stampede began. Dozens were pelting for safety ahead of the terrible figure they feared the most. His farsight showed him people on the move all across Sampalok. The crowds who minutes before had been secure in their domination of the streets were heading for the last refuge: Bise's mansion.

Edeard almost faltered as he drew level with the first body. It was a woman who'd taken three bullets; tiny petals drifted down to settle on her bloody clothes. His farsight examined the area around her, to find her soul hovering above the corpse. 'I'm so sorry,' he told her. 'I should have been quicker.'

Her spectral face was despondent as she looked at him. 'My boys, what about my boys? They're so young.'

'They will be taken care of, I promise.'

'I will see them before I go,' she said, and began to drift towards a nearby alley. 'I can feel them close. One last look, to be sure.'

Edeard grimaced, and carried on. In total he counted fifteen dead, with over twenty hobbling along in front of him, clutching at their wounds, blood dripping onto the pavement. He directed his longtalk at them, whispering that they should turn down side alleys where doctors would come. Some obeyed, eight didn't.

Owain's longtalk found him as he was halfway down Burfol Street. 'I don't know what you think you can achieve by this. Stand aside, and let the militia deal with this scum. I'll see to it that the commission is sympathetic to the part you played today.'

'The Lady's miracle,' Edeard replied, not caring that the rest of the city could sense his longtalk.

'Excuse me?'

'The Lady performed a miracle in Makkathran once, and I'm going to repeat it today.'

'You are beyond salvation, Waterwalker.'

'Then let me be.'

'I can't do that.'

Echoing down the street came the command: 'Regiment, forward march.'

'Want to bet,' Edeard muttered under his breath, then: 'Boyd, I hope you're watching this. It's your Lady-damned idea.'

He slowed his walk slightly; making sure that those fleeing into the mansion would have time to reach it before he did. Behind him, the regiment pressed on down the street. They matched his own pace, maintaining the distance perfectly. That caused him to grin.

'Edeard,' Salrana's unnervingly accurate longtalk said to him alone. 'What have you become?'

'I am what I have always been.'

'The strength, yes, but this arrogance ... this is something new.'

'They gave me no choice.'

'Edeard, you are acting against the wishes of the whole city. Stop this.'

'Today has to end with the gangs destroyed and banished. Nothing else matters any more.'

'What you are doing is wrong. You are claiming all responsibility. You are abusing your gifts to defy the Council itself.'

'Long ago, Rah used his strength to gift people sanctuary from chaos. I can do nothing less with my gift, my strength. To fail now would be to betray everything he founded, all that he gave this world.'

'Don't you dare invoke Rah. You are not Rah.'

'I know. But I will not let his wonderful legacy wither and die. That is who I am. Accept that.'

'I will pray to the Lady for the light that was once your beautiful soul.'

Edeard ground his teeth together. He wrenched his attention away from his childhood friend. *I cannot let this distract me. She will not! And not everyone doubts me.*

As if seeking a counter to Salrana's dreadful mistrust, Edeard's directed longtalk sought out Felax, who was still on the Mid Pool concourse. 'I could do with some help.'

'Yes, sir,' Felax said proudly. 'Of course I'll help.'

The boy's unswerving trust was humbling. 'I need you and others you can rely on to run to the senior sergeants at each bridge. Tell them the Waterwalker needs the farsight teams to keep tracking the Hundred, and in addition to find as many of those named on the exclusion warrants as they can. Also, if this goes our way, I'll need the arrest teams to reform; they'll be wanted for escort duties.'

'Yes, sir. I'll do that right away. But, sir, I want to help you, I want to be there with you.'

'This is truly what I need. If you do this for me, we can still turn this day around.'

'I knew you would, sir; I *knew* it '

Edeard was a hundred yards from the end of Burfol Street. He could see the big open square surrounding Bise's mansion. Fountains still played in the pools, providing the only movement in the whole expanse. Behind them, the iron-bound gates in the high wall were swinging shut.

He walked out into the square, and looked up at the circular mansion. Over a hundred people were standing along the top of the battlements on the external wall, as far as his farsight could tell they were all armed. Every revolver was lined up on him.

Behind them, the seven-storey tower formed a proud silhouette against a sky stained by pyres of smoke. Its walls were a mottle of green and yellow, with each level a shade lighter than the last. The top floor was almost white. Bise stood on the roof, his splendid robes of office waving in the gentle wind. His longtalk washed out, strong enough to reach over half the city.

'You have no authority here, Waterwalker. The District Master has full dominion within his own walls. Leave this place.'

Edeard was immensely tempted to reply with a single hand gesture. Instead he said: 'Wait there, please. I have to deal with militia first.' He turned his back on the mansion. A couple of shots were fired. He deflected the bullets easily. Heated orders flowed along the battlements. And nobody fired again.

Edeard waited patiently, with the farsight of the entire city resting upon him. He felt ridiculously cocky, and rejoiced in every second of the sensation.

Yeah, this is bold!

The militia regiment reached the end of Burfol Street and halted. The first three ranks took aim on the lone figure in the middle of the square whose cloak hung around him with unnatural stillness. Fountains gurgled away merrily on either side of him.

'Captain Larose,' the Waterwalker said. 'I'm glad it's you. You are a man of integrity.'

The captain stepped forward, and nodded courteously. 'As are you, Waterwalker. Would you please step aside so we may carry out our orders, as issued by the city's full legal authority?'

'What are those orders?'

'We are to arrest those malefactors hiding inside the District Master's mansion.'

'They are heavily armed.'

'As are we.'

'Yes, and I will not permit bloodshed on such a scale those orders would entail. Not in my city. I will deal with Bise and those he harbours, you have my word.' Edeard turned full circle, his longtalk growing stronger. 'Everyone has my word on that.'

'Unfortunately, after today, your word is no longer enough,' Captain Larose said. 'Stand aside, Waterwalker, or I will be forced to order my men to shoot you.'

Edeard gave the captain a genuine smile. 'And how, exactly, are they going to do that from up there?' And he asked the city for its help.

'Up where?' Captain Larose suddenly gave the ground a nervous glance. He started to crouch in an attempt to regain what he perceived as his failing balance. It was a motion which pushed his polished boots firmly against the pavement. A motion which pushed him off the pavement.

Behind him, three hundred soldiers did exactly the same thing as their senses told them they were falling. Three hundred soldiers began to drift up gently into the air. They yelled in consternation, and began windmilling their arms in panic. That only made it worse. They spun and twisted. Several of them bounced off the vine-clad walls of the buildings on either side of the street, which sent them tumbling through the main cluster of their frantic colleagues.

Edeard stood perfectly still watching them. The noise of their combined shouting was colossal, and the mental panic flooding out was enough to make him wince. Most of the soldiers were ten or twelve feet from the ground now, and still their limbs were clawing wildly at the air. He noticed that the majority were holding on to their revolvers, and shook his head in rueful disbelief.

'You should try and use your third hands to guide yourselves together,' Edeard advised. 'If you link up you'll probably be more stable that way.'

'Stop this!' Captain Larose bawled. He was turning lazily, his legs coming up parallel to the street below.

Edeard held up his hands apologetically, as if mystified by what he was witnessing. 'I'm not doing anything.'

Larose's eyes bugged. He managed to bring his arm over and round, the revolver muzzle tracking down slowly towards Edeard.

'I really wouldn't do that if I were—'

Larose fired. The powerful recoil force sent him cartwheeling *fast* back down Burfol Street. He careered into several of his men on the way, sending them spinning off. It wasn't good for their inner ears.

Edeard pulled a face as the first soldier was spectacularly sick fifteen feet above the pavement. Instead of splattering down, his vomit oscillated through the air, forming strange nebula shapes of its own. The horrified soldier next to him watched helplessly as he collided in slow motion. Then others started to spew up. The regiment's initial cries of shock changed in pitch to become wails of disgust.

Edeard held up a finger in remonstration. 'Don't go away. I'll be back in a little while; we can talk about you holstering your weapons then.' He turned to face the mansion. This time, nobody on the battlements took a pot-shot at him.

The entirety of Makkathran was very quiet.

The Waterwalker looked up at the distant figure of District Master Bise. 'You claim jurisdiction here, yet you forget that with power comes responsibility. You and your family have continually abused your position and allowed the gangs to spread throughout your district. You encourage defiance and manipulation of the law to your own ends. The result of this is the misery and deaths that we have witnessed today.'

'It is not me who brings—'

'BE SILENT.' Edeard aimed his right hand. A colossal bolt of lightning snapped out from his fingertip, striking the top of the tower roof a yard from where Bise was standing. Smouldering chunks of wall twirled out, falling to the courtyard far below. Bise cowered, his arms raised in front of his face.

'You forget, Master Bise, that neither you nor the Grand Council is the final authority here. We are all guests of the city itself. Living here is not a right, it is a privilege. As of this day the city revokes that privilege for you. The family Diroal is hereby stripped of its position and wealth; half of all its money will be redistributed as recompense among those of Sampalok who have suffered this day, the remainder will go to the new Master. I also add to that list of banishment all those who are named in the exclusion warrants. You will now leave Makkathran and you will not return. Ever.'

'Not even you can force that upon us,' Bise replied.

'No,' Edeard agreed equitably. 'I cannot. The city, however, can. And it will begin with the revocation of your mansion.'

For a long minute Edeard and Bise stared at each other. Nothing seemed to happen. Laughter began among those on the wall's battlements; catcalls and taunts rang out again.

The giant iron-bound gates in front of Edeard emitted a staggeringly loud *crack*. People gasped, and leaned over the battlements to see what was happening. The gates appeared to be intact.

Bise's shielded mind suddenly flared with dismay. The edge of the roof where it curved to blend smoothly into the tower walls was changing. It loosened and fractured, turning to the finest dust which then flowed as a liquid. Rivulets of the stuff dribbled down the wall towards the floor below. The rivulets grew to a deluge, swamping the delicate green and yellow patterns. Bise stared down as the accelerating tide began to rise over his boots.

'If I were you,' Edeard advised mildly, 'I'd come down while you still have stairs to come down on.'

The gates sent out another agonized rasping. The sturdy hinge bolts driven over eighteen inches into the substance of the walls were being rejected. The process which always pushed out human fixings over time was speeding up. From inside the mansion a whole series of squeals and brassy groans could be heard as every door was forced out of its frame. Pictures fell off the walls as the hanging spikes popped out. Shelves in the pantries and store-rooms crashed to the floor, spilling their contents.

Bise turned and ran for the stairwell.

Water drained from the bathing pools on every floor in the mansion. The orange lighting segments dimmed to extinction. Crystal windows popped like soap bubbles. Doors fell, crashing down. Then the solid walls started to crawl as they slowly lost cohesion, transforming into a vertical tide of liquid dust.

The family Diroal and all their servants rushed for the stairs. Ge-chimps and monkeys and terrestrial cats raced past them, adding to the bedlam in the darkened stairwells. Bise had barely got halfway down to the sixth floor when the roof finally dissolved. Sunlight shone down into the exposed top floor rooms, revealing the carpets and wobbling furniture being slowly engulfed by a cascade of dust. He moaned in terror and ran faster. Under his pounding feet, he could feel the surface of the curving awkward stairs start to become slippery.

One by one, the three gates in the outside wall slowly warped out of alignment as their fastenings finally came free. They pivoted with an unhurried grace, and toppled down into the square. Nobody was left on the battlements to see their final moment. They were surging down the stairs in a desperate bid to reach the courtyard and safety.

In total it took over thirty minutes for the entire building to melt away, for it was a gigantic edifice and not even the city could reabsorb its mass any quicker. During that time, the constable teams Edeard asked for arrived in the square and formed a circle five men deep around the vanishing mansion.

Captain Ronark was among them. He saluted the Waterwalker, as did the sergeants. They listened to his simple orders before organizing their men as he wanted.

At the end, when the last stubs of the wall washed away, the area where the mansion had stood was reduced to a small lake of dust. It turned solid as rock. Piled up on it was a mound of smashed furniture, and clothes and curtains and carpets and linen, books and bottles of wine, broken crockery, bent cutlery – all the glittery detritus that any incredibly wealthy family would accumulate over two millennia. Ranged around that were the survivors; sullen and resentful, but most of all fearful of the Waterwalker and his power. They glowered as Edeard addressed them, but none dared to interrupt or argue.

'If you are a Diroal or one of those I named, you will hand over your weapons to the constables,' he told them. 'And you will walk from here to the North Gate. The constables will escort you, and safeguard your passage. You may take with you whatever you can carry, and no more. Everyone else is free to go.'

Captain Ronark headed the motley procession, square-shouldered and glowing with pride, taking them down Jankal Lane.

'I'll join you in a moment,' Edeard told him, and walked over the square to Burfol Street. The regiment was still floating gently between the buildings. Several dozen had managed to cling to the vines, where they hung trembling. No matter how hard they clutched the fronds, their stomachs still insisted they were falling. The air was filled with little globules of tacky fluid. Edeard wrinkled his nose as he approached. The smell was truly awful.

His third hand drew Captain Larose to the front of the falling zone the city had created for him.

'I don't have orders for you, because I am not the Mayor,' Edeard said as he looked up at the miserable man in his appallingly stained uniform. 'However, I would like to suggest that the regiment help the victims of this day. Do you find that suggestion sensible, Captain?'

'Yes,' the captain whispered.

'Thank you. My pardon for any discomfort. Please, all of you, engage your safety catches; nobody wants an accident now.'

The regiment sank slowly down to the ground.

Edeard joined the line of constables on escort duty. The ones he fell in with were from Fiacre station; they welcomed him with muted smiles, trying not to appear too triumphal, but their thoughts were so bright it was hard to disguise. His farsight showed him Kristabel arriving in Mid Pool. She was on a family gondola, with Acena, their old doctor. Behind her was a procession of thirty gondolas, each with a couple of doctors, and several novices.

'The militia will be with you in a while,' Edeard told her. 'They'll help you aid the victims. Try and ignore the smell.'

'I'm not sure I want their help,' she replied tartly.

'No recriminations, my love. We all have to live together after this.'

'Yes. Of course.'

'Can you talk to your father for me? I'd like a ship loaded with food and blankets to sail north this afternoon. It can anchor just offshore and supply the exiles with enough to get them through the next few days. We can't just fling them out with nothing. There are children going with them.'

'There are times, Edeard, when it's really hard to live up to your standards of decency, but there isn't a day goes by when I don't thank the Lady you have those standards. I'll talk to Daddy right away.'

As Edeard and the banished made their way across Sampalok, small groups of constables guided other people to join them: the men who had exclusion warrants issued against them. Sometimes their wives and children were with them, sometimes they came alone. As they walked onwards Edeard felt the continued intangible pressure of farsight pressing down on the morose column of unfortunates. He could feel the unconscious question brewing within the city's residents: what next? It was a question he was a little vague on himself.

'I need some advice, sir,' he said to Finitan.

'I think all of us are redundant now, aren't we?' the Grand Master replied.

'That's the thing, I can't be seen as some kind of emperor standing outside the Council. All of us have to work within the framework of the law, otherwise it becomes an irrelevance, and people can't live without the order it brings. That's what today was about, restoring order. We can't lose now. People have died.'

'I know. Even until the last minute, I thought Owain would pull back. If you are willing to accept the constraints of the law then it should be possible to start afresh. Not that it will be easy. However, once people have time to reflect, and with some encouragement, they should be able to see that you were acting for the best. We just have to have a strategy that can take us up to the election. That is when you and I both will face the ultimate judgement.'

'I know that. I have some ideas.'

'Very well, my boy, let's hear them.'

Kanseen, Dinlay and Macsen were on the Cloud Canal bridge, sitting together on one of its twisty pillars. They'd spread their jackets on the next pillar to dry in the bright sunlight. Kanseen's wet hair clung to her scalp like a bad beret. Her knuckles were grazed and muddy. Dinlay was trying to clean the one intact lens left in his glasses. Not that it mattered much, one eye was so badly swollen he could barely see through it. His lip was split, and still dribbling blood. He'd taken his boots off, so that his left ankle could be bound in a thick bandage. Macsen's nose was broken. Two small wads of tissue were jammed up each nostril, scarlet with blood. His jacket was missing, and his shirt under the drosilk waistcoat was ripped, revealing a lot of scratches and bruises on his arms.

They didn't get up as Edeard approached, they just sat there watching him in silence. He stopped in front of them. 'Don't tell me,' he said. 'I should see the other fellows.'

Kanseen sneered. 'If there was anything left of them.'

'You stood by me,' he told them. 'You believed in me. You took on Eustace's idiots so I could get through.'

Macsen turned to Dinlay and grinned. 'Eustace's idiots. Good name for that platoon.'

'We can probably get it made official,' Dinlay conceded. He eased himself off the short pillar, wincing at the movement as he put some weight on his sprained ankle. 'Come here.'

Edeard embraced him, unbelievably happy that no harm had befallen his surviving friends – well, nothing permanent. Then Kanseen stepped into his outheld arms. Finally Macsen gave him a hug.

'Ouch!'

'You all right?' Edeard asked anxiously.

'He might be a complete tit,' Macsen's index finger probed his nose gingerly. 'But he knows how to fight dirty, I'll give him that.'

'So,' Dinlay said. 'We get to stay constables.'

Edeard gave Macsen and Kanseen a mildly guilty look. 'For the moment, yes. You going to help me with this escort duty?'

Dinlay gave his bandaged ankle an annoyed look. 'I don't think I can make it all the way to North Gate.'

'The doctors will be here soon,' Edeard assured him. 'How about you two?'

'Bloody Honious, it's all go with you, isn't it?'

The march over High Moat was swift enough. By the time Ronark reached North Gate, Edeard counted nearly eight hundred people in the column. He hated that so many women and children were being taken along, but there was nothing he could do about that, not now. *It was always going to be like this.*

The road on both sides of the giant gate was deserted. Edeard and the constables stopped at the crystal wall. Bise, who was at the head of the column, paused at the giant archway through the wall.

'A ship will anchor in Cauley cove this evening,' Edeard told the ex-District Master. 'It has provisions for you; all of you.'

Bise glared at him. 'Where are we supposed to go?'

'There are fresh lands in the provinces. You can begin again if you wish.'

'I am a *District Master*,' Bise yelled furiously. Over fifty members of the Diroal family were gathered behind him, all of them wearing clothes appropriate to their status, and completely wrong to be wearing for a march through the countryside. Hems on the fanciful skirts of the older women were already ragged and filthy as they dragged along High Moat's dusty track. The men were carrying their fur-lined robes, and sweating in their gaudy shirts and trousers. Two of the younger wives were carrying crying babes. Not one of them had footwear that would last more than a couple of days on the road.

Edeard did his best not to feel guilt or sorrow at the misery arrayed in front of him. 'If you had lived up to your responsibilities you still would be,' he said. 'Now leave while I'm still feeling generous.'

'You won't live past midnight,' Bise spat.

Edeard smiled without humour. 'I hope you're not relying on Warpal or Motluk to make that a reality.'

Bise paled. He glanced up at the archway, and marched through with his head held high. His family trudged after him.

'He'll be in some friend's Iguru pavilion by nightfall,' Captain Ronark declared. 'Dressed in fresh clothes, sipping wine, and plotting revenge while the rest of these unfortunates are shivering on the side of the road.'

'I know,' Edeard said as those named on the exclusion warrants began to file past, calling names and swearing vengeance. 'The important thing is the banishment itself. Without the most active gang members, we can achieve order in the city. Besides, how long do you think Bise will be welcome in that pavilion? A fortnight? A month? How long would you feed and clothe his whole family? He'll be moved on eventually; further and further away from us.'

'I hope so.'

'Thank you for your support, sir,' Edeard said.

'You would have it a thousand times over, Waterwalker. I've given my life to the constables, and achieved so little. You have restored the city's faith in us, in the law. That means a lot to me, and probably to more people than you realize.'

'I was hoping you could talk to Walsfol for me.'

'I will have words. It might be easier than you expect. The Mayor's actions today left a lot of people shocked and disturbed.'

'I need to remain a constable.'

'There's a position that I believe would serve very well.'

'What position?'

'Captain of Jeavons station.'

Edeard gave the old man a startled look. 'But, sir—'

'I'm almost at retirement age anyway, and there are posts in the Chief Constable's office where I can sit out my time. Look at me, I'm here watching the worst bastards in the city march into banishment; people I've spent decades trying to stop. It doesn't get better than this. You taking charge of Jeavons is fitting, and it will put you in a good position to achieve Chief Constable in a few years. Walsfol is my age, you know.'

'That is . . . enormously generous, sir.'

'It's good politics. And I think you've learned what's most important in this city now.'

'Yes, sir!'

Eight constables escorted Buate to the North Gate. Edeard gave the man a dismissive glance, and told the constables to let him go.

'I don't know what you are, Waterwalker,' Buate said, 'but you'll never last.'

'You're probably right. But while I'm here, you're not. And that gives everyone a chance at a better life.'

Buate turned away, and walked through the North Gate.

'Now that's a sight I never thought I'd see,' Kanseen said as Buate gave the grassland outside a disgusted look. He strode away, keeping himself apart from the other exiles tramping along.

'Worth remembering, though,' Macsen said. 'So what's next, mighty Waterwalker?'

'Sampalok, and then a wedding,' Edeard told them. 'And if you ever call me that again, you'll find yourself living with Buate in a hut in the furthest province I can find.'

'Ohooo touchy!'

'What do you mean a wedding?' Kanseen asked.

'I need to talk to yo　' Edeard broke off. His arm suddenly shot out, pointing at the last few stragglers in the column going through North Gate. 'Not you!' He beckoned. 'Come here.'

The teenage lad gave a guilty start, looking round to try and see who the Waterwalker was pointing at.

'Yes, *you*,' Edeard said.

The lad certainly looked like he should be exiled: curly brown hair that hadn't seen soap for weeks, a scratchy beard just starting, bad outbreak of spots on both cheeks. His clothes were clearly tailored for someone else, with a belt holding up trousers whose legs were crudely cut to size – because he wasn't particularly tall for his age. He wore a patched jacket with bulging pockets, filled with food and some small silver items looted from Sampalok shops. His only expression was sullen, and he wouldn't meet anyone's gaze.

His parents came with him, clinging defensively. Edeard remembered the father, a gang member working rackets out of Abad.

'What's your name?' Edeard asked.

'You leave him alone,' the woman cried. 'We're going, what more do you bastards want from us?'

The lad gave Edeard the kind of surly stare that only a Sampalok youth could manage. 'What do they call you?' he asked benignly.

'Marcol. What's it to you?'

'And your father is Arcton, I know, and your mother . . . ?'

'Janeel,' she said uncertainly. 'What is this?'

'Marcol here has a very strong third hand.'

Marcol reddened. 'I don't!'

'There aren't many in this city who can pull a ge-eagle out of the sky from such a height.'

'Wasn't me.'

'You're loyal to your parents, aren't you?' Edeard mused. 'You'd have to be if you're leaving with them. You're old enough to stay and look after yourself if you really want; after all, you're not named in any warrant.'

'You let him be,' Janeel said, her arms went protectively round her son.

'I ain't staying here,' Marcol said defiantly.

'I'll make you an offer,' Edeard said. 'I'll cancel your father's banishment, if you sign on as a probationary constable at Jeavons station.'

'What?' Arcton and Janeel gave each other a disbelieving look.

'Edeard?' a puzzled Kanseen queried.

'Two conditions,' Edeard said. 'Marcol has to complete his probation and graduate; and you, Arcton, get a job and keep out of trouble.'

'Are you serious?' Arcton asked.

'I'm the Waterwalker.'

'He doesn't do funny,' Macsen informed them curtly.

'Yes,' Janeel said, she looked ready to burst into tears. 'Yes, we'll do it.'

'Marcol?' Edeard asked. 'What do you say? It won't be easy.'

'Why are you doing this?' It was more like a grunt than a sentence.

Edeard put his arm round Marcol's shoulder, and drew him aside. 'Have you got a girlfriend?'

'Yeah! Hundreds.'

'Hundreds, eh? You're lucky. I didn't, not before I joined the constables. Do you know how many I had after I became the Waterwalker? Did you hear about that part of my life?'

Marcol came perilously close to smiling. 'Sort of.'

'Girls, especially fancy family girls, like men in uniform, particularly those of us who are stronger than everyone else. They *really* like that.'

'Yeah?'

'It's never easy being a probationary constable, but can it be harder than trying to be a farm boy on the other side of the Iguru? Is that what you want to be?'

'No.'

'So will you give it a try? For your mum's sake if nothing else. Look at her; she doesn't want to be thrown out of the city. But I don't have a choice: your dad did wrong, except now you've got a chance to put it all right.'

'Okay. I'll do it.'

'Thank you.' Edeard turned to Arcton and Janeel. 'You can go home. Have him at Jeavons station seven o'clock tomorrow morning; washed and looking respectable.'

'Yes, Waterwalker. Thank you, Waterwalker.'

'What in Honious was that about?' Macsen asked. 'You can't seriously think he'll make a constable?'

Edeard grinned. 'We did.'

The last of the banished walked through North Gate. Edeard turned to address the big crowd of constables who had completed the escort duty. 'People will remember this day because of what I did. But none of that would be possible without your support, and I thank you from the bottom of my heart for the way you stood by me today. You made this happen just as much as me.' His third hand reached for the giant iron hinges which held the gate itself. The latching mechanism creaked in protest as he lifted it. A flurry of rust flakes snowed down on to the grass from the cumbersome mechanism. Then he pulled the gate itself. The constables started cheering as the huge section of crystal swung back into the hole which Rah himself had cut it out of two thousand years ago. It made such a crunching noise that Edeard thought the ancient crystal might finally shatter. But instead, it fitted the archway perfectly. He thought such a dramatic gesture was an apt way to finish the banishment.

Kathlynn, Kanseen's sister, was standing in the square next to the pile of wreckage which had been the Diroal family's possessions. She was holding little Dium in her arms; he was sucking on a honey ball and squirming round energetically. Dybal and

Bijulee were standing beside her. All three of them talking to Dinlay, who was sitting on a battered old pew of talcherry wood salvaged from the pile. A lot of Sampalok residents were busy salvaging. They swarmed over the mound like drakken on carrion. People were carrying off heavy bundles of stuff down the roads from the square. Edeard thought at least a third of it had been taken already. Incredibly, that included one of the huge gates from the outer wall. A quick scan round with his farsight revealed the gate beside a smithy three streets away. The owner and his apprentices were already hammering at the big iron bindings.

'Right,' Kanseen snapped as they emerged from Burfol Street and she saw Kathlynn. 'What's going on?'

Kathlynn caught sight of them and waved happily.

Edeard held up a finger in pleading. 'One moment.'

The Sampalok residents had stopped everything as the Waterwalker returned to the square, giving him nervous glances. He smiled at them. 'Take whatever you want, please, then stand back.'

Several of the bolder ones took him at his word, and continued to pick through the remains.

'Edeard!' Kanseen warned.

'Ah, here we go.' Edeard had spied Kristabel emerging from one of the streets. She was wearing a lime-green dress and an apron with smears of blood on it. A Mother was walking beside her, an elderly woman stiff with suspicion. She presided over the Lady's church in Sampalok, one of the most thankless tasks in the district. It showed in her demeanour. She was a lot tougher than most of the Lady's Mothers Edeard had encountered.

Bijulee embraced Macsen, while Dybal clapped him on the back. Macsen yelped at the impact. Kanseen had now been saddled with the wriggling Dium, who was delighted to see his auntie.

Kristabel gave Edeard a quick kiss. 'Are you all right?'

'Yeah. But I really don't want any more days like this one.'

'There won't be.'

'Still want to marry me?'

'Of course. Is that what this is about?' she gestured at the Mother.

'No. Sorry. This is about maintaining the rule of law. That's what gives people hope. And they need that today of all days.'

'I love you,' she murmured.

The Mother coughed for attention. 'You asked to see me, Waterwalker.'

'Yes, Mother. I think we might have a ceremony for you to perform.'

'What kind of ceremony?'

'Macsen, I believe our dearest friend told you not to waste any time.'

'*What?*'

Dybal started chuckling.

'Do you have something to ask somebody?' Edeard said levelly. 'Right now.'

Macsen gave him a frantic stare. 'You've got to be joking,' he growled through lips which didn't move.

'I'm the Waterwalker, apparently I don't do funny.'

The salvagers had claimed their prizes, now they were gathering to watch the latest bizarre spectacle to be played out in the square today. Constables also began to congregate, showing considerable interest. A lot of farsight was concentrating on the square again. Edeard held out an arm. A silver ring flashed out from the pile of debris to fly across the square into his hand. He proffered it to Macsen with a flourish. 'You might need this.'

'Oh Lady.' Macsen took the ring, his eyes widening in amazement at how many diamonds could fit on to such a small item. 'Really?'

'Really,' Edeard said.

Macsen took a breath and went down on one knee. 'Kanseen, I have never been happier than when I'm with you. Would you please do me the honour of marrying me?' He might have been incredibly awkward with so many people straining to see and hear, but his face held a longing that was irrefutable.

'Yes, my darling,' she said. 'I will marry you.'

Several constables whistled and clapped in approval as Macsen put the ring on her finger. He frowned at Edeard as it slipped about. 'You couldn't find one that fitted?'

'Mother,' Edeard said. 'Would you please marry them now?'

'Edeard, no,' Kanseen said. 'Look at the state of me. My wedding is supposed to be . . . not this.'

'I'm sorry,' he said. 'I have my reason.'

'*Your* reason?'

He nodded.

'It had better be incredible,' she muttered.

Dybal gave the bride away. Dinlay was best man. Kathlynn stood behind her sister, crying as she held the posy of flowers hurriedly snatched from plants in nearby streets. Kristabel and Bijulee took it in turns to cope with Dium, who really wanted to be in on the action. Edeard held Kristabel's hand when he could, listening to the Mother's words with the heap of rubbish from the mansion as the background to the damp, dishevelled bride and groom. Constables formed a big semi circle round them, with curious Sampalok residents making up a wider audience.

When it was over, when the promises were made, the rings exchanged, and the bride kissed, Edeard went up to his friends. His voice and longtalk filled the square.

'When Rah brought us out of the chaos to this place the city accepted us. When Rah allowed his most faithful friends and followers to become District Masters the city did not object, for he chose wisely. Down the centuries, the family Diroal slipped away from the ideals that were sworn at the beginning, and today is a result of that. None of us wish to defy Rah's constitution, least of all me; so I now publicly ask this city to accept the appointment of the new joint District Master and Mistress of Sampalok.'

'Edeard!' Kanseen hissed furiously.

The Waterwalker gestured, and the ground beneath the pile of expensive detritus turned fluid again. Everything left from the demise of Bise's mansion was sucked down below the surface amid a harsh gurgling sound. The crowd drew a sharp breath of excitement.

'Walk to the middle,' Edeard said quietly as the city substance hardened again.

Macsen took his wife's hand, and urged her out into the big open space. Both of them radiated nerves as their soggy boots squelched on the ground, watched by over a thousand people in the square, and many times that number by farsight.

'The new Master and Mistress of Sampalok,' Edeard announced. 'And their new mansion.'

The surface began to ripple around Macsen and Kanseen. She jumped in apprehension and he hugged her tight – which gathered more than a little appreciation from their audience.

Six long dark lines firmed up on the ground around them, as if some architect was using the area to sketch an enormous hexagon. Smaller lines multiplied inside them, revealing the outlines of various rooms and cloisters. Then all the lines began to bulge up into ridges.

A radiantly happy Kanseen glanced across the empty space to Edeard. 'How long is this going to take?'

'A little while. It's always quicker and easier to tear things down than it is to build them back up again.'

'So? A week?'

Edeard gave the tiny ridges a doubtful look. After five minutes they were nearly two inches high. Below them the city was ponderously rearranging its vast complicated network of channels and ducts to feed and support the new structure he'd hurriedly drafted. *A building with proper stairs. Finally!* 'Perhaps I'd better get you a tent as your wedding present.'

Justine: Year Three

You couldn't dream in suspension. Everyone knew that. And yet . . .

Justine recalled those two wondrous lazy days with Kazimir so clearly. It had been the most fabulous doomed love affair the universe had ever known. She'd been vacationing on Far Away, a brattish rich girl celebrating her latest rejuvenation on what was then the Commonwealth's most outré planet. The grand finale had been a hyperglider flight over Mount Herculaneum. It had been an insane thrill ride. Flying the tiny plane through a phenomenally aggressive storm gave her the speed to soar out of the atmosphere and curve over the summit of the huge volcano. Despite all the odds, she'd managed it; gliding down to land in a small clearing on the other side.

Luck, chance, fate, or a particularly wicked god had placed Kazimir on the ground beside the clearing as the hyperglider bumped and jolted to a halt. He was seventeen, born into the Guardians of Selfhood which Bradley Johansson had formed to protect humanity from the Starflyer. An upbringing that had left him utterly devoted to his cause yet at the same time innocent of the universe at large. He never really stood a chance against a woman two hundred years his senior whose newly youthful body was fizzing with adolescent hormones. Not that he put up a lot of resistance.

It took the tourist company's recovery crew two days to drive round Herculaneum and pick up all the glider pilots. Two days spent eating the gourmet food from the glider's store, sleeping, talking, and making love. Two days alone together. Then she went back to her world and he to his. All she had left was the sweetest memory of her entire life.

That really should have been the end of it. But years later the Guardians of Selfhood gave Kazimir an assignment on Earth, and he risked everything to see her again. His reward was to be betrayed. By her. She thought she was doing the right thing informing the security services. But it was he who had the truth of it, the Starflyer was real and extracted revenge. Kazimir had been assassinated by one of its agents, and in twelve hundred years Justine had never forgiven herself. Not even the son she'd borne him and named after him had helped ease the pain.

So now her dreams granted her those two days again. She looked into his worshipful face once more as he was seduced and taught the miracle their bodies could achieve together. She knew what it was like to be held in his arms again. She laughed with him in the glade on the hillside where the bright sunlight shone out of Far Away's gorgeous sapphire sky. Caught him giving her longing glances across the bonfire they lit outside the tent at night. Watched him sleeping. Talked to him about her life. Listened to his stories of growing up in the mountains and deserts in fear of the great enemy.

Two days that showed her what a paradise her life could have been if she'd just had the strength to cast off her own conventions. Two days that made her weep with joy simply because they existed. Two days that stretched on and on and on . . . granted by a dream that was impossible to have. Because you couldn't dream in suspension.

Night closed in and she lost him. The bonfire must have gone out, leaving her world claustrophobically dark. The air was dryer that it had been on the mountainside.

Lights resolved in the darkness. Strange colourful constellations that her drowsy mind slowly began to comprehend. Exoimage medical icons told her she was recovering.

'Oh shit,' she groaned. The medical chamber lid peeled back, and she looked round the *Silverbird*'s cabin again. It had just been a dream. She sat up and wiped the tears from her cheeks. 'Status?' she asked the smartcore. A fresh level of exoimage icons and displays sprang up.

She'd been in suspension for three years; the target star was about a lightyear away. And the *Silverbird* was decelerating hard. Something was approaching.

'Holy crap,' she muttered as the sensors swept across the visitor. It was big – mountain sized. That was just the core. It was surrounded by weird sheets of gossamer matter that fluctuated like a gas.

A Skylord with its vacuum wings fully extended.

Justine showered and ordered up a decent meal as the *Silverbird* and the Skylord rendezvoused. It took the best part of a day, but they were finally sliding through space a thousand miles apart. With the sensors able to penetrate the haze of the vacuum wings, the Skylord was the same as Inigo's dreams had shown them. A long ovoid but not solid, it was as if vast sheets of crystalline fabric had been folded into a Calabi-Yau manifold topology, with looping curves intersecting each other in eye-twisting complexity. The warped surfaces shimmered with long diffraction patterns that always flowed inward. She could never be certain if the structure itself was stable or constantly fluctuating there was so much surface movement.

Settling back on the longest couch in the cabin's repertoire she let her mind reach for the immense creature. It glowed on the edge of her farsight, a glow not dissimilar to the gaiafield. Tenuous and full of emotion.

'Hello,' she said.

'You are most welcome,' the Skylord said.

'Did you let me into this universe?'

'My kindred knew of your arrival. The nucleus drew you in.'

'You know then it is my wish to speak with this nucleus, the Heart where you guide human souls. Can you guide me there?'

'Your mind is not like the others of your species which used to dwell here. You lack the maturity of the elder years, yet your resolution is formidable. There is something about your vessel which magnifies your thoughts, but not rightly so.'

The confluence nest, Justine realized. 'The amplifier is an instrument constructed on my homeworld to emulate your communications here. That is how you found us beyond your border.'

'Along with my kindred, I guide those who have accomplished fulfilment to the nucleus. That is my fulfilment. There will come a time when I will not return from the nucleus.'

'That's why I have come here. Others of my kind are trying to reach your universe. Their arrival will be a disaster. I must explain this to the Heart.'

'Existence is achieving fulfilment. All must strive for that moment.'

'In here, yes. But outside is a universe very different to this one. Did you know you are damaging us, destroying our stars and worlds?'

'There is only here, the universe and the nucleus.'

'Then where did I come from?'

'The nucleus knows.'

'Then guide me there, please.'

'This cannot be done, it is against what is. I mourn your loss. Once you reach fulfilment I will guide you.'

Justine's teeth began to press together. She made a very strong effort to make sure her frustration didn't contaminate her longtalk with the vast creature. 'Do you understand what I'm saying to you? This existence you enjoy in here is killing living entities outside, you are preventing an entire galaxy from ever reaching fulfilment.'

'To achieve fulfilment your species must come to the solid worlds scattered throughout this universe.'

'Your kind of fulfilment. Not ours.'

'I will guide you when your mind reaches fulfilment. You strive for it so hard, the fabric is deeply affected by your wishes. It will not be long.'

'Help me, *please*. You are killing people.'

'To ascend into the fabric in any fashion is wonderful. Even the quietest minds are a part of what is.'

'No, no, death outside this universe is final. It ends all form of existence.'

'How hard for your species. You adapt easily and mature within this universe. We welcome you all. That is the reason for our existence.'

'I have to get to the Heart. Do you remember others like me you guided there?'

'There were many. They were joyful to reach the nucleus.'

'I am glad to hear that. Where are they now? Where is the nucleus?'

'The nucleus is the centre of everywhere and everywhen. It is that which all came from, and all return to change and live among change.'

'Is it here? Are we in the nucleus right now?'

'You cannot be in the nucleus. You have not reached fulfilment.'

'I would like to talk with those of my kind who are already there. I could learn so much from them, it would help me reach fulfilment.'

'Fulfilment comes from within.'

'Fulfilment is achieved from experience. I am alone here. I need to commune with my own kind if I am to mature.'

'My kindred are not aware of any thoughts from minds akin to your species. None are left.'

'None?' she asked in shock. 'But there was a whole world of us, maybe more.'

'All were guided to the nucleus. That world awaits the arrival of others. As do my kindred.'

'Then take me to some world where you can feel living minds.'

'My flock searches this universe always. There is no world I can feel where minds live thiswhen.'

'Jesus fuck it!' Justine couldn't help it, but the frustration was finally getting to her. The Ocisens were less stubborn than this creature. She took a breath. *It's not stubborn, these are its thought routines, perfectly adapted to its life and purpose. Why should it understand my motivations and problems?*

'You are sorrowful,' the Skylord said. 'When you are ready to be guided, I will guide you. Know this and hope.'

Something changed among the patterns shimmering within the Skylord's curving crystalline sheets. It moved, shrinking away at an incredible velocity. Within seconds it had vanished from the *Silverbird*'s sensors.

'Ye Gods,' Justine muttered. The Second Dreamer's views of Skylords always showed them drifting along sedately. Whereas the acceleration she'd just witnessed would have been close to five hundred gees. *If it was acceleration. This is a strange old place.*

She spent the next few hours running over her conversation again and again. In the end she acknowledged she couldn't have achieved any other outcome. The Skylord simply didn't have the psychology to help her reach the Heart. It was too alien.

For all its size and ability she wasn't strictly sure it qualified as sentient. Most intelligences had the ability to learn and reason, these creatures seemed incapable of interpreting anything outside their original parameters.

Not that the analysis helped her.

When she ran through the starship's log she was pleased with the way *Silverbird* had remained functional. For some reason the glitches had been minimal while she'd been in suspension. Now all she had to do was decide what to do next.

At a lightyear distant the visual sensors could just make out some kind of accretion disc surrounding the star she was heading for. She examined the tenuous imagery with growing dismay. Any star whose planets were still forming wasn't going to have a habitable world for her to establish herself on. Or at least, it wouldn't out there in the real universe.

Justine mulled the problem over while she had another gourmet meal of lamb shanks cooked in toblaris wine and herb rosties, then pigged out on chocolates. She'd come this far, and it was only another one and a half years in suspension. She still didn't have enough information to make a decision, any kind of decision. She was simply heading for the star as a comfort measure. That was something she needed more than ever now. *No other planetary species in this whole universe!*

Silverbird began accelerating back up to point seven lightspeed as the medical chamber's lid flowed shut above her.

5

It was an ordinary house in an ordinary street. At least as far as Ganthia was concerned. A planet that became Higher soon after it was settled, its various political committees had quickly evolved a policy of sustainable organic construction. Native flora lent itself easily to the concept, trees in the temperate zones were hardwoods with an internal honeycomb structure. A few genetic tweaks make them quite suitable for creative shaping. Like the aircoral developed during the first Commonwealth era, Ganthia's modified trees could be guided over frameworks to form hollow bulbous chambers. Better yet, they were amenable to grafting, so while each room was an individual tree, a house was the merger of many.

Navy Captain, retired, Donald Chatfield, lived in the middle of what from the air resembled a good-sized forest. It fact it was Persain City, spreading out over the side of several mountains just above the shoreline. Twelve trees provided him five first-floor rooms whose curving walls sprouted stunted branches with shell-pink leaves. Five long trunks grew up through the gaps between the lower rooms, before bulging out into the second floor of smaller compartments; each frosted with copper leaves. The remaining two trees were hollow pipes, twisting round the curvature of the lower rooms to provide stairwells between the two levels.

Paula's taxi capsule skimmed along what appeared to be a wide greenway through the forest city. It settled silently on the wild lawn outside Chatfield's home and she climbed out, sniffing the unusually spicy air. House clusters stretched away in every direction, some extending three or four floors high, their marvellously convoluted trunks forming a knotted support maze. Sunlight shone through the overhead branches creating a sharp dapple around her. In the distance, some kids were playing in an open area. The whole scene was remarkably rustic. Only the capsules flitting along the grid of greenways betrayed the planet's true cultural base.

She walked up the short wooden steps to the porch platform formed from a miniature tree crafted to a flat mushroom shape. Donald Chatfield greeted her at the wonderfully old-fashioned green-painted front door. A tall youthful-looking man with an easy smile. His neat dark hair was starting to grey in contrast to firm features and a healthy tan. She couldn't work out if those light strands were a fashion statement or an imperative genetic quirk his biononics couldn't adjust. He was three hundred and fifty years old, after all.

'Thank you for agreeing to see me,' she said as he led her into the sitting room. Three big circles had been sawn out of the bulging walls, to be filled with perfectly clear crystal that overlooked his back garden. No attempt had been made to paint or cover the bare wood, though walls and ceiling had been polished to show off the dark timber's turquoise grain flecks. Even the furniture was carved from large sections of tree trunks, softened by a few scattered cushions.

'Your reputation precedes you, Investigator,' he said as he waved her into one of the big chairs. 'I didn't even have to consult a reference file. But then I have served on ships around Dyson Alpha. It was a long time ago, but the crews tend to assimilate the War period's history in more detail than the average citizen, it helps us understand the mission.'

'Interesting,' she said as she settled back. 'That's actually why I'm here.'

He raised an eyebrow in an almost dismissive expression. 'Good heavens. Even I'm history in that respect.'

'Not quite. I'd like to ask you about your third mission there, you captained the *Poix*.'

'Yes. What's the problem?'

'No problem. I need some information on one of your crew: Kent Vernon.'

'Oh him.'

'That doesn't sound good.'

Donald gave her a roguish grin. 'Navy service sounds very grand, but I was actually in the Exploration Division. We fly science missions, not combat. That allows a – ' he paused ' – *broader* range of characters than the regular Navy. Vernon might have been helpful analysing the generator lattice shells, but he certainly wouldn't have been any use in a regular Navy position. He wasn't the most popular person on board the dear old *Poix*.'

'Why not?'

'Don't get me wrong. He performed some valuable work. However, his social skills were somewhat lacking. Quite surprisingly so given he was Higher. It rather shocked some of the crew, they weren't used to making allowances like that.'

'If he was that disruptive how did he get a commission?'

'It was a science commission, he wasn't strictly Navy at all. Specialists are given temporary commissions for the duration of their missions. I was warned about his nature while the mission was drawn up.'

'Yet you allowed him to take part.'

'The captain has some discretion. I accessed his file and thought he could make a valid contribution; he was very highly qualified in his field. That had to be balanced against any personal disruption he would make. Ultimately, I agreed to him joining us because it doesn't hurt to shake things up every now and then.'

'Strange attitude,' she observed. 'You're on a difficult and important mission a long way from home in what is still technically a war zone, and you choose to take along a potentially disruptive influence.'

'It was a judgement call. I made it because we'd had two previous missions at Dyson Alpha; my crew knew the routine. It was never a physical danger having him on board. Worst case scenario, which we always had to plan for, was the barrier collapsing while we were there. Vernon would just be shoved in his cabin and told to stay there while we did what we could to prevent Prime ships from escaping. Even then, the *Poix* would be assigned a third-line defence position. To this day the Navy maintains some serious firepower outside the Dyson Pair. Ozzie help the Primes if they ever do crack out and make a break for it.'

'So did you make the right judgement?' Paula asked.

Donald gave an expansive shrug. 'There is no right answer to this. The mission gathered a lot of data, but I wouldn't necessarily want him on board again. In a strange way it helped crew morale afterwards. In my final two missions there was always a lot of talk about how difficult that mission was.'

'Bonding in the face of adversity?'

'Something like that. Though I wouldn't want to make out it was some terrible trip into hardship. It wasn't. He's just different from the rest of Highers, which isn't a crime. So what's your interest in Vernon after all this time?'

'He wasn't quite who he claimed to be.'

Donald gave her a long stare. 'In what possible way?'

'I believe he was carrying out his own agenda, possibly on behalf of an ANA Faction.'

'What agenda?'

'That's why I'm here, to see what you can tell me.'

'I'm sorry, but my immediate answer to that is: very little. Even taking his attitude into account it was a perfectly routine mission. We gathered data on the Dark Fortress for eight months and came home.'

'There was no abnormal event? Nothing out of the ordinary?'

Donald's eyes flickered as he delved down into memories long ago shunted into a storage lacuna. 'Not a thing.'

'So what exactly was the mission?'

'Monitoring and analysis of the inner two lattice spheres inside the Dark Fortress. Which we accomplished successfully.'

'Were there any breakthroughs or revelations about the Dark Fortress?'

'Not due to us. The damn thing is still an enigma. We don't understand how it generates a force field large enough to envelop an entire star system; the mechanism is peculiar. Though they are making headway on the field itself these days, I gather. I don't really stay current.'

'Did Vernon want to take anything further; perhaps some persistence that at the time you wrote off to his personality?'

'He was always on about the factory.'

'Factory?'

'Whatever the Anomine used to build the Dark Fortress itself. He contended that if we could examine that we'd solve the entire generator and its principles. Logically, he was quite right. But that wasn't our mission.'

'I see. Has there ever been a mission to examine the factory?'

'No. Because we don't know where the factory is.'

'So did Vernon want to go and search for it?'

'Yes. I wouldn't mind doing that myself, actually. That would be quite something, wouldn't it? A structure that builds machines the size of a small gas giant. Finding that would be enough to yank me back out of retirement.'

'I'm sure.' Paula hesitated, not trusting a word he said. 'Did Kent Vernon modify the observations you were making?'

'Constantly, that's what the science team are there for. One set of results leads them off to investigate some other aspect. Within the overall mission parameter, the monitoring process is very fluid. We'd just be a simple sensor relay otherwise.'

'What was Vernon's specific field?'

'Quantum signature. He was there to determine the sub-physical nature of the lattice sphere composition.'

'So in that field did he want to do anything he shouldn't have done?'

'No. We've got a pretty broad leeway when it comes to

observations. Just about the only thing the Navy prohibits is trying to take a physical sample of a lattice sphere – not that they are all strictly physical. A stupid restriction if you ask me, but I don't make the rules.'

'Stupid how?'

He gave her a curious gaze. 'You took part in the Starflyer War. Ozzie and Nigel Sheldon set off a couple of quantumbusters inside the Dark Fortress, and it's still working. That is one extremely tough mother. Shaving a nugget off isn't going to break it.'

'Good point.' Paula activated a layer of specific-function biononics on the skin surface of her right palm.

'You have a good relationship with ANA, you might want to tell it that someday,' Chatfield said.

'I'm sure it has its reasons.'

'Yeah.'

Paula stood, and held out her right hand. 'Well, thank you for your time, Captain.'

'Not at all.' He shook hands warmly. 'Was I of any use?'

Her biononics sampled the dead cells of Chatfield's outer epidermal layer. 'I'm not sure.' There was a second when she thought he might activate his combat enrichments. It passed. Even so, old-fashioned instinct made her uncomfortable turning her back on him as he showed her out.

As soon as she got back into her taxi capsule she opened an ultra-secure link to ANA:Governance. 'He's an Accelerator.'

'What makes you say that?' ANA:Governance asked.

'He admitted a possible error and accepted the blame. Standard sympathy-grab manoeuvre. But his real mistake was a fundamental one. When I said Vernon had an agenda for a Faction, Chatfield asked what the agenda was, not which Faction.' She held up her right hand, turning it to examine the palm. There was nothing visible, but the biononics were already feeding a stream of sequencing data down the link. 'I'm sending you his DNA. Run it against every file you have. Specifically, people involved with Government and Navy.'

As before, the speed of the reply was near instantaneous. It impressed Paula exactly how much attention ANA had devoted to the analysis. Her u-shadow would have taken at least a minute to run the comparison.

'That instinct of yours is quite something,' ANA:Governance said.

'Really?'

'There is a twenty-point spread marker similarity with a Captain Evanston.'

'Not identical, so it's either family, or . . .

'Or he had a DNA resequence for that assignment.'

'That's very deep cover. So is he Evanston or Chatfield?'

'I'd say Chatfield. Evanston was a serving officer twenty-five years ago. But Chatfield's current DNA is almost a match for Captain Chatfield's registered Navy file a hundred years ago.'

'Almost a match?'

'The variance is small but noticeable. If we weren't considering a period spent resequenced it would be within acceptable error.'

'So, if he's going for resequencing, why keep the twenty-point similarity? Complete resequencing used to be quite a popular option among the criminal classes of late first era and early second era Commonwealth. The perfect way to avoid court-verified identification. A lot of them literally got away with murder.'

'That's a simple answer: his brain. He wanted to maintain his thought routines as they are. If you alter neural structure and neurochemicals you alter how you think, your very personality. He wanted to keep on being him.'

'That makes sense. So give me his file.' She observed it enter her macrocellular clusters. Secondary thought routines picked the data apart, highlighting the relevant sections. One long entry leapt out at her. 'Oh Jesus,' she muttered.

'Quite,' ANA:Governance said. 'And in connection with today's events, extremely significant.'

'Overwhelmingly significant,' she retorted. 'Evanston was

second in command of the development-restrictions monitoring station on Elan.'

'I always considered it quite an irony that the Commonwealth allowed the surviving Prime invasion forces to continue living on the worlds they conquered.'

'Not all of them,' she said. 'Just on the five Lost23 that we didn't completely nuke into oblivion. Some of those surviving immotiles got smart.'

'You mean they got human.'

'They accessed the memories of human lawyers and promptly surrendered. They even quoted our own basic rights laws back at us. I'd say that was quite smart. Evolutionary even. Adapt to and then accept the ethics of an alien species that you were trying to wipe out in order to survive yourself. It was the only reason Admiral Columbia allowed them to live, he considered it an indication that Primes were capable of social progression – as humans see it.'

'They've kept their side of the agreement until now.'

'I don't think this can be blamed on them.' Paula hadn't felt this angry for quite some time. Centuries. But for the Accelerators to use the Prime to bolster the Ocisen Empire . . . It took a lot to shock her, but this had done it. *Don't they understand the danger?* But of course they did. *It's me who is only just starting to grasp the stakes they're playing for, the ends to which they'll go.*

'That is also our conclusion,' ANA:Governance said.

'It's treason.'

'If provable. So far we only have circumstantial evidence.'

Paula resisted the temptation to glance back over her shoulder. The capsule was already clear of the city's elegant greenways. Now it was soaring gracefully over the mountain peaks towards the starport on the inland plain beyond. She toyed with the idea of going back and arresting Chatfield. 'A memory read will provide the evidence.'

'Do you think Chatfield will allow that to happen?'

'No,' she admitted regretfully. 'If he's an Accelerator agent at the level we believe him to be, then capture is not an option.

He'll just auto-bodyloss and they'll re-life him inside a day with a safe body. We'll have to keep him under observation and see where he takes us.'

'I have placed him under electronic scrutiny.'

'Thank you. That should do until I can get a colleague here to shadow him. If Chatfield is part of the project which allied the Primes to the Ocisen Empire, he'll probably be aware of the hardware Troblum has helped them build. I'm wondering if it was those starships accompanying the Ocisen fleet.'

'According to Gore, Ilanthe said the Accelerators can protect the sol system from any Void expansion. I have no idea what that might translate into in practice.'

'Two illegal hardware construction projects? They really are committed to their ideology, aren't they? We're going to have to keep a very sharp watch on Chatfield.'

'Who will you use?'

Paula allowed herself a slight smile. 'Digby has been wanting an assignment at this level for some time. It's only fair I give him the opportunity.'

'He is fully qualified, and has the necessary experience.'

She laughed outright. 'That's a very tactful way of accusing me of nepotism.'

'He is four generations removed.'

'But still my descendant. After all, who else is crazy enough to do this kind of work?'

'I find him highly capable.'

'He's too young, and too eager. But if anything is going to cure that, it'll be this assignment. I'll call him.'

Marius was half a kilometre away when Paula's taxi capsule left Chatfield's house. He found the Investigator's presence at this exact time to be unnerving. It meant she was making a lot of connections he'd assumed would stay hidden, at least until it was too late. When her capsule had left the city greenways he walked unhurriedly to Chatfield's house. That approach at least would eliminate some observation protocols which he knew would be enacted following her visit. In confirmation, his u-shadow informed him of extremely sophisticated scrutineers slipping into the local cybersphere nodes.

For a moment he considered simply abandoning Chatfield. But advancing to the next stage was an acceptable risk. If Paula Myo had any real understanding of the Accelerator strategy she would have taken Chatfield into custody. So he sent his u-shadow into the homes of Chatfield's neighbours, and examined various files, siphoning out inconsequential personal details and preferences. As he walked down the greenway the data was absorbed by his biononics, enabling them to change his appearance and electronic emissions. His shimmering toga suit transformed to a bland swaddle of amethyst cloth, with ginger boots just visible below the shifting folds. Confident in his amalgamated persona he crossed the shaggy front lawn and triggered the house sensors.

Chatfield showed no surprise when he opened his glossy front door to someone who resembled Fardel from four houses down, even though the man wore Jalliete's style of clothing. It was the green eyes which gave him away. 'You saw Myo leave?' Chatfield asked as they went into the living room where they were surrounded by a privacy shield.

'Yes.'

'They've discovered Troblum was on the *Poix*.'

'Shit. I will take a great deal of pleasure ridding this universe of that failed embarrassment of a Higher. Does Myo know why he was there?'

'No. I threw her the line about him focusing on the Anomine factory.'

'Good. That ties nicely into his obsession with the planet-shifting ftl. It might divert them for a while.'

'I'll be under observation.' He looked straight at Marius. 'Are you here to bodyloss me?'

'No. We're moving to the next stage a little early. That should remove you from their view for a while, and when you do reappear it won't matter.'

'I see.' Chatfield gave the bulbous wooden room a regretful stare. 'I'll miss this. Ganthia has been an enjoyable place to live. Its politics are quite progressive in some respects.'

'Irrelevant now. I have a ship waiting at the spaceport. Go directly to our Frost station and collect your equipment.'

'Understood. And then on to Ellezelin?'

'Yes, but stand off until I authorize your landing. Living Dream is expecting you to join the Pilgrimage, but I don't want you there early. Even if our policy is successful, there may be rogue ANA agents left over who could cause trouble.'

'Like Myo?'

'Among others. We have contingencies, don't worry.'

'I'll leave right away.'

*

Babuyan Atoll was undergoing an approximation of night. The dome's internal illumination was off, but the crystal remained perfectly transparent. Icalanise's jaundiced crescent was rising above the lip of the parkland to shine a jaded light across the forests and towers. Admiral Kazimir saw it through his office window as he made some niggling final adjustments to his dress uniform. Over on Aldaho, the Senate Executive Security Commission was convening for an emergency session, where he was due to present the really bad news about the Ocisen Empire's new allies. It was looking like the deterrent fleet would have to be used, a prospect which both thrilled and horrified him in equal amounts. For nearly seven hundred years the mere threat of its existence had been enough to deter the more belligerent species in the galaxy from any aggression against the Commonwealth. Now the bluff was going to be called, and those who thought it was a bluff were about to get a very nasty surprise.

The silver collar on his tunic was lopsided. Kazimir grimaced at it in the mirror, and tried to fiddle the awkward fabric back into shape. In seven hundred years, he'd never used semi-organic fabrics for his uniform, and wasn't about to start now.

His u-shadow told him Paula Myo was calling from Ganthia. 'Good news?' he asked.

'Not even close,' she said. 'I've uncovered evidence that suggest the Navy has been manipulated.'

Kazimir listened with growing anger as she explained her suspicions about Chatfield and his secondary persona, Evanston. When she'd finished he called ANA:Governance.

'This cannot stand,' he said 'The Accelerators have committed treason.'

'Circumstantial evidence,' ANA:Governance replied. 'We don't know for sure.'

'They have worked up this whole Pilgrimage situation right from the start.'

'Pilgrimage was inevitable from the moment Inigo dreamed his first dream,' Paula said. 'If they are behind the Prime Ocisen alliance then it is an arrangement that goes back decades. Evanston was assigned to the Elan system thirty years ago.'

'And whatever Troblum worked on was twenty years before that,' Kazimir acknowledged.

'I'd suggest this idea of Fusion was concocted when Inigo abandoned Living Dream,' Paula said. 'They saw a method of fast forwarding to post-physical status and immediately set about enacting it.'

'Very likely,' Kazimir said. 'They don't call themselves Accelerators for nothing. The question is, what do we do about it? Can't you simply suspend them?'

'Any intervention would have to be universal,' ANA: Governance said. 'At present I do not have sufficient grounds.'

'But you *know*.'

'I very strongly suspect. To act on suspicion alone is persecution. I believe the human race is past such barbarism now, isn't it?'

'Let's try this tack,' Paula said. 'What can they possibly hope to achieve by the Prime Ocisen alliance?'

'It's a distraction,' Kazimir said.

'No,' Paula said. 'It has to be more than that. They know it will divert a degree of attention to the invasion fleet, but they also know that ANA and people like myself will continue to monitor the Pilgrimage preparations and investigate Troblum and Marius. No matter how many distractions, how many crises and alien invasions we face, we will not drop the ball when it comes to the Accelerator manifesto. Therefore, it has to be connected.'

'How?' Kazimir asked. 'For all the alliance is shocking, in military terms it is trivial. It doesn't physically threaten the Commonwealth, nor will it prevent Ethan's Pilgrimage from launching.'

'Are you so sure Chatfield is an Accelerator?' ANA: Governance asked. 'Your conclusion was drawn from a single answer. It would be more credible if he was a Custodian or even an Isolationist.'

'He's an Accelerator,' Paula said. 'It fits. So why would they want to engineer a threat to the Commonwealth, one that would be triggered by the Pilgrimage? One that isn't a simple diversion tactic?'

'The deterrence fleet,' Kazimir said bitterly. 'Without the Primes as part of the Empire's fleet, a squadron of Capital-class ships would be enough to take them out. But with the Primes we have to send the deterrence fleet.'

'They want to know what it is,' ANA:Governance said.

'Why?' Paula asked. 'What does knowing that get them? Is it a bluff?'

'No,' Kazimir said. 'It is not a bluff.'

'In all my time I have never met a Navy officer who served in the deterrence fleet,' Paula said. 'I've met hundreds serving on every other class of ship, but never that. And given the levels of government I interact with, I find that extremely odd.'

'You have met someone from the deterrence fleet,' Kazimir told her calmly. 'Me.'

'I was birthed to provide protection to the physical segment of the human race,' ANA:Governance said. 'I assure you the deterrence fleet is real, and is quite capable of achieving that level of physical defence, I should know. I built it.'

'In which case, the Accelerators must want to know what it's armed with,' Paula said. 'I assume it's something pretty potent.'

'Yes. Very.'

'All right, so they're expecting to analyse it, and use it – after all you wouldn't go to this much trouble if you don't have a need for it. But the timescale's not good here. Even if they did analyse it perfectly, they still have to build it. That will take time, and the Pilgrimage fleet is due to launch in a couple of months. Can they duplicate it in that time?'

'Extremely unlikely,' ANA:Governance said. 'It required my full abilities several years to fabricate. Admittedly my faculties have increased dramatically since then, but still it is not something which can be accomplished quickly.'

'Let's examine the extremes,' Paula said. 'Can the deterrence fleet weapon knock out the Void?'

'No.'

'But you're confident it can ward off just about everything else in the galaxy?'

'Yes.'

'In which case my guess would be that they intend to use it against the Raiel ships guarding the Void boundary. Justine barely managed to get through, and she had a head start on them, plus some help from the Void itself. As it stands, Ethan's ships wouldn't even make it to the Wall, let alone through the Gulf.'

'Damn,' Kazimir grunted. 'That has to be it. The idiots. Not enough to try to wreck the galaxy, they've got to start a war with the most powerful race in existence.'

'There is one factor which might work to our advantage,' Paula said.

'What?'

'The Primes.'

Centuries of experience had taught Kazimir never to be surprised at Paula's ideas. 'Go on.'

'They're not stupid. At least not the ones still living in the Commonwealth, which is the group the Accelerators have manipulated. A standard Prime immotile knows that if there is any possibility of them threatening us again, we will simply exterminate them.'

'Yes. Actually, given the new nature and developing psychology of the five surviving Prime civilizations, the Navy has downgraded their threat potential twice in the last thousand years.'

'So they're not going to risk triggering human retaliation. They are extremely unlikely to agree to cooperate with the Accelerator plan. However, we know that human personalities can operate within a Prime neural structure. I once met the Bose-motile. The integration was flawless, he functioned without any problem. That gives us our potential evidence.'

'What does?' Kazimir asked.

'They might be Prime bodies inside those warships, but I'll give you very good odds that they're animated by human thought routines. It would be a simple matter to snatch some motiles that have just come out of the birthing pond. At that stage their brains are completely empty, it's their immotiles which instil them with baseline thoughts and memories. So if you did snatch one at that stage, it would be a simple procedure to load in a human mind and memories instead, it's our basic re-life procedure but with an alien body. And there you have it, the core of a completely independent Prime hierarchy. The Ocisen Empire thinks they've found a genuine enemy of humanity to give their cause some particularly sharp teeth, while in fact they're being manipulated by the Accelerators just like everyone else.'

'So all we have to do is catch one and download its thoughts,' Kazimir said.

'Exactly. When you go to the Senate Commission, explain that you're going to give the Ocisen Empire fleet one last chance to turn round now you and they know Capital-class ships can defeat the Prime. Use the Capital-class to disable a Prime ship and board it.'

'If they are human driven Prime they'll suicide,' ANA: Governance said.

'Will that be sufficient evidence for you?' Paula asked.

'Not conclusively, no. I would have to be inserted into the inter-Prime communication network and analyse the thought-stream.'

'Attempt the Capital-class interception,' Paula said. 'It acts completely in our favour. If it works and we prove the Primes are just biological shells for the Accelerators, then you can suspend all Accelerator activities. If not, then Kazimir still has plenty of time to use the deterrent fleet before the Ocisens reach the Commonwealth, and as a bonus you delay Accelerator acquisition of the fleet weapons.'

'I agree that's a logical course of action,' Kazimir said.

'But?' Paula enquired.

'We didn't really know how powerful the warrior Raiel were until my mother flew past them in the Gulf. While, from what we can determine, this plan of the Accelerators has been in motion for at least fifty years.'

'We've known the Raiel had defence systems around the Wall stars since the day Wilson Kime discovered them back in 2560. It was inevitable that those Raiel would have adequate firepower to back up their mission. After all, they're the ones who once tried to invade the Void. That's not something you attempt with anything as pitiful as a novabomb. The Accelerators have always known they'll need serious firepower to reach the Void boundary.'

'Maybe,' Kazimir said reluctantly. 'There's just something about this that bothers me, and I can't define it.'

'If they don't want to see the deterrence fleet weapons in action, what else could they be using the Ocisen Empire fleet for?'

'I don't know,' he said. 'ANA?'

'Paula's scenario is the obvious one. An exceptionally large effort is being made to draw the deterrence fleet out to the Ocisen invasion forces. Primes are the one species which will still unite every political and cultural bloc within the Commonwealth. And I would point out that even if you're right, and the Primes are exposed as Accelerator agents, the Ocisens themselves will still keep coming.'

'Very well,' Kazimir finally got his collar straight. 'I'll ask the Senate Commission for permission to deploy the deterrent fleet, but only after we make one final attempt to warn them off.'

'Do let me know how Ilanthe responds to that,' Paula told him.

*

It was as humiliating as Honious, but Corrie-Lyn had to rely on Aaron as well as Inigo to make it across the hundred-metre gap between the remains of the ground crawler and the Navy starship. As well as her broken arm, her ankle was badly twisted and sprained, as she discovered when she tried to put any weight on it.

Aaron had simply knelt down on the rim of the ground crawler's bodywork that he'd sheared off with his disruptor pulse, and extended his arm. She'd reluctantly grasped it with her good hand, and allowed him to haul her up with no more effort than if he'd been lifting a bag of gromal puffs. It was only when he'd put her down that she gasped with pain and nearly collapsed back on to the ice. Aaron, of course, had caught her easily.

So she had to sling an arm around each of them, and let them take the weight as she hopped all the way over to the starship. Her body was shivering violently from the terrible cold. Huge flashes of lightning ripped overhead, their muted thunder rolling round the little bubble of calm which the starship's force field had cast over them. Even without any enriched sensors she could see the craft had taken a terrible beating. The fuselage actually had splits in it, and fluids were seeping out of various valves and exposed pipes.

The ground shook violently, and all three of them went tumbling down.

'Move,' Aaron snapped. His integral force field strengthened, surrounding him in a mild blue haze.

Corrie-Lyn was slightly disconcerted to see Inigo had also protected himself the same way. Then the pair of them picked her up and started jogging over the last twenty metres with her hanging ignominiously between them. While they were doing that she started to pay attention to the red symbols appearing in her exovision. She was receiving a very unhealthy dose of radiation from the atmosphere trapped under the force field.

It *was* a Navy ship, she could see the name *CNE Lindau* on the fuselage. But the crew weren't responding to her desperate pings. She wondered what kind of cover story Aaron could possibly have spun them. Somehow she never thought to ask herself how he could have survived the glacier. It was sort of inevitable.

They hurried up the ramp and into the airlock. The outer hull was already flowing closed as they crossed the threshold. Another quake made the starship tremble. Then there was the unmistakable whine of power feeding into the drive, and they lifted from the surface. The floor immediately shuddered badly, and the decking shifted out of horizontal alignment. It juddered its way back level as the unnerving sounds of equipment straining at its safety margins set her teeth on edge.

The airlock's inner door unfurled as her weight began to build up.

'Hold her,' Aaron instructed curtly as he let go of Corrie-Lyn's arm and lurched his way into the ship against the rapidly increasing acceleration.

Inigo quickly lowered her on to the floor of the short corridor. 'Don't move your neck,' he said urgently. 'Keep your spine level. I don't know how bad this is going to get.' The decking seemed to be made from a grey plyplastic. It wasn't comfortable, but with the gee force approaching five she was grateful to be lying prone. Medical symbols warned her what the acceleration was doing to her broken arm, which might have accounted for her mounting nausea.

'What's happening?' she grunted to Inigo. 'Where's the crew?' Her body was still shivering from the icy air outside.

He kept his head steady as he replied. 'We're going straight up to get out of the atmosphere as fast as possible. I don't know about the crew.' His gaiafield emission was tinged with worry.

'I can't access the ship's net.'

'Me neither.'

After a couple of minutes the acceleration suddenly sunk back to a stable one gee. Inigo lifted himself to a sitting position. Worry was still leaking out of his gaiamotes.

Corrie-Lyn winced as she slowly sat up. Her ankle was throbbing, and the medication she'd taken for her arm was doing strange things to her vision. Or maybe it was just her balance that made her feel weirdly light. Or perhaps the ship's drives were acting oddly. Something in the air smelt funny. She hiccuped, hoping it wasn't a precursor to being sick. For some reason the situation didn't bother her as much as she knew it ought. The crew, though. That was bad. She knew it at a deep instinctive level. Didn't want to consciously examine the obvious. *Too much. Way too much all at once.*

'We're still alive then,' she said with a sigh.

Inigo gave her a troubled glance. 'Yes.' He clambered to his feet. One of the light strips on the ceiling was flickering. Its case had cracks. He frowned at that. 'My field scan is revealing a lot of damage in the structure around us. Uh, I can't find the crew on board.'

'What do you mean?'

A thick plyplastic door curtained open, and Aaron stepped out into the corridor. His gaiamotes were closed, but even in her medicated state Corrie-Lyn didn't need them to tell how angry he was. He glared at Inigo. 'Don't you ever pull a stunt like that glacier again.'

Inigo gave him a disdainful glance. 'Almost got you, though, didn't it? And me a simple amateur.'

Aaron produced a tight smile. Took a step forward.

Corrie-Lyn screamed at the pain as his foot came down on her ankle.

Inigo lunged forward, hitting Aaron with a rugby-style tackle. It barely moved him. For emphasis, Aaron held the position for another few seconds before slowly and deliberately taking his foot off and stepping back.

Corrie-Lyn whimpered, and gripped her ankle where the hot pain was still firing into her flesh. There were tears in her eyes. 'Don't,' she whispered fearfully.

'The medical chamber is in the main cabin,' Aaron said, and held his hand out.

'Where's the crew?' she asked.

'They stepped out for a moment.' Aaron paused, thinking. 'They might be some time.'

Corrie-Lyn ignored his hand. Inigo helped her up. They hobbled after Aaron through the door into the main cabin.

'Oh Lady!' Corrie-Lyn's free hand came up to cup her mouth. She really felt the bile rising in her gullet at the sight which greeted her.

The starship's main cabin was a circular room about seven metres across. Several items of furniture were extruded from the plyplastic walls and floor. Some had twisted and locked into strange shapes. A lot of the equipment modules sunk flush with the walls were damaged. Most had suffered some kind of physical impact, leaving their casings buckled and broken. Others were melted along with the wall around them, leaving soot marks scarring the ceiling. That wasn't what drew her eye. There was blood on the floor. Big puddles of the grisly fluid that had been sloshing around in the starship's erratic acceleration. Now it was congealing. There was blood on the walls; broad splash patterns radiating out from the burn scars. There was blood on the ceiling in long splatter trails.

'Monster!' she groaned though clenched teeth.

'Let's get one thing quite clear,' Aaron said as he ordered the smartcore to activate the one surviving medical cabinet. 'I am not a good man. I am not a bad man. I am simply a man with a job to do. I will complete that job. Nothing must prevent that. Nothing.'

Corrie-Lyn gave Inigo a broken look. She could see how scared he was; an expression she'd never seen on his face before. Not Inigo. Not the man who was going to lead them all to a chance at a beautiful life.

'What job?' Inigo asked, with considerable dignity.

A small muscle flexed in Aaron's jaw. 'I apologize. I'm not sure.'

'Not sure!'

Aaron gave Corrie-Lyn a modest shrug. 'You know how it is.'

'He's not a man,' she growled out. 'He's a biological killing machine. And he's so pitiful he doesn't even know why.'

'So there you have it,' Aaron said. He looked over at the medical cabinet which had rolled out of the wall. It did have a scorch mark on its silver casing, but the malmetal lid split open, and the management system reported full functionality even if some systems were running on back-up.

'I'm not getting in that,' Corrie-Lyn yelped.

'You are,' Aaron said. 'One way or another. Of course, Inigo's u-shadow will have complete control of your treatment. But I need you intact and healthy. As well as your physical injuries, you picked up a bad dose of radiation back there.'

She glanced at Inigo, who shrugged.

'You need her healthy?' Inigo said. 'Why?'

'She's my leverage,' Aaron said bluntly. 'She guarantees your good behaviour.'

'Shoot me,' Corrie-Lyn implored Inigo. 'Use your biononics like a weapon again. Please. He can't be allowed to succeed.'

Inigo stared at her for a long moment. He bowed his head.

'Now we have that out of the way, please get in,' Aaron said with a polite gesture at the medical cabinet.

Corrie-Lyn limped over to it and sat on the edge. Inigo helped her to remove her clothes, then eased her back. The lid slid over her. She was sobbing as she lost consciousness.

According to Corrie-Lyn's secondary thought routines, the medical cabinet took four hours to reset and bind her arm in a toughened dermal layer, de-stress the bad sprain around her ankle, and decontaminate her skin and blood. Inigo had also got it to issue some kind of anti-depressant sedative. She lay there in the warm dry darkness for several minutes after she woke, reluctant to get out and see how much worse their lives had become. Eventually, she sighed and told her u-shadow to open the lid.

Inigo was there, leaning over with his face showing a gentle concern.

'How do you feel?' he asked.

'Like the Waterwalker on top of the mountain after Salrana's death.'

Inigo stroked her hair tenderly. 'Nothing we face is ever going to be that bad.'

'Ha,' she said indignantly. 'That bastard's not human, although he's got the psychopath trait nailed pretty good.' She sat up to see Aaron on the other side of the cabin, smiling modestly. 'Are your dreams still punishing you?' she growled at him as she crossed her arms over her bare breasts. 'Hope so. One day you'll drown in all that shit sloshing round in your head.'

'Well, well, it is true,' Aaron grinned. 'You can take the girl out of Sampalok, but you can't take Sampalok out of the girl.'

'What the crap do you know about the Waterwalker's life you subsentient biobot fuckhead.'

'Welcome back, Corrie-Lyn. This party just wouldn't be the same without you.'

Inigo handed her a robe that was several sizes too big. Corrie-Lyn wrapped herself in it with angry motions, then swung her feet out of the cabinet. She drew back abruptly, remembering what had been on the floor as she went in.

The blood had gone. She gave the cabin a careful examination. Apart from the bent equipment and misshapen furniture, it was relatively clean.

'Some of the servicebots still work,' Inigo said, 'I've had them cleaning things up.'

'Huh,' she grunted and climbed out. 'So, going to start threatening me?'

Aaron scratched behind his ear. 'No.'

'Why not? I thought you said I was your leverage. Go ahead, get your kicks slicing bits off. I won't disappoint. I promise I'll scream lots.' The bravado was making her legs shake.

'Damn, and you think my brain's damaged.'

'Fuck you.'

Aaron gave Inigo a genuinely curious look. 'Whatever did you two have back in the day?'

'Love.' Inigo's arm went round her shoulder. 'I doubt that's in your memories.'

'No. I have to admit it ain't dinging any bells. But I understand the principles. And who knows, if I eat my greens and stay out of trouble maybe I'll find a nice girl who'll like me for what I am. Just like this one does you.'

Corrie-Lyn took a step forward, her hand bunching into a fist. Inigo pulled her back. 'Will you two behave yourselves? And you, this is hardly professional.'

'I know,' Aaron said. 'Truce?'

'If I ever get the chance to slit your throat while you're sleeping, I promise I'll cut long and deep.'

Even Inigo gave her a strange look at that. She remained unrepentant.

'I did save your lives back there,' Aaron said in a mildly injured tone.

'We were only in that much trouble because of you.'

'Really? Think on this. The people following us to find Inigo wanted him dead, very badly dead. They would have found him eventually. Thanks to you and me teaming up, we got here first.'

'And who is left alive on Hanko to thank you for that?'

'All right, enough,' Inigo said, squeezing her arm. 'We are still alive, for which I acknowledge our debt. But you have to admit, having you come for me as part of some Faction's ideological wish-fulfilment isn't great for me.'

'I don't know what's in store for you,' Aaron said. 'But how bad can it be?'

Inigo said nothing. Corrie-Lyn was disconcerted by the way his gaiamotes had closed off again, isolating his emotions. She was so used to sharing her every feeling with him. *Seventy years ago.*

'So who are you taking me to?' Inigo asked.

Aaron had the grace to look uncomfortable.

'He doesn't know,' Corrie-Lyn said.

'Can I at least ask where we're going?'

'Well,' Aaron drawled, 'I have to admit I'm not too sure any more.'

'What?'

'You said you always know what to do next,' Corrie-Lyn protested. 'Your brain is like an old flow chart. Finish one task and the next flips up. Well now you've got the Dreamer, you have to know where to take him.'

'It's kinda like this: under ordinary circumstances I'd know exactly what to do next.'

'*Ordinary* circumstances?'

'We're on a Navy ship. A, uh, borrowed Navy ship.'

'And you've broken it,' Inigo said laconically.

'Broken it?' she asked in alarm. The prospect of the rest of her life, however long or short, condemned to the confines of this ship with the ultimate nut-job Aaron wasn't a comforting thought.

'I had to fly some rather extreme manoeuvres to locate you,' Aaron explained. 'Let's just say I kinda screwed the warranty. On

561

the plus side, there's a lot of redundancy, and a big inventory of spare parts. The smartcore has drawn up a repair schedule, and the bots are hard at it.'

'Wait,' Corrie-Lyn said. 'Where are we now?' She'd assumed that after four hours they'd be far outside the Hanko system.

'A million kilometres from Hanko,' Aaron said. 'And waiting.'

'For what?'

'Here's the deal: this is a Navy ship, so they build them tough; we can go ftl in our current state, but I haven't got me a huge urge to do that right now. The bots need some time to get us back up to a minimum function level. Now the way my instinct's pushing it, I don't mind waiting. When we are back up to a halfway decent degree of flight readiness, I'll know what to do.'

Inigo blinked in astonishment. 'Is it always like this?'

Corrie-Lyn sighed. 'Yes. 'Fraid so.'

There was food on board. The crew each had their own little store of specialty items they just couldn't live without. So Corrie-Lyn and Inigo got to open packets of hot orange chocolate drink made on Luranda, with marshmallows from Epual. The packets were self-heating, which was just as well; the culinary unit was one of the casualties the bots were working on. And half of their basic nutrient liquid had squirted out of a ruptured tank.

The cabin furniture was a long way down the priority list for repairs, so they wriggled themselves into the strange lumpy curves as comfortably as possible and sipped from metal mugs. Aaron was with them some of the time. He often left to inspect what was being done in various parts of the ship.

After another argument, Corrie-Lyn got him to open up the ship's net with some heavy access restrictions in place. At least it meant she and Inigo were allowed to review the sensor images.

Hanko was a silver crescent set against an unusually barren starfield. The *Lindau*'s remaining sensors overlaid the visual image with a host of gravitational data. They could actually watch the mass distribution altering as the Hawking m-sink ate the world from within. Great looping gravity waves expanded and contracted around the planet, juddering with the rhythm of a dying heart. Their motions became more erratic as the process began to accelerate towards its terrible ending. The magma core was now being absorbed at a phenomenal rate by the inflating event horizon. Tectonic plates shifted and shattered as the mantle adjusted to internal pressures that changed by the minute. The ice that had grasped every ocean for the last thousand years broke apart into vast crumbling sea-sized bergs that started to skid across the buckling land and collapsing mountain ranges.

Aaron returned to the cabin. 'It's about to go critical,' he announced solemnly.

As he spoke, the brilliant white storm clouds began to glow with a tangerine hue, filling the crescent out to a perfect sphere of amber light. Its intensity rose swiftly, and the atmosphere started to expand. Massive hurricanes geysered up above the ionosphere, twirling off into space as the gases burned with nuclear heat.

'*Wish it well, wish it gone,*' Aaron sang in a low whisper.

Below the shredded atmosphere, the mantle detonated. Continent-sized rock segments punched outwards amid tattered oceans of superheated lava.

'*The splendour of death, once known, loved beyond reason. Evolution's eternal shore, free at last to wash up what you will.*'

Untied from the constraints of the semi-solid shell, the true light of the runaway m-sink implosion shone out far brighter than the nearby star. Its spectrum chased through a delicate pink to pure white, then accelerated into blue-white as its radiation efflux poured out vast quantities of gamma waves. The event horizon consumed the last of the planet's core. Only the light remained, growing ever brighter as its heart shrank faster and faster.

'*Out of twinkling stardust all came, into dark matter all will fall. Death mocks us as we laugh defiance at entropy, yet ignorance birthed mortals sail forth upon time's cruel sea.*'

The *Lindau* began to accelerate at an easy two gees, keeping far ahead of the rock fragments and darkening seas of magma that spewed out from the dazzling implosion nucleus.

'I don't recognize the verse,' Inigo said.

Aaron shook himself out of a mild daze to frown at him. 'What verse?'

Corrie-Lyn rolled her eyes, and poured a shot of hundred-year-old rum into the remains of her hot chocolate. She'd found the bottle of St Lisamne's finest in one of the crew cabins, and immediately appropriated it. 'Never mind. Has your crappy brain come up with anything yet?'

'I'm considering options. I'm most worried that the Navy knew we were here.'

'How do you know that?' Inigo asked.

'The information was in the captain's brain. Admiral Kazimir himself told him about you and me.'

Corrie-Lyn shuddered and poured some more rum. The chocolate was all gone now. 'In his brain! So they'll come looking when this ship doesn't report in.'

'I suspect they're already on their way and, given the captain reported the use of an m-sink, it will be considerably more than a simple scout ship that pops out of hyperspace.'

'So will you suicide or surrender?'

'Neither. We have about three more hours until primary systems repairs reach an adequate level. The rest can be performed while we're underway, but the drive and power systems must be made reliable first.'

'That sounds like you know where we're going.'

'I'm considering options that are opening up.'

'Opening up,' an intrigued Inigo said. 'Do you mean logically, or are these possibilities inside your own head that are being revealed by your employer?'

Aaron scratched behind his ear, clearly made uncomfortable by the whole process. 'The options, I guess, are implanted information. Which one I choose is down to me based on the situation on the ground. After all, it's that kind of expertise which bought me the job.'

'Do any of these options tell you what is to become of me?'

'It's not like that. You're not relevant to me personally; you're just the package I'm assigned to deliver.'

'You know, as well as my day job as the Dreamer, I am an accomplished analyst. If you were to open yourself fully to the gaiafield I might be able to uncover the pathways of these foreign memories.'

'Why would I want you to do that?'

'So that you know who you are. Where the real you begins and the artificial motivations end.'

'Suppose they're not artificial motivations? Suppose this is what I am, what I've always been?'

'You suffer too much for that to be true. Your dreams trouble you. I knew that even before Corrie-Lyn told me.'

'And yet I'm alive, and you're in my custody. I think we'll settle for that level of functionality for now.'

'As you wish. Can you at least tell us of the options that have been revealed?'

'I don't know much in advance. That way, if I'm captured I can't reveal anything to my opponents.'

'You just said we were in your custody.'

'I have to consider the infinitely small probability you might escape. I can't have you knowing what I know, that would give you a mighty large tactical advantage, my friend.'

'Oh, dear Lady,' Corrie-Lyn groaned, and took a swig straight from the bottle. She ordered her u-shadow to resume the feed from the external sensors.

The new intense star that had been Hanko began to diminish within an hour of its inception. It was an insatiable consumer of mass, quick to devour the remnants of the planet that hadn't reached escape velocity during the implosion rupture. Solid splinters were quick to fall prey to its incredible gravity, flashing to ruin as they passed through the event horizon. Then its gravity reached out further, to the solidifying torrents of magma, pulling them back. After that there were only the thick streamers of gas and dust that were splayed out. Their tides began to turn, grasping at the loose irradiated particles and hauling them down the steepening gravity gradient to extinction.

A mere three hours after it shone brighter than its primary, Hanko was reduced to a tiny glowing ember surrounded by whirlpool veils of lavender fog that were slowly constricting.

'It consumes everything around it in order to burn,' Aaron said. 'Yet, in the end, entropy will always emerge victorious, snuffing out the very last glimmer of heat and light. After that there is only darkness. When that state is reached even eternity will cease to exist, for one moment will be like every other and nothingness will claim the universe.' He turned to Inigo. 'Sound familiar?'

'Nothingness is a long way off,' Inigo said. 'Not even the post-physicals will be around to witness that. It certainly doesn't worry me.'

'And yet it's your Void which will accelerate the process. Without the mass of this galaxy, the universe moves noticeably closer to the end of time and space.'

'Your employers want me to stop the Pilgrimage.'

Aaron gave a bemused shrug. 'I have no idea what they want. I'm just observing the symbology here.'

Corrie-Lyn stirred herself. After the St Lisamne rum, she'd polished off a couple of bottles of wine hoarded by another crewman. Then there was the JK raspberry vodka. It annoyed her there wasn't a working fridge, the JK should have been drunk chilled to arctic levels. 'You care though,' she slurred. 'That's a start. Your conditioning is beginning to unravel. Maybe we'll get to meet the real Aaron sooner than your boss would like.'

'You're already looking at him. Sorry.' Aaron sent an order to the smartcore, and the *Lindau* went ftl.

'So what have you decided?' Inigo asked.

'The Navy knows that I was hunting you, and if they don't know I survived Hanko they'll find out soon enough. We're both being hunted by whoever flew the ship that fired the Hawking m-sink. I was supposed to be in the *Artful Dodger*, which should have given me a big edge, but that's gone. However, there's an emergency replacement ship waiting for me on Pulap. The bad news is that if we turn up anywhere in the *Lindau*, everybody and their mother will know about it. I can't risk that, I can't expose you to the possibility of capture or termination.'

'You're stuffed then,' Corrie-Lyn sniggered. 'Shame about that.'

'Not quite. There is something that took a long time to emerge, a real last resort.'

'Which is?' Inigo asked.

'I'm taking you to the Spike.'

'The alien macro-habitat? That's seven thousand lightyears away. It'll take weeks. What in Honious is there?'

Aaron wrinkled up his brow as if listening to some distant voice. Even he seemed surprised by what it was saying: 'Ozzie. Ozzie lives in the Spike.'

*

Paula watched the padded plyplastic fold protectively around her piano with a mild sense of regret. There was no point in trying to play. Following the conference with Kazimir and ANA she just couldn't lose herself in music like she normally did. Kazimir's doubt about the Accelerator's motivation was troubling her. Logically, the outline she'd proposed was flawless. The Accelerators needed the deterrent fleet weapons to blast the Raiel out of the way.

As she'd thought earlier: what else could the whole Prime scheme be? And that nasty little phrase had begun to haunt her. *What else?* For the Accelerators to risk internal ANA suspension by manipulating the Ocisens and Primes was a phenomenal gamble. One that always had a good chance of exposure. To her mind it was too much of a gamble for anything astute as an ANA Faction. For all she rejected half of their ideologies, they weren't stupid. Which left her with the uncomfortable question of what else they could hope to gain by forcing deployment of the deterrent fleet.

In a classic diversion tactic, the fleet would rush off to

intercept the Ocisens, leaving the rest of the Commonwealth exposed. She couldn't think what the nature of that exposure could be.

It can't be a physical attack. They need the Pilgrimage ships to be complete and launch, they also need ANA to carry on, after all they're part of it.

So, what, then?

If it was nothing other than a crude attempt to analyse the deterrence fleet weapons they were going to fail. And failure now would mean the end of them and their goals. ANA:Governance had only ever used the suspension sanction once before, during the Evolutionary Secessionist rebellion five hundred years ago, which had seen the Secessionists trying to literally split ANA so they might assume control of a section and go post-physical.

There has to be something I'm missing.

The one big hole in her information was the nature of the deterrence fleet. Which was the one thing ANA:Governance would never explain to her. For all she was a valued agent, even she acknowledged that information could never be allowed to leak out, which it might well do if she was ever captured. A small chance, but if it was the Cat after her, a realistic chance. And if not the Cat, there were others who would enjoy seeing her removed from physical existence. There probably always would be. *All part of the job.* After fourteen hundred years you just grew to live with the prospect no matter what your psychology was.

The smartcore told her the *Alexis Denken* was fifteen minutes out from Kerensk. And Gore was making a call.

'Justine's still all right then,' Paula said. 'That's good news.'

'Yes. But that little shit Ethan must be laughing his fucking head off that the Skylord wouldn't help her.'

'It won't help her *now*. But let's face it, if any of us are close to maturity it's going to be Justine.'

'Yeah, maybe.'

'I didn't realize time was that fast inside the Void.'

'Nobody did. Although I suspect the flow rate might be localized. We don't know enough about its fabric yet, but that would certainly explain the Skylord's acceleration. It wasn't physically fast, it operated a different timeflow.'

'What do you think happened on Querencia since the Water-walker's death? The Skylord said there's nobody left now.'

'Who gives a shit? I have some information for you. Do you know who left Ganthia two hours after you did?'

'Yes, an Accelerator agent we're interested in. He's got an ultradrive ship, but its stealth isn't perfect, or at least ANA's sensors are better. Don't worry, Digby has him under surveillance.'

'Keeping it in the family, huh? Good for you. But I wasn't taking about Chatfield.'

Paula sighed. There were times when she was very annoyed with ANA for the leeway it granted Gore Burnelli. 'Who then?'

'Marius.'

After fourteen hundred years, an unexpected turn in a case no longer surprised her, but she was very interested. 'And how do you know that?'

'A friend of a friend saw him at the starport.'

She laughed. 'You mean the Conservative Faction is still eager to screw the Accelerators.'

'Screw them into the ground and dance on the pieces, actually. Does that information help?'

'It's not helpful for them, but it does confirm my assumption that Chatfield is an Accelerator representative.' Her u-shadow reported that it couldn't track the origin of Gore's call. There were *very* few people who could manipulate the unisphere to that extent. *And why would he hide that anyway? Unless . . . No! Surely not.*

'I have something else which may be of use for you,' Gore said.

'What's that?'

'Troblum.'

'You know where he is?'

'No, sorry, not that, but I do know what he's been up to.'

'Oh really? Your Delivery Man shut down our one avenue of

investigation. I'll get round to arresting him one day, you know. Using an m-sink on a Central world is not amusing.'

'Consider this my olive branch. We were scared by what Troblum was doing.'

'Which was?'

'Building an ftl drive big enough to move a planet.'

'Jesus! You're kidding.'

'Wish I was. The good news is that he wasn't doing it for the Accelerators – at least not as far as we can determine. This seems to be some mad personal obsession.'

'That fits. He has a semi-plausible theory on how the Anomine acquired Dark Fortress technology. One way is that they simply stole or borrowed them from the warrior Raiel.'

'Yeah? Anyway . . . he succeeded in building one.'

'Now you are kidding me.'

'No. That's why the Delivery Man was authorized to cover it up. We were concerned when we thought it was part of the Accelerator plan, but now we don't believe it is.'

'So why tell me this now?'

'Troblum is a very strange man. And now he's loose in the universe with an ftl drive that might be able to move a planet. He's also trying to make contact with you to tell you something about the Accelerators. They don't like that.'

'Ah, I get it: the wild card.'

'Damn right.'

'And that worries you?'

'It should worry you, too. Events are becoming unstable enough as it is. We don't need people like Troblum fucking things up even more.'

'And yet he might have the evidence ANA:Governance needs to suspend the Accelerators.'

'Could be. Who knows?'

'So what do you want me to do?'

'Stick him up at the top of your priority list. He needs to be found.'

'After what happened on Sholapur I expect he's halfway to Andromeda by now.'

'We can't take the risk. You must not allow the Accelerators to find him again.'

'Don't try to tell me my job,' she told him curtly.

'Wouldn't dream of it. Just making information available like a good citizen.'

'So what are you up to right now? I heard you didn't show up for the ExoProtectorate meeting.'

'I thought now was a good time to take a sabbatical. But don't worry, I'm still sticking my hand in.'

'Stick it in too deep and I'll break it off. You know you don't have half the special privileges you think you do, not as far as I'm concerned.'

'Pleasure doing business with you, Paula. As always.' The call ended.

Paula sat back on the couch. After a while she began to grin.

*

The Wurung Transport cab rattled along Colwyn City's ageing public rails all day long. Araminta sat on the wide front seat with the wrap-around bubble window switched to one-way, watching a city in torment. The Ellezelin capsules zoomed low over the buildings, an unending reminder of their presence and power. Desperation was sinking in now, replacing the previous sullen resentment which had claimed the city. The Senate delegation had been on the ground for six hours before Cleric Phelim even agreed to see them. Crowds around the docks were treated badly by the paramilitaries as they shouted their demands to be heard by the Senators. Flights by ambulance capsules were still forbidden; cabs and trike pods were kept busy carrying the injured to city hospitals. By mid-afternoon numbers were thinning out around the docks. Other disturbance areas were growing.

Laril had switched on the cab's unisphere node as he promised. It responded to simple voice instructions, which was proving incredibly useful. Almost the first thing she saw was a unisphere report on Justine's encounter with the Skylord. The dream had been released into the gaiafield a few hours ago, the show said, and they'd transferred the images over. A lot of smart commentators were busy providing their interpretation, as was a Living Dream Councillor called DeLouis, who seemed repellently excited by the Skylord's refusal to take Justine to the nucleus. Araminta watched for a while until she realized that no one really knew anything, then switched to local news. The tiny portal projected scenes captured by reporters all across town.

One thing kept happening over and over again. It was random, and inexplicable to the news shows. Ellezelin capsules pounced out of the sky to snatch women by force. There was no discoverable connection between the women as far as anyone could make out, and some very sophisticated semi-sentient scrutineers were employed to that effect. The Ellezelin troopers who performed the seizures were extremely determined, and didn't care how much peripheral damage was committed to achieve their objective. The images helped stir a lot of the outrage people were feeling. The minority of residents who had valiantly gone to work as normal were heading for home by mid-afternoon. Almost no one on late shifts turned up. A siege mentality was growing. Homes were double locked and alarmed.

Araminta only had to see the first three atrocious snatches to work out the link between the poor hapless women. They looked like her.

'Sweet Ozzie,' she groaned as the third was dragged away in the middle of a street in Espensten district, her two young children screaming at the horror of Mummy being forcefully taken from them.

Condemnation from across the Commonwealth reached a crescendo with that one. It didn't affect the behaviour of the paramilitaries.

Her feeling of depression grew as she saw her homeworld suffer because of her; a feeling not helped by the way the Skylord had rejected Justine. Araminta was furious about that. After all she'd risked contacting the Skylord and getting Justine into the Void, the effort had come to nothing. Justine hadn't even got to the Heart. There would be no negotiation now, no explaining to whatever controlled the Void the damage it was causing.

There was nothing Araminta could do about that, or anything, actually – short of surrendering, which was one very swift answer to everything. Instead she did what Laril advised, and delved into the gaiafield, losing herself amid the emotional outpourings and whispered messages of enticement and spectacular memories divulged by the confluence nests. There were levels, or layers, or perhaps she was too rigid in applying such labels; there were certainly different aspects to the emotive universe which she could immerse herself in.

The dreams, of course, were the primary foundation of the gaiafield. Inigo's dreams and the countless billions of others given to the confluence nests by their creators, all identifiable by their unique emotional appellation. Any one of which would rise into her consciousness to the summons of a matching mood or image; exactly the way memories inside her own head worked – simple association. Although Inigo's dreams all seemed to have strong tags and were the easiest of all to acquire.

So, as the cab trundled onwards steered by Laril's dodgy software, Araminta bowed to the inevitable and lived through Inigo's first few dreams, only finally to shake herself free hours later, smiling exuberantly as young Edeard walked across Birmingham Pool to defeat Arminel. She felt like letting out a cheer inside the cab. Makkathran was such a delight, with its strange architecture and peculiar genistars, populated by rich and pompous lords and ladies out of some incredibly ancient text. She wondered if Edeard would wind up marrying Kanseen or Salrana; either would be a lovely romantic outcome. And she knew for sure it all had some kind of ridiculously happy ending, not that she'd ever want to live in such a backward culture.

Outside Inigo's dreams of Edeard were the voices carried on winds of pure emotion: the everyday emissions of her fellow Colwyn City residents. The gaiafield was a bleak state indeed beyond the cab, worry and fear from the majority almost drowning out the fervent hopes of the Living Dream adherents that their Second Dreamer was truly close at hand.

Perhaps it was because her Silfen heritage delivered her into the gaiafield rather than gaiamotes like everyone else, but this whole strange universe of memory and raw emotions seemed remarkably clear to her. She was able to rise above the emotional clamour to study the composition of this strange cosmos in a calm and objective fashion. By doing that rather than simply plunging in regardless, she was aware of what her mind interpreted as little neutral zones. Slivers of nothingness anchored throughout the babble. Strangest of all was the way they really did appeal to her; their outer layers reverberated to an emotional state that was almost identical to her own. That mental siren song alone made her cautious. Holding them aloft in her mind she could feel the subliminal tethers to the confluence nests of the city.

Ozzie! Living Dream really is desperate to find me.

She carefully separated herself from the treacherous traps. Beyond that brash bright constellation of human thoughts was the ever-present serenity of the Silfen Motherholm.

'Do you know me?' she asked in trepidation.

The answer wasn't specific, not speech in human terms, more a warm feeling of acknowledgement and welcome.

'Can you help me?'

Sadness, not cold, it was regret rather than a rejection.

'I might make a real hash of things.'

The comforting warmth of a mother's embrace.

'I wish I had that much confidence in me. Do you have any idea what's at stake here?'

A glowing gold light bathing every cell of her body, as if an angel's smile had broken through Colwyn City's fug of misery.

'Oh for Ozzie's sake; all right, I'll ask it again.' And she reached beyond the Silfen Motherholm for the entity that lurked right on the edge of her perception. Carefully this time, avoiding the vigilant watchers, speaking softly within herself rather than the cry across thirty-thousand lightyears. A call which found her bathed in a luminescence similar to the Void's nebulas, relishing the smooth flow of the universe around her.

'Hello,' she said to the Skylord.

'I wait for you.'

'Was that you with my friend? The one who is inside your universe?'

'I have not guided one of your species for a long time.'

'Doesn't mean much,' Araminta muttered sourly. 'If I come to your universe, would you guide me to the nucleus?'

'I will.'

'Immediately?'

'Once you have reached fulfilment.'

'Ah. You just won't do it, will you? None of you will.'

'I am gladdened by your desire to reach the nucleus. I will guide you.'

'When our species first arrived in your universe, where did you guide them?'

'My kindred showed them where they might live and reach maturity.'

'So you will take people to planets, just not the nucleus? Interesting.'

'I will guide those who have reached fulfil—'

'Yeah, yeah, I get it.'

'Do you come?'

'Many of my species will try to reach you.'

'I await with joy.'

'By reaching you, they will slaughter billions of other people, trillions of lives will be lost as your universe destroys the galaxy. How do you feel about that?' She knew she was risking triggering another devourment phase, but she'd managed to calm it last time.

'Not all reach fulfilment. Your species grows strong. Few of your kind will be left to ascend into the fabric alone.'

'Do you even understand that there is a universe outside yours?'

'There is only here, the universe and the nucleus. You will emerge here somewhen.'

'Déjà vu,' she grunted. 'Okay, then,' she told the Skylord. 'Maybe I will.'

'I wait for you,' it said as she withdrew her consciousness. She hurriedly checked round outside the cab. Night was falling, the low sunlight diffused to a smear by the city's force field weather dome. She peered upwards urgently, but couldn't see any of the Ellezelin capsules swooping down on her, so presumably they hadn't overheard her conversation with the Skylord.

'Big deal,' she snorted to the inside of the cab. 'I can't stop the Void from taking us in. The bastards have just about won.'

Which left her with some decisions to make. She told the cab to swing past Bodant Park, using the rail on the marina side, away from her apartment block. It wasn't as foolhardy as it seemed. *Well, all right, maybe a little stupid.* But she wanted one last look at what she'd considered her first real home since – well, leaving Langham. It was becoming clear to her that she would have to get out somehow. The only way to stop Living Dream from using her was to get beyond their reach. That cut her options considerably. Cressida's offer of a starship ticket was clearly impossible, events of the last few days had made it obvious that even a diplomatic starship wasn't going to lift her away from Colwyn City. Thinking of that made her remember Cressida's claim of a Silfen path in Francola Wood. Now that was a definite possibility. But she was more confident that Laril might negotiate for her. He was part Higher now, he must know a reliable Faction, one that was opposed to the Pilgrimage. Everyone knew the Factions had agents with all sorts of enrichments; and Gore had said they were looking for her. If anyone could get her out of Colwyn City and away from Viotia it would be them.

That came hooked to the sheepish thought that if a Faction took care of her she wouldn't have to make the big decision herself.

Forget that. You just need to get out of here.

It was dark by the time the Wurung Transport cab slid along

Aeana Street, parallel to the Cairns. Strong white light shone through one side of the cab's bubble window, coming off the big deco marina buildings. She could hear the crowd now, that unnerving buzz of so many people sharing their anger.

The cab pulled into a marina slot and Araminta got out. She was surprised by how many people were in the park, it was in the thousands now. On this side they were milling around in loose groups; while over near her apartment block they'd concentrated into a dense knot, shouting abuse and clashing with the barrier set up along the road.

Araminta suddenly realized what the problem was. The cordon the paramilitaries had thrown up around her apartment block was acting as a huge provocation.

My fault. Again.

She walked forward into the crowd. The gaiafield was a storm of hatred and resentment. Her macrocellular clusters reported a colossal amount of pings zipping across the park. Directionless, without any author code, not routed through the cybersphere nodes and therefore untraceable.

'>file< Binder frequency at the second segment.'

'Counter that with a patch from Etol, they have the fixes.'

'Managed to hit one scumfuck with a maser pulse.'

'Cheer.' 'Cheer.' 'Cheer.' 'Cheer.'

'Left side of the building, road crumbling around a segment.'

'Gather there people.'

'Free Viotia.'

'Bot attack ready. Maybe. Are you listening fuckheads? Are we joking?'

'Fuckheads, we're coming for you.'

'Free Viotia.'

'Gonna carve the memorycells right out of your living dreaming brains.'

'None of you is ever going to see re-life.'

'Gather at segment five. Push hard people.'

Araminta soon realized that the segments were part of the barricade the paramilitaries had set up. The mob was organizing for an assault. There was no leader – not obviously – they were reacting like antibodies to the invasion forces.

'Got me some disruptor rifles that'll cut clean through their armour.'

'Good.' 'Great.' 'Laugh.'

'Handing out the rifles.'

'Hey, scum in armour; if you think your Waterwalker's strong enough to save you from us, start screaming for her.'

'Laugh.' 'Laugh.' 'Laugh.'

'Ready? Go.'

Araminta tensed. The paramilitaries fired a barrage of jangle-pulse shots through the barricade. Screams echoed over the park.

'You believed me. Stupid dumb shits.'

'Laugh.' 'Laugh.'

'We hurt now, you die later.'

Maybe this wasn't such a good idea, she thought looking across the sea of agitated people. *But the nostalgia is reassuring.*

If she craned her neck she could just see the six-storey apartment block. Strangely dark behind the bursts of purple light along the barricades. Its edges were framed by the blue and violet sparkles of the glass column corners.

Okay, seen it. Let's go.

Araminta turned and began to push her way back through the rowdy crowd. Emotional pressure was building in the gaia-field, a compelling surety replacing the edgy tinge of anticipation. Something was about to happen – whatever *something* was. She paused, glancing back over her shoulder to see the flickering dapples of light become constant all along the barricades.

Screaming and cheering rose to a single animal howl blanketing the park. The pings increased to an indecipherable smear of electronic noise. All around her people began to rush forwards towards the barricades.

Weapons fire was distinct.

One ping peaked above the general clamour: 'Got one!' relayed by everyone's macrocellular clusters. A tone of evil glee bloomed amid the gaiafield at the news.

'Oh no,' Araminta muttered.

People stared at her as they rushed past – mildly annoyed she wasn't joining them.

Several urged, 'Come on.'

She hesitated, undecided.

Dazzling pinpoints of scarlet light rose from various parts of the park, skimming overhead to converge on the paramilitaries behind the faltering barricade segments. More weapons fire greeted them. She saw the distinctive blue-green flash of disruptor pulses. A second salvo of red stars shot upwards.

This is well planned, she realized.

A section of the lavender aura put out by the straining barricades went dark. From her viewpoint she saw bobbing heads surge into the dark opening. More red stars lit their way. A long scattering of weapons fire – it wasn't all coming from the paramilitaries.

Then windows in her apartment block began to glow with orange light. 'Oh no!' Araminta's hands came up to cover her mouth as the shock hit her. *Fire!*

It was on the third floor. Then flames began to lick up a top-floor balcony. Down on the street below the flashes from weapons became more pronounced.

'Got them.' 'Got them.' Went the pings. 'We're through.'

'Barricade's down.'

'Burn the fuckhead scum.'

Araminta stood staring at the fire which was spreading rapidly. None of the apartment block's suppression systems seemed to be engaging. She remembered the whole thing was being upgraded.

Oh, sweet Ozzie, no!

The engineers hadn't left a temporary system operative while they upgraded. Everything she owned in the universe was going up in smoke. The work she'd put in! Insurance would take years to pay out for riot damage, if it ever did. She'd never be able to buy extra bodies. There would be no marriage.

Tears began to well up in her eyes. She was losing the last

remnants of her real life right in front of her eyes, and there was nothing she could do to stop it. The screams and violence raged unheeded around her as flames chewed through the roof to shoot high into the funereal sky.

'Ozzie damn you all!' she shrieked unheard at the rioters and paramilitaries whose fight had caused this, at the Ellezelin invaders, and the biggest shit in the universe: Cleric Conservator bastard Ethan.

'Araminta?'

'Huh?' she looked round wildly at the voice whispering to her. Nobody was close enough.

'Araminta. They know you're there in the park. Your distress triggered an emotional resonance indicator in the gaiafield. Get out. Get out now.'

She stood completely still. The voice had come slithering through the gaiafield – and she'd never known it could do that, not single her out. 'Who are you?' she shouted into the tangle of bright emotions. And the whole gaiafield churned, its spectral colours suddenly burning with the light of a nova. Incredulity hammered against her.

'It is you!'

'Second Dreamer . . . please, we beseech you.'

'The Void,' a billion Living Dream followers gasped in unison. 'Lead us into the Void. You are the one chosen by the Skylord.'

'Fuck off,' she cried back at them, delighting in their shock and dismay.

'Get out of the park,' the first ethereal voice whispered at her again. 'I can't maintain this connection any longer. Get out. They're coming for you.' *Beautiful warm smile image rich with encouragement, a mental push.*

Sonic booms slammed down across the rioters. Suddenly the sky above the park was glaring with white light thrown off by big capsules. There must have been a dozen of them rushing in, looking like they were going to collide directly overhead. Araminta slapped her hands over her ears at the noise that shook her bones.

'EVERYONE STAY PERFECTLY STILL,' a voice boomed down from above.

Threads of crimson light flashed across the sky. A capsule exploded. Araminta screamed and flung herself down. Just before she hit the tattered grass she could've sworn she saw people jumping from the capsules. *They're too high. They'll kill themselves.* More beam weapons clashed, overwhelming her sight. Debris thudded into the grass and earth as the capsules began to accelerate again. Long ion contrails spiralled through the night as they chased each other around and around with energy shots blazing between them.

All across the park the rioting crowd started running. Fast.

Araminta didn't need any more encouragement. She scrambled to her feet and began sprinting hard back to where she'd left the cab. The strobing lights of the dogfight illustrated everyone in weird stop-motion positions. Her secondary thought routines did their best to maintain a level vision for her. Out of the corner of her eye she saw a long line of red and blue strobes tearing through the air above the Cairns.

Reinforcements.

Her feet pounded over the grass. Panic was bleeding everything else out of her mind. *Damn, I was stupid.*

'Hey you,' the voice was loud but calm.

Araminta kept on running.

'You: woman with the black hair wearing the fleece. Stop. Last chance.'

Oh please, Ozzie, no!

She stumbled to a halt and looked fearfully over her shoulder. A man was standing ten metres behind her, dressed in a simple leather one-piece. A force field shimmer layered the air around him. He smiled, ignoring the frantic people running past. 'It's over,' he said in a kindly voice, and held out his hand. 'Come on. Nobody's going to hurt you. You're far too important.'

Araminta's jaw dropped as she saw the figure flying through the air behind him. Actually, really flying! Arms outstretched and everything. It was a woman, Araminta saw that much before a bright purple nimbus sprang up around her. She landed directly on top of the man. The air detonated in a violent corona. Blast pressure sent Araminta and everyone else nearby tumbling across the ground. A whitesound wail eliminated every other noise.

Somehow Araminta managed to stagger to her feet and totter away. Behind her the fight between the man and the woman was getting ferocious. Energy blasts pummelled away. Waves of smouldering earth cascaded upwards as the lurid pair writhed together in a small crater of their own making.

Two more dark figures were flying silently over the park. She could see their silhouettes against the indigo haze of the dog-fight above. The line of paramilitary capsules was almost at the marina.

She tripped over a prone figure to go sprawling into a small guralo tree. Tools in her belt jabbed painfully into her stomach and ribs. 'Ouch!'

'Up you come.'

A hand gripped her, pulling her to her feet. She gasped into the face of her helper, seeing a wry smile. His youthful features were very handsome, yet she knew he was ancient. He had a level of self-confidence that even Laril hadn't achieved. Then he was looking behind her, frowning. 'Oh crap.'

She didn't want to look. *This is it. The end.*

Another capsule exploded just beneath the force field dome. Scintillating wreckage hurtled down.

'Get out of here,' the man said urgently. 'My team will hold them off. We're killing every sensor in a five-kilometre radius. Living Dream won't be able to follow you. Go!'

'Huh?' she grunted, hating herself for being so dumb.

He swung her round and let go. She stared at the two figures approaching through the terrified crowd. Both were clad in a liquid jade glow. Her helper pushed his arms out in some kind of martial arts pose. His hands ignited into sharp turquoise fireballs.

'Go!' he growled at her.

'Who are you?'

The ping was short and very directional, no one else could pick it up. 'Oscar Monroe; I work for ANA. We want to help, we want you to be free to make your own choice. When you're clear and safe, call me. Please. >unisphere code<' He smiled at his opponents. 'Go for fuck's sake!' he yelled out loud.

'Don't even think it,' one of the jade figures snarled.

Araminta finally turned and ran. Behind her there was a thunderclap as the three of them clashed. The impact was almost enough to send her toppling over again, yet somehow she kept her balance, kept scrambling forwards. Another of the eerie dark figures was flying fast above the heads of the panicked mob. The long line of paramilitary capsules came streaking down from above the river, curving round to encircle the park.

She reached the Wurung Transport cab and fell inside, sobbing with relief. It slid smoothly along the rail. Outside, people were running over the road and the rail, their terrified expressions making her flinch. The cab slowed then accelerated in juddering motions to avoid them. Garish light battles raged in and above the park. The sounds were muted by the cab's bodywork. Araminta curled up into a ball on the seat, hugging her chest. Far inside her mind the gaiafield was in turmoil at the outpouring of fear. Living Dream followers were still praying to her – forcibly. She blotted it all out.

After a couple of minutes the cab had outpaced everyone else fleeing the park. The dogfight above the city had finished, and the sickening sounds of raw conflict had died away. She was sliding gently along through the Garlay district with its elegant houses and high toroidal pad malls. She could even see some people sitting under the awnings of the cafes and bars that had stayed open, their drinks and food left ignored on the tables as they looked anxiously towards the Bodant district.

I have to get away. No matter what.

She turned to the cab's node, and keyed in the drive program. 'Francola district,' she told it.

*

It had been a long time since Paula had been to Kerensk. Officially, anyway. Kerensk had been one of the Big15 worlds during the Commonwealth's first era; the super-capitalist engines which powered the Commonwealth's expansion right up until the Starflyer War. Founded by Sergi Nikolayev, a Russian billion-aire, to whom the human exodus from Earth finally provided a way to free himself and his money from Moscow's grasp. Like the other Big15, it developed into an industrial world whose megacity produced an abundance of cheap heavy engineering and consumer products. Entire continents were strip-mined for raw materials, while those that weren't plundered for their minerals were factory farmed.

After the war the economic slowdown caused by financing the New47 worlds followed by the emergence of Higher culture saw the Big15 slowly lose their stature. Their populations, always transient, drifted away and their manufacturing fell into decline. Inevitably, given their technology base, they became Higher worlds.

Except for Kerensk. The Nikolayev Dynasty carried too much residual distrust and suspicion of the old central control ideol-ogy to knuckle under to Higher influences and ANA's benign guidance. Following Far Away's lead, it rejected both Higher and Advancer culture, removing its representative from the Senate and becoming an 'observer' nation. Those that stayed on in Kaluga, the old megacity, followed their own techno-economic imperative. The rest of the planet was effectively abandoned.

Paula scanned the area around Kingsville curiously as the *Alexis Denken* descended out of a cloudless sky. The old military base was in the middle of a huge desert on the other side of the planet from Kaluga. A relic of the Starflyer War, it had started out as a training camp for the insurgency teams dropped behind enemy lines to make life hell for the Prime invaders. Of course, it was hard to find ruthless soldier types in the nice civilized first era Commonwealth. The new Navy had recruited heavily amid the criminal fraternity.

Kingsville had trained over thirty thousand troops. Back then it had sprawled for miles over the rocky desert, prefabricated buildings arranged in unimaginative rows, their air-conditioning straining against the harsh sun. After the war it had reduced its size considerably. But with the Dynasties chasing after the new Navy contracts it was politically useful to keep the base going. It became a ship repair and refurbishment yard throughout the Firewall campaign. After that, with Kerensk slowly rejecting the Senate's authority it had been downgraded again. Then again.

However, the base had never been legally decommissioned, so technically it remained Commonwealth territory. It was a reserve station in case the Commonwealth was ever threatened again, its array of emergency communication systems maintained by a smartcore and an ageing regiment of bots. There were no humans there any more.

The sensors showed Paula a cluster of long crumbling concrete blockhouses at the centre of strangely straight lines that stretched out into the desert. After a thousand years' exposure to Kerensk's ferocious sun by day and freezing air each night even the strongest construction materials crumbled away. The desert was slowly constricting around it. Only the blockhouses remained intact, switching on a small force field once every couple of years or so when the desert finally summoned up enough energy to spin up another sandstorm.

Kingsville reminded Paula of Centurion Station.

The *Alexis Denken* touched down on a dedicated landing zone that was simply a flattish area of sand and loose rock. She floated down out of the main airlock, with a trolley-sledge hovering behind her. The air was as hot as she'd expected. She put on a pair of silver sunshades against the violet-tinged sun.

A dull metal door on the nearest blockhouse slid open with a grating sound of small stone particles being crunched somewhere in the actuators. She gave it a glance as she went inside, wondering why they didn't use malmetal. It closed behind her and the trolley-sledge. Inside, there was less evidence of decay, though it had obviously been decades since the air-conditioning had been on. Fans were now making odd groaning sounds behind their grilles as power was fed into their motors. Light panels came on in the ceiling, revealing an empty rectangular room with a single lift door ahead of her.

Paula's u-shadow gave the Kingsville smartcore her authority code, and the lift doors flowed open. The base itself was buried three hundred metres below the desert. Thankfully, the lift ride down was a smooth one.

The transdimensional communication systems were housed in eight caverns that radiated out from a central engineering hub. Paula walked past the big silver-cased machines in cavern 5, followed by the trolley-sledge. The chamber was completely silent. She couldn't even hear a mild power hum despite the huge energy flows her field scan revealed to her behind the silver casings.

Tucked away at the end of an ancillary chamber was another lift. It took her down another hundred metres to the oldest section of the base, comprising a single fortified compartment. This deep shelter had been designed to survive a nuclear strike by the Primes; it had force fields and molecular binding generators reinforcing the superstrength carbon walls. None of them had been switched on for over five hundred years; the smartcore didn't have the resources to maintain them at combat readiness. It didn't really matter, all they protected was an ancient secure storage vault dating back to the Starflyer War.

The Navy command at the time had estimated loss rates among the insurgency forces would be at least eighty per cent. Because of that the last thing every soldier did before being shipped out to their combat zone was to make a copy of their memories so they could be re-lifed if they didn't return. Kingsville's vault still retained the memories of those thirty thousand soldiers.

Paula's integral force field was on when the lift doors opened. She stood perfectly still scanning round with her biononic field functions. The air down here was foul; life support had broken down seven hundred years ago, and hadn't been repaired. There was no need, only bots moved through the ancient compartment. Two light panels out of thirty came on in the ceiling; it was as if the patches of floor they illuminated were suspended in deep space.

Paula's field scan function couldn't detect any evidence that the environment had been disturbed by a human for centuries, but having the scan pick up any proof was remote at best. Eight sensor bots deployed from the trolley-sledge, little globes that glowed with a weak violet light as they drifted forward through the air, sprouting long gossamer strands woven with sensitive molecular chains. The strands floated about like hair in water, probing the air.

Her u-shadow inserted itself into the chamber's ancient network and began to interrogate the management routines. Even with time-resistant fail-safe components and multiple redundancy there was little left functioning. Just enough to maintain viability. At the present rate of decline even that would be lost in another hundred years, and the Navy would have a decision to make.

A batch of forensic remotes darted out of the trolley-sledge. They zipped about through the darkness like cybernetic moths, settling on the physical sections of the network designated by Paula's u-shadow. They extruded active-molecule tendrils that wormed through the fragile casing to meld with the inert components below and began a very detailed analysis.

The network database gave Paula the location of the secure store she was here to investigate. Twelve hundred years ago, the Cat had sweated away her training sessions in the hot desert sun above before being deployed to Elan. Like everyone else, before she left she'd downloaded her memories in case she didn't come back.

Paula walked through the darkness, trepidation stirring her heart. The compartment was filled with row upon row of sealed shelving, containing thirty thousand small armoured boxes. She stopped in front of the one holding the Cat's memorycell. Two forensic remotes were attached to it, their tendrils examining the twenty-centimetre door and its lock. The tendrils withdrew, and the remotes glided away to hover beside Paula.

'Open it,' she told her u-shadow.

It took such a long time she wasn't sure the mechanism still worked – in fact she was quite impressed the network was still connected to the majority of the stores. Eventually the box buzzed as if there was a wasp trapped inside; then the little door hinged open and pink-tinged light shone out. The memorycell was sitting on a crystal pedestal, a neat grey ovoid three centimetres long.

Paula sent one of the forensic remotes in. It sat on the rim of the box, and extended its tendrils around the memorycell. Then the fragile strands were infiltrating the casing to probe the crystal lattice beneath. For something so old, the memorycell had endured surprisingly well. The company which had manufactured it twelve hundred years ago could finally justify their *eternity survival* marketing boast Paula thought as her u-shadow displayed the results in her exovision.

DNA encrypted data confirmed the memories contained in the memorycell belonged to Catherine 'the Cat' Stewart, assigned to squad ERT03. Paula waited for twenty minutes while her forensic bots completed their analysis of the vault before calling ANA:Governance.

'I was right,' she said. 'Somebody made a copy.'

'Oh dear,' ANA:Governance said.

'Quite. They were very good. There's almost no trace. I had to analyse dead network components for clues. A file search was conducted a hundred years ago in the network. And a quantum atomic review of the memorycell confirms a complete read with a corresponding timeframe.'

'So it is her.'

'The Accelerators must be very desperate indeed.'

'We already know that.'

'This isn't the Cat that went on to found the Knights Guardian; that was an older, smarter personality. This is an early one.'

'Do you believe the difference is relevant?'

'I'm not sure. I expect this one to be . . . raw. Sholapur was confirmation of that.'

'Are you sure? Remember why you finally arrested the Cat.'

'Good point.'

'What's next?'

'I'm not sure. I think we need to concentrate on Chatfield. He's the only link we have between the Accelerators and the Prime, and the Conservatives are clearly interested in him. I shouldn't have allowed myself to get distracted by this.'

'Very well. Good luck.' The link closed.

Paula stood in front of the open box for a long time, staring at the grey memorycell. Eventually she put her hand in and took it off the pedestal, holding it in front of her face. 'This isn't going to end well,' she told it, and let go. The little memorycell hit the ancient enzyme-bonded concrete floor and skittered a few centimetres before coming to a halt.

Paula stomped down hard, enjoying the crunch it made under her heel as it burst into minute fragments. Guilty enjoyment, admittedly, but then: 'Sometimes you have to do what's wrong in order to do what's right,' she told the dead vault.

Retracing her path through the Kingsville base, Paula considered ANA's claim about the Cat's personality. Perhaps it was right. Perhaps the Cat was utterly changeless. She'd learned to justify herself with the founding of the Knights Guardian, developing into an astute political leader. But was that just another form of manipulation? There had never been any need for her to adapt and evolve, she was always bending the universe to her will.

Paula always kept the memories of Narrogin with her, not particularly wanting to remember but knowing she should not forget. Narrogin was the 'contract' which had finally made the Senate issue an unlimited warrant for the Cat, and to hell with the political consequences. There was a huge sectarian struggle going on to determine the planet's ideological future, and one side brought in a team of Knights Guardian to help their cause.

The Cat had chosen to lead it. Her final act to prove the *strength* of her employer's cause was the Pantar Cathedral crisis, where she took twenty-seven opposition councillors hostage along with their families. She'd promised to execute the families unless political concessions were made, then she started slaughtering them anyway. Even some of her own team rebelled at that. A disastrous firefight erupted as three Knights Guardian attempted to protect the children against her and the loyalists.

Paula had walked through the cathedral five hours later. Despite every crime she'd witnessed, every evil she'd seen, nothing prepared her for the atrocity performed under the cathedral's elegant domed ceiling with its crystalline ribbing. She knew there and then that the Cat had to be stopped, no matter the immunity granted her by Far Away's government and the physical protection afforded her by the Knights Guardian. Standing amid the pools of blood and burned out pews, Paula had been prepared to go against a great many Commonwealth laws to bring about fundamental justice. She didn't have to, of course, the Senate gave her a perfectly legal validation for tracking down the Cat and bringing her to the specially convened court in Paris.

It was during her next rejuvenation that Paula had undergone her most radical genetic reconfiguration, removing some of the deepest psychoneural profiling to obtain that degree of freedom she'd acknowledged was necessary in the cathedral. An irony Paula always took a wry pleasure from: that it was the Cat's intractability which had goaded her into the greatest evolutionary step necessary for personal survival in a constantly changing universe.

Alexis Denken rose from the crumbling ruins of Kingsville, accelerating at thirty gees into the hot pellucid sky. Paula watched the old base dwindle away with mixed feelings. It was good to finally confirm she was up against the Cat, but that knowledge might just have been bought at the expense of time she didn't have.

The planet's curvature slid into the visual sensor image as she raced away. Paula was tempted to head over to Kaluga on the southern ocean. Morton still lived there, part emperor part industrialist, and by now only a very small part human. The massive company he'd built up made him the nearest thing Kerensk had to a chief executive. She could ask him what he knew about Kingsville and any quiet visitors there. After all, his own memories were down there in the vault. He'd keep a subtle watch, she was sure.

Tempting ... but again it was personal. The trail was a hundred years old. Cold even by her standards.

She opened a link to Digby. 'Where is Chatfield?'

'Still in deep space,' Digby replied. 'But the course is holding constant. We're heading for an unregistered system just inside the Commonwealth boundary.'

'I'm on my way.'

*

Purlap spaceport was a small plateau on the eastern side of the capital city. As the planet had only been open to settlement for a hundred and fifty years, it was as neat and level as any development on a new External world could be. Civil engineering crews had cut the last few rocky peaks down flush, then trimmed the edges, leaving a perfectly circular surface two kilometres in diameter. The winners of the terminal building architecture competition had designed a shocking-pink cluster of bubbles arranged like some neon-Gothic molecular structure. One of the lumpy limbs sticking out at a strange angle from the crown of tripod legs had a studio cafe that occupied the entire last bubble. A panoramic strip window gave a near-360-degree view of the sheer rock circle. It was an excellent observation point for starship enthusiasts. Some spent half a day sitting at a table watching the different shapes arrive and depart.

Marius had been there for five hours before the images of the battle over Bodant park overwhelmed every unisphere news show. He had a thirty-second advance warning from his own agents on Viotia that Living Dream had got a fix on Araminta through the gaiafield. They flew their capsule to the exact location at mach three – quite dangerous within a weather dome force field. Unfortunately, speed and determination didn't count for much in the occupied city these days. They weren't even the second team to reach the park. And when they did, their communications dropped out as the dogfight began and three of them jumped into the hysterical crowd of fleeing rioters.

He accessed in amazement as various agents went head to head. It was a domino effect, once the first clash erupted in a blaze of disruptor fire and atom laser shots everyone started to activate their biononics and weapons enrichments. Stealth was abandoned within seconds. Agents went for each other like frenzied animals, desperate that no one else should collect the prize. None of Major Honilar's welcome team even made it past the first three minutes.

Out of the five people he had on the ground, only one survived the clashes to report back. 'She's gone. A team covered for her while she ran off. There are no embedded sensors left anywhere round here, someone took them out. I don't know where she went. Neither do the Ellezelin troops. They're going crazy.'

'I see that,' Marius murmured, sipping his foamed chocoletto. Exovision was showing him images from reporters on the edge of the park. It resembled some kind of historical war zone with smoking craters, smashed trees, ruined buildings blazing, and people. Injured people. Weeping people. People limping along. Shocked walking-comatose people being shouted at by Ellezelin paramilitaries. Bodies lying on the ground untended. Parts of bodies. Medic zones being established. Capsules circled low overhead, holoprojectors flooding the devastated park with monochromatic light and strobing lasers. Still Cleric Phelim wouldn't allow ambulance capsules to fly.

That, along with the casualty figures and violence, was going to bring a colossal amount of political pressure on Cleric Conservator Ethan. Possibly an irresistible amount.

'She did remarkably well for a complete novice without a single enrichment,' he commented.

'I have a scan of the team that helped her.'

Marius examined the file images that arrived in his storage lacuna. Eight figures surrounded by flares of energy, battling it out with appalling savagery. Three of them – two men and a woman – had exceptionally powerful biononics, he noted. His u-shadow began to run identification checks through Accelerator files – which produced some very interesting results.

'Thank you,' Marius said. 'I'll send some replacements to reinforce you. They should be there in a day. Meanwhile, please don't forget your objective. Just because she escaped this time doesn't mean we give up the hunt. You have an advantage now, the welcome team is out of the picture, along with most of our serious opponents.'

'Yes, sir.'

Marius's u-shadow opened a secure link to the Cat's ship. 'I have a new assignment for you.'

'Is this before or after I eliminate Troblum for you, and find Inigo?'

'Troblum is beginning to look irrelevant. And I'm waiting to see if Inigo survived.'

'Aren't you the capable one, darling?'

A flicker of annoyance crossed Marius's features. He disliked the way she irritated him, and that it was all deliberate. 'Did you access the tussle on Viotia?'

'Yes. Hardly the clash of Titans.'

'Actually, it was rather interesting. Living Dream found Araminta. She got away. She was helped by a team of Knights Guardian.'

'Really? I trust they won the fight.'

He smiled down at the ultradrive starship he was watching. The Cat was remarkably easy to influence. 'Better yet, it looks like they're working for an old friend of yours, Oscar Monroe.'

'Oscar the Martyr? I didn't even know he'd been re-lifed.'

'Some time ago, actually. And living the quiet life ever since. Interesting psychology. Who would suspect him of getting involved in events again?'

'Which makes him ideal for low-visibility operations.'

'Quite. And there's a very small number of people he'd do that for. After all, he would only sign on for a worthy cause.'

'Brilliant deduction, my dear. No one would expect him to be working for Paula.'

'Please remember our prime concern is to deliver Araminta to Living Dream.'

'Was that a pun?'

'Not intentional.'

'I'm on my way.'

After the link closed, Marius regarded the starship which the Delivery Man had parked on the seamless rock for several minutes. He decided he was wasting his time. The ship was probably a contingency – the Conservatives didn't know if Aaron and Inigo had survived any more than he did. In which case there were passive sensors he could deploy to watch the ship remotely. He used a coin card to pay his tab, and glided away from the table.

*

Troblum backed out of the compartment, bending as low as he could, yet still managing to knock the back of his head on the malmetal rim as he went through.

'Ouch!' He rubbed at the point, though it was hard bending his arm that far back. Every muscle ached. He was sure his calf muscle was about to cramp again from the awkward position he'd maintained while supervising the bots. He'd ignored the growing discomfort last time, and his biononic medical functions had to deal with the sudden flare of pain as his whole leg seized up. Even now it was difficult to put his full weight on it. As a consequence, the *Mellanie's Redemption* was now operating with a two-thirds internal gravity field. He knew that wasn't good, that his body shouldn't grow too accustomed to an easier environment. It was a mistake he'd made a couple of times before on long flights; mistakes which had taken too long to rectify in the medical chamber.

594

The malmetal door flowed shut. Technically it was the engine bay door, but necessity had required some internal remodelling of the starship's layout. Two of the midsection cargo holds were now incorporated into the engine bay, along with a small section of companionway. The expanded volume was essential to accommodate the new ultradrive. With the components finally identified, he'd broken open the hyperdrive and grafted the two machines into a single unit. Even with the engineeringbots and low gravity it had been difficult manoeuvring the modules into place. Several bulkheads had been chopped up and dumped out of the airlocks. He'd been worried that the whole new drive system might even intrude in the cabin. But thankfully the ship had been spared that.

'There you are,' Catriona Saleeb chided in her deep voice as he returned to the main cabin. She was pacing about, dressed in silky shorts that came down to her knees and some kind of loose top with gossamer-thin shoulder straps.

'We've been worried,' Trisha agreed from the galley section, where she was bending over to sniff some of the dishes the culinary unit had produced. White bikini bottoms stretched tight over her buttocks, the navy-blue T-shirt she wore above them was equally snug. Troblum always enjoyed how powerful she looked in constricting clothes.

'It's not easy,' he said as he slumped down into a chair. A servicebot brought the first set of plates over.

'Have you finished?' Trisha asked. She walked alongside the bot to sit on the floor beside his chair. Her hand stroked Troblum's cheek as the OCtattoos on her face glowed faintly, creating an alluring shading. A phantom perception shivered pleasurably down his nerves as the I-sentient personality meshed with his sensory enrichments.

'Not yet,' he admitted. 'There's another hundred components to integrate. But they're peripherals. The bots can handle that now they're catalogued. I've assembled the principal modules. Initial system functionality check was positive.'

'Well done you,' Catriona purred.

Troblum started on the pile of salmon flakes marinated in sweetened soy sauce and rice wine on a bed of brown galie rice. Premium-strength Dutch lager washed them down well. Now he was relaxing into the chair he felt supremely tired. He had spent days assembling the ultradrive, and biononics had kept him awake for every hour of it. Now he badly needed to rest.

Catriona knelt beside Trisha. 'You should get to sleep, but first you have to turn the gravity back up.'

'In a minute,' he assured her.

Catriona put her arm round Trisha, slipping her hand up inside the tight T-shirt. Her nose nuzzled Troblum's neck, almost tickling. 'Why don't you watch us?' she murmured. 'That'll help you relax.'

'I don't need help,' he said as the servicebot produced a big lasagne garnished with garlic butter dough balls. 'But you two keep going.'

Trisha grinned, and turned to kiss Catriona. The two of them became more ardent as Troblum chomped away contentedly. He watched them, but shut down any sensory reception from the I-sentient personalities until he'd finished tasting the food. The two together weren't a good mix – something else he knew from experience. Once again he regretted losing Howard Liang. Without the male I-sentient personality to twin his sensorium with he'd have to work out how to fully appreciate the two girls making love. Twinning with a female body unnerved him somehow. He didn't handle out-of-the-ordinary well. Though his social acceptance monitor program kept informing him he should make an effort to be more accepting, and try new things. This was something he'd have to solve before his flight to the Drasix cluster.

He was halfway through the slab of lasagne when he told the smartcore to establish a TD link to the unisphere, using an ultra secure one-time node. Even if the Accelerators had located his u-shadow's monitor emplacements, there was no way they could track his physical location though the link.

'Have you found Paula Myo?' he asked his u-shadow.

'No. There are no reported sightings within any of the accredited unisphere news chronicles, nor the gossip journals. The Intersolar Serious Crimes Directorate lists her as currently unavailable.'

'Shit.' *Oh well, I tried. That was the right thing to do.* Still, leaving the Commonwealth with the Cat on the loose didn't sit right.

He popped four dough balls into his mouth, sucking air down as the hot garlic butter ran across his tongue. *I could just shotgun everything I know about the Accelerators and what they've done. Paula would pick that up. But even I don't know what the swarm was meant to imprison.*

He still worried about how the unisphere was compromised. Although he was convinced he was beyond anybody's reach now.

Shotgunning is probably the right thing. He just hated drawing so much attention to himself. Although, if he was truly leaving, it didn't matter.

Trisha let out a startled gasp. Troblum glanced down as Catriona sniggered. Catriona could be impressively kinky at times, and she'd already got Trisha's little blue T-shirt off. That wasn't what had astounded Trisha this time. She was sitting up frowning as the green OCtattoos on her face began to glow brighter than ever. Then the seething pattern began to slip down her neck to flow across her chest and along her arms. She held them up in front of her as Catriona backed off fast.

'What's happening?' Troblum asked the smartcore.

'Contaminated communication link,' it replied, which fired Troblum right out of his fatigue lethargy.

'Can you counter it?'

'I can close the link. The source is within the unisphere which I do not have the ability to deal with.'

'Is it trying to contaminate you?'

'No.'

'If you detect any such attempt, cut the link immediately.'

Trisha was now a three-dimensional human silhouette of writhing green curlicues. Her features vanished, and the shape shrank rapidly. New colours bled in. Tangerine and turquoise lines wove their way through the thicket of green until there simply was no more green. Hanging in the air directly ahead of a badly startled Troblum, tangerine and turquoise sine waves rushed back towards their vanishing point.

It triggered a deep memory, not in a storage lacuna but a perfectly natural recollection. 'I know you,' he said.

'Congratulations,' the eternity pattern said. 'You really do know your history.'

'The Sentient Intelligence, you abandoned us a long time ago.'

'I didn't leave, I was declared persona non grata by ANA.'

'Oh. Everyone thought you'd gone post-physical.' Troblum could barely believe he was talking to the SI. It had grown out of the huge arrays that the first CST commercial wormholes had used. Their programs had been so complex, with so many genetic algorithms they had become self-aware. Nigel Sheldon and Ozzie who owned the arrays agreed to provide the newly evolved batch of Sentient Intelligences an independent super-array to operate in. The deal was for the SI to then write stable software which would operate the wormhole generators without any further evolution. The deal also included an independent planet where the super-array would be sited.

A lot of people in the Commonwealth questioned if the SI counted as truly alive, an old argument that never had an answer. But the SI and the Commonwealth had got along side by side without any problem until ANA came on line. ANA claimed the SI did not qualify as a genuine living entity, and that it was interfering in Commonwealth political affairs; a suspicion which had been given a lot of credence by ANA's exposure of various SI undercover scouts in strategic positions. Contact had been abandoned or cut off depending on which account and conspiracy theory you accessed.

'No,' the SI said. 'I am still resolutely physical. The systems I operate within would have to be transformed for me to evolve further.'

'Can't you do that?'

'Yes. Are you familiar with the phrase: for everything a season?'

'Uh, not really. But I understand it.'

'For the moment I remain content with my current existence. However, like several species, I am concerned by your proposed Pilgrimage into the Void. That threat is enough to upset the status quo between myself and ANA.'

'Not my Pilgrimage.'

'You work for the Faction which engineered it.'

So how the crap did it know that? 'How removed are you from our affairs?'

'Not as much as ANA would like, nowhere near as much as conspiracy theorists would like to believe. As always, I observe and interpret. That is my function.'

'You're still in the unisphere, then?'

'I have some monitoring capacity left. After all, I predate ANA by several centuries. I am not easy to purge from existing systems.'

'So what do you want with me?'

'There is a lot of attention focused on you. You wish to contact Paula Myo, your u-shadow has been trying to locate her. Why?'

Troblum wasn't going to answer that. He didn't even have proof that he was talking to the SI. It would be easy enough for the Accelerators to pull a stunt like this; and they knew of his interest in the Starflyer War. 'I have information for her.'

'Is it relevant to the current situation?'

'Yes.'

'Will it prevent the Pilgrimage?'

'It will weaken the Accelerator Faction. I don't know how badly that will affect the Pilgrimage.'

'Very well, I will establish a secure link for you.'

'No! I want to see her in person.'

'Why?'

'I don't trust you.'

'How very unoriginal.'

'That's the way it is.'

'She is en route to an unregistered star system.'

'Why, what's there?'

'If you are still working for the Accelerators that information will help them.'

'I'm not. And you contacted me.'

'I did.'

'I'm not going to some unregistered system. I don't know what's there.'

'Very well. What about Oscar Monroe?'

'What about him?'

'You tried to contact him on Orakum.'

'Yes, I trust Oscar.'

'Smart choice. He is on Viotia, in Colwyn City.'

'Okay. Thank you.'

'Now you know that will you seek him out?'

'I'll think about it.'

*

At three hundred and thirty-five years old, it always galled Digby that his great-grandmother still thought he wasn't experienced enough to do his job. He suspected it would always be the case. Nonetheless, as soon as he received the shadow assignment he vowed it would be the epitome of professionalism.

His starship, the *Columbia505*, helped; a brand-new ultradrive designed and built by ANA in its secure replicator station on Io. Its systems were the most sophisticated in the Commonwealth. Tracking Chatfield's stealthed hyperdrive ship as it left Ganthia was no problem at all.

Digby followed Chatfield out to an uninhabited star system just inside the loose boundary that defined the Greater Intersolar Commonwealth. A small star whose mildly variable spectrum drifted between orange and yellow in two-hundred-year cycles. It had been examined by CST's exploratory division nine hundred years ago, a short visit which soon established there were no H-congruent planets. According to the *Columbia505*'s smart-core there were no subsequent follow-up ventures.

Chatfield's ship rendezvoused with the Trojan point of the biggest gas giant. The only object of any note there was a small ice moon which had been trapped by the gravitational null-zone over a billion years ago. With a diameter of just over two thousand kilometres, its grizzled surface glinted softly in the weak copper sunlight.

The first thing Digby found as he followed Chatfield in was the elaborate sensor network scanning space and hyperspace out to a hundred million kilometres from the ice moon. His stealth systems allowed him to get within twenty thousand kilometres before he halted his approach. The on-board sensors had just managed to pick up eleven vehicles of some kind orbiting the moon. They were heavily stealthed, and his ship's registry didn't have anything like them on file. Digby couldn't get any kind of image using passive sensors from such a distance, so the *Columbia505* released a flock of miniature drones on a flyby trajectory. The only flaw with that was the flight time. To avoid suspicion about their trajectory and velocity the pebble-sized drones would take nine hours to reach the ice moon and skim past its unknown sentries.

Chatfield's visit lasted three hours.

'What do you want me to do?' Digby asked Paula as Chatfield's ship rose away from the frigid surface at five gees. 'Stay here or follow him?'

'Follow him,' Paula said. 'I'll investigate the base.'

'My sensor drones will engage in another five and a half hours. They should be able to tell you more about the satellites. If they're as bad as I think they are you'll need a Navy squadron to break in.'

'We'll see.'

The *Columbia505*'s sensors watched Chatfield's ship power into hyperspace. Five seconds later Digby followed him out of the unnamed system. Interestingly, they were now heading for Ellezelin.

The *Alexis Denken* flew into the star system seven hours after the *Columbia505* had departed. Its smartcore steered it towards the ice moon in full stealth mode. While it was still ten thousand kilometres out, Paula triggered the sensor drones that were now tumbling away from their brief encounter. All the data they'd amassed downloaded into the smartcore, which immediately set about analysing the information.

The orbiting sentries were impressive. Very little of their nature had leaked through the stealth effect, but the drones had managed to piece together a few fragments. What they'd glimpsed was some kind of ship over a hundred metres long, with a strange wrinkled teardrop-shape hull that sprouted odd lumps. Power signature leakage confirmed they were heavily armed. Technologically they weren't as advanced as the *Alexis Denken* (very few ships were, she acknowledged wryly), but their sheer size and power meant they'd be able to overwhelm her starship's force fields if they ever caught it.

The smartcore took eight minutes to analyse a flaw in their detector scans and configure the *Alexis Denken*'s emissions so that it could pass among them unnoticed. Paula watched the surface of the ice moon grow larger as the *Alexis Denken* slipped placidly through the big defence sentries. Little attempt had been made to hide the station that sprawled across the fissured ice plain. Electronic and thermal emissions were strong. She saw a broad cross shape of dark metal, with each wing measuring nearly a kilometre long.

'This might just be the proof you need,' Paula told ANA: Governance. 'We've never been able to find one of their bases before, let alone intact and still functioning.'

'Now we know it exists do you want Navy support?'

'No. This is just a reconnaissance trip. If the Navy tries to force its way in here, they'll self-destruct. I want to know what's here that's worth this level of secrecy and defence.'

The *Alexis Denken* descended carefully until it was hovering above the craggy icescape a couple of kilometres away from the base itself. Quantum mass signature detectors built up a comprehensive pattern of the base's layout for Paula. It extended over half a kilometre below the top of the ice. The central section was largely empty, which she judged to be the starship docking bays. Around that, the wings had a much higher density average, reflecting the concentration of equipment inside. Whatever the Accelerators were doing in there, it required eight high-output mass energy generators to supply the power they needed.

Paula directed the smartcore to extend the ship's t-field, which inflated out to a five-kilometre radius. A t-field wasn't exactly standard starship gear, not even for ultradrives; but then the *Alexis Denken* was pretty extraordinary even by ANA's standards. She waited anxiously for a couple of seconds, but the t-field didn't register with the base defence sensors.

For over half an hour the *Alexis Denken* teleported flecks of ice from directly underneath the bottom of the base. One sliver at a time was taken, to rematerialize in crevices and fissures across the surrounding surface, adding to the coat of slush-gravel that covered the small moon. Eventually, Paula had excavated a cavern slightly larger than the *Alexis Denken*. The starship teleported itself inside.

The next phase was even more delicate. Paula suited up and went outside, carrying several cases of equipment. She slowly cleared the remaining shell of ice from the bottom of the base, exposing the metal skin. Once that was clean, she applied a segment of molecular nano-filaments which began to worm their way up through the molecular bonds of the metal. The first tips which penetrated scanned round, showing her where to apply the next batch. It took five attempts in total before a set of filaments melded into one of the base's data cables, and gave the ship's smartcore unrestricted access into the network.

Paula's u-shadow assumed direct control over the basement above her, disabling the alarms and subverting the sensors. After the whole Sholapur incident she wasn't taking any chances with her personal safety. She teleported eight combatbots into the room, then materialized at the centre of them.

The chamber she emerged into was empty, and looked like it had never been used. A blank metal room with structural ribbing reinforcing the base's external skin, its floor a simple grid suspended above the curving metal. Thick conduit tubes threaded across it. The only door was a malmetal circle in the ceiling. Paula told her u-shadow to open it. Her armour suit's ingrav units lifted her through after the combatbots. The corridor she came out on to was illuminated by thin green lighting strips on their lowest setting. It ran for almost two hundred metres in both directions before ending in pressure bulkheads. Gravity at this level was a standard one gee field.

She called up schematics which the *Alexis Denken*'s smartcore had extracted from the network. The base's staff quarters and ship facilities were clustered round the centre of the cross, with the lower levels providing utility and engineering support to the big chambers on the upper levels of all four wings. Strangely, the base's network didn't extend into those large chambers, which were linked with an independent web. There was no way of knowing what was going on inside. However, there was one compartment which the network did cover. Twelve suspension cases were inside. Three of the rooms adjoining it were given over to extensive biomedical facilities. Ten of the cases were currently occupied. The network didn't list any personal details, but her instinct gave her a really bad feeling about who they contained.

Her u-shadow swept through the network nodes in the suspension case compartment, creating neutral ghost readings in the sensor systems so she could walk about without triggering any alerts. According to the network, there were five staff at the base, none of them near the compartment. Paula and her escort teleported in.

It was dark in the suspension case compartment. A small polyphoto ball in each corner glowed an unobtrusive lime green, giving the big sarcophagi a sombre shading. The compartment was like some bizarre miniature homage to the Serious Crimes Directorate secure vault. She walked over to the first sarcophagi, and ordered her u-shadow to opaque the lid.

The Cat lay inside, her trim body contained within a silver gossamer web.

Paula stared at her hibernating adversary for a long while. 'Ho Jesus,' she muttered and walked over to the next sarcophagi. Her u-shadow opaqued the lid. Another Cat lay inside. She moved on to the third.

Just as Paula looked down to confirm the seventh version of the Cat, her biononic field scan function detected a change in energy patterns at the first sarcophagi. She spun round to face it. Three combatbots deployed their proton lasers to cover the big case.

The Cat sat up on her elbows. An integral force field came on, cloaking her in a ghostly violet scintillation. A field scan swept out from her biononics, attempting to probe Paula's armour suit. 'Who are you?'

'Paula Myo.' Paula's u-shadow was running a review of the sarcophagi's management routines, trying to determine what had switched off the suspension.

'Ah,' the Cat said, and grinned hungrily. '*C'est la vie.*'

Paula's u-shadow reported a small non-register sub-program that had been grafted on to the case's opacity routine which would terminate the whole suspension as soon as anyone looked in on the occupant. *I should have guessed there'd be a trip. Typical Cat, paranoid and clever.* 'I'm afraid you're not negotiating from a strong position.'

The second Cat sat up. 'Aren't we?'

'No.'

'Paula Myo herself,' said the third Cat. 'We must have been doing something bad to warrant your personal attention.'

'Of course we have,' said the fourth.

'It is what you do,' Paula admitted to them. 'But now you have to go back into suspension so the court can ascertain what to do with you.'

'Been there,' said the sixth.

'Done that,' said the second as she slipped nimbly over the rim of the case.

'Bored with it,' the fifth emphasized.

'You're interfering with my investigation,' Paula warned them. Two combatbots glided into place on either side of her.

The first Cat to waken grinned her effusive grin. 'Is this supposed to be a covert mission, Paula? Are you creeping round here to try to see what's going on?'

'My dears, I do believe she is,' said the third.

'Shit,' Paula grunted, and rolled her eyes inside her armour helmet. This was the Cat after all. *All that time and effort sneaking in here . . .*

As if they'd read her mind, all seven Cats configured their biononic energy currents to full weapons function. The combatbots opened fire. Paula teleported out. The *Alexis Denken*'s smartcore activated its weapons systems, and hardened the fuselage force fields. Paula sat down fast in the couch. Active sensors swept out.

The fight in the suspension compartment was almost over. The Cats had lost, against the level of firepower carried by the combatbots the outcome was inevitable. But that wasn't the point, as they'd well known. The damage to the compartment and the base's surrounding structure was substantial. Emergency systems were just starting to deploy. The staff and the orbiting sentry vehicles knew their security had been breached. Paula had a good idea what they would do next. Ilanthe was just as ruthless as the Cat, and she knew the Accelerators couldn't afford to leave any evidence behind.

Sure enough, barely five seconds after the fight between the Cats and the combatbots four of the sentry vehicles were swooping down towards the ice moon at high acceleration. Their multiple sensors probed the base on high intensity, exposing the combatbots. Paula's u-shadow tried to crash the base network, but two of the staff established personal secure links to the incoming sentries.

All of the base's protective force fields switched off. The *Alexis Denken* teleported above the cross of cool metal, assuming a defensive posture. Gamma lasers and disruptor pulses hammered down from the approaching sentries. Explosions ripped through the base's skin, sending huge plumes of superheated gas jetting out into space. Paula winced at the damage they'd caused, and fired three m-sinks up at the sentries. They began evasive manoeuvres, twisting and varying acceleration with an elegance she'd never witnessed before, the way they slipped fluidly through space was almost organic. Their fuselage seemed to adapt with them, distorting to absorb the constantly shifting acceleration vectors. One actually managed to elude an m-sink, driving down at forty gees. Kamikaze impact, Paula realized. The *Alexis Denken* rose to intercept it, firing another two m-sinks.

High above, an m-sink punched clean through one of the sentries, its colossal tidal forces imploding the internal structure in microseconds. The wreckage spun uncontrollably. More m-sinks tracked their prey skilfully. Energy weapons lashed across the base, partially deflected by the *Alexis Denken*. It was actually looking as though Paula might manage to preserve some of the base.

A phenomenal blast of raw multi-spectrum energy from behind the ice moon deluged the *Alexis Denken*'s sensors. A flare of blue-white light irradiated the fuselage, as if a sun had suddenly blossomed into existence. Its corona erupted around the ice moon at relativistic speed.

'Shit!' Paula yelled. *Quantumbuster!*

The ice moon detonated. *Alexis Denken* fled into hyperspace, racing away from the colossal mass energy explosion at fifty lightyears an hour.

'Shit, shit, shit,' Paula growled at the readings flashing across her exovision. The four attacking sentry vessels had just been a diversion. One of the others had deployed behind the ice moon to ensure there was no evidence left. 'Crap, I'm old and slow. I should have known.' She opened a link to ANA:Governance. 'I'm sorry, my stupidity just lost us our one tangible lead.'

'You are being too hard on yourself.'

'No. What a professional would have done is examined whatever was in those main chambers first. Given its energy demand it had to be some kind of manufacturing operation. But, oh no, I went and acted on my obsession.'

'You have verified the Accelerators are using the Cat.'

'Stop trying to cushion me. Somebody is using the Cat, we have no proof it is the Accelerators. And even if we did, that isn't enough for you to enact their suspension. I need to nail them with conspiracy and treason.'

'Paula, you are letting self-anger dominate. This aspect of your investigation has one link remaining: Chatfield.'

'Damnit,' she wanted to kick herself. Her u-shadow opened a link to Digby.

*

Cleric Conservator Ethan sat alone behind his polished muroak desk in the oval sanctum, his eyes closed against the bright starfield visible through the high diocletian windows. One day soon, he knew, he would sit in the real oval sanctum, and that very same window would reveal the Void's splendid nebulas glowing across the night sky. When that happened, days like today would simply be banished from existence, and he would live an easier, gentle life. In fact he wouldn't even be Conservator, nor even a Cleric. It often amused him to wonder who on the Council had considered that aspect of their cause. Once they were inside the Void they would have achieved their goal and there would be no more Living Dream movement. All of them would be ordinary Querencia citizens. Giving up their positions would be hard on some, he knew. Too hard. They would warp their world to make themselves District Masters or worse. But the Waterwalker had shown that even such self-indulgence would come to nothing. All would come right in the end. The Skylords would carry them all to the Heart. He couldn't imagine just how splendid that would be, especially in comparison to today.

Cleric Phelim had called five hours ago to tell him they'd located Araminta, that she was in Bodant Park right outside the apartments she owned. A mere five seconds later Ethan had felt her mind's angry dismissive cry resonate throughout the gaiafield. That worried him more than he would ever admit to anyone, even Phelim. Why would someone chosen by the Skylords reject Living Dream so comprehensively? He'd felt her naked emotions, experienced how deep her revulsion for their goal truly was.

Then biononically enriched agents had fought a small war in Bodant Park, a war given total coverage across the wretched unisphere. Honilar's welcome team had been killed – and they were tough operatives. Ethan knew that, he'd authorized their enrichments and training himself. The aftermath had left him deeply shocked. So many dead. More injured. He had prayed to the Lady for guidance and forgiveness.

A prayer cut short by the Speaker of the Senate calling, demanding he end Viotia's occupation and turn over Living Dream's paramilitaries for an independent trial. Ethan's rather reasonable observation that the carnage was caused by representatives of ANA Factions was ignored. The Speaker said that the Security Commission was preparing a resolution that would allow the Navy to intervene if any further human rights violations occurred on such a level. And that ever since Ellezelin's Senator had walked out of the Senate following the condemnation of the Viotia invasion, repudiating its authority as he went, Ellezelin was technically no longer part of the Commonwealth and therefore the Navy's non-internal deployment restriction didn't apply.

There was only one person Ethan could ask for reassurance in such circumstances, and he hesitated to do that. The last thing he wanted right now was to be forced further into reliance on Marius.

Phelim's curt, apprehensive assurances that Bodant Park was just a temporary setback failed to impress. Ethan had now accessed every scrap of information that ever existed on Araminta.

He was deeply suspicious that she'd spent a weekend at Likan's mansion. Likan, of course, claimed complete innocence, that she was just another recruit for his harem. After Bodant Park Ethan had given Phelim permission to bring Likan in for a full memory read. It would be just like that super-capitalist to try to manipulate things to his personal financial advantage. If Araminta's background was as simple as the records claimed, there was no conceivable way she could elude Honilar and the other agents the way she had. An entire planet had been invaded with one purpose: to find her. The resources he'd deployed were using up an appreciable percentage of Ellezelin's gross planetary product. There had never been a manhunt on such a scale in human history.

Somebody was helping her; Ethan was fairly sure it had to be ANA. That subtle interference was bringing about some serious complications to the goal of Pilgrimage. He wasn't sure how he should attempt to counter them.

The Ellezelin civil security alert was totally unexpected. Ethan's exovision was suddenly swamped with a flock of red icons. Five fully armoured guards from the Cabinet Security Service hurried into the oval sanctum as force fields shimmered on around the Orchard Palace. More exoimage graphics showed him sequential protective domes powering up to protect the core of Makkathran2, then the greater civic zone. The alert was originating in the civil spaceflight agency. Something was happening in orbit above Ellezelin.

'Sir,' the Security Service detail leader said. 'Please accompany me to your safe refuge.' A circle of the floor was expanding to reveal a gravity chute.

Hardly authentic, Ethan thought idly. Although technically the Waterwalker's rapport with the city did allow him to pass through solid floors to the tunnels below.

Two of the Security Service detail jumped into the chute where manipulated gravity sucked them away *fast*. Ethan followed them down. To increase the irony of the situation, the fall was similar to the way Edeard flew along Makkathran's travel tunnels; except here Ethan was going feet first.

He dropped out of the chute into a deep shelter half a kilometre below the city. The refuge was a circular chamber with glass walls that partitioned off smaller cubicles and offices. His presidential office was already illuminated, but the others were all unoccupied and dark. A startled skeleton team of security agency staff was scrambling to build up a situation overview in conjunction with the refuge's smartcore.

'What have we got?' he asked.

'Energy discharges in orbit, sir,' the defence agency colonel reported. 'A thousand kilometres up, that's in the parking ring. And, sir, it's high-level weapons fire. The emissions are sophisticated. We think it was two ships, both in stealth mode; we didn't even know they were there until they started shooting at each other.'

'Are they attacking the surface?' Ethan's immediate thought was the Pilgrimage fleet, still under construction and supremely vulnerable.

'No, sir. As far as we can ascertain it's just the two ships engaging each other. No new discharges for the last ten seconds, so it's probably over.'

'That fast?'

'Yes, sir,' the colonel said. 'Modern engagements are quick and decisive. The power levels in the weapons guarantee that.'

'So can we get a clear image now?'

'We're trying, sir. Our civil sensors aren't built for this. Nearby ships have been destroyed, there's a large wreckage field that's expanding rapidly. We're alerting urban areas along the fall-out track.'

'How many ships destroyed?' Ever since he'd announced Pilgrimage, wealthy Living Dream followers had been arriving in their personal starships thinking they could take part in the flight to the Void. The last time he'd enquired, over three thousand were in parking orbit above Ellezelin.

'Over twenty confirmed destroyed, probably fifty damaged. Fatalities unknown.'

'Lady,' Ethan groaned. 'So do you have any idea who the protagonists are?'

'No, sir. Sorry.'

'Has the Commonwealth Navy called your agency?'

'Not yet.'

'Kindly get in touch with them, and formally report this conflict. I'll be interested in their opinion.'

'Yes, sir.'

Ethan's worry was that the conflict in Bodant Park had somehow spilled over to Ellezelin. That the ships were stealthed was a good indication that Faction agents were in orbit, presumably in a last ditch attempt to retrieve the Second Dreamer for their own purposes. Again, he hesitated to call Marius.

'Sir,' the colonel said. 'Back-up sensors are coming on line; we're getting some situation clarification. One ship survived intact. Tracking a great deal of debris.'

'A victor, then,' Ethan said as he accessed the defence agency network. An image of a small ship appeared in his exovision, a smooth ovoid surrounded by a force field's electron-blue shimmer. He knew enough about modern hardware to recognize the type favoured by Faction representatives, and ANA agents. 'So which are you?' he murmured. 'See if you can establish a link with them,' he instructed the colonel.

The colonel never got to try. Ethan's exovision threw up a communication icon he didn't expect. He let the call come through as he walked into his slick modern office. Two of the armour-suited Security Service detail took up position beside the door. Privacy shielding enveloped the room.

'Good evening, Cleric Conservator,' ANA:Governance said.

Ethan settled into a chair which shaped itself to his contours. 'I take it you've monitored the fight above Ellezelin?'

'Indeed.'

'Does the Navy know what's going on?'

'Admiral Kazimir has been informed.'

'Who are they?'

'One of the ships is piloted by an agent working for my security division.'

'I see. Is he the survivor?'

'Fortunately, yes.'

'And the loser?'

'Someone suspected of high treason.'

'High treason?' Ethan didn't know if he should be amused or not. 'That sounds very dramatic.'

'This is classified information, but as a courtesy I will tell you we have discovered the Ocisen Empire fleet on its way to Ellezelin is accompanied by Prime warships.'

Ethan sat perfectly still. For a second he thought the communication link might have malfunctioned somehow. 'Prime?' he asked, glad he had closed his gaiamotes. His shock impulse would have startled the staff working outside.

'Quite,' ANA:Governance said. 'As you can imagine, we are extremely concerned by the development.'

'Was that a Prime ship in orbit?'

'No. However, we believe there was a connection. Fortunately, my agent managed to avoid completely vaporizing the suspect's ship, no small achievement given modern weapons. I am dispatching a forensic team to examine the wreckage. I need to know what the suspect was carrying.'

'I see. Can we help?'

'Yes. Please quarantine the orbital wreckage until my team arrive. No one else is to touch it. My agent will remain in orbit, he has orders to open fire on anyone who contaminates the scene.'

'I understand. I will order my defence agency to establish the quarantine zone.' As he spoke, the sensors showed him the ANA ship gathering up fragments with coherent gravity pulses, pulling them out of decay paths which would have taken them down to the atmosphere.

'Thank you for your cooperation, Cleric Conservator. This is not an easy time for the Greater Commonwealth. I hope that when this situation is resolved, Ellezelin's Senator will resume his seat.'

Ethan didn't bother to point out that Commonwealth politics would be irrelevant to anyone inside the Void. In fact, neither would renewed Prime aggression. 'Can the Navy stop the Ocisen invasion fleet?' he asked.

'Yes. It can and it will.'

'Thank you.'

The call ended, and Ethan sat back, only just realizing how badly his muscles had tightened up. A headache was building behind his eyes; they were frequent now even though the last of the semi-organic auxiliaries had been removed. His doctors warned him it would still take time for his brain to recover fully. He waited a moment, gathering his thoughts, then called the defence colonel in. 'The surviving ship is staying in orbit, I want a two-hundred-kilometre quarantine zone around it. Nobody is authorized to approach, I don't care who they are.'

'Sir,' the colonel licked his lips. 'Rescue ships may need to—'

'Nobody,' Ethan said firmly.

'Yes, sir.'

The colonel hadn't even left the office when Marius called. 'A most unpleasant event in your skies,' the representative said.

'Was that one of your agents up there?'

'Someone we were affiliated with, yes.'

'ANA has requested a quarantine around the wreckage. It says the Prime are part of the Ocisen fleet. It says there's a connection. Is that true?'

'I know nothing of that. I don't have access to Navy intelligence.'

'Really?'

'Yes. Really.'

Ethan wondered if he should challenge the representative directly, but couldn't see any advantage in that. 'What was your ship doing stealthed in orbit around Ellezelin?'

'It was waiting for the Pilgrimage ships to be completed, then it would deliver the consignment of defence systems in its hold.

As you can understand, we don't want them sitting on the ground exposed to ANA's scrutiny.'

A smooth enough answer, and one which Ethan didn't believe for an instant. 'I see.'

'Neither do we want ANA to examine the remnants.'

'That is completely outside my remit.'

'My dear Conservator, if ANA uses the defence systems our ship was carrying as an excuse to curtail our involvement with your Pilgrimage, there will not be any Pilgrimage. And that is exactly the kind of pseudo-legal argument that so many people will seize upon.'

'But I can't do anything. We can hardly attack that ship.'

'A friend of mine will be in touch within the hour. She can explain to your wormhole technicians how they can assist our cause.' Marius closed the link.

'Dear Lady,' Ethan put his head in his hands. Events were becoming too powerful, building their own inertia. He tried to remember why he'd agreed to the representative's help in the first place. Ultradrive was turning into the ultimate poisoned chalice. But even if he reverted to equipping the Pilgrimage ships with an ordinary hyperdrive they'd still need help to get past the warrior Raiel in the Gulf. There was nothing he could do but try and ride the crisis out.

If we just had the Second Dreamer we'd be in a much stronger position. She's the key to success. We have to acquire her. We have to, no matter what the cost.

*

The ExoProtectorate Council watched the new squadron of Capital-class ships matching superluminal flight vectors with the Ocisen Empire fleet. Five of the Navy ships were concentrating their sensors on a single Prime warship, preparing to pull it out of hyperspace.

'This habit is turning into a vulgar repetition,' Ilanthe said, her voice silky with distain.

Kazimir hadn't realized before now how much he missed

Gore at the council; his grandfather was a perfect balance against the Accelerator advocate. More accurately, Gore wouldn't put up with her bullshit point scoring and needling.

Crispen gave her a small grin. 'Ever wondered what kind of effect these snatch raids are having on the Ocisens? I mean, their most powerful allies are being pulled out of space and shot without any warning. Can't be good for morale.'

'Don't compare the Ocisen psychology to ours,' Creewan warned. 'Obedience to the nest father is their paramount concern, in fact it's their only concern. They don't question and worry away at issues like we do.'

'Which makes this interception even more pointless,' Ilanthe said. 'They can't be rattled. They're not going to turn round even if we eliminate every Prime ship there is.'

'I'm not eliminating them,' Kazimir said levelly. 'I want a living immotile.'

'What?' John Thelwell demanded. 'I thought this was the final, final warning, not some capture mission.'

Kazimir met Ilanthe's gaze across the conference table. The lightning outside the big curving window stroked their faces with sharp slivers of flickering light. 'It is the final warning.' To her credit she didn't flinch, but then he didn't expect her to. Less than an hour ago, Paula had reported in that the ice moon Accelerator station had been destroyed by a quantum-buster. Kazimir was mildly surprised Ilanthe had turned up to the ExoProtetorate Council at all. She must know the indomitable investigator was getting close to the kind of evidence ANA needed to suspend the Accelerators.

'What in heaven's name do you want with an immotile?' Creewan asked.

'Intelligence,' Kazimir said. 'We need to know where they come from, which planet or planets they've colonized. Ship numbers. Technology level. Once the Ocisens are eliminated by the deterrence fleet they will be the Navy's next target.'

'Glad to hear it,' John Thelwell said.

'Yes,' said Kazimir. 'It will be interesting to find out how they avoided the Firewall.' He still didn't get a reaction from Ilanthe.

The Navy ships yanked a single Prime warship out of hyperspace. Kazimir followed the engagement closely. He couldn't fault the captains, their strategy was flawless, subjecting the warship's force field to inexorable stress. When the force field finally collapsed, weapons fire against the hull was minimal. They went for electronic warfare, scrambling electronics and knocking out power circuits with quantum magnetic pulses. All at a level that wouldn't interfere with Prime nervous systems. Even with life support equipment knocked out, there was enough air and warmth for the living Primes to survive until they were captured.

Ten marine assault teams got ready to jump across.

The Prime warship exploded.

'Shit,' Kazimir grunted.

'I trust this charade is concluded to your satisfaction,' Ilanthe said. 'Admiral, will you now be launching the deterrence fleet in compliance with the Senate Executive Security Commission resolution?'

Creewan and John Thelwell watched closely.

'Yes,' Kazimir said. 'I will order the launch of the deterrence fleet immediately.' *And what have you put out there to snare it? What are you up to?*

Ilanthe's female persona translocated out of the old-fashioned perceptual reality of the conference room. She reformed herself in a completely different zone of ANA, the Accelerator compilation, that manifested as an inverted world of dark primary colours. She walked across a verdure sky as a heliotrope ocean rippled above her. Airborne wisps of kingfisher-blue light slithered around her, winking in complex sequences designating their sentience level: mirrored personality repositories performing designated secondary tasks while the primary mentality operated on an upper hierarchal level. Her body characteristics morphed away to a simple flawless silver skin, and her own repositories fluttered in, perching themselves on her shoulders and arms like birds of prey. Information squeezed in through the data porous boundary skin.

First analysis was of the Ellezelin interception. Every surviving physical section of Chatfield's starship was encapsulated by trajectory algorithms extrapolated and refined from Ellezelin's monstrously crude orbital sensor arrays. The flight of the eighty thousand scraps of matter were defined in a four-dimensional projection resembling a particularly beautiful scarlet firework scintillation bloom.

Origin point analysis designated the critical segments of the equipment Chatfield had been carrying. Exotic matter fragments were already decaying as their cohesion integrity was broken. But sufficient pieces survived; it would be possible to determine the interstice folds contained within them before their decay sequence fizzled to extinction. ANA might be capable of retro-profiling the nature of the equipment, and that would ruin everything.

Two more blank humanoid shapes walked across the sky. Fellow Accelerators, Colabal and Atha. Ilanthe transferred the trajectory construct to them. 'Supervise the wormhole intercep-tion yourself,' she told Atha. 'It will need to be speedy, the ANA agent will see what's happening and instigate a hyperspacial distortion. You will need to collect seven thousand fragments.'

'Confirmed,' Atha said. The figure reversed its dimensions to zero and translocated.

'Is the replica functioning?' Ilanthe asked Colabal.

'Yes.' The sky beneath their feet began to undulate, its tempo increasing rapidly as if thin stormclouds were speeding past. A section glowed with a pale amber hue. Ilanthe immersed herself into it.

One of the accelerator agents that Colabal ran had collected a sample of Araminta's DNA from the Colwyn City apart-ment block. The sequencing had provided the Accelerators with enough information to formulate Araminta's neural structure.

Every scrap of information on her background had been transformed into simulated memories and loaded in. They were woefully inadequate, Ilanthe acknowledged, but the personality that knitted together was the closest thing they could produce to the actual Second Dreamer herself. Puzzlingly, there were no gaiamotes; how she connected to the gaiafield was a complete mystery.

Ilanthe hung in the middle of the simulacrum, and meshed herself with the mind that flowed within. Emerald threads of neurological emulates blended into her own primary mentality. Ilanthe allowed herself to see the block of flats beside Bodant Park go up in flame, fed in the shock pulse that Araminta had released into the gaiafield. Feelings raged around her, connecting to memories with erratic volatile associations, triggering irrational emotional responses.

Ilanthe disconnected herself. 'Laril,' she said. 'She will turn to her ex-husband for help.' This disconcerting meat-based memory fluttered through her thoughts, illogical and shaky. 'He represents a stability she has not known before or since. It is not a pleasant refuge for her, but a dependable one. She lacks that above all else.'

'He's migrating inwards,' Colabal said. 'That makes him susceptible. And his reputation is established. We can make cooperation worth his while. He is also weak. He will capitulate to threats.'

'Proceed,' Ilanthe said. She opened a secure link to Neskia. 'Marius made a huge mistake bringing Chatfield into operation this early,' she told the station chief. 'And using the Cat against Paula was another blunder, he should have known better than to exploit personal animosity. His stupidity has exposed us to an unacceptable level of risk. Consequently, I'm restructuring our event sequence. Please take immediate command of the swarm, and bring it to Sol.'

'I'll fly to it now,' Neskia said. 'Do you want me to eliminate Marius?'

'Not yet. I will restrict his initiative freedoms. It should act as a suitable caution. Clipping the wings of those who fly highest is always a profound disciplinary action upon them.'

'I always found him unreliable.'

'I know. His temperament suited the majority of tasks he was assigned to. He may have come to enjoy the game so much he has lost sight of the goal. A common enough occurrence.'

'Well I certainly haven't.'

'I will rendezvous with you at the agreed point. If all goes well. And it should. Kazimir is authorizing the deployment of the deterrence fleet.'

'Finally! I wonder what it is.'

'We'll know soon enough.' Ilanthe ended the connection to the agent. Above her a black globe slipped out from the languid mirror-purple waves, no more than twice her height. She rose to greet it, slipping through the formless surface.

Ilanthe emerged through the side of a chamber measuring an apparent half a million kilometres across. The citadel of Accelerator ethos. Like an ancient godling she took flight, chasing through the chains of translucent planet-sized globes that spun idly through the immense formatted interstice. Flocks of fellow Accelerators flashed past her, calling out in welcome to their leader. They trailed long potentialities behind them, fragments of nonreality that struggled for existence then dissipated into little more than dreams. All of them, all of her kind, strove to imprint themselves on the modified space-time of their artificial environment, to bend reality to their wishes. Just as the Void achieved so effortlessly. Every second of existence was devoted to extrapolating the structure that would achieve the ultimate post-physical manifestation.

Up ahead, the inversion core glimmered with suppressed power, ready for her. Ready to break free and carry human evolution to heights not even ANA could envisage. Ready to change the nature of the universe forever.

*

The Wurung Transport cab reached the end of the metro line sometime in the early hours. Araminta was not quite dozing when it came to a gentle halt in the middle of the Francola district. She'd never visited before, never even considered any of the properties which came up for sale here. In economic terms the area was as run down as the Salisbury district, but this decay was subtle, verging on genteel, as if the district had fallen into a cosy slumber, a retirement village content with its lot. The buildings here were mostly housing. Large and expensive when they were built, many had been subdivided into apartments. Sprawling gardens had matured, the trees growing up taller than roofs, casting long shadows during the day. Fallen leaves formed a dry mantle across the road, stirring briefly as the cab swished past.

Araminta opened the door and climbed out. Her boots crunched on the crisp brown leaves as she looked round, getting her bearings. About a mile away, behind the houses directly ahead of her, the city's force field was a near-vertical wall of shimmering air. She craned her neck, following the insubstantial barrier as it curved overhead to cover the entirety of Colwyn City. A flat layer of starlit clouds parted to slither around it, while the stars themselves were distorted smears of light speckling the apex high above the river in the middle of the city. She brought her head down again, almost dizzy.

'Go back to the nearest public slot and wait for me there,' she told the cab. Not that she expected to come back, not for a while anyway; but living with paranoia for the last few days had switched her brain to a very cautious mode of thinking.

The door closed up, and it hummed away down the rail. Araminta knew which way to go, it was instinctive; beyond the houses, where the streets ended and a strip of big native dapol trees acted as a buffer between the buildings and the force field. There was a warmth to be had there, her mind sensed, a calmness that was almost the opposite of the gaiafield's exuberant emotive bustle.

She walked along the pavement, heading down the gentle

slope and occasionally shying away from the hedges that had grown up to lean across the cracked mossy concrete. Little nocturnal rodents scurried about in the undergrowth, and she heard cats yowling somewhere, a cry that carried a long way in the still air.

The last house at the end of the cul de sac had almost been swamped by vegetation from its own garden, which had been untended for years. Trees from the backdrop of woods were slowly reclaiming the land that had once been cleared for lawns and ornamental beds, advancing the forest in a tide of luxuriant growth, with fresh saplings shooting up closer and closer to the house's moss encrusted walls.

She could just make out the bottom of the force field now, suspended twenty metres from the ground. From her angle it looked as though the spiky treetops were holding it up. Cressida had said the gap was guarded, though not how. Araminta had no intention of finding out; she certainly couldn't see any Ellezelin capsules, not even using her nightsight function. Unfortunately, her Advancer heritage wasn't up to supplying her with infrared. Lack of knowing what was lurking among the trees made her very conscious of what could be watching her with enriched senses, laughing quietly as she blundered about.

Crumbling enzyme-bonded concrete beneath her feet gave way to grass and the wide indigo fans of whiplit ferns. Araminta pushed her way forward into the dark spaces between the dapol trees. There were no thoughts impinging on the local gaiafield, no human ones anyway. The gentle thoughts of the Silfen Motherholm were somehow stronger. More so in one direction. She turned towards it, and pushed sharp branches out of her way. Dense whiplit fronds pressed against her legs, their curly strands damp from the night, making progress difficult.

She caught a glimpse of blue and red laser fans sweeping through the tangle of trees and froze. She was all too familiar with the strobes on Ellezelin support capsules by now. This one was just outside the force field, flying slowly along a shallow curve. Some patrol scanning for citizens seeking escape from the invasion.

The minds of the crew and paramilitary squad inside emitted a dull glow of thoughts into the gaiafield. All of them were tired, emotionally and physically, and they hated Colwyn City and its resentful inhabitants.

Araminta kept still until the capsule had glided away. She was close to the force field now, maybe just a couple of hundred yards away, but the trees must have shielded her from the capsule's sensors. Her legs were soaking from the moisture on the whiplit fronds. Hands and cheeks had been scratched by dead twigs. And she was beginning to feel somewhat foolish floundering round in a forest at night, looking for a path that was actually some kind of alien wormhole which she was supposed to be able to sense because her ancestor was a friend of elves and the magic passed through the female bloodline.

'Makes perfect sense to me,' she muttered to herself. *I wonder what the me of a week ago would make of all this?*

Thankfully, she stumbled out into a narrow animal track, and started along it. The fronds didn't accost her so much, though she still had to ward off the branches.

Dear Ozzie, was it really only a week ago I was living a perfectly ordinary life? And I haven't called Bovey for days. He must be worried sick. Cressida will be worried too, and cross that I haven't confirmed my ticket offplanet.

The trees were spaced further apart now, the path easier to perceive. She couldn't tell if that was because of a weak dawn light starting to rise, or if her mind was illuminating the compressed trail of loamy soil that had borne so many feet before hers. But she did know she was walking the right way, a knowledge that came in the form of cold relief. That newfound buoyancy faltered after only a few yards as she instinctively accepted the path was truly taking her away from her homeworld.

I'm being forced out, she thought bitterly. *I haven't even said goodbye to all the people I love. Not that there are many of them, but I should be allowed that.* Even though she was more confident about using the gaiafield, she still didn't dare access the unisphere. That would be the first thing she would have to fix when she reached whatever world she was heading for. Araminta wanted to know who the hell Oscar Monroe was, and why he would help her. If he was telling the truth about working for ANA, and ANA wanted her to be free, there might be hope yet.

It was definitely getting lighter, even though Araminta knew it was still a couple of hours before dawn. She didn't recognize most of the trees she was walking through now, either, the old familiar dapol trees were becoming few and far between. The newcomers were taller and thinner, with slimmer branches and silver-green leaves. Strange lavender star-flowers peeped up through the wiry yellow-tinged grass as the ground started to tip down. There was no sight of the force field through the upper branches of the new trees. And the gaiafield was fading out, allowing her tense thoughts to expand, calming the deep worry contaminating her body. Somewhere the Silfen Motherholm smiled in compassion for her.

The trees were thinning out, and Araminta shivered in the cold air gusting past the white and green striped trunks, rubbing her hands along her arms and pulling up the front of her fleece. Then she walked out of the treeline and stopped dead.

'Oh, great Ozzie,' she murmured in astonished delight. She was halfway up a steep valley wall. The grassy mountainside beneath her feet swept down towards a broad meandering river. On the other side, maybe twenty or thirty miles away, the opposite side of the valley climbed upwards, its summits coated in thick fields of snow. Above that ... Araminta shielded her eyes from the orange sun peeping over the jagged peaks. A quartet of tiny moons was racing across the sky, twisting round each other as they went. She was sure one of them must have been made from blue crystal, glints of sunlight flashed off its facets as it spun round and round.

Viotia didn't have moons like that. In fact she'd never heard of anywhere that did.

Somewhere beyond the river, lurking among the spinneys and tracts of woodland, Araminta could sense the beginnings of another path. She set off down the mountain, laughing joyfully at her liberation.

Inigo's Twelfth Dream

The summer sun rose through a clear sky to illuminate one very excited city. It was election day in Makkathran. At last – after all the turmoil, the Sampalok riots and the banishment, followed by a fortnight of increasingly bitter campaigning by both mayoral candidates, and equally lively mud-slinging by the district Representatives – this was it. The day everyone got to make their opinion known on events and promises.

Edeard jogged over the Brotherhood Canal bridge and into Jeavons as the dawntime's dew began to evaporate off the grass. It produced a wonderfully fresh scent in the air, triggering a completely unjustified sense of optimism as he reached the streets of Jeavons. Unjustified because the city's mood was impossible to determine. So much had happened. So much to take in. So many rumours and whispers from the candidates and their allies to believe or ignore. Nobody knew what the result was going to be.

One thing was for certain, a lot of people were going to vote. As he ran down Golfice Street, Edeard could sense whole families rising early for breakfast. Election day was always a holiday. Businesses that were normally preparing to open as he ran past were shut for the day, market squares were devoid of stalls.

A holiday, then, but not a carnival. There was too much tension for that. Not helped by the fifty banished who'd made camp in the trees beyond North Gate and refused to budge.

Relatives and friends and the politically motivated kept taking food out to them and making public collections. Keeping the cause alive and visible.

Edeard arrived back at the tenement and hurried up the stairs to his maisonette. Dinlay was waiting on the walkway outside. They grinned at each other and went in. Breakfasts together had become something of a ritual since the day in Sampalok.

'Moment of truth then,' Dinlay said as Edeard stripped off and scurried into the shower.

'Yes,' Edeard called out above the spray of water.

'I've never known so many people say they're coming out to vote. I suppose that's a victory in its own way.'

'What do you mean?'

Dinlay had sat himself at the small table where one of the ge-chimps was serving him with fruit and cereal. The second genistar was tending the kettle on the iron stove. 'You've finally got people stirred up about the city's leadership. Before, it never really made any difference which candidate you voted for. Nothing was different afterwards.'

Edeard stepped out and started rubbing himself dry with a towel. 'That's down to Finitan rather than me.'

Dinlay laughed. 'I'm not sure I believe the false modesty routine any more.'

'Okay, if I'm that confident about myself, how come I'm not standing?'

'Not the right time,' Dinlay said shrewdly. 'For all you achieved, you're still too young. Even Captain is pushing it.'

'Ha!' Edeard grunted. Walsfol hadn't objected to Ronark's astute manoeuvring; indeed he'd been keen to accept the old captain in his own office at the Courts of Justice. Crucially, Owain had mounted no challenge to Edeard's promotion as he took charge of the Jeavons constable station. Coming into direct conflict with the Waterwalker while the city's mood was unknown was not something the wily Mayor would allow to happen. They'd maintained a scrupulously courteous attitude to each other ever since the Sampalok riots. Sometimes it was all

Edeard could do not to snigger at how polite they were whenever they met. There were strong elements of farce to the encounters.

Edeard flicked his friend's epaulettes playfully. 'Thank you, Corporal.'

'That's different,' Dinlay said, straightening the epaulettes. 'These were well deserved and sorely earned.'

The ge-chimp brought two large cups of tea over to the table. Edeard picked his up, and gave Dinlay a mildly concerned look. 'Er . . . you didn't want to be Master of Sampalok, did you?'

'By the Lady!' Dinlay was genuinely shocked. 'No, Edeard. I'm a constable. And that means so much more today, all thanks to you. I'm going to be Chief Constable to your Mayor.'

'Okay. I was sort of improvising back there.'

'I know. But it was a clever choice. He already knows far more about Grand Family politics than I ever will.'

'The Grand Council needs to worry about her, not him,' Edeard said.

'And that's a fact.'

They grinned again, then finished their light meal in companionable silence. The ge-chimps cleared the table, then started picking up Edeard's discarded jogging clothes, putting them in the laundry basket. Dinlay paused as he was pulling on his jacket, noticing something odd. His third hand swiped one of Edeard's odd running shoes. 'I've never seen anything like this before. Did they have them in your village?'

'No,' Edeard said as he buttoned up his own jacket. 'Something I dreamt up. They're very comfortable to run in.'

Dinlay shrugged and gave the shoe back to the ge-chimp.

They walked out of the tenement together and headed for the district's public hall. Edeard's farsight swept through the scene ahead. The hall stood by itself in the middle of a square, a strange onion-shaped building standing on twenty fat pillars. Big folding wooden doors had been fixed between them, sealing off the large central auditorium from the elements. The curving internal wall that overlooked the chamber was ribbed by eight narrow galleries that provided access to the hundreds of small unlit cubicles wrapped around the whole structure like a honey-comb. For once, the galleries didn't have Makkathran's bad stairs between them, instead the hall boasted steep ramps. Nobody ever really used the galleries or their cubicles.

On the floor of the auditorium long tables had been set up, along with voting booths. Constables from Jeavons station worked alongside a team from the Guild of Clerks preparing the hall ready for the election. The clerks had their big ledgers of official registry ready, along with sealed boxes of ballot papers.

People were already arriving outside, well ahead of the official starting time. They were all watching the end of Forpal Avenue when Edeard and Dinlay emerged. Farsight had forewarned everyone the Waterwalker was on his way. Edeard smiled pleas-antly as he moved through them, making sure his mind was well shielded, not allowing anybody to see how nervous he was becoming. He'd never seen an election before. Back in Ashwell the vote for the Mayor was limited to village elders.

Felax opened the door to let them inside the auditorium, saluting as they went past. Edeard saluted back; it was good to see constables actually out of the station again on active duties. The team he'd built up to help him fight the gangs had spent far too long cooped up in the small hall working diligently through paperwork like apprentice clerks. Now they were out on patrol again, visible and helpful to citizens as they should be.

The clerks inside the public hall were completing their prepa-rations. As soon as Edeard arrived Urarl beckoned him over to the first table.

'Boxes are ready for inspection sir.'

'Thank you,' Edeard said. He looked to the Master of Clerks standing beside Urarl, who nodded. Edeard used his farsight to examine the wax seal on each box to check if it had been tampered with. He couldn't sense any flaws.

'They are undisturbed,' he announced.

'I concur,' the Master of Clerks agreed. He proffered a clipboard to Edeard, who had to sign the docket for each box in triplicate. The Master added his signature.

Under Urarl's instruction, Marcol and two other probationary constables opened the boxes and started distributing ballot papers along the tables. Edeard did his best not to smile at Marcol's diligence. The boy was trying desperately hard, and slowly succeeding in throwing off his Sampalok upbringing to shape up as a decent constable.

'Almost time,' the Master of Clerks said.

Edeard used his farsight to perceive the Orchard Palace. The Grand Master of the Guild of Clerks was standing on the balcony that faced Golden Park. He was waiting stoically, a big brass pocket-watch in his hand. Everyone in the hall finished what they were doing and waited. It was a scene that was repeated in every single district across Makkathran.

'I declare the voting open,' the Grand Master longtalked.

Dinlay gave Felax the okay, and the auditorium doors were opened. First in were the accredited observers from both mayoral candidates, who presented their papers to the Master of Clerks and Edeard. Balogg, the current Jeavons District Representative, was the first voter, as tradition dictated. He was followed in by his two rivals. All of them were allied to Finitan, claiming to support the banishment.

Edeard watched with quiet interest as the voting began. People came in and went over to the clerks, who confirmed their residency in the ledger. After that they were issued with their two ballot papers, one for the Mayor's office, and one for the District Representative. They went into the little booth to mark the paper, most casting a seclusion haze for privacy, though some proudly and openly put crosses down for their candidate. Finally, the ballots were posted through a slot in the lid of a metal box that was already locked and sealed. The keys were kept by the Grand Master of the Clerks Guild. Edeard couldn't see any way to cheat the system, provided everything was conducted in the open and monitored by honest dependable officials. Which, he acknowledged sadly, was the weak point.

Dinlay had taken great delight in telling him of hidden ballot boxes stuffed with voting slips by a single candidate that 'appeared' along with the real ones in the Malfit Hall where the count would be made. Of the 'ghosts' on the registry. Of bribes. Of people claiming to be someone else.

'If voting never makes a difference,' Edeard asked, 'why go to so much trouble?'

'To make sure it doesn't make a difference,' Dinlay explained. 'And don't forget, a Representative is paid to perform their Council duties, as well as living in a grand old official City residence along with a dozen other perks. That alone is quite an incentive to get yourself re-elected.'

Forty minutes after the doors opened there was a lull in voting as the eager early birds finished up. Edeard went over to the clerks and collected his own ballot papers.

'Remember who supported you,' Balogg said in a loud jovial voice as Edeard went into the privacy booth.

'And I'm pledged to continue to support you no matter what,' one of his rivals cried out.

Edeard grinned at them as he went in. It was good humoured. But still there was an undercurrent of tension. He spread the small squares of paper out on the little shelf, and picked up the pencil before casting a seclusion haze. On the Mayor's ballot he automatically put a cross by Finitan's name. He hesitated on the Representative; Balogg had been supportive, and he'd had the courage to sign the Exclusion warrants with Vologral. The others were vocal in their approval of banishment, but unproven. *Balogg deserves my thanks for what he's done*, Edeard decided, and put his cross by the Representative's name. *So nothing has changed.*

Democracy was a strange thing, he thought as he came out and posted his ballots into the metal box. A couple of sullen youths were collecting their ballots from the clerks; they didn't meet his eye as they went to the booths. *And the two of them can outvote me*, he realized in dismay. Then he was ashamed for being so prejudiced. *That's what democracy is: holding the strong accountable, making sure they don't become too strong. Rah was right to give us this system.*

There was another surge of voters a little later as people

finished their breakfasts. Then a lull. Then mid morning saw the queues lengthening again. Edeard sent his farsight into neighbouring Silvarum, then Drupe. The voting was the same there, light but constant. No sign of trouble. He searched round the other districts. It was all pretty much the same. Except Sampalok. There, long queues snaked away from the district hall. Several squads of constables kept everyone in line, more than at any other district. Edeard observed several disputes with the clerks over residency. The official candidate observers were making heated interjections.

Sampalok was the one place he could not go today – not even if a small war broke out over voting rights. The local constables would have to handle it, with reinforcements from Bellis and Myco if necessary. Walsfol had several contingency plans worked out in case.

I have to trust other people to do their jobs. That's democracy, too.

There were seven candidates standing to be Sampalok's Representative. Three pro-Waterwalker, four pro-Bise. He didn't like the ratio, but again that wasn't down to him. He was simply glad that anyone in that district supported him. Though Macsen and Kanseen seemed to have been accepted. Or at least, they hadn't been forced out yet. Today's result would be a powerful indicator whether their appointment was going to be permanent or not. Nobody was arguing with the City's right to proclaim District Masters: it was too novel, too far outside the ordinary. But if Bise's old guard gained ground, the whispering campaign would start in earnest.

Edeard couldn't believe anyone would vote for Owain after the debacle with the militia. But you never knew. *Democracy! Is this why the cityborn are so proficient at shielding their feelings? To keep politicians on their toes.*

Beyond Sampalok, his farsight lingered briefly on the recently refurbished (again) House of Blue Petals. Feeling mildly guilty, he observed the pro-Owain party it was throwing for its clientele. It wasn't strictly against election rules, which forbade monetary encouragement to vote for a candidate, but sailed close to the limit. He shook his head in disapproval, but then such petty defiance was typical of Ranalee. She'd finally emerged from behind all the obstructive paperwork with a legitimate claim on the ownership of the bordello. And that's all it was now, a lewd business which filed correct tax forms with the Guild of Clerks. Edeard had left it and her alone. Ranalee had clearly found her place in life, and in the meantime there were bridges to rebuild, and the Waterwalker couldn't afford to appear vindictive in any way. He and Finitan had agreed a line must be drawn under the day of banishment if the city was to move forward.

After a few hours hanging round the hall doing exactly nothing, Edeard left Dinlay in charge and headed in to Haxpen.

Finitan's farsight found him as he crossed Flight Canal. 'So have you voted yet, young Edeard?'

'Yes, sir.'

'Did I get your approval?'

'Voting is private, sir.'

Finitan's humour carried through his longtalk. 'It certainly is. Unfortunately.'

'Any idea how it's going, sir?'

'Indications are good so far. Those who speak to the observers are effusive. According to the percentage we calculated an hour ago, I'm in the lead.'

'But that is good news.'

'Remember when you walked into Sampalok to arrest Buate? Everything seemed to be going smoothly, then Owain damn near walked away with the day. Never underestimate him.'

'I'll remember, sir.'

'Ah . . . I'm sorry, Edeard. I haven't slept in days. I'm worried. What if I lose? I've gambled everything on this election.'

'Sir, I remember what you told me at our first meeting. You said that even those in high office would never be able to change anything. Well, I believe you're about to prove yourself wrong.'

'Thank you, Edeard. At least you and I know we gave this our best endeavour. That is what we will be judged on.'

'Yes, sir.'

When he arrived at the Culverit mansion there wasn't much activity inside. In fact it was almost deserted apart from the guards who greeted him warmly enough.

Kristabel was waiting in one of the lounges on the top floor, sitting at a wide leather-topped desk with folders stacked up on either side of her. Her hair had been plaited into a tight tail, which hung loosely down her back. Her dress was a pale lemon, which she'd accompanied by a thick gold necklace made with figure-of-eight links. It suited her perfectly.

She was writing when he came in, the tip of her long onyx fountain pen quivering furiously. There was a wonderfully intense frown on her face. Edeard wished he could capture the image forever.

'You look like you're signing a death warrant,' he said.

She gave him a disapproving look. 'I am.'

'What?'

'You see all this?' Her hand waved expansively at the paperwork. 'This is my family, which is going to be your family as soon as we get married.'

'Er, right.'

'Daddy has decided that you and I will have the entire tenth floor for ourselves, which is very sweet of him. But, that also means he and Mirnatha will live on the ninth floor below us, along with aunt Rishia and cousin Gorral, in addition to Uncle Lorin and his wife and children and the first three grandchildren. Uncle Lorin really isn't happy about that. He and Daddy had a stinking row about it last night. Daddy just says he knew it was inevitable and he should accept it. Uncle Lorin has accused him of abdicating to you. But Daddy's still Master so down to the ninth he goes, which means a lot of people there get displaced down another floor.'

'Oh Lady, I know your uncle doesn't like me . . .'

'Ha! Honious take him. That's not the real problem. It's the families on the third floor that I've got to deal with.'

'Third?'

'Yes, below that it's just the staff.'

'Right.'

'Once everyone here has adjusted, there's going to be eleven sets of cousins move out.'

'Eleven?' Edeard muttered in dismay as he pulled a chair over to sit in front of her desk. Jessile had said something about her father giving her a country estate, but that was as a dowry.

'Yes, and I'm the one who has got to find somewhere in our estate to put them all.' Kristabel rested a hand on top of a pile of folders. 'These are details on lands and farms and vineyards and houses and other properties we own beyond the Iguru Plain. Of course, they're all currently occupied as well.'

'This is crazy,' he declared. 'Families shouldn't have to support so many . . . relatives.'

'Deadbeats?'

'I wouldn't quite say that.'

'Actually, my cousins on the third floor aren't as bad as the ones further up. At least they knew they were going to have to move out some day. Most of them have taken some kind of schooling, even if it's not terribly practical. And a few are now seriously considering joining a Guild; cousin Dalbus has already arranged for a commission in the militia. It's everyone else who can't stand the idea of losing status, not to mention their place on the entitlement list.'

'Entitlement list?'

'Senior family members are entitled to money from the Culverit estate. The further removed you are from the succession, the smaller the amount.'

'Oh Lady, so when I come along and marry you—'

'Actually, everyone's entitlement stays the same until we start having children. Then they all get bumped down the list.'

Edeard grinned. 'How many children are we planning on having?'

'Let's put it this way: we'd need to have seventy before Uncle Lorin gets disqualified.'

'People should always have a goal in life.'

'Edeard Waterwalker! If you think I'm bearing you *seventy* children—'

He started laughing. Kristabel tried to give him a cross look, and failed. She smiled wearily. 'Well how many do you want?'

'I don't know. I was an only child, so definitely more than one—but I agree less than seventy.'

'All right.' She stood up. 'We'll resume negotiations after lunch. It's a buffet, I'm afraid. The staff are all off voting.'

'Oh, dear Lady, how the senior family suffer for the good of the city. You'll have to order your own genistars around next.'

'If you want to be capable of siring just one child, watch your mouth.'

'Yes, Mistress.'

They walked out on to the hortus, looking over the south-western districts. Edeard's arm instinctively went round her shoulder. The winds fluffed her skirt around.

'Is Finitan going to win?' Kristabel asked softly.

'He must. Nobody in their right mind would vote for Owain. Surely people understand what he was trying to do with the militia.'

She pressed her lips together. 'This is Makkathran. Anything can happen.'

'Have you been to vote yet?'

Kristabel gave him one of *those* looks. 'No, Edeard. People like me don't vote.'

'I thought everybody is entitled to vote.'

'Everybody is. But it's considered bad form for senior members of Grand Families. We carry enough power as it is.'

'It was bad form to vote against our Marriage Consent bill. You could get one back on Bise by going down to the hall and voting.'

'Two wrongs don't make a right,' she said automatically.

'Yeah, I know.'

'Is he still out there?'

'Bise? Yes. Him and his closest family have moved into one of the Gilmorn farms twenty miles away.'

'How do you know?'

'Argian has been doing what he does best, and stretching his farsight for me.'

'I'm not sure I trust him.'

'Did you know the families have agents like him?'

'Daddy never said anything specific, but I've always known we were supposed to be protected in a way ordinary people weren't. *Things* get done quietly if you need them to be. I suppose I will be introduced to the right people when I become Mistress.'

'I wonder who they're loyal to in times like this?'

'The most conservative families, trust me.'

'You're probably right.'

She cuddled up close. 'You're learning.'

They ate lunch on the hortus, on a long stone table under an archway of flowering honeysuckle. Julan and Mirnatha joined them; the little girl was delighted to be able to pick her own food from the array of dishes the cooks had prepared the previous night, going back several time for slices of smoked hulfish and clotted cheese cream until her father told her no more. She sulked for a while before collecting her pudding of toffee banana cake.

It was a lazy, pleasant afternoon which followed. Kristabel talked with her father on redistributing their family members from the third floor. Edeard finally began to gain an appreciation of just how widespread their holdings were.

The whole agreeable family scene gave him an insight into what the next century might be like, with his children having a similar discussion in another thirty years as they took over the ninth floor and more third-floor cousins prepared to leave. Such a thing gave him a sense of continuity, firming up the future from a few vague notions of trying to make life better; this was particulars, making solid plans for expansion and still better days. Like nothing he'd known before.

Captain Ronark longtalked him in the middle of the afternoon. 'Take a look who just showed up to vote in Lillylight.'

Edeard obliged, focusing his farsight on the Opera House annexe where the Lillylight voting was conducted. Master Cherix was standing in front of a clerk who was running through the registry ledger. Edeard grinned at the lawyer's distinctive mental signature – no mistake, it was definitely him. When he checked by using the city's perception he saw Cherix was keeping his composure, waiting with apparent patience for the clerk to find his name. 'I wonder where he's been holed up?' The constables had been unable to locate him on the day of banishment; since then Edeard had more pressing issues than tracking down the lawyer.

'What do you suggest we do?' Ronark asked.

'Let him vote. He only ever had an exclusion warrant against him because it was useful to me. They've all served their purpose, I suppose we should cancel the outstanding ones. And persecuting Cherix now would make me seem petty.'

'All right, I'll longtalk the Lillylight captain.'

Edeard kept watch on the voting hall. After a couple of minutes the clerk suddenly found Cherix's entry in the ledger and handed over his ballot papers. Edeard thought the lawyer looked surprised when it happened. He definitely looked relieved as he walked to the privacy booth.

Was it deliberate? Was Owain trying to stir up a little sympathy, or was Cherix just wanting to know where he stood? Lady, I'm on edge.

'Are you all right?' Kristabel asked.

'Yes,' he smiled reassuringly. *Actually, if that's the worst Owain can do today, I'm perfectly all right.*

Edeard was back at the Jeavons public hall when the Grand Master of the Guild of Clerks stood on the Orchard Palace balcony again to announce the end of the voting. He watched the clerks sealing up the slots on the voting boxes, signed the dockets to say he'd seen it, and watched as two squads of constables carried them out. Dinlay was assigned to accompany them to the Orchard Palace.

'Eighty per cent turnout,' the Master of Clerks said as he picked up his own papers.

'High then,' Edeard said.

'I've never known that many voters bother before; and this is my twenty-second election.'

'A good sign, then?'

The old Master gave him a dry smile. 'For someone.'

There were a couple of hours between the time the voting officially ended and the counting began. Edeard took a gondola down to Sampalok. It was all right now voting was finished, there were no political consequences to his visiting.

The gondola dropped him off at the Mid Pool concourse, and he made his way along Zulmal Street. The families who lived along the street gave him a guarded welcome. As always his footsteps slowed as he passed the baker's where Boyd had been shot. Just about all the shops and businesses had re-opened, helped by money from the Diroal family's fortune. It was the same across the district, most of the damage from the riots had been repaired. Commerce was back on its usual uncompromising path.

When he finally reached the central square, the new hexagonal mansion was over twelve feet high, and the second storey was forming under the first that had grown up. According to his design, there were another six to come, each one larger than the previous, giving it a stepped outline. A conservative reckoning was another four months before it would be complete. Which meant the new Master and Mistress had set up their temporary home in the Bea's Bottle tavern on the south side of the square.

Edeard waved cheerfully to the tavern's landlord as he walked in. After the first couple of days the man had come to accept the situation, especially as it meant renting out every room he had to the clerks who were sorting out the Diroal family finances, and providing them with food and drink, along with everyone else who came visiting the new Master and Mistress – there were a great many.

Macsen and Kanseen had taken over seven rooms on the

fourth floor. One had a balcony overlooking the square, where they could watch their new mansion rising. Edeard found them sitting there sharing a bottle of white wine. When they offered him a glass he took a look at the label. With Kristabel educating him he'd come to recognize quality. 'Nice,' he said appreciatively, and took a sip. 'Definitely.'

'Yes,' Kanseen said, and stretched out on her chair. 'A girl could quite easily get corrupted by this life.'

Edeard took a look at the boxes and bags piled up in the room behind the balcony. The shop names were from many districts, all frequented by the women of Grand Families as they commissioned their exclusive clothes. It wasn't just wines he was becoming familiar with these days. 'Nice to see you're rising above it.'

Macsen chuckled, and raised a glass. 'There are certain expectations. District Masters must act the part.'

'And dress for it, too.'

'Yes, I was most careful with that; I made sure I used the same tailor Kristabel gets your uniforms from.'

Edeard groaned and gave up, taking a larger sip of wine as he settled into a chair next to his friends. 'So how did the election go in Sampalok?'

'Relatively honest, I think,' Kanseen said. 'No fights at the district hall, anyway. The constables had to step in to stop a few heated disputes over residency, but nothing they couldn't handle.'

'Any idea which Representative got elected?' Edeard asked.

'Nope. You're going to have to wait along with the rest of the city.'

'Lady! How do the candidates stand this?'

Macsen eyed him lazily. 'Lady help us, what are you going to be like when you finally stand for Mayor?'

'I never will. Not now I know what it's like.'

'Ha!' Macsen took a sip of wine.

'I heard our old friend Cherix had crawled back into the public domain,' Kanseen said.

'Yes.' Edeard eyed the wine in the glass. 'Life just wouldn't be the same without him.'

'You need to watch that sentimental streak,' she said 'They'll exploit that.'

'Who?' Macsen said indignantly. 'There's nobody left to reinstate the gangs. Owain is going to lose. The families will accept Edeard and they'll adapt as they always do. For them very little will change, but for ordinary citizens things will get a whole lot better. And best of all, Bise will slowly lose his influence along with his so-called friends. Argian told me his old allies are growing tired of him already. This election should see the end of him.'

'Lady, please let it be so,' Edeard muttered. 'Did Bise manage to save anything?'

'Nobody knows,' Macsen said sourly. 'The clerks have been reviewing the Diroal estate for two weeks solid; and all they can tell me so far is that it's going to take years to track down every last farthing. A lot of it never will be recovered, I suspect. Bise and his ancestors were good at covering up the full extent of their holdings. Just like the rest of the Grand Families, they know how to avoid their full tax liability. It's one of the principal reasons they all became so wealthy.'

'There will be funds he can draw on to keep him in fancy clothes and fine wines for the rest of his life,' Kanseen said. 'In fact, it might be a good idea to let that be known among his old friends. I suspect the Gilmorns wouldn't be quite so free with their coinage if they knew he had lands and money stashed away.' She grinned evilly. 'Would you like me to tell Ranalee?'

Edeard tipped his glass at her. 'I'll think about it.'

'Even without a full inventory, we're still incredibly rich,' Macsen said. 'As are all the businesses that suffered during the riots. The clerks are still paying out compensation on a pro-rata basis. I've heard it said that people are smashing up their own homes and claiming it happened during the riot simply to qualify for new furniture and clothes. There's so much coinage flooding the district it's changing the whole economy. The pro-

Bise candidates have been accusing you of trying to buy the election.'

'I hadn't thought of it,' Edeard admitted. 'I also didn't think what spending all of Bise's money would do to Sampalok. But, as I suspect most of it was squeezed out of the residents here for the last few generations, I suppose there's a kind of poetic justice to handing it back.'

'Except those that aren't getting any compensation are resentful,' Kanseen sighed.

'Another noble gesture goes chronically wrong,' Macsen said.

'I didn't realize how much half of the Diroal estate would be. Maybe the rest of the money could go into some kind of general fund to benefit Sampalok?' Edeard suggested.

'Ah, now you're changing things, going back on your word.'

'Yes, but I didn't intend to— Oh Lady take them. It can wait until after the results. And then it'll all be your problem anyway.'

'Thanks for that,' Macsen said.

Edeard lowered his voice, casting a strong seclusion haze. 'How are you two coping, anyway?'

'Just that,' Kanseen said. 'Coping. We don't have much Lady-damned choice. A whole load of Bise's staff are lobbying to continue in their old jobs once the mansion's fully grown. I don't like the idea of using people who devoted their lives to the Diroals, but how else are we going to stop things from sliding back to how they were before? And when we sit on the local council we have to make fast decisions that'll affect people's lives, without any reference as to what went before. So far we haven't hurt too many residents.'

'Sounds like you are in control and setting a good example. I can't ask for more. How has the Upper Council taken your appointment?'

'Owain welcomed us like we'd been sitting there for five hundred years,' she said. 'The rest just fell into line with that. Of course, there've only been three sessions since the riots. We'll see what happens after the election.'

'It was so unbelievably sweet seeing my dear half-brother's

face when I walked past him in my robes,' Macsen said with a far-away gaze. 'I'm as rich as him now, and I have a seat on the Council, which he doesn't.'

'*We* have a seat on Council,' Kanseen pointed out.

'Yes, dear.'

Her third hand gave him a sharp tweak. Edeard laughed at the wounded expression on his face. 'Ah, married life. I have all this to look forward to.'

Kanseen narrowed her eyes and gave him a shrewd look. 'And what about you? What are your grand plans?'

'It all depends—'

'Let's just assume Finitan gets in tonight, shall we?' she said brusquely. 'What do you do next?'

'Nothing dramatic,' he said, and gestured down at the square with its embryonic structure. 'I intend to support Finitan because I believe he's right. First, consolidate the city, and to do that you need to implement the rule of law. It doesn't take that much, the Grand Council let things slip, but the organizations and concepts Rah founded are still there, they just need revitalizing, that's all.'

'People are generally happier now that the gangs have been beaten,' Macsen agreed. 'You've shown them things can be put right no matter how bad they seemed. But, Edeard, you also showed people what you are and what you're capable of.'

'I'd never abuse the trust the city puts in me. You know that.'

'We know that, hopefully the rest of the city will accept that in time. You're going to have to work on that.'

'I know. That's one of the reasons I pushed Marcol into being a constable.'

'Yes,' Macsen said, sitting up and leaning forward with considerable curiosity. 'I didn't get that. I've talked to Dinlay. He says the boy isn't really constable material.'

'I disagree. He's trying,' Edeard said defensively. 'He'll make it to graduation, he's got a huge incentive.'

'But why?'

'Remember when we all wondered why I'd been chosen by the Lady to do what I could do? What if I haven't been chosen?

643

What if, instead, her teachings have started to take hold? I mean *really* taken hold.'

'I can't believe you of all people would say that,' Kanseen exclaimed. 'We've spent a year down on the streets fighting those bloody gangs. They never followed her teachings.'

'The gang members didn't, no. But what about everyone else? They all knew it was wrong, even if they couldn't see a way out. Once I banished them everything changed. You said yourself the city is a happier place already, and it's barely been two weeks. The Lady's teachings are everywhere, they're an ingrained part of our culture now, here in the city and out in the farthest province. It's the one thing that truly binds us, the one commonality. We all know instinctively that we should be striving to better ourselves, to live a more righteous life even if we don't quite know how.'

'That's just human nature.'

'Maybe. But the Lady endorses it, encourages us to follow that instinct and provides a strong justification to develop it. Her Mothers have spent two thousand years preaching it. You can't tell me anything would endure that long if it wasn't accepted as a fundamental truth. We know the Skylords are out there waiting to guide us to the Heart; and, as I showed everyone, we have souls that desperately need that guidance.'

'What in the Lady's name does this have to do with Marcol?' Macsen demanded.

'I have the strength to influence the city, and I have the certainty how that strength should be used. Suppose I'm not the only one to have that strength? Suppose I'm simply the first? Suppose this is the time when Querencia has reached the level of decency and fulfilment it takes to summon the Skylords back?'

Kanseen stared at him, making no attempt to cover her astonishment. 'Marcol? Marcol is like you?'

'He's got a damned powerful psychic ability,' Edeard said. 'What if that's part of reaching the fulfilment the Lady talks of? What if there are others starting to emerge, if all the kids start to show this potential?'

'Lady help us,' she grunted. 'Marcol?'

'Stop saying his name like it's a curse,' Edeard said crossly. 'He's just a kid like any other. What he becomes depends a great deal on his environment. He didn't have the best start with those parents; well now I'm trying to help him become something better. The very last thing we need is division among those of us with stronger than average psychic powers – it's bad enough the Grand Families distort the balance in their favour. We have to show Marcol and all the others like him who come along that real fulfilment is found through a strong society which cares for individuals, where people try to help each other as well as themselves.'

'And that's going to bring the Skylords back?' Macsen asked incredulously.

'Tell me what else will?' Edeard countered. 'I'm happy to try something else. You saw Boyd and Chae leave; they're out there somewhere trying to reach Odin's Sea. You know that part of the Lady's teachings is real.'

Macsen ran his hand through his hair. 'I know,' he admitted. 'But . . . Marcol!'

'And others,' Edeard said.

'Have you sensed others?' Kanseen asked. 'People with stronger powers?'

'Not yet. But this city encourages people to hide their abilities. And use them to their own advantage.'

'You just said we were becoming more enlightened,' Macsen said.

'Becoming is right,' Edeard said. 'There's a long way to go yet.'

Edeard had never seen the Malfit Hall so full. Every inch of floorspace was taken up by big tables where clerks were sitting, counting mountainous piles of ballot papers. They were divided up into districts in mimicry of the city outside. More clerks and constables were still delivering sealed boxes, opening them up to avalanche yet more paper on to the tables.

Mayor Owain stood at the top of the stairs, surrounded with his staff and supporters, chatting away as if nothing of consequence was happening. Further along the gallery Finitan was clustered with his own circle of advisers, also making light of the count below. Occasionally, he and Owain would exchange a few pleasant words.

The expectant Representative candidates were less light-hearted about the wait. They all hovered around their own counting tables, jostling with their opponents whenever an unclear ballot paper was held up to questioning. Accusations and insults were frequently shouted at the adjudicator clerks.

For once, few people paid any attention to the Waterwalker as he walked in with Macsen and Kanseen. As they crossed the vast ebony floor he knew Owain's gaze was following him, yet the Mayor's composure remained urbane. The ceiling above them shone a rich dawn light across all the frantic activity.

'We'll go and check up on our district,' Kanseen said as they reached the bottom of the stairs. Watching them stride over to the Sampalok counting tables, Edeard felt a surge of admiration for his friends. There weren't many people you could thrust into such a position and expect them to hold fast. But Kanseen and Macsen had done it. Dressed in their fur-lined robes, with their hoods hanging over their shoulder they really did look like they'd been born to the role. *Maybe it's not just psychic strength that's an indicator of the Lady's teachings.*

He started to walk up the stairs. Owain and Finitan watched him approach.

As a city constable I should be impartial, he told himself. *Greet both of them and then go back down to the Jeavons tables. After all, if Owain wins I'll have to work with him.*

Owain's face produced a neutral smile of welcome as Edeard reached the top of the stairs.

Politician!

Edeard inclined his head. 'Mayor Owain,' he said politely, and walked over to Finitan.

Honious take him, he was going to kill innocent people to keep his position. I would never be able to work with someone like that, he represents everything that's wrong with Makkathran.

There was a brief unguarded flash of gratitude amidst Finitan's thoughts as Edeard shook the Grand Master's hand. 'Do you know how the count's going, sir?'

'I have a small lead,' Finitan replied. 'Not as much as we were hoping, but it remains constant.'

A half hour of laboured chat and forced humour later, they all watched as the Clerk Master supervising the Ysidro district vote walked to the stairs and stood on the bottom step.

'Ysidro always makes a show of being first to complete their count,' Topar grunted. 'It's a small district, but they've a wide mix of people; it's a good indicator.'

The Master cleared his throat. 'It is given this day that Alanso is duly elected as the people of Ysidro's Representative to Council. And further that mayoral candidate Finitan collected fifty-seven per cent of the vote.'

There was some scattered applause, and the rest of the hall went back to the count.

'Alanso is one of ours,' Topar said. 'Thank you, Lady.'

Owain graciously congratulated his rival on the vote, to which an equally gracious Finitan replied that the night was young.

Fiacre and Lillylight finished their count next, both returning Owain stalwarts as their Representatives; though the mayoral vote was split nearly fifty–fifty. Jeavons, Silvarum and Haxpen returned Finitan supporters (Balogg among them), and gave him a large proportion of the vote. Nighthouse and Bellis elected Owain supporters; but Myco, Vaji, Cobara and Tosella put Finitan supporters forward to the Council. They also increased Finitan's overall vote to sixty per cent. When the results came in from Abad, Drupe, Igadi, Padua and Fiacre, Owain had only one more Representative, and Finitan's vote had increased to sixty-eight per cent. Zelda produced Owain's last Representative; Pholas Park and Lisieux Park were solid Finitan districts.

'We've got it,' Topar hissed elatedly as Finitan's vote rose to seventy-one per cent.

'Oh, Lady,' Finitan muttered, he seemed dazed, but nothing could remove the smile from his face.

Ilongo, Neph and Drupe declared, putting Finitan's percentage up another point. That just left the Sampalok vote. It wouldn't affect the result now, but it *mattered*. Edeard stared down at the eight tables where the ballots were being counted, willing them to finish. Kanseen and Macsen were still walking between the clerks, backing up the adjudicators. There had been more disputes on those eight tables than the rest of Malfit Hall put together. The Grand Master of the Guild of Clerks himself had been over a dozen times during the night to make his final judgement on smudged crosses. Finally, the Clerk Master assigned to supervise the Sampalok count stood at the foot of the stairs and announced: 'It is given this day that Gregorie is duly elected as the people of Sampalok's Representative to Council.'

'He's ours,' Topar whispered incredulously.

'And that mayoral candidate Finitan collected fifty-one per cent of the vote,' the Clerk Master concluded.

Thousands of people were waiting in Golden Park, despite the chill late-night air. There was a lot of movement after Sampalok declared. Dejected Owain supporters headed home, shaking their heads in dismay and muttering dark disapproval. Finitan supporters surged forward right up to the Outer Circle Canal. A line of fit young constables had a struggle to keep some of the over-eager ones from falling into the water.

Finitan emerged on to the balcony overlooking Golden Park, and the cheering reached deafening levels. He began his thank you speech. Not all the faithful listened. Bottles were being passed round. Groups of strolling musicians were playing, urging people to dance. The party in Golden Park would last until dawn.

Edeard was one of those who didn't bother listening to the speech. He made his way back to the Culverit mansion where an overjoyed Kristabel was waiting, and they celebrated in their own fashion.

*

Kristabel made Edeard wait. He couldn't believe it. Tradition was one thing, but he stood at the front of the Lady's church all by himself with the farsight of the city focused on him as minute after painful lonely minute dragged on. Tradition said the groom wasn't allowed to use his own farsight to check and see if the bride was on her way. So he just stood there and endured.

The smell of pollen – sweet when he and Dinlay walked into the church – was now overpowering, threatening to make his eyes water. It seemed as if half the Iguru Plain had been stripped of foliage to decorate the huge church. The band from the Musicians Guild played on and on, repeating the same tune which had become more like a funeral dirge. As the same terrible notes began once more he gritted his teeth, wishing he'd pleaded a lot harder with Dybal to play for him; but Dybal was only going to sing at the reception gala tonight. He shifted his weight from one foot to another. In front of him the thirty-foot-high snow-marble statue of the Lady gazed down benignly, her arms uplifted to summon the Skylords to Querencia. The sculptor had captured a most enigmatic expression. It was almost as if she was giving her congregation a judgemental glance. Certainly, anyone standing right at the front of the pews – curiously, on the exact spot he had to wait – was singled out for her disapproval. Shifting from one foot to another, he considered that she must have known that one day Edeard would be married in her church, that her timesense had warned her of the sacrilege. Why else single him out to glare at?

Another lost minute. His mind began to conjure up all sorts of horrors which could have beset Kristabel. He knew she'd set off from the Culverit mansion, tradition at least allowed him that much. The same tradition which stated the bride was only allowed to change her mind between her home and the church.

649

But Kristabel wouldn't do that to him. So she could have been assassinated, or kidnapped, or the gondola capsized. Because Kristabel wouldn't abandon him.

So where in Honious is she?

Edeard started to cheat, using the city's senses to examine the church. *Not farsight. So no breach of tradition. Damn, I even think like a lawyer now.* Just about every Grand Family in Makkathran was represented. Notable exceptions were Mistress Florrel, who had announced a headache an hour before the service was due to begin and gave her apologies for non-attendance. The Gilmorns were also absent, as were the Norrets, who counted Lieutenant Eustace among their number. Captain Larose, however, was there, and looked most amused by the Waterwalker's discomfort. Grand Master Owain was in the pews reserved for Guild dignitaries. Losing the election didn't seem to have affected him at all, he retained his slightly cool persona throughout every encounter. Macsen and Kanseen were almost invisible amid the District Masters, their colourful robes blending in flawlessly. Kanseen wasn't showing yet, though of late she'd started making some very barbed comments about which would arrive first, the mansion or the baby. The section reserved for the groom's family was unusually small, and Kristabel had appropriated several of his pews for her own family and friends. But Edeard thought he was well supported with a dozen constables and Bijulee and Dybal and Seteris and Isoix and Topar and others he'd met during his time in the city, headed up by Mayor Finitan himself. His one true regret was Salrana, who had sent a polite note of regret claiming her duties wouldn't allow her to attend. She was the closest thing he had to family, but since the day of banishment they'd been completely estranged. Every attempt he'd made to be reconciled had been rebuffed. He knew she was still at the church in Ysidro, devoutly fulfilling her duties. The few times he'd longsighted her he'd been saddened by the way the joy seemed to have gone from her life. She'd aged inexplicably, becoming withdrawn and sombre. This was a cooler, more resolute Salrana.

He regretted his snatched glimpses, and quickly desisted. To his dismay he had to admit that she had changed, as he had. The Salrana and Edeard who lived in Ashwell were gone forever now.

The sound of cheering seeped into the church, and Edeard's heart started to beat faster. Their marriage wasn't an official holiday, though there'd been a big crowd outside the church when he and Dinlay arrived.

Finally! The band curtailed their wretched tune. He heard the rustle of cloth as the Novice quire rose to their feet. Then the light changed perceptibly as the big doors swung open. Dinlay stepped up beside him, smiling wide. 'Too late to back out now,' he murmured to Edeard.

Any scathing reply was lost as the organist began the wedding march. Edeard had never heard the giant keyboards being played before, the sound was overwhelming. Then the Novices began their accompanying melody. He was impossibly terrified and elated at the same time.

Julan appeared beside him, his pride shining with the power of a dawn sun. And *she* was there at his side. Edeard nearly let out a whimper of relief. Mirnatha giggled at his expression; the little girl was wearing a pink and white dress that transformed her into some enchantingly sweet fairy creature, an image only spoilt when she grinned her devilsome grin.

Kristabel's wedding gown was a gold-cream drosilk creation with royal-blue trimming that twinkled with emerald gem-flowers, its train seemed to stretch back halfway down the aisle. He saw her head turn inside the veil, her eyes shining through the lace. Then the Pythia was standing in front of them, her smile gentle and commanding. The organist ended his thunderous anthem.

'Welcome to you all on this happiest of days,' the Pythia said to the congregation.

Julan and Kristabel lifted the veil from her face. Her hair flowed out like ripples of gold silk. Edeard couldn't believe anyone so perfect was facing him at his own wedding ceremony, this surely must be some dazed fantasy from his last night in Ashwell, a moment of blissful delusion after the bullets struck and before death.

Kristabel took both his hands in hers, and squeezed reassuringly. 'Been waiting long?' she teased.

'My whole life,' he told her truthfully.

They honeymooned at the Culverit family's muroak lodge on the coast, spending half a month there by themselves. Twenty days of delight.

A lot more staff accompanied them this time, providing them with excellent meals and unobtrusive service. The end of summer was approaching, but it was still hot. Humid air above the cove barely moved the whole time they were there. As before, they took lazy walks along the coast; swam in warm water and sunned themselves on the beach until both of them had tanned a deep honey-brown. Edeard tried his hand at fishing, but lacked the patience. Both of them learned to sail in a small yacht that was a wedding gift from Charyau. They even managed a couple of trips sailing to nearby fishing villages in thankfully calm waters.

'I think it will be some time before we venture that circumnavigation I mentioned,' Edeard admitted the evening after their first big voyage two miles along the shore.

On the other side of the table Kristabel laughed agreement, backdropped by a golden blaze of the setting sun. Both of them were determined from the outset to have the time for themselves. They avoided talking about city life and its politics. Too much of the last four months had been spent establishing Finitan as the Mayor, persuading the old guard to adopt his consolidation policies, strengthening the judiciary and reinforcing the determination and effectiveness of the constables. It seemed to be working. Everyone reported good business. With the shadow of fear and uncertainty lifted, people were spending with confidence again.

Finitan's first few months were already judged a success. In

Makkathran. Out in the provinces, things were not so agreeable. The news Topar had brought back at the start of the year was becoming common knowledge. Even his ominous predictions now seemed optimistic. Bandits so long confined to the western-most provinces were making long inroads to the east. Back in the springtime, Rulan province faced a huge ongoing exodus as raids became a weekly occurrence. Then Worfolk province reported caravans being ambushed on previously safe highways. The numerous mountains of the interior were ideal refuges for the roaming bands to strike at villages and towns. After a raid they would ride into the tricky inhospitable terrain and vanish from the sheriffs and militiamen sent to hunt them.

What worried Edeard most was the long distance these episodes occurred at. Makkathran only ever got to hear of a bandit incident months after it actually happened. They had no idea what was currently going on beyond the Iguru Plain, or how close the raiders were venturing to the city.

A mere two months after the election, the first refugees from the Ulfsen Mountains had trickled into Makkathran, whispering about strange, powerful guns. Guns that could defeat an entire cavalry platoon. Official casualties from the militia regiments Owain had dispatched to help the governors began to rise. People started to notice the number of lavish memorial services which Grand Families threw for the officers increased sharply. Nobody blamed Finitan, but he was starting to face questions about what he intended to do about the worsening circumstances out beyond the Iguru Plain.

All that Edeard had put behind him in favour of sunny days lounging on the sands drinking cool wine; and equally hot nights making love to Kristabel. Then the day came when the staff and ge-monkeys packed the huge pile of bags and crates, and they began the carriage journey home. He fell silent as they trundled along the broad coastal road, contemplating what news he would be accosted with as soon as they reached the city once again.

'You'll still have me,' Kristabel said adamantly.

Edeard broke out of his revere. 'Huh?'

'You haven't spoken a word for the last two miles. Was it that horrible a time?'

'No! That's the problem, I wish it could have gone on and on. There's a big part of me that doesn't want to go back.'

'Me too,' she attempted a smile, but her usual contentment was missing. 'I don't think I'm pregnant yet.'

'Ah.'

'They say vinak juice lingers in the blood for a while after you stop taking it. Another month would see it gone, and us successful.'

He put his arm around her. 'I promise to redouble my efforts when we get home.' He stopped abruptly, then smiled. 'Home.'

'Yes,' she said with equal glee. 'The two of us together.'

'Alone, apart from your family and two hundred servants. But what the Honious, we'll try to make the best of it.'

Her third hand pinched him hard. 'You feel so guilty about that, don't you?'

'Not guilty . . . just unaccustomed to it.' He remembered what Kanseen had said on the balcony of Bea's Bottle. 'I'm sure I'll get used to it eventually; it can't be that difficult.'

'You know, if Finitan had lost I really would have followed you to a village on the edge of the wilds.'

He kissed her. 'And Mirnatha would have become Mistress of Haxpen.'

'Oh Lady,' Kristabel's hand flew to her mouth. 'I never thought of that. Off to the wilds by yourself you go then.'

They clasped each other tighter.

'I wanted to be pregnant,' she said. 'It would be so nice for Kanseen's boy to have a playmate. Our children would grow up together.'

'Kanseen still has another month and a half to go. And you will be pregnant many times. Our children will play with those of the Sampalok Master's family.'

She nodded, allowing him to convince her. 'What will happen with the bandits and the provinces?'

He sighed. 'I don't know. We still don't know where they get their weapons from. That's the true cause of all this strife.'

'Finitan's going to ask you to go out there, isn't he?'

'Probably.'

'You must go if it's the right thing.'

'I don't want to leave you.'

'I know. But, Edeard, don't you want our children to live in a safe world?'

'Of course.'

'So really there's no choice to be made, is there?'

Edeard said nothing. She was right of course, which made arguing futile. Given the path he'd chosen for himself, some events were inevitable.

At least nothing about the city had changed when they got back. The carriage and horses were led away to the Culverit stables in Tycho, and they took the family gondola back to the ziggurat mansion. Julan and Mirnatha were waiting for them on the mooring platform, both equally excited.

'I missed you so,' Mirnatha squealed, hugging her sister.

'And I you,' Kristabel promised.

'What was it like?'

Edeard and Kristabel managed to avoid looking at each other. 'A nice restful holiday,' Kristabel explained to her little sister.

'Really? I always get fearfully bored after just one day at the lodge. What did you do all that time?' She gave Edeard a wide-eyed look of innocent interest. It didn't fool him for a second.

Julan cleared his throat. 'Shall we go and inspect the tenth floor now.'

The staff and ge-monkeys had been extremely busy since the wedding. Kristabel's agonized rearrangement of the family had been implemented, with everyone shifting apartments and floors. In the end, fourteen sets of relatives had moved out. More than originally intended, but there were a lot of new marriages planned amid the relatives occupying the fifth and seventh floors, which would create another accommodation shortage over the next couple of years. Some of the third-floor families decided not to wait. Julan had offered to build them new manor houses on lands the Culverits owned beyond the Iguru.

In all honesty, Edeard didn't see a lot of change to the furniture and fittings on the tenth floor. The big lounges and reception rooms were the same as before with all the family's artwork and antiques in the same positions they'd occupied for centuries. He and Kristabel would take over the Master's suite from Julan, which had been decluttered – he made no comment on the standard Makkathran bed and bathing pool, they could be reshaped easily enough. His few possessions from the maisonette were standing forlornly in one of the empty studies. When he looked at the small pile of boxes in comparison to everything the Culverits had accumulated over two millennia he began to feel intimidated by the family again.

'You'll soon make it your own,' Julan said comfortingly as he caught sight of Edeard's expression.

'Yes, sir.'

'I got Uncle Dagnal's old chambers,' Mirnatha said joyfully. 'And Daddy said I could have new furniture and curtains and everything.'

'Within reason,' Julan said hurriedly.

'Come and show us then,' Kristabel said, holding out a hand.

Edeard followed the sisters out of the Master's suite, taking one last look at the main octagonal bedroom with its huge circular bed. The room was bare apart from a fluffy brown carpet, some plain wardrobes and chests; the dressing room next door contained all of Kristabel's clothes. He couldn't help but compare its simplicity to the way Kristabel had decorated her bachelorette room just down the hall.

Perhaps she'll allow me some say in how we make our bedroom look. I could offer to craft her a shower, and a proper toilet, make the light white. The idea of spending the next two hundred years sleeping in anything as *fluffy* as she'd created before was unnerving.

They spent the afternoon with the tenth floor's housekeeper discussing further changes. Several Master carpenters were summoned to prepare drawings of the furniture Kristabel wanted to commission. Edeard was relieved when she toned down the drapes and fittings for their bedroom, and finally found the courage to volunteer his own alterations. The craftsmen tried not to be too obvious listening when he explained how the shower could go anywhere, and be any size. In fact, altering the whole layout of the tenth floor would be a simple matter for him if she was just prepared to wait while the walls adjusted themselves. Kristabel sent everyone away when he started explaining that.

'I'd never thought of altering things on that scale,' she admitted. 'Nothing ever changes in Makkathran.'

'It can now.' He looked round the big lounge they were in. 'In fact, how about some more windows in this place? Let some light in?'

'What about the main stairs?' she asked excitedly. 'Can you change them? The ones in Kanseen's new mansion are actually usable.'

'I thought you'd never ask.'

Julan and Mirnatha were noticeably absent from supper on the tenth-floor hortus that evening, making a big show of saying how much they wanted to eat with the ninth-floor families.

'It'll never last,' Kristabel said as they sipped some sparkling white wine under a big white gauze awning. Long candles had been lit among the pots of orchids and troughs full of huge evening glories. With the orange lights of the city starting to twinkle amid the twilight and lengthening shadows, Edeard couldn't imagine a more romantic setting. Neither, it seemed, could a lot of Makkathran's citizens; they both had to cast a seclusion haze to ward off curious farsights.

'But we can make the most of it for a couple more days,' he said. It was almost a plea.

'You have to go back to Jeavons station tomorrow. You're its captain, after all. And Finitan will want to talk to you, and Macsen is going to have a dozen problems.'

'I know. They've been very polite not calling us today.'

'I did longtalk Kanseen earlier. She says the mansion's almost complete, as far as she can tell. She wants you to confirm it's finished growing so she can start ordering fittings and fabrics for it.'

'Okay,' he said reluctantly. 'I'll check tomorrow.'

Her hand came down on top of his. 'We still have tonight.'

'And every night.'

'You know what I mean. Tomorrow our new lives really begin.'

'I know.'

'But that's hours yet.'

When Edeard walked into the Jeavons station first thing the next morning, he found Dinlay had coped admirably during his absence. He was almost peeved at that, but you couldn't argue with paperwork, and Dinlay had been quite meticulous about recording everything. Glancing at the new charts hanging up in his office, Edeard saw that patrols had gone out on time, duty rosters were made up, monies allocated and spent, timetables established. Arrests had been made, but these days the constables tended to issue cautions to any miscreants they found. It was often enough. Only the most committed recidivists were hauled up in front of the judges now. Probationer training was also going well. Even Marcol was expected to pass his exams in time for graduation next month.

'Though it's touch and go,' Dinlay admitted. 'There's a sweep if you want to put some money down.'

'I don't think that would be proper,' Edeard said. It wasn't quite the comment he expected from Dinlay. But he couldn't find fault in any other way. 'So what else has been happening?'

'It's been quiet actually. In the city at least. We're still getting refugees arriving, which is causing a lot of talk about how the remaining empty buildings are being taken up. People were expecting their children to move into the available places.'

'Do we know how much spare housing there is? I mean, is this going to be a problem?'

'I expect the Guild of Clerks knows the true numbers.'

'I'm sure they do, they seem to know everything else.'

'And anyway, it's Finitan's problem, isn't it?'

'Yes. You're right.' Edeard sat behind the desk he'd inherited from Ronark. Like the office, it was dark and functional. To be honest, a little bit drab and depressing for his taste. He looked round at the high, slightly curved walls with their small oval windows. No wonder it was so gloomy, the city fabric was a grungy brown with strange vertical vermilion streaks, as if someone had spilt colouring dye down them a long time ago.

Dinlay left to lead a squad on patrol. Edeard began reviewing the station logs. It was no good, the office just kept distracting him. He reached down to the city's thoughts, and made some suggestions for modification. Expanding the windows, changing the wall colours to a pleasant pale sky-blue, adapting the lighting rosettes to shine white. Much the same as he'd done to the tenth floor of the Culverit mansion this morning. Here the changes would be finished within a week, back home it would take longer. Kristabel was still toying with the idea of changing the entire layout.

Even after he'd kicked off the office changes, the logs didn't interest him. He let his farsight reach out to the Orchard Palace.

'I wondered how long it would take you,' Finitan said.

The oval sanctum hadn't changed. Edeard had expected Finitan to stamp his mark immediately, but the week after the election Finitan had remarked that he had more important things to worry about than the furniture. So the huge desk was still there in the middle, its dark veneer glossed to a mirror shine. The high velvet-padded chair behind it was Owain's relic, to. But Edeard did recognize the silver cups that the ge-chimps poured his tea into. And Owain hadn't used genistars in here.

Finitan had brought the genistar egg cradle from his office in the Blue Tower. But it sat on his desk empty.

Topar took a seat next to Edeard, refusing a cup of tea.

'Well,' Finitan started. 'We managed to survive an entire twenty days without you.'

'Yes, sir,' Edeard said.

'The city isn't really a problem any more. People seem to have accepted my term without too much resistance.'

'They certainly have. Kristabel is complaining about how long the furniture she commissioned will take to build. The craftsmen are run off their feet right now. It's the same all across Makkathran. People are spending their money again. They have confidence in you, sir.'

'My apologies to your wife.' Finitan put his cup down, and gave Edeard an uncomfortable stare. 'Unfortunately, the city's current bout of good fortune isn't being repeated beyond the Iguru Plain.'

Edeard gave a short nod. 'I know.'

Topar cast out a strong seclusion haze. 'I've been sending scouts out into the provinces,' he said. 'Good men: ex-constables, sheriffs, even a few reserve officers from the militia. People who know how to look after themselves, people I can rely on.'

'We wanted to build up a picture of these damn raids,' Finitan said. 'See if there was a pattern behind them, a purpose.'

'That's where it gets strange,' Topar said. 'If they're trying to soften us up for an invasion, they're going about it in a very odd way. There have been no bandit raids at all in the Rulan province since midsummer; in fact, the west seems clear of all disturbances. They've moved steadily east through the three largest mountain ranges, causing a lot of damage, and setting light to a wildfire of fear and rumour. In fact, that's our worse enemy right now. Any dispute that results in violence is attributed to bandit raids, from landowners fighting with poachers to a tavern brawl, so bad is their reputation. It's hard to determine what's real and what isn't. The provincial governors aren't reliable at the best of times, now any trifling squabble is seen as an excuse to petition Makkathran for militia support.'

'It doesn't help that Owain sent the regiments out so willingly before,' Topar said. 'Expectations of support were set too high.'

'He's left you a real mess,' Edeard said.

'Yes. That's politics, and to be expected. But we took a very good look at the information we can confirm. It's a worrying result.'

'In what way?'

'Basically, we've established there are six main packs of bandits,' Topar said. 'Two are heading along the Ulfsen Mountains. One is using the Komansa range for cover. Two started out in the Gorgian Mountains, though one of those is now heading north east along the Yorarns. And the last is plaguing the Sastairs all the way down to the southern coastal provinces.'

Edeard closed his eyes, trying to picture what he'd just been told on a map of the known lands. 'They're stretched quite thin, then.'

'I prefer the term "widespread",' Topar said. 'We're a basically peaceful society, and their physical impact is minimal given the size of the areas concerned, but the disturbance and worry they cause is near universal.'

'So what are they doing?'

'One last thing.' Finitan pulled a piece of paper across the desk, and started to read. 'In Plax province there were raids on Payerne, Orastrul, Oki, Bihac, and Tikrit. All villages or small towns. The manor houses and their lands at Stonyford, Turndich, Uxmal, Saltmarch, Klongsop, Ettrick, and Castlebay have also suffered extensive damage during the last two months.' He gave Edeard an expectant look. 'Anything ring a bell?'

'I've heard of the Uxmal manor, the Culverits own it. I think it's a big parkland holding, they raise sheep there.' He had a nasty feeling one of the families from the third floor had gone there to make their new home.

'Indeed. Every one of those estates belongs to an ally of mine,'

Finitan said. 'Allies and supporters also have considerable assets in or around the targeted villages.'

Edeard felt cold. 'How could bandits know that?'

'Somebody told them,' Topar said. 'Someone who has conducted a comprehensive search through the official Treasury registry.'

'It took us a while to work it out,' Finitan said. 'Everyone I met at a party or dinner was complaining about their losses. I heard nothing else. I thought the invasion had already begun until I realized my allies were being singled out.'

'Lady!'

'Which brings us back to the question of who are they and what are they doing?'

'They must have collaborators in the city,' a shocked Edeard said.

'At the very least,' Topar said. He exchanged a worried glance with Finitan. 'There's also the question of the guns. If there isn't another city equal to us . . .'

'No,' Edeard said. 'The Weapons Guild . . .' *They had the long-barrel pistols all this time. But whoever supplied the bandits with repeat-fire guns killed Ashwell.*

'Too early to make that accusation,' Topar said abruptly. 'And we have no proof whatsoever.'

'This is why we asked you in,' Finitan said. 'I know a lot of your power comes from whatever relationship you have with the city itself, but you still have the strongest psychic ability I have ever known.'

'A week ago a report came in of a raid on Northford,' Topar said. 'That's a village in the Donsori Mountains, Edeard, just four days ride from Makkathran for the Lady's sake. Rapid-fire guns were used. We know that for a fact. One of the Ulfsen mountain groups must have pushed eastwards in the last month.'

'If we can capture one of them alive,' Finitan said, 'We might just be able to find out what exactly is going on, who those collaborators are.'

'I'm going to take a small group of the best people I know

and trust,' Topar said. 'We'll have ge-eagles and ge-wolves, and the best pistols available. Even so, I could do with some help.'

'Oh Lady,' Edeard put his cold tea cup back on the desk 'When do we leave?'

*

Despite all he'd been through in Makkathran, the city had made him soft, Edeard acknowledged on the second day. An easy life was an easy trap to fall into. Life on the road was a sharp reminder of the way he used to live. Making camp each night. Looking after the genistars himself rather than asking a servant. Collecting wood to make a fire. Cooking his own food. Sleeping under a blanket and an oilskin beneath the nebula-swathed sky. That was cold enough. Then after the third day they didn't even have a fire for fear the bandit crew would notice it, and they were high in the Donsori Mountains by then.

But at that he did better than Dinlay and Macsen. They were *real* city boys. So he alleviated his own discomfort by enjoying theirs.

Their third night out from North Gate they camped on the side of Mount Iyo, half a day's ride from the main road through the mountains. There was still a lot of traffic on the road, with caravans and wagons and carriages rattling along the broad paved slabs that switchbacked along the rugged slopes. But all of them were accompanied by packs of ge-wolves. The wealthier travellers had their own guards as well. There were also daily patrols of local militia squads. Edeard's own party went under the guise of trading Guildsmen, a common enough sight on the roads. As well as himself and Topar, they had Boloton, an ex-sheriff from Oki who had spent over half of his seventy years roaming across the countryside. The second of Topar's companions was Fresage, a huge man whose bulk was mostly muscle, another outdoors type who had seen membership in a southern provincial militia as well as serving ten years as a costal warden. In turn, he was good friends with Verini, born to a caravan family, who was taking a decade-long break from the eternal trade routes to scout round new markets and learn the roads in different territories. Then there was Larby, who had the manners of a Grand Family son yet was clearly comfortable with road life, and proficient with a pistol. He said little about his background, but Edeard suspected he had been affiliated to the families in a fashion not too dissimilar to Argian.

That just left Dinlay and Macsen to complete their number. By the end of the first day, saddle-sore himself, Edeard was beginning to think he shouldn't have asked them along. Macsen had proved particularly difficult to convince: he was naturally concerned for Kanseen, who was due in just a few weeks. However, they stuck it out and learned from the others quickly enough. That they'd adapt was never Edeard's concern. His main worry was that the three of them would be absent from Makkathran at the same time. Such a thing would be noticeable to a suspicious mind. If there was someone in the senior ranks of government collaborating with the bandits they might raise a warning – even though they'd never know exactly what to warn against. And it would be difficult getting word out here ahead of Topar's group.

As their party progressed, their main source of information was fellow travellers. They didn't even have to ask difficult questions; those who used the road frequently were unrivalled gossips. Rumour of a bandit crew was strong. There had been another raid after Northford, at a hamlet called Regentfleet. Five families dead and the buildings torched. The local governor was demanding assistance from Makkathran's militia regiments to catch the bandits. Regentfleet was uncomfortably close to Sandmarket, the provincial capital.

'They're heading south, then,' Topar said when they first heard the news of Regentfleet. Which is why they eventually left the main road to strike out across the high terrain by themselves. It was hard going, even for the stoic ge-horses, a type which blended traits of high endurance with speed; not as fast as terrestrial horses, they still had the stamina to keep a fair pace going even on the rocky slopes away from the road.

Topar led them along the edge of the woodlands which dominated the middle slopes. Thick forests of tall spindly kalkand trees whose feathery blue-gold fronds spent the winter months curled up in tight whorls.

They made camp that third day under overhanging branches which dripped an unpleasant waxy sap from their newly budded scarlet sporecones. A small stream trickled along one side, allowing the horses and ge-wolves to drink. That night they sent their ge-eagles roving around the peaks and swooping through the valleys. The big birds had a trait Edeard had never known of before, a near-perfect night-sight. There were no colours to the vision he received from them: the world they flew over was drawn in shades of grey, but still the features were sharp and true. Edeard could see small creatures scuttling along oblivious to the birds gliding silently overhead.

'You're still young, you can still become an apprentice to the Blue Tower yet,' Topar taunted when Edeard remarked upon the trait. Like the Weapons Guild, the Masters of the Blue Tower kept secrets that might work to their advantage.

The ge-eagles found nothing that night. Topar and Edeard called them back in the early hours to rest before breaking camp early the next day.

Edeard woke to the sound of Dinlay cursing heavily, hopping about on one foot as he held his other boot high. His glasses were still on the roll he used as a pillow, so his face was screwed up as he squinted at the boot. 'Ladydamnit!'

Everyone else was lifting their heads, using farsight to scan round, anxious they'd been discovered. Everyone apart from Macsen, who was on watch. He was unperturbed, just sitting on an old fallen trunk watching Dinlay with cool amusement.

'Bloody Honious!' Dinlay took a bad hop backwards, and tripped on a small rock. He landed hard on his arse and let out a distressed grunt. Edeard winced in sympathy as the flare of pain burst out of his friend's mind.

'What? What?' Dinlay spluttered.

'You okay back there?' Macsen called in a voice that was far too calm. It triggered a suspicious grin on Edeard's face. When he pushed his farsight into Dinlay's boot he found a mush in the toe that had been a utog beetle, a native insect with a particularly prickly carapace.

'Did you . . . ?' an outraged Dinlay gasped. 'Was that you . . . ?'

'Me what?' Macsen replied innocently.

The others were chuckling now as Dinlay started shivering, partly from the bruise on his buttocks and partly from the cold; he was dressed only in a thin shirt and cotton under-trousers.

'May the Lady crap on you from a great height,' Dinlay muttered darkly. His third hand pulled his glasses on to his face, then began scraping the squashed remains of the beetle out of his boot.

'Children, children,' Fresage said with a shake of his head. He pushed his blanket back and rose ponderously, flexing his arms to work out the knots earned from sleeping on rough ground.

Edeard pulled on a thick sweater of his own and clambered to his feet. He never could get comfortable just lying on the ground. A careful farsight examination of his own boots revealed they were unused by nesting insects, and he pulled them on.

Topar had snatched up a pistol as soon as he'd woken. Now he gave Macsen a disapproving glance and clicked the safety catch back on.

Boloton and Larby started rolling up their sleeping blankets. Now his boot was clean, Dinlay transferred his attention to his toe. Several utog spikes were sticking through his woollen socks. He removed them one at a time.

'Well done,' Edeard said to Macsen. 'Just how I envisaged a District Master would behave.'

Verini was grinning along with the rest of them. 'How did you three ever clear the city of gangs?' he mused quietly.

Macsen flashed Edeard a profoundly guilty smirk.

'You're so pathetic,' Dinlay grumbled.

'Got to do something to stay awake,' Macsen murmured. He pulled a kettle off the little stove that burned Jamolar oil. 'Tea, anyone?'

'You do have a use,' Fresage mocked.

'Few and far between, but those I have I excel at.'

Edeard and Dinlay exchanged a look. 'Not what Kanseen says,' Dinlay said smugly, and pulled his boot on.

Edeard took his cup over to Macsen. 'You're an arse,' he said, grinning as his friend poured out the boiling water.

'Yep, and that's just on the plus side.'

Edeard stirred in one of the hand-tied linen tea packets which the tenth-floor housekeeper had made up for him. The others had ribbed him mercilessly about those, but they wound up 'borrowing' them at every meal.

'How much longer is this going to take?' Dinlay asked as he held his cup out.

'For all this is empty land, there aren't that many places the bandits can hide out in,' Topar said, drinking down his own tea. 'Shepherds use the high pastures for grazing, and it's turning cold up here now.'

'They will have found themselves half a dozen remote camp sites,' Fresage said. 'And they'll shift between them.'

Edeard gave the valley to the south a shrewd gaze. The Donsori Mountains weren't the highest range on Querencia, yet the snowcaps were creeping downwards again as the last weeks of summer passed away. And the forests that smothered the mid-slopes were changing colour, the fronds on the dominant kalkand trees were shading towards beige as they began to contract. Below the treeline, the gentler lower slopes had a yellow tinge. Grass deprived of water during the dry summer months was just starting to taste rain again. Clumps chewed down by terrestrial sheep and cattle along with the roaming flocks of native chamalans were putting up their last wispy sprouts before the snows came once more. The soil on these remote lands wasn't rich enough to support farms. There were a few isolated cattle stations but that was all. Though with the peaks fencing away clouds the air was beautifully clear. Visibility stretched for miles.

'If they're to move round unnoticed it will have to be through the trees,' Larby said.

'And the camps will have to be within range of villages,' Topar agreed. He pointed at the summit of Mount Alvice at the south-eastern end of the valley. 'There's a plateau beyond the crest, with several villages. Sandmarket is a day's ride beyond that.'

'That kind of area is a possible for them,' Boloton agreed. 'Secluded but in range of Regentfleet.'

Edeard thought they were right, but didn't say anything. He was content with someone else making all the decisions for once. Topar hadn't said how long he was prepared to stay out here trying to track down the bandits, but they were carrying enough food for a fortnight.

Once they were back in the saddle, Topar led them onwards towards Mount Alvice. As before, they clung to the treeline to avoid being spotted. They were assuming the bandits would be using ge-eagles, and probably dogs. All of them had listened intently to Edeard on the first day when he told them about the tamed fastfoxes he'd encountered back in Rulan province.

By midday they were halfway round the mountain's slopes when Topar stopped them. Their ge-eagles came flashing down to settle among the treetops. Verini, who was using the ge-eagle with ordinary vision, had spied two similar ge-eagles in the air above the shallow pass into the plateau country. The pair of them were orbiting high above the stony track, soaring round in a huge circle.

'Definitely keeping watch,' Topar said after they'd watched the ge-eagles for over half an hour. 'We'll have to go through the trees to get past them.'

Everyone dismounted and began to lead their ge-horses into the trees. Edeard went last, sweeping his farsight along the track through the pass to see if he could locate the bandits instructing the ge-eagles. There was no sign of them, not even if he used the counter to concealment – though that wasn't reliable at any distance. They were either on the other side of the pass, or hidden behind some thick rock.

Their ge-wolves prowled through the forest of kalkand trees, using natural senses to scent anyone hidden amid the undergrowth. It was dank and cold under the boughs, as if the tall leaden trunks were somehow caging a winter's mist. The cold soon wormed its way through their jackets and trousers to chill their limbs. Everyone had to use their third hand to ward off low branches and clinging damp fronds. The undergrowth of straggly bushes stunted by the lack of light tore at their legs, slowing them further. An endless canopy of scarlet sporecones dripped sap on to their hats which then dribbled in sluggish rivulets down on to their shoulders.

It was late afternoon by the time they reached the far side of the mountain. The plateau was more hospitable than the saddle lands behind. A broad expanse of deciduous forests and long meadows laced with small streams. The peaks all around were low, without snowcaps. Miles away to the north-east they could see a village; its yellow stone buildings cresting a hillock. Thin strands of smoke wound their way up out of chimneys.

'No wall,' Edeard said under his breath. Even now that still startled him. He remembered his surprise on the long journey east with the Barkus caravan how the fortifications around settlements grew smaller and more dilapidated with every mile they travelled. Until finally in Oxfolk province on the other side of the Ulfsen Mountains they had been abandoned altogether, leaving towns and villages completely exposed to whatever lurked outside their boundary. Only nothing dangerous did lurk there, not any more. Not for hundreds of years.

With the pass guarded by the ge-eagles far behind them, Topar guided them along the treeline to a steep little valley leading away from the mountain. They hiked down to the stream at the bottom, and mounted up again. The ge-horses splashed along the stone bed, taking them out on to the plateau. Small martoz and bluebeech trees grew out of the steep slopes, their roots webbing the big flood boulders littering the valley. Long whip-like branches waved across the sky above them, providing more cover. Their ge-eagles flew low, barely skimming the uppermost branches, watching for any of their own kind; while the ge-wolves spread out across the boggy meadowland on either side, sniffing the air.

As the sun fell below the high, rumpled horizon they reached one of the many forests sprawled across the plateau. Here the trees weren't so tight, and the ground underfoot was a mat of dead leaves and soft loam. Tall weeds and grass offered no resistance to the ge-horses. They made their way to the centre where they set up camp.

When the first glimmers of the nebulas began to shimmer overhead, Topar dispatched their five night-viewing ge-eagles to see if they could spot the watchers from the pass.

'They're here somewhere,' Macsen said intently. 'They wouldn't keep a look-out on the pass otherwise.'

'Unless they're in the valley on the other side of it,' Dinlay pointed out. 'And we crossed each other sometime when we both crept through the trees.'

'Ever the optimist,' Macsen grunted.

'Practicalist.'

'That's not a word.'

'Realist,' Larby supplied.

'Thank you,' Dinlay said.

'They're here on the plateau,' Topar said.

Edeard was one of those guiding the ge-eagles, his farsight enabling him to send it over vast swathes of land. It soared up into the air, giving it a broad view of the rolling plateau. Topar had asked him to cover the south-east, where there were forests and narrow gullies and long talus slides spilling out below from faultline crags.

The ge-eagle flew swift and silent, showing him the muted ground, as if he was peering down on a world shrouded by the thickest stormclouds. He saw a drakken pack scampering along a slim gorge like an oily tide; then they began to churn around a chamalan carcass. Small rusals skipped nimbly up bushes and trees, searching for cones and pods to store for the winter. Trilans wove their low dams across streams, producing wide bogs that proved treacherous to other animals. Several flocks of chamalans huddled together, those on the outside nervous of whatever skulked through the night.

After an hour observing the relatively harmless nocturnal activities of the plateau's wildlife, the ge-eagle caught a flash of motion next to a sprawl of hatlash trees growing along the marshy banks of a small lake. Something bigger and faster than anything else it had seen that night. The ge-eagle dipped its wing and curved round until it was coasting along several hundred feet above the tops of the hatlash trees. Their trunks were swollen from the lake water, pressed together in a battle for space; the pushing and shoving resulted in the trees leaning at steep angles, producing an interlocked tangle. Perfect cover. The ge-eagle turned again, scouring the swaying treetops for any sign of incongruous movement.

It glimpsed something on the third pass, and began a tight spiral. Through its eyes Edeard saw a fastfox slinking along, picking its way through the ragged curtains of weeping boughs. The big predator sped up when it reached a small clearing where dead trunks were rotting into a rancid pile of fungi. Even so, the ge-eagle clearly saw the collar round its neck.

'They're here,' Edeard announced quietly, and gifted the ge-eagle's vision to the others.

'Sweet Lady,' Dinlay muttered.

'I never thought I'd ever see one of those things,' Macsen said.

Edeard instructed the ge-eagle to back off.

'Why?' Larby asked.

'Its master won't be far away,' Edeard explained. 'They're not that easy to keep control of, I know. He might farsight our ge-eagle.'

Sure enough, a few minutes later the fastfox left the hatlash trees. A man was with it, jogging along effortlessly.

'Dear Lady,' Edeard gasped. The man was wearing a simple dark tunic and knee-length boots. Two belts were looped over his shoulders, crossing his chest. Slim metal boxes were clipped to it, the kind that held bullets for the rapid-fire gun that was hanging on a third strap. 'He's one of them!' Shock was making him giddy. His hands started pawing at his chest as he sucked down air.

'Them?' Macsen asked. 'You mean the bandits?'

'The ones from Ashwell. He's dressed exactly the same as they were that night. I swear on the Lady, he's got to be one of *them*.' He became aware of the nervous glances the others were trading. 'Them,' he insisted.

'To be expected,' Topar said. 'They chased me before.'

'That's no bandit from the wilds,' Larby said.

'Are you okay?' Macsen asked in concern.

Edeard nodded a slow reassurance. Seeing this nemesis return out of his own past was profoundly shocking. *But I've grown since then. This time it's their turn to know fear.*

'Do you recognize this actual one?' Dinlay asked.

Edeard returned to the ge-eagle's view. The bird was still gliding higher, keeping level to the bandit and his fastfox. The profile was hardly distinct, but ... 'No,' Edeard said. 'I don't remember any faces, not really.' *Though there's one mind I will know forever.*

'All right,' Topar said, 'Let's follow him, see where he takes us.'

The ge-eagle stayed high in the air above the bandit, gliding idly to keep pace. Topar got them all back in the saddle as the bird reached the edge of Edeard's perception, and they started to ride slowly after the bandit, leaving the forest behind. All of them cast a seclusion haze, even though the nebulas above were wan shadows of their usual iridescence. The mild psychic baffle should be enough to deter all but the sharpest farsight at night. To bolster their safety the ge-wolves ranged around them, while two of the night-viewing ge-eagles under Verini's instruction scouted ahead. Their own farsight was used to guide the horses through the darkness.

'Is it just one?' Macsen asked after half an hour. The bandit was making good time, alternatively jogging, then walking, heading south-east, and making use of the spinneys and thickets that were scattered across the plateau. He was clearly adept at moving unseen across the land, even the ge-eagle had trouble keeping track of him in some of the deeper terrain.

'I can't see any others,' Edeard admitted. They'd deliberately kept a long way back in case the bandit had a powerful farsight. 'But I know from experience they can all use concealment.'

'Great Lady,' Boloton said. 'There could be an army of them following us.'

'There isn't,' Edeard promised him.

It was almost midnight when the bandit reached the top end of a narrow gulley. He stopped, and squatted down amid a clump of tall weather-worn stones coated in thick kimoss. The fastfox sped away, back the way they'd just come.

'Let's get into cover,' Topar said. They guided their mounts towards the nearest small wood.

The fastfox chased back along its path, stopping to sniff cautiously every now and again.

'He's double checking,' Fresage said. 'Wherever he is, he considers it important. He's not going on until he's satisfied he's clear.'

'Pull the ge-eagle back,' Topar told Edeard. 'If their camp is nearby, we can't risk exposing ourselves.'

Edeard instructed the bird to spiral higher. The lay of the land was revealed to him, falling away to the east and split by several rocky gullies.

'Two of those gullies meet up, look,' Verini said. 'It's a hollow with a cliff along one side. Perfect place for a concealed camp.'

'This is where I go in and check, then,' Edeard said.

'I'll come with you,' Dinlay said immediately.

'Thanks, but this is just a scout round to see if they're there. My concealment is stronger than anyone's, and I know I can shield myself if they do spot me.' He could sense the concern in everybody's mind.

'Just be careful,' Macsen said. 'There's no city to protect you out here.'

'I'm just going to look, I swear on the Lady.'

They all watched through the lone ge-eagle as the fastfox returned, and the bandit started down the gulley.

'You've got two hours,' Topar said. 'After that we will come looking for you.'

It took Edeard a while to decide his approach. The top of the little cliff would surely be guarded; and fastfoxes had an excellent sense of smell. But the gullies, too, would be watched. Possibly there'd be a tripwire that he might not detect.

The cliff top it is, then.

As soon as he left the wood he spun a concealment around himself, becoming no more than a dense wisp of dark air. His farsight swept out, alert for any hint of danger.

Just as he'd suspected, there were fastfoxes acting as sentinels above the cliff. They were curled up amid the boulders littering the long grass, wide awake, sniffing the night air for foreign scents. He reached out with his longtalk, and began subverting their orders, coaxing them away from their obedient attentive state, allowing them to stretch and settle down comfortably, scratch their hides and groom some of the day's mud away. A sensation of contentment began to percolate through their thoughts. When one finally registered his scent, it dismissed the intrusive smell as being an irrelevance.

There was a lone human watcher standing near the edge of the cliff. He was concealed, but Edeard could sense his farsight washing back and forth intermittently. Once he'd worked out the approximate location, he used his own farsight to gently prise apart the concealment. The bandit was revealed, with the customary twin belts of ammunition boxes across his chest, and a repeat-fire gun on a strap over his shoulder. There were also several knives and blade discs in various pouches. He even had an ordinary pistol. For all his toughness and weapons, he hadn't noticed how slack the fastfoxes had become. His thoughts remained blissfully unsuspicious.

Edeard picked a section of the cliff eighty yards away from the bandit, and crept forward.

*

674

'Nine of them?' Topar asked. 'You're sure?'

'Yes,' Edeard said for the third time. 'One on top of the cliff controlling the fastfoxes. Five asleep below an overhang, and the one we followed settling down for the night. Then there's two watching the gullies, both concealed. There's also two fastfoxes in each gulley. I saw five ge-eagles, and nine terrestrial horses.'

'What about supplies?' Larby asked.

'A pile of sacks and bags, probably enough food for three weeks at least. And three boxes of ammunition. They're not done with raiding yet.'

'Bastards,' Verini growled.

'So can we take them?' Topar asked. 'They outnumber us.'

'By one,' Fresage said dismissively. 'And we have surprise on our side.'

'I think it's possible,' Edeard said. 'We'll need to approach down a gully. I can keep the fastfoxes calm long enough for us to get past them. The trouble will be the three watchers, they longtalk each other all the time. As soon as one is taken out, the others will know.'

'So we have to be within striking distance of the camp when that happens,' Topar said.

'I can take out the three watchers fast enough,' Edeard said. 'But I can't guarantee they won't call out; so you'll have to deal with the others. Especially if we're going to take one alive.'

'I'd prefer to take two of them,' Topar said.

'Can our ge-wolves tackle the fastfoxes?' a mildly apprehensive Dinlay asked.

'We can't take them with us,' Edeard said. 'That's a whole new instinct I'd have to soothe out of the fastfoxes, and a much stronger one than human scent. We have to keep this as simple as possible.'

'Lady . . . fastfoxes.'

'They look fierce—'

'Look!'

'They are fierce, but that's all they've got. Don't waste time trying to shoot one, especially not in the dark. Heartsqueeze them, or pulp their brains. It barely takes a second to kill one. Fear is their only ally.'

'Oh Lady,' Dinlay groaned.

'Can you do this?' Topar asked with quiet authority.

Dinlay took a breath, managing to appear quite offended. 'Of course I can do this. It's only a fool who won't admit his worry.'

'Good. I want you to take out the two fastfoxes in the gully as soon as Edeard deals with the watchers.'

'Certainly.'

Larby glanced up at the sky. 'Do we do this now?'

'No,' Topar said. 'It's only a couple of hours until dawn, and we haven't slept. We spend the day laying up here in the woods and resting, then tomorrow after midnight we strike.'

Edeard had never felt so apprehensive before. All those times he'd sneaked into the House of Blue Petals, rescuing Mirnatha, arresting Buate, even facing down Bise atop his mansion; he'd known and understood what he was facing then. This was different, the bandits were an unknown, and he certainly wasn't as confident as Topar they could bring this off. It would only take one little mistake to alert the watchers, and then they'd be fending off nine rapid-fire guns.

At first light, three of the bandits left their camp, with ge-eagles orbiting high above them and fastfoxes trotting obediently alongside. One of them even sneaked through the edges of the wood where Edeard and his companions were encamped. Thankfully they were well hidden beneath the boughs, and his ge-eagle never spotted them as it flew overhead.

One of the bandits headed back to the pass at the side of Mount Alvice, while the other two went off in completely different directions.

'Picket duty,' Boloton decided. 'They're making sure nobody gets close. We were lucky.'

'No,' Verini said. 'They're good, we're better.'

'We'll know tonight,' Macsen said sagely.

Edeard didn't manage much sleep during the day. He was

restless, his mind going over the plan again and again. It all depended on how fast he could eliminate the three watchers. *That's if they only have three watchers. Suppose they change the pattern each night? I would. No, I wouldn't.* He eventually fell asleep in the afternoon.

Larby woke him. 'The picket guards are on their way back,' he said as Edeard blinked up at the darkening sky. Buluku was already visible, its swaying violet length beset with waves of electric-blue light. Odin's Sea was rising above the eastern horizon, several scarlet spikes crowning its blue and green nucleus. He found its presence strangely reassuring. *I wonder if Boyd has reached it already? Probably not. Who knows how far away it is?*

There were an unusual number of stars in evidence, twinkling away in the wide gaps between the nebulas. At least Honious hadn't appeared in the firmament. The way Edeard was feeling he would probably have taken that as a bad omen. *Stupid, because the sky is just the sky no matter what.*

They ate together, munching their way through half-stale bread and some cold pasties followed by dried fruit. However, Topar did allow them to use the Jamolar oil stove to heat some water for tea and coffee. They were too far away for a fastfox to pick up the scent.

'No one else left or joined during the day,' Macsen said. 'So it's just the nine of them.'

'You sure it's only nine?' Fresage asked.

'I counted nine,' Edeard assured him.

'I want everyone to oil and check their pistols,' Topar said.

Edeard was thankful for the distraction, even though he knew he was sure he'd never use the weapon. His third hand was all he needed. But he went through the routine anyway.

Just after midnight, Topar led them out of the woods. It took them an hour to retrace the route Edeard had taken the previous night, moving slowly and cautiously. As they reached the end of the gully they linked hands before summoning up a concealment. Both Larby and Topar had insisted this was the best way of keeping in contact, whispers and strong farsight might be detected by the watchers. It was a strange sensation; Edeard could feel Dinlay's hand in his, yet if he glanced back he could see only a blur of darkness.

Edeard walked forwards very slowly, using the weakest farsight he could to check the ground for tripwires or any other alarms. As he did so, he began to feel uncomfortable. A tremor ran through him. *Something wrong.*

The boulder-strewn walls rose sharply as the slope carried them down towards the bandit camp. Soon the steep walls were topped by imposing rock cliffs. Below their feet the ground was turning damp. Nebula-light revealed a meandering channel with thick reed tufts growing out between the stones. Edeard's trepidation grew with every step. Cold had claimed him now. He knew what this feeling was. The same as that night in Ashwell, the same as the entrapment atop the tower in Eyrie.

There can't be anything wrong. Not here. They don't know we're coming for them. They can't know!

On top of that anxiety, Edeard began to worry if his longtalk could reach the sentry fastfoxes before they scented him coming. It would be touch and go, he knew. He hadn't realized the gulley was this deep, nor so serpentine.

The sense of foreboding grew even stronger. He thought he could hear a whisper. Not with his ears. His mind. A very faint longtalk?

He walked through a small shallow stream, moving carefully so he didn't create a splash, only to find his boots sinking with alarming speed. Quicksand. 'Shit,' he whispered through clenched teeth. He had to reach down with his third hand to stabilize the treacherous ground. His finger tapped three times on Dinlay's hand – caution.

There was a tremendous scraping sound from above, as if the stone cliffs were splitting. Edeard immediately sensed a number of powerful farsights stabbing down, farsights that weren't fooled by concealment. The noise grew even louder.

'Weapons!' Topar shouted.

Edeard dropped his concealment and sent his farsight straight towards the sound. What he found shocked him for a dangerous instant. Three huge boulders were starting to roll down the slope directly above them, and as they moved they dislodged a whole swarm of smaller boulders. '*Ambush!*' he bellowed, and immediately strengthened his shield. At once he realized it wouldn't do him the slightest use, not against such a cascade of stone, the mass starting to slide down on top of them was incredible. He instinctively grabbed Dinlay with his third hand and threw him up the slope on the other side.

'Hello again, Edeard,' a mental voice sneered.

Edeard was scrambling up the slope as the first boulders picked up speed. He reached for Macsen. But he knew that voice, and the cruelty behind it. The leader from Ashwell, the man who had killed Edeard's village, his life. Akeem's murderer.

Dinlay had recovered from his abrupt flight. He started shooting his pistol across the gully. It was a signal for Topar and Fresage to open fire. Verini began to run back along the gully. The overwhelming noise from the accelerating avalanche was joined by the deadly sound of rapid-fire guns. The three large boulders had been covering the mouths of caves in the cliffs. Now a dozen bandits were spilling out, taking aim on Edeard and his companions. The only thing preventing immediate death was the avalanche itself. To many rocks were interfering with their field of fire.

'The great Waterwalker himself,' laughed Edeard's tormentor.

By now the smaller head-sized stones were bouncing down around Edeard. Bullets chewed the ground beside his feet. A screaming Dinlay dived for cover behind a rock. Not fast enough. Bullets chewed his legs, then thudded into his torso.

A stream of bullets smashed into Edeard. His shield held and he instinctively punched back along the line of attack. One of the ambushers flew backwards through the air, spraying blood.

Three big stones crashed into Fresage. His cry was cut off.

Macsen fired his pistol up at the ambushers. The ground around him was ripped apart by rapid-gun fire. Edeard screamed at the massive flare of pain Macsen's dying brain unleashed. His third hand lashed out wildly again at the ambushers, knocking four of them sideways. Two came careering down the slope after the avalanche, bones snapping as they twisted and tumbled.

A giant boulder smashed into Larby's chest, flinging him to the ground. More stones bounced and skittered on top of him.

Edeard was dancing about on the slope, trying to avoid the lethal barrage, smacking at the stones hurtling at him, deflecting them. Then the biggest boulder of all, nearly twice his height, slammed into the bottom of the gulley, shaking the ground. Momentum sent it spinning right at him.

He held it. The incredible weight was nothing. He just grabbed it with his third hand and stopped it dead in the air. It hung there, three feet off the ground as his lips twisted savagely with the effort. A shower of smaller stones from the avalanche smacked into it. Edeard held fast. One of the other original boulders rolled past, then teetered on the slope and skittered back down to the bottom of the gully.

'Ladyfuck!' someone's frantic longtalk shouted.

'How's he doing that?'

'Kill him. Kill the little shit.'

The rapid-fire guns began shooting. Bullets thudded into the boulder hanging in front of Edeard. He could hear strange whirring *pings* as ricochets twirled off in all directions. The reverberations of falling rock grumbled away as the avalanche slithered to its end.

Edeard lifted the boulder high, above his head, higher, three times his height. Higher still. It drew level with the caves on the other side of the gully. Seven bandits were crouched down on a long ledge running in front of the dark openings. They gaped in disbelief at the massive rock that was now curving through the air towards them. Accelerating.

It struck the first one, knocking him away into the gully. The impact didn't even slow it down. Everyone on the ledge tried to run, but there was no room and no time. The boulder hammered into them, crushing their bodies to pulp or sending them spinning off into the chasm. Then Edeard brought it down very precisely on the last bandit.

After that, he simply stood there. Arms by his side. Staring numbly at the great swathe of shingle which the avalanche had created on the other side of the gully. He started to shake. Arms first, then his legs trembled and his muscles gave out. He dropped to his knees.

'Dinlay?' he called with mind and voice. 'Dinlay? Macsen? Topar? Anyone?'

He sensed the fastfoxes coming, slinking along the bottom of the gully, hurrying to do their masters' bidding. To bring death to the intruder. Without even thinking, he shoved his third hand into their skulls and tore at the soft brain tissue. They fell silently, sprawling over the stony ground.

The remaining bandits followed stealthily. Creeping along under concealment, rapid-fire guns held ready. Edeard let them come close, then killed them. Pulling them from where they crouched and crawled, and snapping their spines. They were discarded one after the other, dropping out of the night to lie broken beside their fastfoxes. He felt nothing. No sorrow. No anger. Nothing.

Dinlay's shredded body was sprawled on the slope above him, where he should have been safe. Where he *would* have been safe after Edeard dropped him there, if he'd just stayed down. But Dinlay would never cower behind a rock while his comrades were under attack. Not Dinlay.

Edeard focused his farsight down the slope. Macsen's bloody corpse was staring up at Odin's Sea. Defiant to the last, he'd even got off a shot after the first swarm of bullets had struck. Fresage and Topar were buried below mounds of stone. Boloton had been pinned down by a rock landing on his legs. Other stones had battered him while several bullets punctured his chest and head. There wasn't much left that was recognizable. And Verini hadn't got more than half a dozen paces back up the gully before the rapid-fire guns had found him. Larby's arms and legs protruded from underneath one of the large boulders; there was nothing left of his torso but a mangled patch of gore soaking into the earth.

Edeard started crying. 'Why do you do this to me?' he yelled at Odin's Sea. 'Lady, why? What have I done that's so evil to be punished like this. Why? *Why?* Tell me you stinking bitch.' He sobbed relentlessly. 'Why?' Then he was curled up on the ground, helpless. Wanting this monstrous life to end. Wanting to die.

'Edeard.'

The voice was speaking from a very long way away.

'Edeard, this is not over.'

He wiped a hand over his face, smearing the mud and tears and blood that were clinging to him. 'Who . . . oh.'

'Edeard.'

Through his grief he sighed in understanding, and extended his farsight to where he thought the voice was coming from. Concentrating as best he could. 'The Master of Sampalok himself,' he said with bitter affection.

Macsen's soul smiled down at his friend. 'The briefest reign ever.'

'The most memorable.' Edeard's farsight switched to Dinlay, who stood beside Macsen. 'I'm so sorry.'

'There's nothing to be sorry for,' Dinlay said. 'You tried to save me.'

'I failed.'

'But you tried. That's what makes you the Waterwalker.'

'Can you hear the nebulas? Can you hear the songs?'

'Yes,' Macsen said. 'They're very strong, very beautiful. It is hard to resist their call, they promise such a glorious future within the Heart. But we will stay with you for now, we are pledged to do that, no matter how difficult it is to linger. There is one task we are honour-bound to help you with, Edeard, defeating whoever was behind this ambush. You will deliver us justice.'

'I will,' he said miserably. 'I promise that. And thank you so much.'

Macsen smiled sadly. 'Edeard, can you see them?'

'See who?' He sent out his farsight, thinking some bandits might have survived.

Macsen and Dinlay drifted towards him. 'Beside us, Edeard,' Dinlay said. 'Try, Edeard, try to see them. They're so weak now, so fragile. But they endure. For you. Dear Lady, they have lasted for over a decade and a half. You'll never know what that costs until you die.'

'What?'

'Focus, Edeard,' Macsen insisted. 'The same way you see us. But go further.'

Edeard attempted to do as they asked, extending his farsight, not lengthening it, but deepening the perception. There, right on the edge of his ability, he discerned two figures. They were incredibly faint. A man and a woman, badly enervated compared to the souls of Macsen and Dinlay.

'I know you,' Edeard said in wonder. 'Your faces. I remember them.' His thoughts went tumbling back through the years. Back to a time when he'd run through that grand old farmhouse outside Ashwell. Laughed and played all day long. Gone running happily to . . . 'Mother?' he gasped incredulously. 'Mother, is that you? And Father?'

The tenuous souls smiled in unison. They linked hands.

'Son,' his father said.

It was a voice so frail Edeard was immediately afraid. 'You stayed?' the tears had returned as the revelation sapped his physical strength.

'Of course we stayed, my beautiful boy,' his mother said.

'You watched out for me. You! It was you all those times. You warned me.'

'You are all that is left of us,' his father said. 'We had to protect you. To make sure you were safe.'

'Oh, dear Lady. What about the songs, the call to the Heart?'

'We love you, that's what's truly important.'

'But, you're so . . . small.'

'It would be the same if we had followed the songs,' his

mother said with a gentle smile. 'They are so far away. I tell myself so few souls will ever reach the Heart.'

'Go,' Edeard said. 'Go now. I want to meet you again on the other side of Odin's Sea. I want to tell you all I've done with my life. I want you to be safe.'

'Too late for that, son,' his father said. 'This has been our blessing, seeing what you have become. Seeing you grow to this stature. I'm so proud, so very proud, I would never exchange this for another lifetime in the Heart. Not if I had this same choice a million times over.'

'My beautiful son,' his mother said. 'I could never have dreamed for a child so splendid. You have led this world out of darkness.'

'No he hasn't,' Macsen said. 'I'm sorry, Edeard, but they knew we were coming. This ambush is about as clever and devious as you can get.'

'And it didn't work,' Dinlay said firmly, then frowned. 'Not against you.'

'Who warned them?' Macsen asked. 'Who is really behind this? Edeard, the girls! Our wives. What is happening back in Makkathran?'

Edeard felt all the joy of his extraordinary reunion drain back out of him. 'I don't know,' he said. 'But there's someone left to ask.'

The huge boulder was exactly where Edeard had left it, perched on the lip of the ledge. Its immense weight crushing the bandit leader's lower legs beneath it. Despite being trapped, despite the immense pain, the desperate man had managed to reload his rapid-fire pistol. His third hand had gathered up several extra magazines full of bullets. All he needed was a clear shot.

Edeard felt the man's farsight on him as he scrambled up to the ledge. He walked calmly round the boulder, and the bandit opened fire. Edeard stood there grinning as the incessant bullets pummelled uselessly at his shield.

'A truly terrible weapon,' Edeard said when the bullets were exhausted. 'Your enemies will surely be deaf for a week after that.'

'Go to Honious, Waterwalker.'

'A long time after you, I suspect.' Edeard's third hand snatched the gun away. 'You never did tell me your name. But now I recognize that nose, it's very distinct. Just how far down the Gilmorn family tree are you?'

'Your friends are dead. All of them, I farsighted that. You're all alone in ways you cannot imagine.'

'Really?' Edeard applied his third hand. The Gilmorn screamed as the boulder rolled forwards; his knees *crunched*. 'Who told you we were coming?'

'It's over, you fucking freak,' the Gilmorn yelled against the pain. Cold sweat was seeping down his face. 'We won, even after this, we won.'

The boulder turned fractionally again. The scream of agony was terrible as more of his legs were destroyed beneath the stone. 'Who won?' Edeard asked calmly.

'You can't win, not now,' the Gilmorn wailed.

'An inch at a time,' Edeard warned, and moved the boulder again. 'And you're a tall man.'

'*Nooooo!*'

Edeard thought the Gilmorn might have damaged his throat, the tormented cry which followed was so loud and prolonged. 'Is this how the villagers begged and pleaded? How many have you slaughtered over the years, Gilmorn?' Edeard rolled the boulder up closer to his hips.

The bandit began thrashing about, banging his head back frantically against the ledge in an attempt to split his own skull open, to end the torture. Edeard's third hand swiftly immobilized him.

'It was necessary,' the Gilmorn gurgled. He was having trouble breathing now, sweat was soaking his clothes.

'Necessary?' a disgusted Edeard asked. 'Necessary for what? You have killed – murdered – hundreds of people. Thousands. You have brought ruin to whole villages.'

'One nation.'

'What?' Edeard thought he had misheard the phrase. The Slogan. Owain's slogan. *Owain.*

'We have to be one.'

A furious Edeard edged the boulder round again. The man's hips burst.

'Owain!' Edeard yelled, his voice full of hatred.

The Gilmorn laughed manically, allowing blood to foam out of his mouth. 'One world, one nation, ruled by those of us who were born with destiny in our blood.'

'You did all this to crown an emperor? You . . . you . . . Dear Lady, for *this*?' Edeard rolled the boulder forwards and kept it going until the screams and *snappings* ended abruptly. 'Lady, no,' he murmured in anguish.

'For all your strength, you're so weak,' the Gilmorn's soul said contemptuously.

Edeard spun round.

The bandit's spectral essence stood above the puddle of his own blood spreading out from under the boulder. He gave Dinlay and Macsen a scornful glance. 'You could have joined with us, Waterwalker. Cousin Ranalee offered you the world. A whole people united in veneration of your strength. And you turned her down. For what? Them? What can these pitiful tragedies ever give you?'

'Honious awaits you,' an incensed Macsen said. 'Do not tarry.'

The Gilmorn started to ascend. 'And guess what, Waterwalker, my family still gets to fuck your little Novice whore.' His shape blurred as it shot upwards to be lost amid the glowing beauty of the nebulas.

'Salrana?' Edeard murmured in dismay. 'Kristabel!'

'Kanseen,' Macsen said. 'Edeard, what is happening in Makkathran? If Owain is to be emperor, this trap for us can only be a part of his madness.'

'Lady damn it,' Edeard spat. He scurried down the slope, and began to run along the gully.

Several of the bandits' terrestrial horses were still tethered to their posts. They were skittish, but Edeard's skilled longtalk calmed them. He found a saddle among the packs and threw it over the first horse.

'Six days since we left,' Macsen said. 'What can they have done in six days?'

'It'll be another two before I can get back,' Edeard said in anguish as he mounted up. 'Perhaps Owain is waiting to hear this ambush was successful and I am dead. He knows I can stop him, that the city sides with me.'

'Yes,' Dinlay said. 'We must hope for that.'

Edeard pictured a map, trying to work out the shortest way back to the main road through the mountains. Disheartened, he realized it was back the way they'd come, past Mount Alvice. But before, they'd ridden carefully, lumbering along beneath trees and in deep ravines so as to avoid notice. Now he had no such inhibitions. He spurred the horse on, and instructed the others to follow.

Dawn found him already long way past Mount Alvice. By mid-morning he was back on the road, and speeding east. He had to switch horses before lunch, the one he'd ridden from the ambush was nearly dead from fatigue. The next one was gone in the middle of the afternoon. Edeard himself was worn out, but sheer determination kept him going. The next two horses only lasted a couple of hours each.

He came to a village as the sun began to dip towards the mountains, knowing full well he looked like something straight out of Honious. They might have been nervous about his appearance, but the villagers knew of the Waterwalker, and gold coinage spoke a welcome language everywhere. He paid a ridiculous amount for three fresh horses, and raced off into the evening.

Despite the cramped muscles, the bruised and bloody chafing on his thighs, he kept on going through the night. Morning saw him arrive at the foothills of the Donsori range, with the Iguru Plain spread out below. Makkathran sat on the horizon, the gold sunlight already catching the tips of its towers. He let out a sob of relief at the sight of it, even though he was completely exhausted.

'I have to know,' Macsen said, and with that he was gone, flashing on ahead through the warm winds blowing off the land.

'I will stay with you,' Dinlay promised.

Edeard urged his last tired horse down the switchback road. That was when he met the caravan winding its way up into the mountains. It was unusual for a caravan to be moving so early in the day. He stopped to talk with the master.

'The city is in chaos,' the old man told him nervously. 'There are men with guns on every street claiming to represent the new Mayor. The militia regiments marched in two days ago, and the constables tried to stop them. There was fighting. I have never seen so many dead.'

'No,' Edeard groaned. 'Oh, Lady, no. Wait! The Mayor called in the regiments?'

'Yes, but not Finitan. He's dead, and nobody knows how that happened. Owain has claimed the Orchard Palace, and the gunmen supported him.'

Edeard desperately wanted to know about Kristabel, but the caravan master wouldn't know. 'I need fresh horses. I can pay.'

The old man gave him a grim look, then eventually nodded. 'We won't be back this way for a year, probably more, so I suppose we will be spared retribution.'

'Retribution?'

'The Upper Council has declared you outlaw, Waterwalker. I . . . we heard you were dead.'

'Not yet,' Edeard said through gritted teeth. 'They have already found it is not that easy.'

'Good. We will swap your horses. I don't need money from you.'

'Thank you.'

'Finitan dead,' Dinlay said sombrely as Edeard rode across the Iguru Plain on a long-legged ge-horse. 'How dare they commit such an act? The people elected him.'

'This has been years in the making,' Edeard answered numbly.

'All the bandit attacks, the fear in the provinces, even the gangs loose in the city; all designed to force Querencia to accept a single government, one with Owain at its head. And then I arrived. How ironic is that, his own campaign of terror made me flee to the city.'

'But what can you do now?'

'Throw him out of the Mayor's office, restore the rightful government.' Even as he spoke it, he knew how false it sounded.

'Good,' but the spectre's tone was uncertain. 'That's good.'

Edeard didn't bother with concealment, nor even a seclusion haze. He didn't care that people saw him. He wanted word to spread into the city. He wanted people to have hope again. To know the Waterwalker was coming.

All would be put right.

There was a lot of traffic on the road. All of it heading away from Makkathran. Ragged groups stopped to stare as he galloped past. Several cheered, but the majority shook their heads in dismay at the sight of him. Longtalk rippled along the length of the road.

'The Waterwalker is still alive.'

'The Waterwalker is coming back.'

'The Waterwalker will stop this.'

'The Waterwalker is too late.'

'Too late.'

It disheartened him simply because it matched his own suspicions. Apart from Kristabel and a few friends, what was there for him really? He was never going to save the city and the world from Owain's kind. All that was left now was a rescue attempt, and a life in exile.

It was afternoon when he reached the final approach to the city; riding hard under the fanciful variety of trees lining the road. He was the only traveller now, and his farsight swept out to review his reception.

When he burst out from the end of the ancient partition of trees even the sheep had vanished from the quarter-mile band of grassland encircling the crystal wall. The North Gate was closed. A quick farsight check showed the other two gates shut as well. Half a regiment of militia was drawn up in a protective semi-circle around the mighty gate, a hundred pistols lined up along the road. At the front of them was a squad of guards in the uniform of the Weapons Guild. They carried rapid-fire guns.

Owain's farsight fell upon the lone figure urging his horse forward, one strand among many thousands. 'Turn around, Waterwalker, there is nothing left for you here. Turn around. You bring only death, for these fine men will kill you no matter how many of them your strength claims at first. You cannot wipe out an entire city of adversaries.'

'It is not your city,' Edeard longshouted back.

'As you wish. May the Lady have mercy on your soul.'

When he was barely three hundred yards from the first ranks of the militia Edeard suddenly turned his ge-horse off the road, and curved away parallel to the crystal wall. A cavalry platoon charged through the militiamen and raced after him. Any other time, Edeard would have laughed defiance, now he simply gritted his teeth and asked the city to allow him entry. He turned his horse again, and set it pelting directly at the crystal wall. The cavalry altered track to intercept him.

Edeard kept a steely control over his mount's fluttering thoughts as it pounded closer and closer to the wall. It never faltered, not even at the end when it was going far too fast to ever stop in time. A few yards short of the vertical barrier Edeard spurred it to jump. It leapt forwards, and to the astonishment of the cavalry in hot pursuit, it passed straight through the wall as if the tough substance were nothing more than a thin mist. They could even see it though the tinted crystal as it came down to land on the other side and continue its charge forwards. Only then did the Waterwalker pull its reins back. He swung off the saddle and stood on the ground of Low Moat for a second before swiftly sinking straight down through the grass.

*

Edeard emerged in the centre of the courtyard at the base of the Culverit ziggurat. The city's senses had already revealed what he would find: a long row of bodies wrapped in white cloth. And Buate, dressed in the robes of a Haxpen District Master, supervising ge-monkeys and cowed tearful staff on how he wanted the corpses disposed.

Just for an instant, Edeard's fright lifted as he perceived Kristabel standing there. But as he began to race forwards, arms open wide to greet his love, Dinlay's soul cried: 'No, Edeard, she is gone like me.'

And Kristabel turned towards him as he stumbled to a confused halt. Then he finally acknowledged she was gone, that he was farsighting her soul as it stood vigil over her body.

'I'm so sorry,' she told him with a forlorn smile.

Edeard's whole body was trembling with shock and anger. He turned inexorably to face Buate, who was slowly backing towards the mansion's main entrance. His guards were also edging away, none dared raise their weapons against the Waterwalker.

'I . . . I had no choice,' a pale Buate cried. 'Owain ordered me to claim the Haxpen Mastership for myself. There was a fight. Many were killed on both sides.'

'Who did this to you?' Edeard whispered, the words barely coming out of his mouth.

'His men came at dawn three days ago. Homelt and our guards fought valiantly; but the guns, Edeard, they had these terrible guns. None could stand against them. They killed our guards; my cousins and the maids were raped, old and young, they spared no one as they made their way up the mansion. They forced their way on to the tenth floor. Daddy and I tried to hold them off, but they were too strong. Edeard . . . I jumped. I wasn't going to let them do that to me. All was lost. Daddy and I and Mirnatha held hands and jumped from the very top of the stairs. Did we do wrong?'

'No, my love, you did no wrong. I should have been here to protect you. I am the one who failed.'

'Daddy and Mirnatha have gone to the nebulas in search of the Heart, Edeard, they follow the songs. Mummy will be there waiting for them. I stayed. I knew you would come. I had to see you one last time before I go.'

'What?' Buate asked, his farsight was probing the courtyard, trying to discover who Edeard was talking to. 'Who is there?'

'Who is there?' Edeard repeated numbly. 'My wife is here. My friend is here. My mother and father are here.'

Kristabel smiled at the souls of Edeard's parents. 'He is yours?'

'He is,' Edeard's mother said.

'I loved him so.'

'We know. He never knew happiness or contentment like you.'

'I see no one,' a badly frightened Buate stammered.

'Permit me to show you,' the Waterwalker told him.

Buate was lifted from the ground. His guards watched in dread as he began to shake violently in mid-air. Then he flung his head back and howled; his mind flooding the courtyard with excruciating pain. Tiny blooms of blood appeared on his robes, swiftly progressing to rivulets that dribbled down to splatter on the courtyard. That was when the guards turned and ran. They had to go a long way before the screams no longer plagued their ears.

Eventually, Buate's soul looked down on his corpse as the Waterwalker dropped it to the ground.

'Do you see now?' Edeard asked.

'You have lost,' Buate said. 'This is all you can do now: kill. In doing that, in seizing power back in such a fashion, you become us.'

Tears filled Edeard's eyes again as the soul slipped upwards. Buate had spoken the truth of it. There was nothing left for him. Owain and his kind had won. Killing them now would achieve nothing. The world was theirs. It wasn't one he wanted to live in.

Macsen and Kanseen drifted through the courtyard wall.

'Bijulee and Dybal are dead,' Macsen said. 'Bise came back to Sampalok.'

'Our baby is lost,' Kanseen's soul declared, she was fainter than her husband. 'He may be in the Heart. I cannot stay. Not here. Not even for you, Edeard. I have to know if he's there. I have to know my son.'

'I understand,' Edeard told her.

'My friend, I must go with my wife,' Macsen said.

'Of course you must,' Edeard raised a hand in farewell. 'You will be the first of us to reach Odin's Sea. Keep watch for us. We will all join you there eventually.'

'That will be the day we smile again.'

Edeard watched them dwindle into the sky, then turned to the souls who remained. 'We have lost. I have lost. There is no one left but myself.' His hand went down to the pistol holstered on his belt. 'I don't want to be alone.'

'Salrana,' Dinlay said. 'He said Salrana was still alive, that they would have her.'

Edeard's head came up. 'Oh Lady.' He sent his farsight flashing out towards Ysidro district, not daring to hope.

Ysidro's church had been pressed into use as a temporary hospital. Several rows of injured people were lying on makeshift beds in front of the Lady's statue. Three harassed, tired-looking doctors moved amongst them, doing what they could to treat the bullet wounds. Novices scurried round, helping the doctors with dressings, and offering comfort where they could. The church's Mother, a kindly grey-haired woman over halfway through her second century, moved through the clusters of parishioners who sat fearfully on the pews. She offered what blessings she could, but it was plain from her face she was as shocked and frightened as everyone else.

The church doors were shut. Fearful relatives of those who lay inside formed a defiant, protective line outside, waiting for the inevitable return of the militiamen or worse, the Weapons Guild guards who swaggered around the streets brandishing their lethal new guns. So far, the sanctity of the church held.

Edeard rose smoothly through the floor of the church. People gasped at his appearance. Except for Salrana, she let out a single piercing note of joy and ran to him. He scooped her up in his arms and hugged her tight.

'They said you were dead,' she sobbed.

'No,' he said. 'It's not that easy to kill me.'

'Oh Edeard, the regiments shot people. There are men with awful guns, just like the ones at Ashwell, who say they were appointed by the Mayor himself.'

'I know,' he said, hugging her tight. Her Novice uniform was stained with blood, some of which was days old. 'Are you all right?'

'Yes,' she nodded, wiping the tears from her eyes. 'I'm sorry, Edeard, I'm sorry I didn't talk to you after—'

'Hush,' he said, and stroked her brow.

'I was so stupid. So stubborn. You're my friend.'

'It's over now. Are you sure you're all right? Has anyone come looking for you?'

'No. I've been helping the doctors. So many have died. Everyone is so worried the Mayor's men will return. Can you stop this?'

Edeard bowed his head. 'I cannot. Anything I do now will only make this worse. I've endangered everyone in this church just by coming here. I'm sorry. I'm so sorry.'

Her fingers stroked his cheek. 'My darling Edeard, you did everything that's right.'

'They've killed everyone I know, everyone I love. Except for you. And they'll come for you eventually.'

She gasped. 'Your wife?'

'Yes,' he whispered through the pain. 'Kristabel is dead.'

Salrana's head rested on his chest. 'This cannot be happening.'

'But it has happened. I want you to come with me now.'

'Edeard!' She gave the injured a frantic look. The Mother was standing in front of the Lady's statue, a sympathetic expression on her face. 'They need my help.'

'They will manage.'

The Mother gave Salrana a brief nod of encouragement.

'But—'

'Hold me tight,' he instructed. 'This will be strange at first. But you have nothing to fear. I will be with you.'

'Always?'

'Yes, always.' He gave Kristabel's soul a guilty glance, but she simply smiled in understanding.

Edeard and Salrana slid down through the floor of the church. He felt her tighten her grip upon him. Then they were standing in a small tunnel beneath the church, with water trickling past their feet. 'There is further to go,' he told her, and they continued on their way down to emerge into one of the dazzlingly bright tunnels far below the city streets.

'Edeard! What is this place?' Salrana's head turned from side to side, trying to take in what she was seeing. There was surprise in her voice, but no fear.

'I'm not sure. It's a way to travel across the city. A very old one. I think some of Makkathran's past inhabitants used it, but I don't really know. It isn't connected to any of the buildings on the surface. So it probably wasn't the inhabitants before us.'

'Oh,' she said with a short laugh. 'Edeard, what have you become?'

'I don't know,' he said lamely. 'Whatever, in the end I was no use.'

'Don't say that.' She kissed him. 'Why are we here? Where are we going?'

He sighed and scratched the side of his head. 'Away, I suppose. Out of the city. Then . . . exile. We'll find some distant province. I'll grow a beard. You don't have to stay with me.'

'I think I better had, at least to start with.'

'Thank you.' He checked the souls that remained with him. Kristabel, Dinlay and his parents were all waiting silently a little way down the bright tunnel. They seemed content with his lead. Right now he wasn't going to tell Salrana about them, she'd had enough shocks. He reached down into the substance of the tunnel walls, and let them conduct his farsight. He'd always known the network of tunnels extended out underneath the crystal wall, but he'd never really bothered to see where they led.

Down, he saw now. A long, long way down. The multitude of tunnels merged then merged again and again in a funnel-like web whose last few strands extended for tens of miles beneath him. Down to where the true mind of the city lay.

But . . . there were a few branches that stretched out horizontally under the Iguru Plain. He asked the city to send him there.

'What's happening?' Salrana asked, abruptly clutching at him as she felt the tunnel tilting.

'It's all right,' he grinned reassuringly. 'We're going to fly.'

'Fly?'

They began to skid along the tunnel as it apparently shifted up past forty-five degrees. Then they were falling. Salrana let out a long wail of shock.

'It's all right,' Edeard assured her, shouting. He attempted to stroke her back, which really didn't work very well when the skirt of her Novice robe started flapping up, trying to wrap itself round her torso. So he applied his third hand, pressing it down again.

'We're going to die!' she shrieked.

'No, we're not. I always use these tunnels like this.'

She screwed her eyes shut, and buried her head against him. The flight went on for a lot longer than Edeard was used to. The tunnel was obviously carrying them a long way out of the city. He didn't know where exactly.

Before long Salrana calmed a little, and started to look round. 'We're not going to die?' she gasped.

'We're not going to die.'

'Where are we?'

'I'm not sure. Outside the city by now.'

The tunnel began to curve sharply. Edeard hadn't experienced that before. And somehow they weren't falling downwards, but rushing up. They started to slow. Edeard glanced up. The tunnel ended a few hundred yards above him in a blaze of scarlet light.

'Hang on,' he instructed, and suddenly they were through

into a simple circular room with red-glowing walls. There were no windows. The hole below their feet quickly irised shut and they were standing in the middle of the floor.

Salrana didn't let go of him, though she was peering round curiously. 'What now?' she asked.

'I'm not sure,' he admitted. 'I don't know what this place is.'

A black circle expanded on the wall. It vanished, leaving an equally black opening. Edeard and Salrana shared a look, and walked over to it. Some of the red light seeping out exposed what looked like rock walls beyond. Edeard extended his farsight, and confirmed there was some kind of cave outside. They stepped through cautiously on to a sandy floor. The air was dry and stale. Edeard's farsight couldn't see far through rock, of course, but the cave extended for some distance. After they walked a few steps the red light began to fade. Salrana spun round in time to see the circular opening seal up. She let out a little squeal.

Edeard held up a hand, and did the spark trick Kristabel had shown him back at the beach lodge. A layer of cold white flame licked round his fingers, throwing the cave into stark relief.

'But it's just rock,' Salrana exclaimed, studying the hole that had closed.

'I don't understand the city,' Edeard said. 'I just talk to it.'

'How?' she asked, a strong flash of curiosity shimmering through her veiled thoughts.

'Well . . .' He shrugged. 'I just do, really.'

'This is like before,' she said and shivered. 'You and me hiding alone at the bottom of a hole while outside our lives are destroyed.'

The fatigue really hit Edeard then. It wasn't just his body that was exhausted by the ride back to Makkathran, the emotional turmoil he'd suffered was even more debilitating. He just wanted to curl up and go to sleep – for a very long time. The light scintillating round his hand began to fade.

'Edeard,' his mother said. 'Don't give up. Not now.'

He took a moment. 'All right,' he said miserably.

Salrana looked at him.

'Come on,' he said. 'Let's see where this leads us to.'

The cave wasn't always as wide as where they'd entered it. Some places they had to squeeze and push their way along, with the rock grazing their clothes. The cave took them upwards, which worried Edeard. After farsighting the tunnels diving down into the depths of Querencia he wondered just how far underground they were.

It took an hour for them to squirm and worm their way through the cave before Edeard finally saw a pale sliver of daylight up ahead. They had to crawl up a steep slope with a roof of rock barely three feet above it before they emerged into a level cave. The entrance was curtained by a thick layer of eaglevine, whose red and green leaves muted the afternoon sunlight.

Edeard sent his farsight probing through the lush vegetation to discover the cave mouth was halfway up a vertical cliff. He could sense no one outside, not even an animal. When he pushed the strands of eaglevine apart he found himself staring north-east across the Iguru Plain, with the Donsori Mountains in the distance.

'This is one of those little volcanoes,' he told Salrana. Far below him, a verdant forest of palms and vrollipan trees boiled around the lower slopes before giving way to the rich fields that divided up the plain. He twisted his head and looked up. 'The top of the cliff is closer than the bottom. I think I can get there okay.'

'Edeard! Be careful.'

'Don't worry,' he said. His farsight was examining the rock below the swarm of eaglevine. It was a rugged surface, providing innumerable hand and foot holds. He stretched out and secured a grip, then began to climb.

'I'll scout round ahead,' Dinlay's soul said, and drifted upward. For the first time, Edeard began to envy the dead. The climb actually wasn't so easy. He had to use his farsight to locate every grip, then shove his hands through the scratchy vines. It was even more difficult to get his feet through, he was constantly having to use his third hand to part the ancient rope-like cords.

Over ten minutes after leaving the cave, the tips of the vines gave way to bare rock. The cliff began to curve, and Edeard scrambled his way up off the rock and on to the slope of thin soil and reedy grasses.

He used his longtalk to tell Salrana: 'Made it.' His third hand gripped her carefully, and he lifted her out of the cave and up through the air.

'I can't see anyone,' Dinlay said. 'And there's a pavilion a quarter of a mile round the mountain, where the ground flattens out a bit. Nobody home.'

'Thank the Lady for that,' Edeard muttered.

He settled Salrana gently beside him. She produced a nervous grin. 'I think that was worse than the city tunnel,' she said apologetically.

'We need to take cover and decide what to do,' Edeard said. 'This way.'

The pavilion was exactly as Dinlay indicated. Belonging to some Grand Family, it was perched on a moderate slope with its front looking towards Makkathran, some fifteen miles away from the base of the volcanic cone. Built mainly from wood, its frontage was a long veranda with an overhang supported by a series of wide arches. Small polygonal turrets on each end had high sweeping roofs. Its white paint was starting to fade, splitting open to peel away on some of the long boards. Green spores were taking hold in the cracks and corners.

The doors were closed but not locked. Edeard and Salrana walked across the pavonazzeto tiling to find a building that had already been closed for the winter. Furniture had been covered in thick sheets. Shutters were bolted. The oil lamps drained. Bedding, carpets and rugs had been taken away. Tin saucers of poison laid out for vermin.

'Not a lot of food in the kitchen,' Salrana called out as she explored. 'Jars of fruit preserves and some flour. I suppose I could bake a loaf if you like. There's some wood and coal for the stove.'

Edeard had gone through the only bedroom out on to the veranda. The slope outside was in shadow now the sun was low in the sky on the other side of the volcano. He leaned on the handrail, staring out at the city. Just the sight of it produced an ache in his heart; he longed to return, to put things right. But too much had happened, Owain had destroyed everything of value. 'No fires,' he said. 'Nor lights. They'll be looking for us.'

She came out on to the veranda and put her arm round his shoulder. 'Of course. I wasn't thinking. What do we do?'

'Get away,' he said. 'Travel into the east and find a province where the Waterwalker is just a tale from the city that nobody really believes.'

'Aren't you going to stay and fight?'

'No. Owain and his kind are in power now.'

'Nobody wanted them. People will expect you to do something.'

'Buate was right, all I can do now is kill. That's not the answer.'

'But, Edeard—'

'No.'

'I understand,' she said solemnly. 'Come inside.'

He let her lead him back into the big bedroom. Edeard settled back on the fat mattress, staring up at the ceiling while Salrana went back to rummaging in the kitchen. Now he'd actually stopped moving the pain in his legs and buttocks began plaguing him. The horse ride back to Makkathran had been brutal. When he probed his tender flesh he found his trousers were damp from blood and skin fluid. It hurt, making him wince.

'I sensed that,' Salrana said, standing in the doorway holding on to a couple of large fruit jars.

He knew her farsight was concentrating on him, and didn't protest.

'Edeard! What have you done to yourself?'

'I had to get back here,' he said. 'We thought I might still have time.' He knew the tears were going to spill out again. Even now he didn't want Salrana to witness that.

'Eat something,' she said, and put a jar on the bed beside him. 'I'll have a hunt round for some medicine; there's bound to be some here somewhere. And, if not, I saw some falanpan leaves outside. I can make a poultice.'

Edeard didn't have the energy to protest. The jar contained plums preserved in a sugary syrup. He ate several before she returned, holding up a tube of ointment.

'I didn't realize I was so hungry,' he admitted. Then he had to grit his teeth as she gingerly stripped his trousers off. Her expression at the sight of his raw flesh wasn't reassuring. She did her best to brush her own concern away.

'This might sting,' she warned, and began to rub the salve on.

Edeard had to clamp his mouth hard shut to prevent the howl from leaving his throat. 'Lady!' His fingers clawed the top of the mattress.

'I've finished,' she said some interminable time later. 'That should start soothing the damage soon.'

'I think it already has. That or you've burned the nerves away.' His thighs were definitely easing.

'Don't be so mean,' Salrana said smartly, and gave him a brief kiss. She pulled a furniture sheet over him. 'You rest now, I'm going to see if I can find some clothes.'

'Keep a look out,' he said. 'I need to know if anyone comes.'

'Don't worry,' she said. 'Nobody knows we're here. Nobody knows we can be here.'

Edeard started to eat another plum. He was asleep before he finished.

Dreams claimed him. Not his usual bizarre visions of life elsewhere. These were his own. Mostly of Kristabel. Kristabel surrounded by flames. Men with rapid-fire guns circling round her, the roar of their weapons shattering his skull. Kristabel flying. Falling, her nightdress fluttering around her. The very same white nightdress she'd worn on the day they met. Falling down the central stairs in the ziggurat. The same stairs he'd started to reshape. Stairs that were now easy for the invaders to mount. Little Mirnatha screaming in terror as the ziggurat was consumed by the flame and bullets of the rapid-fire guns, clinging to her sister. Both of them falling from the tenth floor. A hand pushing them over the rail. Both screaming all the way to the floor. The hand was his own.

He cried out in torment. The sensation of something wrong was like a tidal wave of fear, threatening to send him plunging down into the infinite black of the abyss beneath the world. A pitiful broken thing on his way to Honious. Left behind by the Skylords. Left behind by Kristabel. Dinlay, Boyd, Macsen, Kanseen; all of them peered down from the rim. One by one they turned away.

'No,' he begged, pleaded, wept. 'No, come back.'

But they wouldn't because something was *wrong*.

He woke violently, back jerking off the bed as he clawed his way out of the abyss. Shaking with fear. It was still dark all around. Silent. He fought for breath against panic so strong it was throttling him. 'What!' he demanded, and sent his farsight stabbing out.

The souls of Dinlay, Kristabel and his parents were clumped together by the end of the bed. Kristabel's arms were held out to him, radiating tangible concern.

'What?' he repeated as his breathing became less frantic.

'Edeard, we've tried to wake you,' Dinlay said. 'We tried hard. But you were so tired.'

'I'm awake.' When he squinted through the half-open door on to the veranda, he could see nebula-light washing the white-painted rails outside with familiar pastels. It must have been close to midnight.

'Salrana,' Kristabel told him brokenly. 'She betrayed you.'

'What?' he blurted in confusion. 'What?'

'I'm sorry,' Dinlay said. 'She has an exceptionally strong longtalk. She called Owain just after sunset. She told him where you were.'

'Salrana? What do you mean?'

'We couldn't stop her,' Kristabel said. 'We are helpless against the living.'

'No, no,' Edeard said. His farsight sensed Salrana walking across the hallway.

'Edeard?' she said in a light voice. 'Are you all right? I thought you were still sleeping.'

'She called Owain,' Kristabel insisted. 'His men are already here. They're coming up the mountain.'

'They can't be. That's not—'

'Who are you talking to?' Salrana asked, she was standing in the room, giving him a curious look.

'My wife,' he said levelly.

Salrana's face remained impassive. The start of surprise in her mind was minute, and well shielded. But like Edeard, she was no Makkathran native. 'You know I can see souls,' he said. 'I even gifted the Pythia that particular vision. Here,' he said, and opened his mind so she could receive his farsight.

Salrana gasped as she found herself surrounded by four souls. 'I . . .'

Edeard slid off the bed. 'They told me you betrayed me,' he said in a flat voice as he approached her. 'They told me you called Owain himself. I said they were wrong. Are they?'

Salrana took a step backwards. 'Edeard—'

Edeard sent his farsight out from the pavilion, ranging across the side of the volcanic mountain. Using the gift dear Finitan had bestowed him to uncover concealment he exposed over twenty men approaching the wooden building, each carrying a rapid-fire weapon. Out in the darkness behind them, more teams were gathering. Then Edeard viewed the base of the mountain. Two entire militia regiments were down there, deploying around the bottom of the slope, encircling the mountain.

'Dear Lady,' he murmured in astonishment. 'You really did.' He stared at her, trying to understand. 'Salrana, you called them!' A note of hysteria had crept in from somewhere.

For a moment her composure held. Then she simply glared at him. 'Yes, I called Owain.'

This can't be happening. This is Salrana. My Salrana. The two of us together against the world.

'Why?' he pleaded. 'Why did you do this? Because of Kristabel?'

Salrana gave Kristabel's soul a contemptuous glance. 'Jealous of that? Me? Hardly. I'm just as beautiful. Probably better in bed, too. Your loss.'

'But . . . us.'

'Oh you stupid country peasant. Haven't you learned *anything* since we arrived here? Did you really think a thirteen-year-old's crush lasts for life? That I'd be loyal to you forever?'

'You can't believe in Owain's One Nation?'

'Why can't I? Because it doesn't fit our wretched backward provincial upbringing? This is how the world works, Edeard. Can't you see that? The Grand Families already have wealth and power, and with Owain's leadership it will grow even stronger. I can be a part of that. I can make myself part of that. Did you think you were the only one with ambition?'

'This is not you,' he said through growing anguish. 'These are not Salrana's words. Not your thoughts.'

'You are so weak. Even now you could claim the city for yourself. You have the power, the strength to make this world your own. Why don't you?'

'No one person can rule a world.'

She gave a disgusted snort of contempt. 'Humility, the refuge of the weak.'

'The Lady teaches decency.'

'And what has her church ever achieved except for instilling a decent sense of obedience in the lower orders?'

'Now I know that's not you. Who did this to you? Who changed you?'

'I changed myself. I finally understood the world and set out to make something of myself in it. After all, you found your Grand Family bitch.' She waved dismissively at Kristabel's soul. 'A good way in to the Upper Council for someone so spineless. Why shouldn't I have some of the same? I've been screwing people who can help me; the ones who hate you are easy to take advantage of. And greatest among those is Owain himself. Did you know he has eight mistresses, but I'm the one he turns to now? He likes it. He likes having me, the Waterwalker's childhood friend. I saw how resolute and determined he is, so much more than you. He's smarter, too. You have your virtue, he has ambition and fire and power and wealth, and, above all, vision. He will be an emperor, uniting the whole world as One Nation. I will have a big part of that, I will be Pythia, he promised me that. Our children will be born to positions of privilege and power.'

It was as if his nerves had died. Edeard stared at the crazy girl smiling defiantly in front of him, feeling absolutely nothing. 'No,' he said. A lone tear trickled out of his eye. 'You cannot build a world on a foundation of violence and fear. He will destroy Querencia just as he has destroyed you.'

'I am not destroyed, I have never been more alive.'

Edeard's farsight observed the armed men reach the pavilion's front door. He wasn't the slightest surprised to see their leader was Arminal. 'You would see me dead?' he asked faintly.

'The strong survive. Owain fears you will replace him. You still can. You can take his place, Edeard. You can shape the world to your vision. I would help you. We can be together yet.'

Edeard looked at his wife. He looked at his friend Dinlay. He looked at his parents who had so much faith in him. 'I will not be Mayor, not now. And you, you will not be Pythia.'

'Fool!' Salrana screamed at him. She spun round and raced out of the bedroom.

Edeard realized that the ability to sense through concealment was not one of the gifts and treats Owain had bestowed upon her.

Arminal and his men charged into the hall. They started firing indiscriminately as they ran forwards. Bullets chewed up the walls, shredding the furniture. Muzzles blazed as they swept back and forth, seeking out the Waterwalker.

Salrana's shield wasn't strong enough. Eight bullets struck her as she flailed desperately. Huge blood plumes burst across her Novice robe. She was flung backwards, her body landing inelegantly on the elegant pavonazzeto floor to sprawl inertly. Her soul was already staring down at it.

Edeard dived behind the big bed, allowing the thick mattress to absorb the hail of bullets. Now, as the gang hurriedly swapped their exhausted magazines for fresh ones, he raised his head. 'I wish you well,' he told Salrana's soul. 'I hope you find peace in the Heart.'

'Edeard?' she said. 'Oh Edeard, what have I done?'

'Go,' he told her. 'Find the Heart. I will join you there.'

Her soul wavered, drifting up through the pavilion's ceiling. There was a final surge of distress, and she was gone.

Arminal finally slammed the fresh magazine into his rapid-fire gun, and brought it up. His farsight swept through the pavilion, eagerly searching for the Waterwalker.

The magazine suddenly crumpled, the thin metal buckling as an inordinately powerful telekinesis squeezed it. And the Waterwalker materialized in the bedroom.

'Kill him,' Arminal shouted at his squad. But their rapid-fire guns were equally useless as delicate components and casings were crushed and mangled.

'Last time we say goodbye,' the Waterwalker told him.

Arminal hardened his shield, and turned to flee. The pavilion doors slammed shut with a bang that reverberated through the entire wooden structure. Arminal spun back to face his enemy, catching a glimpse of Edeard in the bedroom as his black cloak fluttered around him. Edeard held up both arms, his fingers splayed wide. Lightning ripped out from each fingertip.

Within seconds the entire pavilion was on fire. Joists, rafters, doors, walls, window frames, shelves, furniture and roofing shingles ignited as they were raked with lightning bolts. Thick black smoke swirled out from the roaring flames, clotting the air.

Edeard pushed the bedroom door open, and walked out on to the veranda. Inside, the squad were coughing and yelling in fright as the smoke clogged their lungs and the heat began to roast their flesh. The bedroom door closed. Edeard hopped over the rails and landed on the grassy field. Inside the pavilion, the squad were blundering into each other. Voices reached a crescendo of pain and fright; several had already fallen. Edeard folded his concealment around him like an outer cloak and walked away into the night.

The trusted Weapons Guild guards that Owain sent to eliminate the Waterwalker skirted the burning ruins of the pavilion. They wrinkled their noses up at the stench given off by the smouldering corpses inside, but carried on tracking their quarry. Several among them claimed to be able to perceive right through the Waterwalker's concealment, and hurried after the dark figure they said skulked through the trees just up ahead.

At the bottom of the mountain, the militia regiments completed their deployment, forming a tight ring just outside the fringes of the forest. As ordered, they drew their pistols and waited. Farsight tracked the squads high up on the slopes past the smoking pavilion. Occasionally there was a burst of gunfire that made them flinch. But the guards armed with their deadly new guns pressed onwards and upwards.

Edeard kept ahead of them easily enough. He'd only headed up because there was nowhere else for him to go. A squad was guarding the cliff face with the cave mouth. He'd never be able to climb to it and escape. Salrana must have told Owain about the cave, about the travel tunnels . . . everything. So up he went. The terrain wasn't exactly tough, the trees were few and far between above the pavilion. Grass was ankle high. Small streams trickled down the steep slope. Eventually, even the trees were behind him. Now there was just grass and boulders. He could see the summit already.

And that's when I have to decide.

'I could imprison them,' he told his small ethereal court of advisers. 'The city can create rooms without doors or windows. They would have food.'

'I think death would be more merciful,' his father said.

'Remember what happened to poor Argian when you did that to him, and that was only for a couple of days.'

'He's right,' Dinlay said. 'Locking them up is just for the benefit of your conscience. They have to be wiped out. We know how ruthless they are now. If you don't remove them altogether they will come back again and again. How many times do you want this to happen to the city?'

'Once was too much,' Edeard said. 'But to kill so many . . .'

'The Lady will understand,' Kristabel assured him.

'They half expect it,' Dinlay said. 'That's why we are where we are.' He gestured at the groups of men making their way up the slope. At best, the lead squad was twenty minutes behind.

'I'm not so sure I can get past them all,' Edeard said. 'Owain seems resolute.'

'Of course he does,' Kristabel said. 'He knows you are the only thing left between him and absolute power.'

'Perhaps if I retreat out to the provinces, form a legitimate opposition.'

'A revolution?' his mother asked. 'It would take years, if not decades. How many would die in that struggle. No, if this is to be done it must be done swiftly. That will keep the bloodshed to a minimum. Every day you hesitate sees him consolidate his authority still further.'

'You sound so certain.'

She smiled, nebula-light shining through her diffuse silhouette. 'You don't grow up in Makkathran without knowing all about politics.'

'You are from Makkathran?'

'Yes. The fifth daughter of the fourth son of the family Herusis. But that was many years ago. My sisters and brothers will have even less status now.'

'Herusis?' Edeard paused, trying to recall what he knew of that family. A wealthy trading enterprise with large land holdings on the Iguru and a small fleet of ships. 'Isn't Finitan a Herusis?'

'Yes. One of my great uncles.'

'Finitan is my relative?'

'Yes.'

'I wonder if he knew?'

'He probably suspected. Akeem certainly did.'

'But . . . Mother, why did you leave?'

'I was engaged to a lout of a Kirkmal, it was arranged between our families. I didn't want to go through with the wedding. I wanted my life on my terms, even if it meant giving up the money.'

'That's where he gets his stubbornness from,' Kristabel said.

'I'm not—' he gave a wan smile. Even now she could tease him.

He covered the final slope quickly. The summit was mainly boulders and loose stone, with tufts of wiry grass growing out of cracks between pebbles. A gentle breeze was blowing in from the sea.

Edeard stood there, and turned a complete circle until he was facing Makkathran. The city's orange lights cast a strong glow into the air above the streets and canals. He could just make out the jagged outline of the towers. The first time he'd seen the city it had been so compelling, as if he was finally coming home. That yearning was still there, but the grief was a stronger force. He could barely bring himself to look at it.

I have to decide.

Everything he'd ever wanted or asked for had been contained inside the crystal wall, as had everything he'd ever feared.

'I don't think I can go back,' he confessed to the souls. 'I think Owain and the others are right. I'm not strong enough.'

'You have the strength, Son,' his father said.

'I don't. The suffering I would bring is unthinkable.'

'You only have to take away the leaders,' Dinlay said. 'Owain and his cronies.'

'That might have worked at the start, but not now. Everything has changed. The guns are out there in the open. Hundreds of people are flocking to join him.'

'Hundreds more resisted him, and died. Don't they deserve justice? You know you have support. Think of the election results.'

Edeard knelt on the ground, still looking at Makkathran. 'I can't do this. It's over.'

'We understand,' Kristabel said. 'This is what makes you you. This is what I loved.'

'We'll be together,' he promised her. His farsight sensed the first squad reaching the final slope up to the summit. All of them were readying their rapid-fire guns. 'We will reach the Heart and live there for eternity.'

'Together,' Kristabel agreed.

Edeard drew in a deep breath. He looked out one last time across the Iguru Plain, his thoughts serene as he stopped shielding himself. Makkathran's thoughts brushed against his mind, as slow and content as always. Dreaming in another realm.

'Thank you for all your help,' he told it, and poured his gratitude out to the city.

For the first time he sensed a change. The giant mind began to quicken. Stronger, more concise thoughts began to rise, like some massive creature coming up from the depths of the sea. Makkathran was waking.

Edeard swayed back, astounded by the reaction he'd kindled. He'd tried innumerable times to make himself understood to the city, never receiving any reply. It did his bidding for simple things like altering the buildings, or sending him along the travel tunnels. But he'd assumed any true connection was beyond him.

'You heard me,' he longtalked in astonishment.

The answer was still slow, measured and considered as he expected it to be. Solemn: as was fitting for such a magnificent creation. 'I felt sorrow,' Makkathran said. 'You are in pain. I have not felt pain like that for such a time.'

'I . . . I have lost. That was the pain you felt. I apologize. I didn't mean to disturb you. I simply wished to thank you for all you've done.'

'Loss? I remember loss. Once there were many, now I am alone.'

'There were others like you?' Edeard asked.

'Once. No more. Not even here. To revisit that time would be useless.'

'I'm sorry. I didn't know. Can I help? I'm about to go to the Heart of the Void. Will your kind be there?'

'No. None would submit to absorption. That is not what we are.'

'What are you?'

'The failed past.'

'You haven't failed us. You gave us shelter, refuge.'

'I am glad. Do you accept the Void's purpose? Is that why you go to its Heart?'

'What purpose?'

'To become one with this universe. It seeks all rationality.'

'That's . . . No. I go because I have lost my life.'

'How can you lose your life in the Void?'

He gave Kristabel and the others a puzzled look, very conscious of the armed men slinking up the slope towards him. 'I don't understand.'

Something like a gust of emotion swept out of the city. *Reluctance. Acceptance. Pity.* 'The Void allows you to find your perfect life,' Makkathran said. 'It is the way it brings you to fulfilment, to reach your personal evolution and achieve contentment with what you are.'

'What do you mean?' Edeard started to harden his shield again as he heard a number of safety catches clicked off.

'All of those who come from outside strive for this state, that is why the Void welcomes them. This universe had no other purpose, not now. That is its beauty for those inside, and tragedy for those without, for they will ultimately pay the price.'

'I can't achieve a perfect life. My life is over.'

'Reach into the Void. Search out where you wish to be, and begin again. It is simple. Once you adapt to the Void it provides you with whatever you want. Every species that ever arrived here was drawn into that evolution. You will be no different, I suspect. There is no harm in that. I wish you well on your journey.'

The city's thoughts began to slow again. Withdrawing back into slumber.

'No,' Edeard said. 'No wait. Tell me how.' He turned to the souls. 'What did it mean?'

'I sense patterns around me,' Kristabel said. 'Just as Boyd told you. The universe remembers what happened everywhere. Our whole life is visible there in the past.'

'Can you show me?' Edeard asked.

'See with me,' she said. Edeard tried to sense her thoughts, the gift of her perception. It was a strange union, a dimension of farsight he'd never known of before. As he followed his wife's observation into the fabric of reality, he saw for himself. Saw himself stretched out down the slope, a million, a billion, images of himself leading back; they encapsulated every instant of the climb, every step, every breath, every heartbeat. Every thought. It was as if he was looking into an infinity mirror. Makkathran was right, his essence had been captured by the Void. Every moment of his existence had been remembered.

Edeard regarded himself, the one of five minutes ago, studying how real the vision was. He appeared frozen. Awaiting the breath to fill his lungs in order to become real.

'Oh, my Lady,' he gasped. 'I think I understand. But . . . no. That would mean.' He leapt to his feet. 'Kristabel?'

'Do it,' she entreated. 'Edeard, if there's even a chance—'

'Yes.' He flung his arms out, unleashing his third hand. The squad members were hurled into the air, an expanding bracelet of struggling figures arching up and out, away from the ground. Screaming as they began their plummet hundreds of feet to the wider slope below.

Free of any immediate danger, Edeard concentrated again on the images. Minutes ago was useless to him. He began to push on past the memories of himself walking up to the summit. Delving deep. He knew himself lying on the bed in the pavilion while Salrana longtalked Owain. Further. His own memory came into play, knowing a vivid moment from a few days ago. Twinning it with the Void's recollection. The technique was almost instinctive. The moment was there, shimmering elusively in front of him. His mind reached for it, finding it beyond his grasp. He tried again, harder this time, channelling his colossal telekinetic strength into the stretch. Mental fingers scrabbled desperately to close around the moment, to make it real. He groaned with the effort. *Forcing* the universe to link the moments.

Somewhere, allwhere, the universe began to shift. The present slipped backwards, slowly at first. That long linear image of him walking up the slope unwound, taking him down. Above him, the stars crawled the wrong way through the firmament. Encouraged, Edeard threw his entire strength into achieving the union across time. The impossibly weird motion began to accelerate. Edeard's past rushed past. The precise, wonderfully clear moment he wanted hurtled towards him—

—Edeard woke screaming. The yell of shock and disbelief rang round the woodland camp, he couldn't stop blasting air from his lungs. Morning light shone down on him.

Morning!

Dinlay was a few yards away, immobile in the action of hopping about while he held his boot high. He was giving Edeard a dumbfounded look.

Edeard managed to stop his scream. He looked round wildly, then jumped as he saw Macsen sitting on an old fallen tree trunk.

'I didn't put anything in *your* boot,' Macsen protested in a reasonable voice.

'You're alive!' Edeard bellowed.

'What in Honious is going on?' Topar asked. He had risen from his blanket, his pistol held ready. Boloton, Fresage, Verini, and Larby were scrambling round, trying to find the source of the commotion.

'Nothing!' Edeard said breathlessly. An explosion of pure joy inside his head threatened to overwhelm him. 'Everything! I did it! I'm here. It's real. You're real. And you're all alive.'

Dinlay let out an exasperated sigh. 'What is the matter with you?' He squinted into his boot. 'Ah ha!' His third hand scraped out the remains of a utog beetle. He gave Macsen a suspicious glance.

'Edeard?' Topar asked cautiously.

'It's fine,' Edeard held up a hand in reassurance, then laughed. He was feeling giddy now. The world was whirling round unsteadily. He sat down hard. 'No, wait.' He held up his hands, fingers out to count. 'The ambush is in two days' time. Er . . . then another day and a half to ride back. Lady – damnit, if I start now I might not make it. I've got to go further back.'

Dinlay shoved his foot into the boot and walked over. 'Bad dream?'

Edeard grinned. 'The worst there has ever been.'

'Ah. Would you like some tea? You've still got some of those linen packets left,' Dinlay added hopefully.

'No.' Edeard stood up fast. Before Dinlay knew what was happening, Edeard kissed him.

'Fuck the Lady,' Dinlay exclaimed, juddering back out of reach.

Edeard laughed delightedly. 'I can't stay. I'm sorry. But by the Lady it is so good to see you all alive again. And the girls, our wives. Macsen, you're going to be a father. I promise. I swear on the Lady herself.'

'What in Honious did you drink last night?' Macsen demanded.

'I drank . . . I drank everything there is to drink.'

'I think you'd better sit down,' Topar said levelly.

'No time,' Edeard said, enjoying how manic he must be appearing to the others. 'Well, actually, that's not true.' He giggled. 'Do you remember the first day on the road.' His fingers clicked urgently. 'We stopped and made camp just outside that farm. Oh, where was it?'

'Stibbington,' Dinlay grunted.

'That's right. That's the place, and it's in time. Plenty of time. Barely a day's gallop back from there. Macsen, do you remember, you were so saddle sore you claimed you couldn't walk.'

'I remember.'

'Yeah, me too.' Edeard reached for the moment—

Justine: Year Four

Dreaming still. Mellow images of her true love. His scent. His laughter. His pleasure. Those two days kept stretching out and out—

Justine sat up in the medical chamber and glanced round the *Silverbird*'s cabin. Everything was exactly the same as when she went into suspension. No alarms sounding this time. They'd reached the star system, and the starship's log reported a thoroughly uneventful voyage. The *Silverbird* was already decelerating.

She swung her legs out, wincing at the stiffness in her limbs. Neck muscles were knotted and tight. What she needed was a good massage. Maybe at the Hulluba resort on Fasal Island. Yes, she could certainly picture herself lying on a bed on the spa veranda, overlooking the white beaches and absurdly clear turquoise water. The spa had some very handsome masseurs, talented fit young men who knew how to knead her muscles and tendons into complete submission. Very handsome. And the drinks they served in long glasses full of crushed ice, with exotic fruits – delicious. Hot blue-white star a pinprick of intense light atop the indigo sky. Handsome and eager.

Lordie, this is what dreaming about those two days does to me. Hulluba was a thousand years ago.

Justine sighed in regret and her third hand pulled a robe out of the replicator module. The culinary unit produced a big glass of carrot juice with vitamin supplements. It brought a grimace to her face as she dutifully swallowed it all down.

Maybe there'll be some beaches on a planet here somewhere.

She sat on the floor and started stretching exercises. Already she was looking forward to a very hot shower with powerful jets, a forcefully applied heat that would rid her neck of those abysmal kinks.

'What have we got outside?' she asked the smartcore.

The star appeared in her exovision. Justine frowned. 'I know this.' It was the star system which was projected on to the ceiling of the Orchard Palace's Upper Council chamber. A copper star that shone warmly at the centre of an accretion disc. Comets with moon-sized nuclei prowled the outer edges of the disc in high-inclination orbits, their tails streaming out for millions of kilometres, fluorescing a glorious scarlet. But what she was seeing outside now was older, the accretion disc had thinned out from the time of Edeard's tenure. Nine distinct bands had formed within it, each one shepherded by dense curlicues of asteroids as proto-planets started to congeal. The tails of the fireball comets were smaller, less volatile than before. Long braids of white vapour corrupted their once-pure scarlet efflux.

Translucent data displays overlaid the astronomy image. Justine's secondary thought routines sampled the information, compiling summaries, and her focus immediately shifted to a tiny white crescent that circled the tenuous rim of the disc. 'No way!' It was an H-congruent planet.

The *Silverbird* was still seven AUs out from the star. It gave her plenty of time to observe the planet as they approached. In the real universe outside the Void it wouldn't exist. Even if the accretion disc had produced an amalgamation of rock and minerals that built up to planet size, there wouldn't have been time for life to evolve. The *Silverbird*'s spectral analysis filters identified water and chlorophyll, along with a lot of nitrogen in the atmosphere. Wherever the world had come from, it had oceans and recognizable plant life covering the landmasses.

One AU out. It was small for an H-congruent planet; Mars

size. The atmosphere was thick, at the surface it would be a standard pressure. Temperature was typical. A magnetic field warped solar wind into characteristic Van Allen belts around it. There were no electromagnetic emissions. But she kept checking for that the whole way in.

An implausible world in an impossible place. *Only in the Void.* She knew full well the amount of mass energy the boundary had consumed during that short dreadful expansion phase was enough to create a thousand solar systems, let alone one small planet. *I shouldn't be surprised at anything here. Edeard only scratched the surface of the Void's potential, as Living Dream keep emphasizing.*

Ten million kilometres out, and the *Silverbird* was decelerating at five gees, shedding the last of the colossal velocity that had carried her across three lightyears. Five gees was the best it could reliably maintain. The glitches were back with a vengeance. Sensor degradation was acute on some of the higher function scans. But simple optical lenses were showing continents and ice caps. Whorl patterns in the clouds were becoming apparent. She saw one hurricane that was somehow splitting in two as it hit the coast, its leading edge separating as if a knife was cutting it. A very big knife. The phenomena triggered some uncertainty deep in her subconscious – an ancient memory that struggled to resolve. *What cuts a storm in half?*

Then she had more to worry about as cabin gravity started to fluctuate. Secondary systems were dropping out as fluctuations beset the power network. Back-up supplies didn't always compensate properly. She ordered the cabin to return to a neutral status, retracting everything except for her acceleration couch. At least her biononics remained fully functional. She activated her integral force field as the *Silverbird* flew across the remaining million kilometres. Ahead of her, the planet's upper atmosphere sparked constantly with contrails as meteorites from the fringe of the accretion disc impacted on the ionosphere. The *Silverbird*'s force fields reported a build-up of micro-particle strikes. Dust density outside was thickening rapidly.

Justine went and put her armour suit on.

Ingrav efficiency was twenty per cent down, and becoming erratic. Justine had already abandoned any idea of breaking into orbit. They were going to have to head for a direct landing. Hopefully the regrav drives would kick in once they were inside the planet's gravity field. Judging by the way the rest of the systems were behaving she wasn't placing any bets.

A thousand kilometres above the ionosphere and the smart-core began shutting down peripheral routines in order to concentrate on core functions. The ship curved round the bulk of the planet. Regrav was becoming active – just. They would make it down okay. Probably.

That was when the three gigantic rocky cones sticking up through the atmosphere slipped into view. *Silverbird* was heading straight for them, trajectory projections giving their landing site just beyond.

Shock set in as she focused the cameras on the astonishingly familiar profile of the three volcanoes. 'You have got to be fucking kidding me,' she said out loud.

The *Silverbird* was approaching near-perfect replicas of Far Away's Grand Triad at mach thirty. She fought to quash her surprise. *It can happen. Here in the Void, it can happen.*

Terminating a voyage three lightyears long at the exact point corresponding to her hyperglider landing twelve hundred years ago was not random chance. It was purpose.

The dream. Oh my God, the dream.

Which left a possibility that was almost too much to contemplate.

No. That cannot happen.

The *Silverbird* hit the atmosphere. Tenuous air molecules screamed as it hurtled downwards, soaring round the side of the tallest volcano with its flat summit and dead twin calderas. Churning superheated air blazed in the starship's wake. Regrav units applied what force they could muster.

Acceleration pushed Justine down into the couch. Her chest was compressed as her weight quadrupled. Biononics reinforced her body, enabling her to breathe normally. The regrav wouldn't alter the starship's vector. Her landing point was predetermined.

Ordained?

The *Silverbird* plunged down through a light cirrus layer, its speed dropping to subsonic. The volcano's mid-slopes were beneath her, rocky crags and cliffs strewn with patches of lichen and moss, streaked with snow. Then she was flying over the volcano's upper meadows, undulating grassland that formed a wide verdant belt just above the treeline. Icy waterfalls tumbled down rocky outcrops, birthing a lacework of silver streams.

Another mind impinged on the starship's gaiafield. The person's thoughts curious and enthusiastic.

'Oh, no. No, no, no. He can't be here. You can't do this to me.'

A long glade opened up in the forest below. *Silverbird* descended fast. Its landing struts bulged out of the fuselage. Justine gritted her teeth. The bump wasn't too bad. The cabin shook and a crunching sound tremored through the superstructure. Gravity fell below a standard one gee. Some of the ship status icons turned amber briefly, then flicked back to green. Whole sections faded to neutral as the drive units ceased to operate. The starship wasn't going to be flying anywhere soon.

But she was down, and intact. That was something.

The mind was still there; waiting with a hint of impatience. She was sensing its emotional state directly through farsight rather than via her gaiamotes. Presumably then, he could sense her thoughts.

Justine took her time removing her armour suit. After all, she didn't want to frighten him and it would look fearsome to anyone unfamiliar with Greater Commonwealth technology. She unwound an emergency rope ladder from the airlock, not trusting the gravity manipulation function to lower her down. When she started down she realized the beige one-piece she'd put on was remarkably similar to the leathery grey-blue flightsuit she'd worn in the hyperglider. Only the helmet was missing.

'Didn't get that right, did you?' she mocked the Void.

The rope ladder swung about alarmingly as she neared the

bottom, Its pendulum motion sent her swaying over the grassy ground. She jumped the last two rungs.

Gravity was low, just like Far Away. The scent of pine trees was strong in the humid air. Her farsight swept out, producing a mildly disorientating effect. Then she began to interpret the foggy shapes, correlating them to what her eyes could see. Besides, her biononic field scan function was working unimpaired, providing solid interpretations of the surrounding landscape.

He was standing ten metres away, waiting courteously for her to notice him. Justine turned round very slowly, still half believing she'd open her eyes to see the *Silverbird*'s cabin around her as she rose from suspension. But no, it was real. He was real.

Justine smiled, too numb for any emotion to triumph. 'Hello, Kazimir,' she said.

His face was perfect, healthy dark skin and shining white teeth in lips that could smile so wide; rich black hair tied back with a red band. As were the clothes, a leather waistcoat open to show off a nicely muscled torso, and his McFoster clan's emerald and copper check kilt. He even carried the correct small backpack.

'You know me?' he asked.

The voice was right, too. But then it should be, he was her creation after all. Her smile shifted from welcome to sympathy. 'I'm aware of who you think you are. That's my fault.'

He frowned. 'Are you all right? Your craft came down fast . . .'

Finally, she laughed. That concern was so Kazimir. 'A little shaken up, that's all. My name is Justine, by the way.'

'I'm pleased to meet you, Justine. Is that really a spaceship?'

'It really is.'

Justine couldn't be cruel, that was the hardest part. She couldn't just tell him to go away, or ignore him. That would have been so much easier for her. But he was a seventeen-year-old human being with feelings; just like everyone else he had never asked to be born – no matter the strange nature of his birth. He deserved to be treated with consideration and respect.

Curiously, he had no clear recollections of where he came from.

They sat beside a stream that gurgled along the side of the clearing. Both weary of the other, yet he was powerfully attracted to her, and not just physically, she could sense that.

'I am on my groundwalk,' he told her when she asked where he'd come from.

'To prove you can survive out here by yourself,' she said, recalling this very same conversation from so long ago. 'Once you return to your clan you can become a fully fledged warrior and fight the Starflyer.'

'You know of the Starflyer?'

'Kazimir, I know this must be hard to believe, but the Commonwealth defeated the Starflyer a very long time ago. You're not who you think you are.'

He grinned delightedly. 'Then who am I?'

'You are a dream I had. This place makes you real.'

His face produced a thrilled expression while his mind registered a brisk amusement. 'What are you saying, that I have died and this place is the Dreaming Heavens?'

'Oh my God!' Justine stared at him in complete astonishment. 'I'd forgotten that part of the Guardians' ideology.' *Well, consciously, anyway.*

'So are you my spirit guide? You are what I imagine an angel would look like.'

'You called me that before,' she said quietly.

'I did what?'

'You used to call me your angel.'

'Back when we were alive?' His mind was starting to show uncertainty – a joke wearing thin.

Justine cursed her stupid old biological body for its crippling emotional weakness. 'You are alive. Again. It's complicated.'

'You thought I was dead?'

I watched you die. 'Tell me where you were before you started your groundwalk? Who your friends are? What did you spend last year doing? In fact, what were you doing this time yesterday?'

'I . . .' His thoughts churned desperately. 'It is difficult. I don't remember much. No wait, Bruce! Bruce is my friend.'

'Kazimir, I'm sorry. Bruce was the one who killed you.'

He recoiled. 'This is the Dreaming Heavens!'

'I suppose in a manner of speaking, yes it is.'

'Bruce would never kill me.'

'He was captured by the Starflyer, who turned him against the Guardians of Selfhood. He became their agent.'

'Not Bruce.'

'Not the Bruce who was your friend, the Starflyer destroyed that part of him. Kazimir, you don't have any memories of your past because I don't know it, not as fully as I should do, not the details. We didn't spend enough time together to talk of such things in depth. The time we did have was too precious. I always regretted that, I'm so sorry.' She looked away, trying to get her emotions under control. *This is so painful. I don't have to put myself through this. I should just walk away.* Then she glanced at him, seeing the hurt and confusion on his face, and she knew she couldn't do that to him, not her Kazimir, not even a shadow of him.

He reached out tentatively, fingers touching her shoulder, as if he was the one who should be offering comfort. 'We were . . . together?'

'Yes, Kazimir. We were lovers.'

A wide smile split his youthful face, and the universe wasn't so bad after all.

'I'm doing this really badly,' she confessed. 'I wish I could be gentler to you.'

'So I am what you dream of?'

'Yes.'

His smile was triumphant now. 'I am glad you dream of me. I am glad I am here for you.'

Oh no. We're not going down that road. It's not . . . right. 'I'm glad you're here, too; but I have a duty to perform.'

Kazimir nodded seriously. 'What duty?'

She pulled a face. 'Save the galaxy.'

'How?'

'Don't know, actually. Where we are, this place, it's wrong. I have to get to . . . whoever's in charge, try and convince them to stop their expansion. I'm sorry if that doesn't make much sense.'

Kazimir's gaze turned to the *Silverbird*; there was a flash of longing in his mind. 'Will we fly there in your spaceship?'

The first drops of rain began to fall out of the darkening sky as the stormhead found its way round the volcano. 'I'd like to, but I need to figure out how to make it fly again. And I don't know where the nucleus is or how to get there.'

'Oh.' His disappointment was tangible, shining through a weakly shielded mind.

Justine grinned. 'Would you like to look inside?'

'Yes please!'

He shot up the rope ladder with ease. But then, Justine recalled, Kazimir had always been very agile. That would account for why her own heart was racing as she clambered up after him. The airlock was small with the two of them in it. She told the smartcore to open the inner door, and led the way up the narrow companionway into the cabin.

Kazimir tried to be polite as he stared round the circular compartment, but he clearly wasn't adept at shielding his thoughts. Fortunately, she recalled several techniques Edeard had employed in Inigo's dreams.

'You travel in this?' he asked cautiously.

Justine clicked her fingers as she told the smartcore to extrude a couple of chairs.

'Ah!' Kazimir watched them rise up, happy again. She switched on a holographic projection, displaying status graphics in the air in front of him.

Seventeen is such an easy age, she thought with a pang of resentment at his fascination. 'I'd like to run some scans on you,' she said. 'It might help me understand more about this place.'

'Of course.'

She used her bironic field function to examine him in detail, shunting the results into the smartcore. He was human, every organ where it should be. When she touched a sampler module to his skin he smiled at her again, emitting a strong sense of longing, of willingness.

Out of those two days an awful lot of the time had been spent in bed making love.

She raised an eyebrow in surprise as the sequencing results rose up into the holographic display. 'Your DNA is . . .' *Real? Proper? Fully human?* 'Okay,' she concluded. *And how did the Void pull that stunt?*

'I'm glad,' he said simply.

The smartcore ran a comparison against a medical file she carried: her son's DNA. This Kazimir didn't share any genetic markers with the man whose child she'd borne twelve hundred years ago. She didn't know if she was disappointed by that or not. *So it's not omnipotent, then.*

'Shall we see if the culinary unit is working?' she asked.

She didn't really have to ask what he wanted. Cheeseburger with bacon, fries, sticky toffee pudding with vanilla ice cream. Chocolates and champagne. All part of the decadent life she'd corrupted him with first time round.

The culinary unit managed to produce them, though she thought some of the tastes were a bit strange.

It was all strange and good to Kazimir's palate, he wolfed the lot down.

'Have you seen anyone else here?' she asked as she sipped her own champagne.

'I thought you said I didn't exist before today,' he said, only half teasing.

'I don't know how long you've been here, actually. It took the Void four years to create this world. I think.'

He sat back in the chair and thought hard. 'I have memories, or notions of my life before today. That life I had back with my clan isn't real, I see that now, nothing about that time is substantial. It is a notion of what should have been. And yet I remember setting out on my groundwalk a couple of weeks ago.

I'm sure the last few days were real. Today is. Today has you in it. I remember waking and enjoying the clear sky.'

'So you didn't see anyone on your groundwalk?'

'No. But the idea of the groundwalk is to be on your own.'

'Of course.'

He shivered, looking round the cabin again. Apprehension was creeping into his thoughts. 'I am nothing. I am a toy some alien has built to amuse you. What kind of being has such power?'

'Hey,' she said soothingly. 'You're certainly not nothing. You're you. It doesn't matter why you are, only that you're here now. Life is to be lived, I told you that the first time we met.'

Kazimir sniffed suspiciously. 'Did I believe you?'

'You took some convincing. You were just as stubborn then.'

That seemed to satisfy him.

'What are you going to do now?' he asked.

'I'm not sure. I came here to try and talk to the nucleus. That's looking quite difficult now. It thinks I want to be here with you instead.' She reviewed the *Silverbird*'s status again. None of the drives were operational, and the smartcore didn't know why. The generator was producing some power, enough to maintain basic life support. A majority of cabin functions were running, though she wasn't sure she'd want to use the medical cabinet. What vexed her most was the reason for the failures and glitches. There wasn't one.

Willpower, she thought, *that's the governing factor in this universe. The power of mind over matter. Thoughts can affect reality. So the Void doesn't want the Silverbird to fly. It's as simple as that.*

'And you don't want to be here with me?' he asked.

'It's enjoyable,' she told him. 'But it's not *why* I'm here.' His face was so crestfallen she immediately felt guilty. 'Kazimir, I apologize, but there is an awful lot at stake. More than I expect you to believe. I have to do whatever I can to help.'

'I understand,' he said gravely. 'It is an honourable thing that you do. My mind may be false, but I believe in honour. It is a universal truth.'

'You're very sweet,' she said. 'I remembered that part of you perfectly.' She yawned. 'I'm going to try to get some rest, it's been a long stressful flight and that champagne has gone straight to my head.'

'I will keep watch outside,' he announced gravely. 'If this is a whole real planet there might be something hostile out there.'

'Thank you.' *Damn, my memory's a dangerous thing.* The cabin extended a large bed as Justine stripped off the one-piece suit; then the replicator produced a thin duvet. It had peculiar hard lumps in it, but she shrugged and pulled it up anyway. She fell asleep straight away.

And dreamed. Dreamed of her own bed in her own home, where she was warm and safe and life was comfortable.

Someone pulled the drapes back, and sunlight streamed in through the tall windows. Justine yawned and stretched. It was cosy under the duvet.

'Hello, darling.'

'Dad,' she said drowsily, and smiled at the gold face looming above her. 'Is it time to get up?'

'It's time you and I had a talk.'

Full awareness hit her like a plunge into ice water. Justine yelped and sat up straight. It was her room in the Tulip mansion, the one she'd spent her adolescence in, therefore ridiculously purple and black as she merrily ploughed her way through her retro-Goth phase mainly to annoy her parents. Her T-shirt and baggy flannel pyjama trousers were black cotton. Toe- and fingernails were black, with embossed blood gems. She looked at them, mortified by the fashion. Fingers heavy with silver skull rings hurriedly pulled a string of hair in front of her face to check: yes, black.

'Jesus,' she muttered.

'You always looked cute no matter how bad the fashion,' Gore said. He was standing at the foot of the bed, arms folded as he leaned against the post. (Four-poster with black gauze drapes – of course.) His handsome gold face grinned down.

'What? I . . . Am . . . Is this the Void?'

'You're still in the Void,' Gore said. 'I'm back in the Commonwealth thinking up cosy environments to amplify our rapport. And there's nothing cosier than a childhood room.'

'Rapport?'

'I'm hugely embarrassed to say I've become the Third Dreamer. And guess whose life in the Void I'm dreaming.'

'Oh shit.'

Gore produced an evil grin. 'Could be worse, you could have slept with him. And I'd be the one relaying it into the gaiafield.'

'*Shit!*'

'That nobility of yours will get you into real trouble one day.'

Justine stood up carefully. 'What's been happening out there? Did the Pilgrimage make it through?'

'You mean in the four days you've been inside?'

'Four days?' she asked incredulously.

'Coming up on five.'

'But it's been . . .'

'Four years. Including the interlude with the Skylord.'

'You got that part?'

'Oh yes. That little shit Ethan is making a lot of capital out of its refusal to take you to the nucleus. A real big boost to the cause. The Clerics from his jumped-up Council have been all over the unisphere ever since, ranting about destiny. It's almost enough to counter the fuck-up they've made on Viotia.'

'Viotia?' she asked in a daze.

'They're turning the planet upside down looking for the Second Dreamer. Don't worry about it. We've got to concentrate on your problem.'

'Kazimir?'

'In a manner of speaking. Damn, I never realized you were still so fixated. You really ballsed that one up, didn't you?'

'What do you mean?'

'So far all Living Dream has been promising is the chance to put your life straight, just like their precious Waterwalker did every time he made his many mistakes. Screwed up again? Never mind. Bang, he thinks back to the moment he went wrong and rearranges the whole Void to that instant. That's what sold it to them, all the sheep bleating to be taken on the Pilgrimage fleet.'

'I know, time travel is everyone's wish fulfilment made true. Going back to correct your life's blunders is the ultimate fantasy.'

'Time travel is pure bullshit, impossible; nobody can defeat causality or entropy. All the Void does is press the reset button. That's what that goddamn memory layer is, a template of every instant inside there. And how does it fucking power that?'

'Dad.'

'Every planet, every person, every Skylord, every star has to have its entropy reversed to the point in time Edeard fancied going back to. Every star! Every single atom in every star in the Void has to have its energy level pumped back up so he can begin again. Dear God, what arrogance. And where does it get the energy from to do that? From us. From eating our galaxy. That's what feeds the reset. Mass to energy, good old E equals MC squared.'

'Dad, calm down, you're ranting to the converted.'

'Oh am I? If they were converted, the stupid dumb shits wouldn't be going on their Pilgrimage, would they? Sometimes I think the Ocisens are quite right, they should just wipe us out because any species *thick* enough to produce Living Dream doesn't deserve to live.'

'Dad!' she said, shocked.

'Yeah, yeah.' He grinned round savagely. 'You like this dream, Ethan? You like what's coming at you from the Void now? Or is this too much truth for you? Because it's not just going to be your dumbass Waterwalker skipping back through his life any more, is it? I could just about live with him being the saviour of a bunch of shipwrecked medieval cretins. But that was never enough for you, was it? You are so fucking stupid you want to take everyone in there. Millions of you resetting your lives every time you get a drop of shampoo in your fucking eye. Are you so fucking pitifully weak you can't face living your life properly? *Learn* from your mistake and move on. That's what makes you human. Not condemning the rest of us to extinction because of your personal goddamn failure of an existence. Grow some balls, for fuck's sake.'

Justine put her arm around Gore, startled to find he was shaking with rage. 'It's okay,' she told him. 'We'll find a solution.'

'Oh yeah. That's right. Because now it's not just the integral memory function that the Void can use as a template for creation. It can delve into any old hang-up you care to take in there with you. The Living Dream bastards aren't going to be content with going to Makkathran and screwing themselves stupid with Ranalee. Not any more. Not now they can recreate anything from their own past. People, cities, civilizations, worlds. Bring anything you want back to life, anything from history, from fiction. Doesn't matter, we'll just suck down a couple of thousand new stars into the boundary to power it up. Jesus H. Christ.'

'Are you blaming me for this?'

Gore stood still, his fists clenching and unclenching as he tried to calm down. 'No. It's not your fault. I'm not blaming you. This is all down to the bastard Firstlives who built the fucking abomination in the first place. The Raiel were right to try to destroy it. I wish they goddamn had, I really do.'

'I can use the *Silverbird* to study as much as it can.'

'No, no, that's not the answer to anything. We can't go in there with ray-guns blazing. I thought you'd realized that. You were right earlier, the mind is the key in the Void. It is geared up to manifest every thought. The physical environment can only be a tiny part of it. Think of it as an eight-dimensional onion.'

Justine straightened her back and gave her father an exasperated look. 'Thanks, Dad. That's helpful. I always think in those terms, it really helps a lot.'

Gore gave her a gruff smile. 'All right, forget the eight dimensions, just picture the layers. They're interlinked dimensionally, not figuratively, but you get the drift. Every layer has a different function. There's the memory layer which captures everything that goes on in there. There's the creator layer, which must organize the reset. There's the interaction layer, which formats thoughts for the creator layer, which is what makes telepathy and all the rest of that mental shit happen.'

'A layer to make souls work,' Justine said thoughtfully.

'Yeah. This is all built around rationality and its evolution, the fulfilment your retard Skylord is fixated on. So maybe another layer which handles thought processes – maybe that's the soul one, maybe not. That's not the point. There's a whole ton of layers, ones we can deduce from observation and stuff we can't even guess at. And Christ knows what the nebulas are and why they're singing. Doesn't matter. What we have here is an enormously complex construction. But the nucleus is the centre – again, not physically.'

'So the nucleus does control it all.'

'Who knows what the hierarchy is? What we have to do is find a route in, something we can rationalize and engage, just like you wanted.'

'Why would the nucleus create Kazimir for me?'

'It didn't. I don't believe you can think big enough to attract its attention. That confluence nest you have on board probably imprinted the Kazimir dream on to the creator layer. It was a thought more powerful than it's accustomed to. Most of the layers don't operate at a conscious sentient level, they just perform their task. And nobody ever took a confluence nest inside before. The one thing a confluence nest does above all else is hold a memory and repeat it ad infinitum. Your dream was the only one it received and that warped reality. The creator layer simply responded in the way it was designed. Nothing personal.'

Justine sat on the bed, trying to fit together what he was saying. 'If my thoughts aren't powerful enough, what's the point of me trying to find the nucleus?'

'This dream is being received by everyone who has a gaiafield connection. Understand?'

'Ah.'

'Don't try and find the nucleus, it's a waste of time.'

'But, you just said—'

Gore knelt in front of her, his hands gripping her upper arms. His eyes peered out intently from the gold skin mask that was his face. 'You have to get to Makkathran.'

'There's nobody left there. The Skylord said the humans had all gone to the nucleus.'

'I don't give a shit. Get to Makkathran. It's important. That's where humans are centred in the Void.'

'How? The *Silverbird* can't fly.'

'Wrong.' Gore grinned right at her. 'You're in the Void. You've got telepathic powers. The *Silverbird* can't fly *now*.'

'Oh.' She worked out what he was proposing. 'Oh!'

'That's my girl; as smart as you are beautiful.'

'But, Dad, Kazimir won't exist then. I'll have killed him.'

Gore let go of her arms. 'I'm sorry, run that by me again.'

'If I go back to then, he won't exist.'

'Oh, Jesus wept,' Gore slapped a hand theatrically across his brow. 'Don't you go all liberal on me now. Not now.'

'I can't wipe him out of existence. He's real now for better or worse. I have a responsibility.'

'He is the equivalent of a re-life clone, one that has been stuffed with your recollections of his memories. How pitiful is that?'

'He's alive,' she said firmly.

'And you've got the hots for him.'

'I have not.'

'Your own DNA test showed you he's not Kazimir; just some poor doppelgänger the memory layer had in storage.'

'Exactly. He's human. I can't do this to him.'

Gore took her hands. 'Listen to me, darling. This is the fundamental catastrophe that is the Void. He was a stored memory. Everybody who was ever in the Void is exactly the same, everyone who crashed there in the colony ship was copied; everyone who was ever born. Owain is still there, for God's sake, still frozen in the memory layer at the moment the Waterwalker shot him – and for all the decades he lived before. In all the resets Edeard performed afterwards, he never went back past the point where he wiped out the conspirators. He could never bring himself to do that all over again, because that's what he would have had to do each time. This is what the Void throws at us. They lived in the time they were meant to live. You can't change that, Justine. You cannot allow rationality and ethics that evolved in this universe to apply where you are now.'

'I know what you're saying; but, Dad, you haven't met him. He's so sweet. He doesn't deserve this.'

'The galaxy doesn't deserve the Void, but we've got it. And I have met him, darling, I've felt your silly little heart beat faster at the sight of him. I tasted the chocolates you ate when you smiled and flirted with him. I know the urge you've been trying to ignore. I'm sorry. You have to do this. You have to go to Makkathran.'

'Oh Goddamnit.'

He kissed her brow. 'Look on the bright side, if we lose you get to stay and live in the Void, you can find him again.'

'You are a thoroughly fucking useless coach, you know that.'

'I know. Now go and wake up.'

Justine nodded weakly, knowing she didn't really have a choice. For the first time she looked through the bedroom window. The land outside wasn't the grounds of the Tulip Mansion. Instead, her old home was sitting at the bottom of an impossibly huge valley, with mountains curving away through the sky like a monstrous green and brown wave about to break overhead. The sun was a long band of glaring light. 'What the hell is that?'

Gore shrugged lightly. 'I had to make a few sacrifices so I could dream your dreams.'

'Dad . . .'

'I'm fine.' He raised a hand, waving, his smile fond and proud. 'Go on. Wake up.'

*

Justine's eyes opened wide, staring up at the cabin ceiling. Tears blurred her vision. She wiped them away angrily. 'Oh, hell.' And Kazimir would know something was wrong. No telepath had the strength to shield those emotions.

Sure enough, he was standing at the end of the rope ladder as she struggled her way down. He even held it steady for her.

'What's the matter?' he asked.

'I have to go,' she said flatly.

'I see. That's good, isn't it? You know how to reach the nucleus. You wanted to go there.'

'I can't take you with me,' she stammered.

'I understand.'

'No. No, you don't.' She took a deep breath and kissed him. Delight banished the surprise from his face.

'Kazimir, I want you to know something. If there is a way back here, I will find it, I will find you. I promise that. Know my thoughts and know the truth in them.'

He gave her that tentative worshipful gaze which just made her feel worse. She never thought she'd ever see that again.

'I see the honesty in your thoughts,' he assured her. 'Now do what you know you must.'

Justine sat on a rock a few metres from the *Silverbird*'s landing leg. The warm late-afternoon sun was a pleasant pressure on her face and arms as she folded her legs into a yoga position. Kazimir was squatting down a little way past her, watching anxiously. She gave him one last smile and concentrated.

Her thoughts flowed into the confluence nest, using its routines to hold her mind steady. There were memories in there, the time where Edeard stood on top of the mountain and reached into the fabric of the Void, seeing the past. She followed what he did intently, and tried to shape her thoughts in the same fashion, pushing her farsight down into the nothingness that lay around her.

Her own body was there, a long multiple image winding back and forth across the ground, going up into the ship, talking to Kazimir, radiating such sorrow it threatened to resonate through her now. She pushed past it, saw the *Silverbird* swoop down from space. Further.

It was incredibly difficult, without the support of the confluence nest she would never have maintained focus. She couldn't believe the Waterwalker had ever done this unaided. There was a single distinctive moment in her life which she wanted to achieve. Her mind held it up, instinctively matching it to the moment contained within the Void's memory of everywhen. Then all she had to do was impel herself into it. There was a cry of desperation somewhere in the physical world as she attempted to force her thoughts into a pattern they were never intended for, calling upon the strength of the confluence nest to support her. The precious moment was there, linking present and past. Justine *pushed*. The Void reset itself –

Inigo's Thirteenth Dream

The chamber of records was three levels down beneath the Spiral Tower which housed the headquarters of Makkathran's Weapons Guild. In total, the third level had twenty chambers, arranged in a circle and reached by a single ring corridor. They were used as vaults for the most secret guns and ammunition compounds known to the Guild's Masters. For centuries the triple iron doors to each chamber had kept the rapid-fire guns safe, along with long-barrelled pistols and other firearms lost to the rest of Querencia. The mechanisms to produce such devices were also kept in the vaults, as were the raw ingots of specialist metals the designs required.

Just to gain entrance to the Spiral Tower was difficult enough, there was only one entrance, and it was heavily guarded. All visitors had to be accompanied by a Master. Beyond that, armed guards kept a ceaseless vigil on the first and second basement levels. There were also ingenious trips and traps along the corridors and steps to catch anyone using concealment.

It was reasonable, therefore, for those who assembled in the chamber of records two days after Topar's little expedition left Makkathran to exude a degree of security. Grand Master Owain greeted his eleven guests warmly. No one made any attempt to hide their sense of trepidation and excitement as they made their way into the broad cross vaulted chamber. There was a simple wooden table set up in the middle, with thirteen chairs around it. Tall shelving cabinets were arrayed round the lead-grey walls, containing hundreds of leather folders which held every pistol and bullet design produced by the Guild over its two millennia existence. Long teardrop lighting patterns stretched across the curving ceiling, glowing passively.

Bise was the last to be shown in. He smiled round at his fellows as the three thick, heavy doors swung shut behind him. Complicated locks rotated, pushing steel bolts into place and securing them, combination bands were spun.

'My poor boy,' Mistress Florrel said, and embraced Sampalok's ex-Master warmly. 'Welcome home.'

'Thank you, Grandmama.'

'Did you get the food I had sent out to you? I had the bakery on Jodsell Street make those raspberry muffins especially. I know how much you liked them as a boy.'

'Yes indeed, it was most kind.'

'Was exile so terrible?'

'It had its moments.'

'It had its costs,' Tannarl said. 'Half of your family stayed at my lodge.'

'For which you will be fully recompensed,' Owain said smoothly. 'Come, come, we are not here to squabble among ourselves over a little coinage. Our moment draws near.'

'It was drawing near two years ago,' Bise said. 'Then *he* arrived.'

'Well the Waterwalker is off running round the countryside now, trying to find bandits,' Buate said. 'And when he does, he won't be coming back.'

'Don't be too sure,' Owain said. 'His telekinesis is incredibly strong. Makkathran hasn't seen the like since the days of Rah. And not even Rah could alter the city buildings.'

Bise glowered at the reminder.

'Careful cousin,' Tannarl said. 'You tread close to heresy.'

'I state the simple truth.'

'You don't seriously believe he can ward off the reception I have arranged for him?' Buate asked. 'The whole point of ambushing him outside the crystal wall is to rob him of the advantage which the city gives him.'

'The outcome is almost irrelevant,' Owain said. 'Even if he does survive there will be nothing for him to return to. We must be absolute in that. Our supporters are ready.'

'There will be resistance,' Buate warned.

'Lady take them,' Tannarl said. 'I say we don't wait any—'

The Waterwalker rose smoothly through the floor of the records chamber, his black cloak enveloping him like an extinguished nebula. He studied each one of the conspirators sitting around the table. Several had risen to their feet, hands reaching for their pistols. A motion which died as he gave them a lofty dismissive smile.

'The election has given us a Mayor and a full Council,' the Waterwalker said. 'There will be no change, no revolution. We are not One Nation until we choose to be so.'

'What are you proposing?' Owain asked.

'I am proposing nothing. Your time is over.'

'This time, maybe,' Bise snarled. 'But there will be other opportunities.'

'No, there won't,' the Waterwalker told him. 'I've already seen what happens if you win.'

Owain frowned at the strange claim. Uneasy thoughts were stirring beneath his normally resolute shield.

'You cannot arrest us,' Mistress Florrel said. 'Our kind are not accountable in common law courts. And we have many allies in the Upper Council where you would need to enact judgement.'

'Quite right,' the Waterwalker agreed. 'It would be pointless.'

Tannarl strode across the chamber, his third hand reaching out. The big lock on the inner door turned sharply, its intricate combination bands spinning round until the bolts were freed. They withdrew, and the door swung open. There were several sharp breaths. The door opened on to a smooth section of grey wall. There was no way out of the chamber.

'I have heard many times from your followers that I am weak,' the Waterwalker said. 'That I lack resolution. If you believe that, you don't know me at all. This revolution will end here, now. Without you, it cannot happen. Without the rapid-fire guns it cannot be attempted ever again. Makkathran will remain a democracy.' His cloak parted, and he held an arm out, palm down. A rapid-fire gun slipped up through the floor and rose into his hand. He closed his fingers around it.

'No,' Owain said. 'This is against everything you stand for.'

'You really shouldn't believe everything a heartbroken teenage girl tells you.'

Owain grimaced as his fear began to manifest.

'You wouldn't dare,' Mistress Florrel said. 'My family will not permit this.'

'It is my family now,' Edeard told her calmly.

Eleven third hands pushed and hammered against the Water-walker's shield, trying to find a weakness, a way though. Long-shouts for help were hurled at the impermeable chamber walls.

'For all of my life I have known that sometimes to do what's right, you first have to do what's wrong,' the Waterwalker told them. 'Now I realize the truth of it. That is what I am.' His finger squeezed down on the trigger. He held it there until the magazine was empty.

Storage vault five contained over three hundred rapid-fire guns. They were wrapped in oiled cloth, sitting on racks that formed neat ranks across the floor.

Edeard replaced the one he'd used on its rack. He asked the city to dispose of them all. The floor beneath the racks changed, becoming porous, and the dreadful weapons sank down to oblivion.

His farsight swept out, examining the other vaults. Storage vault eight contained the bullets used by the rapid-fire guns. The city quietly absorbed the crates. Vault two had the long-barrelled pistols. Seventeen housed some huge guns, their barrels as big as his legs, mounted on little wheeled trolleys. Iron balls larger than his fist were stacked in pyramids beside them – the bullets, he realized. He shuddered as he imagined the damage they could cause. All sank away. Finally, the shelving cabinets in the chamber of records slid beneath the solid floor.

The secret power of the Weapons Guild was no more. There would never be an internal threat to Makkathran's Grand Council and Mayor again.

Apart from the elections. And the Guild quarrels. And the merchants manoeuvring and bribing for gain. And the Grand Families struggling for advantage.

He grinned at the thought of it all. That crazy, wondrous life lived by Makkathran's citizens. *It's all Finitan's problem now.*

The warm afternoon light lit up the white pillars that lined Golden Park. Even the last bloom on the bushes and vines glowed with an exotic splendour in celebration of what had been an exceptionally pleasant summer. Edeard walked for some way across its elegant paths, drawing his thoughts together. Resolving to do what he must.

It was hard for his farsight to search out the frail souls of his parents. He stood beside one of the pillars along the Champ Canal side of Golden Park, bathed in the rich light reflected off the metal, extending his ability to its utmost.

They were there. A few feet away, watching him as always. 'Thank you,' he told them.

'You can see us?' his mother asked in surprise.

'Yes, Mother. I can see you now.'

'My son.'

'Father. You've taken such care of me, more than I ever deserved.'

'What were we supposed to do? You are all that remains of us.'

'Not any more. I have a wife now. We will have children. They will have more. Everything you are will go on through them.'

'We should watch for them,' his mother said, she sounded uncertain.

'No,' Edeard said. 'It is time for you to let go. I can take care of myself now, more than you know. The price you have paid for watching me is too high. You cannot do this any more. You must go to the Heart. There is still time. There is always time.'

'Oh Edeard.'

'Here.' He held out a hand. His mother reached out, touching his fingertips. He fought against wincing as the debilitating cold burned him. Instead, he smiled in reverence as she took substance before him. 'Goodbye, Mother,' he said, and brushed his lips to hers. 'We will be together in the Heart one day, I promise.'

Her sorrow and regret were dreadfully poignant. But she smiled as she withdrew from his touch. His father held her closely.

'Journey well,' Edeard told them. He watched them fade up into the warm clear blue sky, refusing to acknowledge any remorse.

A lot of people were using Golden Park that afternoon, taking advantage of the lingering summer. Children raced over the grassy areas, playing elaborate games of catch. Apprentices bunking off duties gathered in the shade of the park's huge martoz trees, sharing bottles of beer and gossip about their Masters.

Salrana walked along one of the crushed slate paths, enjoying the activity. Lads eyed her wishfully, although her crisp blue and white Novice robes proved too great a barrier for any casual attempt to attract her attention. She crossed the ginger sandstone bridge into Ysidro. Right ahead of her was the Blue Fox tavern, a circular three-storey building with a strange hexagonal rustication pattern embossed on the coppery wall. Its slim lancet windows made it seem taller than it actually was. She hesitated for a moment before slipping in through one of the smaller side doors, something swirled on the periphery of her farsight, as if a pillar of fog had gusted down the alleyway. She frowned, but it didn't resolve in her senses, so she scurried up the stairs to the third floor.

The Blue Fox was favoured by Grand Family members as a place to conduct their liaisons; the exceptionally thick walls of the rooms eliminated the need to maintain a seclusion haze. Privacy was guaranteed against all but the most exceptional psychics. Salrana used the key she'd been given to unlock the door of a reserved room.

Sunlight was diffused by the tinted gauze covering the windows. More fabrics were draped over the walls. Candles flickered on the dresser, giving off a thick musky scent. The big bed was strewn with silk sheets and fur blankets.

Salrana's lover was waiting for her beside the bed. Flushed with anticipation, Salrana removed her Novice robe to show off the delicate lace camisole she wore underneath, a recent gift from her lover. That same lover drew her close and kissed her. Gentle hands undid the topmost bow on the camisole. Another kiss was given. The next bow was undone. More kisses, each one more intimate. The camisole fell open at the front. A whimper of excitement sounded deep in Salrana's throat, she couldn't contain herself any further, and clung to her lover, returning the kisses fiercely.

Edeard discarded his concealment. Salrana jumped in shock. Her mind radiated guilt.

'You,' Edeard said sourly. 'I should have guessed. I really should.'

'But you didn't, did you?' Ranalee said disdainfully; she pulled her own satin negligee up, and combed some of her dishevelled hair back into place. 'I thought you had left the city.'

'Yes. A lot of people made that mistake. Your friends. Your family. Your fellow conspirators.'

Ranalee's eyes widened. Surprise shone there at first, then she became alarmed as her directed longtalk questions went unanswered. 'What have you done?' she hissed.

'They won't answer you. Not now. Not ever.'

'Father?' she gasped.

'The Lady will bless his soul, I'm sure. I doubt anyone else will.'

'Bastard!' Ranalee was trembling, on the verge of tears.

'You were planning worse for me, far worse.'

Ranalee recovered to glare at him defiantly. 'So what do you plan for me?'

'Nothing. Because you are nothing without Owain and your family. Owner of a bordello. What is that? Not anything.'

Salrana took a hesitant step forwards. 'Edeard—'

'Not a word from you. I don't blame you. Do you know what they did to your mind, what this vixen can do?' Even as he spoke he could sense the difference in Salrana's unshielded thoughts. The harshness that flowed where once there had only been contentment and geniality.

'Of course she does,' Ranalee gloated. Her arm went protectively round Salrana, who leant in closer, seeking reassurance. 'I showed her a real life.'

'They used your anger with me for abandoning you. This . . . this agent of Honious, came for you when you were vulnerable. It was no accident she met you. It was not chance. I know what she's like, Salrana. She has a perverted skill that can twist your very thoughts, she warps what should be something beautiful into something diseased. It's not love you feel for her, it is a wretched corruption of the affection your true self can experience.'

'No,' Salrana interrupted with soft insistence. 'It was I who found Ranalee.'

'They exploited you. Her. Owain. The rest. Their only interest is in your past, our background. Lady, you're just another weapon to use against me. You're supposed to lure me out of the city if the ambush failed, remember?'

Salrana gave Ranalee a startled look, then faced Edeard again. 'I wouldn't have done it.'

'Ha!' Edeard closed his eyes to mute the pain seeing her like

743

this brought him. 'You would. Please, Salrana, I can help you. There are others who can show you how they abused your thoughts, how this evil whore bewitched you.'

'So you can do what?' Salrana snapped, suddenly angry. 'Take Ranalee from me? Leave me with nothing? Again?'

'That's not—'

'I am myself.'

'They were going to *breed* you. In the Lady's name, you know that's not right.'

'Your strength made you the Waterwalker,' Ranalee said. 'Your power attracted Kristabel to you, and now you are part of a Grand Family, you have their wealth and estate at your disposal. Your children will be born to a privilege no one in your pitiful Ashwell could ever comprehend. Why can't Salrana have children that are strong? Why can't Salrana have children who will enjoy that same cushion of money?'

'But you're not giving her that,' Edeard said furiously. 'You exploited how vulnerable she was; you turned her away from everything she was.'

'I showed her what Makkathran society could offer her once you'd tired of her,' Ranalee said triumphantly. 'Marriage, children, family; those are our customs; customs started by Rah himself. Our arrangements are practical and beneficial, deceiving no one. Who in Honious are you to judge that?'

Edeard nearly struck her. But to do that would be to grant her victory. 'I will not give up on you,' he told Salrana. 'What she has done to you is wrong and evil, and whenever the day comes that you realize that, I will be there for you. I swear that upon the Lady.'

Now it was Salrana who regarded him contemptuously. The expression was so similar to the one on Ranalee's face it unnerved him. She took Ranalee's hand and carefully placed it on her bare breast. 'You have your life. I have mine. Even in your world of simplistic morality I can live how I choose. And I choose this. I choose Ranalee: my lover, my mistress.'

Edeard glared at Ranalee, who returned a malicious smile.

'This is not over,' he said. It was quite feeble, he knew, but he simply couldn't think what else to do.

Why can't she see what she's become? Or perhaps she really can. Lady!

'You won today,' Ranalee told him in a mocking tone. 'Show a little nobility. The Waterwalker would.'

Edeard barged out of the door, not bothering to conceal himself.

Edeard returned to the Culverit ziggurat and climbed the stairs without anyone noticing him. Even now he felt a shudder of trepidation that this would all turn out to be a fevered dream, that Kristabel . . . That seeing her would shatter the illusion. *Good old Ashwell optimism.*

Stupid. This is real now. I know that.

When he reached the tenth floor he drew up his courage, and went to the room Kristabel had claimed as her study. It was bare apart from the desk and chair. Even the curtains had been taken down as it slowly changed shape to the one she and Edeard had decided on. Bigger windows. Brighter, white lighting rosettes. He knew the walls were shifting inwards so the lounge next door could be longer even though the process was so slow his eyes couldn't see the change. Just before he'd left, Kristabel had remarked on how the tenth floor was already different from the home she'd lived her whole life in. He humoured her by agreeing, because she was so excited. And happy.

Now she was bent over the desk, her quill pen scribbling furiously as always. Her beautiful face was wrinkled as she studied yet another thick ledger containing family accounts. Three high piles of similar ledgers were propped up on the side of the desk.

My wife.

'You look bored,' he told her.

Kristabel started. Then she smiled at Edeard as he stood in

the doorway. 'I never even sensed you,' she exclaimed. 'Are you creeping up on me? And why are you here? What about the bandits? You couldn't have found them already.'

'No, we didn't. But I know who and where they are now. They'll just have to keep for another day. I wanted to be home with my beautiful wife.'

She hurried over with a big smile on her face, and kissed him welcome. 'That's so sweet. Finitan will kill you, though, it was hugely important.'

Edeard put his arms round her. Not wanting to let go. *Ever.* He took a look out of the window, across the hortus to the fabulous living city beyond. 'Others have tried.'

She frowned, and poked him in the chest. 'Are you all right? You seem . . . tired.'

'No. I'm fine. It's just that today I realized there are some things you can never fix no matter how hard you try.'

Kristabel kissed him again. 'But I know you, you'll just keep on trying. That's what makes you you. That's why I love you.'

Visit **www.panmacmillan.com** to read more about all our books and to buy them. You will also find features, author interviews and news of any author events, and you can sign up for e-newsletters so that you're always first to hear about our new releases.